PENGUIN CLASSICS

THE MANUSCRIPT FOUND IN SARAGOSSA

'A Polish classic . . . constructed like a Chinese box of tales . . . It reads like the most brilliant modern novel' – Salman Rushdie in the *Guardian*

'One of the great masterpieces of European literature . . . this new translation offers us the work as a whole in English for the first time, in the dizzyingly elaborate form envisioned by the author's extraordinary imagination' – Larry Wolff in *The New York Times Book Review*

'The translation by Ian Maclean is crisp, lucid and unfussy . . . A beautiful volume, underlining Potocki's forgotten masterpiece as a work of real substance' – James Woodall in *The Times*

'A picaresque ramble through Islam and the inquisition . . . This is the stuff of reading on a grand scale, fiction of enduring splendour' – David Hughes in the *Mail on Sunday*

'Impossible to put down' – Katherine A. Powers in the *Boston Globe*

'A bravura translation . . . the 100 or so stories told over 66 "Days" are fantastic, ghostly, erotic, comic, ghoulish, philosophical and Munchausenly tall' – David Coward in the *Sunday Telegraph*

'This volume is excellent value, two dozen fresh and ingenious tales for the price of a novel' – Julian Duplain in the *Times Literary Supplement*

'At its most magical *The Manuscript Found in Saragossa* reads like *The Arabian Nights*, at its most italianate like something from *The Decameron* . . . a masterwork of European romanticism' – Michael Dirda in the *Washington Post Book World*

'One of the strangest books ever written can at last take its rightful place in world literature' – Kola Krauze in the *Guardian*

ABOUT THE AUTHOR AND TRANSLATOR

JAN POTOCKI was born in Poland in 1761 into a very great aristocratic family, which owned vast estates. He was educated in Geneva and Lausanne, served twice in the army and spent some time as a novice Knight of Malta. During his lifetime he was an indefatigable traveller and travel-writer, an Egyptologist and pioneering ethnologist, an occultist and an historian of the pre-Slavic peoples. He was a political activist and probably a freemason, although he seems to have espoused a bafflingly wide range of political causes, some of them patriotic. Among his other exploits were an ascent in a balloon over Warsaw with the aeronaut Blanchard and the provision of the first free press in that city.

Potocki was proficient in many different languages, and his extensive travels led him through the Mediterranean, the Balkans, the Caucasus and China. He married twice (the first marriage ending in divorce) and had five children: scandalous rumours surrounded both of his marriages. In 1812 he retired to his estates in Poland, suffering from chronic ill health, melancholia and disillusionment. He committed suicide in 1815. Although the exact details of his end are uncertain, the most credible story is that he blew his brains out with a silver bullet, which was modelled from the knob of his sugar-bowl and first blessed by the castle chaplain.

IAN MACLEAN is Reader in French at the University of Oxford and a Fellow of the Queen's College.

The Manuscript Found in Saragossa

JAN POTOCKI

TRANSLATED BY IAN MACLEAN

PENGUIN BOOKS

in memoriam absentium
J. N. M. M.   J. W. M.   E. M. D.   E. M. M.   W. B. H.

PENGUIN BOOKS

Published by the Penguin Group
Penguin Books Ltd, 27 Wrights Lane, London W8 5TZ, England
Penguin Putnam Inc., 375 Hudson Street, New York, New York 10014, USA
Penguin Books Australia Ltd, Ringwood, Victoria, Australia
Penguin Books Canada Ltd, 10 Alcorn Avenue, Toronto, Ontario, Canada M4V 3B2
Penguin Books (NZ) Ltd, Private Bag 102902, NSMC, Auckland, New Zealand

Penguin Books Ltd, Registered Offices: Harmondsworth, Middlesex, England

First modern edition published in French 1989
This translation first published by Viking 1995
Published in Penguin Books 1996
4

Contents

Contents

Contents

Contents

Introduction

The Manuscript Found in Saragossa is a complex interweaving of tales narrated by a young army officer called Alphonse van Worden, who kept a diary of his experiences in the Sierra Morena in 1739, recording both the events which he witnessed and the stories he was told by the company in which he found himself. In 1769 or thereabouts, his diary was sealed by him (so the story goes) in a casket; forty years later, it was found by a French officer while out looting after the fall of the city of Saragossa. He didn't know much Spanish, but he realized that what he had come upon was a story about brigands, ghosts, cabbalists, smugglers, gypsies, haunted gallows and no doubt much else besides. It was an intriguing mystery: intriguing enough to persuade him to keep the book in his possession, to attempt to hang on to it when he was captured and, later, to inveigle his captor into translating it for him. The same intriguing mystery awaits the reader of this translation: or rather the same complicated web of mysteries. The French officer of the foreword was careful not to spoil the story by revealing too much about it in his preface, and in this introduction I shall be just as discreet; but without giving away too much, I can suggest where the mysteries of the book are to be found.

There are in fact three enigmatic aspects to the book: its author, its composition and its contents. Its author, Count Jan Potocki (1761–1815), was a member of a very great Polish family who lived at a time of considerable literary and political turbulence throughout Europe. His life was spent in travelling, writing, political intrigue and scholarly research. He received a solid education in Geneva and Lausanne, had two spells in the army as an officer in the engineers, and spent some time on a galley as a novice Knight of Malta. He was among the first to make an ascent in a balloon (in 1790), which brought him much public acclaim; he was a tireless political activist,

xi

consorting with patriots in Poland, Jacobins in France and the court of Alexander I of Russia. He appears to have been a freemason. All this activity cannot easily be ascribed to a single set of beliefs: at certain times he applauded, at others condemned the French Revolution; he fought against the Russians yet served the Tsar, and accepted a commission to fight alongside the Austrians while declaring himself their political enemy. His travels at different periods of his life took in Italy, Sicily, Spain, Tunisia, Turkey, Egypt, France, Holland, England, Germany, Russia, even Mongolia; he wrote lively accounts of most of these journeys, and while on them engaged in historical, linguistic and ethnographical researches. His published writings helped found the discipline of ethnology. He compounded his scholarly activity with an interest in publishing, establishing an independent press in Warsaw in 1788 and a free reading room there four years later. As well as writing and publishing scholarly works and pamphlets, he wrote a play, a set of sketches ('parades'), and, of course, *The Manuscript Found in Saragossa*. He married twice, and had five children; he was divorced from his second wife in 1808. There were rumours of incest. By 1812, politically disillusioned and in poor health, he had retired to his castle at Uładówka in Podolia. On 2 December or 11 December 1815 (depending on the source), he committed suicide, although whether out of political despair, mental depression or a desire to be released from a highly painful chronic condition is not clear. Many stories are told about his death. He is said to have fashioned a silver bullet himself out of the knob of his teapot (or the handle of a sugar-bowl bequeathed to him by his mother); he had it blessed by the chaplain of the castle, and then used it to blow out his brains in his library (or his bedroom), having written his own epitaph (or, according to other sources, drawn a caricature of himself). The macabre stories about his end, his equivocal political career and personal life, his polymathy and his restless wanderings all contribute to the composite picture of an Enlightenment thinker and a romantic figure *par excellence*, commensurate with his one great literary work.

The controversies surrounding the composition of his novel *The Manuscript Found in Saragossa* are scarcely less dramatic than those surrounding his life. For a long time its authorship was disputed;

indeed, the editor of a very recent partial translation still maintains (against conclusive evidence) that Potocki may not have written it. Its publishing history is highly complex. A set of proofs of the first ten or so days appeared in St Petersburg in 1805; this was followed by the story of Avadoro, the gypsy chief, extracted from the framework of the novel, which appeared almost certainly with Potocki's permission in Paris in 1813; the following year saw a republication of the first ten days, linked to the story of the gypsy chief. If one looks closely at these Paris publications, it is clear that Potocki had still not completely decided in which form to publish his novel, nor whether it would please the public; his death in 1815 put an end to further flotations on the book market of the French capital. But that did not prevent his published work from being plagiarized three times in the next quarter-century, and even becoming the subject of a lawsuit.

It is not clear when Potocki conceived of his novel or when he finished it; the best informed opinion seems to suggest that he began it in the 1790s and completed it in the last year of his life. If one looks, however, at the details included in the first day, one sees that the outcome of the novel is already carefully prepared, which suggests that by 1805 Potocki knew more or less where he wanted to go. The whole text was composed in French; but in spite of assiduous researches in Polish family archives, not all of it appears to have survived in this form. About a fifth of the text is only available in a Polish translation from a lost French manuscript of the whole book, made by Edmund Chojecki in 1847. For a long time, it was hoped that a complete original version would be discovered; but in 1989 René Radrizzani cut the Gordian knot of speculations as to what and where this might be by publishing the complete story in French for the first time, having supplied a French translation of the missing parts from Chojecki's Polish version. Radrizzani's French edition includes all the variants relating to the different surviving manuscripts and printed versions; there are, however, only one or two (very minor) points where they are necessary for the understanding of the text, and these have been recorded in footnotes. Critical controversy still rages in France, and it is possible that a new edition by a much respected Potocki scholar may appear in the near future; but, even if it does, it is unlikely to modify much of Radrizzani's text, although it might bring new manuscripts to bear on Chojecki's Polish version and make different editorial choices with respect to the existing material. Like the author's life, the text of his masterpiece leaves many questions unanswered, or unanswerable.

What is the novel about? At a simple level, it is a novel of frames; the preface, supposedly written in 1809, encapsulates the narrative of Alphonse van Worden, a young Walloon officer about to join the Spanish army, who for two months in 1739 is diverted from his journey to Madrid, and obliged to spend this time in the company of the Muslims, cabbalists, Spanish noblemen, thieves and gypsies whose stories are recorded by him as they are told to him. These story-tellers adopt the first person not only to tell their own tales, but also to relate stories they have heard from others: at one point even, the gypsy chief Avadoro (or Pandesowna, as he is also known) tells a story within a story within a story within a story, much to the annoyance of one of the more literal-minded members of his audience. These stories are loosely linked to events in European history between about 1700 and 1740, although it is not necessary to know about the historical background to understand them. An epilogue, also written by Alphonse van Worden in about 1769, closes the novel and ties up the loose ends. All this self-conscious and often highly sophisticated story-telling may suggest that the book is demanding, even difficult to read, in the way that modern experimental fiction can be: but this is not the case. It cannot be denied that by the middle of the novel there are several different stories being related at the same time, and that their enmeshment is such that the characters in the novel them-selves are made to complain about its complexity. But, this fact apart, Potocki's novel has much in common with other epics of entertaining story-telling such as Boccaccio's *Decameron* or *The Thousand and One Nights*, with which its first readers compared it. Like those works, each story is complete in itself, even though there is an overall design which enhances the pleasure of reading by the many coincidences, patterns and recurrent figures which help bind the whole text together.

Potocki seems at one time to have thought of his work in terms of the Gothic novel ('*à la* Radcliffe', as he said in a letter to a friend), and indeed there is no shortage of macabre, sinister, ghastly and horrific events; but it also has affinities with many other literary modes: the picaresque, in the story of Avadoro-Pandesowna's semi-criminal youth; the adventure story, in its evocation of inexhaustible gold-mines and grand international conspiracies; the pastoral, in its disabused portrayal of court life and its celebration of the beauties of nature; the libertine novel, in its imaginative exploration of the erotic; the *conte philosophique*, in the dry satirical tone of much of the text and its moral, political, religious and scientific discussions; the fantastic, in its intermingling of the supernatural and the ordinary (although how much remains supernatural at the end is for the reader to decide); the *Bildungsroman*, in the process by which the naïve Alphonse van Worden is brought to maturity. These affinities have led critics to compare it to *Don Quixote*, *Gil Blas*, even *Nathan der Weise*; but as well as all of this, it is a novel of portraits, a veritable gallery of eccentrics, boors, wits, fools, pedants, philosophers, tricksters, boon companions, cowards and brave men, coquettes and (more rarely) virtuous women. Some of these portraits are just vignettes, others are extensive and profound; some add their colourful voices to the rich texture of the novel, others are no more than the objects of picturesque description.

Leitmotifs run through the work, adding to its pleasure. There are erotic encounters involving sometimes two, sometimes three, sometimes four participants, some told naively, some urbanely, some with a tortured conscience; authoritarian fathers (van Worden, Velásquez, Soarez) repeatedly appear to imprint on their sons their own strange philosophies of life; characters are metamorphosed or transform themselves from Christians into Muslims or Jews, from men into women, from beautiful girls into hideous corpses. Dreadful scourges in the shape of implacable persecutors (the principino, Sedekias, Busqueros) haunt the lives of the protagonists. There is a great deal of impersonation and acting, of illusion and delusion, throughout the novel: much of this has to do with strange, convoluted, even barbaric and cruel rites of initiation, which the major characters – Alphonse van Worden, Juan Avadoro-Pandesowna, the Great Sheikh of the Gomelez – all undergo. Other, more mysterious, patterns can be traced, not only in the succession and balance of the stories, but also in the recurrent tableaux, which, as some scholars have pointed out, seem to have affinities with the tarot pack. These motifs are there to be enjoyed, whatever significance may be attached to them by critics.

Does the book have a message? Certain commentators have seen in it an answer to Chateaubriand's *Génie du Christianisme*, a sort of Enlightenment celebration of reason and toleration. Others have opted for the rationalism implicit in the younger Velásquez's mathematization of the human being; yet others for the materialism to which the elder Hervas turns in despair at the end of his life. *The Manuscript Found in Saragossa* could be seen as a novel of social and political conservatism, or a savage indictment of the social order and of all political activity, or a plea for pragmatism and liberalism. In a certain sense, all of these apparently contradictory views are true, for different parts of the text can be used to support different theories about it. Nowhere is this seen more clearly than in the contrast between the heartfelt confession of Enrique de Velásquez, the proponent of selflessness, and the measured Mephistophelian speeches of Don Belial, who propounds a philosophy based on egoism. A recurrent moral theme is that of honour: various versions are explored, and all are subtly and mercilessly satirized. There is the lunatic delicacy of the Walloon officer Juan van Worden, who will fight any number of duels to satisfy a nightmare punctiliousness about aristocratic honour which is almost never shared by his reluctant adversaries; we encounter the bandit Zoto, whose scrupulous and much-praised observance of the niceties of brigandry and murder perplexes Juan's naïve son; Pedro de Velásquez's obsession with science and mathematics spills over into his bizarre courtship of the person known as Rebecca de Uzeda; the sanguinary fanaticism of the Gomelez family contrasts with the Uzedas' readiness to submit to any requirements of outward observance, in a spirit akin to that of the Vicar of Bray; yet more relaxed ethical postures can be detected in such figures as the Knight of Toledo and Señora Uscariz. Do all these value systems have a single root, in the same way that the novel suggests (at certain points) that all religions spring indifferently from one source? Do they constitute the bundle of contradictions – integrity and duplicity, flesh and spirit, rigidity and suppleness, youth and maturity, indulgence and asceticism, prolixity and silence, folly and wisdom – which go to make up the human being? Could this be the hidden message of the book?

Every reader will no doubt find certain passages or aspects more significant than others. There are moments when a reader may detect a lyrical or passionate note breaking through Potocki's characteristically witty, detached, satirical prose, which is dominated by the humane, worldly-wise, ironic voice of Avadoro-Pandesowna. On two occasions, it seems to me, his tone changes: once, towards the end of his life story, when he speaks of the loves of a young man, in which the individual figures of his mistresses merge into a composite evocation of the tenderness, excitement, adventure and pleasures of love; the other occasion, and to my mind the more telling, when he describes a specifically Spanish mode of social intercourse. The French had at this time, as is well known, the reputation for brilliant, flirtatious, urbane conversation between social equals of different sexes in the context of the salon (Carlos de Velásquez practises it in this novel); at the same time, the Spaniards were known for their taciturnity. Avadoro's father, the implausible progenitor of the articulate figure whose narrative voice dominates the novel, scarcely utters a single word in the whole of his adult life; his granddaughter, the mysterious elfin Ondina, is almost as uncommunicative. But between these zones of silence, the gypsy chief himself revels in speech, both his own and that of others, which he relays to his motley band of listeners. This celebration of polyphony, of unfettered human intercourse, has been linked to the enlightened, tolerant exchanges of freemasonry, but Avadoro-Pandesowna offers it as a specifically Spanish experience, arising from the institution of the highway inn, which makes no distinction of class, is not bound by the stiff etiquette of Spanish polite society, brings together all sexes and ages, is unpredictable, jolly, communal; if Potocki's novel has a message, this seems to me to be it. It is to this that Avadoro-Pandesowna gives expression in his nostalgic description of the Spanish hostelry on the twelfth day:

The beasts were at the rack in the stables and the travellers were at the other end in the kitchen, separated from the stable by two stone steps. At that time, this was the normal arrangement in nearly all Spanish inns. The whole building was but one long room of which the greater part was occupied by the mules and the lesser by the humans. But it was all the merrier for that. As the *zagal* (muleteer) saw to the pack animals, he kept up a steady stream of repartee with the innkeeper's wife, who replied with all the liveliness of her sex and station until the more serious-minded innkeeper came between them and interrupted the exchanges. They soon started up again, however. The inn rang to the sound of the castanets played by the maids, who danced to the raucous singing of a goatherd. Travellers made each other's acquaintance and invited each other to supper. Everyone gathered round the stove, said who they were, where they were going and sometimes told stories. Those were the good old days; now our inns are more comfortable, but the boisterous social life which the travellers of those days led had a charm I cannot describe to you.

Not just here, but for much of the novel, we are vicariously transported into the atmosphere of an early-eighteenth-century Spanish hostelry (or, if we abandon the fictional framework, an inn in 1780, when Potocki visited Spain), listening to the stories of men and women, some rich, some poor, some law-abiding, some criminal, some naïve, some worldly-wise; how can such a cornucopia of narratives be brought to an end? Some critics have said that the resolution of this particular novel is disappointing, but it may be that no novel of this sort can resolve the problem of an ending which must be indefinitely deferred if the entertainment is to continue: for when the voices are stilled and the party breaks up, silence, solitude, absence, even a sort of death supervenes. But for as long as the book remains open, inviting the reader into the imaginary hostelry of its pages, it can prove itself to be the most lively and entertaining of companions.

Translator's Note

Potocki's text poses a number of problems in respect of the titles of address and courtesy, which are rendered by Potocki from an original language (usually Spanish) into French (e.g. 'Señor caballero' becomes 'Seigneur cavalier'). I have thought it appropriate to revert to the original, rather than find an English equivalent for the French, and to leave foreign titles of nobility in the most usual form, depending on the context. In some cases, this leads to mixed usage (e.g. both 'Duque' and 'Duke'); in others the use of the lower case (in referring to characters by title). I have not translated the many terms for different currencies (pieces of eight, darics, piastres, piastres fortes, sequins, pistoles, reals, and others besides); their context makes their value clear enough. I have also left the various horse-driven modes of transport (carrosses, chaises, chaises roulantes, litters, calèches, etc.) in their original form for the most part. I have provided footnotes for the foreign words and phrases which Potocki left in his text, and have also noted historical events where it seemed to me to be enlightening; but not all of Radrizzani's own notes have been reproduced, nor has his critical apparatus (variant readings, alternative versions of days, etc.) been included. The occasional textual inconsistencies or errors have also been recorded in footnotes.

It gives me great pleasure to place on record the debts I owe to Pauline, my wife, and to Paul Foote, for having read whole drafts of the translation, to Roger Pearson, for his astute advice about the Introduction, and to Peter Southwell, Ron Truman, John Rutherford, Peter Neumann, Peter Robbins, John Baines and Peter Miller for guidance on specific points of the text. Siegbert Prawer generously lent me invaluable books to which I was able to refer while undertaking this translation; but his advice and encouragement over many years has been more valuable still, and it gives me particular pleasure to record it here. Jan Lewendon and Fleur Walsh put up with my presence in their office for long periods of time with more good humour than was my due, and generously provided me with liquid sustenance and technical advice. Pat Lloyd heroically typed a first draft from a scratchy dictaphone; without her help, *my* manuscript would perhaps never have seen the light of day.

A Note on the Geographical Location

Potocki refers to a number of places and geographical features in Andalusia in the course of his story: a brief glance at a map will reveal that he has deliberately mixed up his locations. The Venta de Cárdenas is indeed the most northerly inn in the Sierra Morena on the road to Madrid; but the Venta Quemada is a fiction, perhaps suggested by the village of Aldeaquemada, which is west of the Venta de Cárdenas. The settlement called La Carlota is not north of Andújar, but more than sixty miles to the south-west, on the other side of Córdoba; the river Guadalquivir does indeed rush down from the mountains in the way described by Potocki, but only in the spring, and not in the Sierra Morena, but the Sierra de Cazorla, far to the east of the place where he situates it. Although in the book there is a lake of volcanic origin called La Frita, there does not seem to be one at all in the region; but Potocki's description of the countryside north of Andújar corresponds quite well to what is to be found there today. In the spring there is a profusion of wild flowers, aromatic herbs and flowering shrubs in a landscape of bizarrely shaped and weathered rocks and some caves; certainly attractive enough to engender the feelings of Rousseauistic enthusiasm for natural beauty which are attributed to Alphonse van Worden. Further south, however, in the putative site of the Baetican gold mine, the scrubby uplands are less appealing; for the most part they have been reclaimed for use as extensive olive plantations, a feature of the whole region today.

Glossary

———————— ∽ ————————

Only those words which recur in the text have been included in this list: in other cases, a footnote gives the meaning.

agour!, good day! (an invention of Potocki's)

alcalde, mayor

alguazil, policeman

barigel, gaoler

contador, comptroller of accounts

corregidor, senior official of the crown, with legal and administrative functions

fray, brother

gonilla, Spanish ruff

hidalgo, gentleman

oidor, judge

olla, pot

olla podrida, stew

pelota, outdoor ball game

presepe, crib

quinta, farm

sbiro, policeman appointed by the community or government

seguidilla, a Spanish song form

tirana, ancient Spanish song form

venta, inn

virreina, wife of viceroy

zagal, muleteer

A Guide to the Stories

◦

For those who may wish to follow particular stories without having to engage with the full complexity of Potocki's interwoven narrations, the following index is a guide to the principal stories, with page references:

xxiii

The Manuscript Found in Saragossa

Foreword

As an officer in the French army, I found myself at the siege of Saragossa.[1] A few days after its fall, I was proceeding towards a remote corner of the town when I noticed a small, well-built house which appeared to me not to have been searched as yet by any Frenchmen.

Curiosity prompted me to go in. I knocked on the door but, seeing that it was not closed, I pushed it open. I called out, and searched everywhere, but found nobody. It looked to me as though everything of value had been removed already; the objects left behind on tables and in cupboards were of little worth. But in the corner several handwritten notebooks caught my eye; I cast my eyes over the contents of the manuscript. It was in Spanish; I knew very little of that language, but I knew enough to see that the book might well be entertaining. It was all about brigands, ghosts and cabbalists; nothing could be more suitable to divert my mind from the rigours of the campaign than to read a novel full of strange adventures. As I was convinced that the book could no longer be restored to its rightful owner, I did not hesitate to possess myself of it.

Later we were forced to abandon Saragossa. I found myself by mischance separated from the main body of the army, and was taken prisoner by the enemy together with my detachment. I thought that was the end of me. Once we had reached the place where they were taking us, the Spanish began to strip us of our possessions. I pleaded to be allowed to keep only one object, which could not be of any use to them: it was the manuscript I had found. They at first raised objections, but in the end consulted their captain who, having cast his eyes over the book, came to me and thanked me for preserving intact

1 Saragossa capitulated on 20 February 1809.

3

a work to which he attached great value, as it contained the history of his ancestors. I told him how it had fallen into my hands. He then took me away with him, and during my quite lengthy stay in his house, where I was treated civilly, I asked him to translate the work for me into French. I wrote what follows as he dictated it.

The First Day

At the time of which I speak, the Count of Olivarez had not yet established new settlements in the lowering mountain range of the Sierra Morena, which separates the provinces of Andalusia and La Mancha.[1] They were then only inhabited by smugglers, bandits and some gypsies who were said to murder travellers and then eat them: which is the origin of the Spanish proverb 'Las gitanas de la Sierra Morena quieren carne de hombres.'[2]

But that was not all. Travellers who ventured into that wild country found themselves assailed, it was said, by countless terrors which would make even the stoutest of hearts tremble. Piteous wailing could be heard above the roar of the torrents and the howling of the storm; travellers were lured from their path by will-of-the-wisps, and invisible hands propelled them towards bottomless abysses.

There were in fact a few *ventas*[3] or isolated hostelries scattered along that calamitous route, but ghosts who were even more diabolical than the innkeepers themselves had forced these last to flee and to leave them in control. Such ghosts struck bargains with the innkeepers, who retired to more peaceful parts of the country where they were disturbed only by the pangs of their consciences. The innkeeper at Andújar swore by St James of Compostella to the truth of these fantastic stories; he went on to say that the constables of the Holy Inquisition had refused to undertake any expedition into the Sierra Morena, and that travellers took the road through Jaen or Estramadura.

I replied to him that this choice of route might suit ordinary

1 The Sierra Morena was colonized by the Conde de Olivarez between 1767 and 1776.

2 'The gypsy women of the Sierra Morena are keen on the flesh of men.'

3 Inns.

travellers, but that as King Philip V[4] had graciously bestowed on me a commission in the Walloon Guards, I was bound by the sacred laws of honour to take the shortest route to Madrid without considering whether it was the most dangerous.

'Señor,' the innkeeper said, 'a young military gentleman such as yourself will permit me to point out that if the king has entrusted him with a company of Walloon Guards at an age at which his chin is still as smooth as a girl's, it would be wise of him to show prudence in such matters; now I maintain that once devils have taken over part of the country . . .'

He would have gone on, but I spurred my horse forward and did not stop until I thought I was out of earshot of his protestations. Only then did I turn round, and saw that, though distant, he was still indicating by his gesticulations that I should take the Estramadura road. My valet Lopez and my *zagal*[5] Mosquito gave me pathetic looks which carried roughly the same meaning. I pretended not to understand them, and pressed on into the heathland in which the settlement called La Carlota has since been built.

Where there now stands a post-house, there was then a shelter which was well known to muleteers, who called it Los Alcornoques or the holm oaks, because two fine specimens of that tree gave shade to a copious spring which flowed into a marble trough. It was the only water and shade to be found between Andújar and the hostelry called the Venta Quemada, which was built in the middle of a wilderness, although it was tall and spacious. It was in fact an old Moorish fort which the Marqués de Peña Quemada had had repaired: hence the name Venta Quemada. The marqués had leased it to a citizen of Murcia who had turned it into an inn, the finest indeed of all the inns on that route. It was usual for travellers to leave Andújar in the morning, stop at Los Alcornoques in the middle of the day to consume the provisions they had brought with them, and pass the night, and often the following day as well, at the Venta Quemada, to prepare for the crossing of the mountains and to take

4 Philip V reigned from 1700 to 1746.
5 Muleteer.

6

on fresh provisions. That was the way I had planned my journey too.

But as we came close to the holm oaks and I was speaking to Lopez about the light meal that we were counting on eating there, I noticed that Mosquito was no longer with us; nor was the mule bearing our provisions. Lopez told me that Mosquito had stopped about a hundred paces back to adjust the saddle of his horse. We waited for him; we then took a few paces forward; we stopped to wait for him again; we called him; we turned back to look for him, but all to no avail. Mosquito had vanished and had taken with him our most cherished hopes, that is to say, our lunch. I alone had not eaten at all, for Lopez had been gnawing away throughout the journey at a Toboso cheese with which he had provided himself; but he was no more the merrier for that, and did not stop muttering under his breath that the innkeeper at Andújar had warned us, and that devils had surely carried off the unfortunate Mosquito.

When we reached Los Alcornoques, I found a basket full of vine leaves on the trough; it appeared to have once been full of fruit, and to have been left behind by a traveller. I plunged my hand into it out of curiosity and discovered to my delight four fine figs and an orange. I offered two figs to Lopez, but he declined them, saying that he could wait until evening; so I ate the fruit myself, and then turned to a nearby spring to quench my thirst. Lopez stopped me, however, claiming that the water would be bad for me after the fruit, and said that he had a little Alicante wine left which he could offer me. I accepted, but no sooner had I swallowed the wine than I felt a great heaviness come over me, and earth and sky began to spin round and round my head. I should certainly have fainted if Lopez had not hurriedly come to my assistance; he helped me recover from my attack of dizziness and told me that it was only the effects of exhaustion and lack of food, and nothing to be disturbed about.

Indeed, not only did I soon recover completely, but I found myself in a state of restless energy which was almost uncanny. The countryside appeared to me to be painted in the most glowing colours; as I looked at them, objects sparkled like stars in a summer night; I could feel my pulse pounding in my temples and my neck.

Lopez saw that my momentary weakness was past and could not restrain himself from continuing his lamentations. 'Alas!' he said.

'Why didn't I listen to Fray[6] Gerónimo de la Trinidad, monk, preacher and confessor, the oracle of our family? He is the brother-in-law of the sister-in-law of the father-in-law of my mother-in-law, and therefore is the closest relative we have; so nothing is done in our family without his advice. I refused to follow his counsel, and now am being justly punished for it. He warned me that the officers of the Walloon Guards were all heretics, as can clearly be seen from their fair hair, blue eyes and pink cheeks; proper Christians have the complexion of Our Lady of Atocha as depicted by St Luke.'[7]

I put a stop to this torrent of impertinent remarks by ordering Lopez to give me my double-barrelled gun and to stay with the horses while I found some nearby outcrop from which to look for Mosquito, or at least signs of where he had gone. At this suggestion Lopez burst into tears and, throwing himself at my knees, begged me by all the saints not to leave him alone in a place so full of danger. I offered to look after the horses while he went to look for Mosquito, but he seemed even more terrified by this proposal. I gave him, however, so many good reasons for searching for Mosquito that he let me go. Then he took a rosary from his pocket and began to pray beside the trough.

The heights which I intended to climb were more distant than I had thought. It took me nearly an hour to reach them, and, when I got there, I saw nothing but a wild and desolate plain; there were no signs of men, animals or dwellings, no road apart from that by which I had come, and no other travellers in sight; nothing but a deep all-pervading silence which I broke with my shouts. Only the echoes of my own voice in the distance replied. At last I turned back and retraced my steps to the trough; there I found my horse tied to a tree, but Lopez had vanished.

Two courses of action were open to me: to return to Andújar or to continue on my journey. I did not even consider the former. I

6 Brother.

7 The church of Nuestra Señora de Atocha was a place of pilgrimage in Madrid.

8

jumped on my horse and, spurring it to a gallop, reached in two hours the banks of the Guadalquivir, which is not at this point in its course the calm river which flows majestically round the walls of the city of Seville, but rather, as it emerges from the mountains, a deep, powerful, roaring torrent, difficult of access, constantly thundering against the rocks which confine it.

The valley of Los Hermanos[8] begins where the Guadalquivir joins the plain. This valley is so called because three brothers, even more united by their taste for banditry than by their ties of blood, had for a long time made it the scene of their exploits. Two of the three brothers had been caught and their bodies could be seen hanging from the gallows at the entrance to the valley; Zoto, the eldest, had escaped from prison in Córdoba and was thought to have taken refuge in the Alpujarras mountains.

Very strange tales were told about the two brothers who had been hanged; they were not said to be ghosts, but it was claimed that at night nameless demons would possess their bodies, which would break free from the gallows and set out to torment the living. This was taken to be so well attested that a theologian from Salamanca had written a thesis proving that the two hanged brothers were species of vampire, and that the supposition that one of them should be a vampire was no less implausible than that the other should be so: an argument that even the most sceptical were forced to agree was sound. There was also a widespread rumour that the two brothers were innocent and that, having been unjustly executed, they took vengeance on travellers and other wayfarers with the consent of heaven. As I had heard these stories in Córdoba, curiosity prompted me to approach the gallows. The spectacle that met my eyes was made all the more revolting by the fact that the ghastly corpses were swung in eerie gyrations in the wind, while hideous vultures tore at their flesh. Horrified, I averted my gaze and hurried along the track leading to the mountains.

8 'The Brothers': Potocki gives one origin of the name in the text (Zoto's brothers), but the Inquisition ('la santa Hermandad', as it is referred to at the beginning of this chapter) is also known as 'los Hermanos'; their role in the story will become clear in due course.

The valley of Los Hermanos, it must be acknowledged, seemed very well suited to fostering the activities of bandits and affording them refuge. The way forward was barred here and there by large boulders which had fallen down the mountainside, and by trees uprooted by storms. The track frequently crossed river-beds or passed by the mouths of ominous-looking deep caves which put travellers on their guard.

I emerged from that valley and entered another in which I saw the *venta* which was to serve as my resting-place; but from the moment I caught sight of it in the distance, I was filled with foreboding. For, as I could see, it had no windows or shutters, no smoke was rising from the chimneys, there were no signs of life nearby and no dogs barking to mark my approach. I concluded from this that the inn was one of those which had been abandoned, as the innkeeper at Andújar had told me. It seemed to me that the closer I came to the *venta*, the deeper the silence grew. When finally I reached it, I saw an alms box on which the following words were inscribed: 'Good travellers, of your charity pray for the soul of Gonzalez of Murcia, sometime innkeeper of the Venta Quemada. I entreat you above all else to continue on your way and not to spend the night here, for any reason.'

I decided at once to face the dangers with which the inscription threatened me. It was not that I did not believe in ghosts, but, as will subsequently become clear, honour had been the focal point of my whole upbringing, and I took honour to mean that one should never show any signs of fear.

As the sun had only just set, I wanted to take advantage of the fading light to explore all the hidden recesses of the building, less to reassure myself about any infernal powers which might have seized possession of it than to look for food, for the little I had eaten at Los Alcornoques had dulled but not satisfied the great hunger which I then felt. I passed through many rooms and apartments. Most were decorated with mosaic up to the height of a man; the ceilings were fashioned in that beautiful panelling which is the splendour of Moorish buildings. I searched the kitchens, store-rooms and cellars, which were hewn out of the solid rock. Some were connected to underground passages which appeared to lead far into the mountain. But nowhere did I come across any food.

Eventually, as the last light was fading from the sky, I went to fetch my horse, which I had tethered in the courtyard, and led it to a stable in which I had seen some hay. I myself settled down in the room in which was the only pallet bed left in the whole inn. I would very much have liked to have had a light, but the one good thing about the hunger which still tormented me was that it prevented me sleeping.

None the less, as the night grew darker, my thoughts grew also more sombre. For some of the time my mind was occupied by the disappearance of my two servants; at other moments by thoughts of how I might obtain food. I formed the opinion that robbers had jumped out from behind some bushes or had emerged from some underground hiding-place and had taken Mosquito and Lopez captive one after the other; I had only been spared, I thought, because my military uniform had suggested that I might not have been so easily overpowered. My hunger preoccupied me more than all the rest of my thoughts. I had noticed some goats on the mountainside; they must be tended by a goatherd who would no doubt have a small amount of bread to eat with his milk. I was also counting somewhat on my gun. But the one thing I was not prepared to do was to turn back and face the mockery of the innkeeper of Andújar. On the contrary, I was resolutely set on continuing my journey.

Having exhausted all my thoughts on such matters, I could not stop myself going over in my mind the well-known tale of the counterfeiters and others of the same kind which I had been told at bedtime when I was a child. I also thought about the inscription on the alms box. I did not believe that the devil had wrung the neck of the innkeeper, but I could not make any sense of his tragic end.

Hours went by in this way in deep silence, when suddenly the unexpected chiming of a bell made me start up with surprise. It tolled twelve, and as everyone knows, ghosts are only active from midnight to cock crow. I say that I started up with surprise; I had good reason to, for the bell had not tolled the other hours, and as well as that, it seemed to me that there was something lugubrious about its tolling.

A moment later the bedroom door opened and I saw a totally black figure come in; not a frightening apparition, however, but a beautiful, half-naked negress holding a torch in each hand.

She came up to me, bowed low and said in very good Spanish, 'Señor caballero, you are invited to partake in the supper of two foreign ladies who are spending the night at this hostelry. Please be so good as to follow me.'

I followed the negress along corridor after corridor until we reached a well-lit room in the middle of which stood a table laden with oriental bowls and carafes made of rock crystal, with three places set. At the end of the room was a magnificent bed. Many negresses were there, all eager to be of service; I saw them fall back respectfully as two ladies came in, whose pink-and-white complexions formed a perfect contrast with the ebony hue of their maidservants. They were holding each other by the hand. Both were dressed in a strange manner: strange, that is, as it then seemed to me, but in fact the style of their dress is common to several towns on the Barbary coast, as I have since discovered on my travels. Their attire was as follows: it consisted of a shift and a bodice. The shift was made of linen above the waist, but of Meknes gauze below it; such a gauze as would be wholly transparent if broad silk ribbons woven into its fabric had not caused it to veil those feminine charms which are best imagined and not seen. The sleeveless bodice, richly embroidered with pearls and adorned with diamond clasps, moulded itself closely to the bosom. The gauze sleeves of the shift were lifted back and fastened in a knot behind the neck. On their bare arms the ladies wore bracelets, both at the wrist and above the elbow. Had they been she-devils, their feet would have been cloven or armed with talons; they were not at all like that, but bare, and encased in small em-broidered slippers. Their legs were adorned with anklets studded with large diamonds.

The two strangers approached me with an easy and sociable air. They were perfect beauties; one was tall, slim, dazzling; the other tender and shy. The elder was statuesque; she had a fine figure, with fine features to match. The younger of the two was well-rounded, with slightly pouting lips and half-closed eyelids, revealing but a small part of the pupils through extraordinarily long lashes.

The elder addressed me in Castilian: 'Señor caballero, we are grateful for the kindness you have shown in accepting our invitation to share this light repast. If I am not mistaken, you must be in need of it.'

She said these last words in such a mischievous way that I almost suspected her of having contrived the abduction of my pack animal; but the proffered meal was such a good substitute for my provisions that I could not find it in my heart to be angry with her.

We sat down to table; the same lady moved an oriental bowl towards me and said, 'Señor caballero, you will find in here an *olla podrida*[9] containing all sorts of meat with one exception, for we are of the number of the faithful, that is to say, we are Muslims.'

'Fair stranger,' I replied, 'I think you have spoken the truth; you are indeed of the number of the faithful, but of those who profess the religion of love. Please satisfy my curiosity before my hunger, and tell me who you are.'

'Please eat, Señor caballero,' said the Moorish beauty. 'We will not conceal our identity from you. I am Emina and this is my sister Zubeida; we come from Tunis, but our family is originally from Granada, and some of our relatives have stayed behind in Spain, where they continue to profess in secret the religion of their fathers. We left Tunis a week ago; we came ashore near Málaga on a deserted beach. We travelled up into the mountains between Loja and Antequera and have since come to this isolated spot to change our attire and to take such precautions as are necessary for our safety. As you can see, Señor caballero, the fact that we have journeyed here is an important secret which we have disclosed to you; we rely upon your discretion.'

I assured the two ladies that they had no indiscretion to fear on my part, and began to eat, somewhat greedily, it is true, but with the restraint and good manners which befit a young gentleman finding himself alone in the company of women.

When it was clear that the edge of my hunger had been blunted and that I had turned my attention to what in Spain are called *los dulces*,[10] Emina told the negresses to perform for me the dance of their country. There could have been no command more agreeable to them; they obeyed with an abandon which approached licentiousness. I

9 Stew.
10 Sweetmeats.

13

even believe that it would have been difficult to bring their dance to an end if I had not asked their beautiful mistresses whether they also did not occasionally dance. They did not reply to my question, but rose up and asked for castanets. The steps they danced resembled the Murcia *bolera* and the *fofa* as it is performed in the Algarve. I say this to give people from those places an idea of their dance; but even then they will not be able to picture the charm which the grace and beauty of the two African strangers, enhanced as it was by their diaphanous garments, added to their movements.

I watched them for some time almost dispassionately; but their movements became more rapid and insistent, and everything both in me and around me – the hypnotic effect of the Moorish music, my heightened senses inflamed by the unexpected repast – conspired to befuddle my mind. I no longer knew whether I was in the company of women or of seductive succubi. I neither dared nor desired to watch them; I covered my eyes with my hands, and felt overcome by dizziness.

The two sisters came over to me; each took one of my hands. Emina asked me whether I felt unwell. I assured her that I did not. Zubeida then asked me what the medallion was she saw on my chest and whether it was a portrait of my beloved.

'It is a locket,' I replied, 'which was given to me by my mother, and which I have promised always to wear; it contains a fragment of the true cross.'

I saw Zubeida recoil and grow pale as I uttered these words.

'You are upset,' I said to her, 'but the true cross only inspires dread in the spirit of darkness.'

Emina replied on her sister's behalf and said, 'Señor caballero, we are Muslims, as you know; you must not be surprised that my sister was visibly distressed. I am also troubled; we are both extremely displeased to discover that you, our closest relative, are a Christian. I see that my words have amazed you; but was not your mother a Gomelez? We are members of the same family, which itself is but one branch of the Abencerrages. But let us sit down on the sofa, and I will tell you more.'

The negresses withdrew. Emina had me sit on one end of the sofa, and sat down next to me, her legs folded under her. Zubeida sat on my other side, leaning on my cushion. We were so close to each other that their breath mingled with mine.

For a moment Emina seemed lost in thought; then she looked at me with great attention, took my hand and said, 'Dear Alphonse, there is no point in hiding from you that it was not chance which brought us here. We have been waiting for you; and if fear had made you choose another route, you would have lost our esteem for ever.'

'You flatter me, Emina,' I retorted. 'What possible interest could you have in whether I am courageous or not?'

'We take a deep interest in you,' the Moorish beauty replied. 'But you may well be less flattered when you learn that you are practically the first man we have ever met. What I have just said has astonished you, and you seem to doubt it. I promised to tell you the story of our ancestors; perhaps it would be better if I began with our own.'

THE STORY OF EMINA AND HER SISTER
∽ ZUBEIDA ∽

We are the daughters of Gasir Gomelez, the maternal uncle of the reigning Dey of Tunis; we have no brothers, we did not know our father and have been kept confined within the walls of the harem, so that we have no idea of what men are like. However, we were both born with an extremely affectionate nature and have always loved each other passionately. This attachment began in our infancy. We would cry if people tried to separate us, even for the shortest of times; if one of us was scolded, the other would burst into tears. We would spend whole days playing at the same table, and we slept in the same bed.

This strong attachment seemed to grow as we did; it was strengthened by an incident which I shall tell you about. I was then sixteen, and my sister was fourteen years old. For a long time we had been aware that there were books which my mother carefully hid from us. At first we paid little attention to them, being profoundly bored by the ones used to teach us to read; but as we grew older, we became curious. On the first occasion when the forbidden cupboard was left open, we seized our opportunity and removed a small book which turned out to be *The Loves of Madjnoun and Leïla*,[11] translated from the Persian by ben Omri. This sublime work, which describes in ardent terms the joys of love, inflamed our young imaginations. We were not able to understand it perfectly, because we had never encountered members of your sex, but we tried out on each other its expressions. We learned to speak the language of these lovers, and resolved eventually to court each other in the way they did. I played the part of Madjnoun, and my sister took that of Leïla. First, I declared my passion for her by arranging flowers in a certain way; this is a sort of secret code much used throughout Asia. Then I made my glances eloquent, I prostrated myself before her, I kissed the ground where her feet had trod, I begged the gentle breezes to carry to her my amorous complaint; I even thought that I could set them alight with the ardour of my sighs.

Zubeida faithfully followed the lessons of the author and allowed me to meet her. I threw myself down before her, kissed her hands, and bathed her feet with my tears; my mistress began by resisting gently, then allowed me to steal some favours and finally abandoned herself altogether to my eager passion. Our souls seemed really to melt one into the other and even now I do not know what could make us happier than we were then.

I can't remember for how long we enjoyed these passionate interludes, but in the end we allowed calmer sentiments to take their place. We acquired a taste for study, especially for the study of plants, which we pursued in the writings of the celebrated Averroës.

My mother, who believed that one couldn't do too much to ward off the tedium of harem life, saw with pleasure that we had acquired a taste for occupying ourselves. She summoned from Mecca a saintly person whose very name, Hazareta, meant 'most holy'. Hazareta taught us the law of the prophet in that pure and harmonious language which the tribe of Koraish[12] speak. We could never grow tired of listening to her, and we learned by heart almost all the Koran. Then my mother taught us herself about the history of our family,

---

11 A novel by the Persian writer Nizami, written in the late twelfth century.
12 The tribe of Muhammad.

16

and placed in our hands a great number of memoirs, some in Arabic, some in Spanish. How odious your law seemed to us, dear Alphonse! How we hated your priests and their persecutions! And how strongly we sympathized on the other hand with their many illustrious victims whose blood flowed in our veins!

Sometimes our hearts went out to Said Gomelez, who suffered martyrdom in the prisons of the Inquisition, sometimes to his nephew Leiss, who for a long time lived a primitive life in the mountains which was scarcely different from that of a wild animal. Such persons predisposed us to love men; we would have loved to meet some, and we would often climb up to our terrace to gaze from afar at those embarking on the lake of La Goulette, or those on their way to the baths at Hammam Nef. And if we hadn't altogether forgotten the teachings of Madjnoun the lover, at least we did not rehearse them to each other any more. It even seemed to me that my love for my sister no longer had the character of a passion, but a fresh incident proved to me that I was wrong.

One day my mother introduced an older lady to us who was a princess from Tafilet. We received her as best we could. After she had left, my mother told me that she had asked for my hand for her son, and that my sister would marry a member of the Gomelez family. We were thunderstruck by this news, and our shock caused us to lose the power of speech. Then the misery of living apart from each other impressed itself with such force on our minds that we gave way to the most terrible despair. We tore out our hair, and filled the harem with the sound of our sobbing. Eventually these demonstrations of our distress became so extreme that my mother was alarmed by them and promised not to force us to do something contrary to our desires. She assured us that we could either remain unmarried or both marry the same man. These assurances brought us a measure of calm.

Some time later, my mother came to tell us that she had spoken to the head of our family, who had given his approval that we should marry the same husband, provided that he was of the Gomelez blood.

We did not respond to this at once, but as the days went by, we grew more and more attracted to the idea of having the same husband. We had never seen a man, whether old or young, except from far off, but as young women seemed to us more pleasant than

17

old women, we decided that we would like a young husband. We hoped also that he would explain to us some passages of ben Omri's book whose meaning was not clear to us . . .

At this Zubeida interrupted her sister, and, clasping me in her arms, said, 'Dear Alphonse, what a pity it is that you are not a Muslim! What a pleasure it would be for me to see you in the arms of Emina, to add to your raptures, to join in with your embraces! For, dear Alphonse, in our family as in that of the prophet, the maternal line has the same rights as the paternal one. You could perhaps become the head of our family, which is dying out, if you decided to. All you would have to do is to acknowledge the holy truths of our law.'

This seemed so much like a temptation of Satan himself that I almost believed that I could see horns sprouting out of Zubeida's pretty forehead. I stammered out a few religious phrases. The two sisters drew back a little.

Emina then assumed a serious expression and spoke again. 'Señor Alphonse, I have talked too much about my sister and myself, which was not my intention. I only set out to tell you the history of the Gomelez family, from which you are descended in the female line. This, then, is what I had to tell you:

THE STORY OF THE CASTLE OF
৩ CASSAR GOMELEZ ৩

The forefather of our race was Massoud ben Taher, brother of Youssuf ben Taher, who invaded Spain at the head of the Arabs and gave his name to the mountain of Gebat Taher, which you call Gibraltar. Massoud, who had contributed much to their military success, obtained from the Caliph of Baghdad[13] the governorship of Granada, where he stayed until his brother's death. He would have stayed there longer for he was much loved both by Muslims and

13 The Caliph of Baghdad was the head of the Shi'ite sect (those who, *inter alia*, recognize only the descendants of Ali, the cousin of Muhammad and husband of his daughter Fatima, as the rightful leaders of Islam).

Mosarabs, that is, Christians still living under Arab rule, alike. But Massoud had enemies in Baghdad who turned the caliph against him. Knowing he was doomed, he decided to leave. Massoud gathered his own men together and retreated to the Alpujarras mountains, which are, as you know, a continuation of the Sierra Morena range, which separates the kingdoms of Granada and Valencia.

The Visigoths from whom we conquered Spain had never ventured into the Alpujarras. Most of the valleys were unpopulated. Only three were inhabited by the descendants of an ancient Spanish race called the Turdules. They did not recognize either Muhammad or your Nazarene prophet. Their religious beliefs and law were contained in songs and were passed down from parents to children. They once had sacred books, but they had been lost.

Massoud won over the Turdules more by persuasion than by force. He learned their language and taught them the holy law of Islam. The two races intermarried and became mixed. We owe our high colouring, which is the distinguishing mark of daughters of the Gomelez family, to this mixture as much as to the bracing mountain air. Many Moorish women are also fair-skinned but they are always pale of complexion.

Massoud took the title of sheikh and built a castle stronghold, which he called Cassar Gomelez. He made it his duty to be always accessible to his tribe, to whom he was more a judge than a ruler. But on the last Friday of every month he took leave of his family and shut himself up in an underground part of the castle where he stayed immured until the following Friday. These absences gave rise to much speculation. Some said that their sheikh was conversing with the twelfth imam, who we believe will reappear at the end of time.[14] Others believed that the Antichrist was kept chained in the cellars of the castle. Yet others thought that the seven sleepers of Ephesus were resting there with their dog, Caleb.[15] Massoud took no notice of these

14 According to Shi'ite belief, the 'twelfth imam' will reappear at the end of time and inaugurate the age of peace and justice.

15 According to legend, seven young Ephesians hid in a cave in 251 CE to avoid religious persecution, taking their dog with them. They fell asleep and reawoke several centuries later.

rumours but continued to govern his little people for as long as his strength permitted. At length he chose the most prudent man of the tribe and named him successor. He gave him the keys to the underground part of the castle and retired to a hermitage, where he lived on for many years.

The new sheikh ruled in the same way as his predecessor and absented himself in the same way on the last Friday of every month. Everything went on on the same footing until the time when Córdoba obtained its own sheikhs, who were no longer subject to those in Baghdad. Then the mountain people of the Alpujarras who had played their part in this revolution began to settle in the plains, where they came to be known as the Abencerrages, while those who remained attached to the Sheikh of Cassar Gomelez kept the name of Gomelez.

The Abencerrages in the meanwhile purchased the best land in the kingdom of Granada and the best houses in the town. Their riches attracted public attention. There was speculation that the underground domains of the sheikh contained immense treasures, but it was not possible to establish this as the Abencerrages did not know themselves what the source of their wealth was.

Eventually, these fine kingdoms called down on themselves the vengeance of heaven and fell into the hands of the infidels. Granada was captured and a week later the illustrious Gonzalo de Córdoba entered the Alpujarras at the head of three thousand of his men.[16] Hatem Gomelez was then our sheikh. He went out to meet Gonzalo and presented him with the keys of his castle. The Spaniard asked for those which gave access to the underground parts. The sheikh gave them to him without demur. Gonzalo decided to go down into them himself but he found only a tomb and some books there. He poured public scorn on the stories he had been told about them and returned to Valladolid, attracted by the prospect of gallantry and amorous intrigues.

Peace then reigned in our mountains until Charles V came to the throne.[17] At that time our sheikh was Sefi Gomelez, who for reasons

16 Granada fell in 1492 to Gonzalo of Córdoba (1453–1515).
17 In 1516.

which have never been well understood sent word to the new emperor that he would reveal to him an important secret if he were to dispatch to him a trustworthy nobleman. Within fifteen days Don Ruiz de Toledo presented himself to the Gomelez in His Majesty's name, only to discover the sheikh had been murdered the day before. Don Ruiz pursued some individuals, but soon became tired of this and returned to court.

Meanwhile the secret of the sheikhs remained with Sefi's murderer, whose name was Billah Gomelez. He called together the elders of the tribe and proved to them that such an important secret required new precautions to be taken to safeguard it. It was decided that a number of the Gomelez family would be told of it but that each one would only be initiated into part of the secret and then only after having given ample proof of his courage, prudence and loyalty.

Here Zubeida interrupted her sister again and said, 'Dear Emina, don't you think Alphonse would have been equal to all these ordeals? Who could doubt it? Oh Alphonse, why aren't you a Muslim! Immense wealth might be in your hands!'

This sounded just like the work of the spirit of darkness. Having failed to make me succumb to the temptation of lechery, now it was trying to make me succumb to the lure of gold. Yet as these two beautiful creatures pressed closer to me it seemed to me that I was touching not spirits but flesh and blood.

After a moment of silence Emina took up her story again.

'You will know well enough, dear Alphonse,' she continued, 'what persecutions we suffered during the reign of Philip, son of Charles V.[18] Children were carried off and brought up as Christians. They were given the possessions of their parents who had remained faithful to the prophet. It was during this time that a Gomelez was received into the *takiat*[19] of the dervishes of St Dominic and rose to the rank of Grand Inquisitor.'

At that moment we heard a cock crow, and Emina stopped

18 Philip II reigned from 1556 to 1598.
19 Monastery.

talking. The cock crowed a second time and a superstitious man might have expected the two beautiful girls to fly away up the chimney. This they did not do; but they none the less looked absent and preoccupied.

Emina was the first to break the silence.

'Dear Alphonse,' she said to me, 'the day is about to dawn and the time we are able to spend together is too precious to be passed in telling stories. We can only become your wives if you embrace our religion. But you can consort with us in your dreams. Would you consent to this?'

I consented to everything.

'But we need more than your consent,' continued Emina with great solemnity. 'You must swear by the sacred laws of honour never to betray our names, our existence or anything you know about us. Are you bold enough to dare to take this solemn pledge?'

I promised all they asked.

'Enough,' said Emina. 'Bring the sacred cup of Massoud, our forefather, here.'

While Zubeida went to fetch the magic receptacle, Emina had prostrated herself and was reciting prayers in Arabic. Zubeida reappeared bearing a cup which seemed to me to have been fashioned from a single emerald. She moistened her lips in it as did Emina, and then ordered me to drain the cup at a single draught.

I did as she asked.

Emina thanked me for my compliance and embraced me tenderly.

Then Zubeida pressed her lips to mine in a seemingly unending kiss. At last they left me, telling me that I would soon see them again; and they advised me to fall asleep as soon as possible.

So many strange incidents and fantastic stories and such unexpected emotions would normally perhaps have led me to reflect upon them all night, but I confess that I was most interested in the dreams I had been promised. I undressed in haste and lay down on the bed which had been prepared for me. Once there, I noted with pleasure that my bed was very wide – wide enough, indeed, to accommodate more than just dreams. But I had scarcely had time to note this before my eyelids were closed by an irresistible drowsiness and the fantasies of the night overtook my senses. I was under the magic power of wayward fancies and my thoughts, transported on the wings of desire, carried me into the midst of African harems, where I contemplated the charms of those confined within their walls, rapturously enjoying them again and again in my imagination. I felt as though I was dreaming, but I was aware at the same time that it was not the creatures of dreams that I was embracing. I revelled in vague and wanton fancies, never leaving the company of my beautiful cousins. I fell asleep on their breasts and awoke again in their arms.

I do not know how often I passed from one sweet illusion to the other . . .

The Second Day

When at length I awoke, the sun was burning my eyelids. I could scarcely open them. I saw the sky and I saw I was in the open air. But my eyes were still heavy with sleep. I was not really asleep but neither was I properly awake. Images of torture flashed through my mind one after the other. Terror took hold of me. I rose with a start and sat up.

How can I express in words the horror which filled me then? I was lying below the gibbet of Los Hermanos. The corpses of Zoto's two brothers were not hanging from it but were lying on either side of me. I had apparently spent the night with them. I was lying on pieces of rope, fragments of wheels and human remains and the revolting rags which had fallen from them as they had rotted.

I thought that I was not fully awake and prey still to unpleasant dreams. I closed my eyes and tried to remember where I had been the night before. It was then that I felt claws sink into my side and saw a vulture had perched on me and was devouring one of my bedfellows. The pain caused by its talons as they dug into me woke me up altogether. I saw my clothes to hand and hastily put them on. Once dressed, I resolved to leave the gallows enclosure but found the door nailed fast and tried in vain to break it down. I was forced to scale its gloomy walls. I reached the top and, leaning on one of the uprights of the gallows, surveyed the surrounding countryside. I easily recognized where I was. I was indeed at the entrance of the valley of Los Hermanos and not far from the banks of the Guadalquivir.

As I watched, I caught sight of two travellers near the river, one preparing a repast, the other holding two horses by their bridles. I was so overjoyed to see my fellow man that my first impulse was to shout

24

at them 'Agour! Agour!', which in Spanish means 'Good-day' or 'Greetings'.[1]

On seeing themselves greeted thus from the top of a gallows, the two travellers seemed for an instant undecided what to do. They then suddenly jumped on their horses and urged them into a full gallop, taking the road to Los Alcornoques.

I shouted to them to stop but to no avail. The more I shouted the more they spurred their horses on. When they were lost to sight, I thought about leaving my eerie vantage point. I jumped down and in jumping down did myself a small injury.

Limping badly, I reached the banks of the Guadalquivir and found there the meal abandoned by the two travellers. Nothing could have been more welcome to me for I felt exhausted. There was chocolate still cooking, with *esponajas*[2] steeped in Alicante wine, bread and eggs. The first thing I did was to recover my strength. Then I thought about what had happened to me the previous night. My recollections were confused but I remembered with great clarity that I had given my word of honour to keep what had happened a secret, and I was firmly determined to do so. Once I had resolved this it only remained to decide what I should do at that instant; that is to say, which way I ought to go. And it seemed to me that I was more than ever honour bound to go by way of the Sierra Morena.

It may come as a surprise that I was so much preoccupied with my reputation and so little with the events of the previous evening. But my manner of thinking was a consequence of the education which I had received, as will become clear in the course of my story. For the moment I shall return to that of my journey.

I was very eager to find out what those devils of the previous evening had done with my horse, which I had left at the Venta Quemada. As the inn was on my way, I decided to pass by. I had to walk the full length of the valley of Los Hermanos and that of the

---

1 This word, which is not Spanish, seems to have been an invention of Potocki's.

2 Sponge cakes.

venta itself, which duly tired me out and made me dearly hope to find my horse again, as indeed happened. It was in the same stable where I had left it and seemed frisky, in good shape and recently groomed. I had no idea who could have looked after the animal, but I had seen so many extraordinary things that this did not preoccupy me for long. I should have set out immediately on my journey if I had not been curious to search the inn one more time. I found the room in which I had slept, but however much I looked I could not find the one in which I had seen the two beautiful African girls. I grew tired of the search after a while, mounted my horse and continued on my journey.

When I had awoken beneath the gallows of Los Hermanos, the sun had already run half its course. I had then taken over two hours to reach the *venta*, so that after I had ridden for about two leagues, I had to turn my mind to finding shelter for the night. None was in sight, so I rode on. At last I saw a Gothic chapel in the distance, together with a cabin which looked like the dwelling of a hermit. Both were far from the road, but I turned unhesitatingly from my path as I was beginning to feel hungry and wanted to obtain food. I knocked at the door of the hermitage and a monk with a most venerable face emerged. He embraced me in a warm paternal way and said:

'Come in, my son. Do not linger! Do not spend the night outside! Beware of the tempter! The Lord has withdrawn his protection from us.'

I thanked the hermit for the kindness he had shown me and said that I was sorely pressed by hunger.

'Think rather of your soul, my son. Go into the chapel. Prostrate yourself before the cross. I shall take care of the needs of your body. It will only be a frugal meal, such as you might expect of a hermit.'

I went into the chapel and did indeed pray, for I was no free-thinker and did not even know then of their existence. This again was an effect of the way I had been brought up.

The hermit came to fetch me after about a quarter of an hour and led me to the cabin, where I found the table already laid in a wholesome if simple way. There were excellent olives, chards pickled in vinegar, sweet onions in sauce and biscuits instead of bread. There was even a small bottle of wine. The hermit assured me that he never drank any but only kept it for the celebration of Mass. So I did not drink any more wine than did the hermit, although I greatly enjoyed the rest of my supper. As I was doing justice to it I saw a person of yet more terrifying aspect than any I had seen up to then come to the cabin. It was a man still young-looking but hideously emaciated. His hair stood on end and from the socket of his missing eye blood was oozing. A slobbery froth dribbled from his tongue, which hung out of his mouth. He was dressed in a respectable black habit but this was all he wore, having neither shirt nor hose.

This horrendous apparition did not address either of us but squatted in a corner, where he remained without moving as though he was a statue, his eye fixed on a crucifix which he held in his hand. When I had finished eating, I asked the hermit who this man was.

'My son,' he replied. 'He is possessed of a devil whom I am exorcizing. His terrible story proves the dread tyranny that the angel of darkness exercises over this unfortunate land. His story may help you to win your salvation and I shall command him to tell it to you.'

Then turning to the possessed man he said, 'Pacheco, Pacheco, in the name of your Redeemer, I command you to tell your story.'

Pacheco uttered a terrible cry and began as follows:

ᴥ THE STORY OF PACHECO THE DEMONIAC ᴥ

I was born in Córdoba, where my father lived a more than comfortable existence. Three years ago my mother died. At first my father seemed to mourn greatly for her but, after several months, having occasion to travel to Seville, he fell in love with a young widow whose name was Camilla de Tormes. She did not enjoy a very good reputation and some of my father's friends tried to keep him from her company, but in spite of their assiduous efforts my father married her two years after the death of my mother. The wedding took place in Seville and a few days later my father returned to Córdoba with Camilla, his new wife, and one of her sisters, called Inesilla.

My new stepmother lived up to her bad reputation in every way and began by trying to make me fall in love with her, in which she did not succeed. But I did fall in love, not with her but with her sister Inesilla. Soon my passion grew so strong that I went to see my father, threw myself at his feet and asked for the hand of his sister-in-law in marriage.

My father gently raised me to my feet and said, 'My son, I forbid you to think of such a match, for three reasons. First, it would be undignified for you to become in a sort of way the brother-in-law of your father. Second, the sacred canons of the Church do not give their blessing to such unions. Third, I do not wish you to marry Inesilla.'

Having informed me of these three reasons, my father turned his back on me and went away.

I retired to my bedchamber, where I succumbed to despair. My father had at once told my stepmother what had happened. She came to see me and told me that I was wrong to be so upset; if I could not become the husband of Inesilla then at least I could become her *cortejo*, that is, her lover, and that she would arrange this for me. But at the same time she declared her own love for me and stressed the sacrifice she was making in surrendering me to her sister. I was only too ready to listen to what she said, for it flattered my own desires. But Inesilla was so modest that it seemed to me impossible to bring her ever to return my love.

At about that time my father decided to travel to Madrid to solicit the position of *corregidor*[3] of Córdoba, and took his wife and sister-in-law with him. His absence was only to last two months but the time seemed interminable to me, because I was separated from Inesilla.

After about two months I received a letter from my father, telling me to come to meet him and to wait for him at the Venta Quemada in the foothills of the Sierra Morena. Some weeks before I would not readily have taken the decision to travel through the Sierra Morena, but Zoto's two brothers had just been hanged. His band had been dispersed and the roads were said to be reasonably safe.

So I set out from Córdoba just before ten in the morning and reached Andújar, where I stayed the night with one of the most talkative innkeepers in Andalusia. I ordered a large supper at his inn, of which I ate part and kept what remained for the rest of the journey.

The next day I had a midday meal at Los Alcornoques, consisting

---

3 Senior official of the Crown, with judicial and administrative functions.

of what I had kept from the night before, and arrived that same evening at the Venta Quemada. I did not find my father there, but as he had told me in his letter to wait for him, I decided to do so, all the more willingly because I found myself in a spacious and comfortable hostelry. The innkeeper at that time was a certain Gonzalez de Murcia, a decent sort of fellow even if given to boasting. He duly promised me a supper worthy of a Spanish grandee. As he set about preparing it I went for a walk along the banks of the Guadalquivir, and on returning to the hostelry I found the supper laid out. And indeed it was not at all bad.

After eating I told Gonzalez to make up my bed. I saw at once that I had upset him. What he said to me in reply did not make much sense. In the end he confessed to me that the inn was haunted by ghosts and that he and his family slept in a little farmhouse on the banks of the river, adding that if I should care to sleep there also he would make up a bed for me next to his own.

What he proposed seemed unsuitable to me and I told him that he could go and sleep where he wished, but that he should send my servants to me. Gonzalez obeyed me and went off shaking his head and shrugging his shoulders.

My servants arrived a moment later. They had also heard talk of ghosts and tried to persuade me to spend the night at the farmhouse. I dismissed their advice somewhat curtly and ordered them to make up my bed in the same room in which I had eaten my supper. They obeyed me, albeit unwillingly, and when the bed had been made up pleaded with me again with tears in their eyes to come with them to sleep at the farmhouse. On this occasion their remonstrations made me really impatient and I allowed myself to show it in a way which made them all flee. As it was not a habit of mine to be undressed by my servants, I was able easily to do without them and to get ready for bed. They for their part had been more attentive to my needs than my treatment of them deserved, and had left next to my bed a lighted candle with another in reserve, a pair of pistols and some books to keep me awake. But the truth of the matter was that I lost all desire for sleep.

I spent two hours reading, tossing and turning in my bed. Eventually I heard the sound of a bell or a clock strike midnight. This surprised me for I had not heard it strike the other hours. Soon after, the door opened and, as I watched, my stepmother came in, wearing night garments and bearing a candlestick. She tiptoed up to me, a finger on her lips as if to ensure that I remained silent. Placing the candlestick on my bedside table, she sat down on my bed, took one of my hands in her own and spoke to me as follows:

'Dear Pacheco, the moment has come when I can give you the pleasures which I promised you. We reached the inn an hour ago. Your father has gone to sleep at the farm, but on learning that you were here I have obtained his permission to sleep here with my sister Inesilla. She is waiting for you and is disposed to refuse you nothing, but you must first know the conditions I have placed on your happiness. You love Inesilla and I love you. Of the three of us, two must not be happy at the expense of the third. I intend therefore that we should all share one bed tonight. Come.'

My stepmother did not give me time to reply. She took me by the hand and led me through one corridor after another, until we at last arrived at a door where she bent down to look through the keyhole.

Having looked for long enough she said, 'All is well, see for yourself.'

I took her place at the keyhole, and indeed I saw the charming Inesilla in her bed. But she was far from the modest girl I had known. Everything – the expression in her eyes, her heaving bosom, her heightened complexion, her posture – indicated to me that she was expecting a lover.

Having let me watch for some time, Camilla said to me, 'Pacheco, stay here at this door. When it is time for you to come in I shall come and get you.'

After she had entered I put my eye to the keyhole again and saw many things which I find it difficult here to relate. First Camilla undressed in more or less the usual way and, getting into bed with her sister, she said to her:

'My poor Inesilla, do you really want a lover? My poor child, you have no idea of the pain that he will cause you. He will first throw you down, then press himself upon you, and crush you, and tear you apart.'

When Camilla thought that her pupil had received enough instruc-

30

tion, she opened the door to me and led me to the bed where her sister was lying, and lay down beside us.

What can I tell you about that fateful night? I drank the cup of criminal passion to the last drop. I long fought against my natural desire for sleep in order to prolong my sinful pleasures. I fell asleep at last and awoke the next day under the gallows of Zoto's brothers, lying between their foul corpses.

The hermit interrupted the demoniac to say to me, 'Well, my son, what do you think of that? You would have been terrified, I think, to find yourself lying between two hanged men.'

I replied: 'You have offended me, Father. A gentleman must never feel fear, let alone a gentleman who has the honour of being a captain in the Walloon Guards.'

'But have you ever heard, my son, of a similar adventure befalling anyone?' continued the hermit.

I hesitated a moment before replying. 'If this adventure befell Señor Pacheco, father, it could have befallen others. I will be better placed to pass judgement if you would kindly command him to carry on with his story.'

The hermit turned to the possessed man and said to him, 'Pacheco, Pacheco, in the name of your Redeemer, I command you to continue your story.'

Pacheco uttered a ghastly howl and continued as follows:

I was half-dead when I left the gallows. I dragged myself along without knowing where I was going. In the end I met some travellers who took pity on me and brought me back to the Venta Quemada. There I found the innkeeper and my servants, who were deeply worried about me. I asked them whether my father had slept at the farm. They told me that no one had come there.

I was unable to bring myself to stay longer at the *venta* and took the road back to Andújar, where I arrived after sunset. The inn was full, so a bed was made up for me in the kitchen, where I lay down; but I was unable to sleep for I could not banish from my mind the horrors of the previous night.

I had left the candle lit in the chimney of the kitchen. Suddenly it

31

went out and I felt immediately something like a mortal shiver, which froze my blood.

There was a tug at my blanket and I heard a little voice say, 'I am Camilla, your stepmother. I am cold, dear heart. Let me join you under your blanket.'

Then another little voice said, 'I am Inesilla. Let me come into your bed, for I am cold, so cold.'

Then I felt an icy hand grasp me under the chin. I drew together all of my strength and said aloud, 'Get thee behind me, Satan.'

Then the little voices said, 'Why are you driving us away? Are you not our dear little husband? We are cold and we are going to light a little fire.'

And indeed a moment later I saw a flame appear in the kitchen hearth. It gradually grew brighter and I was able to make out not Inesilla and Camilla but Zoto's two brothers hanging in the fireplace.

These apparitions drove me out of my mind. I sprang from my bed, jumped through the window and began to rush about in the open country. For a moment I flattered myself with the hope that I had outrun all these horrors, but then I turned round, only to see that the two hanged men were pursuing me. I broke into a run again and soon saw that I had left Zoto's brothers behind. But my joy was short-lived. Those foul creatures began to cartwheel towards me and were on me in a flash. I went on running, but in the end all my strength deserted me.

Then I felt one of the hanged men seize my left ankle. I tried to shake myself free but the other one cut off my escape. He loomed up in front of me, staring at me with terrible eyes and poking out his tongue, which was as red as iron straight from the furnace. I pleaded for mercy but in vain. With one hand he grasped me by the throat, and with the other he tore out my eye, the one that I am now missing. He darted his burning tongue into my eye-socket and licked my brains, which made me bellow with pain.

Then the other one, who had grasped my left leg, decided to use his claws. First he tickled the sole of the foot he was holding, then that monster tore off my skin, separated out all the sinews, laid them bare and tried to play a tune on them as though on a musical instrument. But as my sinews did not give out a sound which pleased

32

him, he stuck his claw into my calf, pinched the tendons and began to twist them round as one does in order to tune a harp. Eventually he began to play on my leg, which he had turned into a sort of psaltery. I could hear his diabolical laughter. As the pain made me groan horribly the screams of hell chanted in chorus. And as I listened to the wails of the damned it seemed to me that every fibre in my body was being crushed in their teeth. Eventually I lost consciousness.

The next day a herdsman found me in open countryside and brought me to this hermitage, where I confessed my sins and where I have found some relief from my suffering at the foot of the cross.

At this point the demoniac uttered a ghastly howl and fell silent.

Then the hermit spoke and said to me: 'Young man, you see the power of Satan. Pray and weep. But it is getting late. We must each go his own way. I do not suggest that you should sleep in my cell, for Pacheco's screams during the night might disturb you. Go and sleep in the chapel. There you will be under the protection of the cross, which triumphs over demons.'

I replied to the hermit that I would sleep where he wanted me to. We carried a little camp bed to the chapel, where I lay down. The hermit wished me good-night.

Once alone, Pacheco's story came back to my mind. In it I found much in common with my own adventures and was still thinking about them when I heard midnight strike. I did not know whether it was the hermit striking midnight or whether I was dealing with ghosts again. Then I heard a scratching at my door. I went to the door and asked who was there.

A little voice replied to me, 'We are cold. Open the door for us. We are your little wives.'

'Away with you, damned gallows-birds!' I replied. 'Go back to your gibbet and leave me to sleep.'

Then the little voice said, 'You are defying us because you are in a chapel. Why don't you come out here?'

'I shall do that this very moment,' I replied at once.

I went to fetch my sword, but when I tried to go outside I found the door locked. I informed the ghosts of this but they did not reply. So I went back to my bed and slept until daybreak.

The Third Day

I was roused by the hermit, who seemed delighted to find me safe and sound. He embraced me, bathed my cheeks with his tears and said to me:

'My son, strange things happened last night. Tell me the truth. Did you sleep at the Venta Quemada? Did you fall into the clutches of demons? There is still a remedy. Come with me to the foot of the altar and confess your sins! Repent!'

The hermit repeated again and again his pious exhortations. Then he fell silent and waited for me to reply.

'Father,' I said to him, 'I went to confession before I left Cadiz. Since then I do not believe that I have committed any mortal sin except perhaps in my dreams. It is true that I slept at the Venta Quemada, but if I was witness to anything there I have good reason for not speaking about it.'

This reply seemed to take the hermit aback. He accused me of being possessed by the demon of pride and tried to persuade me that I should make a confession of all my sins. But on seeing that I was steadfastly opposed to this, he abandoned his apostolic tone and said to me in a much more natural manner:

'Your courage amazes me, my son. Who are you? What sort of upbringing have you had? Do you or do you not believe in ghosts? I beg you not to refuse to satisfy my curiosity.'

'Father,' I replied, 'your desire to know more about me can only do me honour. And for this I am grateful to you as is only fitting. Allow me to get up and I shall join you in the hermitage, where I shall tell you all you want to know about me.'

The hermit embraced me again and left the room.

Once dressed I went to look for him. He was warming up some goat's milk which he then gave me, together with some sugar and bread. He himself ate only a few boiled roots.

34

When we had broken our fast the hermit turned to the possessed man and said:

'Pacheco, Pacheco, in the name of your Redeemer I command you to lead my goats up the mountain.'

Pacheco uttered a terrible cry and went out.

Then I began my story, which I told as follows:

∽ THE STORY OF ALPHONSE VAN WORDEN ∽

I am descended from a very ancient family, but one which has achieved very little fame and acquired even less wealth. Our whole patrimony has never consisted of more than Worden, a noble fief which fell within the jurisdiction of Burgundy and is situated in the middle of the Ardennes.

My father had an elder brother and had to be satisfied with a tiny legacy which, none the less, was enough to support him honourably in the army. He fought throughout the War of the Spanish Succession,[1] and when peace came Philip V promoted him to the rank of lieutenant-colonel in the Walloon Guards.

At that time in the Spanish army there was a strong sense of honour which was sometimes taken to extremes: my father went even further. For which in truth he cannot be blamed, since honour is properly speaking the life and soul of a military man. Not a duel was fought in Madrid whose ceremonial he did not supervise, and once he had said that satisfaction had been obtained, all parties declared themselves satisfied. But if by chance someone said that he was not satisfied then he had to contend with my father himself, who never failed to uphold the rightness of his decisions by the point of a sword. Moreover, my father kept a blank book in which he wrote down the history of every duel with all its attendant circumstances. This gave him a great advantage when it came to passing judgement on difficult cases.

My father was almost completely taken up with this tribunal of blood and had not shown himself to be much susceptible to the charms of love. But in the end even his heart was moved by the

1 1701–1714

35

beauty of a young lady called Mouraque de Gomelez, who was a daughter of the *oidor*[2] of Granada and the descendant of the ancient rulers of that province. Mutual friends soon brought the interested parties together and the marriage was arranged.

My father thought it appropriate to invite to his wedding all the men with whom he had fought duels (I only mean those, of course, whom he had not killed). A hundred and twenty-two came to the wedding feast. Thirteen of those absent were away from Madrid, and it had been impossible to trace a further thirty-three whom he had fought while in the army. My mother told me on more than one occasion that the feast had been extraordinarily merry and that there was an atmosphere of great cordiality. I do not find this difficult to believe, for my father had at bottom an excellent heart and was much loved by everyone.

For his part, my father was deeply attached to Spain and would never have left it, but two months after his marriage he received a letter signed by the magistrates of the town of Bouillon informing him that his brother had died without heirs and that the fief of Worden had reverted to him. This news distressed my father greatly. And my mother has since told me that he was so preoccupied that he could not be brought to speak about it. Eventually he consulted his chronicle of duels, chose twelve men from Madrid who had fought the greatest number, invited them to his house and spoke to them as follows.

'My dear brothers in arms. You know well enough how often I have set your consciences at rest on matters in which honour seemed to have been compromised. Today I find myself constrained to defer to your judgement because I fear that my own judgement may prove to be at fault, or rather that it will be clouded by partiality. Here is the letter written to me by the magistrates of Bouillon, whose testimony is worthy of respect although they are not noblemen. Tell me whether honour requires that I should return to live in my ancestral castle or whether I should continue to serve King Philip, who has overwhelmed me with favours and has just promoted me to

2 Judge.

the rank of brigadier-general. I shall leave the letter on the table and withdraw. In half an hour I shall come back and hear your decision.'

Having thus spoken my father did indeed leave the room, and returned in half an hour to hear the verdict. He found that five had voted that he should remain in the army and seven had voted that he should go to live in the Ardennes. Without demur my father accepted the majority verdict.

My mother would have preferred to stay in Spain, but she was so devoted to her husband that he failed even to notice how averse she was to leaving her native land. At last all that remained to be done was to prepare for the journey and to arrange for the small number of those who were to accompany them to be the representatives of Spain in the Ardennes. Although I had not yet been born my father was sure that I would be, and thought that it was time to arrange for me to have a master-at-arms. His choice fell on Garcías Hierro, the best fencing master in Madrid. This young man, who had had his fill of parrying blows in the Plaza de la Cebada, accepted with alacrity. For her part my mother, not wishing to leave without a chaplain, chose Iñigo Vélez, a theology graduate from Cuenca. He was later to instruct me in the Catholic religion and the Spanish language. All these arrangements for my education were made a year and a half before my birth.

When my father was ready to depart, he went to take leave of the king and in accordance with Spanish custom he knelt on one knee to kiss his monarch's hand. But he found this so upsetting that he fainted and had to be carried back to his house. The next day he went to take leave of Don Fernando de Lara, who was then prime minister. This gentleman received him with great respect and informed him that the king had granted him a pension of 12,000 reals and the rank of sargento-general, which is the same as major-general. My father would have given half his life's blood to satisfy his desire to kneel again before his royal master, but as he had already taken leave, he confined himself to expressing his heartfelt feelings in a letter. Eventually he left Madrid, having shed many a tear.

My father chose to pass through Catalonia so that he could again visit the lands over which he had fought and bid farewell to some of his former companions in arms who held commands on the frontier. He then entered France by way of Perpignan.

As far as Lyon his journey was not troubled by any untoward incident. But on leaving that town with his post horses he was overtaken by a chaise which, being lighter, arrived at the post house before him. Reaching there a few minutes later, my father noted that the horses were already being harnessed to the carriage. He at once took up his sword and, going up to the traveller, asked him for the honour of a brief conversation. The traveller, who was a colonel in the French army, saw that my father was wearing the uniform of a general officer and also took up his sword out of respect for his rank. They went into the inn, which was across the road from the post house, and asked for a room.

When they were alone my father said to the traveller, 'Señor, your carriage overtook mine and arrived at the post house before me. This act, which does not itself constitute an insult, none the less has something disobliging about it for which I feel obliged to ask you for an explanation.'

The colonel was very taken aback by this and placed the blame on his postilions, assuring my father that he had no part in it.

'Señor caballero,' continued my father, 'I also do not wish to make anything serious of this. And so I shall be satisfied by first blood.' In saying this he drew his sword.

'One moment,' said the Frenchman. 'It seems to me that it was not my postilions who overtook yours but rather yours who by lingering fell behind mine.'

My father thought about this for a moment and then said to the colonel, 'Señor, I think you are quite right. If you had made this observation to me earlier, before I had drawn my sword, I think we would not have had to fight each other. But you must realize that now things have gone this far some blood must be drawn.'

The colonel, who probably thought this last argument good enough, also drew his sword. The duel did not last long. On feeling himself wounded my father at once lowered the point of his sword and apologized to the colonel for the trouble to which he had put him. He replied in turn by offering my father his services and gave an address in Paris where he could be found. Then he stepped back into his chaise and left.

My father first thought that he was only lightly wounded, but he was so covered with scars that any new cut could not fail to open up an old one. In this case the colonel's blow had reopened an old musket wound from which the bullet had not been extracted. The lead ball began to work its way to the surface and came out after the wound had been treated for two months. Only then could the journey continue.

On arriving in Paris my father's first thought was to present his compliments to the colonel, whose name was the Marquis d'Urfé. He was one of the most respected members of the French court. He received my father with great kindness and offered to introduce him to the minister as well as to the best circles. My father thanked him but asked only to be presented to the Duc de Tavannes, who was then the doyen of the maréchaux, because he wanted to be apprised of all that concerned this tribunal, which he held in the highest regard and about which he had often spoken as a very judicious institution that he would have liked to see introduced into Spain. The duke received my father with great civility and recommended him in turn to the Chevalier de Belièvre, the senior officer of the maréchaux and recorder of their tribunal.

In the course of his frequent visits to my father the chevalier came to hear of his chronicle of duels. This work seemed to have no precedent in its kind and he asked permission to show it to the maréchaux who, like their senior officer, thought it unique and asked my father for the favour of a copy that would be kept in the registry of their tribunal. No request could have flattered my father more or given him greater pleasure.

To my father, such marks of esteem made the stay in Paris highly agreeable, but my mother took a different view of it. She had made it a rule not only not to learn French but also never to listen to it when it was spoken. Her confessor, Iñigo Vélez, repeatedly passed acerbic comments about the freedoms of the Gallican Church and Garcías Hierro ended all conversations by declaring the French to be miserable worms.

At last they left Paris and after four days' journey arrived in

39

Bouillon. My father made himself known to the magistrate and went to take possession of his fief.

On being abandoned by its masters, the ancestral roof had also been abandoned by a fair number of its tiles, so that it rained in the bedrooms as much as in the courtyard, the difference being that the paving stones of the courtyard dried very quickly whereas the water formed puddles in the bedroom that never disappeared. These domestic floods did not displease my father since they reminded him of the siege of Lerida, where he had spent three weeks knee-deep in water.

His first concern, however, was to put his wife's bed in a dry place. There was a fireplace in the Flemish style in the state room, around which fifteen people could easily warm themselves. The mantel of the fireplace consisted of a sort of roof supported by two columns on either side. My father had the flue blocked up and my mother's bed placed in the hearth underneath the mantel, together with her bedside table and a chair. Since the hearth was a foot higher than what surrounded it, it formed a nearly inaccessible island.

My father settled himself at the other end of the room on two tables linked by planks. A jetty was constructed from his bed to that of my mother, buttressed in the middle by a sort of coffer-dam built from trunks and chests. This construction was completed on the very day they arrived at the castle. Exactly nine months later to the day, I came into the world.

While work on the most urgent repairs was proceeding at a feverish pace, my father received a letter which filled him with joy. It was signed by the Maréchal de Tavannes, and in it this gentleman asked his opinion on a point of honour which was then occupying the tribunal. This genuine sign of favour seemed so important to my father that he resolved to celebrate it by giving a feast to the whole neighbourhood. But as we had no neighbours the revels were restricted to a fandango performed by the fencing master and Señora Frasca, who was my mother's first chambermaid.

In his reply to the maréchal my father asked if he could be permitted to see in due course the résumé of the tribunal's deliberations on matters placed before it. This favour was granted him, and on the first day of every month he received a dispatch which provided the subject-matter for four weeks' conversation and small talk. In winter this took place around the great fireplace and in summer on two seats placed in front of the castle door.

Throughout my mother's pregnancy my father spoke to her about the son she would have and thought about the choice of godfather. My mother suggested the Maréchal de Tavannes or the Marquis d'Urfé. My father agreed that such a choice would do us great honour. But he was afraid that these great noblemen might consider that they were doing him too great an honour, and decided with thoughtfulness and tact to ask the Chevalier de Belièvre, who for his part was honoured and grateful to accept.

At last I was born. At the age of three years I could already hold a little foil, and at six I was able to discharge a pistol without blinking. I was about seven when my godfather visited me. This gentleman had married at Tournai, where he occupied the post of lieutenant to the high constable and recorder of the tribunal which settled matters of honour. Both posts go back to the time of trial by champions. Later they were transferred to the tribunal of maréchaux.

Madame de Belièvre was of delicate health and her husband used to accompany her to Spa for the waters. Both took me to their hearts and, not having children themselves, they implored my father to entrust them with my education, which could not have been properly attended to in as remote a place as the castle of Worden. My father agreed, persuaded above all by the office of recorder of the tribunal settling matters of honour, which ensured that in his house I could not fail to be imbued at an early age with the principles that should govern my conduct when I grew up.

At first there was talk of Garcías Hierro accompanying me, because my father considered that the most noble manner of combat was to fight with a sword in the right hand and a dagger in the left, this way of fencing being wholly unknown in France. But as my father had become accustomed to fencing on the battlements every morning with Hierro and this exercise had become necessary for his health, he thought that he could not do without him.

There was talk also of the theologian Iñigo Vélez going with me. But as my mother still only spoke Spanish, naturally she could not do without a confessor who understood that language. So it turned out

41

that neither of the men who had been chosen to provide me with an education came with me. But I was given a Spanish manservant whose duty it was to instruct me in the Spanish language.

I set out for Spa with my godfather and spent two months there. We travelled on to Holland and arrived back in Tournai towards the end of autumn. The Chevalier de Belièvre lived up to the trust placed in him by my father in every way, and for six years neglected nothing that might contribute to making me one day an excellent officer. Then Madame de Belièvre died and her husband left Flanders and took up residence in Paris, while I was recalled to my father's house.

After a journey which was made wearisome by the lateness of the season, I reached the castle about two hours after sunset and found its inhabitants gathered around the great fireplace. My father was overjoyed to see me but did not give himself over to those demonstrations of affection which might have compromised what you Spaniards would call his *gravedad*. My mother wept copiously over me. The theologian Iñigo Vélez gave me his blessing and the fencing master Hierro presented me with a foil. We then fought and I acquitted myself in a manner beyond my years. My father was too well versed in such things not to notice, and his gravity gave way to great warmth and affection. Supper was served and everyone was jolly.

After supper everyone reassembled around the fireplace and my father said to the theologian: 'Reverend Don Iñigo, be so kind as to fetch your great book, in which there are many fantastic tales, and read us one.'

The theologian went up to his bedroom and returned carrying a folio volume bound in white parchment which was yellowed with age. He opened it at random and read aloud the following tale:

✑ THE STORY OF TRIVULZIO OF RAVENNA ✑

Once upon a time, in an Italian town called Ravenna, there lived a young man whose name was Trivulzio. He was handsome, rich and had a very high opinion of himself. The girls of Ravenna would come to their windows to see him go by, but none of them took his fancy. Or rather, if one or other of them *did* attract him, he did not let it show for fear of showing her too much honour. But in the end all his conceit was not a match for the charms of the young and beautiful Nina dei Gieraci. Trivulzio deigned to declare his love for her. Nina replied that she was touched; Signor Trivulzio did her much honour, but since her childhood she had been in love with her cousin, Tebaldo dei Gieraci, and would, she was sure, never love anyone but him.

At this unexpected reply, Trivulzio departed, showing signs of extreme rage.

A week later, on a Sunday, as all the citizens of Ravenna were on their way to the metropolitan church of S. Pietro, Trivulzio caught sight of Tebaldo in the crowd with his cousin on his arm. He covered his face with his cloak and followed them. They went into the church, where it is not permitted to cover your face with a cloak, and the two lovers might easily have noticed Trivulzio following them had it not been for the fact that they could only think of their love for each other to the exclusion even of the Mass, which is a great sin.

Meanwhile, Trivulzio had sat behind them in a pew. He could hear what they were saying to each other and this made him more and more furious. Then a priest went up into the pulpit and said, 'Brethren, I am here to publish the banns of the marriage of Tebaldo and Nina dei Gieraci. If any of you know cause or impediment why these two persons should not be joined together in holy matrimony ye are to declare it.'

'I know of cause and impediment!' cried Trivulzio, who, as he spoke, stabbed the two lovers twenty times. An attempt was made to arrest him but, striking out with his dagger, he fled from the church, left the town and crossed the border into the state of Venice.

Trivulzio was conceited and spoiled but he had a sensitive soul. Remorse avenged his victims and he lived a miserable existence, moving from one town to the next. After some years his family settled matters and he came back to Ravenna, but he was not the Trivulzio of old, beaming with happiness and proud of his privileges. He was in fact so changed that not even his nurse recognized him.

On the very first day of his return Trivulzio asked where Nina had been buried. He was told that her tomb and that of her cousin were in the church of S. Pietro, very close to the spot where they had been murdered. Trembling, Trivulzio went there, and on reaching the tomb kissed it and wept copiously.

Whatever the grief which the unhappy murderer suffered at that moment, he felt that the tears had brought him some relief. He therefore gave his purse to the sacristan and obtained leave from him to enter the church whenever he wanted. This resulted in his coming every evening, and the sacristan soon became accustomed to this and paid little attention to him.

One evening Trivulzio, who had not slept the night before, fell asleep at the tomb. When he woke up he found the church locked. He readily decided to spend the night there because he was not averse to indulging his grief and wallowing in his melancholy. He heard the hours strike one after another. At each one he wished that his own last hour had come.

At last midnight tolled. At that moment the door of the sacristy opened and Trivulzio saw the sacristan enter, carrying his lantern in one hand and a broom in the other. This sacristan, however, was a skeleton. He had a small amount of skin still on his face and he seemed to have deep-sunken eyes. But his surplice, which clung to his bones, showed plainly that there was no flesh on them.

The ghastly sacristan put his lantern down on the high altar and lit the candles as though for vespers. Then he began to sweep the church and dust the pews. He passed close to Trivulzio on several occasions but did not appear to see him.

At last he went to the sacristy door and rang a little bell that is always found there. Thereupon the tombs opened up, the dead rose up still wrapped in their shrouds and began to intone the litany in a doleful way.

After they had chanted in this manner for a certain time one of the dead, wearing a surplice and stole, went up into the pulpit and said, 'Brethren, I am here to publish the banns of the marriage of Tebaldo and Nina dei Gieraci. Accursed Trivulzio, do you find cause and impediment to it?'

My father interrupted the theologian at this point and, turning to me, said, 'Alphonse, my son, if you had been Trivulzio, would you have been afraid?'

I replied, 'Dear father, I imagine that I would have been terrified.'

At this my father rose up in fury, reached for his sword and tried to run me through with it. Someone came between us and eventually he calmed down a little.

When he had taken his seat again, however, he shot a terrible glance at me and said, 'Unworthy son of mine, your cowardice is a disgrace to the regiment of Walloon Guards, which I intended you to join.'

These harsh words, at which I nearly died with shame, were succeeded by a long silence, which Garcías eventually broke by addressing my father.

'My lord,' he said, 'if I may be so bold as to give my opinion on this matter to Your Excellency, I would say that it should be demonstrated to your son that there are not, and cannot be, ghosts or spectres or dead men singing litanies. He then wouldn't be afraid of them.'

'Señor Hierro,' said my father somewhat sharply, 'you have clearly forgotten that yesterday I had the honour of showing you a story about ghosts written in my great-grandfather's own hand.'

'My lord,' replied Garcías, 'it is not my place to challenge Your Excellency's great-grandfather's word.'

'What do you mean by "It is not my place to challenge your great-grandfather's word?"' replied my father. 'Do you realize that such an expression presupposes that you could call my great-grandfather's word into question?'

'My lord,' replied Garcías, 'I am well aware that I am of too little consequence for your noble great-grandfather to wish to demand satisfaction of me.'

Then my father looked even more terrible and said, 'Hierro, heaven preserve you from excusing yourself, for to excuse yourself is to imply that you have given offence.'

'It only remains for me then to submit myself to whatever punishment it pleases Your Excellency to inflict upon me in the name of your great-grandfather. But for the honour of my profession I would wish that this penalty might be administered by our chaplain so that it could be seen by me to be religious penance.'

'That is not a bad idea,' said my father in calmer tones. 'I remember

45

having written some time ago a little treatise on acceptable ways of giving satisfaction when a duel is out of the question. I'll think about it.'

At first my father appeared to be considering the matter, but one thought led to another and he eventually dropped off to sleep in his chair. My mother was already asleep, as was the theologian, and García's was not long in following their example. At that point I thought it incumbent on me to retire. And that is how the first day after I returned to my paternal home was spent.

The next day I fenced with García's and went hunting. We had supper together, and after we had risen from table my father again asked the theologian to fetch his great book. The reverend gentleman obliged, opened it at random and read aloud the story which I am about to relate:

৶ THE STORY OF LANDULPHO OF FERRARA ৶

There was once a young man whose name was Landulpho, who lived in a town in Italy called Ferrara. He was a free-thinker and a rake and was looked upon with horror by all the good souls in the town. This abominable man was addicted to the company of prostitutes and he had gone the rounds of all those living in Ferrara. The one who pleased him most was Bianca de Rossi because she was the most depraved of all of them.

Bianca was not only debauched, grasping and depraved, but she also required that her lovers should commit dishonourable acts to please her. And in Landulpho's case she demanded that he take her home with him every evening to eat supper with his mother and sister. Landulpho at once went to his mother and told her what was proposed as though it was the most respectable thing in the world. This good soul burst into tears and implored her son to think of the effect of this on his sister's reputation. Landulpho was deaf to her entreaties and only undertook to keep the affair as secret as possible. Then he went to fetch Bianca and brought her home with him.

His mother and sister received the prostitute much better than she deserved. Seeing their kindness, she became all the more insolent. During supper she made outrageously suggestive remarks and offered advice to her lover's sister which she could have well done without. Eventually she made it clear to both daughter and mother that they would do well to withdraw because she wanted to be alone with her lover.

Next day the prostitute Bianca spread her story all over town and for a few days people spoke of nothing else. In the end Odoardo Zampi, the brother of Landulpho's mother, came to hear these public rumours. Odoardo was a man who would not permit any insult to go unpunished. He considered himself insulted in the person of his sister and he had the infamous Bianca murdered that very day. When Landulpho went to call on his mistress he found her stabbed to death and lying in a pool of her own blood. He soon learned that this was the work of his uncle. He rushed to his house to punish him for it. He found it surrounded by the stalwarts of the town, who jeered at his rage.

Not knowing on whom to vent his wrath Landulpho rushed to his mother's house, intending to heap insults on her. The poor woman was with her daughter and was just about to sit down to table when she saw her son come in. She asked him whether Bianca was coming to eat with them.

'May she come and drag you off to hell,' said Landulpho. 'You, your brother and all the Zampi family.'

His poor mother fell to her knees and said, 'Dear God, forgive him his blasphemy.'

At that moment the door crashed open and a pallid spectre entered, covered with stab wounds yet still bearing a ghastly likeness to Bianca.

Mother and daughter began at once to pray and God gave them the strength to endure such an apparition without dying of fright.

The phantom walked slowly forwards and sat down at table as though to dine. With a courage that could only have been inspired by the devil, Landulpho boldly took up a dish and presented it to her. The phantom opened her mouth so wide that her head seemed to split in two. A reddish flame issued forth from it. Then, with a hand that had been most horribly burnt, she took a morsel of food and swallowed it. It was heard to fall under the table. In this way she devoured the whole dish and all the morsels fell to the floor. When the dish was empty the phantom stared at Landulpho with terrible eyes and said to him, 'Landulpho, whenever I dine here I sleep here also. Come to bed.'

At this point my father interrupted the chaplain and, turning to me, said, 'Alphonse, my son, would you have been afraid if you had been Landulpho?'

I replied, 'Dear father, I assure you that I would not have felt even the slightest twinge of fear.'

This reply seemed to satisfy my father and he was very jolly for the rest of the evening.

So we spent our days with nothing to change their pattern except that in summer we sat down not around the fireplace but on the seats in front of the castle door. Six years passed in such sweet tranquillity. They seem to me now like so many weeks.

When I had completed my seventeenth year my father decided to enter me in the Walloon Guards and wrote on this matter to his trustworthy old comrades. Those worthy and respectable officers together exerted on my behalf all the influence they possessed and managed to obtain for me a captain's commission. When my father learned of this, he suffered a seizure so severe that his life was thought to be in danger. But he soon recovered and turned his mind to preparing for my departure. He wanted me to go by sea so that I might enter Spain by way of Cadiz and present myself to Don Enrique de Sa, the commandant of the Walloons, who was the person who had contributed most to my preferment.

Even as the post-chaise was waiting drawn up and ready to leave in the courtyard of the castle, my father led me away to his bedroom and having closed the door behind us said, 'My dear Alphonse, I am going to confide in you a secret which came down to me from my father and which you must pass on to your son, but only if he shows himself worthy of it.'

As I was sure it was about some hidden treasure I replied that I had never looked on gold except as a means of helping the poor and needy.

But my father said, 'No, dear Alphonse, it is not about gold or silver. I want to teach you a secret pass in which by counter-parrying and following with a flaconade you are sure to disarm your adversary.'

He then took up two foils, showed me the pass, gave me his blessing and led me to my waiting carriage. I kissed my mother's hand again and departed.

I travelled by post-chaise to Flushing, where I found a vessel to take me to Cadiz. Don Enrique de Sa received me as though I were his own son. He set me up with a horse and recommended two men to serve me, one called Lopez and the other Mosquito. From Cadiz I went to Seville, from Seville to Córdoba and then I went on to Andújar, where I took the road to the Sierra Morena. I suffered the misfortune of being separated from my servants near the drinking trough at Los Alcornoques. Yet I went on to the Venta Quemada the same day and yesterday evening reached your hermitage.

'My son,' said the hermit to me, 'I have found your story absorbing and I am very grateful to you for being so good as to tell it to me. I can now well see that from your upbringing fear is an emotion which must remain completely alien to you. But since you did sleep at the Venta Quemada I am afraid that you were exposed to haunting by the two hanged men and that you have suffered the same fate as the demoniacal Pacheco.'

'Father,' I replied to the anchorite, 'I have thought long and hard about the story of Señor Pacheco. Although he is possessed, he is none the less a gentleman and hence incapable of failing in his duty to tell the truth. But Iñigo Vélez, our castle chaplain, told me that although there were cases of possession in the first centuries of the Christian era there are no more nowadays, and I take his testimony to be all the more worthy of belief as my father commanded me to believe what Iñigo said on all matters concerning religion.'

'But,' said the hermit, 'did not you see for yourself the ghastly face of the possessed man and how demons had blinded him in one eye?'

'Father,' I replied, 'Señor Pacheco could well have lost his eye in another way. Besides, I defer on such matters as these to those who know more about them than I. It is enough for me to show no fear of ghosts or vampires. However, if you would like to give me some holy relic as a protection against their snares I undertake to wear it faithfully and reverently.'

I thought the hermit smiled at my naivety. Then he said to me, 'I can see, my son, that you still have faith, but I fear that you may lose it. The Gomelez family from which you are descended on your mother's side are all recent converts. It is even said that some are still Muslims at heart. If they offered you a vast fortune to change religion would you accept it?'

'Certainly not!' I replied. 'It seems to me that to renounce one's religion is as dishonourable as to desert one's colours.'

At this the hermit smiled again and said, 'I am sorry to see that your virtues are based on an exaggerated sense of honour. I warn you that you will not find Madrid as swashbuckling as in your father's time. Virtues also can have more secure foundations. But I do not want to hold you up any longer for you have a hard day's travelling ahead before you reach the Venta del Peñon, or the inn of the rock. The innkeeper is still there in spite of robbers because he relies on the protection of a band of gypsies who are encamped close by. The day after tomorrow you will reach the Venta de Cárdenas and you will have passed through the Sierra Morena. I have put some provisions in your saddle-bags.'

After these words the hermit embraced me affectionately. But he did not give me a relic to ward off demons. I did not like to mention it again so I got on my horse.

As I rode along I began to think about the precepts I had just heard, but I could not imagine any sounder basis for virtue than a sense of honour, which seemed to me in itself to contain all the virtues.

I was ruminating on these matters when a horseman suddenly shot out from behind a rock, cut me off and said, 'Is your name Alphonse van Worden?'

I replied that it was.

'In that case,' said the horseman, 'I arrest you in the name of the king and the Holy Inquisition. Give me your sword.'

I obeyed without a word. Then the horseman whistled and I saw armed men bearing down on me from all sides. They tied my hands behind my back and we set off into the mountains up a side track which led after about an hour to a heavily fortified castle. The drawbridge was lowered and we went in. While we were still under the shadow of the keep, a little side door was opened and I was thrown into a cell, without anyone bothering to untie me.

It was pitch-black in the cell and, not having my hands free to feel my way forward, I would have found it difficult to walk about without banging my nose on the walls. So I sat down where I was and, as one may well imagine, began to wonder what could have caused me to be imprisoned. My first and only thought was that the Inquisition had captured my beautiful cousins and that their black servants had reported everything that had happened at the Venta Quemada. Supposing that I was going to be interrogated about the two African girls, I was faced with the alternative of either betraying them and thus breaking my solemn word of honour, or of denying that I knew them, which would embark me on a series of shameful lies. After some thought as to how I should behave, I decided to maintain absolute silence and I firmly resolved to say nothing in reply to any interrogation.

Once I had settled these doubts in my mind I began to ponder the events of the previous two days. I did not doubt that my cousins were creatures of flesh and blood. I was convinced of this by an intuition stronger than all that I have been told about the powers of demons, and, as for the trick of transporting me to lie under the gallows, I was extremely indignant about it.

Meanwhile the hours passed by. I began to feel hungry, and as I had heard that cells are sometimes supplied with bread and a jug of water I set about looking for something of the sort by feeling about with my legs and feet. And indeed I soon felt an object of some kind, which turned out to be a loaf. My problem was how to raise it to my mouth. I lay down beside the loaf and tried to seize it between my teeth, but it slipped away from me since there was nothing there to push against. I pushed it so far in the end that it came up against the wall. I was then able to eat it as the loaf was cut down the middle. If it had been whole I would not have been able to bite into it. I found the jug of water too but was not able to drink from it. No sooner had I sipped a little than the jug tipped over and the water ran away.

I explored further and found some straw in a corner on which I could lie down. My hands were tied together in a very clever way, that is, tightly but not painfully, so that I had no difficulty in falling asleep.

The Fourth Day

When I was woken up it seemed to me that I had slept for several hours. I saw a Dominican monk enter my cell, followed by several men of evil countenance. Some carried torches, others objects which I had never seen before but which I imagined were instruments of torture. I reminded myself of my resolutions and bound myself again to keep them. I thought of my father. He had never suffered torture, but had he not suffered many painful operations at the hands of surgeons? I knew that he had borne them without a single cry of pain. I decided to follow his example and neither to utter a single word nor to let out a single groan.

The inquisitor had a chair brought for him, sat down beside me and in a gentle and wheedling tone spoke to me in more or less these words:

'My dear child, my sweet child, thank heaven for having brought you to this dungeon. But tell me, why are you here? What sins have you committed? Confess. Pour out your tears on my breast. What? No reply? Alas, my child, you are wrong. We do not practise interrogation, that is not our method. We allow the guilty party to accuse himself. Such a confession, if somewhat forced, is not without value, especially if the guilty party denounces his accomplices. What? No reply? So much the worse for you! We will have to set you on the right path. Do you know two princesses from Tunis or rather two infamous witches, two execrable vampires, two demons incarnate? You still remain silent. Have the two infantas of Lucifer's court brought in.'

At this point my two cousins were led in. They, like me, had their hands tied behind their backs.

Then the inquisitor continued as follows: 'Do you recognize them, my son? Still no reply! My dear child, do not be alarmed by what I am going to tell you. We are going to hurt you a little. You see these

53

two boards. Your legs will be placed between them and they will be tied tightly with ropes. Then we will drive these wedges, which you see here, between your legs and they will be hammered into place. At first your feet will swell up, then blood will spurt from your toes and all your toe-nails will drop off. Then the soles of your feet will split open and from them will issue thick gouts of fat and mangled flesh. That will hurt you a great deal. Still you say nothing. But I am only talking of the standard torture so far. All this will make you faint. Here we have bottles filled with various spirits to bring you round again. When you have regained your senses the wedges will be taken away and these bigger ones will be put in their place. At the first hammer blow your knees and calves will break. At the second your legs will split open all the way up and a mixture of marrow and blood will flow out on to the straw. You will not speak? Well then, apply the thumbscrews.'

The torturers grabbed hold of my legs and fastened them between the boards.

'Still no reply? Drive in the wedge! Still no reply? Hammers at the ready!'

At that very moment a gunshot was heard and Emina cried, 'Oh Muhammad, we are saved! Zoto has come to rescue us!'

And Zoto and his band did indeed burst in, chased off the torturers and chained the inquisitor up to a ring on one of the walls of the dungeon. The Moorish princesses and I were then untied. The first use they made of their arms when they were freed was to throw themselves into mine. We were prised apart. Zoto told me to mount and ride ahead of the rest and reassured me that he would follow shortly with the two ladies.

The advance party with which I left consisted of four horsemen. At daybreak we arrived in a very deserted spot, where we found fresh horses. Then we rode up into the high mountains along snow-covered ridges.

Towards four o'clock in the afternoon we reached some hollows in the rock where we were to pass the night. I was very glad to have got there before nightfall because the view was truly remarkable, especially to someone like myself who had only ever seen the Ardennes and Zeeland. At my feet stretched out the beautiful plain of Granada,

54

which its inhabitants ironically call 'la nuestra vegilla'.[1] I saw all of it, with its six towns, its forty villages, the tortuous course of the river Genil, its torrents which tumbled down from the Alpujarras mountains, its groves and shady thickets, its buildings, its gardens and its many *quintas*, or farms. I gave myself up to rapt contemplation of so many fine objects which my eyes could embrace all at once, and felt myself falling in love with nature itself. I forgot about my cousins, but they soon arrived on litters borne by horses.

They sat down on the flagstones in the cave, and when they had rested a little I said to them, 'Ladies, I have no complaint about the night I spent at the Venta Quemada but I must tell you that it ended in a way which I found most displeasing.'

Emina replied, 'Dear Alphonse, blame us only for the nice part of your dreams. In any case, why complain? Did you not have an opportunity to show superhuman courage?'

'What?' I replied. 'Is there someone who doubts my courage? If I knew where to find him I would fight him: on a cloak or with a handkerchief stuffed in my mouth if he wanted.'

Emina replied, 'I have no idea what you mean with your cloak and your handkerchief. There are things I am not able to tell you and others which I do not know myself. I act only on the orders of the head of my family, the successor of Sheikh Massoud, who knows all the secrets of Cassar Gomelez. All I can tell you is that you are our very close relative. The *oidor* of Granada, your mother's father, had a son who was found worthy of being initiated. He embraced the Muslim faith and married the four daughters of the reigning Dey of Tunis. Only the youngest had any children. She is our mother. Soon after the birth of Zubeida, our father and his three other wives died of the plague which at that time was ravaging the whole Barbary coast. But let us no longer speak of such things, things you will perhaps yourself know one day. Let us speak of you, of our gratitude to you or rather our admiration for your courage. How steadfastly you gazed upon the instruments of torture! How faithfully you kept your

1 'Our little meadow'.

word! Dear Alphonse, you are greater than all the heroes of our race and we now belong to you.'

Zubeida, who was willing to let her sister speak when the subject of conversation was serious, reclaimed her rights when it took a sentimental turn. In short, I was flattered, caressed and pleased with myself and others. The negresses appeared, and supper was served by Zoto himself, who showed us every mark of respect. Then the negresses made a tolerable bed for my cousins in a sort of grotto. I went to sleep in another grotto and we all enjoyed the rest we needed.

The Fifth Day

———————— ∽ ————————

The next day the caravan made an early start. We came down from the mountains and wound our way into deep, narrow valleys or rather ravines, which seemed to go down to the very bowels of the earth. They cut across the mountain range in so many different ways that it was impossible not to lose one's sense of direction. One did not know which way one was heading at any one time.

We proceeded in this way for six hours till we reached the ruins of a desolate and abandoned town. There Zoto had us dismount. He led me up to a well and said:

'Señor Alphonse, look down into this well and tell me what you think of it.'

I replied that I could see water in it and judged it to be a well.

'Well,' said Zoto, 'you are wrong, for it is the entrance to my palace.'

Having said this, he thrust his head down the well and shouted in a certain way. First I saw planks come out from one side of the well, a few feet above the water-line. Then an armed man emerged from the opening, followed by another. They climbed out of the well. When they got to the top Zoto said to me:

'Señor Alphonse, I have the honour of presenting to you my two brothers, Cicio and Momo. You may have seen their bodies hanging from a certain gallows, but they are in good health for all that and will always loyally serve you since they, like me, are in the service and in the pay of the Great Sheikh of the Gomelez.'

I replied that I was delighted to meet the brothers of a man who appeared to have done me such great service.

We all had to steel ourselves to climb down into the well. A rope-ladder was brought, and the two sisters used it with greater agility than I expected. I went down after them. When we reached the planks we found a little door on one side through which we could

57

only proceed by bending low. Thereafter we found ourselves at the head of a very grand staircase, cut into the rock, which was lit by lamps. We went down more than two hundred steps and came at last to an underground residence made up of many rooms and chambers. The walls of the living-rooms were all covered with cork to protect them from the damp. I have since visited the monastery at Cintra, near Lisbon, which has similar wall coverings.[1] It is known for this reason as the cork monastery.

In addition, strategically placed and well-stoked fires made the temperature of Zoto's underground dwelling very pleasant. The horses which he used for his men were dispersed here and there in the surrounding countryside. But even these could if necessary be brought down into the underground chambers through an opening which came out in a neighbouring valley. There was equipment for hoisting them up but it was very rarely used.

'All these marvels are the work of the Gomelez,' Emina told me. 'They excavated the rock when they were the masters of this region, or rather they finished off the excavation, much of which had been undertaken by the heathens who were living in the Alpujarras when the Gomelez invaded. Learned historians claim that this is the site of the mines of virgin gold of classical Baetica, and ancient prophecies predict that the whole region will one day return to the control of the Gomelez. What do you say to that, Alphonse? What a fine inheritance that would be!'

Emina's words seemed to me in very poor taste, and I let her know as much. Changing the subject, I asked what her future plans might be.

Emina replied that after what had happened she and her sister could not remain in Spain, but they had resolved to have a little rest until arrangements could be made for their sailing.

We were given a lavish dinner with a great deal of venison and preserves. The three brothers served us most attentively. I commented to my cousins that it would be impossible to find more obliging hanged men anywhere. Emina agreed and, turning to Zoto, said to

1 Potocki is referring to the Convent of the Holy Cross, founded in 1560.

him, 'You and your brothers must have had some very strange adventures. We should be delighted to hear about them.'

After some coaxing, Zoto sat down beside us and began as follows:

⌘ ZOTO'S STORY ⌘

I was born in the city of Benevento, the capital of the duchy of that name. My father, who was also called Zoto, was a skilled armourer. But as there were two other even more renowned armourers in the city, his trade barely provided an adequate living for himself, his wife and his three children, that is, my two brothers and myself.

Three years after my father's wedding a younger sister of my mother married an oil merchant called Lunardo, who gave her as a wedding present gold earrings and a gold chain to wear round her neck. On her return from the wedding, my mother seemed sunk in deep gloom. Her husband tried to find out why but she refused for a long time to tell him. Eventually she admitted that she was dying of envy, wishing to possess earrings and a necklace like her sister's. My father said nothing, but he had a finely chased hunting-piece with two pistols, and a hunting-knife of similar workmanship. The gun could be fired four times without reloading. It had taken my father four years to make it. He valued it at three hundred ounces of Naples gold. He went to see a collector, to whom he sold the whole set for eighty ounces. Then he bought the jewels that my mother coveted and took them to her. That very day my mother went to show them off to the wife of Lunardo. Her earrings were considered to be a little more valuable than those of her sister, which gave her great pleasure.

But a week later Lunardo's wife paid a visit to my mother. She had had her hair braided and coiled, and it was held in place by a golden pin, the head of which was a filigree rose with a little ruby inset. This golden rose drove a cruel thorn in my mother's heart. She relapsed into melancholy until my father promised her a pin like that of her sister. However, as my father had no money and no means of procuring any, and as such a pin cost forty-five gold ounces, he became as gloomy as my mother had been a few days before.

While this was going on, my father was visited by a local stalwart called Grillo Monaldi, who came to him to have his pistols cleaned.

Seeing my father so depressed, Monaldi asked him why and my father told him. Monaldi, having thought for a moment, spoke to him as follows:

'Signor Zoto, I am indebted to you more than you know. A few days ago my dagger was by chance found in the body of a man who had been murdered on the road to Naples. The police took this dagger to all the armourers, and you nobly testified that it was unknown to you. And yet it was a weapon which you had made and sold to me. If you had told the truth, it could have caused me some embarrassment. So here are the forty-five gold ounces you need, and if you need more my purse will always be open to you.'

My father accepted gratefully and went to buy a gold pin studded with a ruby. He took it to my mother, who duly showed it off that very day to her haughty sister.

When she came home, my mother had no doubt that she would soon see Signora Lunardo wearing some new jewel. But her sister had other plans. She resolved to go to church followed by a hired lackey in livery, and she suggested this to her husband. Lunardo, who was very miserly, had not jibbed at buying an object in gold, which seemed to him to be as safe an investment on the head of his wife as in his coffers. But it was quite another matter to be asked to give some wretch an ounce of gold to do no more than stand behind his wife's pew for an hour. But Signora Lunardo nagged him about it so often and so violently that he finally decided to walk behind her himself, wearing livery. Signora Lunardo thought her husband would do as well as anyone else in such a role, and she decided the very next Sunday to make an appearance in the parish with this new style of lackey in her train. Her neighbours sniggered a little at such a masquerade but my aunt attributed their teasing to the envy that was consuming them.

As she approached the church, the beggars hooted and jeered and shouted out in their dialect, 'Mira Lunardu che fa lu criadu de sua mugiera!'[2]

But beggars do not push their boldness beyond a certain limit, and

2 'Look at Lunardo, who's playing the lackey to his wife!'

60

Signora Lunardo entered into the church unmolested, where she was accorded all sorts of honours. She was offered holy water and led to a pew, whereas my mother was left to stand lost in a crowd of women of the lowest class.

When she got back home my mother took out my father's blue coat and began to decorate the sleeves with pieces of a yellow bandolier which had once belonged to a bandit's cartridge belt. My father was taken aback by this and asked what she was doing. My mother told him what her sister had done and how her husband had obliged her by following her in the livery of a lackey.

My father informed her that he would never oblige her in this way. But the following Sunday he paid one ounce of gold to a hired lackey to walk behind my mother to church, where she cut an even finer figure than had Signora Lunardo the previous Sunday.

Immediately after Mass on the same day, Monaldi came up to my father and spoke as follows:

'My dear Zoto, I have been told about the extreme lengths to which the rivalry between your wife and her sister has been taken. If you don't do anything about it you will be unhappy as long as you live. There are only two courses of action open to you: either to beat your wife or to adopt a manner of life which will allow you to satisfy her expensive tastes. If you decide to adopt the first course I will give you a hazelwood stick which I used on my late wife when she was alive. There are other hazelwood sticks which, when you grasp them by both ends, turn in your hand to indicate where water or even treasure is to be found underground. This stick does not possess these properties. But if you take it by one end and apply the other to your wife's shoulders, I can assure you that it will cure her of her various whims. But if on the other hand you choose the second course and indulge all your wife's fancies, then I will give you the friendship of the bravest men in all Italy. They often gather in Benevento because it is on the frontier. I think you understand me. So think it over.'

After these words Monaldi left the hazelwood stick on my father's work-bench and went away.

Meanwhile my mother had gone after Mass to show off her lackey on the Corso and at various of her friends' houses. Eventually she returned, glowing with triumph, and my father received her in a way

61

she did not expect at all. With his left hand he grasped her left arm and proceeded to put into effect Monaldi's advice. His wife fainted. My father cursed the hazelwood stick and asked for forgiveness; he obtained it and peace was restored.

A few days later my father sought Monaldi out and told him that the hazelwood stick had not had the desired effect and that he placed himself at the disposal of the brave men of whom Monaldi had spoken.

'Signor Zoto,' Monaldi replied, 'it is somewhat surprising that you have not got the heart to administer any punishment at all to your wife but you are prepared to waylay men at the edge of a wood. But everything is possible and this is far from the only such contradiction hidden in the human heart. I am ready to introduce you to my friends but you must first commit at least one murder. So every evening when you have finished your work, take a long sword and put a dagger in your belt and swagger up and down near the Madonna gate. You may find employment that way. Farewell, and may heaven bless your ventures.'

Father followed Monaldi's advice and soon observed that various gentlemen equipped like himself and the local *sbiri*[3] were greeting him with knowing looks.

After doing this for a fortnight my father was accosted by a well-dressed man who said to him, 'Signor Zoto, here are eleven ounces of gold. In half an hour you will see two young gentlemen go by with white feathers in their hats. Go after them as though you had a confidential message to pass on and then whisper, "Which of you is the Marchese Feltri?" One of them will reply, "It's me." Stab him in the heart. The other young gentleman, who is a coward, will take to his heels. Finish Feltri off. When it's all over, do not take sanctuary in a church but calmly return home. I shall be just behind you.'

My father followed the instructions to the letter, and he had just got home when he saw the stranger arrive whose grievance he had satisfied.

'Signor Zoto,' he said to my father, 'I appreciate very much what

3 Policemen appointed by the community or government.

you have done for me. Here is a purse containing a hundred gold ounces which I would like you to accept, and another containing the same sum which you must give to the first officer of the law who comes to your house.'

Having uttered these words, the stranger left.

Soon after, the chief of the *sbiri* came to see my father, who immediately gave him the hundred gold ounces destined for the law. Thereupon the chief invited my father to take supper at his house in the company of his friends. They went to a lodging which backed on to the public prison and there they found their fellow-guests to be the *barigel*[4] and the prison chaplain. My father was somewhat upset, as is commonly the case after one has committed one's first murder.

The priest noticed his distress and said to him, 'Come now, Signor Zoto, no sadness. It costs twelve tari to have a Mass said at the cathedral. I hear that the Marchese Feltri has been murdered. If you have twenty or so Masses said for the repose of his soul you will be given a general absolution into the bargain.'

No further reference was made after that to what had happened and supper was merry enough.

The next day Monaldi came to see my father and complimented him on the way he had conducted himself. My father tried to give back the forty-five ounces of gold that he had received but Monaldi said to him:

'Zoto, you are offending my finer feelings. If you speak to me again about the money, I shall think that you are chiding me for not having given you enough. My purse is yours to dispose of. You have won my friendship. I will no longer conceal from you the fact that I am myself the head of the band which I told you about. It is made up of men of honour and the strictest integrity. If you want to join us, say that you are going to Breschia to buy rifle barrels and come and join us in Capua. Take a room at the Golden Cross and leave the rest to us.'

My father left three days later and conducted a campaign as honourable as it was lucrative.

4 Gaoler.

Although the climate of Benevento is very mild, my father, who was not yet hardened to the rigours of his new employment, decided not to work during the cold weather. His winter quarters were at home with his family, and his wife had a lackey every Sunday, gold clasps on her black bodice and a gold fastening from which her keys hung.

As spring approached, it happened that my father was accosted in the street by a servant he did not know, who asked him to follow him to the gates of the town. There, an elderly gentleman was waiting with four men on horseback.

The gentleman said, 'Signor Zoto, here is a purse containing fifty sequins. I would be obliged if you would follow me to a nearby castle and allow your eyes to be blindfolded.'

My father agreed to this, and after a long ride and several detours they all arrived at the old gentleman's castle. He was led up the steps and his blindfold was removed. He then saw a masked and gagged woman tied to a chair.

The old gentleman said to him, 'Signor Zoto, here are a hundred more sequins. Be so good as to stab my wife to death.'

My father, however, replied, 'Signor, you are mistaken about me. I lie in wait for people at street corners or I attack them in a wood as befits a man of honour, but I do not undertake the office of public executioner.'

With these words my father threw down the two purses at the feet of the vindictive husband, who did not persist in his request but had my father's eyes blindfolded again and ordered his servant to take him back to the town gates. This noble and generous action brought great honour on my father, and later he did another which was even more widely acclaimed.

In Benevento there were two gentlemen, one called Count Montalto, and the other the Marchese Serra. Count Montalto summoned my father and promised to give him five hundred sequins if he would assassinate Serra. My father took the commission but asked for time to carry it out because he knew the marchese was very much on his guard.

Two days later the Marchese Serra summoned my father to a lonely spot and said to him, 'Zoto, here is a purse containing five hundred sequins. It is yours. Give me your word of honour that you will murder Montalto.'

My father took the purse and replied, 'My lord, I give you my word of honour that I will kill Montalto, but I must tell you that I have given my word to him that I will kill you.'

The marchese laughed and said, 'I sincerely hope that you won't do so.'

My father gravely replied, 'I am very sorry, my lord, I have given my word and I will keep it.'

The marchese leapt back and drew his sword, but my father drew a pistol from his belt and blew the marchese's brains out. He then went to Montalto and told him that his enemy was no more. The count embraced him and gave him the five hundred sequins. My father then admitted to him with some embarrassment that before dying, the marchese had given him five hundred sequins to murder the count.

Montalto said that he was delighted to have forestalled his enemy.

'My lord,' replied my father, 'that is neither here nor there. I have given my word.'

And with these words, he struck him down with his dagger. As he fell, the count gave a cry which brought his servants to the scene. My father disposed of them with his dagger and fled to the mountains where he rejoined Monaldi's band, whose worthy members vied with each other in praising such strict adherence to one's word of honour. I can assure you that this act is still, as one might say, on everyone's lips, and that it will be a talking point for a long time to come in Benevento.

Just as Zoto reached this point in his father's story, one of his brothers came to tell him that instructions were needed for the embarkation. So he left us, asking permission to continue his story the next day. But his words had given me much to think about. He had repeatedly praised the honour, delicacy and integrity of people for whom hanging was not a severe enough punishment. His misuse of these words, which he uttered with such conviction, completely bewildered me.

Emina, who noticed my perplexity, asked me what had caused it. I replied that the story of Zoto's father reminded me of the words that a certain hermit had uttered to me two days earlier, namely that there were surer foundations for virtue than a sense of honour.

'Dear Alphonse,' Emina replied, 'respect the hermit, believe what he has told you. You are going to encounter him more than once in your lifetime.'

Then the two sisters rose and withdrew with the negresses into the inner recesses of their apartment, or rather that part of the subterranean dwelling which had been set aside for them. They came back for supper and then everyone went to bed.

When all was quiet in the caves I saw Emina come into my room, holding a lamp in one hand like Psyche, and leading her younger sister, who was more beautiful than love itself, by the other. The shape of my bed allowed them both to sit down.

Emina then said to me, 'Dear Alphonse, I have told you that we are yours. May the great sheikh forgive us if we anticipate his permission somewhat.'

'Fair Emina,' I replied, 'forgive me in turn, for if this is another test of my virtue, I don't think I shall come out of it very well, I'm afraid.'

'That has already been foreseen,' the African girl replied. She took my hand, put it on her hip and made me feel a belt which, although it owed much to the art and skill of Vulcan, Venus's husband, owed nothing to Venus herself. The belt was secured by a lock whose key was not in my cousins' possession, or that at least is what they said.

With modesty's innermost sanctum thus protected, the sisters did not dream of denying me access to their more accessible charms. Zubeida recalled what she did when she acted the part of the beloved with her sister. Emina saw her sister, once the object of her feigned passion, in my arms, and indulged in the sensual delights of such sweet contemplation. Her younger sister was supple, lively, ardent; her discreet skills consumed me and her caresses transfixed me. We filled our time together in the most charming manner, talking about plans which were never worked out in detail, in that sweet converse which young people indulge in between the memories of recent joy and the hope of future happiness.

At last, sleep weighed down the pretty eyelids of my cousins and they went back to their own apartments. When I was alone, the thought struck me that it would be very unpleasant to wake up under the gallows again. I laughed this thought away but it still occupied my mind till the moment I fell asleep.

The Sixth Day

---------------- ∽ ----------------

I was woken up by Zoto, who told me I had slept a long time and that dinner was ready. I hurriedly dressed and joined my cousins, who were waiting for me in the dining room. They continued to caress me with their eyes. And they seemed more occupied with memories of the previous night than the meal which they were served. When the table had been cleared, Zoto sat down with us and went on with his story as follows:

∽ ZOTO'S STORY CONTINUED ∽

I may have been seven when my father went off to join the Monaldi band. I remember that my mother, my two brothers and I were taken to prison. But it was only for form's sake. As my father had never failed to pay his dues to the officers of the law, they did not require much convincing that we were in no way connected with his activities.

The chief of the *sbiri* was particularly attentive to us during our incarceration and even shortened its term. On her release, my mother was well received by the women living immediately nearby and by the whole neighbourhood, for in southern Italy bandits are popular heroes, much as smugglers are in Spain. We also had our share of public esteem, and I more than my brothers was considered the prince of the urchins of our street.

At about this time Monaldi was killed in a skirmish and my father took over the command of the band. As he wanted to begin with a brilliant action, he lay in wait on the road to Salerno for the consignment of money being sent by the viceroy of Sicily. The ambush came off but my father was wounded by a musket shot in the back, which soon put an end to his career. The moment of parting from the band was extraordinarily moving. It is even said that some of the bandits wept. I would find this difficult to believe if I had not once in my life wept after having stabbed my mistress to death, as you will discover in due course.

The band soon dispersed. Some of its stalwarts went to Tuscany, where they got themselves hanged. Others went to join Testalunga, who was then gaining a reputation for himself in Sicily.[1] My father himself crossed the straits and went to Messina, where he sought asylum in the Monastery of the Augustinians del Monte. He placed his savings in the hands of the fathers, did public penance and settled down under the portals of their church, where he lived a very pleasant life with the freedom to wander in the gardens and courtyards of the monastery. The monks gave him soup and he sent out to a nearby chop-house for a cooked dish or two. The lay brother of the order even dressed his wounds into the bargain.

I suppose that my father used to send us large sums of money, for we had more than we needed for our household. My mother took part in the carnival, and during Lent she had a *presepe*, or crib, made up of little dolls, sugar castles and similar childish things which are very much in fashion in the kingdom of Naples and are luxuries indulged in by the citizens. My aunt, Signora Lunardo, would also have a *presepe*, but not nearly as fine as ours.

From what I can remember of my mother, she seemed to me to be very tender-hearted and we often saw her weep when she thought of the dangers to which her husband was exposed. But a few triumphs over her sister or her neighbours soon dried her tears. The satisfaction she obtained from her splendid crib was the last such pleasure she was able to enjoy. I don't know how, but she caught pleurisy, from which she died a few days later.

After her death we would not have known what to do if the *barigel* had not taken us in. We spent a few days in his house, after which we were entrusted to a muleteer who took us right across Calabria. On the fourteenth day we arrived at Messina. My father had already been told of the death of his wife. He welcomed us with great affection,

1 A historical figure, cited also by Diderot in his story *Les deux amis de Bourbonne*.

69

had bedding put down for us next to his and introduced us to the monks, who enrolled us as altar boys. We served at Mass, we snuffed candles and lit lamps, but apart from that we were the same shameless street urchins that we had been in Benevento. After we had eaten the monks' soup, my father gave each of us a tari with which we would buy chestnuts and cracknel, and we would then go down to play in the port until nightfall, when we would return. And we went on being happy ragamuffins until an event occurred which changed my life and which even now I cannot recall without feelings of rage.

One Sunday, shortly before vespers, I came back to the church gates laden with chestnuts, which I had bought for my brothers and myself. I was sharing them out when a splendid carriage drove up. It was drawn by six white horses and preceded by two other horses of the same colour which were not hitched to the carriage, a display of wealth I have only ever seen in Italy. The door of the carriage opened. First a *bracciere*[2] emerged, who gave his arm to a beautiful lady. Next came a cleric and finally a boy of my age with a charming face, magnificently dressed in the Hungarian style, which then was not uncommon among children. His little winter coat was made of blue velvet embroidered with gold and trimmed with sable. It came down below his knees and even covered the top of his light brown morocco-leather boots. His cap, which was also trimmed with sable, was of the same blue velvet. At its peak there was a tassel of pearls which fell on to one shoulder. His belt was hung with gold tassels and cords and his miniature sabre was studded with jewels. Finally he had in his hand a prayer-book with gold mounts.

I was so amazed to see a boy of my age with such fine clothes that without thinking very much about what I was doing, I went up to him and presented two chestnuts to him which I had in my hand. But instead of responding to my gesture of kindness, the unworthy little wretch hit me in the face with his prayer-book with the full force of his arm. My left eye was badly bruised, and the clasp on the book caught my nostril and ripped it so that I was instantly covered in blood. It seems to me now that I then heard the lordling wailing

2 Gentleman-in-waiting.

horribly, but I had more or less fainted. And when I came to my senses I found myself near the fountain in the garden, surrounded by my father and brothers, who were washing my face and trying to staunch the flow of blood.

In the meantime, while I was still bleeding profusely, the lordling came back, followed by the cleric, the gentleman from the coach and two footmen carrying a bundle of sticks. The gentleman tersely stated that Her Excellency the Princess de Rocca Fiorita demanded that I be beaten till I bled as a punishment for having frightened her darling son, the principino. The footmen at once began carrying out the sentence.

My father, who was afraid that he would lose his sanctuary, did not dare say anything at first, but seeing that I was being mercilessly flayed he could not contain himself any longer and, turning to the gentleman, said in a voice which betrayed his stifled rage, 'Stop this at once, or remember that I have murdered men worth ten the likes of you!'

The gentleman saw the sense of these words and gave the order to stop beating me further. But while I was still face down on the ground the principino came up to me, kicked me in the face and said, 'Managia la tua facia de banditu.'[3]

This last insult drove me wild with rage. I can even say that at that moment my childhood came to an end, or at least that I ceased from then on to enjoy childhood's pleasures. And it was a long time before I could look at a richly dressed man and not lose my composure.

Vengeance must be the original sin of our country, for even though I was only eight years old at the time, night and day I thought of nothing else than of ways to punish the principino. I would wake up with a start from a dream in which I held him by the hair and rained down blows on him. By day I thought of how I could hurt him from a distance, for I suspected that I would not be allowed to get near to him and I intended to make good my escape, having done the deed. Eventually I decided to throw a stone in his face, this being an exercise in which I was adept. To perfect

3 'Damn your eyes, you little bandit!'

my technique I chose a target on which I practised all day long.

My father once asked me what I was doing. I told him that it was my intention to smash the face of the principino, to make good my escape and then to turn bandit. My father gave the impression of not believing me but he smiled at me in a way which strengthened my resolve.

At last came the Sunday which was to be my day of vengeance. The carriage appeared, its occupants got out. I was very nervous but I brought myself under control. My little enemy caught sight of me in the crowd. He poked his tongue out at me. I threw the stone I was holding and he fell backwards. I ran off at once and did not stop until I reached the other end of town. There I met a young chimney sweep I knew, who asked me where I was going. I told him what I had done and he at once took me to his master, who was short of boys and did not know how to procure them for such an arduous job. He greeted my arrival with pleasure. He told me that no one would recognize me when my face was smeared with soot and that knowing how to climb chimneys was a useful talent. He was quite right about that. I have often owed my life to the skill I acquired then.

At first I found chimney dust and the smell of soot very unpleasant, but I got used to them for I was of an age when one can accustom oneself to anything. I had been working as a chimney sweep for six months when the adventure I am about to relate befell me.

I was on a roof listening to hear from which flue my master's voice would come out. I thought I heard him shouting out of the nearest chimney to me. I went down it but found that the flue separated into two just below the roof. I should have called out myself then but did not do so. Instead I decided rashly to take one of the flues at random. I slipped down it and found myself in a handsome drawing-room. The first thing I saw was the principino, wearing only a shirt, playing with a shuttlecock.

Although the little fool had probably seen chimney sweeps before, he took it into his head to take me for the devil. He fell to his knees, begging me not to carry him off and promising to be good. I might have been moved by his entreaties but I had my sweep's brush in my hand and the temptation to make use of it had grown too strong. Although I had avenged myself for the blow the principino had given me with his prayer-book, and in part for the beating I had received, I still resented the kick in the face and the words 'Managia la tua facia de banditu,' and when all is said and done, Neapolitans prefer to take a little more than a little less revenge.

I pulled a fistful of switches from my broom, ripped apart the principino's shirt and, when his back was exposed, I ripped that apart too, or at least gave it severe treatment. But the strangest part of it was that fear prevented him crying out.

When I thought I had done enough I wiped my face clean and said to him, 'Ciucio maledetto, io no zuno lu diavolu, io zuno lu piciolu banditu delli Augustini.'[4] At that the principino recovered the use of his voice and started to yell for help. But I did not wait to see whether anyone came. I climbed back up the way I had come down.

When I reached the roof I could hear my master's voice calling me but thought it inadvisable to reply. I started to run from roof to roof until I came above the stables, in front of which stood a haywain. I jumped down from the roof on to the hay and from the hay to the ground. Then I ran all the way to the portal of the Augustinian monastery, where I told my father what had happened.

My father listened with great interest and then said to me, 'Zoto, Zoto, già vegio che tu sarai banditu.'[5]

Then, turning to a man who was standing beside him, he said, 'Padron Lettereo, prendete lo chiutosto vui.'[6]

Lettereo is a baptismal name peculiar to Messina. It comes from the letter which the Virgin is said to have written to the townspeople and which she is said to have dated in 'the one thousand four hundred and fifty-second year from the birth of my Son'. The inhabitants of Messina venerate this letter as much as the Neapolitans venerate the blood of St Januarius.[7] I mention this detail because a year and a half

4 'You damned ass, I'm not the devil, I'm the little bandit from the Augustinians.'

5 'Zoto, Zoto, I can see already that you're going to become a bandit.'

6 'Captain Lettereo, you'd better take him with you.'

7 The blood of St Januarius, Bishop of Benevento, who died in 305, is said to liquefy three times a year.

later I said what I thought would be the last prayer of my life to the Madonna della Lettera.

Now Padron Lettereo was the captain of an armed pink which was supposedly equipped for coral fishing but was actually used for smuggling and even piracy if a good opportunity arose, which was not very often because it carried no cannon and had to take ships by surprise off deserted beaches.

All this was public knowledge in Messina; Lettereo smuggled on behalf of the city's leading merchants. The customs officers also had a share in it. Besides, Padron Lettereo had the reputation of being very free with the *coltellade*,[8] which made an impression on those who might have liked to make trouble for him. He was indeed an impressive figure of a man. His great chest and shoulders alone would have set him apart from others. But the rest of his appearance was so singular that timid souls could not look on him without feeling a surge of fear. His deeply bronzed face was made darker still by the scorch marks of gunpowder, which had left many small scars, and his sallow skin was decorated with many strange designs. Nearly all Mediterranean sailors have themselves tattooed on their arms and chests with letters, galleys, crosses and other such decorations. Lettereo had gone further. On one cheek he had the tattoo of a crucifix, on the other a madonna. Only the top of these images was visible, the bottom being hidden by a thick beard which no razor ever touched and which scissors alone kept within certain bounds. Add to this gold earrings, a red bonnet and belt, a sleeveless jerkin, sailor's trousers, bare arms and feet and pockets full of gold and you have an idea of what the padron looked like.

It was said that in his youth he had enjoyed the favours of ladies of the highest circles and that he was the darling of the women of his own class and the scourge of their husbands.

Finally, to complete this portrait of Lettereo, I should tell you that he had been the best friend of a man of true merit who has since acquired a reputation under the name of Captain Pepo. Pepo and Lettereo had both served with the corsairs of Malta, but whereas Pepo

8 Blows with a dagger.

74

had then entered the service of his king, Lettereo, who cared less for honour than for money, had decided to acquire wealth in any sort of way. At the same time he had become the sworn enemy of his former comrade.

As my father had nothing else to do in his sanctuary than to tend his wound, which he no longer expected to heal completely, he was glad to converse with heroes of his own kind. That is why he befriended Lettereo, and in recommending me to him he had grounds to believe that I would not be turned down. Nor was he mistaken. Lettereo was even quite touched by such a sign of trust. He promised my father that my apprenticeship would be less harsh than that of a ship's boy normally would be. And he assured him that as I had been a chimney sweep it would only take me two days to learn to climb the rigging.

For my part I was delighted, since my new profession seemed to me more noble than cleaning chimneys. I kissed my father and brothers goodbye and cheerfully set off with Lettereo to join his ship. When we had boarded her the padron called together his crew, which numbered twenty men all similar in appearance to him. He introduced me to these gentlemen and said to them, 'Anime managie, quista criadura e lu filiu de Zotu. Se uno de vui a outri li mette la mano sopra is li mangio l'anima.'[9] This speech had the intended effect. It was even decided that I should mess together with the others, but I saw that two ship's boys of my age served the sailors and ate the leftovers, so I did the same. This they accepted and they liked me the better for it. But when they saw how I climbed the lateen yard they all were quick to congratulate me. The lateen yard on lateen-rigged boats takes the place of the main yard; but it is much less dangerous to perch on main yards because they are always in the horizontal position.

We set sail and on the third day we reached the straits of S. Bonifacio, which separate Sardinia and Corsica. There were more than sixty boats there fishing for coral. We also started to fish, or

---

9 'You damned scum, this lad is the son of Zoto. If one of you or anyone else lays a hand on him I'll do for him.'

75

rather pretended to. But I personally learned a great deal, for after four days there I could swim and dive as well as the boldest of my companions.

After a week the little fleet was scattered by a gregale – that is what the stiff north-easterly wind is known as in the Mediterranean. Each boat made for safety as best it could. We reached an anchorage known as the Roads of St Peter, which is a deserted beach on the Sardinian coast. There we came across a Venetian polacca which seemed to have suffered a great deal of damage during the storm. Our padron at once had designs on the boat and dropped anchor close to it. He sent part of the crew down to the hold so as to make it appear that few men were on board. This was a more or less pointless precaution since lateen-rigged boats always had more men than others.

Lettereo kept a close watch on the Venetian crew and established that it was composed of no more than a captain, a mate, six sailors and a boy. He also noticed that the topsail was torn and had been taken down to be mended since merchant ships never carry spare sails. Having gathered this information, he put eight guns and as many sailors in the longboat, hid them under a tarpaulin and settled down to wait for the right moment.

When the weather improved the sailors duly climbed the topmast to unfurl the sail, but as they did not set about this in the right way, the mate, followed by the captain, climbed up too. Lettereo then had the ship's boat lowered, stealthily embarked with seven other sailors and boarded the stern of the polacca, whose captain shouted down from the mainsail, 'A larga ladron, a larga.'[10]

But Lettereo aimed the gun at him and threatened to kill the first man who tried to climb down. The captain, who had the appearance of a resolute fellow, threw himself down into the shrouds, but Lettereo shot him in mid air. He fell into the water and was not seen again.

The sailors begged for mercy. Lettereo left four men to guard them and with the three others he searched the vessel. In the captain's room he found a barrel of the sort used to store olives, but as it was rather

10 'Keep off, you thieves, keep off!'

heavy and was carefully hooped he guessed that it might contain things other than olives. He opened it and was gratified to find several bags of gold. That was enough for him and he sounded the retreat. The boarding party returned and we set sail. As we passed by the stern of the Venetian boat we shouted out mockingly, 'Viva San Marco!'

Five days later we reached Livorno. The padron at once called on the Neapolitan consul with two of his men and made a formal declaration that his crew had picked a fight with that of the Venetian polacca and that by misfortune the captain of that ship had been pushed by a sailor and had fallen into the sea. A small part of the contents of the olive barrel were used to enhance the plausibility of this story.

Lettereo had a marked taste for piracy and would doubtless have continued to engage in similar enterprises, but at Livorno he was offered the opportunity of engaging in a different kind of trade, one that he preferred. A Jew, whose name was Nathan Levi, had noticed how much profit the pope and the King of Naples had obtained from their copper coinage and decided to share it. So he had counterfeit coins struck in an English town called Birmingham, and when there was a sufficient quantity he set up an agent in La Lariola, a fishing village on the border of the two states. Lettereo undertook to transport and unload the merchandise there.

The profits were considerable and we plied to and fro with cargoes of Roman and Neapolitan coins for more than a year. We might have been able to continue our voyages even longer but Lettereo, who had a genius for speculation, suggested to the Jew that he should produce gold and silver coinage too. Nathan Levi followed his advice and established at Livorno a small factory which produced sequins and scudi. The profits we were making aroused the jealousy of the authorities. One day when Lettereo was in Livorno and about to set sail, he was informed that Captain Pepo had been ordered by the King of Naples to seize his ship but that he was not able to put to sea until the end of that month. This false rumour was a trick on the part of Pepo, who had been at sea for four days. Lettereo fell for it. The wind was favourable. He reckoned that he could make one more journey and so set sail.

At daybreak on the next day we found ourselves in the midst of Pepo's flotilla, comprised of two galiots and two light vessels known as *scampavie*. We were surrounded, with no means of escape. With death in his heart, Lettereo broke out all sails and set a course for Pepo's vessel. Pepo was on the bridge, giving orders to board our ship.

Lettereo took a gun, took aim and hit Pepo in the arm. All this happened in a few seconds.

Soon after, the four ships bore down on us and we could hear from all sides the shout, 'Mayna ladro, mayna can senza fede.'[11]

Lettereo close-hauled, with the result that our side skimmed the surface of the water. Then, addressing the crew, he said:

'Anime managie, io in galera non ci vado. Pregate per me la santissima Madonna della Lettera.'[12]

We all knelt down. Lettereo put cannon-balls into his pocket. We thought that he had decided to throw himself into the sea but the crafty pirate had other plans. There was a large barrel full of copper lashed to the windward side. Lettereo cut the ropes with an axe. At once the barrel rolled to the other side of the ship, and as the ship was already listing quite far it had the effect of capsizing it. At first the crew, who were on their knees, fell into the sails, and when the ship went down we were fortunately thrown a fair distance clear on the other side by the sails' elasticity.

Pepo fished us all out of the sea with the exception of the captain, a sailor and a ship's boy. As we were hauled aboard, we were tied up and thrown into Pepo's hold. We put into Messina four days later. Pepo let the authorities know that he had some objects worthy of their attention to deliver to them. Our disembarkation did not lack a certain pomp. It happened to be at the time of the Corso when all the nobility walk up and down what is known as La Marina. We solemnly processed along, with *sbiri* behind us and *sbiri* in front of us.

The principino was among the spectators and recognized me as

11 'Haul down your flag, you double-dealing rascal!'

12 'You damned scum, I'm not going to the galleys. Pray for me to the most holy Madonna della Lettera.'

soon as he saw me, crying out, 'Ecco lo picolu banditu delli Augustini.'[13]

As he did this, he leapt at me and grabbed me by the hair and scratched my face. Since my hands were tied behind my back, I had difficulty in defending myself.

However, I remembered a trick I had seen done on some English sailors at Livorno. I freed my head and butted the principino in the stomach. He fell over backwards, got up boiling with rage, drew a little knife from his pocket and tried to strike me with it. I dodged and tripped him up, causing him to fall heavily, and even to cut himself on the knife he was holding. The princess arrived on the scene at this moment, and again wanted to have me beaten by her servants, but the *sbiri* would not allow this and led us off to prison.

The trial of the crew did not take long. The sailors were sentenced to the *strappado* and then to spend the rest of their days in the galleys. As for me and the other ship's boy who had survived, we were set free because we were under age. As soon as we were released, I went to the Augustinian monastery but found that my father was no longer there. The brother porter told me that he had died and that my brothers were cabin-boys on a Spanish ship. I asked to speak to the prior. I was taken to him and I told him my little story, not forgetting to mention the head-butt, and the tripping up of the principino.

His Reverence listened to me kindly and said, 'My son, your father left a considerable sum of money to the monastery on his death. It was ill-gotten gains to which you had no right. It is now in the hands of God and is destined to be used to provide for his servants. However, we have ventured to set aside a few gold pieces which we gave to the Spanish captain who was taking charge of your brothers. As for you, we are unable to give you sanctuary in this house out of respect for la Principessa de Rocca Fiorita, who is our illustrious benefactress. But, my child, you can go to the farm that we have at the foot of Mount Etna, where you can quietly spend your childhood years.'

13 'There's the little bandit from the Augustinians!'

After these words the prior sent for a lay brother and gave instructions concerning my future.

The next day I set out with the lay brother. We arrived at the farm, where I settled down. From time to time I was sent to town on errands which had to do with the running of the farm. On these trips I did all that I could to avoid the principino. One time, however, as I was buying chestnuts in the street, he happened to pass, recognized me and had me beaten by his lackeys. Soon after, I gained access to his house by means of a disguise and it would probably have been easy for me to kill him. I will never cease to regret not having done so, but I was not then familiar with such procedures and I was content to do no more than thrash him. Throughout my early years, six months did not pass, nor even four, without my meeting that damned principino, who often had the advantage of numbers over me. At last I reached the age of fifteen, still a boy in years and in reason, but almost a man in strength and courage, which is hardly surprising when you think of the sea air and then the mountain air which strengthened my constitution.

So I was fifteen when I first met the brave and worthy Testalunga, the most honourable and virtuous bandit there has ever been in Sicily. Tomorrow, if you will allow me, I will tell you all about this man whose memory will live on for ever in my heart, but now I must leave you. The management of my cavern requires careful supervision to which I must now devote myself.

Zoto left us, and we all discussed his story in ways which reflected our own characters. I confessed that I could not but feel some respect for men as courageous as Zoto described them. Emina maintained that courage is only worthy of our esteem if it is put to ends which bring virtue into good repute. Zubeida said that a little bandit of sixteen years of age was certainly capable of inspiring love.

We had supper and made our way to bed. The two sisters came to me again, catching me unawares.

Emina said to me, 'Dear Alphonse, would you be able to make a sacrifice for us? It is in your interest more than in ours.'

'Fair cousin,' I replied, 'these preambles are quite unnecessary. Tell me simply what you want.'

'Dear Alphonse,' said Emina, 'we are shocked, even horrified, by the jewel which you carry round your neck and which you call a piece of the true cross.'

'Oh no, as to that jewel, don't ask me for it,' I promptly replied. 'I promised my mother that I would never be parted from it and I keep my promises, as you very well know.'

My cousins remained silent and sulked a little, but they were soon mollified and that night was spent in much the same way as the night before, which is to say that their belts were left in place.

The Seventh Day

The next morning I woke earlier than the day before and went to see my cousins. Emina was reading the Koran, Zubeida was trying on some pearls and jewels. I interrupted these serious occupations with gentle caresses which were almost as much caresses of friendship as of love. Then we dined. After our meal Zoto came back to continue his story, which he did as follows:

ZOTO'S STORY CONTINUED

I promised to tell you about Testalunga and I will keep my word. My friend was a peaceful inhabitant of Val Castera, a village at the foot of Mount Etna. He had a charming wife. The young Prince of Val Castera, while visiting his estates, met his wife, who had come to greet him with other wives of leading citizens. Far from appreciating the homage offered to him by his vassals in the persons of their beautiful wives, the presumptuous young man had eyes only for the charms of Signora Testalunga. He bluntly told her the effect she had on his senses and put his hand inside her bodice. At that moment her husband was standing behind her. He drew a dagger from his pocket and plunged it into the heart of the young prince. Any man of honour would have done the same, I think.

After committing this act Testalunga fled to a church, where he stayed until nightfall. But deeming it necessary to take other measures for the future, he decided to join a small group of bandits who had recently taken refuge high up on Etna. There he went, and the group acknowledged him as their leader.

At that time Etna had just spewed out a vast quantity of lava. Testalunga established his band in the midst of those fiery torrents in a hiding-place the access to which was known only to him. After he had seen to his own safety, that brave leader wrote to the viceroy to

82

ask him for a pardon for himself and his companions. The government refused, fearing, I suppose, that their authority would be compromised.

So Testalunga negotiated with the principal farmers in the neighbouring district. 'Let us all steal together,' he said. 'I shall come and ask you for things, you will let me have what you will and you will still be blameless in the eyes of your masters.'

It was still stealing, but Testalunga shared everything with his companions and kept back for himself only what he absolutely needed. On the other hand, whenever he passed through a village he paid twice the proper price for everything, so that he soon became the idol of the people of the two Sicilies.

I have already told you that some of my father's band had joined Testalunga, who for several years was based on the southern slopes of Mount Etna, from which he raided the Val di Noto and the Val di Mazara. But at the time of which I am now talking, that is, when I was fifteen years old, the band came back to the Val Demoni, and one fine day we saw it arrive at the monks' farm.

In panache and brilliance Testalunga's men surpassed by far anything you could imagine. They were dressed as for the fray in brigands' clothes, with their hair in silk nets, belts bristling with pistols and daggers, long swords and long-barrelled guns. They stayed for three days, eating our chickens and drinking our wine. On the fourth they were informed that a detachment of dragoons from Syracuse was making towards them with a view to surrounding them. This news made them all laugh heartily. They set up an ambush in the sunken road, attacked the detachment and put it to flight. There were ten of them to every bandit but every bandit carried ten firearms all of the highest quality.

After this victory the bandits came back to our farm and I, having seen the fight from a distance, was so carried away with enthusiasm that I threw myself at their leader's feet and begged him to take me into his band. Testalunga asked me who I was. I replied that I was a son of Zoto the bandit.

On hearing this much-loved name, all those who had served under my father shouted for joy. One of them carried me in his arms to a table and, placing me on it, said, 'Comrades, Testalunga's lieutenant has been killed in the fight and we are at a loss to replace him. Let little Zoto be our lieutenant. Haven't we all seen the sons of dukes and princes put in charge of regiments? Let's do for the son of Zoto the brave what is done for them. I'll guarantee that he'll prove worthy of this honour.'

This speech earned rousing applause for the speaker and I was elected unanimously.

My rank was no more than a joke at first, and all the bandits would burst out laughing when they called me 'Signor tenente', but they soon changed their tune. Not only did I always lead the attacks and was the last to cover the retreat, but no one could match me when it came to spying out the enemy's movements and ensuring that the band was safe from attack. Sometimes I would climb on top of the rocks to overlook whole stretches of country and make the agreed signals. At other times, I would spend whole days in the very midst of our enemies. It often came about that I would stay all night up the tallest chestnut trees on Mount Etna and then, when I couldn't keep awake any longer, I would tie myself to the branches with a strap. Such things were not difficult for me as I had been both a ship's boy and a chimney sweep.

So well did I do that in the end I was entrusted with the overall security of the band. Testalunga loved me like a son and, if I may say so, I acquired a reputation which almost outshone his. The exploits of little Zoto became the talk of the two Sicilies. Such a reputation did not make me indifferent to the sweet pleasures of young men of my age. I have already told you that bandits were the heroes of the people. You can well imagine that the shepherdesses on Mount Etna would not have refused me their hearts. But mine was fated to yield to more delicate charms: love was reserving for me a more flattering conquest.

I had been a lieutenant for two years and had completed my seventeenth year of life when our band was forced to move south again because a new eruption had destroyed our usual hideouts. After four days' journey we reached a castle called Rocca Fiorita, the fief and family seat of my enemy the principino.

I hardly ever thought any more about the insults I had suffered at his hands, but the name of the place brought back all my rancour.

84

This should not surprise you, for in our climes hearts are implacable. If the principino had been in his castle, I believe I would have put it to fire and sword. But I confined myself to inflicting as much damage as I could, and my comrades, who knew why I was doing it, helped me to the best of their ability. The castle servants, who at first had put up some resistance, failed to resist the good wine of their master, which we caused to flow freely. They joined our side. In short we turned Rocca Fiorita into a land of plenty.

We lived in this way for five days. On the sixth our spies warned us that a whole Syracuse regiment was going to attack us and that afterwards the principino would arrive with his mother and ladies from Messina. I ordered my band to retreat but stayed behind myself out of curiosity. I settled myself down in the crown of a leafy oak which was at one end of the castle's gardens, having taken the precaution of making a hole in the garden wall through which I could make good my escape.

I duly saw the regiment arrive and set up camp in front of the castle, having posted sentries all around. Then a procession of litters arrived with the ladies in front and the principino at the back, lying on a pile of cushions. He got down with difficulty, helped by two young gentlemen of his household, and ordered a company of soldiers to march on ahead. When he was sure that none of us had remained behind in the castle he went in himself with the ladies and some gentlemen of his retinue.

At the foot of my tree there was a freshwater spring, a marble table and some garden seats. It was the most ornamental part of the garden. I guessed that the party in the castle would not be long in coming there and decided to wait to get a better look at them. And indeed, after about half an hour, a young girl of about my age appeared. Angels are not more beautiful than she was. The impression she made on me was so sudden and so strong that I would have fallen from my tree if I had not attached myself to it with my belt, something I did from time to time in order to rest in greater safety.

The young girl's eyes were cast down and she looked extremely dejected. She sat down on the seat, leaned over the marble table and wept copiously. Scarcely knowing what I was doing, I slid down the tree and positioned myself so that I could see her without being seen.

Then I saw the principino approaching with a bouquet of flowers in his hand. It was nearly three years since I had last seen him. He had grown up. His face, while handsome, was somewhat weak.

When the young girl caught sight of him her expression betrayed a contempt for which I felt deeply grateful to her.

Meanwhile the principino, looking self-satisfied, came up to her and said, 'My dear betrothed wife, here is a bouquet which is yours if you can promise never to mention that little wretch Zoto again.'

The young lady replied, 'Your Highness, I think that you are wrong to attach conditions to your favours, and in any case, even if I were not to mention charming Zoto to you, your whole household would be talking to you about him. Did not your nurse even say that she had never seen such a pretty boy? And you were there at the time!'

The principino was stung by this and retorted, 'Signora Sylvia, do not forget that you are my promised bride.'

Sylvia did not reply but burst into tears.

Then the principino flew into a rage and said, 'You contemptible creature. Seeing that you are in love with a bandit, this is what you deserve.' And with that, he slapped her face.

Then the young lady cried out, 'Zoto, why aren't you here to punish this coward?'

Scarcely had she uttered these words than I appeared and said to the prince, 'You recognize me, I am sure. I am a bandit. I could kill you. But I respect the signora who has done me the honour of summoning me to her assistance. However, I am prepared to fight as you nobles do.'

I had two daggers and four pistols on me. I divided them up into two lots, set them ten paces apart and offered the choice of weapons to the principino. He meanwhile collapsed on a seat in a faint.

Sylvia then spoke and said, 'Brave Zoto, I am of noble birth and poor. I was bound tomorrow to marry the prince or be sent to a convent. I shall do neither. I want to be yours for the rest of my life.' And she threw herself in my arms.

As you can well imagine, I needed no persuading, but I had to stop the prince from impeding our flight. I took a dagger and, using a stone as a hammer, I nailed his hand to the seat on which he was sitting. He screamed and fainted again.

We escaped through the hole that I had made in the wall and reached the high mountains.

All my comrades had mistresses and they were delighted that I should have found one. Their ladies swore complete obedience to mine.

I had lived with Sylvia for four months when I was forced to leave her to reconnoitre the area to the north, which had been changed by the last eruption. During this journey I found in nature delights that I had not noticed before. I saw grassy meadows, grottoes, and shady groves where before I had only seen places for ambushes or defensive positions. Sylvia had at last softened the heart of a brigand, but that heart was soon to regain all its ferocity.

I returned from my journey to the north of the mountain. I say the mountain because Sicilians always say 'il Monte', meaning the mountain *par excellence* when speaking of Etna. I made my way towards what we call the Philosopher's Tower[1] but could not reach it. A chasm which had opened up on the side of the volcano had belched forth a lava flow which had divided into two just above the tower and come back together about a mile below it, forming a completely inaccessible island.

I realized at once the value of this position. Moreover, we had a store of chestnuts in the tower which I did not want to lose. I eventually located, after much searching, an underground passage which I used on other occasions and which led me to the foot of the tower, or rather right inside it. I at once decided to install all our womenfolk on this island. I had huts built out of foliage and made one as attractive as I could. Then I went south again and brought the whole colony back with me. They were delighted with their new refuge.

Now, when I think back to the time I passed in that happy place, it seems to me an island in the middle of the cruel tempests which have assailed my life. Rivers of fire separated us from the rest of mankind. Our senses were inflamed by fires of love. All obeyed my orders and

1 This tower, which was built in the time of Hadrian, was linked by legend to the Greek philosopher Empedocles, who was said to have thrown himself into the crater of Etna.

87

all were subject to my dear Sylvia; and to crown my happiness my two brothers came to join me. They both had had interesting adventures, and I think I can assure you that if you wanted ever to hear an account of them you would derive more satisfaction from theirs than you have from mine.

Few men cannot count some days of perfect happiness, but I do not know whether any can count happiness in years. Mine did not last one whole year. The members of my band behaved honourably towards each other and none would even so much as look at the mistress of another, still less at mine. Jealousy was therefore banished from our island, or rather it was in temporary exile. For that fury can all too easily find a way to places where love dwells.

A young bandit called Antonino fell in love with Sylvia. His was so strong a passion that he could not hide it. I myself noticed it, but seeing that he was very sad I supposed that my mistress had given him no ground for hope and so was not concerned about it. But I would have liked to cure Antonino because I liked him for his courage. There was another member in the band, called Moro, whom I hated on the other hand for his cowardice. If Testalunga had listened to me, he would have driven him out long before then.

Moro wormed his way into the confidence of young Antonino and promised to serve him in his love. He also managed to persuade Sylvia to listen to him, and he made her believe that I had a mistress in the neighbouring village. Sylvia was afraid to bring the matter up with me but she began to act in an unnatural way, which I attributed to a change in her feelings for me. Meanwhile Antonino, on Moro's advice, had increased his attentions to Sylvia and went around with a satisfied air, which suggested to me that she was making him happy.

I had had no experience in dealing with intrigues of this sort, so I stabbed Sylvia and Antonino to death. The latter, who did not die at once, revealed Moro's treachery to me. I sought out the wretch, my bloody dagger still in my hand. The sight of this terrified him. He fell to his knees and confessed that the Prince of Rocca Fiorita had paid him to do away with Sylvia and me and that he had joined my band with the intention of accomplishing that end. I stabbed him to death. Then I went to Messina and, having gained access to the principino's house by means of a disguise, I dispatched him to the other world to join his henchman and my two other victims. Such was the end of my happiness and also of my glory. My courage now turned into an utter indifference for my own life, and as I manifested the same indifference for the lives of my comrades, I soon lost their trust. Since then I have become, I can assure you, the most ordinary of brigands.

Soon after, Testalunga died of pleurisy and his whole band broke up. My brothers, who knew Spain well, persuaded me to go there. At the head of a dozen men I went down to the Bay of Taormina and hid for three days. On the fourth we snatched a vessel, a snow, which carried us to the shores of Andalusia.

Although in Spain there was more than one mountain range which might have offered us favourable hiding-places, I chose the Sierra Morena and have not had cause to regret my decision. I captured two convoys of piastres and was responsible for a number of other feats on this scale.

In the end my successes caused offence at court. The Governor of Cadiz was ordered to take us dead or alive and sent out several regiments. But from another quarter the Sheikh of the Gomelez invited me to enter his service and allowed me to use these caves as a hiding-place. I had no hesitation in accepting.

The court in Granada did not want to admit defeat. So, seeing that we could not be found, it had two shepherds from the valley arrested, and hanged them under the names of Zoto's two brothers. I was acquainted with the two men and know that they had committed several murders. It is said, however, that they were vexed at being hanged in our stead and that at night they get down from the gallows and cause all sorts of mischief. I have not been witness to this and do not know what comment to make about it. However, it is true that I have had occasion to go by the gallows at night, and when the moon has been out, I have noted that the hanged men were no longer there although by morning they had reappeared.

And that, my dear sirs, is the story you asked of me. I believe that my brothers, whose lives have not been so wild, would have more interesting tales to tell you, but they will not have the time as we are ready to embark and I have had firm orders that this should take place tomorrow morning.

*

89

Zoto withdrew, and fair Emina said in a sad voice, 'That man is quite right. In any human life the time of happiness is very short. We have had three days here such as we may never see again.'

Supper was mournful and I hastened to say good-night to my cousins, for I hoped to see them again in my bedchamber and to be more successful in dispelling their melancholy.

They came back earlier than usual, and to my great delight carried their belts in their hands. The meaning of this gesture was not difficult to grasp. Emina took the trouble to explain it to me.

She said, 'Dear Alphonse, you have set no limit to your loyalty to us. We wish to set no limit to our gratitude. We may be parted for ever. For other women this would be a reason to refuse you their favours. But we wish to live on in your memory, and even if the women whom you will meet in Madrid surpass us in beauty of mind or face, at least you will not find that they outdo us in love and passion. But you must renew your oath never to betray us, dear Alphonse, and swear also that whatever ill is said of us you will not believe it.'

I could not help laughing at this last request but promised what they wished and was rewarded with the sweetest caresses.

Then Emina continued, 'My dear Alphonse, the relic around your neck bothers us. Couldn't you take it off for a little while?'

I refused, but Zubeida had a pair of scissors in her hand and, holding them behind my neck, cut the ribbon from behind. Emina seized the relic and threw it into a crevice in the rock.

'You can get it back tomorrow,' she declared. 'Meanwhile, put this tress of hair around your neck. It has been woven from my hair and that of my sister and the talisman which is attached to it wards off inconstancy in lovers, if anything is capable of doing such a thing.'

Then Emina pulled out a gold pin which held her hair in place and used it to close up the curtains around my bed tight together.

I shall do as she did and draw a veil over the rest of this scene. You need only know that my charming companions became my wives. There are doubtless cases where it is a crime violently to shed innocent blood, but there are others where such cruelty enhances innocence by making it appear in all its lustre. That is what happened to us. And I am led to conclude that my cousins played no real part in my dreams at the Venta Quemada.

Eventually our passions were spent and we lay peacefully together, when a fateful bell began to strike midnight. I could not repress a shiver of horror, and said to my cousins that I feared that some sinister event hung over us.

'I fear so, too,' said Emina. 'The danger is near. But listen carefully to what I am now saying to you. Do not believe any ill that is spoken of us. Do not even believe the evidence of your eyes.'

At that moment the curtains of my bed were ripped open and I saw a man of majestic height standing there in Moorish dress. In one hand he held the Koran, in the other a sabre. My cousins threw themselves at his feet and said:

'Oh mighty Sheikh of the Gomelez, forgive us.'

The sheikh replied in a terrible voice, 'Adonde están los fajas?'[2] Then he turned to me and said, 'Damn you, Christian wretch. You have dishonoured the blood of the Gomelez. You must become a Muslim or die.'

I heard a ghastly howl and caught sight of Pacheco the demoniac making signs at me from the corner of the room. My cousins also saw him, and in a terrible rage they got up, took hold of him and dragged him out of the room.

'Miserable Nazarene,' continued the Sheikh of the Gomelez, 'drink at a single draught the liquid contained in this cup or you will die a shameful death and your body will hang between those of Zoto's brothers; it will be prey to the vultures and the plaything of the infernal spirits who will use it for their diabolical charades.'

It seemed to me that in such circumstances honour dictated that I should commit suicide. I cried out in anguish, 'Oh father, in my place you would have done as I did.'

Then I took the cup and drained it at one draught. I felt a terrible pain and lost consciousness.

2 'Where are the belts?'

The Eighth Day

Since I have the honour of telling you this story, you will know that I did not die of the poison I thought I had drunk but only fainted, and I do not know how long I was unconscious. All I know is that I awoke under the gallows of Los Hermanos and this time came to my senses with a feeling of pleasure, for at least I had the satisfaction of knowing that I was not dead. Nor did I find myself lying between two hanged men. This time I was on their left, and to their right I saw another man who I thought had also been hanged as he looked dead and had a rope around his neck. But I soon realized that he was only sleeping and I woke him up.

When the stranger saw where he was, he started to laugh and said, 'It must be admitted that in studying the cabbala one is subject to annoying delusions. Evil spirits can take on so many shapes that one doesn't know whom one is dealing with.

'But,' he added, 'why have I got a rope around my neck? I thought I had a tress of hair.'

Then he caught sight of me and said, 'You are young for a cabbalist but you too have a rope around your neck.'

And so I did. I remembered that Emina had put a plait woven from her hair and that of her sister around my neck. And I did not know what to make of it.

The cabbalist stared at me for a moment and then said, 'No, you are not one of us. Your name is Alphonse and your mother was a Gomelez. You are a captain in the Walloon Guards and you are brave but still a bit naïve. Never mind. We must get out of here and then we'll see what is to be done.'

The gallows gate stood open and we went out. Once more I saw the accursed valley of Los Hermanos. The cabbalist asked me where I wanted to go. I told him that I had decided to take the road to Madrid.

'Good,' he said, 'I am also going that way. But we will begin by taking a little nourishment.'

He pulled out of his pocket a gilt cup, a pot filled with an opiate substance and a crystal phial, which contained a brownish liquor. He put a spoonful of the opiate in the cup, added a few drops of the liquor and told me to drink it all down. He did not need to repeat his request for I was faint with hunger. The elixir was marvellous. I felt so much better that I did not hesitate to set out on our journey on foot, which I would have found very difficult to do otherwise.

The sun was already quite high in the sky when the ill-fated Venta Quemada came into view.

The cabbalist stopped and said, 'There's an inn where a very cruel trick was played on me last night. However, we shall have to venture into it. I have left some provisions there which will do us good.'

So we went into that terrible *venta*, and in the dining room we found a table ready laid, on which there was a partridge pâté with two bottles of wine. The cabbalist seemed to have a healthy appetite and he encouraged me by his example. If he had not, I do not think that I could have brought myself to eat anything, for all that I had seen over the last few days had so perplexed my mind that I no longer knew what I was doing, and if anyone had tried they could have made me doubt my own existence.

When we had eaten we went from room to room and came to where I had slept on the day I left Andújar. I recognized my miserable pallet bed, sat down on it and began reflecting on all that had happened to me and especially on the events in the caves. I did not forget that Emina had warned me not to believe any ill which might be said of her.

I was absorbed in these thoughts when the cabbalist pointed out to me something which was glinting between the loose-fitting planks of the floor. I looked more closely and saw that it was the relic which the two sisters had removed from my neck. I had seen them throw it into a crevice in the rock and now I discovered it in a gap in the floorboards. I began to believe that I had never left that damned inn, and the hermit, the inquisitor and Zoto's brothers were so many ghostly apparitions produced by magical spells. Meanwhile with the help of my sword I recovered the relic and put it round my neck again.

The cabbalist started to laugh and said, 'So it belonged to you, Señor caballero! If you slept here, I am not at all surprised that you woke up under the gallows. Never mind, we must be on our way and we will reach the hermitage this evening.'

We set out and were only half-way there when we met the hermit, who seemed to be finding great difficulty in walking. He caught sight of us from afar and shouted out, 'Ah, my young friend, I was looking for you! Come back to the hermitage. Snatch your soul from Satan's clutches! But first lend me your arm. I have exerted myself cruelly on your behalf.'

We rested for a while and then set off again. The old man could only keep up by leaning on one or the other of us in turn. Eventually we reached the hermitage.

The first thing I saw was Pacheco stretched out in the middle of the room. He seemed at death's door, or rather his chest was racked by that terrible rattle which is the harbinger of imminent demise. I tried to speak to him but he did not recognize me.

The hermit took holy water, sprinkled it over the possessed man and said to him, 'Pacheco, Pacheco, in the name of your Redeemer, I order you to tell me what happened to you last night.'

Pacheco shuddered, let out a long wail and spoke as follows:

✎ PACHECO'S STORY ✎

You were in the chapel, Father, and were intoning a litany when I heard a knocking on the door and a bleating which sounded exactly like our white nanny-goat. So I thought that it was she and that I had forgotten to milk her and she had come to remind me. It was all the more easy to think this as the same thing had really happened a few days before. So I went out of your hut and indeed saw our white nanny-goat with her back to me, showing me her swollen udders. I tried to get hold of her to perform the service she asked of me but she slipped through my hands and, repeatedly stopping and then running

94

off, she led me to the edge of the precipice which is close to your hermitage.

When we reached the edge the white nanny-goat turned into a black billy-goat. I was very frightened by this transformation and tried to run back to where we live, but the goat cut off my retreat, and, rearing up on its hind legs and glaring at me with bloodshot eyes, it so frightened me that my senses froze.

Then the cursed goat started to butt me and push me back towards the precipice. When I reached the very edge it stopped to enjoy the sight of my mortal anguish. Then it pushed me over.

I thought that I would be dashed to pieces, but the goat reached the bottom of the pit before I did and I landed on its back without doing myself an injury.

New horrors soon assailed me. As soon as the cursed goat felt my weight on its back it galloped off in an extraordinary manner. It sprang at one single leap from one mountain top to the next, across deep, deep valleys as if they were mere ditches. In the end it shook itself and I fell somehow into the bottom of a cave. There I saw the young horseman who two days ago had slept at our hermitage. He was in his bed and beside him were two very beautiful girls dressed in Moorish clothes. These two young persons first caressed him, then removed from his neck a relic that was round it. As soon as they did this, their beauty vanished before my eyes and I saw them to be the two hanged men from the valley of Los Hermanos. But the young gentleman still took them to be beautiful young creatures and called them the most affectionate names. Then one of the two hanged men took the rope from around his neck and put it round the neck of the gentleman, who showed his gratitude by renewed caresses. In the end they shut the bed-curtains, and I do not know what they did next although I imagine that it was some horrible sin.

I tried to call out but could not make a sound. This lasted some time, then a bell struck midnight and soon after I saw a demon come in with fiery horns and a flaming tail, which was carried behind him by a number of little imps.

The demon held a book in one hand and a pitchfork in the other. He threatened to kill the young gentleman if he did not embrace the faith of Islam. Seeing this danger to a Christian soul, I made a great effort and think I was able to make myself understood, but at the same moment the two hanged men leapt on me, and dragged me out of the cave. There I found the black goat again. One of the two hanged men sat astride the goat, the other sat astride my neck and they forced us to gallop up hill and down dale.

The hanged man I was carrying on my neck kept poking me in the ribs with his claws, but on finding that I was still not fast enough for his taste he gathered up two scorpions as we ran along and attached them to his feet as though they were spurs. He then began to tear at my sides in a most barbarous way. When we at last reached the door of the hermitage he left me. That is where you found me lying unconscious this morning, Father. I thought I was saved when I woke up in your arms, but the scorpions' venom has got into my bloodstream and is tearing at my entrails. I shall not survive.

At this point the possessed man let out a terrible howl and fell silent.

Then the hermit said to me, 'My son, you have heard what he has said. Is it possible that you had carnal knowledge of two demons? Come, confess! Admit your guilt! The mercy of God is infinite. What? No reply? Has your heart become hardened?'

After having thought for a moment I replied: 'Father, this demoniacal gentleman saw things that I did not see. One of us has been bewitched. Perhaps both of us were suffering from delusions. But here is a gentleman, a cabbalist, who also slept at the Venta Quemada. If he will consent to tell us what happened perhaps we will gain new insight into the events which have been occupying us for the last few days.'

'Señor Alphonse,' replied the cabbalist, 'people who, like me, concern themselves with the occult sciences cannot disclose everything. I will try, however, to satisfy your curiosity to the best of my ability. But not this evening. Let us now eat supper and go to bed. Tomorrow our imaginations will be less excitable.'

The hermit served us a frugal supper, after which everyone only thought of bed. The cabbalist claimed that he had good reasons for sleeping beside the possessed man. I was sent off to the chapel as before. My bed of moss was still there and I lay down on it. The hermit wished me good-night and warned me that he would lock the door on his way out for greater safety.

When I found myself alone I reflected on Pacheco's story. I was sure that I had seen him in the caves and sure that I had seen my two cousins leap on him and drag him out of the bedchamber. But Emina had warned me not to think ill of her or her sister. In any case, the demons who had seized Pacheco could also have confused his mind and assailed him with all kinds of visions. I was still looking for reasons to justify my cousins and continue to love them when I heard midnight strike.

Soon after, I heard a knock at the door and what sounded like the bleating of a goat. I took my sword, went to the door and said in a loud voice, 'If you are the devil, try opening the door, for the hermit has locked it.'

The goat fell silent. I went back to my bed and slept until the next day.

The Ninth Day

The hermit came to wake me up, sat down on my bed and said, 'My child, my unfortunate hermitage was assailed last night by more devilment. The solitaries of the Thebaid[1] themselves were not more exposed to Satan's malice than we are. I also do not know what to make of the man who accompanied you here. You said he is a cabbalist. He has undertaken to cure Pacheco and has indeed done him some good. But he did not use the rites of exorcism prescribed by the holy Church. Come with me to my hut. We shall breakfast and then we shall ask him to tell us his story, which he promised us yesterday evening.'

I got up and followed the hermit. I indeed found Pacheco to be in a more tolerable state, and his face was less hideous. He was still blind in one eye but his tongue was no longer hanging out. He was not foaming at the mouth, and his one eye looked less wild. I complimented the cabbalist, who replied that it was only a very small demonstration of his power. Then the hermit brought us breakfast, consisting of hot milk and chestnuts.

As we were eating, we saw a gaunt, lean man come in. There was something frightening about his face, but it was impossible to say precisely what it was about him which inspired such horror. The stranger knelt before me and took off his hat. I saw then that he wore a headband. He presented his hat to me as if asking for alms. So I tossed a gold piece into it.

The extraordinary beggar thanked me and added, 'Señor Alphonse, your good deed will not go unrewarded. I am able to tell you that an

---

1 Monks who practised the most extreme form of asceticism in the upper part of the Nile Valley, inspired by the example of St Paul of Thebes (c. 230–341).

98

important letter is waiting for you at Puerto Lapiche. Do not enter Castile until you have read it.'

Having told me this, the stranger knelt before the hermit, who filled his hat with chestnuts.

Then he knelt before the cabbalist, who stood up at once and said to him, 'I want nothing of you, and if you say who I am, you will regret it.'

The beggar then left the hut.

When he had gone out the cabbalist began to laugh and said to us, 'In order to show you what little importance I attach to that man's threats, I shall first tell you who he is. He is the Wandering Jew of whom you may have heard. For about seventeen hundred years he has neither sat down, nor lain down, nor rested, nor slept. As he walks along he will eat your chestnuts and he will have covered sixty leagues between now and tomorrow morning. Normally he wanders all across the vast deserts of Africa. He lives off wild fruit. Wild animals cannot harm him because on his forehead is branded the sacred sign of Tau, which he hides under a headband as you have seen. He rarely appears in these lands unless forced to do so by the conjuration of some cabbalist. For the rest I assure you that I did not summon him here, for I detest him, but I admit that he is well informed about many things and I advise you not to ignore the information he has given you, Señor Alphonse.'

'Señor Cabbalist,' I replied, 'the Jew told me that there was a letter for me at Puerto Lapiche. I hope to reach there the day after tomorrow and I'll be sure to ask for it.'

'You will not have to wait so long,' said the cabbalist. 'I would have very little power over the world of genii if I could not arrange for you to have your letter earlier.'

He then turned his head towards his right shoulder and uttered a few words in a commanding tone. Five minutes later a thick letter addressed to me fell on the table in front of our very eyes. I opened it and read as follows:

Don Alphonse,

On behalf of King Ferdinand IV, I am instructed to command you not to enter Castile at present. You may attribute this severe ruling to the misfortune you have suffered of having displeased the holy tribunal whose duty it is to preserve the purity of the faith in Spanish lands. Do not let your zeal to serve the king slacken. You will find herewith a permit of leave for three months. Spend the time on the frontiers of Castile and Andalusia without making your presence conspicuous in either province. We have seen to it that your honourable father's mind has been set at rest and that he will look on this affair in a way which will not cause him too much distress.

Yours affectionately,

Don Sancho de Tor de Peñas, Minister of War.

The letter was accompanied by a three months' leave in due form and provided with the customary signatures and seals.

We complimented the cabbalist on the speed of his couriers. Then we entreated him to keep his promise and tell us what had happened the night before at the Venta Quemada. He replied as before that there would be things in his account which we would not be able to understand. Then, after having pondered for a moment, he began to tell his story.

∽ THE CABBALIST'S STORY ∽

In Spain I am known as Don Pedro de Uzeda and it is under this name that I own a fine castle a league away from here. But my real name is Rabbi Zadok ben Mamoun, and I am a Jew. This is a somewhat dangerous admission to make in Spain, but apart from the fact that I trust your integrity, I warn you that it would not be very easy to do me harm.

The influence of the stars on my destiny began to show itself as soon as I was born. My father, who cast my horoscope, was filled with joy when he saw that I had come into the world at the very moment that the sun entered the sign of Virgo. He had indeed employed all his skill to bring about this result but he had not expected to have achieved his goal with such precision. I do not have to tell you that my father, Mamoun, was the leading astrologer of his age. But knowledge of the constellations was one of the least difficult arts that he possessed, for he had gone further into the cabbala than any rabbi before him.

Four years after I was born, my father had a daughter, who was born under the sign of Gemini. Despite this difference between us, we received the same education. Before I was twelve and my sister eight years of age, we already knew Hebrew, Chaldean, Syro-Chaldean, Samaritan, Coptic, Abyssinian and several other dead or dying languages. As well as this, we could without the aid of a pencil combine all the letters of a word in all the ways prescribed by the rules of the cabbala.

It was also at the end of my twelfth year that we were both placed under strict discipline, and so that the modesty of the sign under which I was born should not be offended, we were only given meat from virgin animals, with the added nicety that I was to eat only the flesh of male animals and my sister only that of female.

When I reached the age of sixteen, my father began to initiate us into the mysteries of the cabbala of Sephiroth. First, he gave us to read the *Sepher ha-Zohar*, or book of splendour, which is so called because nothing can be understood of it at all, for it sheds so bright a light that it dazzles the eyes of the mind. Next, we studied the *Siphra di-Zaniutha*, or book of concealment, which at its most explicit might well be thought to be written in riddles. Finally, we were shown the *Idra Rabba* and the *Idra Sutha*, also known as the greater and lesser *Sanhedrin*.[2] These are dialogues in which Rabbi Simon bar Jochaï, who wrote the two preceding books, simplifies his style to the conversational, pretends to instruct his friends in the most basic knowledge but actually reveals to them the most astonishing mysteries; or rather, all the revelations that come to us directly from the prophet Elijah, who secretly left heaven to join Simon and his friends under the pseudonym of Rabbi Abba.

You non-initiates may think that you have got some idea of all this Holy Writ from the Latin translation which was printed together

2 The *Sephiroth* are the ten manifestations of divine power presented in the form of a geometrical configuration. The *Sepher ha-Zohar* was written in Aramaic towards the end of the thirteenth century by Moses ben Chemtob (1250–1305), who attributed it to the Talmudic scholar Simon bar Jochaï (90–160). Among the texts associated with it are the *Idra Rabba* and the *Idra Sutha*.

with the original Chaldean in 1684 in a small German town called Frankfurt.[3] But we cabbalists laugh at the presumption of those who believe that all that is needed in order to read are the physical organs of sight. That may suffice for some modern languages, but in Hebrew every letter is a number, every word a learned combination of signs, every phrase a terrible formula, which, when correctly pronounced with all the appropriate aspirates and stresses, could cause mountains to crumble and rivers to dry up. I do not need to tell you that Adonai created the world by the Word and then made himself into a Word.

Words strike the air and the mind, they act on the senses and on the soul. Although you are not initiates, you can easily grasp that they are the true intermediaries between matter and every order of intelligence. All that I may tell you is that every day we were growing not only in knowledge but also in power. If we did not dare to make use of this, we at least had the satisfaction of being aware of our new faculties and being inwardly convinced of their potency.

But our cabbalistic pleasures were soon interrupted by the most fateful of all events. As the days went by, we noticed, my sister and I, that our father Mamoun was losing his strength. He looked like a pure spirit who had only taken on human form so as to be perceptible to the vulgar senses of terrestrial beings.

Finally he called us one day into his study. His appearance was so venerable and divine that we both instinctively felt unease. He did not ask us to rise but, showing us an hour-glass, said, 'Before the sand in the glass shall have run out, I shall be no more. Listen carefully to every one of my words.

'I shall first address myself to you, my son. I have chosen celestial brides for you, daughters of Solomon and the Queen of Sheba. Their fate was to be born no more than mere mortals, but Solomon revealed to the Queen of Sheba the great name of He-who-is and the queen uttered it at the moment of giving birth. The spirits of the Grand Orient[4] hastened to the scene and caught the twins before they

3 Potocki is referring to Knorr von Rosenroth's *Kabbala denudata*, first printed in fact in Salzburg in 1677–8.

4 The name given to the part of the Temple of Jerusalem where the Holy of Holies was located.

had come into contact with that impure place known as earth. They bore them off to the sphere of the daughters of Elohim, where they received the gift of immortality and the power to pass it on to the person they chose as their common husband. It was these two ineffable brides which their father had in mind when he wrote his *Shir ha-Shirim*, or Song of Songs. You must study this divine epithalamium in groups of nine verses.

'As for you, my daughter, you are destined for an even more splendid match. The two Thamim[5] which the Greeks knew by the name of Dioscuri and the Phoenicians Cabiri, in other words, the celestial Gemini, will be your husbands. What can I say? With your tender heart I fear that a mortal . . . the sand has run out . . . I die.'

After these words my father faded away, and all we found on the spot where he was standing was a small pile of light and shining ashes. I gathered up these precious remains, put them in an urn and placed the urn in a tabernacle within our house under the wings of the cherubim.

As you may well imagine, the hope of enjoying immortality and possessing two celestial brides increased my enthusiasm for the cabbalistic sciences. But it was years before I could contemplate such lofty heights. At first I was content to summon up spirits of the eighteenth order. But by slow degrees I grew bolder, and last year attempted an exercise on the first verses of the Song of Songs. I had scarcely completed one line when there was a terrible noise and my castle seemed to shake apart on its foundations. This did not alarm me. On the contrary, I concluded that I had performed the correct operation. I passed on to the second line. When it was finished, a lamp I had on my table jumped up and dropped to the floor, bounced across it and placed itself in front of a tall mirror at the back of the room. I gazed into it and saw the tips of a girl's dainty feet and then two more little feet. I flattered myself that these charming feet belonged to the celestial daughters of Solomon but thought that I had proceeded far enough with my exercises.

I started anew the next night and saw the four little feet up to the

5 Perfect ones (in Hebrew).

103

ankle. The next night I saw the legs up to the knee. But then the sun left the house of Virgo and I was obliged to stop.

When the sun entered the sign of Gemini my sister carried out similar exercises to mine and saw a no less astonishing vision, which I will not tell you about, as it has nothing to do with my story.

This year I was getting ready to begin again when I learnt that a famous adept was due to pass through Córdoba. A discussion I had about this with my sister made me decide to go and see him on his way through. I was a little late in leaving and that day only got as far as the Venta Quemada. I found the inn abandoned because of the fear of ghosts. But as I do not fear them I settled down in the dining room and ordered little Nemrael to bring me supper. Nemrael is an abject, insignificant genie whom I use for such errands. It was he who fetched your letter from Puerto Lapiche. He went to Andújar, where a Benedictine prior was staying the night, unceremoniously removed his supper and brought it to me. It consisted of that partridge pâté which you found there the next day. I was so tired that I hardly touched it. I sent Nemrael back to my sister and went to bed.

In the middle of the night I was woken by a bell which tolled twelve times. After this prelude I expected to see some ghost or other. I got ready to send it away, because in general they are a tiresome nuisance. That was my frame of mind when I saw a bright light appear on the table in the middle of the room, in which a little sky-blue rabbi manifested himself, bobbing up and down in front of a desk in the way rabbis do when they pray. He was no more than one foot tall, and not only his clothing but also his face, his beard, his desk and his book were all blue. I soon realized that he was not a ghost but a genie of the twenty-seventh order. I did not know his name and had never come across him before. But I was able to use a formula which has some power over all spirits in general.

Then the little sky-blue rabbi turned to me and said, 'You have begun your operations backwards. That is why the daughters of Solomon have appeared to you feet first. Begin with the last verses and start by looking for the names of those two celestial beauties.'

Having uttered these words the rabbi vanished. What he told me contradicted all the laws of the cabbala. But I weakly followed his advice. I started at the last verse of the *Shir ha-Shirim* and by dint of looking there found the names of the two immortal sisters, which were Emina and Zubeida. This surprised me greatly but I began my invocation none the less. Then the earth shook terrifyingly beneath my feet. I thought I saw the skies falling down upon my head and I lost consciousness.

When I came round I found myself in a place radiant with light, in the arms of two young men more beautiful than angels.

One of them said to me, 'Son of Adam, come back to your senses. You are in the home of those who have not died. Our governor is the patriarch Enoch,[6] who walks before Elohim and was raised up from the earth. The prophet Elijah is our high priest. And his chariot will always be at your service whenever you want to visit one of the planets. As for us, we are Grigori born of the conjunction of Elohim's sons with mortal women. Among us there are some Nephilim but they are few in number.[7] Come, and we will introduce you to our sovereign.'

I followed them to the foot of the throne on which Enoch sat. I could not bear the sight of the fire which radiated from his eyes. I dared not raise mine higher than his beard, which was quite like the pale light which can be seen around the moon on rainy nights.

I was afraid that my ears would not be able to bear the noise of his voice. But his voice was more gentle than that of celestial organs. He softened it yet more to say to me, 'Son of Adam, your spouses will be brought to you.'

Then I saw the prophet Elijah come in, leading two beautiful women by the hand. Their charms were beyond mortal imagination. They were so delicate that they were transparent: one could see their souls and the fire of their passions as they flowed into their veins and mingled with their blood. Behind came two Nephilim, carrying a tripod made of a metal as superior to gold as gold is more precious than lead. My hands were placed in those of the daughters of Solomon, and around my neck was placed a plait woven from their hair. A pure bright flame

6 See Genesis 5:21–4.

7 According to the *Book of the Secrets of Enoch*, Grigori are angels who fathered, with the daughters of Seth son of Adam, the giants known as Nephilim. See also Genesis 6:1–4.

issuing from the tripod consumed in an instant my mortal being.

We were led to a couch resplendent with glory and burning with love. A large window was opened onto the skies of the third heaven[8] and angelic music carried me to the pinnacles of ecstasy . . .

Do I need to tell you that I woke next day under the gallows of Los Hermanos, lying next to their two foul corpses, as was this gentleman here? From this I conclude that I had encountered two very wicked spirits whose true nature is not well known to me. Indeed I am very much afraid that this adventure will prejudice my chances with the real daughters of Solomon, whose feet alone I have seen.

'You blind wretch!' cried the hermit. 'Do you have no remorse? All is but illusion in your baleful art. The cursed succubi have tricked you and inflicted the most terrible torments on poor Pacheco, and a similar fate may well await this young gentleman who, through a fatal hardness of heart, refuses to confess his faults. Alphonse, my son, oh Alphonse, repent! There is still time.'

I disliked intensely the hermit's persistence in asking of me a confession which I did not want to make. I replied to him coldly that although I respected his saintly exhortations, the code of honour was my guide. Then we spoke of other matters.

The cabbalist said to me, 'Don Alphonse, since you are being pursued by the Inquisition and the king has ordered you to spend three months in this remote part of the country, let me offer you refuge in my castle. There you will meet my sister, Rebecca, who is almost as beautiful as she is learned. Do come. You are a descendant of the Gomelez and all that family has a claim to our attentions.'

I looked at the hermit to read in his eyes what he thought of this proposal.

The cabbalist seemed to guess my thoughts because he turned to the hermit and said, 'Father, I know you better than you think. Your faith has given you great powers. My methods are not as holy but they are not diabolical. Why don't you come too, with Pacheco, whose cure I will complete?'

---

8 The *Book of the Secrets of Enoch* refers to seven heavens in all.

The hermit did not reply at once but began to pray. Then, having reflected a moment, he came across to us and with a cheerful look on his face told us that he was prepared to follow us.

The cabbalist turned his head towards his right shoulder; then he gave the order for the horses to be brought. A moment later two appeared at the door of the hermitage, together with two mules, which the hermit and Pacheco mounted. Although the castle was a day's ride away, according to ben Mamoun, we reached it within the hour.

On the way, ben Mamoun had spoken a great deal to me about his learned sister, and I expected to meet a black-haired Medea with a wand in her hand, muttering some incomprehensible words under her breath. But my image of her was quite wrong. Sweet Rebecca met us at the gate of the castle. She was the most adorable and engaging blonde. Her golden locks fell naturally down to her shoulders. She was dressed in a simple white dress secured by priceless clasps. Her outward appearance suggested someone who gave no thought to what she wore, but had she thought more about it, it would have been difficult for her to achieve a better effect.

Rebecca threw her arms around her brother's neck and said, 'You have given me a terrible fright. You always kept in touch except for the first night. What happened to you?'

'I'll tell you all about it,' said ben Mamoun, 'but for the moment think only of receiving the guests I have brought with me. This is the hermit from the valley, and this young man is a Gomelez.'

Rebecca glanced at the hermit with some indifference, but when she caught sight of me she seemed to blush and said with an air of sadness, 'I hope for the sake of your happiness that you are not one of us.'

We went in and the drawbridge was raised behind us. The castle was quite immense and seemed in excellent order. There seemed to be only two servants: a young mulatto and a girl of the same age and race. Ben Mamoun first took us to his library, a little rotunda which served also as a dining room. The mulatto laid the table-cloth, brought in an *olla podrida* and set four places, for the fair Rebecca did not sit down to table with us. The hermit ate more than usual for him and seemed also to become more human. Pacheco, who still only had one eye, did not seem to think himself possessed any more, although he was grave and remained silent. Ben Mamoun had a healthy appetite, but he seemed preoccupied and admitted that his adventure of the previous day had given him much to reflect upon.

As soon as we got up from table he said, 'Dear guests, here are books to keep you entertained, and my negro servant will gladly attend to all your desires. But I hope that you will allow me to withdraw with my sister. There is important work to be done. You will not see us again before the midday meal tomorrow.'

Ben Mamoun then duly withdrew and left us as it were in charge of the house.

The hermit took down from the bookcase an account of the lives of the Desert Fathers and told Pacheco to read some chapters aloud to him. I went out on to the terrace, which overlooked a precipice in whose unseen depth there flowed a raging river, which could be heard roaring below. However desolate the countryside looked, it gave me great pleasure to contemplate it, or rather to give myself over to the feeling which it inspired in me as I looked at it. This was not melancholy but rather an annihilation of all my faculties brought about by the many violent emotions to which I had been a prey for the last few days. Having thought much about what had happened to me and having come to no understanding of it, I no longer dared to dwell on it any more for fear of losing my reason. The prospect of spending a few quiet days in the castle of Uzeda was what gave me most hope. I left the terrace and went back into the library.

Then the young mulatto served a light meal of dried fruit and cold meats, none from unclean animals. Thereafter we went our own separate ways. The hermit and Pacheco were taken to one bedroom, I to another.

I lay down and fell asleep.

Shortly afterwards I was awoken by the fair Rebecca, who said to me, 'Señor Alphonse, forgive me for interrupting your rest. I have come from my brother's apartment. We have tried the most terrible invocations in order to discover who the two spirits were with whom he dealt at the *venta*, but without success. We think that he was tricked by baalim[9] over whom we have no power. Yet the dwelling

9 Pagan divinities.

108

of Enoch is indeed as he saw it. All this is of the highest importance to us and I beg you to tell us what you know.'

Having said this, Rebecca sat down on my bed, but she sat down only for that purpose and seemed only concerned with the information that she was asking of me. But she did not obtain it for I confined myself to telling her that I had given my word never to speak about the matter.

'But Señor Alphonse,' continued Rebecca, 'how can you believe that a promise given to two demons can be binding on you? Now we know already that there are two female demons there called Emina and Zubeida, but we don't know very much about the nature of these demons because in our art as in all others one cannot know everything.'

I stuck to my refusal and asked the beautiful girl not to speak any more about the matter.

She then looked at me with a kind of benevolence and said, 'How lucky you are to have principles of virtue which guide you in all your actions and which keep your conscience clear! How different is our own fate! We have striven to see what mortal eyes are not given to see and to know what mortal reason may not comprehend. I was not meant for such sublime knowledge. I care little for my futile authority over demons. I would have been well satisfied to rule over the heart of a husband but my father decided otherwise and I must bow to my destiny.'

As she spoke these words Rebecca drew out a handkerchief, apparently to hide her tears. Then she continued, 'Señor Alphonse, please allow me to return tomorrow at the same time and try again to overcome your stubbornness or, as you would call it, your steadfast attachment to your word. Soon the sun will enter the sign of Virgo. It will be too late then and what will happen, will happen.'

In taking leave of me, Rebecca shook my hand in a friendly way and seemed reluctant to go back to her cabbalistic exercises.

The Tenth Day

———————————— ✍ ————————————

I woke earlier than usual and went out on to the terrace to get a breath of fresh air before the sun had made the atmosphere too hot. There was no wind and above the roar of the river, which seemed now less furious, the chant of bird-song could be heard.

The peace of the elements stole into my soul and I was able to reflect with some tranquillity on what had happened to me since I left Cadiz. A few passing comments of Don Enrique de Sa, the governor of that city, which then came to my mind, led me to think that he also was part of the mysterious existence of the Gomelez and that he too knew part of their secret. He it was who had recommended to me my two valets, Lopez and Mosquito. I suppose it was on his orders that they deserted me at the entrance to the disastrous valley of Los Hermanos. My cousins had often led me to believe that I would be tested. I conjectured that I had been given a sleeping draught at the *venta* and that I had been carried under the gallows as I slept. Pacheco could have lost an eye in a quite different way than by an amorous liaison with two hanged men, and his terrifying story might be no more than a fable. The hermit, who was continually trying to discover my secret by means of the sacrament of confession, seemed to me then to be an agent of the Gomelez seeking to test my discretion.

At last, just as I thought I was beginning to understand better what had happened to me and to be able to explain it without having recourse to supernatural beings, I heard in the distance merry music which seemed to be coming from round the mountain. The music soon became more distinct and I saw a jolly band of gypsies who were marching along in step, singing and accompanying themselves on their *sonajas* and *cascarras*.[1] They set up their little temporary camp

---

1 Drums and handbells.

near the terrace, giving me the opportunity of observing the clothes and accoutrements which gave them so elegant an appearance. I supposed that these were the same gypsy thieves under whose protection the innkeeper of the Venta de Cárdenas had placed himself, as the hermit had told me. But they seemed too gallant to be brigands. As I was observing them, they set up their tents, placed their *ollas* over their fires and hung their babies' cradles from the branches of nearby trees. When all these preparations had been completed, they devoted themselves again to the pleasures of their nomadic existence, the greatest of which in their eyes was doing nothing.

The tent of their leader was distinguished from the others not only by the pole topped by a great silver knob which was planted at its entrance but also by its excellent condition and rich ornamental fringe, which is not usually seen on gypsies' tents. But you can imagine my surprise on seeing the tent open and my two cousins come out, wearing the elegant costume which in Spain is known as *a la gitana maja*. They came up to the terrace without, however, seeming to see me. Then they hailed their companions and began to dance that well-known *polo* to the words:

> Cuando mi Paco me alce
> las palmas para bailar
> se me pone el cuerpecito
> como hecho de mazapan, etc.[2]

If affectionate Emina and sweet Zubeida had turned my head when dressed in their Moorish simars, they delighted me no less in this new costume. But I thought that they had a sly, mocking air about them of the kind which suited fortune-tellers and which seemed to suggest that they were plotting some new trick on me by appearing before me in this new and unexpected guise.

The cabbalist's castle was carefully locked up. He alone held the keys, so I was unable to join the gypsies; but by taking a tunnel which led to the river and which was shut off by an iron gate, I was able to

2 'When my Paco lifts / my palms to dance / my little body / becomes like marzipan . . .'

take a close look at them, and even speak to them without being seen by those in the castle. So I went down to this secret gate and found myself separated from the dancers by no more than the bed of the river. They turned out not to be my cousins. They even appeared to me to have a somewhat common air typical of their station in life.

Ashamed of my mistake, I went slowly back up to the terrace. When I reached it, I looked down again and recognized my cousins. They seemed to recognize me too, burst out laughing and then retired to their tent.

I was indignant. Heavens above, I said to myself, can it be possible that two such adorable and adoring creatures should be two sprites who are in the habit of playing tricks on mortals by taking on many forms and shapes? Or even two witches? Or, what would be even more horrible, vampires which heaven has allowed to assume the hideous bodies of the hanged men in the valley? It seemed to me a moment ago that all my experiences could have had a natural explanation, but now I was not so sure.

As these thoughts were passing through my mind I returned to the library, where I found a thick tome on the table, written in Gothic script, entitled *Curious Stories by Happelius*. The book lay open and the page seemed to have been folded over deliberately to mark the beginning of a chapter in which I read the following story:[3]

✒ THE STORY OF THIBAUD DE LA JACQUIÈRE ✒

Once upon a time in France, in the town of Lyon, situated on the river Rhône, there was a wealthy merchant whose name was Jacques de la Jacquière; or rather he only took the name de la Jacquière after he had retired from commerce to become the provost of the city, which is an office the people of Lyon only give to men of great personal fortune and spotless reputation. Such was the good Provost de la Jacquière. He was charitable to the poor and a benefactor of monks and other religions, who are according to the law the true poor.

---

3 The story of Thibaud de la Jacquière appeared in 1687, in volume three of this eight-volume work, with the title 'Die stinckende Buhlschaft'.

But the provost's only son, Thibaud de la Jacquière, ensign in the king's men-at-arms, was not at all like his father. A stout campaigner who was always ready to draw his sword, a lusty seducer of girls, a shaker of dice, breaker of windows, smasher of lanterns, blasphemer and swearer, who often collared citizens in the street and swapped his old coat for a new one and his hat for a better one. So it was not long before Messire Thibaud was the talk of the town in Paris, in Blois, in Fontainebleau and in the other royal residences. Now our good king of saintly memory, François I, came eventually to be displeased by the behaviour of the young officer and sent him back to Lyon to do penance in the house of his father, the good Provost de la Jacquière, who lived at that time on the corner of the Place de Bellecour at the top of the Rue St Ramond.

Young Thibaud was received back into his father's house with as much joy as if he had come bearing all the indulgences in Rome. Not only was the fatted calf killed for him, but the good provost gave a banquet for his friends that cost more gold ecus than there were guests. And that is not all. The young stalwart's health was drunk and everyone wished him wisdom and true repentance.

But these charitable wishes displeased him. He took a golden cup from the table, filled it with wine and said, 'By the bloody death of the great devil himself, I pledge my body and my soul in this wine if ever I become a better man than I am now.'

These terrible words made the guests' hair stand on end. They crossed themselves and some of them rose from the table.

Thibaud also rose and went to take the air on the Place de Bellecour, where he ran into two of his former companions, who were rakes like himself. He embraced them, took them home with him and had them served many flasks of wine, without sparing a thought for his father and the other guests.

What Thibaud had done on the day he arrived he did the next day too, and all the days after that. The goodly provost's heart was broken and he resolved to commend himself to his patron saint, St James, and to place before the saint's image a candle weighing ten pounds which was decorated with two gold rings, each worth five marks. But as the provost tried to put the candle on the altar, he dropped it and upset a silver lamp which was burning in front of the saint. The provost had

had this candle made for another purpose, but nothing was closer to his heart than his son's conversion and he joyfully made the offering. However, when he saw the candle on the ground and the upset lamp he interpreted this as a bad omen and sadly made his way home.

On that same day Messire Thibaud again entertained his friends. They tossed back many a flask of wine, and when the night was already far advanced and it was pitch-black they went out to take the air on the Place de Bellecour. Once there, they linked arms and swaggered up and down like young men who think they will attract the attention of the girls in this way. But on this occasion it was to no avail, for neither girl nor woman passed by and they could not be seen from the windows because it was a dark night, as I have already said. So young Thibaud, in a louder voice than before and swearing his customary oath, said, 'By the bloody death of the great devil himself I promise to give him my soul and body if the great she-devil, his daughter, were to pass by and I had my way with her. For this wine has made my blood hot.'

These words displeased Thibaud's two companions, who were not as great sinners as he. One of them said, 'Messire, my good friend, remember that the devil is the eternal enemy of mankind and he does enough mischief without being invited and his name being invoked.'

But to this Thibaud only replied, 'I shall do what I have said.'

As he spoke the three rakes saw a lady wearing a veil, with the charming figure of one still very young, come out of a nearby street. She was pursued by a little black servant, who tripped, fell on his face and broke his lantern. The young lady seemed very frightened and did not know what to do. Then Messire Thibaud went up to her and as politely as he could he offered her his arm to accompany her home. After protesting a little, our poor damsel in distress accepted, and Thibaud turned to his companions and whispered to them, 'There, you see that the one I invoked hasn't kept me waiting. I bid you good-night.'

The two friends realized what he wanted and took their leave of him, laughing and wishing him joy and happiness.

Thibaud gave his arm to the fair young maiden, and the little negro whose lantern had gone out walked in front of them. The young lady seemed so distressed at first that she could hardly stand, but her courage returned little by little and she leaned more boldly on her escort's arm. From time to time she stumbled and even held tight to his arm to save herself from falling over. Then her escort would support her and press her arm against his breast, which he did, however, with great discretion so as not to startle his quarry.

So they walked and walked for such a long time that in the end it seemed to Thibaud that they had lost their way in the streets of Lyon. But he was not in the least displeased about this for it seemed to him that he would have his will all the more easily with his pretty lady, who had lost her way. But desiring to know whom he was dealing with, he asked her to sit down on a stone seat which he caught sight of near a doorway. She agreed and he sat down next to her. He then took one of her hands in a gallant manner and wittily said to her, 'Oh lovely wandering star, since my star brought it about that we have met tonight, be so kind as to tell me who you are and where you live.'

The young lady seemed at first very shy, but gradually grew in confidence and spoke as follows:

THE STORY OF THE FAIR MAIDEN OF ∽ THE CASTLE OF SOMBRE ∽

My name is Orlandine, or at least that is what I was called by the few people who lived with me in the Château de Sombre in the Pyrenees. There the only human beings I ever saw were my governess, who was deaf, and a maidservant, who stammered so badly that she could well have been called mute, and an old gatekeeper, who was blind.

The gatekeeper did not have much to do, since he only had to open the castle gates once a year to admit a gentleman who only visited us to take me by the chin and speak to my duenna in Basque, which I do not understand. Fortunately, I could speak when I was locked away in the castle of Sombre, for I certainly would not have learnt to speak from my two companions in that prison. As for the blind gatekeeper, I only ever saw him when he came to pass our meals through the bars of our only window. To be fair, my deaf governess shouted moral advice in my ears, but I made so little of it that I might have been as deaf as she, for she spoke of the duties of marriage without telling me what marriage was. She spoke in the same way about many other things which she refused to explain. Often my stammering maidservant tried to tell me some story that she assured me was very funny, but since she would never get beyond the first sentence she was forced to give up, stammering out excuses, which she managed to do no better than she could tell stories.

As I have told you, we had only one window, by which I mean only one looked out on to the courtyard of the castle. The others looked on to another courtyard which, as there were trees planted there, could pass for a garden, and to which there was only one way out, which led through my bedroom. I grew a few flowers there. It was my one pastime.

I am not telling you the whole truth, for I had another pastime as innocent as the first. There was a tall mirror in which I went to look at myself as soon as I had got up. Indeed on getting out of bed, my governess, as little dressed as I was, went to look at herself in it also and it amused me to compare my figure with hers. I would also indulge myself in this distraction before going to bed and after my governess was already asleep. Sometimes I imagined that I saw in the mirror a companion of my own age, who responded to my gestures and shared my feelings. The more I indulged in this make-believe, the more I found pleasure in it.

I have told you that a gentleman came once a year to take me by the chin and to speak Basque to my governess. One day, instead of taking me by the chin, this gentleman took me by the hand, led me to a closed carriage and shut me up inside it with my governess. Shut me up is the right expression, because the only light to enter the coach came from above. We were not let out until the third day, or rather the third night, for it was very late on in the evening.

A man opened the door and said, 'You are now in the Place de Bellecour at the end of the Rue St Ramond. Here is the house of Provost de la Jacquière. Where do you want to be taken?'

'Enter the first gateway after the provost's,' replied the governess.

At this young Thibaud pricked up his ears, because he was indeed the neighbour of a gentleman called the Sieur de Sombre, who had the reputation of being very jealous. And the aforesaid Sieur de Sombre had often boasted in Thibaud's presence that he would demonstrate one day that it was possible to ensure the fidelity of one's wife, and that he was bringing up a young maiden in his castle who would become his wife and prove his claim. But young Thibaud did not know she had reached Lyon and was delighted to have her in his hands.

Meanwhile Orlandine continued as follows:

So we went through the gateway of the house, and I was taken up to some beautiful great rooms, and from there up a spiral staircase to a tower from which it seemed to me that one could have seen the whole city of Lyon if it had been daytime. But even by day one would not have seen anything, because the windows were covered with very heavy green cloth. For the rest, the tower was lit by a fine crystal chandelier set in enamel. My duenna sat me down on a chair, gave me her rosary beads to play with and then went out, triple-locking the door behind her.

When I found myself alone I threw down the beads, took hold of the scissors I had on my belt and cut a hole in the green cloth covering the window. Through it I saw another window very close to mine, and through that window I saw a brightly lit room in which three young gentlemen and three young girls were eating supper. They were more handsome and merrier than anything imaginable. They sang, they drank, they laughed, they hugged each other. They even took each other by the chin sometimes, but in a very different way from the gentleman at the castle of Sombre, who none the less came to do just that. What is more the gentlemen and the ladies took off more and more clothes, as I used to do in front of my tall mirror in the evening. And truthfully speaking this suited them just as well, not like my governess.

At this point Messire Thibaud realized that she was talking about the supper party he had given the day before with his two companions. He put his arm round the plump and supple waist of Orlandine and pressed her to his heart.

'Yes,' she said, 'that is exactly what the young gentlemen were doing. Truthfully it seemed to me that they all loved each other very much. But one of the young gentlemen claimed that he was a better lover than the others. "No, I am. No, I am," cried the other two. So the one who had boasted of being the best lover thought of a very curious way of proving that he was right.'

At this point Thibaud remembered what had happened at supper and nearly choked with laughter.

'Well, pretty Orlandine,' he said. 'What was it that the young gentleman thought of?'

'Oh, do not laugh, sir,' replied Orlandine. 'I assure you it was a very good idea and I watched it closely until I heard someone opening the door. Immediately I returned to my rosary and my governess came in.

'Silently she took me by the hand and led me down to a carriage which was not closed as was the first, so that from it I could have seen the town, but it was after dark and all I saw was that we went very far and came eventually to a stretch of countryside on the very edge of town. We stopped at the last house in the suburbs. It looked like a simple hut and it was even thatched, but inside was very pretty, as you will see if the little negro knows the way, for I see he has found a light and is lighting his lantern again.'

So Orlandine's story ended. Thibaud kissed her hand and said, 'Pretty lady who has lost her way, pray tell me, do you live alone in this house?'

'All alone,' said the fair maiden, 'with the little negro and my governess. But I don't think that she will come back to this house this evening. The gentleman who used to take me by the chin sent word to me to join him with my governess at the house of one of his sisters, but added that he could not send his carriage as it had gone to fetch a priest. So we set out on foot. Someone stopped us to tell me how pretty I looked. My governess, who is deaf, thought that he was insulting me and so she insulted him in turn. Others arrived on the scene and joined in the squabble. I took fright and began to run, and the little negro ran after me. He fell over, his lantern broke and it was then, kind sir, that I had the good fortune to meet you.'

Messire Thibaud was charmed by the naivety of this account and was about to make a gallant reply when the little black servant came back with his lighted lantern. As its light fell on Thibaud's face,

Orlandine exclaimed, 'What do I see? It's the same gentleman who thought up the clever idea!'

'It is, indeed,' said Thibaud, 'and I assure you that what I did was nothing to what a charming and respectable young lady might expect. For my female companions were anything but that.'

'But you certainly looked as though you loved all three of them,' said Orlandine.

'That's because I didn't love any of them,' replied Thibaud.

And so he talked and she talked and, walking and chatting all the while, they reached the outskirts of the town and came to an isolated hut whose door the little black servant opened with a key he carried on his belt.

The interior of the house was not cottage-like at all, for there were Flemish tapestries with figures so well worked and exquisitely drawn that they seemed alive, chandeliers whose arms were made in fine, solid silver, rich furniture in ivory and ebony, armchairs covered in Genoese velvet and trimmed with gold tassels, and a bed in Venetian moiré. But all this did not catch the attention of Messire Thibaud. He had eyes only for Orlandine and would have liked there and then to have reached the climax of his own plot.

Then the little negro arrived to lay the table, and Thibaud saw that he was not a child, as he had first thought, but rather an old, coal-black dwarf with a hideous face. But the midget brought something that was in no way ugly. It was a silver-gilt dish on which there were four appetizing and well-prepared partridges still steaming from the oven. Under his arm he had a flask of hippocras. No sooner had Thibaud eaten and drunk than he felt as though liquid fire was coursing through his veins. Orlandine ate little and gazed at her guest, sometimes with a tender, naïve expression and sometimes with eyes so full of mischief that the young man was almost unnerved by them.

Eventually the little negro came to clear the table. Then Orlandine took Thibaud's hand and said, 'Handsome sir, how would you like us to spend the rest of the evening?'

Thibaud did not know what to reply.

'I've an idea,' said Orlandine. 'Here is a tall mirror. Let us play the game I played at the castle of Sombre. There I amused myself by seeing whether my governess was built differently from me. I'd like now to see whether I am differently built from you.'

Orlandine placed two chairs in front of the mirror. Then she unlaced Thibaud's ruff and said, 'Your neck is more or less the same as mine. So are your shoulders, but what a difference in our chests! Mine was like yours last year, but I have become so plump there that I hardly recognize myself any more. Take off your belt, undo your doublet. What are all these laces for?'

Thibaud could not control himself any longer and carried Orlandine over to the bed of Venetian moiré, where he thought himself the happiest of men . . .

But he soon changed his mind when he felt something like claws digging into his back.

'Orlandine, Orlandine, what is the meaning of this?'

Orlandine was no more. In her place Thibaud saw only a revolting mass of strange and hideous forms.

'I am not Orlandine,' said the monster in a terrible voice. 'I am Beelzebub. Tomorrow you will see what body I assumed to seduce you.'

Thibaud tried to invoke the name of Jesus but Satan guessed his intention and seized his throat with his teeth, preventing him from uttering that holy name.

Next day, peasants who were on the way to market to sell their vegetables heard groans coming from an abandoned shack which was close by the road and was used as a rubbish dump. They went inside and found Thibaud lying on a half-decomposed corpse. They lifted him up, laid him across their baskets and in this way carried him home to the Provost of Lyon. The unhappy la Jacquière identified his son.

The young man was put to bed. Soon after he seemed to regain his senses to some extent, for he said in a weak, almost unintelligible voice, 'Open the door to the holy hermit. Open the door to the holy hermit.'

At first he was not understood. Finally the door was opened and a venerable monk came in, asking to be left alone with Thibaud. His request was granted and the door was shut behind them. For a long while the hermit's exhortations could be heard, to which Thibaud replied in a strong voice, 'Yes, Father, I repent and I trust in God's mercy.'

Eventually nothing more was heard and it seemed right to go in. The hermit had disappeared and Thibaud was found dead with a crucifix in his hands.

No sooner had I finished this story than the cabbalist came in and seemed to want to read in my eyes the impression the story had made on me. The truth is that it had made a deep impression. But I did not want him to see this, so I retired to my own room. Once there I thought about everything that had happened to me, and I almost came to believe that demons had assumed the corpses of two hanged men to trick me and that I was a second la Jacquière. The bell for dinner sounded. The cabbalist was not at table. Everyone seemed preoccupied to me because I was preoccupied myself.

After dinner I went back to the terrace. The gypsies had pitched their camp some distance from the castle. The enigmatic gypsy girls did not appear. Night fell and I retired to my bedroom. For a long time I waited for Rebecca. She did not come and I fell asleep.

The Eleventh Day

I was awoken by Rebecca. As I opened my eyes the Jewish girl was already installed on my bed and was holding one of my hands.

'Brave Alphonse,' she said. 'You wanted yesterday to accost the two gypsy girls but the river gate was closed. I have brought you the key. If they approach the castle today, I beg you to follow them even into their camp. I assure you that you would greatly please my brother if you gave him information about them. As for me,' she added in a melancholy tone, 'I must depart. My fate so ordains, my strange fate. Oh my father, why didn't you leave me with an ordinary destiny? I could then have loved what is real and not what is in a mirror.'

'What do you mean, in a mirror?'

'Nothing, nothing,' replied Rebecca. 'One day you will know. Farewell. Farewell.'

The Jewish girl left in great distress and I could not help thinking that she would find it very difficult to preserve her purity with the celestial twins whose bride she was destined to be, according to her brother.

I went out on to the terrace. The gypsies had moved even further away than the day before. I took a book from the library but hardly read at all. I felt distracted and preoccupied. At last we sat down to table. As usual, the conversation turned on spirits, spectres and vampires. Our host told us that in antiquity people had no clear notion of them and called them empusae, larvae and lamiae, but that the ancient cabbalists were at least as good as modern ones even though they were known as philosophers, a name they shared with people who knew nothing about the hermetic arts.

The hermit spoke about Simon Magus,[1] but Uzeda claimed that

---

1 Simon Magus was said to be the founder of a gnostic sect (see Acts 8:9–24).

122

Apollonius of Tyana should be considered the greatest cabbalist of those times since he possessed extraordinary powers over all the spirits of the whole world of demons. On saying this, he went to fetch a copy of the 1608 edition of Philostratus printed by Morel,[2] and cast his eyes over the Greek text. Then, without showing the slightest difficulty in understanding it, he read aloud in Spanish the following:

✐ THE STORY OF MENIPPUS OF LYCIA ✐

In Corinth, there was once a Lycian called Menippus. He was twenty-five years old, handsome and intelligent. It was said in the town that he was loved by a beautiful and very wealthy foreign lady whose acquaintance he owed solely to chance. He had met her on the road to Cenchreae. She had come up to him and said most charmingly, 'Menippus, I have long been in love with you. I am a Phoenician and I live on the edge of the suburbs of Corinth, not far from here. If you come to my home you will hear me sing. You will drink wine such as you have never drunk before, you will not have to fear any rival and you will find me always as faithful as I believe you to be wholly honest.'

Although a philosopher, the young man did not resist these blandishments issuing from such beautiful lips, and became devoted to his new mistress.

When Apollonius saw Menippus for the first time he studied him as carefully as a sculptor who had undertaken to make a bust of him. Then he said, 'Handsome young man, you are caressing a serpent and the serpent is caressing you.'

Menippus was surprised by these words. Apollonius went on, 'You are loved by a woman who cannot be your wife. Do you think that she loves you?'

'Without doubt,' said the young man. 'She loves me very much.'

'Will you marry her?' asked Apollonius.

---

2 The story of Menippus of Lycia is to be found in book three of Philostratus's *Life of Apollonius of Tyana*, written in the third century CE.

'It would please me very much to marry a woman that I love,' said the young man.

'When will the wedding be?' said Apollonius.

'Perhaps tomorrow,' said the young man.

Apollonius took note of the hour of the ceremony, and when the guests were assembled he went into the room and said, 'Where is the good lady who is giving this feast?'

Menippus said, 'She is not far away.'

And then rather shamefacedly he stood up.

Apollonius then said, 'All this gold, all this silver, all these ornaments in the room – are they yours or the woman's?'

Menippus said, 'They belong to the woman. All I possess is my philosopher's cloak.'

Then Apollonius said, 'Have you ever seen the gardens of Tantalus, which exist and yet do not exist?'

The guests replied, 'We have found them depicted in Homer. We have not gone down into the underworld.'

Then Apollonius said to them, 'All that you can see here is like those gardens. It is all appearance without any reality. In order to make you realize the truth of what I am saying let me tell you that the woman is one of those empusae normally called larvae or lamiae. They are desperate not for the pleasures of love but for human flesh. The way they attract those they want to devour is by exciting their lust.'

The bogus Phoenician then said, 'Hold your tongue.'

Next, showing signs of her annoyance, she fulminated against philosophers and called them madmen. But at Apollonius's words the gold and silver cutlery disappeared; at the same time the cup-bearers and cooks also vanished. Then the empusa pretended to cry and begged Apollonius to torment her no longer. But he continued to press her until she finally admitted who she was and said that she had satisfied Menippus's desires only to devour him in due course, and that she liked eating handsome young men because their blood did her a lot of good.

'In my view,' said the hermit, 'it was Menippus's soul rather than his body that she wanted to devour. This empusa was no more than the demon of lust. But I can't imagine what the words were which gave so great powers to Apollonius. For after all, he was not a Christian and could not deploy the awesome arsenal which the Church has placed in our hands. Moreover, philosophers may have managed to gain some power over demons before the birth of Christ, but the Cross itself, which silenced all their oracles, must have destroyed all other powers of idolaters. And I think that Apollonius, far from being able to drive out the most paltry of demons, could not even have had authority over the least ghost, because such spirits only return to earth by divine permission and only do so to ask for Masses, a proof in itself that there weren't any ghosts in pagan times.'

Uzeda was of a different opinion. He maintained that pagans had been plagued by ghosts as much as Christians, although no doubt for different reasons, and to prove it he picked up a volume of Pliny's letters, from which he read the following:[3]

THE STORY OF ATHENAGORAS
✒ THE PHILOSOPHER ✒

There was in Athens a large house which would have been pleasant to live in, but which was ill-famed and deserted. Often in the silent watches of the night a noise of iron striking iron was heard, and if one listened more closely one could hear a rattle of chains which seemed to start in the distance and then come nearer. Soon a spectre would make its appearance in the shape of a thin, downcast old man with a long beard, hair standing on end and irons on his feet and hands which he rattled in a terrifying way. This ghastly apparition caused insomnia in those who set eyes on it, and insomnia is the cause of many illnesses which have a tragic outcome. For although the spectre did not appear by day, the visual image he made did not fade from one's eyes and the terror was just as great, even though the object which had caused it had vanished. In the end the house was abandoned and given over altogether to the phantom. A board was none the less put up to make it known that the house was for sale or to let, in the hope that a

---

3 From the twenty-seventh letter of book seven.

person not informed about so terrible an inconvenience might be fooled into living there.

At that time Athenagoras the philosopher came to Athens, saw the board and asked the price of the house. The reasonableness of the asking price aroused his suspicions. He made inquiries and was told the story, but far from making him withdraw, it encouraged him to complete the purchase without delay. He moved into the house, and that evening he ordered his bed to be laid out in the front room, called for writing-tables and a light and told his servants to retire to the back of the house. Fearing that his all-too-active imagination might succumb to baseless fear and produce idle phantoms, he concentrated his mind, his eyes and his hands on his writing.

During the first part of the night silence reigned in the house as everywhere else. But a little later he heard the clanking of iron on iron and the rattling of chains. He did not raise his eyes. He did not put down his pen. But he steeled himself and tried as it were to blot out all noise.

But the noise grew louder and seemed to be coming first from the door of his room, then from inside the room itself. He looked up and saw the spectre just as it had been described. The spectre was standing and beckoning to him. Athenagoras gestured to him to wait a little and went on writing as though nothing untoward had happened. The spectre then started to rattle his chains again in the very ears of the philosopher.

Athenagoras turned round and saw the spectre beckoning again. He got up, took the light and followed the phantom, who walked ahead with a slow tread as though weighed down by the chains. When he reached the courtyard of the house he suddenly disappeared, leaving our philosopher on his own. Athenagoras then picked some leaves and grass and put them on the spot where the spectre had left him, so that he would find it again. The next day he went to the magistrates and asked them to have the spot excavated. This was done. Fleshless bones bound up in chains were found. Time and the dampness of the earth had caused the flesh to rot away, leaving only bones in the fetters. The remains were collected together and the town assumed the responsibility of burying them. And ever since the corpse was paid its last respects it no longer disturbed the peace of the house.

When the cabbalist finished reading he added, 'Ghosts have appeared throughout history, Reverend Father, as we see from the history of the Witch of Endor,[4] and cabbalists have always had the power to summon them up. But I admit that in other ways there have been great changes in the world of demons. Vampires, among others, are new inventions, if I may put it that way. I myself distinguish two species: the vampires of Hungary and Poland, who are corpses which leave their tombs at night to suck human blood, and the vampires of Spain, who are foul spirits which assume the first dead body they come across, turn it into any imaginable shape and . . .'

Realizing what the cabbalist was getting at, I left the table with a haste which was somewhat discourteous and went out on to the terrace. I had been there for less than half an hour when I saw my two gypsy girls, who appeared to be coming towards the castle and from that distance looked just like Emina and Zubeida. I immediately decided to use my key. I went into my bedroom, fetched my sword and cloak and then hurried down to the river gate but, having opened it, the hardest part was yet to come, for I had still to cross the river. To do so, I had to edge along the retaining wall of the terrace, holding on to the iron rings which had been placed there for that purpose. I eventually reached the bed of stones and by leaping from one to the next I reached the other bank and came face to face with the gypsy girls. They were not my cousins. They did not have their refinement although they were not as common and vulgar as the women of their race usually are. It almost seemed as if they were only playing at being gypsies. They wanted first to tell my fortune. One opened out my hand and the other pretended to see my future in it, saying:

'Ah, Señor, que veja en vuestra bast? Dirvanos kamela ma por quien? Por demonios!'

4 See Samuel I 28:7–19.

That is to say, 'Ah, sir, what do I see in your hand? Much love but for whom? For demons!'

As you may well imagine, I would never have guessed that 'dirvanos kamela' meant 'much love' in the gypsy tongue. But they took the trouble to explain it to me and then they each took one of my arms and led me to their camp, where they introduced me to a healthy-looking and still robust old man who they said was their father.

The old man said in a mischievous way, 'Do you know, Señor caballero, that you are in the midst of a band of which some ill is spoken in these parts? Are you not a little afraid of us?'

At the word 'afraid' my hand went to the hilt of my sword, but the old gypsy held out his hand in a friendly manner and said, 'I am sorry, Señor caballero, I did not mean to offend you. Indeed such a thought was so far from my mind that I am inviting you to spend a few days in our company. If a journey in these mountains is something which may interest you, we can promise to show you their most beautiful and their most awesome valleys, the most agreeable parts and, hard by them, what are called their picturesque horrors. And if you enjoy hunting, you will have plenty of free time to satisfy your taste for it.'

I accepted this offer all the more eagerly because I was beginning to be bored by the cabbalist's lectures and the isolation of his castle.

Then the old gypsy led me to his tent and said, 'Señor caballero, this tent will be your quarters for as long as you choose to spend time with us. And I'll have a small open tent erected right next to it for me to sleep in so that I can better see to your security.'

I replied to the old man that as I had the honour of being a captain in the Walloon Guards I was bound to rely for my protection on my sword alone.

This reply made him laugh and he said, 'Señor caballero, the muskets of the bandits in these parts could kill a captain in the Walloon Guards as easily as anyone else. Once they have been told about you, you will even be able to leave our band and go off on your own, but until then it would be imprudent to try.'

The old man was quite right and I felt somewhat ashamed at my bravado.

We spent the evening wandering around the camp and talking to the young gypsy girls, who seemed to me to be the most wanton and also the happiest women in the world. Then supper was served. The table was laid in the shade of a carob tree near the chief's tent. We stretched out on deerskins and the food was served on a buffalo hide, which had been treated to resemble Morocco leather, and which took the place of a table-cloth. The food was good, especially the game. The chief's daughters poured out the wine, but I preferred to drink water from a spring which flowed from the rock a few paces away. The chief kept the conversation going pleasantly. He seemed to know all about my adventures and predicted that I would have more.

At last it was time to go to bed. One was made up for me in the chief's tent and a guard was posted at the door. But towards the middle of the night I was awoken with a start. Then I sensed that my blanket was being lifted from both sides at the same time, and I felt two bodies pressing against mine. 'Merciful God,' I said to myself. 'Will I have to wake up again between two hanged men?'

But this idea soon left my head. I supposed that what was happening was an aspect of gypsy hospitality and that it would be hardly right for a soldier of my age not to go along with it. Later I fell asleep in the firm conviction that my companions were not two hanged men.

The Twelfth Day

Indeed, I did not wake up under the gallows of Los Hermanos but in my bed, roused by the noises the gypsies made as they struck camp.

'Get up, Señor caballero,' said the chief to me. 'We must cover a lot of ground today. You will ride on a mule which has not its equal in all Spain. You will not even feel yourself going along.'

I hastily dressed and mounted my mule. We went ahead with four gypsies all armed to the teeth. The rest of the band followed at a distance, led by the two girls with whom I thought I had spent the night. Sometimes the zigzags the paths made in the mountains caused me to pass several hundred feet above or below them. I stopped to look at them and they then seemed to me to be my cousins. The old chief seemed amused by my perplexity.

After about four hours of strenuous progress we reached a plateau high up in the mountains and found there a large number of bales, which the old chief checked off. Then he said:

'Señor caballero, this is merchandise from England and Brazil; enough to supply the four kingdoms of Andalusia, Granada, Valencia and Catalonia. The king loses somewhat by our little enterprise but he gets it back in another way, as a little smuggling consoles his people and keeps them happy. Besides, in Spain everyone is involved in it. Some of these bales will find their way to military barracks, some to monastic cells and yet others to the vaults of the dead. The bales marked in red are due to be seized by the *alguaziles*,[1] who will thereby gain credit with the customs officers and will be all the more devoted to our interests.'

Having said this, the gypsy chief hid the bales in different hollows in the rock. Then he had a meal served in a cave, the view from

1 Policemen.

130

which stretched much further than the eye could see, by which I mean that the horizon was so distant that it seemed to blend into the sky. As I had been coming to appreciate the beauties of nature more and more, this sight sent me into a veritable ecstasy which was dispelled by the chief's two daughters, who brought the food. At close quarters, as I have said, they did not look at all like my cousins. Their furtive glances seemed to indicate that they were well pleased with me, but something in me told me that it was not they who had come to visit me in the night.

The girls brought a hot *olla* which some men who had been sent out in advance had been simmering the whole morning. The old chief and I ate copiously, the difference being that he interrupted his eating with the frequent embraces he gave to a skin filled with good wine whereas I was content with water from a nearby spring.

When we had satisfied our appetite I indicated to him that I was curious to know more about him. He demurred but I insisted, and eventually he agreed to tell me his story, which he began as follows:

THE STORY OF PANDESOWNA,
✍ THE GYPSY CHIEF ✍

All the gypsies in Spain know me by the name of Pandesowna, that is, the translation into their language of my surname, Avadoro, for I was not born a gypsy.

My father's name was Don Felipe Avadoro. He had the reputation of being the most serious and methodical man of his age. He was so methodical, in fact, that if I told you the story of one of his days you would at once know his whole life's history, or at least the history of the time between his two marriages, the first to which I owe my existence and the second which caused his death by the irregularity it introduced into his style of life.

While my father was still living in his own father's house he grew deeply attached to a distant relative, whom he married once he had become the head of the family. She died giving birth to me. My father was inconsolable at her loss and shut himself away in his house for several months, refusing even to receive those who were close to him. Time, which heals all things, assuaged his grief too, and eventually he appeared at the door of his balcony, which looked out on the Calle de Toledo. There he breathed in the fresh air for a quarter of an hour and then opened a window which looked out on to the side-street. He saw some of his acquaintances in a house across the street and greeted them quite cheerfully. He was seen to do the same thing in the days which followed, and this change in his way of life finally reached the ears of my mother's maternal uncle, Fray Gerónimo Sántez, a Theatine monk.[2]

This monk called on my father, congratulated him on his return to health, spoke a little about the consolation which religion affords us and much more about my father's need for recreation. He even went so far as to suggest that he should go to the theatre. My father had the greatest confidence in Fray Gerónimo and went that very evening to the Teatro de la Cruz. A new play was being performed there which had the support of the whole Pollacos, while the Sorices were trying to ensure that it flopped. The rivalry between these two theatrical factions interested my father so much that from that time on he never willingly missed a single performance. He even made a point of supporting the Pollacos and would only go to the Teatro del Príncipe when the Teatro de la Cruz was closed.

After the performance he would join the end of the double line which the men formed to compel the women to file past one by one. But he did not do so as the others did to be able to inspect them at his leisure. On the contrary, he showed little interest in them and once the last woman had gone by he would make his way to The Cross of Malta, where he would partake of a light supper before returning home.

The first task of the morning for my father would be to open the door of the balcony which looked out over the Calle de Toledo. There he would breathe in the fresh air for a quarter of an hour; then he would open the window which looked out on to the side-street. If there was anyone at the window opposite he would greet them courteously, saying 'Agour', then close the window. 'Agour' was sometimes the only word he would utter all day, for although he was

---

2 The Theatines were an austere order founded in 1524 in Rome.

passionately interested in the fate of all the plays performed at the Teatro de la Cruz he would only manifest this interest by clapping, never by speaking. If no one was at the window opposite he would wait patiently for someone to appear so that he could perform his courteous greeting.

Next, my father would go to Mass in the Theatine house. On his return he would find the room had been cleaned by the maidservant of the house. He himself took particular care to see that every piece of furniture was put back in exactly the same place it had been in the day before. He was extraordinarily careful about this and was quick to discover the tiniest piece of straw or speck of dust which had escaped the maidservant's broom.

When my father was satisfied that his room was in order, he would take a pair of compasses and a pair of scissors, cut up twenty-four pieces of paper of equal size and, filling each of them with a pinch of Brazilian tobacco, would make twenty-four cigarettes which were so well-rolled and so uniform in size that they could be considered the most perfect cigarettes in all Spain. He would smoke six of these masterpieces while counting the tiles on the roof of the palacio de Alba, six more in counting the people coming through the Toledo gate, then he would fix his gaze on the door of his room until his dinner was brought to him.

After dinner he would smoke the remaining twelve cigarettes. Then he would stare at the mantel clock until it struck the hour of the day's theatrical performance, and if there was no performance that day he would go to Moreno's bookshop to listen to the men of letters who used to assemble there at that time. But he would never join in the conversation. Whenever he was ill he would send to Moreno's for the play that was being performed at the Teatro de la Cruz, and at the time the performance was due to begin, he would begin to read the play, not forgetting to clap at all the passages which the Pollacos claque had the habit of applauding.

This was a very innocent life, but my father, wishing to fulfil his religious duties, asked the Theatines for a confessor. They sent him my great-uncle, Fray Gerónimo Sántez, who took this opportunity of reminding him that I was alive and living in the house of Doña Felisa Dalanosa, my late mother's sister. Whether my father feared that the sight of me would revive memories of the beloved person whose death I had unwittingly caused or whether he did not want my infant cries to disturb his silent habits, it is a fact that he asked Fray Gerónimo never to let me come near him. At the same time, however, he did see to my needs by making over to me the income from a *quinta* or farm near Madrid which he owned, and he made me a ward of the Procurator of the Theatines.

It seems, alas, that my father, in keeping us apart, had some inkling of the tremendous difference which nature had set between our two characters. You have heard how methodical and orderly he was in the way he lived. I venture to claim that it would be almost impossible to find a more inconstant man than I am and have always been.

I have even been inconstant in my inconstancy, because in my travels and wanderings I have always been haunted by the idea of tranquil happiness and a life of retirement, and the taste of something new has always lured me from such a life, so that now that I finally know myself for what I am I have put an end to these restless alternatives by settling down with this gypsy band. In one way it is a sort of retirement to an orderly way of life, but at least I do not have the misfortune of always looking out on the same trees and rocks or, what would be even more intolerable, the same streets, the same walls and the same roofs.

Here I interrupted and said to the storyteller, 'Señor Avadoro – or Pandesowna – I imagine that such a wandering life must have brought you many strange adventures.'

The gypsy replied, 'Señor caballero, I have indeed seen some extraordinary things since I have lived in these remote parts. As for the rest of my life, however, it only comprises quite humdrum events, in which all that is remarkable is the infatuation I showed for experiencing different forms of life, though without embracing any one of them for more than a year or two at a time.'

Having given me this reply, the gypsy continued as follows:

I have already told you that my Aunt Dalanosa had taken me in to live with her. She herself had no children and showed me, it seemed, all the indulgence of an aunt together with that of a mother. In a word, I was a spoilt child. Indeed, I became daily more spoilt, for as I grew in strength and intelligence, I was also more tempted to take advantage of the kindness I was shown. But on the other hand, since I scarcely ever encountered obstacles to my own desires, I in turn scarcely ever resisted the wishes of others. And this made me seem almost docile. In any case, my aunt always accompanied her orders with a certain tender and affectionate smile, and I never refused them. In short, such as I was, the good Dalanosa was pleased to believe that in me Nature had produced with her aid a veritable masterpiece. But her happiness was in one crucial respect incomplete, because she was not able to bring to my father's attention my so-called progress and persuade him of my accomplishments, for he steadfastly refused to see me.

But is there any obstinacy which a woman cannot overcome? Señora Dalanosa's pressure on her uncle Gerónimo was so persistent and effective that he decided in the end to take advantage of my father's next confession to tax his conscience with the heartless indifference he was showing to a child who could not possibly have done him any harm.

Father Gerónimo did as he had promised my aunt to do, but my father was highly alarmed at the idea of receiving me in his own room. Father Gerónimo suggested a meeting in the Jardín del Buen Retiro. But a walk to the garden did not form part of the regular and methodical routine from which my father never departed. Rather than make such a departure, my father consented to meet me in his own house. Father Gerónimo then went to announce the good news to my aunt, who thought she would die of joy.

I must tell you at this point that ten years of hypochondria had left their mark on my father's home life, which was very eccentric. Among other fads, he had acquired that of making ink. This is how it came about:

One day he was at Moreno's bookshop in the company of several lawyers and some of the finest minds in Spain when the conversation turned to the difficulty of obtaining good ink. Everyone said that none could be found or that he had tried in vain to make some. Moreno said that he had in his bookshop a collection of recipes from which it would be possible to inform oneself on the subject. He went off to look for the volume, which he did not find straight away, and when he returned, the topic of conversation had changed. There were heated exchanges about the fortunes of a recent play, and no one wanted to talk about ink or listen to someone reading from a book about it. Not so my father. He picked up the book, located at once the recipe for ink and was amazed to discover that he could easily understand something which the greatest minds in Spain considered to be very difficult. Indeed, all that was involved was to mix a tincture of nutgall with a solution of vitriol and then add gum to it. The author pointed out, however, that it was not possible to produce good ink unless a large quantity was made at one time and the mixture was kept hot and stirred frequently, because the gum had no affinity with metallic substances and tended to separate out. Moreover, the gum itself tended to dissolve and putrefy, and the only way to prevent this was to add a small amount of alcohol to it.

My father bought the book and the next day procured the necessary ingredients, scales for weighing out the amounts and the largest flask he could find in Madrid, because the author had recommended the ink should be made in as great a volume as possible at any one time. The process worked perfectly. My father took a bottle of his ink to the great minds who met in Moreno's bookshop. They all declared it excellent and wanted to have some.

In the course of his quiet, retiring life my father had never had occasion to gratify anyone and even less to receive praise. He found it pleasant to be able to oblige others and pleasanter still to be praised, and so he devoted himself wholeheartedly to making a substance which brought him such gratifying pleasures. Seeing that the great minds of Madrid emptied in a twinkling the largest flasks that he could find in the city, my father sent to Barcelona for a demijohn, one of those in which the Mediterranean sailors store their wine. With this he was able to make twenty bottles of ink, which the great minds of Madrid used up as they had the first batch, heaping praises and thanks on my father all the while.

But the larger the glass bottles the more difficult they were to use. It was not possible to heat the mixture up in them, still more difficult to stir it and it was above all else difficult to decant it. So my father decided to send to Toboso for one of those great earthenware jars which are used in the manufacture of saltpetre. When it arrived, he had it set above a little stove which was kept constantly hot with a few live coals. A tap fitted to the base of the jar was used to draw off the liquid, and by climbing up on the stove it was fairly easy to stir the mixture with a wooden pestle. Jars of this sort are taller than a man, so you can easily imagine how much ink my father made at any one time, and he was careful to top the jar up with as much as he drew off.

It gave him real pleasure to witness the arrival of a maidservant or valet of some famous man of letters coming to ask for ink. And whenever the famous man published a literary work that was talked about in Moreno's bookshop, my father smiled with pride and pleasure as though he had contributed something to it. Indeed, to complete this account, I should tell you that my father came to be known throughout the city as Don Felipe del Tintero Largo or Don Felipe of the Large Inkpot, and his surname Avadoro was known only to a few.

I knew all of this. I had heard about the eccentricity of my father, the tidiness of his room and his great jar of ink, and I was very eager to see it all for myself. My aunt, for her part, believed firmly that as soon as my father had the pleasure of meeting me he would give up all his fads and devote himself solely to admiring me from morning till night. At last a day was set for the introduction. My father confessed to Father Gerónimo on the last Sunday of every month. The priest was going to strengthen him in his resolve to meet me, tell him that I was waiting for him at his house and accompany my father there. In telling us about these arrangements Father Gerónimo strongly recommended that I should not touch anything in his room. I promised to do as I was told and my aunt promised to keep an eye on me.

At last the much-awaited Sunday came. My aunt dressed me in a pink *majo*[3] suit with silver trimming and buttons of Brazilian topaz. She assured me that I looked like Cupid himself and that my father could not fail to go wild with joy at the sight of me. Full of hopes and flattering expectations, we merrily made our way across the Calle de las Ursulinas and reached the Prado, where several women stopped

3 Stylish, elegant, respectable.

to caress me. At last we reached the calle de Toledo and the house of my father. We were shown into his room and my aunt, who was nervous about my excitable state, sat me down on a chair, seated herself opposite me and seized hold of the fringes of my scarf to stop me getting up and touching anything.

At first I made up for this restraint by looking all around the room, whose tidiness and cleanliness I much admired. The corner used for making ink was as clean and tidy as the rest. The great Toboso jar looked almost ornamental, and next to it stood a tall, glass-fronted cupboard in which all the necessary ingredients and instruments were kept.

The sight of this tall, narrow cupboard next to the stove and jar gave me a sudden irresistible desire to climb up on it. I thought that nothing would be more amusing than to watch my father looking for me vainly everywhere in the room before catching sight of me in my hiding-place above his head. Quick as a flash, I slipped off the scarf by which my aunt was holding on to me, jumped on to the stove and from there climbed on to the cupboard. At first my aunt could not stop herself applauding my skill, then she pleaded with me to come down.

At that moment we were told that my father was coming up the stairs. My aunt fell to her knees and begged me to come down from my vantage-point. I was unable to resist her gentle entreaties, but in trying to climb down on the stove I felt my foot touch the rim of the jar; I tried to hold on to where I was but sensed that I would bring down the cupboard with me, so I let go with my hands and fell into the jar of ink. I would have drowned in it had not my aunt grabbed the pestle which was used to stir the ink and hit the jar very hard with it. It broke into a thousand pieces.

At that moment my father came in. He saw a river of ink flooding his room and a black figure filling it with appalling shrieks. He rushed down the staircase, twisted his foot and fell down in a faint.

As for me, I did not shriek for long. The ink I had swallowed made me very ill. I passed out, and only fully recovered consciousness after a long illness that was followed by a long convalescence. What contributed most to my recovery was my aunt's announcement that we were to leave Madrid and set up house in Burgos. I was so excited

138

by the idea of a journey that it was feared I would lose my reason, but my intense pleasure was spoilt when my aunt asked me whether I preferred to travel in her chaise or in a litter.

'Neither one nor the other,' I replied in a violent rage. 'I am not a woman. I want to travel on horseback, or at least on a mule, with a fine Segovia rifle attached to my saddle, two pistols in my belt and a long sword. I refuse to go unless you give me all of this. Anyway, it is in your interest to give it to me as it is my duty to protect you.'

I uttered many similar silly remarks which seemed wholly reasonable to me but which were, of course, highly amusing coming from the mouth of an eleven-year-old.

The preparations for the journey gave me cause to engage in frenzied activity. I came and went, carrying things upstairs and downstairs, and gave orders. I was the proverbial busy bee. And there was indeed much for me to do, for my aunt was taking all of her furniture with her to set up house in Burgos. At last the happy day arrived on which we were to leave. We sent the heavy baggage by way of Parenda and ourselves took the road to Valladolid.

At first my aunt had wanted to travel in a chaise but, seeing that I was determined to ride a mule, she did the same. In the place of a saddle a comfortable little seat was made for her which was attached to a pack saddle and shaded by a parasol. A *zagal* walked ahead of her so as to ward off the least semblance of danger. The rest of our train, which consisted of twelve mules, looked very smart. And I, who considered myself the leader of this elegant caravan, sometimes rode at the front, sometimes brought up the rear. I always had one of my weapons in my hand, especially at bends in the road and other suspicious places.

As you may well imagine, no opportunity arose for me to show my mettle and we reached Alabajos without incident. There we met up with two caravans as large as ours. The beasts were at the rack in the stables and the travellers were at the other end in the kitchen, separated from the stable by two stone steps. At that time, this was the normal arrangement in nearly all Spanish inns. The whole building was but one long room of which the greater part was occupied by the mules and the lesser by the humans. But it was all the merrier for that. As the *zagal* saw to the pack animals, he kept up a steady stream of repartee with the innkeeper's wife, who replied with all the liveliness of her sex and station until the more serious-minded innkeeper came between them and interrupted the exchanges. They soon started up again, however. The inn rang to the sound of the castanets played by the maids, who danced to the raucous singing of a goatherd. Travellers made each other's acquaintance and invited each other to supper. Everyone gathered round the stove, said who they were, where they were going and sometimes told stories. Those were the good old days; now our inns are more comfortable, but the boisterous social life which the travellers of those days led had a charm I cannot describe to you. All I can tell you is that on that very day I was so captivated by it that I took it into my little head to travel all my life, which is what I have done.

But one particular incident confirmed me in this decision. After supper, when all the travellers grouped round the stove had given some account of the country through which they had passed, one of them, who had so far remained silent, said:

'Everything that has happened to you on your journeys has been of interest to listen to and to think about. For my part, I would wish nothing worse to have befallen me, but travelling through Calabria I had such an extraordinary, odd and terrifying adventure that I cannot get it out of my mind. It pursues me, haunts me, poisons all the pleasures I might have, and it still fills me with such melancholy that it has almost robbed me of my sanity.'

This prelude greatly roused the curiosity of those present, who urged the traveller to unburden himself by telling them what extraordinary things had happened to him. It took a lot to persuade him, but at last he began his story as follows:

THE STORY OF GIULIO ROMATI AND
∽ THE PRINCIPESSA DI MONTE SALERNO ∽

My name is Giulio Romati. My father, Pietro Romati, is the most famous lawyer in Palermo and indeed in all Sicily. As you might imagine, he is very attached to a profession which provides him with a respectable living, but he is even more attached to philosophy, to which he devotes all the time he can steal from his legal affairs.

I can say without undue boasting that I have followed in his footsteps in both his careers, for I was a doctor of law at the age of twenty-two and, having since applied myself to mathematics and astronomy, I have advanced so far as to be able to write commentaries on Copernicus and Galileo. I am not telling you this to vaunt myself, but because I am about to relate to you a most amazing adventure and do not want to be taken for a gullible or superstitious person. Indeed, I am so far from superstition and credulity that theology is perhaps the only branch of knowledge that I have consistently neglected. As for the rest, I devoted myself to them with untiring enthusiasm, since the only recreation I found congenial was in turning from one branch of knowledge to another. So much study affected my health and my father, who could not think of any distraction which would suit me, suggested that I should make a tour of Europe and only return to Sicily after four years' absence.

At first it was very hard for me to leave my books, my study and my observatory. But my father insisted and I had to obey him. I had no sooner begun my journey than I took a turn for the better. I recovered my appetite, my energies – in a word, my health. At first I had travelled in a litter but from the third day I rode a mule and was none the worse for it.

Many people know the whole world except for their own country. I had decided that my own country would not be able to reproach me with similar failings, so I began my journey by visiting the marvels which nature had so lavishly bestowed on our island. Instead of following the coast of Palermo to Messina, I went by Castro Novo, Caltanisetta and reached the foot of Etna at a village whose name I have forgotten. There I made preparations for the trip up the mountain, to which I intended to devote a month. And indeed that is how long I spent, principally attempting to confirm the number of experiments which had recently been done on barometers. At night I observed the heavens and had the great pleasure of sighting two stars which were not visible from the observatory in Palermo because they were below the horizon.

It was with genuine regret that I left that place in which I almost felt as though I could share the ethereal light and sublime harmony of the heavenly bodies whose laws I had studied so deeply. Besides, it is a fact that the rarefied air of high mountains acts on our bodies in a very special way, quickening our pulses and our breathing. Eventually I left the mountain and I came down it on the side of Catania.

Catania is inhabited by gentry as famous as that of Palermo but more enlightened. Not that the mathematical sciences have more adherents in Catania than elsewhere on our island, but a great deal of attention was paid to the arts, to antiquities, to ancient and modern history and to the history of all the peoples who have inhabited Sicily. The excavations and the artefacts found in them were a universal subject of conversation.

At that time, as it happens, a very beautiful marble tablet, covered with strange writing, had just been recovered from deep under the earth. Having looked at it closely, I realized that the inscription was in Carthaginian and, knowing Hebrew quite well, I was able to decipher it to the satisfaction of all concerned. This success won me a flattering welcome. The most distinguished persons in town tried to keep me there with attractive financial offers, but I had left my family with other purposes in mind so I refused them and took the road to Messina. I stayed in this city, which is famous for its commercial activity, for one whole week, after which I crossed the straits and landed at Reggio.

Up to then the journey had been no more than a pleasant trip, but at Reggio the undertaking became more difficult. A bandit called Zoto was at that time laying waste to Calabria and the sea was infested by Tripolitan pirates. I had absolutely no idea how to get to Naples and I would have returned to Palermo, if a sense of shame had not prevented me from doing so.

I had already spent a week in Reggio, full of uncertainty as to what to do, when one day, having walked up and down the port for some time, I sat down on some rocks on the least frequented part of the beach.

There I was accosted by a handsome-looking man wearing a red cloak. He sat down by me without greeting me and then spoke to me as follows: 'Is Signor Romati busy with some algebraic problem or some question of astronomy?'

'Not at all,' I replied. 'All that Signor Romati would like to do is to travel from Reggio to Naples, and the problem that is bothering him at the moment is how to escape the clutches of Signor Zoto's band.'

Then the stranger looked very solemn and said, 'Signor Romati, your talents already do honour to your country, and you will bring it yet more honour after the journeys that you are undertaking have extended the range of your knowledge. Zoto is too much of a gentleman to wish to hinder you in so noble a venture. Take these red feathers and put one in your hat, give the others to your servants and then boldly set out, for I am that Zoto whom you so much fear, and so that you can have no doubt on this score I am going to show you the instruments of my profession.'

At this, he opened his cloak and showed me a belt bristling with pistols and daggers. Then he shook my hand and vanished.

At this point I interrupted the gypsy chief and told him that I had heard of Zoto and had made the acquaintance of his two brothers.

'I know them too,' said Pandesowna. 'Like me, they are in the service of the Great Sheikh of the Gomelez.'

'What? You too are in his service?' I cried in great astonishment.

At that moment a gypsy came up and whispered in the chief's ear. He at once rose and left me to reflect on what I had just learned.

What, I wondered, is this powerful conspiracy which seems to have no other purpose than to hide some secret or other from me or to dazzle my eyes with magic, parts of which I think I can guess, only to be thrown shortly after into confusion by new happenings? It is obvious that I myself form part of this invisible plot and it is clear that others are trying to keep me here with ever closer bonds.

My thoughts were interrupted by the chief's two daughters, who came to suggest that we went for a walk together. I accepted and followed them. The conversation was in correct Spanish, unadulterated by *jerigonza* or gypsy language. Their minds were cultivated and they were of a cheerful and open temperament. After the stroll we took supper and then went to bed.

But that night, no cousins.

The Thirteenth Day

The gypsy chief had me brought an ample breakfast and then said, 'Señor caballero, the enemy – that is to say, the customs officers – are closing in. It is only right to abandon the battlefield to them. There, they will find the bales intended for them; the rest is already safely hidden away. Take your time over breakfast, then we shall leave.'

As the customs men could already be seen on the other side of the valley, I ate hastily while the majority of the band went on ahead. We made our way from one mountain to the next, going deeper and deeper into the wilderness of the Sierra Morena. At last we stopped in a deep valley where some of the band were already waiting for us and had prepared our meal. After we had eaten I asked the chief to continue the story of his life, which he did as follows:

∽ THE GYPSY CHIEF'S STORY CONTINUED ∽

You left me listening attentively to the remarkable tale of Giulio Romati. This, more or less, is how he went on:

∽ GIULIO ROMATI'S STORY CONTINUED ∽

Zoto's character was well known and I had complete confidence in the assurances he had given me. I happily returned to my inn and sent for muleteers. Several came forward. The bandits do not harm them or their beasts. I chose the man amongst them with the best reputation. I took a mule for myself, one for my valet and two for my baggage. The head muleteer also had his mule and two servants, who followed on foot.

Next day I left at daybreak, and as I was on my way I noticed members of Zoto's band who seemed to be following us at a distance and passed us on to fresh relays as we proceeded. As you can well imagine, no harm could possibly come to me in this way.

I had a very pleasant journey, during which my health improved from day to day. I was only two days from Naples when the idea of making a detour through Salerno occurred to me. My curiosity to see this place was quite natural, as I was very interested in the history of Renaissance art, the cradle of which, in Italy, had been the school of Salerno. I don't know what evil fate led me to make this ill-starred journey.

I left the high road at Monte Brugio and a guide from the village led me into an unimaginable wilderness. At about midday we reached a tumbledown hovel which the guide assured me was an inn, though it was not noticeable from the way in which the innkeeper greeted me. Far from offering me food, he begged me to share any provisions I had with him. I did in fact have some cold meat, which I shared with him, my guide and my valet, as the muleteers had stayed behind in Monte Brugio.

I left this poor hostelry about two hours after midday and soon caught sight of an immense castle perched on a mountain top. I asked my guide what it was called and whether it was inhabited. He replied that in those parts it was known simply as lo Monte or lo Castello. The castle was completely deserted and in ruins. Inside its walls, however, a chapel and several cells had been built, in which the Franciscans of Salerno usually maintained a community of five or six monks. He added naïvely:

'There are many strange stories about the castle, but I cannot tell you any of them because as soon as anyone speaks of it, I run out of the kitchen and go to my sister-in-law Pepa's house, where I am sure to find a Franciscan Father who will let me kiss his scapular.'

I asked the guide whether we were going to pass close by the castle, and he replied that our path would pass halfway up the mountain on which it was built.

Meanwhile the sky had clouded over and towards evening a terrible storm burst over our heads. At that point we were on the back of a mountain which offered no shelter. My guide said that he knew of a cave where we could take cover but that it was difficult to reach. I accepted the risk, but no sooner had we begun to make our way through the rocks than lightning struck close by us. My mule collapsed under me and I fell some distance down the mountainside. I grabbed hold of a tree, and when I felt that I was safe I shouted to my travelling companions, but none of them answered.

The flashes of lightning were so frequent that I could distinguish the objects around me and could move with some degree of safety. By holding on to trees I was able to go forward and to reach a little cave, which, since no beaten path led up to it, could not have been the one to which my guide had tried to take me.

The rain, the wind and thunder continued unabated. I was shivering in my wet clothes and was forced to spend several hours in this uncomfortable situation. Then suddenly I thought I caught sight of torches moving about in the valley bottom, and heard voices. Thinking that these were my companions, I shouted out and there was a reply.

Soon a good-looking young man appeared, followed by several valets, some with torches, some with bundles of clothing.

He greeted me ceremoniously and said, 'Signor Romati, we are members of the household of la Principessa di Monte Salerno. The guide whom you engaged in Monte Brugio said that you were lost in the mountains, and we have been searching for you on the princess's orders. Take these clothes and follow us to the castle.'

'What?' I said. 'Do you propose to take me to that uninhabited castle on top of the mountain?'

'Not at all,' said the young man in turn. 'You will see a superb palace which is only two hundred paces away.'

I supposed that some local princess kept a house close by. I changed my clothes and followed the young man. We soon arrived at a black marble portal, but as the torches cast no light on the façade I was unable to form any judgement about it. We went in. The young man left me at the bottom of the staircase. After climbing one flight I met a remarkably beautiful lady, who said, 'Signor Romati, la Principessa di Monte Salerno has charged me to show you the beauties of this house.'

I replied that if the princess was anything like her ladies-in-waiting I had already formed a very high opinion of her.

Indeed, the lady whose task it was to accompany me was, as I have said, flawlessly beautiful, and had so noble an air about her that I at first took her to be the princess herself. I also noticed that she was dressed in more or less the same way as were the family portraits of the last century, but I merely assumed that this was how Neapolitan ladies dressed and that they had gone back to fashions of former times.

We went first into a room in which everything was made of solid silver. There were silver floor tiles, some with matt, some with polished surfaces. Solid silver wall-hangings were made to look like damask, having a polished silver background and the patterns of leaves and branches in matt. The ceiling was carved like the wood-work of ancient castles. Finally, the panelling, the edges of the wall-hangings, the chandeliers, the picture-frames and the tables were all masterpieces of the silversmith's art.

'Signor Romati,' said the supposed lady-in-waiting, 'this silverwork seems to delay you for an unduly long time. We are only in the antechamber of the footmen of la Signora Principessa.'

I made no reply, and we passed on to a room similar to the first except that all was silver gilt, with ornaments in that shade of gold that was fashionable some fifty years ago.

'This room is the antechamber of the gentlemen-in-waiting, the major-domo and the other officers of the household. We will see neither gold nor silver in the princess's apartment. Her own taste is solely for simplicity, as you can see from this dining room.' Where-upon she opened the side-door and we went into a room with walls covered with coloured marble, surmounted by a magnificent white marble bas-relief frieze. There were also handsome sideboards covered with rock-crystal vases and Indian porcelain bowls of the highest quality.

We then went back through the officers' antechamber to reach the grand salon.

'You may care to admire this room,' said the lady-in-waiting.

And indeed I did admire it. My first astonished glance was for the floor, which was made of lapis lazuli encrusted with hard stones in a style of a Florentine mosaic, in which it takes several years even to make a table. There was an overall pattern in the way the stones were arranged which created an effect of harmonious unity. But a close inspection of the different sections revealed a great variety in the detail, which none the less did nothing to detract from the effect of symmetry. Indeed, although the same pattern repeated itself, in some places it took the form of delicately drawn flowers, elsewhere of exquisite enamel shells, in yet other places of butterflies and humming-birds. In it the most precious stones in the world had been used to imitate nature's most beautiful creatures. In the centre of this magnificent floor there was a picture of a casket which had been made from stones of every colour and surrounded by festoons of large pearls. Everything seemed to have depth and substance, as on Florentine tables.

'Signor Romati,' said the lady, 'if you linger everywhere we will never get to the end.'

I raised my eyes, and the first thing I saw was a picture by Raphael which may well have been his first sketch for the *School of Athens*, but in more striking colour since it was painted in oils.

Then I noted the *Hercules at the feet of Omphale*. The Hercules was by Michelangelo and the brush of Guido[1] had evidently executed the female figure. In short, every picture in the salon was of better quality than any I had seen before. The wall-hangings were made of plain green velvet, the colour of which enhanced the beauty of the pictures. On either side of the doors there were statues a little less than life-size. There were four in all. One was the famous depiction of Venus by Phidias, whose sacrifice Phryne demanded. Another was the Faun by the same artist. The third was the original Venus by Praxiteles, of which the Medicis possess only a copy. The last was an Antinoüs of extraordinary beauty. There were other groups in every window.

All around the salon there were commodes with drawers, which instead of the usual bronze furniture were covered with the most beautifully fashioned jewels, which had been used to frame cameos of the kind found only in the private apartments of kings. The commodes contained a series of gold medallions of the highest denominations.

'This is where the princess spends the time after dinner,' said the lady. 'Examining this collection gives rise to conversations as instruc-

1 Guido Reni (1575–1642).

tive as they are pleasurable. But there are still many things to see. Follow me.'

We then entered the bedchamber, which was octagonal. It contained four alcoves, each with a bed of impressive dimensions. There was no panelling, no wall-hangings, no decorated ceiling, but everything was covered in Indian muslin draped with remarkable taste, embroidered with extraordinary skill and so fine that it could have been taken to be a mist which Arachne herself[2] had managed to trap in this delicate needlework.

'Why four beds?' I asked the lady.

'So that one can move from one to the next during nights when one is hot and cannot sleep,' she replied.

'And why are the beds so large?' I continued.

'That is because the princess is joined in them by her ladies-in-waiting whenever she feels like chatting before she goes to sleep. But let us pass on to the bathroom.'

It was a rotunda lined and edged with mother-of-pearl of different kinds. The upper parts of the wall were decorated with a wide net of pearls instead of draperies, and had a fringe of pearls all of the same size and colour. The ceiling consisted in a single mirror in which Chinese goldfish could be seen swimming. Instead of a bath there was a circular pool surrounded by artificial foam, in which had been set the most beautiful shells from the Indian Ocean.

Here I could no longer contain my feelings of wonderment and said, 'Oh Signora, paradise itself cannot be more beautiful.'

'Paradise?' cried the lady with an expression of madness and despair. 'Paradise, did he not mention paradise? Signor Romati, I beg of you, do not use that word again. I am in deadly earnest. Follow me.'

We then came to an aviary full of tropical birds and songbirds from our own clime. There we found a table laid for me alone.

'Oh Signora,' I said to my beautiful guide, 'how can you think of eating in such a heavenly dwelling? I see that you do not intend to take your place at table. I could never bring myself to sit down alone

---

2 The seamstress who, according to the myth, defeated Athena in a sewing contest and was turned into a spider.

149

except on condition that you would be so kind as to tell me about the princess who owns such marvels.'

The lady graciously smiled, served me, sat down and began as follows.

'I am the daughter of the last Prince of Monte Salerno.'

'Who? You, Signora?'

'I meant to say the princess was his daughter. Do not interrupt me again.'

THE PRINCIPESSA DI MONTE SALERNO'S
∽ STORY ∽

The Principe de Monte Salerno, who was descended from the ancient Dukes of Salerno, was a grandee of Spain, High Constable, Grand Admiral, Master of the King's Horse, Royal Chamberlain and Master of the Royal Hunt. In short, he united in his person all the grand offices of state in the kingdom of Naples. Although he was himself in the service of his king he maintained a household of gentlemen which included several titled persons. Among these was the Marchese di Spinaverde, the first gentleman-in-waiting of the prince, a man who enjoyed the prince's complete confidence, which he shared with his wife, the Marchesa di Spinaverde, the first lady-in-waiting of the princess.

I was ten years old . . . or rather, I meant to say, the prince's only daughter was ten years old when her mother died. At that time, too, the Spinaverdes left the prince's household. The marchese took charge of the administration of his fiefs and the marchesa took charge of my education. They left behind them in Naples their elder daughter, Laura, who occupied a somewhat irregular place in the prince's household. Her mother and the young princess came to live at Monte Salerno.

Little attention was paid to Elfrida's upbringing, but a great deal was lavished on training those around her. They were taught to anticipate my every whim.

'*Your* every whim?' I said to the lady.

'I asked you not to interrupt me,' she replied angrily. Then she continued:

★

I enjoyed putting the obedience of my ladies-in-waiting to all sorts of tests. I would give them contradictory orders, only half of which they could ever carry out, and then I punished them either by pinching them or sticking pins into their arms or thighs. They did not stay long. The Marchesa di Spinaverde appointed others, who also soon left me.

While all this was going on, my father fell ill and we travelled to Naples. I did not see much of him but the Marchese di Spinaverde and his wife never left his side. Eventually he died, having drawn up a will in which Spinaverde was made the sole guardian of his daughter and the administrator of his estates and other possessions.

The arrangements for the funeral took up several weeks, after which we returned to Monte Salerno, where I resumed pinching my ladies-in-waiting. Four years went by in these innocent pastimes, which were all the sweeter to me because the Marchesa di Spinaverde assured me that I was right; it was the duty of everyone to obey me, and those who were slow to do so or did not carry out my orders well enough deserved to be punished in every way.

Eventually, however, all my ladies left me one after the other, and one night I found that I had almost reached the point of having to undress myself. I wept with rage and ran to the Marchesa di Spinaverde, who said, 'Dear, sweet princess, dry your pretty eyes. Tonight I will undress you and tomorrow I will bring you six more ladies-in-waiting, whom you will, I am sure, find satisfactory.'

When I awoke the next morning, the marchesa presented six beautiful young girls to me. The sight of them moved me in a strange way, and they also seemed to be affected. I was the first to recover, and leapt from my bed, dressed only in my nightgown. I embraced them one after the other and assured them that they would never be scolded or pinched. And, indeed, even if they were clumsy in dressing me or dared to contradict me, I never lost my temper with them.

'But, Signora,' I said to the princess, 'they might have been young boys dressed up as young girls.'

The princess said with a majestic air, 'Signor Romati, I have asked you not to interrupt me.'

Then she resumed her story.

★

On my sixteenth birthday I was told that I had distinguished visitors. They were a secretary of state, the Spanish ambassador, and the Duke of Guadarrama. The duke had come to ask my hand in marriage. The other two were only there to offer their support. The young duke was as handsome as it is possible to be, and I cannot deny that he made an impression on me.

That evening it was suggested that we might like to stroll in the grounds of the castle. We had scarcely set out when a mad bull rushed out of a clump of trees and charged directly at us. The duke ran towards it, his cloak in one hand and a sword in the other. The bull hesitated a second, then charged the duke, impaled itself on his sword and fell dead at his feet. I believed that I owed my life to the duke's courage and skill. But the next day I learned that the bull had been deliberately planted there by the duke's equerry, and that his master had arranged the whole episode to pay me a gallant compliment in the manner of his country. Far from being grateful for this, I found it impossible to forgive him for having caused me such a fright and I refused to marry him.

The Marchesa di Spinaverde was grateful that I had refused. She took the opportunity to make me aware of the advantages I possessed and to stress how much I would lose if I changed my state and gave myself to a lord and master. Some time after that, the same secretary of state came to see me again in the company of another ambassador and the reigning prince of Noudel-Hansberg. This ruler was a fat, podgy, pale, fair-skinned, pasty-faced grandee, who wanted to tell me about his entailed estates in the lands of the Holy Roman Empire, but when he spoke Italian, he did so with the accent of the Tyrol. I began to mimic his accent and as I did so I assured him that his presence was indispensable in his entailed estates. He went away somewhat miffed. The Marchesa di Spinaverde covered me with kisses, and to make sure of keeping me at Monte Salerno she made all of the improvements which you have seen.

'Well,' I exclaimed, 'she certainly succeeded in what she did. This place could be called paradise on earth.' At these words the princess rose up indignantly and said, 'Romati, I asked you not to use that term again.'

And then she began to laugh, a convulsive, horrible laugh, saying again and again, 'Oh yes, paradise, paradise. It's all very well for him to talk of paradise.'

The scene was becoming distressing. Eventually the princess recovered herself, threw me a severe glance and ordered me to follow her.

She opened the door and we found ourselves in underground vaults, beyond which was what looked like a silver lake, but was actually a lake of quicksilver. The princess clapped her hands, and a boat propelled by a yellow dwarf appeared. We stepped into the boat, and I saw that the dwarf's face was of gold, with diamond eyes and a coral mouth. In other words it was an automaton who rowed through the quicksilver with his little oars and skilfully made the boat skim along. This novel pilot took us to the foot of a rock which opened up to allow us to pass into another chamber, in which there was the amazing spectacle of countless other automata: peacocks spreading enamel tails which were studded with jewels, parrots with emeralds for plumage flying above our heads, negroes made of ebony proffering golden platters laden with ruby cherries and sapphire grapes. There were numerous other astonishing objects in these magical vaults which stretched further than the eye could see.

At that moment I was unaccountably tempted to repeat the word 'paradise' to see what effect it would have on the princess. I yielded to this fatal curiosity and said, 'Signora, one can truthfully say that you are living in paradise on earth.'

The princess smiled in the most charming manner and said, 'So that you can better judge the delights of this place, I shall introduce you to my six ladies-in-waiting.'

She took a golden key from her belt and opened a huge chest which was covered in black velvet and decorated with solid silver.

When the chest was opened, a skeleton appeared, who came towards me in a menacing way. I drew my sword. The skeleton ripped off its left arm and, using it as a weapon, launched a furious attack on me. I put up a good fight, but a second skeleton emerged from the chest, tore a rib off the first skeleton and hit me over the head with it. I grabbed it by the throat but it clasped me in its fleshless arms and tried to throw me to the ground. I managed to get clear of it, but a third skeleton emerged from the trunk to join the other two. Then the other three appeared. Seeing no chance of coming away alive from so unequal a combat, I fell to my knees and begged the princess to spare me.

The princess ordered the skeletons to return to the chest, then said, 'Romati, never forget as long as you live what you have seen here.'

As she said this she grasped my arm. I felt it burn to the bone and I fainted.

I do not know how long I remained in that state. When eventually I came round, I heard chanting nearby and saw that I was in the midst of vast ruins. I tried to get out and I came to an inner courtyard where I saw a chapel, and monks singing matins. When the service was over the superior invited me into his cell. I followed him there and tried to pull my wits together and tell him what had happened to me. When I had finished my account the superior said, 'My son, do you bear a mark on your arm where the princess grasped it?'

I drew up my sleeve and indeed saw that my arm was burnt and that it bore the marks of the princess's five fingers.

Then the superior opened a chest which was by his bed and took an old parchment from it. 'Here is the bull of our foundation,' he said. 'It may explain to you what you have seen.'

I rolled out the parchment scroll and read the following:

In the one thousand, five hundred and third year of Our Lord, and the ninth year of the reign of Frederick, King of Naples and Sicily, Elfrida de Monte Salerno, in an act of outrageous impiety, boasted publicly that she possessed paradise on earth and of her own free will renounced the one we all await in the life eternal. But during the night between Maundy Thursday and Good Friday an earthquake destroyed her palace, and their ruins have become an abode of Satan and a place in which the enemy of mankind has lodged countless demons, who for long have haunted and continue to haunt by numerous devilish devices not only those who dare to approach Monte Salerno but even good Christians living close by. We, Pius III, Servant of Servants, etc., therefore authorize by these presents the foundation of a chapel in the precincts of the ruined castle etc.

I do not remember the rest of the bull. All I recall is that the superior assured me that such hauntings had become much less frequent, though they did still recur from time to time, especially in the night between Maundy Thursday and Good Friday. At the same time he advised me to have Masses said for the repose of the soul of the princess and to attend them myself. I followed his advice and then continued on my journey, but what I saw on that fateful night has left me with an impression of melancholy so deep that nothing can dispel it. And my arm is still very painful.

Having said this, Romati drew back his sleeve and showed us his arm, on which we could see the marks of the princess's fingers and something like the scars from a burn.

At this point I interrupted the gypsy chief to tell him that I had glanced through Happelius's collection of tales whilst staying with the cabbalist, and that I had found a more or less identical story among them.[3]

'Perhaps that is so,' said the chief. 'Perhaps Romati took his story from that book. He may have made it up. But what is certain is that his tale contributed greatly to giving me a taste for travel as well as a vague hope that strange adventures might befall me, which they never have. But such is the force of the impressions we receive in childhood that this unreasonable hope obsessed me for a long time, and I have never been wholly cured of it.'

'Señor Pandesowna,' I said to the gypsy chief, 'didn't you lead me to think that since you have been living in these mountains you have seen things which might be called marvellous?'

'That is so,' he replied. 'I have seen things which have reminded me of Romati's story.'

At that moment a gypsy came and interrupted us. After that, we dined, and then as the chief had other things to do I took my gun and went hunting. I climbed several peaks. From one of them I looked down into the valley which stretched out below my feet and thought

3 It appears in volume three, with the title 'Das seltzahme Lucenser-Gespenst'.

that I recognized the ill-starred gallows of Zoto's brothers. The sight of this made me curious. I hastened down and indeed came to the foot of the gallows from which the two hanged men were suspended.

I looked away and sadly climbed back up to the camp. The gypsy chief asked where I had been. I replied that I had been down to the gallows of Zoto's two brothers.

'Were they there?' asked the gypsy.

'What do you mean?' I replied. 'Are they in the habit of absenting themselves?'

'Often,' said the gypsy chief, 'especially at night.'

These few words made me very pensive. I found myself once again in the neighbourhood of those damned ghosts and whether or not they were vampires or had been used to persecute me, I believed that I had much to fear from them. I was morose for the rest of the day, did not eat supper and went to bed, where I dreamed of vampires, phantoms, nightmares, spectres and hanged men.

The Fourteenth Day

The gypsy girls brought me my chocolate and were good enough to take breakfast with me. Then I took my gun and was drawn by some fatal attraction to the gallows of Zoto's two brothers. They had been taken down. I went through the gallows gate and found the two corpses stretched out, and between them was a young girl whom I recognized as Rebecca. I woke her as gently as I could. However, the shock which I could not entirely spare her reduced her to a piteous state. She went into convulsions, wept and then fainted. I picked her up in my arms and carried her to a nearby spring. I splashed water on her face and she slowly came round. I would never have dared to ask her how she came to be under the gallows, but it was she who spoke first.

'I clearly foresaw,' she said, 'that your discretion would be disastrous for us. You refused to tell us what happened to you so, like you, I have fallen victim to those accursed vampires. I can hardly bring myself to believe the horrors of last night. I shall, however, try to recall them and relate them to you, but you will not be able to understand them fully unless I start my story from an earlier point in my life.'

Rebecca pondered for a few moments and then began as follows:

✑ REBECCA'S STORY ✑

In telling you his story my brother has also told you part of mine. My father had intended him to be the husband of the Queen of Sheba's two daughters and he wanted me to marry the two spirits who preside over the constellation of the Gemini. My brother was flattered by his promised marriage and became much keener to acquire the science of the cabbala, but of me the opposite was true: to marry two genii at the same time seemed to me to be a very

157

frightening prospect. Simply thinking about it upset me so much that I could not bring myself to compose two lines of cabbala. Every day I postponed my task to the next until in the end I had forgotten that art which is as difficult as it is dangerous.

It was not long before my brother noticed my neglect of the cabbala and bitterly reproached me for it. I promised to be better but did nothing about it. In the end he threatened to complain to my father about me. I begged him to spare me this. He promised to wait until the following Saturday. But as I had still done nothing by then he came into my room at midnight, woke me up and told me that he was going to invoke the shade of my father, the terrible Mamoun. I fell to my knees, I begged him to show pity, but he was inexorable. I then heard him utter the terrible formula invented long ago by the Witch of Endor. At once my father appeared, seated on an ivory throne. In his terrible glance was the threat of death. I was afraid that I would not survive the first word which came forth from his lips. Yet he spoke the name of the God of Abraham and Jacob. He dared to utter that awesome invocation.

At this point the young Jewess covered her face with her hand and seemed to tremble at the mere thought of that cruel scene. After a while she pulled herself together and continued as follows:

I did not hear the end of what my father said. I had fainted before he had finished speaking. When I regained consciousness I saw my brother holding out the book of Sephiroth to me. I thought I would faint again but I had to bow to his will. My brother, who rightly suspected that I would have to go back to first principles, had the patience to remind me of them one by one. I started with the composition of syllables, then went on to words and formulae. In the end I became devoted to that sublime science and would spend my nights in the study that had been my father's observatory; I would go to bed only when first light interrupted my exercises. By then I was dropping off to sleep. Zulica, my mulatto maidservant, would undress me almost without my noticing. I would sleep for several hours and then return to the pursuits which were not meant for me, as you will see.

You know Zulica and you have been able to judge her charms for yourself. She is very beautiful, her eyes are full of tenderness, her mouth has the most pretty smile and her figure is perfectly shaped. One morning, on returning from the observatory, I summoned her to undress me. She did not hear me. I went into her room, which is next to mine, and saw her leaning, half-undressed, out of the window, making signs across the valley and blowing kisses from her hand that seemed to carry her whole heart with them. I had no idea what love was. For the first time I saw this emotion expressed before my eyes. I was so disturbed and shocked that I remained motionless like a statue. Zulica turned round and a deep pink blush suffused the dusky skin of her breast and spread to her whole body. I blushed too, then went pale and seemed on the point of fainting. Zulica caught me in her arms and her heart, which I could feel beating against mine, transmitted to me the turmoil of her senses.

Zulica hurriedly undressed me, and when I was in bed she seemed glad to withdraw and gladder still to close the door behind her. Soon after, I heard the footsteps of someone going into her room. I was drawn by an impulse as swift as it was involuntary to run to her door and put my eye to the keyhole. I saw Tanzai, the young mulatto servant. He walked towards Zulica, carrying a basket of flowers which he had just gathered in the fields. Zulica ran towards him, took bunches of flowers in her hands and pressed them to her breast. Tanzai drew closer to smell their scent, which mingled with his mistress's sighs. I clearly saw a deep shiver run through Zulica's whole being. I seemed to feel it with her. She fell into Tanzai's arms. I returned to my bed, there to hide my shame and weakness.

My bed was wet with my tears, sobs choked me and in my great distress I cried out, 'Oh my one hundred and twelve times great-grandmother, whose name I bear, sweet and tender wife of Isaac, if from the bosom of your father-in-law you can see the state I am in, appease the shade of Mamoun and tell him that his daughter is not worthy of the honour for which he has destined her.'

My cries had awoken my brother. He came into my bedroom, and believing me to be ill, made me take a sedative. He returned at midday and, finding my pulse was racing, offered himself to continue my cabbalistic exercises for me. I was glad to accept his suggestion for I was in no fit state to work on them. I fell asleep towards evening and my dreams were very different from those I had had until then. The next day I dreamed while fully awake, or at least I was so absent-minded that I might well have given that impression.

One night my brother came into my bedroom. He had the book of Sephiroth under his arm and a star-spangled scarf in his hand, on which were written the seventy-two names which Zoroaster gave to the constellation of the Gemini.

'Rebecca, Rebecca,' he said to me, 'shake off this state of mind which dishonours you. It is time for you to try your powers on elemental beings and on infernal spirits. This bandeau with its stars will protect you from their mischief. Choose a spot in the nearby mountains that you think the most suitable for your exercises. Do not forget that your fate depends on the outcome.'

With these words my brother dragged me out of the castle gates and shut them behind me.

Left to myself, I summoned up my courage. It was a dark night. I was in my nightgown, barefoot, with my hair loose and my book in my hand. I made for the mountain that seemed to me to be nearest. A shepherd tried to lay hands on my person, but I pushed him away with the hand in which I held the book and he fell dead at my feet. This will not surprise you once you learn that the cover of my book was made of the wood of the ark and that it had the property of killing anything that touched it.

The sun was just rising when I reached the mountain top which I had chosen for my operations. I could not begin them until midnight on the following day, so I took shelter in a cave, in which I found a she-bear with her cubs. She hurled herself at me but the cover of my book did its work: she fell dead at my feet. Her swollen teats reminded me that I was dying of hunger and I still did not have a single genie at my command, not even the humblest will-o'-the-wisp. So I decided to lie down beside the bear and suck her milk. The she-bear was still warm and this made my meal less revolting, but I had to fight off the bear-cubs. Just imagine, Alphonse, a sixteen-year-old-girl, who had never left the walls within which she had been born, in such a dreadful situation. I had fearsome weapons at my disposal but I had never used them and the least lapse of concentration could turn them against me.

Meanwhile I saw the grass wither, the air fill with a fiery vapour and birds falling dead in mid-flight. I inferred that the demons, forewarned, were gathering. A tree spontaneously burst into flames; from it emerged swirls of smoke which did not rise but surrounded my cave and plunged me into darkness. The she-bear lying at my feet seemed to come back to life again. Her eyes sparkled with fire which momentarily dispelled the darkness. An evil spirit emerged from her mouth in the shape of a winged serpent. It was Nemrael, a demon of the lowest order, who had been chosen to serve me. Soon after, I heard words uttered in the language of the Grigori, the most famous of the fallen angels, and I realized that they were honouring me by their presence at my induction into the world of intermediary beings. Their language is also found in the first book of Enoch, a work of which I have made a special study.

Eventually Semiamas, Prince of the Grigori, came and told me that it was time to begin. I emerged from my cave and formed my star-spangled scarf into a circle, opened my book and spoke aloud the terrible formulae which I had until then only dared read silently to myself. As you will appreciate, Señor Alphonse, I cannot tell you what happened next. In any case, you would not understand. All I will tell you is that I acquired some considerable power over spirits and that I was taught how to contact the heavenly twins. At about the same time my brother succeeded in seeing the tips of the feet of Solomon's daughters. I waited for the sun to enter the sign of Gemini and performed my operations in turn. On that day, or rather night, I worked prodigiously hard and in the end was overcome by sleep and forced to give in to it.

The next morning Zulica brought my mirror and in it I caught sight of two human forms which seemed to be behind me. I turned round and saw nothing. I looked back in the mirror and saw them again. I should add that this apparition was in no way frightening. I saw two young men who were slightly taller than human beings. Their shoulders were a little broader and were rounded in the way women's shoulders are. Their torso was also feminine in form but they did not have breasts. Their arms, plump and perfectly shaped, were resting at their sides in the posture that Egyptian statues have. The heavy curls of their blue and gold hair fell down to their shoulders. I will not describe their faces to you. You can well imagine how handsome demi-gods are for these were indeed the heavenly twins. I recognized them by the little flames which burned above their heads.

'How were these demi-gods dressed?' I asked Rebecca.

'They wore nothing at all,' she replied. 'Each one had four wings, two lying on their shoulders and two folded and crossed around their waists. These wings were actually as transparent as those of a fly, but woven through with gold and blue veins which hid from sight anything which might have shocked my modesty.'

'So here they are,' I said to myself, 'the heavenly spouses to whom I am promised.' I could not help privately comparing them to the young mulatto who adored Zulica. But I was ashamed of the thought. I looked in the mirror and thought that I saw two demi-gods looking severely at me, as though they had been able to read my mind and had taken offence at the involuntary comparison I had made.

For several days I did not raise my eyes to the mirror, but at last I ventured to do so. The divine twins had their arms crossed on their chests and dispelled my shyness by their gentle air. Yet I did not know what to say to them. To escape my predicament, I fetched a volume of the works of Edris, whom you call Atlas.[1] It is the most beautiful poetry that we have. The harmony of Edris's verse imitates that of the heavenly bodies. I was not familiar with the poet's language and, fearing that I had not read it well, I surreptitiously looked into the mirror to see what effect I was having on my audience. I had every reason to be pleased. The Thamim were looking at each other as though they approved of what I was doing, and from time to time they shot glances into the mirror that I could not meet without feeling disturbed.

My brother came in at that moment and the vision disappeared. He told me about Solomon's daughters, the tips of whose feet he had seen. He was exhilarated, and I shared his joy. I felt myself at that

---

1 A prophet mentioned in the Koran.

moment imbued with an emotion which until then I had not known. The private thrill which usually accompanied cabbalistic exercises imperceptibly gave way to an indescribable, sweet abandon, the like of which I had not known before.

My brother had the castle gates opened. They had been shut since my excursion into the mountains. We enjoyed the pleasures of a walk together. The countryside seemed to me to be painted with the most vivid colours. I could see my brother's eyes burning with a sort of fire, different from the passion for knowledge. We made our way deep into an orange grove. I went off to muse by myself. He went his own way. We were still occupied by our reveries on our return.

In preparing me for bed, Zulica brought me a mirror. I saw that I was not alone. I had the mirror taken away, thinking like an ostrich that I would not be seen if I could not see. I lay down and fell asleep, but some strange dreams took hold of my imagination. I thought I saw in the vast abyss of the heavens two brilliant stars travelling majestically across the zodiac. They suddenly left it and then reappeared, bearing with them the nebula from the belt of Andromeda.

These three heavenly bodies continued together on their ethereal course. They then stopped and took on the appearance of a fiery meteor. Next they appeared to me in the form of three luminous rings which, having spun round for a certain time, settled around the same centre. After that they changed into a sort of halo or aureola around a sapphire throne. I saw the twins holding out their arms to me and pointing me to the place I should occupy between them. I tried to rise up to them, but it seemed to me at that moment as though Tanzai the mulatto was stopping me by gripping me round the waist. I was indeed very gripped by all this and as a result woke up with a start.

It was dark in my bedroom but I saw through the chink in the door that there was a light in Zulica's room. I heard her moan and thought that she was ill. I should have called to her but I did not. I cannot say what guilty, rash impulse led me to resort again to the keyhole. I saw Tanzai the mulatto taking liberties with Zulica's person that froze me with horror. My eyes closed and I fell down in a faint.

When I came round, my brother and Zulica were standing beside my bed. I gave her a withering look and told her never to appear again in my presence. My brother asked me what had caused me to be so severe. I blushingly told him what had happened to me. He replied that he had married them the previous evening and that he was very upset at not having foreseen what would happen. It was true that only my sight had been profaned, but the extreme sensitivity of the Thamim made him uneasy. As for me, the only emotion I felt was shame. I would have died rather than look in the mirror.

My brother did not know the nature of my relations with the Thamim but he knew that I was no longer a stranger to them, and, seeing me sinking into a sort of melancholy, he feared that I would neglect the exercises I had begun. When the sun was on the point of leaving the sign of Gemini he thought it was his duty to warn me. I woke as from a dream. I trembled at the thought of not seeing my gods again, of being separated from them for eleven months without even knowing what they thought of me or whether I had made myself wholly unworthy of their attention.

I decided to go to a high-ceilinged room in the castle where there was a ten-foot-high Venetian mirror. So as not to lose countenance, I took with me a volume of the works of Edris, which included his poem on the creation of the world. I sat down a very long way from the mirror and began to read aloud.

Then I broke off my reading and, raising my voice, ventured to ask the Thamim whether they had witnessed these marvels. At that the Venetian mirror left the wall to which it was attached and positioned itself in front of me. I saw the Gemini smile at me with an air of satisfaction, and both nodded to indicate to me that they had indeed been present at the creation of the world and that it had all happened just as Edris had described it.

I then grew bolder. I shut my book, and looked into the eyes of my divine lovers. This moment of abandonment nearly cost me dear. I was still too close to common humanity to be able to endure such intimate communication. The heavenly flame which shone in their eyes threatened to consume me. I lowered my gaze and, when I had recovered a little, continued to read aloud. But I happened to turn to the second canto in which this poet of poets describes the loves of the sons of Elohim for the daughters of mortals. Today it is impossible to imagine the ways of love in the first age of the earth. The exaggerated descriptions which I scarcely understood made me hesitate again and again. At those moments my eyes were instinctively drawn to the mirror and I thought that I could see the Thamim taking an increasingly great pleasure from the reading. They stretched out their arms to me and came close to my chair. I saw the shining wings at their shoulders unfold and even detected a slight fluttering in those which girded them. I thought that they were going to spread these too and covered up my eyes with my hand. Just then I felt a kiss on that hand and on the other, which held the book. Also at the same instant I heard the mirror shatter into a thousand pieces. I realized that the sun had left the sign of Gemini and that they had taken their leave of me in this way.

The next day I noticed in another mirror something like two shadows, or rather a faint outline of my divine lovers' forms. The day after, I saw nothing. To while away the tedium caused by their absence I spent my nights in the observatory where, with my eyes glued to the telescope, I followed my lovers until they set. Even when they had dropped below the horizon I still thought I could see them. When finally the tail of Cancer disappeared from sight I retired to bed myself, and my bed was often wet with involuntary tears which I shed for no reason. Meanwhile, filled with love and hope, my brother devoted himself more than ever to the study of the occult sciences. One day he came to me and said that from certain signs he had seen in the heavens he had learned that a famous adept, who for two hundred years had been living in the pyramid of Soufi, had left for America and that he would pass through Córdoba on the twenty-third day of our month Thybi[2] at 7.42 precisely.

I went that evening to the observatory and found him to be right. But my calculations produced a slightly different result. My brother insisted that his own were right and, as he is very confident in his opinions, he decided to go himself to Córdoba to prove to me that he was right and I was wrong. My brother could have made the journey in as little time as I take in relating it to you. But he wanted to enjoy the pleasures of the excursion and followed the contours of the hills,

2 February (in the Coptic calendar).

165

having chosen a route with the most attractive views to afford him delight as he went along. He reached the Venta Quemada by this route. For company he had taken Nemrael with him, that evil spirit who appeared to me in the cave. He told him to bring him supper. Nemrael stole the meal of a Benedictine prior and brought it to the *venta*. Then my brother sent Nemrael back to me, having no more need of him. At that moment I was in the observatory and saw signs in the heavens which made me tremble for my brother. I ordered Nemrael to return to the inn and not to leave his master's side. He set off, but came back a moment later to tell me that he had been prevented from entering the inn by a power greater than his own. My anxiety reached new heights, but at last I saw you arrive with my brother.

I detected in your features an assurance and a serenity which proved to me that you were not a cabbalist. My father had predicted that I would suffer greatly at the hands of a mortal. I feared that you were that mortal, but soon other worries occupied my mind. My brother told me what had happened to Pacheco and what had befallen him. But he added, to my great surprise, that he did not know with what sort of demons he had been dealing. We waited for nightfall with great impatience. When night came we uttered the most fearsome spells, but in vain. We were not able to determine the nature of these two beings nor whether my brother had lost his right to immortality through them. I thought that we might be able to obtain some enlightenment from you but you refused to say anything, bound by some promise or other.

Then, in order to help my brother and to calm his anxieties, I decided myself to spend the night at the Venta Quemada. I set out yesterday and didn't reach the entrance to the valley until long after nightfall. I brought together some swirls of vapour which I formed into a will-o'-the-wisp and I ordered it to guide me. This is a secret which has been kept in our family. Using similar means Moses, the blood-brother of my seventy-third times great-grandfather, produced the pillar of fire which led the Israelites through the desert.

My will-o'-the-wisp grew very bright and moved ahead of me to guide me, but it did not take the shortest route. I noticed this act of disobedience but did not pay enough attention to it.

It was midnight when I reached the *venta*. As I came into the courtyard I saw light in the middle room and heard melodious music. I sat on a stone seat and performed some cabbalistic exercises, which had no effect whatsoever. It is true that the music charmed and delighted me to such a degree that as I speak to you now I do not know whether my exercises were correctly performed, and I suppose that I must have left out some essential element. But I believed then I had performed them correctly. Deducing that there were neither demons nor spirits in the inn, I reached the conclusion that there were only men there and gave myself over to the pleasure of hearing them sing. There were two voices accompanied by a stringed instrument. They were so perfectly in tune and so harmonious an ensemble that no earthly music could compare with theirs.

The airs sung by these voices inspired a tenderness so alluring that I cannot describe it. For a long time I remained on my seat, listening to them. But in the end I had to go in, having come for that sole purpose. I went up the stairs. In the middle room I found two young gentlemen, both tall and handsome, sitting at table, eating, drinking and singing lustily. Their dress was oriental: they wore turbans, their chests and arms were bare, and they had costly weapons in their belts.

The two strangers, whom I took to be Turks, rose, drew up a chair for me, filled my plate and then my glass and started singing again to the accompaniment of a theorbo, which they took it in turns to play.

Their easy manner was infectious. They did not stand on ceremony, so neither did I. I was hungry, so I ate. There was no water, so I drank wine. Then the fancy took me to sing with the young Turks, who seemed to listen to me with delight. I sang a Spanish *seguidilla*. They replied, using the same rhythm and the same theme.

I asked them where they had learnt Spanish.

One of them replied, 'We were born in Morea and are sailors by profession. We have found it easy to learn the language of the ports we visit. But enough of *seguidillas*. Listen to the songs of our native land.'

What can I say, Alphonse? Their songs had tunes which drew from the soul every nuance of feeling. Just when they had moved you almost to extremes of tenderness, an unexpected twist in the music would restore you to the most wanton merriment.

I was not fooled by this performance. On inspecting these bogus sailors closely it struck me that they were remarkably like each other and remarkably like my own divine twins.

'So you are Turks born in Morea?' I said to them.

'Not at all,' replied the one who had as yet not spoken. 'We are Greeks born in Sparta of the same egg.'

'Of the same egg?'

'Ah, divine Rebecca,' said the other. 'How can you fail to recognize us? I am Pollux and this is my brother.'

I jumped up from my chair and fled to a corner of the room. The supposed twins took on the form in which they appeared in the mirror and spread their wings. I felt myself borne aloft, but by a happy inspiration I uttered a sacred name which only my brother and I of all cabbalists know. At the same instant I was thrown back to earth. My fall made me lose consciousness. Your kind offices restored it to me. An intuition that I trust tells me that I have not lost what it was most important for me to preserve intact. But I have grown tired of such marvels. Oh divine twins, I am not worthy of you, I feel it! I was born to remain a mere mortal!

Rebecca ended her story at this point, and my first thought was that she had been making fun of me throughout, and that her only aim had been to take advantage of my credulity. I took my leave of her without ceremony and started to reflect on what she had told me. 'Either this woman is in league with the Gomelez to test me and convert me to Islam,' I said to myself, 'or else she has some other motive for extracting from me my cousins' secret. Or else they are demons. Or else if they are acting on the orders of the Gomelez . . .' I was still going over these conjectures in my mind when I caught sight of Rebecca drawing circles in the air and performing other magical hocus-pocus. A moment later she came over to me and said, 'I have let my brother know where I am, so he is sure to be here by this evening. While we wait, let's go and join the gypsies in their camp.'

She boldly leant on my arm, and we soon rejoined the old gypsy chief, who greeted the Jewess with many marks of respect. Throughout the whole day Rebecca behaved very naturally and seemed to have forgotten all about the occult sciences. Her brother arrived before nightfall. They went off together and I went to bed. Once there, I thought again about Rebecca's story. I think it was the first time I had heard talk of the cabbala, of genii, and of celestial signs. In what I had heard, there was nothing concrete I could find to disagree with, and so I fell asleep in a state of perplexity.

The Fifteenth Day

I awoke quite early and went for a walk to while away the time before breakfast. Some way off, I caught sight of the cabbalist and his sister, who seemed to be having a somewhat heated exchange. I turned aside from my path, not wishing to interrupt them, but soon saw the cabbalist disappearing in the direction of the camp and Rebecca hurrying towards me. In a few paces I was by her side and we continued our walk with scarcely a word between us.

At last the fair Israelite broke the silence and said, 'Señor Alphonse, I am going to tell you a secret which will not leave you unmoved if you have any interest at all in my fate. I have just decided to give up studying the cabbala. I spent last night thinking hard about this. What is the vain immortality worth which my father wanted to confer on me? Are we not all immortal? Are we not all bound for the heavenly dwellings of the just? I want to live this short life to the full. I want to spend it with a husband, not in the company of two stars. I want children; I want to see the children of my children and then, tired and sated with living, I want to fall asleep in their arms and fly to the bosom of Abraham. What do you think of my plan?'

'I approve of it very much,' I replied to Rebecca, 'but what does your brother have to say about it?'

'He was furious at first,' she admitted, 'but in the end he promised me that if he was forced to give up all hope of Solomon's daughters, he would do the same. He will wait until the sun has entered the sign of Virgo and then will make his decision. Meanwhile he wants to know who the vampires are who tricked him in the *venta*, whose names, according to him, are Emina and Zubeida. He has given up all thought of questioning you about them, because he claims that you don't know any more than he does. But this evening he plans to summon up the Wandering Jew, whom you saw at the hermit's house. He hopes to obtain some information from him.'

170

As Rebecca reached this point in what she was saying, we were met by others, to be told that breakfast was ready. It had been laid out in a spacious cave into which the tents had also been brought, because the sky was beginning to cloud over. In no time, we heard the storm break. Seeing that we were condemned to spend the rest of the day in the cave, I asked the old gypsy chief to continue with his story, which he did as follows:

༄ THE GYPSY CHIEF'S STORY CONTINUED ༄

You remember, Señor Alphonse, the story of the Principessa di Monte Salerno, which was related by Romati. Well, I told you how great an impression she had made on me. Once we had lain down to sleep, the bedchamber was lit only by the dim light of a lamp. I did not dare to look into the darkest corners of the room, and was especially careful to avoid casting my eyes on a certain chest in which the innkeeper habitually kept his supplies of barley. I was afraid at any moment that I would see the princess's six skeletons emerging from it. I buried my head under the blankets to avoid seeing anything and soon fell asleep.

The tinkling of the mule bells woke me early next morning, and I was one of the first to get up. I forgot all about Romati and his princess, and thought only of the pleasure of continuing on our journey, which turned out indeed to be very agreeable; we were not too incommoded by the sun, which was to some degree veiled by clouds, and the muleteers decided to travel the whole day without a break, only stopping at the watering place known as Dos Leones, at the junction of the roads to Segovia and to Madrid. Here there is plenty of shade, and the two lions from which water gushes into the marble trough add considerably to the beauty of the place.

It was midday when we got there, and we had hardly arrived before we saw other travellers approaching on the Segovia road. Riding on the lead mule was a girl who looked about my age, although in fact she was a little older, and the *zagal* who was leading the mule was also young; he was a handsome seventeen-year-old lad who was well turned-out, even though only wearing what muleteers ordinarily wear. Behind him came a middle-aged lady, who could have been taken for my Aunt Dalanosa, not because she physically resembled her, but because she had precisely the same manner, and in particular the same kindly expression that showed in every feature in just the same way. She was followed in turn by a number of servants.

As we had reached the spot first, we invited the newcomers to partake of the meal which was being laid out under the trees. They accepted, but in a very morose way; the girl seemed especially sad. From time to time she cast tender glances at the young muleteer, who was very assiduous in serving her. The middle-aged lady looked at them with compassion; there were tears in her eyes. I noticed their general air of sadness, and would have liked to have said something to console them, but not knowing how to go about it, I concentrated on my meal.

We set off again; my aunt rode alongside the other lady, and I caught up with the girl. I clearly saw the young *zagal* touch her hand or her foot as he pretended to adjust her saddle; once he even kissed her foot.

After two hours on the road we arrived at Olmedo, where it was intended we should spend the night. My aunt had chairs placed at the front door of the inn, where she sat down with the other lady. Shortly after she told me to order some chocolate. I went into the inn in pursuit of our servants, and found myself in a room where I could see the young man and the girl holding each other tight and weeping piteously. It was heart-rending to see; I threw my arms round the neck of the young man, and cried so much that I could scarcely breathe. While this was going on, the two ladies had come in, and my aunt, herself very moved, led me out of the room and asked me why I was crying. As I didn't know the cause of all this weeping, I was unable to tell her. Once she knew that I had been crying without knowing why, she could not help smiling. Meanwhile, the other lady had shut herself in the room with the girl, and we could hear them sobbing; they did not come out at supper time.

The meal was neither merry nor long.

When the dishes had been cleared away, my aunt turned to the older lady and said, 'Señora, heaven forbid that I should think ill of my neighbour, and especially not of you, for you seem to me to be a kind and Christian person. But, well, I have had the honour to eat with you, and it will certainly be an honour to do so whenever the occasion presents itself; yet here's my nephew, who saw this young lady embracing this admittedly good-looking muleteer; there's nothing to reproach him for on that score. And of course I have no right ... but, having had the honour to eat with you ... and since the journey to Burgos is still before us ...'

At this point my aunt became so embarrassed that she would never have been able to finish her sentence, but the other lady broke in at just the right moment. 'You are quite right, Señora,' she said, 'after what you have seen, you are wholly justified in inquiring why I am so tolerant. I have a thousand reasons not to tell you, but I can see that it is my duty to do so.'

The good lady then drew out her handkerchief, wiped her eyes, and spoke as follows:

‿ MARIA DE TORRES'S STORY ‿

I am the daughter of Don Emanuel de Noruña, the *oidor* of the court of Segovia. I was married at the age of eighteen years to Don Enrique de Torres, a colonel who had retired from active service. My mother had died many years before. We lost my father two months after our marriage, and took into our household my younger sister, Elvira de Noruña, who, although not yet fourteen years old, was already famed for her beauty. My father left practically nothing; as for my husband, he was quite well off, but we were obliged for family reasons to pay the pensions of five knights of Malta and the dowries of six nuns who were related to us, so that our income was only sufficient to provide us with the bare necessities. But a pension which my husband had been granted by the court made our lives somewhat easier.

At that time there were a good number of noble houses in Segovia which were no better off than we were; drawn together by this common interest, they had introduced a method of saving money. They rarely visited each other; ladies showed themselves at their windows, and gentlemen remained in the street below. There was a great deal of playing of the guitar, and even more amorous sighing, neither of which cost a penny. Manufacturers of vicuña cloth lived in luxury; we could not emulate them, so we took our revenge by despising and ridiculing them.

As my sister grew older, the street below grew more and more congested with guitars. Some sighed while others strummed, or else they strummed and sighed at the same time. The other beauties of the town were in torments of jealousy, but the object of all these attentions took no notice of them. My sister almost never showed herself; so as not to be impolite, I remained at the window and spoke a few obliging words to everyone. This courtesy was a duty which I could not have foregone, but when the last strummer had departed, I took indescribable pleasure in closing the window. My husband and sister were waiting for me in the dining room, where we partook of a frugal supper which we spiced with endless jokes at the expense of the suitors. Everyone was ridiculed in turn, and I am sure that if they had been listening behind the door, not one would have come back. These conversations were hardly charitable, but we took such pleasure in them that we continued them sometimes long into the night.

One evening, as we were talking about our favourite subject, Elvira became more serious and said to me, 'Have you noticed, sister, that when all the strummers have left the street and the light has gone from our drawing room, one can still hear one or two *seguidillas* which are sung and accompanied as though by a professional player rather than an amateur?'

My husband confirmed that it was true, and that he had noticed the same thing. I replied in similar terms, and we teased my sister about her new suitor. But we thought that she responded less well to these jokes than was usual.

The next day, after having bid farewell to the strummers and closed the window, I put the light out and stayed in the room. I could soon hear the voice of which my sister had spoken. At first there was a very elaborate prelude, and then a couplet was sung about the pleasures of secrecy, followed by one on love that is shy; I heard nothing after that. As I left the drawing room, I saw that my sister had been behind the door, listening. I did not reveal that I had seen her, but I noticed that she seemed preoccupied and abstracted.

The mysterious singer carried on with his serenades, and we grew so used to them that we would wait to hear them before going to supper.

Elvira was made curious by this persistent mystery, but her heart was not touched by it. Meanwhile Segovia witnessed the arrival of a new personage, causing heads to turn and fortunes to topple. It was the Conde de Rovellas, an exile from the court and therefore a man of importance in the eyes of provincials.

Rovellas had been born in Vera Cruz. His Mexican mother had brought an immense fortune to his family, and as Americans were at that time well looked-upon at court, he crossed the ocean to acquire the rank of grandee. As you may well imagine, he was bound to have but little knowledge of the manners of the Old World, having been born in the New. But he lived in great luxury, and even the king deigned to be amused by his naïve behaviour. However, as it nearly all stemmed from the high opinion he had of himself, he became in the end an object of mockery.

It was at that time the practice among the young gentlemen of the court to choose a lady to whom to dedicate their thoughts. They would wear her colours, and on certain occasions, as for example at the *parejos*, which are a kind of joust, they would sport a symbol representing her.

Rovellas, who was very arrogant, wore the symbol of the Princess of the Asturias. The king found this to be a very amusing gesture, but the princess found it offensive; so an *alguazil de corte* arrested the count in his own house and escorted him to the tower of Segovia. He spent a week there, and then was confined to the town itself. The reason for this exile was hardly very honourable, but it was in the nature of the count to boast about everything; so he took to speaking of his 'disgrace' and to insinuating that the princess was secretly in league with him.

Indeed, Rovellas was possessed of every sort of vanity. He thought that he knew about everything and that he would succeed in everything he undertook. His greatest pretensions were reserved, however, for bullfighting, singing and dancing.

His fellow men were not impolite enough to cast doubt on the latter two talents, but the bulls were less forbearing. None the less, the count, with the help of his picadors, thought himself invincible.

Our houses, as I told you, were not open to callers, except for the first visit, to which we were always at home. As my husband was distinguished by birth and military career, Rovellas felt it incumbent upon him to begin his visits at our house. I received him on my dais; he remained below, as it is the custom of our province to keep a considerable distance between us women and the men who call upon us.

Rovellas spoke fluently and at great length. As he was holding forth, my sister came in and sat down beside me. The count was so struck by her beauty that he was turned to stone. He stammered a few words which made little sense, and then asked her what her favourite colour was. She replied that she did not have one.

'Señora,' said the count, 'since you show such indifference on the subject, it befits me to display only a colour consistent with such melancholy; brown shall henceforth be my colour.'

My sister was not used to such compliments and did not know how to respond. Rovellas rose and took his leave. That very evening we learnt that he had done nothing but speak of Elvira's beauty during all the visits he had made, and the following day we found out that he had ordered forty brown liveries, embroidered in gold and black.

And from that evening on we no more heard the singing that had so moved us.

Having found out that it was not the custom of the noble houses of Segovia to receive regularly, Rovellas resigned himself to spending all his evenings under our windows in the company of the other gentlemen who did us the same honour. As he was not a grandee of Spain, and the other young noblemen were of Castilian origin, they thought themselves his equal and treated him accordingly. But gradually wealth reasserted its real power; all the guitars fell silent when confronted with his, and just as he dominated conversations, so did he the music-making under our windows.

But this pre-eminence did not satisfy Rovellas. He was desperate to fight bulls with us there to see him, and to dance with my sister. So he told us, not without pomposity, that he had had a hundred bulls brought from Guadarrama to Segovia, and that he was going to have a public square a hundred paces from the bullring floored over, where the nights following the bullfights would be spent dancing. This announcement, although brief, had a great effect in Segovia: the effect of turning heads and, if not toppling fortunes, at least causing great inroads to be made into them.

No sooner had the news of the bullfight got out than young gentlemen were to be seen running about like madmen, adopting the postures associated with this sort of fighting, and ordering the traditional golden costumes and scarlet cloaks. I do not need to tell you what the women got up to. Of course, they tried on the whole of their wardrobe of dresses and wigs; but they also summoned tailors and milliners, and their orders, as yet unpaid-for, added to the general prosperity.

The day after this celebrated announcement, Rovellas appeared beneath our windows at the usual time and told us that he had summoned twenty-five confectioners of sweets and lemonade, on whose talents he invited us to comment. And at that very moment, our street was filled with servants in brown and gold livery carrying refreshments on gold-plated platters.

The next day the same thing happened, and my husband quite rightly took offence. It did not seem honourable to him that our house should become a place of public assembly. He was kind enough to consult me on the subject. As always, I was of his opinion, and we decided to retire to the little village of Villaca, where we had a house and estate. We found a further great advantage in doing this: that of saving money. Thanks to this arrangement, we were able to miss some of Rovellas's bullfights and balls, which saved us the cost of as many new dresses. However, since the house at Villaca needed some restoration, we had to delay our departure for three weeks. As soon as our plan was announced, Rovellas made known how sad it had made him, and how passionate were the feelings which my sister had inspired in him. As for Elvira herself, she seemed to me to have forgotten the singer who had so moved us each evening; but for all that, Rovellas's attentions left her completely unmoved.

I should already have told you that at this time my son was two years old, and this son is none other than the little muleteer whom you have seen with us. The child, whom we called Lonzeto, was our pride and joy. Elvira loved him almost as much as I did, and I can assure you that he was our only consolation when we had wearied of the inanities going on below our windows. No sooner had we decided to go to Villaca than Lonzeto caught smallpox. You can imagine our grief. We passed our days and nights caring for him, and during this time the singer who had so moved us began again to sing. Elvira would blush as soon as the prelude began, but thereafter gave all her attention to Lonzeto. Once he had recovered we opened our window again to the suitors below, and the mysterious singer fell silent again.

Once we had again opened the window, Rovellas did not fail to reappear. He told us that we were the only reason for the bullfight's postponement, and he asked us to suggest a date for it. We replied to this courtesy as we were bound to, and so at last the date for this famous event was fixed for the following Sunday, which came only too soon for the unfortunate Rovellas.

I shall not describe the spectacle to you; to have seen one, is to have seen a thousand of them. Of course, you are aware that gentlemen do not attack the bull as do those of lower rank; they begin on horseback with a *rejon*, or lance. Once they have struck the first blow, they have to receive one in turn; but as their horses are trained in this exercise, it is just a glancing blow on their hindquarters. The nobleman must then dismount and continue the fight sword in hand. For this to turn out well, it is necessary to have *toros francos*, or bulls with trustworthy natures who are not devious. But the count's picadors had made the mistake of bringing him a *marrajo*[1] bull, which had been kept for other purposes. The connoisseurs noticed the error that had been made, but Rovellas was already in the arena and there was no means of retreating. He seemed not to be aware of the risk he was running. He paraded around the animal and struck it in the right shoulder with his lance, with his arm extended and his whole body leaning forward between the horns of his adversary, as the rules of the art dictate.

The wounded bull seemed to flee in the direction of the gate, but suddenly turned round, charged Rovellas and tossed him with such violence that the horse fell beyond the fenced enclosure and Rovellas inside it. After that, the bull turned on him, caught him up with its horn by the collar of his cloak, swung him round in the air and then

---

1 'vicious'.

threw him to the other side of the arena. Having lost sight of its victim, the animal looked for him everywhere, and having eventually spotted him, glared at him with rising anger, pawing the ground and swishing its tail furiously. At that very moment, a young man leapt over the fence, seized hold of Rovellas's sword and scarlet cloak and set himself before the bull. The crafty animal tried a number of feints, but could not disconcert its unknown adversary. At last, it charged him with its horns low to the ground, impaled itself on his sword and fell stone dead at his feet. At that, the victor threw the sword and the cloak over the bull, looked in the direction of our box, bowed to us, leaped back over the fence and was lost in the crowd. Elvira clasped my hand and said, 'I am sure that he is our mysterious singer.'

As the gypsy chief reached this point in his story, one of his henchmen came across to speak to him. He asked us to allow him to postpone to the next day the rest of the story, and disappeared to see to the needs of his little realm.

'I am very put out by this interruption,' said Rebecca. 'Our chief has left the Conde de Rovellas in a very sorry state, and if he has to remain in the arena until tomorrow, help will come too late for him.'

'Don't be upset,' I replied. 'You may be sure that rich men never are left abandoned, and you can trust his picadors to do what is necessary.'

'Of course you are right,' said the Jewess. 'So it's not that which is upsetting me; what I want to know is the name of the slayer of the bull, and whether he is the same as the mysterious singer.'

'But Señora,' I said, 'I thought that nothing was hidden from you.'

'Alphonse,' she retorted, 'I forbid you to speak to me about the occult sciences; from now on, I only want to know what I am told, and I want no other art than that of making the man I shall love happy.'

'So you have made your choice?'

'Certainly not; such a choice is very difficult. I don't know why, but I do not think that I shall be easily satisfied by a man of my own religion. I shall under no circumstances marry someone of yours, which only leaves a Muslim. It is said that men from Tunis and Fez

179

are handsome and agreeable. That will do for me, provided that I can find one who is affectionate.'

'But why do you so hate Christians?' I asked Rebecca.

'Please do not ask me,' she replied. 'All you need to know is that apart from my own religion, Islam is the only one I could embrace.'

We carried on in this vein for some time, but after a while the conversation began to pall, and I took my leave of the young Israelite. I spent the rest of the day hunting, and came back at supper time. I found everyone in a pretty good mood. The cabbalist was talking about the Wandering Jew; he said that he was already on his way and would arrive shortly from deepest Africa. Rebecca then said to me, 'Señor Alphonse, you will shortly meet someone who knew personally the Saviour whom you adore.'

Such words could not but displease me, so I changed the subject. We would all have liked that very evening to have had the gypsy chief continue his story, but he asked to be allowed to put this off to the next day. So we all went to bed, and I enjoyed an unbroken night's sleep.

The Sixteenth Day

I was awoken just after dawn by the chirping of the cicadas, which is particularly lively and cheerful in Andalusia. I had become sensitive to the beauties of nature. I left my tent to see the effect of the first rays of the sun on the vast horizon. My thoughts turned to Rebecca. 'She is right,' I said to myself, 'to prefer the concrete joys of this mortal life to idle speculation about an ideal world to which we shall all sooner or later belong. Does not this world offer us physical sensations and pleasurable impressions in enough variety to occupy us during the time of our short life?' I was carried away for a moment by such thoughts, though they were no more than day-dreams. Then, seeing that others were on their way to breakfast in the cave, I made my way there also. We ate like people who had slept in the fresh mountain air, and when our appetite had been satisfied we asked the gypsy chief to take up again the thread of his story, which he did as follows:

⟶ THE GYPSY CHIEF'S STORY CONTINUED ⟵

I told you, Señores, that two nights out from Madrid on the way to Burgos we were in the company of a young girl who was in love with Maria de Torres's son, who was dressed up as a muleteer. This same Maria was telling us that the Conde de Rovellas had been left for dead at one end of the arena, while at the other a mysterious young stranger had killed the bull which threatened to put an end to his life. So it's Maria de Torres who will continue her story.

⟶ MARIA DE TORRES'S STORY CONTINUED ⟵

Once the fearsome bull lay wallowing in its own blood, the count's equerries rushed into the arena to come to his assistance. He gave no sign of life. He was lifted on to a stretcher and was carried to his house. The spectacle did not go ahead, as you may well imagine, and everyone returned home. But that very evening we learnt that Rovellas was out of danger. My husband sent our page out for news of him. It was a long time before he returned. At last he brought us the following letter.

Señor Coronel Don Enrique de Torres,

Your honour will see from this letter that the Creator's mercy has deigned to leave me still in possession of some of my powers. But a great pain which I feel in my chest leads me to doubt whether I shall recover completely. You know, Señor Don Enrique, that providence lavished upon me worldly goods. I hereby bequeath a share of these to the noble stranger who risked his life to save mine. As for the remainder, I could not make better use of it than to lay it at the feet of Elvira de Noruña, your incomparable sister-in-law. I beg you to make known to her the respectful and honourable feelings she has inspired in one who will shortly perhaps be no more than dust and ashes, and whom heaven still grants the strength to call himself, Conde de Rovellas, Marqués de Vera Lonza, y Cruz Velada, Hereditary Commander of Tallaverde, y Rio Floro, Señor de Tolesquez, y Riga Fuera, y Mendez, y Lonzos, and so on, and so on, and so on, and so on.

You will be surprised that I can remember so many of his titles but we used to attribute them to my sister one after another as a joke and in this way we ended up by learning them.

As soon as my husband received this letter he let us know its contents and asked my sister what reply he should make to it. Elvira replied that she would not act without having first heard the advice of my husband, but she confessed that the count's good qualities had impressed her less than the excessive vanity which was apparent in all his words and actions.

My husband easily grasped the tenor of this reply, and so he replied to the count that although Elvira was too young to appreciate the proposals of His Excellency, she joined with all the household in wishing him restored to health. The count did not take this to be a refusal. He even spoke of his marriage with Elvira as settled. In the meanwhile we left for Villaca.

Our house was situated at one end of the village and was more or less in the country. Its situation was charming and it had moreover been very prettily restored. But exactly opposite it stood a peasant's house which had been decorated in unusually good taste. There were flowerpots on the front steps, fine windows and an aviary, together with some other pleasant, refined features. We were told that the house had just been bought by a *labrador* from Murcia. The farmers to whom are given the name of *labradores* in our province are a class of persons midway between the nobles and the peasants.

It was late when we arrived at Villaca. We began by going over the whole house from cellar to attic. Then we had chairs placed at the front door and partook of chocolate. My husband teased Elvira about the poverty of the house, which was unworthy to receive a future Countess of Rovellas. She took these jokes in good part. Soon after, we saw a cart pulled by four powerful oxen returning from work in the fields. They were led by a farm-hand, followed by a young man with a young woman on his arm. The young man was remarkable for his height. When he came close Elvira and I recognized the person who had saved Rovellas. My husband paid no attention to him, but my sister shot a glance at me which I clearly understood. The young man greeted us like a person who did not wish to make our acquaintance and went into the house opposite. The young woman seemed to observe us very closely.

'What a handsome couple,' said our housekeeper, Doña Manuela.

'What do you mean, a handsome couple?' said Elvira. 'Are they married?'

'Indeed, they are,' said Doña Manuela. 'To tell you the truth, they were married against the wishes of their parents. The girl was abducted. No one around here is under any misapprehension about it. We could well see they are not peasants.'

My husband asked Elvira why she had made so much of it and added, 'He might well be the mysterious singer.'

At that moment we heard a prelude on the guitar coming from the house opposite, and the voice that accompanied it confirmed the suspicions of my husband. 'That's strange,' he said. 'But since he's married, the serenades were perhaps intended for one of our neighbours.'

'Actually,' said Elvira, 'I believe they were intended for me.'

This naïve comment made us smile and then we fell silent on the matter. Throughout the six weeks of our stay at Villaca the blinds of the house opposite remained closed, and we did not catch sight of our neighbours. I even think that they left Villaca before us.

At the end of our stay we learned that the Conde de Rovellas was well on the road to recovery and that the bullfights were going to begin again, although he himself would not take part. We returned to Segovia. Festivity followed festivity, and ingeniously contrived social event followed ingeniously contrived social event. In the end the count's attentions touched Elvira's heart and the wedding was celebrated with the greatest magnificence.

The count had only been married three weeks when he learned that his exile was over. He had permission once again to appear at court. The idea of taking my sister there gave him very great pleasure, but before leaving Segovia he wanted to discover the name of the person who had saved his life. So he had the town crier announce that anyone giving news of the person who had saved him would receive a reward of a hundred pieces of eight, each worth eight pistoles. The next day he received the following letter:

Señor Conde,

Your Excellency is putting himself out to no purpose. Give up your plan of discovering the man who saved your life and satisfy yourself with the thought that you have taken his from him.

Rovellas showed this letter to my husband and said in a very haughty way that this missive could only have come from a rival, but that he had not known that Elvira had had previous affairs of the heart. If he had known this he would not have married her. My husband begged the count to be more circumspect in what he said and never again called on him.

Going to court was no longer in question. Rovellas became sombre and violent. All his vanity had turned into jealousy and his jealousy turned into sustained fury. My husband had communicated to me the contents of the anonymous letter. We concluded that the farmer from

Villaca must have been a suitor in disguise. We sent for information about him, but he had disappeared and the house had been sold.

Elvira was pregnant. We carefully hid from her what we knew about the change in her husband's feelings. She noticed it and did not know to what to attribute it. The count declared that for fear of incommoding his wife he would sleep in a separate bed. He only saw her at mealtimes. Conversation then was awkward and nearly always conducted in an ironic tone.

As my sister was in her ninth month of pregnancy, Rovellas left on the pretext of business which called him to Cadiz. A week later, a notary appeared who gave Elvira a letter and asked her to read it in front of witnesses. We all foregathered. These were the contents of the letter:

Señora,

I have discovered your amorous intrigue with Don Sancho de Peña Sombra. I have long harboured suspicions about it. His stay at Villaca proves your infidelity, which was ineptly disguised by the presence of Don Sancho's sister, whom he passed off as his wife. I expect that I was preferred because of my wealth. You will have no part of it. We will never again live together. I will provide for your needs but I will not recognize as mine the child to whom you will give birth.

Elvira did not hear the end of the letter. She had fainted after the first lines. My husband left that evening to avenge the offence done to my sister. Rovellas had just set sail for America. My husband left on another ship. A sudden storm claimed both their lives. Elvira gave birth to the girl who is here with me today, and died two days later. How did it come about that I too did not die? I really do not know. I believe that the very excess of my grief gave me the strength to endure it.

I gave the little girl the name of Elvira and tried to establish her right to succeed her father. I was told that I had to address myself to the court of Mexico. I wrote to America. I was told that the inheritance had been divided between twenty collateral relations and that it was well known that Rovellas had refused to recognize my sister's child as his. My whole income would not have been sufficient to pay for as much as twenty pages of legal representations so I contented myself with declaring Elvira's birth and parentage at Segovia. I sold the house I possessed in the town and retired to Villaca with my little Lonzeto, who was soon to be three, and my little Elvira, who was as many months old. My greatest regret was to have always in my sight the house where the accursed stranger with his mysterious passion had taken up residence. In the end I became accustomed to it and my children were a consolation.

I had been in retirement in Villaca for less than a year when I received the following letter from America:

Señora,

This letter is addressed to you by the unhappy person whose respectful passion caused the ills which have befallen your house. My respect for the incomparable Elvira was, if such a thing were possible, even greater than the love she inspired in me at first sight. I did not therefore venture to air my sighs and to play the guitar until after the street had been abandoned and there were no longer any witnesses to my audacity.

As soon as the Conde de Rovellas declared himself the slave of the charms which had conquered my heart, I thought it my duty to lock away in my bosom even the slightest sparks of a potentially blameworthy love. But when I learned that you planned to spend some time at Villaca I was so bold as to buy a house in that place, and there, hidden behind the blinds, I risked gazing on the person to whom I should never have dared to speak, still less declare my love. With me was my sister, whom I passed off as my wife, so that not the slightest suspicion could arise that I might be a lover in disguise.

The danger to the health of our much-loved mother made us rush to her side.

On my return I discovered that Elvira now bore the name of Condesa de Rovellas. I wept at the loss of a prize to which I could, however, never have aspired, and I set off deep into the forests of another hemisphere to hide my sufferings. There I learned of the indignities which I had innocently caused and the horrors of which my respectful love had been accused. I declare therefore that the late Conde de Rovellas lied when he suggested that my respect for the incomparable Elvira could have made me the father of the child she was carrying in her womb.

I declare that this is a falsehood and I swear on my faith and on my salvation never to marry anyone other than the daughter of the incomparable Elvira, which must prove that she is not my child. In witness of this truth I invoke the Blessed Virgin and the sacred blood of her Son. Let them be my succour at my last hour.

Don Sancho de Peña Sombra.

PS I have had this letter countersigned by the *corregidor* of Acapulco and several witnesses. Please have it formally recorded and legalized by the court of Segovia.

No sooner had I finished reading the letter than I liberally cursed Peña Sombra and his respectful passion. 'You wretched, preposterous, mad demon! You Lucifer! Why did the bull which you killed before our very eyes not tear your stomach out? Your cursed respect has caused the death of my husband and my sister. You have condemned me to spend my life in tears and poverty and now you dare to ask for the hand of a ten-month-old infant in marriage. Let heaven ... Let ...' Well, I gave vent to everything that my anger inspired me to say and then I went to Segovia and legalized Don Sancho's letter. I found my affairs in a terrible state on my arrival in that town. The payments from the house I had sold had been stopped to meet arrears of the pensions which we had to pay to the five knights of Malta. And my husband's pension had been suppressed. I made a final settlement with the five knights and six nuns, after which all I had left was the little estate at Villaca which became all the more dear to me, and my delight in going back there all the greater.

I found my children healthy and happy. I kept on the woman who had been looking after them and she, together with a lackey and a carter, comprised my whole household. I lived thus without wanting for anything.

My birth and my husband's rank gave me a certain position in the village. Everybody served me as best they could. Six years passed in this way. I hope never to have ones less pleasant.

One day the *alcalde*[1] of the village came to see me. He knew about Don Sancho's extraordinary declaration. He brought me the gazette and said, 'Señora, please allow me to congratulate you on the brilliant marriage that your niece will one day make. Read this article.'

Don Sancho de Peña Sombra, having done the king outstanding service not only by conquering two provinces rich in silver mines to the north of New Mexico but also by the skill and judgement with which he ended the Cuzco rebellion, has been raised to the dignity of grandee of Spain with the title Conde de Peña Vélez. He has just been sent to the Philippines as captain-general.

'Praise be to God!' I said to the *alcalde*. 'Elvira will have if not a husband then at least a protector. May he return without mishap from the Philippines, be made viceroy of Mexico and cause our property to be restored to us.'

And indeed what I so ardently desired came about four years later. The Conde de Peña Vélez was made viceroy, and I wrote to him on behalf of my niece. He replied to me that I had deeply insulted him in thinking that he would ever forget the daughter of the incomparable Elvira; but far from being guilty of such forgetfulness he had already taken the necessary steps at the court of Mexico. But the case would last a very long time and he dared not force the pace because, as he desired no other wife than my niece, it would not be fitting that he should cause an exception to the way justice was administered to be made in her favour. I then realized that the count had not weakened in his resolve. Soon after, a Cadiz banker sent me a thousand pieces of eight and refused to tell me from whom the sum came. I suspected that it came from the viceroy. But a sense of delicacy prevented my accepting the money or even touching it. I asked the banker to invest it in the Asiento Bank.

I kept all this as secret as I could, but everything is discovered in the end, and so in Villaca it became known what the viceroy's

1 Mayor.

intentions towards my niece were. And she was then called nothing other than the little wife of the viceroy.

My little Elvira was then eleven years old, and any other girl of her age would have had her head turned by all this. But I only discovered too late that her mind and heart were of a disposition which prevented vanity from acting on them. From her earliest childhood, she had already, as it were, been stammering words of love and affection. The object of these precocious feelings was her little cousin, Lonzeto. I often thought of separating them but didn't know what to do with my son. So I scolded my niece, but all that I achieved was to make her hide things from me.

As you know, in the provinces our reading matter consists only of novels, novellas and romances, which are recited to the accompaniment of a guitar. We had a score of such fine literary works at Villaca and those who were keen on them lent them to each other. I forbade Elvira to read a single page, but by the time I thought of imposing this prohibition she had long since got to know them all by heart.

What is unusual is that my little Lonzeto had the same romantic turn of mind. They had a perfect understanding between them, especially when it came to hiding things from me, which wasn't very difficult. For, as you know, mothers and aunts are about as observant in these matters as husbands are. But I had some inkling of their complicity and wanted to send Elvira to a convent. I didn't have enough, however, to pay for her board. It seems now that I did nothing I ought to have done. It came about that instead of being delighted with the title of *virreina* (viceroy's wife), the girl had taken to the notion of playing the star-crossed lover and illustrious victim of fate. This fancy she conveyed to her cousin, and the pair of them decided to uphold the sacred rights of love against the tyrannical decrees of fortune. This went on for three months without my having the slightest suspicion of it.

One fine day I came upon them in my chicken-house in the most tragic attitude. Elvira was lying on a cage of chickens, holding a handkerchief and weeping copiously. Lonzeto was on his knees a dozen yards away and was also weeping his heart out. I asked them what they were doing there and they replied that they were rehearsing a scene from the novel *Fuen de Rozas y Linda Mora*.

On this occasion I was not taken in by them and saw that in their play-acting there was real love. I did not let them see that I understood, but went to our priest to ask him what I should do. The priest, having thought a little, said that he would write to a friend of his, also a priest, who might be able to take Lonzeto in, and that in the meanwhile I should say novenas to the Blessed Virgin and carefully lock the door of the bedroom where Elvira slept.

I thanked the priest, said the novenas and locked Elvira's door. But unfortunately I didn't lock the window. One night I heard a noise in Elvira's room. I opened the door and found her in bed with Lonzeto. They leapt out in their night-clothes, threw themselves at my feet and said that they were married.

'Who married you?' I exclaimed. 'Which priest can have committed so unworthy an act?'

'No, Señora,' replied Lonzeto gravely, 'no priest has been involved. We married each other under the great chestnut tree. The god of nature received our sacred vows in the presence of the first rays of dawn and the birds all around us were witnesses to our joy. That, Señora, is how the beautiful Linda Mora became the wife of the happy Fuen de Rozas. It is set down in print on the pages of their story.'

'Oh, wretched children!' I said. 'You are not married, nor could you ever be. You are cousins german.' I was so cast down with grief that I did not even have the strength to scold them. I told Lonzeto to leave and I threw myself on Elvira's bed, which I bathed with my tears.

When the gypsy chief reached this point in his story, he remembered some business that required his presence and asked permission to leave.

Once he had gone, Rebecca said to me, 'These children interest me. Love looked charming in the mulatto features of Tanzai and Zulica. It must have been even more beguiling when it enlivened the faces of handsome Lonzeto and tender Elvira. It's like the statue of Cupid and Psyche.'

'What a well-chosen comparison!' I replied. 'It shows that you are making as much progress in the art of Ovid as you have made in the writings of Enoch and Atlas.'

'I believe,' Rebecca said, 'that the art of which you speak is as dangerous as that with which I was involved up to now. Love has its own magic as well as the cabbala.'

'On the subject of the cabbala,' said ben Mamoun, 'I am able to tell you that the Wandering Jew has tonight crossed the mountains of Armenia and is hurrying towards us.'

I was so tired of the subject that I scarcely listened any more when the conversation turned to that subject. So I left the company and went hunting. I returned towards evening. The gypsy chief had gone off somewhere. I supped with his daughters for neither the cabbalist nor his sister appeared. I felt some embarrassment at being alone with these two young persons. But it seemed to me that they were not the girls who had been in my tent at night. They seemed to me to be my cousins. But what I could not work out for myself was who precisely these cousins or demons were.

The Seventeenth Day

When I saw the company assembling in the cave I made my way there too. We had a hurried meal. Rebecca was the first to ask for news of Maria de Torres. The gypsy chief needed no persuasion to go on, and began as follows:

✍ MARIA DE TORRES'S STORY CONTINUED ✍

Having wept for a long time on Elvira's bed, I returned to my own to weep yet more. My distress would perhaps have been less acute if I could have asked someone for advice. But I did not dare to reveal my children's shame, and I was dying of shame myself since I considered myself alone to be guilty. So I spent two whole days weeping continuously. On the third, I saw a long train of horses and mules draw up in front of my house. The *corregidor* of Segovia was announced. After the usual greetings, the magistrate told me that the Conde de Peña Vélez, grandee of Spain and Viceroy of Mexico, had sent a letter which he had commanded to be delivered to me, and that the high esteem in which he held the noble gentleman had led him to deliver it himself into my hands. I duly thanked him and took the letter, which was expressed in the following terms:

Señora,

Thirteen years and two months ago, I had the honour of writing to you that I would have no other wife than Elvira de Noruña, who on the day that the letter was written from America was seven and a half months old. The respect which I then felt for this charming person has grown with her beauty. I intended to hurry to Villaca to prostrate myself at her feet, but the supreme orders of His Majesty obliged me not to come within fifty leagues of Madrid. For that reason, I expect to see

Your Graces on the road which goes from Segovia to Biscay.

I am respectfully Your Grace's faithful servant,

Don Sancho Peña Vélez.

Such was the letter of the respectful viceroy. Distressed as I was, I could not help but smile a little at it. The *corregidor* placed into my hands a wallet containing the sum I had deposited at the Asiento Bank. He then took leave of me and, after dining with the *alcalde*, left for Segovia.

As for me, I remained frozen like a statue, holding the letter in one hand and the wallet in the other. I had still not recovered from my surprise when the *alcalde* came to tell me that he had escorted the *corregidor* to the frontier of the territory of Villaca and that he was at my service to obtain mules, muleteers, guides, saddles and provisions; in other words, everything needed for me to undertake the journey.

I let the good *alcalde* make the arrangements. Thanks to his assiduous help we were ready to leave the following day. We passed last night at Villa Verde and here we now are. Tomorrow we will reach Villa Real, where the respectful viceroy will be waiting for us. But what shall I say to him? What will he himself say when he sees the tears of Elvira? I did not dare leave my son at home for fear of raising suspicions, and if the truth be told I was unable to resist his pleading to be allowed to come. So I have disguised him as a muleteer. Heaven alone knows what will happen. I fear and wish at the same time that all will be revealed. I shall of course have to meet the viceroy. I must find out from him what he has done to recover Elvira's property. If she is no longer worthy to become his wife I want him to take sufficient interest in her to take her under his protection. But how shall I at my age dare to confess my negligence to him? In truth, if I were not a Christian, I would prefer death to such a moment.

The good lady finished her story at this point and gave in to her distress. Tears streamed down her face. My good aunt drew out her handkerchief too and started to cry. I wept also. Elvira sobbed to the point where she had to be unlaced and put to bed. And that caused everyone to retire.

∽ THE GYPSY CHIEF'S STORY CONTINUED ∽

I lay down and fell asleep. The sun had not yet risen when I felt someone grasp my arm. I woke up and tried to cry out.

'Speak quietly!' said a voice. 'It's Lonzeto. Elvira and I have thought of a way out of our predicament, at least for a few days. Here are my cousin's clothes. Put them on and Elvira will take yours. My mother is so kind-hearted that she will forgive us. And as for the muleteers and servants who accompanied us from Villaca, they will not be able to betray us because they have just been replaced by others sent by the viceroy. The maid is in league with us. Get dressed quickly and you can go to sleep in Elvira's bed. And she will sleep in yours.'

I saw no reason to object to Lonzeto's plan so I dressed as quickly as I could. I was twelve and tall for my age, so that the clothes of a fourteen-year-old Castilian girl fitted me perfectly, for, as you know, Castilian women are generally shorter than those from Andalusia.

When I had dressed I lay down in Elvira's bed. Soon after, I heard her aunt being told that the major-domo of the viceroy was waiting for her in the kitchen of the inn, which served as the common-room.

A moment later Elvira was summoned, and I went down in her place. Her aunt raised her hands to heaven and fell back on a chair behind her, but the major-domo did not notice her. He knelt, assured me of his master's respect for me and presented me with a casket. I accepted it graciously and commanded him to stand up. At that moment many of the viceroy's retinue came in to greet me and shouted three times, 'Viva la nuestra virreina!'

My own aunt then came in, followed by Elvira, dressed as a boy. She made signs to Maria de Torres to show that she knew what was going on and felt sympathy with her, meaning that there was nothing else to do than to let us go on with our plan.

The major-domo asked me who the lady was. I told him that she was from Madrid and was on her way to Burgos to enter her nephew in the Theatine College. The major-domo invited her to travel in the viceroy's litters. My aunt asked for one for her nephew, who was very delicate and worn out by travelling. The major-domo arranged for this to be done. He then offered me his gloved hand and handed me up into the litter. I was in front. The whole procession then set off.

So now I was a future virreina with a diamond-studded casket in my hand, being transported in a gilded litter drawn by two white mules, with an escort of two equerries parading on either side of my carriage. In this situation, very singular for a boy of my age, I started to think about marriage, a bond whose nature was not altogether known to me. Yet I knew enough to be sure that the viceroy could not marry me and that the best thing I could do would be to keep him in ignorance of the truth for as long as possible, giving my friend Lonzeto time to think up some way of extricating himself from his predicament. To be of service to a friend seemed to me to be a very fine thing. In short, I decided to act the part of a young girl, and I practised by lying back in my litter, simpering and giving myself airs. I remembered also that I had to avoid taking long strides when I walked and generally stop myself from making any expansive movements.

I had reached that point in my thoughts when a great whirlwind of dust heralded the arrival of the viceroy. The major-domo had me step down from the litter and told me to take his arm. The viceroy dismounted, knelt down and said, 'Señora, be so gracious as to accept these tokens of a love which began when you were born and will not end until I die.' He then kissed my hand and, without waiting for a reply, installed me again in my litter, remounted and ordered us on our way.

As he was prancing alongside my litter, scarcely looking at me, I had the leisure to examine him closely. He was no longer the young man who had looked so handsome to Maria de Torres when he killed the bull or when he returned with his cart to the village of Villaca. The viceroy could still pass for handsome, but his complexion had been burnt by the equatorial sun and it was closer to black than white in colour. His eyebrows, which hung low over his eyes, gave his face so fearsome an expression that all the efforts he took to soften it merely produced a grimace which had nothing friendly about it. When he addressed men, his voice was like thunder, when he spoke to women, it was a falsetto you couldn't hear without laughing. When he addressed his servants, he seemed to be commanding an army, when he spoke to me, he seemed to be taking orders from me for a military expedition.

The more I observed the viceroy, the less comfortable I felt. The thought came to me that the moment he discovered that I was a boy would herald a beating the very idea of which made me quake. I did not therefore need to pretend to be shy. I was trembling in all my limbs and did not dare to raise my eyes to anyone.

We reached Valladolid. The major-domo gave me his hand and led me to the apartment which had been prepared for me. I was followed by my two aunts. Elvira wanted to come in but she was sent off as if she was an over-inquisitive boy. As for Lonzeto, he was with the ostlers.

As soon as I saw that I was alone with my aunts I threw myself at their feet, begging them not to betray me. I described to them the punishments to which the slightest indiscretion would expose me. The idea of my being whipped drove my aunt to despair. She also pleaded on my behalf, but her entreaties were unnecessary. Maria de Torres was as frightened as we were and sought only to delay the climax of the story for as long as possible.

At last dinner was announced. The viceroy received me at the door of the dining room, led me to my place and sat me on his left. 'Señora,' he said, 'the anonymity which I am presently keeping merely suspends the dignity of viceroy: it does not annul it. For this reason I venture to place myself on your right, just as the august master whom I represent sits on the right of the queen.'

Then the major-domo disposed the other guests according to rank, giving the highest place to Maria de Torres.

We ate for a long time in silence. Then the viceroy spoke to Maria de Torres. 'Señora,' he said, 'it gave me great distress to note that in the letter which you wrote to me in America you seemed to doubt that I would fulfil the promise that I made to you thirteen years and a few months ago.'

'Your Highness,' said Maria, 'my niece would seem, and would indeed be, more worthy of your high office if I had thought that you were more serious about it.'

'It is obvious that you are from Europe,' said the viceroy. 'In the New World everyone knows that I do not speak in jest.'

Then the conversation died and did not revive. When we rose from table the viceroy escorted me to the door of my apartment. The two aunts went to fetch the real Elvira, who had eaten at the major-domo's table, and I stayed with the maid, who was now mine. She knew I was a boy but was no less assiduous in my service, yet she too was petrified by the viceroy. We bolstered each other's courage and ended up by laughing heartily.

My aunts came back. As the viceroy had let it be known that he would not see us again that day, they secretly brought Elvira and Lonzeto to join us. My joy was then complete. We laughed like madmen and our aunts, delighted to have some respite from their sorrows, almost shared our merriment.

Quite late in that evening we heard a guitar and saw the amorous viceroy wrapped in a dark cloak, half-hidden behind a neighbouring house. His was no longer a young man's voice but it was still quite beautiful. He sang in tune and it was obvious that he had devoted a lot of time to music.

Little Elvira, who knew how to behave gallantly, took off one of my gloves and threw it into the street. The viceroy picked it up, kissed it and placed it in his bosom. But no sooner had I accorded him this favour than the thought struck me that I would receive an extra hundred strokes of the cane for it once the viceroy found out what sort of Elvira I was. This made me so sad that all I wanted to do was to go to bed. Elvira and Lonzeto wept a little as they took leave of me.

'Till tomorrow,' I said.

'Perhaps,' said Lonzeto.

Then I slept in the same room as my new aunt. I undressed as modestly as I could, and she did the same.

Next day, we were woken by my Aunt Dalanosa who informed us that Elvira and Lonzeto had run away during the night and that no one knew what had become of them. This news struck Maria de Torres like a thunderbolt. As for me, I realized at once that the only course of action I could follow was to become virreina in Elvira's place.

As the gypsy chief reached this point in his story, a gypsy came to speak to him about business. He rose and asked our permission to postpone the next part of his story until the next day.

Rebecca observed with some impatience that the story was always broken off just as it was reaching the most interesting point. Then we spoke of other matters. The cabbalist said that he had had news of the Wandering Jew, who had crossed the Balkans and would soon be in Spain. I can't remember what we did for the rest of that day, which is why I shall now pass to the next, which was more eventful.

The Eighteenth Day

———————— ✍ ————————

I rose before dawn, and on a whim decided to walk to the disastrous gallows of Los Hermanos to see whether I might not find a new victim there. My journey was not fruitless. There was indeed a man lying between the two hanged men. He seemed as lifeless as they. I touched his hands, which were stiff but still retained a little warmth. I fetched some water from the river and threw it in his face. Seeing that he then gave some signs of life, I picked him up in my arms and carried him outside the gallows enclosure. He came to his senses, and stared at me with wild eyes. Then, breaking free from my grasp, he ran off into the countryside. I watched him for some time but, seeing that he would be lost to sight among the bushes and might stray into the wilderness, I felt bound to run after him and fetch him back. He turned round and, seeing me pursuing him, ran even faster – eventually falling over, giving himself an injury above the temple. I used my handkerchief to dress the wound and then tore off a bit of my shirt to bind his hand. Silently, he let me do this. Seeing that he was so docile, I felt that it was my duty to take him back to the gypsy camp. I offered him my arm, which he accepted, and he walked at my side without my being able to coax a single word out of him.

When I reached the cave everyone had assembled for breakfast. A place had been kept for me. Another was laid for the stranger and no one asked who he was. Such are the laws of hospitality which are rarely broken in Spain. The stranger took the chocolate beverage like a man in need of refreshment. The gypsy chief asked me whether my companion had been wounded by thieves.

'Not at all,' I replied. 'I found this gentleman unconscious under the gallows of Los Hermanos. As soon as he came round, he ran off into the countryside. Fearing that he might lose his way in the heath land, I ran after him. The more I tried to catch up with him, the faster he ran to escape me. Which is why he did himself such an injury.'

199

At this, the stranger set down his spoon and, turning to me, said gravely, 'Señor, you express yourself badly. I suspect that you have not been inculcated with the right principles.'

You can well imagine what sort of effect these words had on me. But I kept my temper and replied, 'Señor caballero, whom I don't know, I venture to assure you that I have been brought up in the best possible way and that my education has been all the more essential to me in that I have the honour to be a captain in the Walloon Guards.'

'Señor,' replied the stranger, 'I spoke of the principles, about which you may have been taught, which govern the acceleration of heavy bodies when this occurs on an inclined plane. Actually, since you wanted to talk about my fall and give an account of its cause, you might have observed that, as the gallows was placed on top of a hill, I was running down an inclined plane, and from that you should have considered my path to be the hypotenuse of a right-angled triangle with its base parallel to the horizon, and its right angle formed by that same base and the perpendicular which met the point of the right angle, that is to say, the foot of the gallows. You might then have said that my acceleration along the inclined plane was to the acceleration I would have had by falling down the perpendicular as that same perpendicular was to the hypotenuse. It was an acceleration calculated in this way which led me to fall over so hard, not the fact that my speed increased because I was trying to escape from you. But all that doesn't prevent you being a captain in the Walloon Guards.'

With these words, the stranger took up his spoon and set about consuming the chocolate beverage again, leaving me uncertain how I ought to react to his reasoning and whether he had been serious or making fun of me.

Seeing that I was on the point of taking offence, the gypsy chief decided to change the subject and said, 'This gentleman, who seems very well instructed in geometry, must be in need of rest. It would be indiscreet to ask him to tell us anything today and that is why, if the company consents, I shall continue with the story I began yesterday.'

Rebecca said that nothing would please her more. And so the gypsy chief spoke as follows:

✑ THE GYPSY CHIEF'S STORY CONTINUED ✑

At the moment we were interrupted yesterday, I was just relating to you how my Aunt Dalanosa had come to tell us that Lonzeto had run off with Elvira, who was dressed as a boy, and how we were plunged into consternation by this news. Aunt Torres, who had lost both a niece and a son, was in an unimaginable state of distress. As for me, I thought that all that remained now that Elvira had abandoned me would either be to become the virreina in her place or to receive a beating that I feared more than death itself. I was contemplating these unpleasant alternatives when the major-domo came to tell me that it was time to go and offered me his arm to escort me downstairs. I was so persuaded in my mind of the necessity of becoming the virreina that I instinctively adopted a haughty air and took the major-domo's arm with such dignity and modesty that my aunts laughed in spite of their distress.

That day the viceroy did not prance alongside my litter. We met him again at the door of the inn at Torquemada. The favour I had bestowed on him the day before had emboldened him. He showed me the glove hidden in his bosom, he offered me his hand to help me down from the litter and gently squeezed and kissed mine. I could not prevent myself feeling a certain pleasure at being so treated by a viceroy, but the idea of the whipping which would probably follow all these signs of respect still troubled me.

We spent a short time in the apartment set aside for the ladies. Then dinner was announced. We were seated more or less as on the previous evening. The first course was eaten in complete silence. As the second was brought the viceroy turned to Señora Dalanosa and said:

'I have learnt, Señora, of the trick played upon you by your nephew and that impudent little muleteer. If we were now in Mexico they would soon be in my hands. Anyway, I have given orders for them to be pursued. If they are found, your nephew will be solemnly whipped in the courtyard of the Theatines and the muleteer will have a tour of duty in the galleys.'

The mention of the galleys and the thought of her son made Maria de Torres faint on the spot, and the idea of being whipped in the Theatines' courtyard made me fall off my chair.

In coming to my assistance, the viceroy was most assiduous and gallant. I recovered somewhat and put on a brave enough face for the rest of the meal. When we had risen from table the viceroy, instead of escorting me to my apartment, led me, together with my two aunts, under the trees opposite the inn, sat us down and said:

'Señoras, I notice that today you took exception to an apparent hardness which I seemed to possess and which I might be thought to have acquired in the course of the various offices of state I have occupied. It occurred to me also that all you could know about me relates to a very few aspects of my life whose course and guiding-force are unknown to you. It seems to me, therefore, that you will want to know the story of my life and that it would be fitting for me to relate it to you. I hope at least that by knowing me better you will no longer have the same fear of me as I witnessed today.'

Having said this, the viceroy fell silent and awaited our reply. We expressed our great desire to know him better. He thanked us for this token of interest in him and began as follows:

✍ THE CONDE DE PEÑA VÉLEZ'S STORY ✍

I was born in the beautiful countryside around Granada, in a country house my father possessed on the banks of the romantic Genil river. As you know, Spanish poets set all their pastoral scenes against the background of our province, and they have so convinced us that our climate is bound to inspire love that hardly a single inhabitant fails to pass his youth, and sometimes his whole life, in amorous pursuits.

When one of our young men enters society his first concern is to seek out a lady to serve. If she accepts his homage he then declares himself her *embebecido*, or slave of her charms. In receiving him as such, the lady enters into a tacit agreement not to entrust her gloves and hand to any other than he. She also gives him precedence over others when a glass of water is to be fetched for her. The *embebecido* then kneels before her to give it to her. He also has the right to parade on horseback by the doors of her carriage and to offer her holy water in church and some other privileges of equal importance. Husbands are not jealous of these relationships and indeed they would be quite wrong to be so; primarily, because their wives do not receive visitors in their houses, where, in any case, they are surrounded by duennas and ladies-in-waiting, but also, to be completely frank, because those of our women who decide to be unfaithful to their husbands do not choose their *embebecidos*. They look rather to some young relative who has access to the house, and those who are most infamous take lovers from among the lower classes.

This was the style of gallantry in Granada when I first joined polite society, but I was not taken by this style. It wasn't that I had no feelings for the opposite sex: far from it. My heart had felt the sweet influence of our climate more strongly than any other, and my first youthful feelings were a need for love.

I was soon convinced that love was something quite different from the insipid exchanges in which ladies in our society engaged with their *embebecidos*. These exchanges were indeed in no way guilty, but their effect was to interest the female heart in a man who was destined never to possess her, and to weaken feelings for the man to whom her person and heart belonged. This division revolted me. Love and marriage seemed to me to be necessarily but one, and Hymen with Venus's features became the most secret and dearest of my thoughts and the idol of my imagination. In short, I must confess to you that by cherishing this favourite notion, all my mental faculties became absorbed to the point where my reason itself was affected and that sometimes I could have been taken for a genuine *embebecido*.

Whenever I went into a house, far from taking an interest in the conversation going on there, I indulged myself in the fancy that the house was mine and my wife lived there. I would furnish her drawing-room with the finest tapestries from the Indies, as well as Chinese mats and Persian carpets on which I imagined that I could already see her footprints. I saw also the favourite tiled seat on which she would sit. Whenever she went out to take the air she would find a balcony, decorated with the most beautiful flowers, on which there would be a birdcage filled with the most exotic birds. As for her bedroom, I did not dare think of it except as a temple which my imagination feared to profane. While I was occupied with these thoughts the conversation followed its course. I took part only when I was spoken to, when I would reply at cross-purposes and always with a somewhat ill grace because I disliked being disturbed while making these arrangements.

Such was the strange manner in which I behaved during such visits. The same aberrant behaviour occurred on walks. If I had to cross a stream, I would wade into the water up to my knees and my wife would walk across the stepping-stones, leaning on my arm, rewarding my attentions with a heavenly smile. Children delighted me. There was not one I met whom I did not cover with caresses. A woman giving the breast to her infant seemed to me to be nature's crowning glory.

At this the viceroy turned towards me and said, tenderly and respectfully, 'I have not changed my mind on this matter and I am sure that adorable Elvira will not allow the blood of her children to be sullied by the milk of a paid wet-nurse.'

This proposition disconcerted me more than you could imagine. I clasped my hands together and said, 'Your Excellency, in heaven's name, do not speak to me of such matters for they are beyond my understanding.'

The viceroy replied, 'Señora, I am most sorry to have thus shocked your innocence. I shall continue with my story without making a similar mistake.'

And indeed he did continue as follows:

My frequent bouts of absent-mindedness led Granada society to believe that I had lost my sanity. There was indeed something in this. Or rather I seemed mad because my own madness was not of the same sort as that of my fellow-citizens. I would have been called wise if I could have brought myself to be the mad *embebecido* of some lady of Granada. However, a reputation for madness is not flattering and I decided to leave my native province. I was resolved to do this for yet another reason. I wanted to be happy with my wife and happy on her account. If I had married a lady from Granada she would have thought herself free to accept the homage of an *embebecido* on the authority of local custom. You have heard that that did not suit me at all.

So I decided to leave, and I went to court. There I found the same fatuous practices under different names. That of *embebecido*, which has today passed from Granada to Madrid, was not then used. The court ladies called their favoured but unrewarded lover their *cortejo*. They called *galanes* those who were even less well treated, rewarded at most with a smile and then only once or twice a month. But all their lovers without exception sported the colours of their lady and paraded alongside her carriage daily, raising a dust on the Prado that made the streets adjoining this beautiful promenade impossible to live in.

I had neither enough wealth nor high enough birth to be singled out at court. But I made my name there by my skill in fighting bulls. The king himself spoke to me on several occasions and grandees did me the honour of seeking my friendship. I was very well known to the Conde de Rovellas among others, but when I killed his bull he was unconscious and hence unable to recognize me. Two of his picadors certainly knew me well, but I must suppose they were busy elsewhere, otherwise they would not have failed to claim the thousand pieces of eight[1] promised by the count to the person who could give him information about his rescuer.

One day, when I was dining at the house of the Minister of *Haciendas* (or finance) I found myself sitting next to Don Enrique de Torres, your worthy husband, Señora. He had come to Madrid on business. It was the first time I had had the honour of speaking to him, but his manner inspired confidence and I soon turned the conversation to my favourite topic: that of marriage and affairs of the heart. I asked Don Enrique if the ladies of Segovia had *embebecidos*, *cortejos* or *galanes*, too.

'No,' he replied. 'Such figures have as yet not been accepted in our customs. When ladies go walking on the promenade known as Zocodover they are half-veiled, and it is not the custom to accost them whether they be on foot or in their carriages. Nor do we receive in our houses, except for the first visit by a gentleman or a lady, but it is the custom to spend the evenings on balconies which

---

1 The figure given by Maria de Torres in The Sixteenth Day (p. 184 above) and later on p. 210 is one hundred.

are a little above the level of the street. The older gentlemen stop to speak to persons of their acquaintance, younger men wander from balcony to balcony and end their evening in front of a house where there is a marriageable girl.

'But of all the balconies of Segovia,' added Señor de Torres, 'mine receives the most homage thanks to my sister-in-law, Elvira de Noruña, who, as well as all the excellent qualities of my wife, possesses a beauty which is not equalled in all of Spain.'

Señor de Torres's speech made a deep impression on me. A person who was so beautiful, so richly endowed with excellent qualities and living in a part of the country where there were no *embebecidos* seemed to me to be destined to be the person who would make my happiness. Some Segovians whom I induced to speak on the same topic confirmed that Elvira's beauty was incomparable. So I decided to judge with my own eyes.

Even before I left Madrid my passion for Elvira had already grown. But so had my shyness. So that when I reached Segovia I could not bring myself to visit Señor de Torres or others whose acquaintance I had made in Madrid. I would have liked someone to predispose Elvira in my favour as I had been predisposed in hers. I envied those whose great name or brilliant qualities herald their arrival and I thought that if I failed to make a favourable impression on Elvira at our first meeting it would be impossible for me to be preferred in her eyes to the others.

I spent several days at my inn, seeing no one. At last I had myself shown the street in which Señor de Torres lived. I saw a board on the house opposite and asked there whether there was a room to let. I was shown one under the roof. I was lodged there for two reals a month. I took the name of Alonzo and said that business had brought me to Segovia.

But in fact all the business I did was confined to peeping through a blind. Towards evening I saw you emerge with the incomparable Elvira. Dare I say it – I thought at first that she was no more than an average beauty. But after a short glance I clearly saw that the perfect harmony of her features did make her seem less strikingly beautiful, though as soon as she was compared to another woman her superiority was clear. I would even go so far as to say to you, Señora de Torres, who were very beautiful, that you could not stand comparison with her.

From my attic room I was pleased to note that Elvira was perfectly indifferent to all the homage paid to her and that she seemed even bored by it. But this observation took away all desire to swell the numbers of her admirers – that is to say, those gentlemen who bored her. So I decided to observe from my window until some favourable opportunity arose to make myself known. If I am perfectly honest, I was placing my hopes on bullfights.

As you will remember, Señora, I had then quite a good voice and could not resist the desire to make it heard. When all the suitors had returned to their homes I went down into the street and, accompanied by my guitar, sang a *seguidilla* as well as I could. I did this several evenings in a row and observed in due course that you did not retire from the balcony until you had heard my song. This filled my heart with ineffably sweet feelings, which were, however, still far from being feelings of hope.

I then learnt that Rovellas had been banished to Segovia. This made me despair. I did not for a moment doubt that he would fall in love with Elvira, nor was I wrong. Thinking himself still in Madrid, he declared himself openly to be the *cortejo* of your sister, took her colours, or what he imagined her colours to be, and embroidered them on his livery. From high up in my attic I was for long a witness of his fatuousness and impertinence and it gave me great pleasure to see that Elvira judged him on his personal attributes rather than the splendour with which he surrounded himself. But he was rich and on the point of becoming a grandee. What could I offer which could compete with such advantages? Perhaps nothing. Indeed I was so convinced of this and loved Elvira so selflessly that I ended up by wishing sincerely that she would marry Rovellas. I gave up all thought of introducing myself and stopped singing my tender *tiranas*.[2]

Meanwhile Rovellas expressed his passion only by his gallant behaviour. He made no formal approach to obtain Elvira's hand. I even learned that Señor de Torres intended to retire to Villaca. I had become used to the agreeableness of living opposite his house in town

---

2 An ancient, popular Spanish song form.

and decided to enjoy the same advantage in the country. I went to Villaca and assumed the name of a *labrador* from Murcia. I bought the house opposite yours and furnished it in my own taste. But since lovers in disguise are always easy to recognize, I had the idea of fetching my sister from Granada and passing her off as my wife, which, it seemed to me, would dispel any suspicions. When I had made all these arrangements I went back to Segovia, where I learnt that Rovellas was preparing to stage a magnificent bullfight. But, Señora de Torres, you then had a two-year-old son. Might I not have news of him?

Aunt Torres remembered that this child was the same muleteer whom the viceroy had proposed condemning to the galleys an hour before, and was at a loss to reply. She drew out her handkerchief and burst into tears.

'Please forgive me,' said the viceroy. 'I can see that I have revived some cruel memories. But for me to continue my story I must speak to you of that unfortunate child.

'As you will remember, he was then suffering from smallpox. You showered the tenderest attentions on him and I know that Elvira too would spend days and nights at the bedside of the young patient. I could not resist the pleasure of letting you know that there was another mortal who shared your grief. So every night, close to your windows, I would sing some melancholy romances. Do you remember this, I wonder, Señora de Torres?'

'I remember it very well,' she replied. 'Only yesterday I was telling this lady about it.'

The viceroy then continued.

The illness of Lonzeto was talked about all over town, for it was the cause of the delay in the festival of bullfighting. The child's recovery gave rise to universal rejoicing. The festival took place. It did not last long, for Rovellas was severely mauled by the first bull. When I plunged my sword into the animal's side, I looked up to your box and saw Elvira leaning towards you and speaking about me with an expression on her face which gave me pleasure. Meanwhile I disappeared into the crowd.

The next day Rovellas had recovered somewhat and asked for Elvira's hand in marriage. It was said that he had been refused. He averred that he had been accepted. But as I learned that you were preparing to leave for Villaca I myself concluded that he had been refused. I left myself for Villaca, where I took on all the habits of a *labrador*, driving my cart myself or at least pretending to, for in fact I left all that to my farm-hand.

After some days, as I was following my oxen home, with my sister, who was taken for my wife, on my arm, I caught sight of you with Elvira and your husband. You were sitting at the front door of your house drinking chocolate. You recognized me, as did your sister, but I did not reveal who I was. But to excite your curiosity I had the cunning idea, as I went into my house, of playing some of the songs which I had played to you during Lonzeto's illness. I was only waiting to be sure that Elvira had refused Rovellas before declaring my love.

'Ah, Your Excellency,' said Maria de Torres, 'it is true that you had succeeded in attracting Elvira's attention and it is a fact that she had refused Rovellas. If she did in fact marry him afterwards it was perhaps because she believed you to be married.'

'Señora,' said the viceroy, 'providence no doubt had other plans for my unworthy person. Indeed, if I had obtained Elvira's hand in marriage, the Assiniboins and the Chiricahua Apaches would not have been converted to Christianity and the cross, the holy sign of our redemption, would not have been planted three degrees north of the Mar Bermejo.[3]'

'That may be so,' said Maria de Torres. 'But my sister and husband would still be alive. None the less, Excellency, please continue your story.'

A few days after you came to Villaca, a special messenger from Granada informed me that my mother was dangerously ill. Love gave way to filial affection, so I left with my sister. My mother's illness

3 The French has 'Mer vermeille' : it is not clear which sea Potocki has in mind.

lasted two months. She breathed her last in our arms. I mourned her not long enough perhaps and then went back to Segovia, where I learned that Elvira had become the Condesa de Rovellas. I learned at the same time that the count had promised a reward of a hundred pieces of eight to anyone who revealed the identity of his rescuer. I replied by an anonymous letter and left for Madrid, where I sought employment in America. I obtained this and left as soon as I could. My stay in Villaca was a mystery known only to my sister and myself, or so I believed. But our servants are born spies who miss nothing. A valet, who would not follow me to the New World, entered Rovellas's service and told the whole story of the house at Villaca and my disguise. He confided in the chambermaid of the duenna major of the countess. She in turn told the duenna, and the duenna, to ingratiate herself through her diligence, told the count. He, putting together the disguise, the anonymous letter, my skill in bullfighting and my departure for America, reached the conclusion that I really had been the lover of his wife. In due course I was informed of all these facts, but on my arrival in America I was astonished to receive the following letter:

Señor Don Sancho de Peña Sombra!

I have been told of the secret affair you have had with the infamous person whom I no longer recognize as the Condesa de Rovellas. You may, if you think it fitting, send for the child which will be born to her. As for me, I will shortly be following you to America, where I hope that I shall see you for the last time in my life.

This letter drove me to despair. And my grief could not have been greater when I learned of the death of Elvira, your husband and Rovellas, whom I had hoped to convince of his injustice. Meanwhile I did all that was in my power to refute the calumny and establish the rights of his daughter. I therefore took a solemn oath to marry her as soon as she was old enough to be married. Having fulfilled this duty, I believed myself at liberty to seek the death which my religion did not allow me to inflict on myself.

A savage people allied to Spain were then at war with their neighbours. I had myself accepted into the tribe. To be admitted, I had to allow a tattoo of a serpent and tortoise to be pricked on to my whole body with a needle. The head of a serpent was drawn on my right shoulder, its body wound round mine sixteen times, with the end of its tail inscribed on the toe of my left foot.

During the ceremony the savage who does the drawing deliberately pricks the bones of the leg, and other sensitive parts, and the recipient is not allowed to let out the slightest cry. As I was being tortured in this way, the war cries of the savages who were our enemy were already resounding in the plain, and my tribe intoned a chant of death. I tore myself free from the hands of the priests, armed myself with a mace and rushed into battle. We brought back two hundred and thirty scalps and I was chosen to be cacique on the battlefield. Two years later the tribes of the New World had been converted to Christianity and brought under the crown of Spain. You must know more or less the rest of my story. I have reached the highest dignity to which a subject of the King of Spain can be raised. But, dear Elvira, I must tell you that you will never be the wife of a viceroy. It is the policy of the Council of Madrid not to permit a married man to have such great power in the New World. At the moment at which you deign to marry me, I shall cease to be viceroy. All I can lay at your feet is my title of grandee of Spain and a fortune about which I shall give you a few details. It will be held in common.

When I had conquered the two provinces to the north of New Mexico the king granted me the right to exploit a silver mine of my choosing. I took as my associate a private citizen from Vera Cruz. In the first year we shared a dividend of three million piastres fortes. However, as the grant was in my name I received six hundred thousand piastres more than my associate in the first year.

The stranger then interrupted. 'Señor, the share of the viceroy was one million, eight hundred thousand piastres and that of his associate one million, two hundred thousand.'

'That may well be,' said the gypsy chief.

'That is half the sum plus half the difference,' the stranger went on. 'Everyone knows that.'

'Capital!' said the gypsy chief, and carried on with his story.

'The viceroy, still wanting to tell me about the state of my fortune, said, 'In the second year we mined deeper into the ground and we had to build galleries, sumps and tunnels. The costs of exploitation, which had been only a quarter, now rose by an eighth and the quantity of ore diminished by a sixth.'

At this point the geometer[4] drew out of his pocket some writing tablets and a pencil, but thinking it was a quill pen he had in his hand he plunged it into the chocolate. Seeing then that the chocolate did not allow him to write as he wanted to, he decided to wipe the pen on his black coat but instead wiped it on Rebecca's skirt. Then he started writing down figures on his tablets. We all smiled at his absent-mindedness. The gypsy chief then went on.

'Our problems grew greater in the third year. We were obliged to bring in miners from Peru, to whom we gave a fifteenth of the profit without counting the expenses, which, that year, increased by two-fifteenths. But the ore increased by ten and a quarter times in respect of what we had obtained in the second year.'

I was well aware that the gypsy was trying to upset the geometer's calculations. In fact, pretending to turn his story into a mathematical problem, he continued as follows:

'Since then, Señora, our dividends diminished every year by two-seventeenths. As I obtained interest on the money from the mine, which I compounded with the capital, the result is that I have a fortune of fifty million piastres, which I place at your feet together with my titles, my heart and my hand.'

At this the stranger rose and, still writing figures on his tablets, took the path by which we had come, but instead of following it he went off on a track used by the gypsy women to fetch water. A moment later we heard him fall into the torrent. I ran to his assistance. I plunged into the water and, having struggled hard against the current,

4 I have used 'geometer' to translate the French 'geomètre', although 'mathematician' or even 'mathematical philosopher' might be closer in sense, because 'geometer' as a description seems to me to retain something of the angularity of Potocki's usage.

was lucky enough to bring the absent-minded stranger to the bank. We made him regurgitate the water he had swallowed, and lit a great fire; then he said to us, staring at us with eyes which betrayed his enfeebled state:

'Señores, the fact is that the fortune of the viceroy amounted to sixty million, twenty-five thousand and a hundred and sixty-one piastres, on the assumption that the share of the viceroy was to that of his associate as eighteen hundred is to twelve hundred or three is to two.'

Having uttered these words, the geometer fell into a sort of lethargy from which we were loath to rouse him, since it seemed to us that he now needed sleep. He slept in fact until six o'clock that evening, but he only emerged from his lethargy to lapse into an endless succession of absent-minded remarks.

First, he asked who had fallen into the water. He was told that *he* had fallen into the water and that I had dragged him out.

He then turned to me with great courtesy and friendliness and said, 'I really didn't know that I could swim so well. I am delighted that I have saved for the king one of his best officers, for *you* are a captain in the Walloon Guards. You told me that and I never forget anything.'

Everyone laughed. But that didn't put the geometer off. He went on amusing us with his absent-mindedness.

The cabbalist seemed scarcely less distracted himself. He spoke only of the Wandering Jew, who was to give him information about the two demons called Emina and Zubeida.

Rebecca took my arm and led me to a place where we could not be overheard. 'Señor Alphonse,' she said, 'I urge you to tell me what you think of all you have heard and seen since you have been in these mountains, and to let me know what your thoughts are on the cursed hanged men who keep playing such nasty tricks on us.'

'Señora,' I replied, 'I am much put out by your question. What interests your brother is a secret which is unknown to me. As for myself, I am convinced that I was carried under the gallows after I had been drugged by a sleeping draught. And you it was who told me about the power that the Gomelez secretly exercise in this part of the country.'

'Yes, indeed,' said Rebecca. 'I think they want to convert you to Islam. Perhaps it would be a good idea to give in to their desires.'

'What?' I cried. 'Are you a party to their plans?'

'No,' she replied. 'Perhaps I am following my own. I have already told you that I will never love a man of my religion or a Christian. But let's rejoin the company. We'll talk about this another time.'

Rebecca went to find her brother and I went on my own way, pondering on what I had seen and heard. But the harder I thought about it, the less I could understand it.

The Nineteenth Day

The whole company met together early in the cave. But the gypsy chief was not among them. The geometer had recovered very well. He was still convinced that he had pulled me out of the water. He would look at me with that proprietorial air that we reserve for those for whom we have performed important services.

Rebecca noticed it and thought it very funny. When we had eaten she said, 'Señores, we are losing a great deal by the chief's absence, for I am dying to know how he received the offer of the hand and fortune of the viceroy. But we have in our midst a gentleman who could make up for it by telling us his own story, which must be very interesting. He seems to have cultivated sciences which are not unknown to me, and anything about a man like that must please me greatly.'

'Señora,' the stranger replied, 'I do not think that you have applied yourself to the same sciences that I have, since most women are incapable of understanding even their rudiments. But since you have received me so hospitably it is my duty to tell you all about myself. So to begin with, I shall tell you that my name is ... my name is ...'

'What?' said Rebecca, 'are you so absent-minded that you can forget your own name?'

'Not at all,' said the geometer. 'I am not absent-minded by nature at all. But my father had one great moment of absent-mindedness in his life. He signed his brother's name in the place of his own and that act of absent-mindedness caused him to lose his wife, his fortune and the reward for his labours at a single stroke. So in order to prevent a similar thing happening to me, I have written my name on my writing-tablets. And when I want to sign it I copy what is written there.'

'But,' said Rebecca, 'it's a matter here of saying your name, not signing it.'

'You are quite right,' said the stranger. So he put his tablets back in his pocket and began.

∽ VELÁSQUEZ THE GEOMETER'S STORY ∽

My name is Don Pedro de Velásquez. I am descended from the famous house of the Marquesses of Velásquez, who, since the invention of gunpowder, have all served in the artillery and have given Spain the finest officers they have ever had in that army. Don Ramiro Velásquez, Grand Master of Artillery to Philip IV,[1] was made a grandee by his successor. He had two sons, both of whom married. The older branch retained the family fortune and the title of grandee, but far from giving themselves up to the soft life of court office, the heads of our family always remained devoted to the glorious work to which they owe their reputation. And, what is more, they made it their duty to support and protect the cadet branch.

This lasted down as far as Don Sancho, fifth Duke of Velásquez, great-grandson of the elder son of Ramiro. This worthy gentleman was, like several of his ancestors, endowed with the office and dignity of grand master of artillery. He was, moreover, the Governor of Galicia and resided in that province. He married a daughter of the Duke of Alba, and this marriage gave him as much happiness as it brought honour to our family through an alliance with the house of Alba. The duchess was not, however, as fertile as her husband had hoped. She had but one child, a daughter named Blanca. The duke intended her to be the wife of a Velásquez of the younger branch, to which she would bring the older branch's title of grandee and the family fortune.

My father, whose name was Don Enrique, and his brother, Don Carlos, had just lost their father, who was descended in the same degree as the duke from Don Ramiro. The duke took them both into his household. My father was twelve at the time and his brother eleven. Their characters were very different. My father was earnest, studious, over-sensitive. His brother was frivolous, rash and incapable

1 Philip IV reigned from 1621 to 1665.

of applying himself to anything. The duke perceived these contrary dispositions, decided that my father should be his son-in-law and, to prevent Blanca's heart making a choice different from his own, he sent Don Carlos to Paris to have him educated under the supervision of his relative, the conde de la Hereira, who was then ambassador in France.

By the excellent qualities of his heart and extraordinary hard work, my father won daily more and more of the goodwill of the duke and of Blanca, who knew that she was intended for him and became more and more attached to the choice her father had made. She even shared the tastes of her young suitor and followed from afar his career as a scientist. Imagine a young man whose precocious genius encompassed all human knowledge at an age when others were only just acquiring its rudiments. Imagine next that this young man was in love with a young girl of his age, of superior intelligence, eager to understand him and pleased to share as she thought in his success. This will give you some idea of the happiness enjoyed by my father in that short period of his life. How could Blanca not have loved him? He was the pride and joy of the old duke and the darling of the whole province. Before he was twenty years old his reputation began to spread beyond the confines of Spain.

Blanca loved her betrothed with passion and vanity. But Enrique, who was all heart and soul, loved her only with affection. He loved the duke almost as much as his daughter and often thought of his brother Don Carlos.

'My dear Blanca,' he would say to his mistress, 'don't you think our happiness is incomplete without Carlos? There are many lovely girls here who could settle him down. He is very inconstant. He rarely writes to me, but a sweet, tender wife would cultivate his heart. Dear Blanca, I adore you, I love your father but, since nature has given me a brother, why must we always be apart?'

One day, the duke summoned my father and said, 'Don Enrique, I have just received from the king, our master, a letter whose contents I wish to communicate to you. This is what it says:

Cousin,
We in our council have resolved to redesign the strongholds

217

which serve to defend our kingdom. We note that Europe is divided between the systems of Vauban and Coehoorn.[2] Employ the best minds among our subjects to write on this matter. Send their written proposals to us. If we find one which satisfies us, its author will himself be given the task of executing the design he shall have put forward. And our royal magnificence will reward him accordingly. Whereupon we pray God to keep you under his holy protection.

I, the king.

'Well, my dear Enrique,' said the duke, 'do you feel yourself able to enter the lists? I warn you that I will set you as rivals the most skilled engineers not only from Spain but from all Europe.'

My father thought for a moment about what the duke had told him, then said with confidence, 'Yes, Your Excellency, I shall enter the lists and will not cause you to feel ashamed.'

'Very well,' said the duke. 'Do your best, and when the task has been completed there will be no further postponement of your happiness. Blanca will be yours.'

You can imagine how ardently my father set himself to work. He laboured night and day, and when his exhausted mind forced him to take some rest he would spend his free time in Blanca's company speaking about their future happiness and often, too, of the pleasure he would have in seeing Carlos again. A year passed in this way.

At last, various proposals came in from every corner of Spain and all over Europe. They were sealed and deposited in the duke's chancellery. My father saw that it was time to put the finishing touches to his work and he brought it to a pitch of perfection of which I can only give you a very faint idea. He began by establishing broad principles of attack and defence. He showed how Coehoorn had conformed to these principles and how he had departed from them. He placed Vauban well above Coehoorn but predicted that he would change his system a second time. History has confirmed his

2 Sebastien Le Prestre de Vauban (1633–1707) and Menno van Coehoorn (1641–1704): the most famous military engineers of their day.

prediction. All these arguments were not only supported by learned theory but also by details of localities, estimates of expenditure and above all else by such calculations as would frighten even specialists.

When my father had written the last lines of his proposal, it seemed to him that he could see a thousand previously undetected faults in it. Trembling, he presented it to the duke, who returned it to him the next day with the words, 'My dear nephew, the prize is yours. All you need to think about now is your marriage. It will soon be celebrated.'

My father threw himself at the duke's feet and said, 'Your Excellency, I beg you to be so kind as to summon my brother. My happiness will not be complete unless I am granted that of embracing him after so long an absence.'

The duke frowned and said, 'I foresee that Carlos will bore us to tears with the greatness of Louis XIV and the splendour of his court. But since it is your wish, let's summon him.'

My father kissed the duke's hand and went to see his betrothed. Geometry was no longer in question. Love filled all his moments and all the faculties of his soul.

Meanwhile the king, who was very keen on the fortification project, commanded that all the proposals should be read and examined. It was unanimously decided that my father's had won. He received from the minister a letter informing him of the satisfaction of the king and telling him that it was the king's wish that he name his own reward. In a separate letter, addressed to the duke, the minister intimated that if the young man were to ask for the commission of colonel-general of artillery he might obtain it.

My father took his letter to the duke, who informed him of the contents of the one he had received. My father declared that he could not solicit a rank which he did not think he deserved and begged the duke to reply on his behalf. The duke refused.

'It was to you that the minister wrote and it is you who must reply,' he said. 'The minister must surely have his reasons and, as he calls you "young man" in the letter he wrote to me, it may be surmised that your youth interests the king and that the minister wants to place before his eyes a letter from the young man himself.

We will, I am sure, find some turn of expression to prevent the letter appearing too presumptuous.'

Having said this, the duke went to his secretary and wrote the following letter:

Your Excellency,

The satisfaction of the king, of which Your Excellency informed me, is reward enough for any Castilian nobleman. However, emboldened by your kind remarks, I dare to ask for His Majesty's consent to my marriage with Blanca de Velásquez, the heiress of our family fortune and title. This settlement will not lessen in any way my zeal to serve the king. I should indeed be happy if one day I might deserve by my efforts the office and rank of colonel-general of artillery, which several of my ancestors have filled with honour.

I am Your Excellency's humble servant, etc. etc.

My father thanked the duke for the pains he had taken, and took the letter to his apartment and copied it out verbatim, but as he was on the point of signing it he heard someone shouting in the courtyard, 'Don Carlos has arrived! Don Carlos has arrived!'

'Who? My brother? Where is he? I want to embrace him.'

'Sign the letter, Don Enrique,' said the courier who was to take it to the minister. My father, pressed by the courier and full of joy at the arrival of his brother, wrote 'Don Carlos de Velásquez' instead of 'Don Enrique de Velásquez', sealed the letter and rushed into the arms of his brother.

The two brothers then embraced. Don Carlos stepped back at once, laughed heartily and said, 'My dear Enrique, you are the image of Scaramouche in Italian comedy. Your *gonilla*[3] cuts across your chin like a shaving-dish. But I like you like that. Let's go in and see the old man.'

They went up to see the old duke, whom Don Carlos nearly hugged to death, as was then fashionable at the court of France. Then he said, 'Dear uncle, that ambassador chap gave me a letter for you

3 Spanish ruff.

but I took good care to leave it with my bathing attendant. In any case it doesn't matter. Grammont and Roquelaure and all the other old fellows send you their greetings.'

'My dear Carlos,' said the duke, 'I don't know any of these gentlemen.'

'Too bad,' said Carlos. 'They are great to know. But where's my future sister-in-law? She must be quite a beauty now.'

Blanca came in at that moment. Don Carlos went up to her in a casual way and said, 'Ah, divine sister! In Paris it is the custom to kiss the ladies!' So he kissed her, to the astonishment of Enrique, who had never seen Blanca except in the company of her duennas and never even dared kiss her hand.

Don Carlos said many other indecorous things, which deeply upset Enrique and caused the duke to frown. In the end the duke said to him, 'Go and change the clothes you have been wearing on your journey. There will be a ball this evening, and remember that what is taken to be proper behaviour the other side of the mountains is taken for impudence here.'

Carlos, who was not at all disconcerted, replied, 'Dear uncle, I'll go and put on the new uniform which Louis XIV has prescribed for his courtiers. You'll see that this prince is great in all he undertakes. I'll mark my beautiful cousin's card for a saraband. It's a Spanish dance but you'll see what the French have done with it.'

With these words, Carlos went out, humming a tune by Lully. His brother, deeply upset by his misbehaviour, tried to apologize for it to the duke and to Blanca. But he was wasting his time. The duke was already too prejudiced against him and Blanca not at all. At last the ball commenced.

Blanca made her appearance dressed not in Spanish but French fashion, which surprised everyone. She said that her dress had been sent to her by her great-uncle the ambassador and that her cousin had brought it with him. This explanation was found inadequate and could not fail to cause surprise.

Don Carlos kept everyone waiting a long time. At last he too appeared, dressed in the manner of Louis XIV's court. He wore a blue jacket embroidered with silver, a white satin scarf and lace, also embroidered with silver, a collar in an Alençon needlepoint and an extremely voluminous blond wig. This manner of dress, magnificent in itself, appeared all the more so because the last Hapsburg king had introduced a very mean costume into Spain. Even the ruff, which would have brightened it up a bit, had been abandoned in favour of a *gonilla* of the kind that nowadays is worn by *alguaziles* and legal officers, and that indeed resembled Scaramouche's costume, as Don Carlos had aptly observed. My rash relative, already quite distinct from the Spanish gentlemen by his dress, became even more so by the manner in which he made his entry to the ball. Instead of bowing or greeting anyone at all, he shouted out to the musicians for all to hear, 'Stop playing, you rascals! If you don't at once play a saraband for me I'll wrap your violins round your ears!' Then he handed round the musical scores he had brought with him, went to find Blanca and led her to the middle of the ballroom to dance with her.

My father admits that Carlos danced wonderfully well and that Blanca, who was naturally very graceful, surpassed herself on this occasion. When the saraband was finished, all the ladies at once rose to compliment Blanca on her dancing. But as they were lavishing praise on her, they turned their eyes to Carlos to let him see that *he* was really the object of their admiration. Blanca was not deceived by this and the tacit approval of the ladies raised the young gentleman in her esteem.

For the rest of the evening, Carlos did not leave Blanca's side. When his brother approached her, he said, 'Enrique, my friend, go away and solve some problems of algebra. You will have all the time in the world to bore Blanca when she's your wife.' Blanca would encourage Carlos in these insulting remarks by laughing at them immoderately and poor Enrique would retire in confusion.

When supper was served, Don Carlos gave Blanca his hand and led her to the top of the table, where he too sat down. The duke frowned but Enrique begged him not to upset his brother.

At supper, Don Carlos told the assembled company of the festivities which Louis XIV put on, and above all of the ballet *L'Olympe Amoureux*, in which the king himself had played the part of the sun. Carlos said he knew this particular dance well and that Blanca would make an excellent Diana. He then allocated the other parts, and before the company had risen from table Louis XIV's ballet was arranged. Enrique left the ball. Blanca did not notice that he had gone.

Next day, my father went at the appointed time to call upon Blanca and found her practising a dance-step with Carlos. Three weeks went by in this manner. The duke became sombre. Enrique hid his distress. Carlos uttered countless impertinent remarks which were recorded as though they were oracles by the ladies of the town. Blanca's head was filled with Paris and the ballets of Louis XIV. She was wholly unaware of what was going on around her.

One day when all were at table, the duke received a dispatch from the court. It was the following letter from the minister:

Your Excellency,

The king our master approves the marriage of your daughter with Don Carlos de Velásquez, confirms him in the rank of grandee and grants him the office of colonel-general of artillery.

Yours affectionately, etc., etc.

'What's this?' exclaimed the duke furiously. 'What's the name of Carlos doing on this letter? Blanca is betrothed to Enrique.'

My father begged the duke patiently to listen to him, then he said, 'Señor, I don't know how Carlos's name comes to be in place of mine but I am sure that it isn't my brother's fault, or rather it's nobody's fault. That this name should be changed was decreed by providence. And indeed you must have noticed that Señora Blanca is not at all fond of me but is on the other hand very fond of Carlos. So her hand, her person and her titles belong to him. I no longer have any right to them.'

The duke turned to his daughter and said, 'Blanca, Blanca, is it true that your heart is inconstant and wanton?'

Blanca fainted, wept and in the end admitted that she loved Carlos.

The duke said to my father in desperation, 'Dear Enrique, if he has taken away your beloved he can't take away the office of colonel-general of artillery. You deserve it and I will associate part of my fortune with it.'

'Señor,' replied Enrique, 'all your fortune belongs to your daughter, and as for the office of colonel-general, the king has given it to my brother and indeed has done well to do so. For the state my heart is in

223

does not permit me to serve in this or any other rank. Let me retire. I shall seek some holy asylum in which to cast my sorrows before the altar and offer them as a sacrifice to Him who suffered for us.'

My father left the duke's house and entered a Camaldolese monastery, taking the habit of novice. Don Carlos married Blanca. The wedding was a quiet affair. The duke dispensed himself from attending. Blanca, having caused her father to despair, was saddened by the ills she had caused, and Carlos for all his impertinence was somewhat put out himself by the general mood of gloom.

Soon after, the duke suffered an acute attack of gout and sensed that he did not have long to live. He sent word to the Camaldolese monastery to ask leave to see Brother Enrique once more. Alvarez, the duke's major-domo, went to the convent and delivered the message. The Camaldolese monks did not reply because their rule imposes silence on them, but they took him to Enrique's cell. Alvarez found him lying on straw, dressed in rags and chained round the middle of his body.

My father recognized Alvarez and said, 'Friend Alvar, how did you find the saraband I danced yesterday? Louis XIV was delighted with it. But those rascals of musicians didn't play it at all well. And what does Blanca have to say about it? Blanca, Blanca, answer me, you rogue!' Then my father shook his chains, bit himself in the arm and flew into a terrifying rage. Alvarez burst into tears, withdrew and went to tell the duke the sad news.

The next day the duke's gout spread to his stomach and all hope was given up of his life. Close to death, he turned to his daughter and said, 'Blanca, Blanca, Enrique will soon follow me. We both forgive you.' Those were the duke's last words. They insinuated themselves into Blanca's soul and carried there the poison of remorse. She fell into terrible melancholy.

The new duke did what he could to divert his young wife but he was unsuccessful. So he left her to her sadness and summoned a famous courtesan from Paris, called La Jardin. Blanca retreated to a convent. The office of colonel-general of artillery did not suit the duke though he tried for a while to fill it; not being able to do so with honour, however, he resigned his commission and asked the king for an office at court. The king made him chief gentleman of the bedchamber and he set up house in Madrid with La Jardin.

My father spent three years with the Camaldolese monks. The good fathers managed by means of assiduous care and angelic patience to restore to him the use of his reason. He then went to Madrid and called on the minister. This gentleman called him into his office and said, 'Señor Don Enrique, your affair has come to the ears of the king, who has blamed this mistake on me and on my office. But I showed him your letter signed Don Carlos and here it is. Please tell me why you didn't put your own name on it.'

My father took the letter, recognized his handwriting and said to the minister, 'Alas, Your Excellency, I now remember that at the moment of signing the letter my brother's arrival was announced. The joy of hearing his name must have made me put it in the place of mine. But it isn't this mistake which caused my misfortunes. Even if the commission of colonel-general had been sent in my name, I would not have been able to exercise the office. Today my sanity has been restored and I now feel able to carry out the plan which the king then had.'

'My dear Enrique,' said the minister, 'all the proposals for fortification have been abandoned and at court it is not the custom to mention again things which have been forgotten about. All I can offer you is the office of commandant of Ceuta. That is the only vacancy I have. And you will have to leave for Ceuta without seeing the king. I admit that this office is beneath your talents and it is moreover unkind at your age to be confined to a rock in Africa.'

'That is precisely what attracts me to the post,' replied my father. 'It seems to me that I shall escape my cruel fate by leaving Europe; by going to another part of the world, I shall become as it were another man, and shall at last find peace and happiness there under the influence of more favourable stars.'

My father quickly collected his orders as commandant, went to Algeciras, from where he set sail, and arrived without mishap in Ceuta. As he disembarked there, he experienced a delicious feeling. It seemed to him that he had reached port after many long days of stormy weather.

The first task of the new commandant was to get to know his

duties, not only in order to fulfil them but to exceed them. Much as he liked fortifications, he did not concern himself much about them where he was because, although the place was surrounded by barbaric enemies, it was already disposed well enough to resist them. Instead he devoted all the resources of his genius to improving the lot of the garrison and population and to procuring for them all such pleasures as their situation allowed, while, to achieve this end, he gave up all the privileges and benefits which the commandants had hitherto enjoyed. This course of action made him the idol of the little colony. My father also took infinite pains with the political prisoners who were in his care and sometimes he bent the strict rules in his instructions in their favour, either letting them communicate with their families or procuring for them other little benefits.

When everything had been improved as much as it could be at Ceuta, my father began again to devote himself to the study of the exact sciences. At that time the world of science was ringing with the debate between the Bernouilli brothers.[4] My father jokingly called them Eteocles and Polynices, but he also took a serious interest in them and often joined in the debate with anonymous treatises which lent unexpected support to one or the other party. When the great problem of isoperimeters was submitted to the arbitration of the four greatest geometers of Europe, my father communicated to them methods of analysis which can be considered as masterpieces of mathematical inventiveness. But no one thought that their author would actually decide to withhold his name and so in every case they were attributed to one or the other of the brothers. Everyone was wrong. My father loved science, not the reputation which science brings. His misfortunes had made him shy and timid.

Jacques Bernouilli died at the moment of winning an absolute victory and his brother remained master of the field of battle. My father clearly saw that he was wrong to consider only two elements of the curve but he did not want to prolong a war which had so upset the scientific community. Meanwhile Jean Bernouilli could not endure

4 Jakob Bernouilli (1654–1705) and Johann Bernouilli (1667–1747), the mathematicians.

living in peace. He declared war first on the Marquis de l'Hospital,[5] whose discoveries he claimed as his own, and later attacked Newton himself. The subject of these new battles was infinitesimal calculus, which Leibniz had discovered at the same time as Newton and which all England had made into a national issue.

In this way my father spent the best years of his life watching from afar the great battles fought by the greatest minds of the world, with the sharpest weapons the spirit of mankind has ever forged.

The love which my father had for the exact sciences did not however make him neglect the others. The rocks of Ceuta harbour many marine creatures which have much in common with the nature of plants and which form a sort of bridge between these two great realms. My father always kept some of these creatures confined in specimen jars and took delight in observing the marvels of their organisms. He also had with him a library of Latin books, or books translated into Latin, which he considered as historical sources. He had made this collection with the intention of supporting with empirical evidence the principles of probability developed by Bernouilli in his book entitled *Ars Conjectandi*.

So my father, living the life of the mind, passed in turn from observation to meditation, nearly always confined to his residence. The continual efforts to which he subjected his intellect made him often forget that cruel period of his life when his reason had given way under the weight of his misfortunes. But often, too, the past would claim its due. This would occur mostly in the evenings, after the labours of the day had exhausted his mind. Then, since he was not used to seeking distractions outside his own company, he would climb up to the terrace and look across the sea to the horizon, edged in the distance by the coasts of Spain. This view reminded him of those glorious and happy days when he was cherished by his family, loved by his mistress, admired by men of worth, and his soul, burning with the fire of youth and lit by the wisdom of a mature intellect, opened itself to all those feelings that are the delight of human life and all those thoughts that dignify the human spirit.

Then he remembered his brother robbing him of his mistress, his fortune and his rank and himself lying on the straw, deprived of his reason. Sometimes he took up his violin and played the fatal saraband which decided Blanca in favour of Carlos. This music provoked him to tears. When he had cried he felt relief. Fifteen years went by in this manner.

One evening the Lieutenant-Governor of Ceuta, having some business to transact with my father, visited him quite late and found him in one of his melancholy moods. Having thought for a moment, he said, 'My dear commandant, I beg you to pay attention to me. You are unhappy and you are sorrowful. That is no secret. We know it and so does my daughter. She was five when you came to Ceuta and since then not a day has passed without her hearing you spoken of with adoration, for you are the tutelary deity of our little colony. Often she has said to me, "Our dear commandant only feels his sorrows so deeply because he has no one to share them with." Come and see us, Don Enrique. It will do you more good than counting the waves of the sea.'

So my father let himself be taken to Inés de Cadanza. He married her six months later, and I was born ten months after their marriage.

When the weak child that I was first saw the light of day, my father took me in his arms, raised his eyes to heaven and said, 'Oh almighty power, whose exponent is immensity, oh last term of all ascending series, oh my God, behold another sensible being projected into space. If he is destined to be as unhappy as his father may you in your mercy mark him with the sign of subtraction.'

Having thus prayed, my father kissed me passionately and said, 'No, my poor child, you will not be as unhappy as I have been. I swear by the holy name of God that I will never teach you mathematics but you will know the saraband, the ballets of Louis XIV and every other form of impertinence which comes to my attention.' Then my father bathed me in his tears and gave me back to the midwife.

Now I beg you to note the strangeness of my fate. My father swears never to teach me mathematics and swears to teach me to dance. Well, the reverse happened. It has turned out that I know a great deal about the exact sciences and I am incapable of learning, I won't say the saraband because that's no longer in fashion, but any other dance. In fact, I cannot conceive how one can remember the steps of the quadrille. There are indeed no dance steps which are produced by a point of origin whose sequence is governed by a consistent rule. They cannot be represented by formulas and it seems inconceivable to me that there are people who can retain them in their memory.

As Don Pedro de Velásquez reached this point in his story, the gypsy chief came into the cave and said that it was in the interests of the band to move on and retire further into the Alpujarras mountains.

'Capital,' said the cabbalist. 'We'll meet up with the Wandering Jew all the sooner and, as he is not allowed to rest, he will come along with us on our journey and we will have all the more pleasure from conversing with him. He has witnessed much. No one can have experienced more than he.'

Then the gypsy chief turned to Velásquez and said, 'And you, Señor caballero, do you want to stay with us or would you prefer to be escorted to a nearby town?'

Velásquez thought for a moment and then said, 'I left some papers next to the mean bed where I slept the day before yesterday, before waking up under the gallows where this gentleman who is a captain in the Walloon Guards found me. Please send to the Venta Quemada. If I have not got my papers there is no point in my continuing on my journey. I shall have to go back to Ceuta. But while you are sending someone back to the *venta* I can still travel along with you.'

'All my people are at your service,' said the gypsy. 'I'll send some of them to the *venta* and they will catch us up when we next pitch camp.'

Everyone packed up. We covered six leagues and passed the night on a remote mountain top.

The Twentieth Day

—— ✍ ——

We spent the morning waiting for those whom the gypsy chief had sent to the *venta* to fetch Velásquez's papers. Prompted by an idleness which I believe to be natural to all the human race, we stared down the path along which they were to come. All except Velásquez who, having found on the hillside a slate slab polished by the action of the water, had covered it with x's, y's and z's. When he had had his fill of calculations he turned to us and asked us why we were impatient. We told him that it was because his papers hadn't yet arrived. He replied that it was very good of us to be impatient on his behalf and that he would wait impatiently with us once he had finished his calculations. Then he completed his equation and asked us what we were waiting for, and why we weren't leaving.

'Good Lord,' said the cabbalist to Señor Don de Velásquez the geometer, 'if you don't yourself know the feeling of impatience you must have observed it occasionally in those with whom you have had dealings.'

'That is so,' replied Velásquez. 'I have often observed impatience in others, and it seems to me to be a feeling of unease which never ceases growing, without there appearing to be any law that governs its growth. One may say, however, that in general terms it is in inverse ratio to the square of the force of inertia. So that if I am twice as difficult to move to impatience as you are, I will only suffer one degree of it at the end of the first hour while you will suffer four. The same applies to all the emotions which can be looked on as motive forces.'

'It seems,' said Rebecca, 'that you perfectly understand the springs of the human heart and that geometry is the surest way to achieve happiness.'

'Señora,' said Velásquez, 'the pursuit of happiness can, it seems to me, be compared to the solution of a quadratic or cubic equation.

You know the last term and you know that it is the product of all the roots, but before having exhausted all the divisors you reach a certain number of imaginary roots. Meanwhile the day goes by and you have had the pleasure of engaging in calculation. The same is true of human life. You also reach imaginary quantities which you have taken for real values. But in the meantime you have lived and moreover acted. Now activity is a universal law of nature. Nothing is at rest. This rock seems to be at rest because the ground on which it rests opposes a force to it greater than the pressure it exerts. But if you put your foot on this rock you will soon see how it acts.'

'But,' said Rebecca, 'can you submit the movement which we call love to calculation? It is claimed, for example, that with familiarity love grows smaller in men and it grows greater in women. Can you tell me why?'

'The problem that you have set me, Señora,' said Velásquez, 'presupposes that one of the two loves grows and the other diminishes. So that there will necessarily be a moment when the two lovers love each other equally, one in exactly the same degree as the other. In this way the problem can be brought under the rule of maxima and minima and can be represented by a curve. I have thought up a very elegant proof for problems of this kind. Let x . . .'

As Velásquez reached this point in his analysis, the men sent to the *venta* came into sight. They brought with them papers which Velásquez examined carefully, after which he said, 'All my papers are here with the exception of one, which in fact is not very important but with which I was busy the night I was taken to lie under the gallows. It doesn't matter, let me not hold you up.'

So we did in fact go on. We travelled for part of the day, then stopped and assembled in the gypsy chief's tent. After eating supper, we asked him to continue the story of his life, which he did as follows:

∽ THE GYPSY CHIEF'S STORY CONTINUED ∽

You had left me in the company of the terrible viceroy, who was deigning to tell me about his wealth.

★

231

'Whom I well remember,' said Velásquez. 'His fortune amounted to sixty million, twenty-five thousand, one hundred and sixty-one piastres.'

'Splendid!' said the gypsy, and carried on with his story.

If the viceroy had frightened me when I first saw him, he frightened me even more when I learned that he had been decorated by a serpent, pricked into him with a needle, that went round his body sixteen times and ended on the toe of his left foot. So I didn't pay much attention to what he said about the state of his worldly affairs. But that wasn't the case with Aunt Torres. She summoned up all of her courage and said to the viceroy, 'Your Excellency, your fortune is no doubt very big, but that of this young lady must also be considerable.

'Señora,' replied the viceroy. 'The Conde de Rovellas's prodigality had eaten a long way into his fortune. And although I took upon myself all the costs of the action, I was only able to retrieve the following from what he left: sixteen plantations on San Domingo, twenty-two shares in the San Lugar silver-mine, twelve in the Philippines Company, fifty-six in the Asiento Bank and some minor effects, the total sum amounting to twenty-seven million piastres fortes more or less.'

Then the viceroy summoned his secretary and had brought to him a casket made of precious wood from the Indies. Then he knelt and said to me, 'Charming daughter of a mother whom my heart still adores, be so gracious as to receive the fruit of thirteen years' effort. For it has taken me all that time to extract this wealth from the hands of your greedy collateral relatives.'

At first I wanted to take the casket with a gracious and tender air, but the idea of having at my feet a man who had smashed the heads of so many Indians, or perhaps the shame of having to play a part which was alien to my sex, or some other emotion, made me nearly faint. But Aunt Torres, whose courage had been considerably bolstered by the twenty-seven million piastres, supported me in her arms, seized the casket with a gesture which betrayed a certain greed and said to the viceroy, 'Señor, this young girl has never seen a man kneeling before her. I beg you to allow her to withdraw to her apartment.'

Once there, we double-locked the door and Aunt Torres gave herself over to raptures of joy, kissing the casket again and again and thanking heaven that Elvira would have not only a safe but also a brilliant future.

A moment later, there was a knock at the door. We saw the count's secretary enter with a notary, who made an inventory of the papers contained in the casket and required Maria de Torres to give a receipt for them. He added that as I was a minor my signature was not necessary.

Then my aunts and I once again shut ourselves in. 'Señoras,' I said. 'Elvira's future is secure but how are we going to get the bogus Elvira de Rovellas admitted to the Theatine College? And where are we going to find the real one?'

No sooner had I uttered these words than the two ladies heaved many a sigh of woe, with Señora Dalanosa picturing me already suffering the whip and Maria de Torres fearing for her niece and her son, hapless children who were exposed to so many dangers of different kinds, wandering in the world without guidance or support. Each went sorrowfully to bed. I thought for a long time about how to extract myself from my predicament. I could have fled but the viceroy would have sent people after me in all directions. I fell asleep without having thought of anything. We were then only a day away from Burgos. The part I was to play there caused me great anxiety; however, I had to step once more into my litter and the viceroy took again to parading alongside it, softening from time to time the habitual severity of his features with tender expressions which made me feel very uneasy.

In this manner we reached the deep shade of a watering-place, where we found that refreshments had been laid out for us by the citizens of Burgos.

The viceroy handed me down from my litter. But rather than lead me to the meal he took me aside, sat me down in the shade, seated himself next to me and said, 'Charming Elvira, the more that I have the good fortune to be near you, the more I am convinced that heaven has intended you to gild the evening of a stormy life dedicated to the good of my country and the glory of my king. I have secured the possession of the archipelago of the Philippines for Spain. I have

233

discovered half of New Mexico. I have brought the turbulent Inca people back to the path of duty. I have had ceaselessly to fight for my life against stormy seas, the inclement weather of the equator and the deadly fumes from the mines I have had opened up. Who will compensate me for this number of years, the best years of my life? I could devote them to retirement, to agreeable pleasures, to friendship and to other sweet feelings. But perhaps the King of Spain and the Indies, powerful though he is, is not powerful enough to give me this reward. But you, adorable Elvira, this reward is in your power. With your fate united to mine, I could wish for nothing else, passing my days with no other occupation than to be attentive to your dear heart's desires. I should be made happy by a single smile and transported with ecstasy at the tiniest sign of affection it may please you to grant me.

'The idea of this peaceful future coming after the turmoil of my past life has so captivated me that this very night I took the decision to bring forward the moment when you will be mine. So I shall leave you now, fair Elvira. But only to go on to Burgos, where you will witness the effects of my impatience.'

After these words the viceroy knelt before me, kissed my hands, remounted and galloped off.

I do not need to tell you what sort of anguish I felt. I anticipated the most unpleasant scenes, and this desperate prospect would always end in the whipping which I would not fail to undergo in the Theatines' courtyard. I rejoined my aunts, who were eating their meal. I wanted to tell them of the viceroy's latest declaration but there was no way of doing so. The inexorable major-domo urged me to step back into the litter and I had to obey.

At the gates of Burgos we were met by one of my future husband's pages, who told us that we were expected at the bishop's palace. Icy beads of sweat which I felt running down my forehead told me that I was still alive, for in all other respects fear had plunged me into a state of prostration from which I did not emerge until I found myself in front of the archbishop. The prelate was sitting in an armchair opposite the viceroy. His clergy were placed below him. The leading citizens of Burgos were sitting next to the viceroy. At the other end of the room there stood an altar dressed for the ceremony. The archbishop rose, blessed me and kissed me on the forehead.

Overcome by all the emotions that welled up in my heart, I fell at the archbishop's feet, and at that moment I don't know what presence of mind inspired me to say to him, 'Your Grace, have pity on me! I want to become a nun! I want to become a nun!'

After making this declaration, which rang throughout the room, I thought it proper to faint. I only recovered to fall into the arms of my aunts, who were finding it difficult not to collapse themselves, such was their distress. Through half-closed eyes I could see the archbishop standing respectfully in front of the viceroy, waiting for him to make his mind up what to do.

The viceroy asked the archbishop to sit down again and to give him time to reflect. As the archbishop therefore sat down, I could again see the face of my august lover, whose expression was even more severe than usual. It would have caused the boldest to quake. For some time he seemed absorbed in his thoughts, then he proudly got to his feet, put on his hat and said, 'I shall no longer remain incognito, I am the Viceroy of Mexico. The archbishop may remain seated.' All the other persons present rose to their feet respectfully.

'Señores,' said the viceroy, 'fourteen years ago vile slanderers accused me of being the father of this young person. I could think of no other way of silencing them than to engage myself to marry her once she should have reached the requisite age. While she grew in grace and virtue the king, acknowledging my services, caused me to rise in rank and eventually clothed me in the high dignity which has brought me close to the throne. Meanwhile the time to fulfil my promise had come. I asked the king for permission to return to Spain and to marry. The reply of the council of Madrid was that I could come but that I would not be given the honour due to a viceroy unless I gave up the idea of marriage. At the same time I was forbidden to come within fifty leagues of Madrid. I understood clearly that I had to give up the idea of marriage or renounce my master's favour. But I had promised and I did not even hesitate.

'When I saw charming Elvira I thought that heaven had taken me away from the paths of honour to enjoy a new felicity in the peaceful enjoyment of my retirement. But since heaven jealously calls to itself a soul of which the earth was not worthy, I place this soul back in your charge. Have her taken to the convent of the Annunciads, let her begin her noviciate. I shall write to the king and ask his permission to come to Madrid.'

With these words the terrible viceroy greeted those present, replaced his hat, pulled it down over his eyes with an expression of the greatest severity and returned to his coach. He was accompanied by the archbishop, magistrates, clergy and all their retinue. We were left alone in the room with a few sacristans, who undressed the altar. Then, with my two aunts, I fled into a neighbouring room and ran to the window to see whether there was no way for me to escape and avoid the convent.

The window looked out on to an interior courtyard where there was a fountain. I saw two small exhausted boys in rags, who seemed eager to slake their thirst. On one of them I recognized the clothes I had exchanged with Elvira. Then I recognized her. The other ragged child was Lonzeto. I shouted for joy. There were four doors in the chamber in which we found ourselves. The first one I opened gave on to a staircase which led down into the interior courtyard where those ragamuffins were. I ran and brought them back. Good Maria de Torres thought she would die with joy as she hugged them in her arms.

At that moment we heard the archbishop coming back, after having seen the viceroy off, to fetch me and take me to the convent of the Annunciads. I only just had time to throw myself at the door and close it. My aunt cried out that the young girl had fainted again and was not in a state to receive anyone. We once more hurriedly exchanged our clothes. Elvira's head was bandaged as though she had hurt herself falling over, and part of her face was carefully hidden so that it would be more difficult to detect the substitution.

When all was ready, I fled with Lonzeto and the door was opened. The archbishop was no longer there but he had left his vicar-general behind, who escorted Elvira and Maria de Torres to the convent. Aunt Dalanosa went to the Venta de las Rosas, having told me to meet her there. We took an apartment, and for eight days thought of nothing but rejoicing in the happy outcome of this adventure and the anguish it had caused us. Lonzeto, no longer a muleteer, shared our lodgings. He was known as Maria de Torres's son.

My aunt made several visits to the convent of the Annunciads. It was agreed that Elvira would at first evince a great desire for the religious life, but that the fervour of her vocation would decline to the point where she would be removed from the convent and Rome would be asked for the necessary dispensation to allow her to marry her cousin german. Soon after, we learned that the viceroy had been to Madrid and that he had been received with great honour. He even obtained the approval of the king to transfer his fortune and title to his nephew, the son of the sister whom he had taken with him to Villaca. A little later he set sail for America.

As for me, the excitement of so unusual a journey had done much to develop the frivolous and vagabond side of my nature, and I dreaded the moment that I would have to be cloistered with the Theatines. But that was what my great-uncle had decided, and after employing all the delaying tactics I could think of, I had to accept the idea too.

As the gypsy chief reached this point in his story someone came to fetch him away. We all had reflections to make on so strange an adventure. But the cabbalist promised us even more bizarre tales which the Wandering Jew would tell us, and he assured us that the next day without fail we would meet that extraordinary person.

The Twenty-first Day

We set off again. Having promised us the Wandering Jew's company for that day, the cabbalist was unable to keep in check his impatience at not seeing him appear. At last we caught sight of a man on a distant mountain top, walking quickly, without bothering to follow a beaten path. 'Aha, do you see him?' said Uzeda. 'The lazy oaf, the rascal! Fancy taking a week to get here from deepest Africa!'

A moment later the Wandering Jew reached us. When he was within hailing distance, the cabbalist shouted to him, 'Well, can I still aspire to Solomon's daughters?'

'No, no,' the Jew shouted back. 'You have no right to them any more, and you have even lost the power you had over spirits above the twenty-second class. And I trust you won't keep the power you acquired over me much longer.'

The cabbalist seemed plunged in thought for a few moments and then said, 'Very well. I'll do as my sister. We'll speak about this another time. Meanwhile, Señor Traveller, I command you to walk between the mule of this young officer and the mule carrying this other young gentleman, the glory of geometry. Tell them the story of your life. And I warn you, do so honestly and straightforwardly.'

The Jew seemed to want to refuse but the cabbalist addressed a few unintelligible words to him and the hapless wanderer began as follows:

∾ THE WANDERING JEW'S STORY ∾

My family was among those who followed the priest Onias and with the permission of Ptolemy Philometor built a temple in Lower

238

Egypt.[1] My grandfather was called Hiskias. When the famous Cleopatra married her brother Ptolemy Denys, Hiskias joined her household as the queen's jeweller. But he also had the task of buying cloth and ornaments, and later he it was also who organized the festivities. In short, I can assure you that my grandfather was a very important person at the court of Alexandria. I don't say this to boast. What would I get out of that? He has been dead seventeen hundred years or a little more because he died in the forty-first year of Augustus's reign. I was then very young and scarcely remember that someone called Dellius often talked to me about all that went on then.

Velásquez interrupted the Wandering Jew at this point to ask him whether this was the Dellius who was Cleopatra's musician and is often referred to by Flavius Joseph and Plutarch.[2]

'The very one,' said the Jew. Then he continued as follows:

Ptolemy was unable to have children by his sister and believed her to be barren. He repudiated her after three years of marriage. Cleopatra retired to a port on the Red Sea. My grandfather followed her into exile, and it was then that he had occasion to buy for his mistress the two pearls, one of which was dissolved at a feast and swallowed by Mark Antony.

Meanwhile, civil war broke out throughout the Roman Empire. Pompey sought asylum with Ptolemy Denys, who had him beheaded. This act of treachery, which was designed to bring him Caesar's favour, had the opposite effect. Caesar decided to put Cleopatra back on the throne. The inhabitants of Alexandria took the side of their king with a zeal which has scarcely been equalled in history. But he drowned in an accident. Nothing then stood in the way of Cleopatra's ambition and her gratitude was unbounded.

Before Caesar left Egypt he married Cleopatra to young Ptolemy,

1 The legend of the Wandering Jew is very ancient: the first full written account of it appeared in 1602, in Leiden. Onias is a historical figure, as is Ptolemy Philometor, who reigned from 181 to 145 BCE.

2 Flavius Joseph (37–100) is the author of a history of the Jews.

239

who was both her brother and brother-in-law, being the younger brother of Ptolemy Denys, to whom she had first been married. This prince was then eleven years old. Cleopatra was pregnant. Her child was called Caesarion so that there would be no doubt about his paternity.

My grandfather, who was then twenty-five, then considered marriage himself. That is late for a Jew, but he had a strong disinclination to choose a wife from an Alexandrian family. Not that we were looked upon as schismatic by the Jews of Jerusalem, but there could only be one temple according to our religion and the general opinion was that our Egyptian temple, founded by Onias, would lead to schism as had the temple of Samaria, which the Jews looked upon as the abomination of desolation.

These pious motives and feelings of distaste which are never absent from court life, made my father want to retire to the sacred city of the Lord and marry there. But at about that time a Jew from Jerusalem, called Hillel, came to Alexandria with his family on business. My grandfather's choice fell on his elder daughter, Melea. The wedding was celebrated with extraordinary magnificence. Cleopatra and her husband honoured it with their presence.

A few days later the queen summoned my grandfather and said to him, 'My dear Hiskias, I have just learnt that Caesar has been appointed perpetual dictator. He is the master of the race which conquered the world and fortune has placed him higher than she has placed any mortal up till now, far above Belus, Sesostris, Cyrus and Alexander. I am more proud than ever of loving the father of my little Caesarion. The child will soon be four years old. I want Caesar to see him and to hold him in his arms. Within two months I want to have left for Rome. As you will appreciate, I must make my appearance there as a queen. I want the least of my slaves to be dressed in gold cloth and the meanest of my furniture to be made of solid gold encrusted with jewels. As for me, I shall only wear pearls and my dress will be made of the lightest weave of the finest Byssus silk. Take all my caskets and all the gold there is in my palace. My treasurer will give you a hundred thousand golden talents. It is the price of two provinces which I have sold to the King of the Arabs. Go, and be ready in two months.'

Cleopatra was then twenty-five years old. Her young brother, whom she had married four years before, was then only fifteen years old. He loved her with an extraordinarily violent passion. When he discovered that she was to go away he broke out in the most dreadful despair, and when he took leave of the queen and saw her ship sail off, he was in such distress that people feared for his life.

Cleopatra set sail and arrived at the port of Ostia in less than three weeks. She found there magnificent gondolas waiting to take her up the Tiber, and it would be fair to say that she entered in triumph into that very city which monarchs rarely entered except chained to the chariots of Roman generals.

Caesar, who was the most gallant of men as well as the greatest, received Cleopatra with boundless courtesy but with a little less affection than she expected. The queen, who set greater store by ambition than she did by feelings, took little notice of this, desiring only to get to know Rome. As she was not lacking in perception she was quick to notice the dangers threatening the dictator. She spoke to him of them, but anything resembling fear can have no place in the hearts of heroes. Seeing that Caesar refused to listen to her, Cleopatra thought of benefiting herself from what she had observed. It seemed to her certain that Caesar would end up the victim of a conspiracy and that the Roman world would then be divided into two factions. One was the Friends of Liberty, which had as its figurehead the aged Cicero, a man of great vanity who thought that he had achieved great things because he had made great speeches, and who would have liked not only to devote himself to his leisurely studies in his retreat at Tusculum but also to enjoy all the reputation attached to the active life of statesmen. All the members of this party desired the good but could not bring it about because they were ignorant of human nature. The other party was the Friends of Caesar, brave warriors and still more valiant drinkers, who abandoned themselves to their passions and knew how to exploit those of others. Cleopatra was not slow in choosing between them. She showed great respect for Antony and very little for Cicero, who never forgave her for this, as you can see from several letters that he wrote at this time to Atticus.

Cleopatra did not want to witness the denouement of the drama whose plot she had already fathomed. So she departed for Alexandria.

Her young husband greeted her return with excessive transports of joy. The people of Alexandria were drunk with happiness. By looking as though she shared the delight which she inspired, Cleopatra completely won over the hearts of the Alexandrians. But those who knew her well realized that her effusions were largely founded on political calculation, and that her feelings were more affected than sincere. And indeed when she thought that she could be sure of Alexandria she went to Memphis, where she appeared dressed as Isis, wearing the horns of a cow, which won the affections of the Egyptians there. She even made herself popular with the Nabataeans, the Libyans and all those peoples whose lands border Egypt.

At last the queen returned to Alexandria. Caesar was murdered and civil war broke out in all the provinces of the empire. From that moment on, Cleopatra seemed plunged in sombre thoughts. Those who were closest to her discovered her plan, which was to marry Antony and reign in Rome.

One morning my grandfather went to the queen and presented her with jewels which had just arrived from the Indies. She seemed delighted with them, praised my grandfather's taste and extolled his zeal. She then said to him:

'My dear Hiskias, here are some excellent crystallized bananas which I believe were brought from India by the same Serendib merchants from whom you obtained these precious stones. Please be so kind as to take these fruits to my young husband and tell him to eat them for the love of me.'

My grandfather did as he was asked and the young king said to him, 'Since the queen wants me to eat these confections for the love of her, I want you to be witness to the fact that I shall consume them all.'

But before he had eaten three bananas his features became contorted and his eyes seemed to bulge out of his head. He cried out in pain and then fell dead on the floor. My grandfather realized at once that he had been used as the instrument of the most terrible of all crimes. He withdrew, rent his garments, put on sackcloth and covered his head with ashes.

Six weeks later the queen summoned him and said, 'My dear Hiskias, you must have heard that Octavius, Antony and Lepidus have divided the empire of the world between them. The East has fallen to my dear Antony. I have decided to join him in Silicia. I want you, my dear Hiskias, to build me a boat in the form of a conch shell lined with mother-of-pearl inside and out. I want the deck to be draped all over with a fine net of gold, through which I will be seen with the attributes of Venus surrounded by graces and cherubs. Go now and carry out my orders with your usual intelligence.'

My grandfather then threw himself at the queen's feet and said, 'Your Highness, please consider that I am a Jew; anything to do with Greek divinities is in my eyes sacrilegious, and I am bound to have no dealings with them.'

'I understand,' said the queen. 'You feel remorse for the death of my young husband. Your sorrow is justified. I feel it myself more than I would have expected. Hiskias, you were not meant for the life of the court. I dispense you from appearing at it.'

My grandfather needed no further persuasion. He went home, packed up and retired to a house that he possessed on the shores of Lake Mareotis. Once there he devoted himself entirely to putting his affairs in order, so as to be able to carry out the plan which he had long been considering of setting up house in Jerusalem as soon as possible. He lived in complete retirement and received no one whom he had known at court, with the exception of Dellius the musician, for whom he had always felt great friendship.

Meanwhile Cleopatra had had the ship built more or less in accordance with her wishes and had set sail for Silicia, whose people really took her to be Venus. And Mark Antony, who thought that the Silicians were not that far wrong, followed Cleopatra back to Egypt, where their marriage was celebrated with a magnificence beyond description.

As the Wandering Jew reached this point in his story the cabbalist said to him, 'My friend, that is enough for today. We have reached our resting-place. You must spend the night walking round and round this mountain. Tomorrow you will join us on our travels. As for what I have to discuss with you, we'll leave that to another time.'

The Jew shot the cabbalist a terrible glance, plunged into a valley and was soon lost to sight.

The Twenty-second Day

We set out quite early and after we had gone a few leagues we were joined by the Wandering Jew who without further instructions took up his place between my horse and Velásquez's mule and began as follows:

THE WANDERING JEW'S STORY CONTINUED

Once she had become Antony's wife, Cleopatra realized that to keep his affections she would have to play the part of Phryne rather than Artemis,[1] or rather this resourceful woman would easily slip from the role of courtesan into that of a queen and even play to perfection the faithful, loving wife. She knew that Antony was the most sensual of men, so it was principally through the exquisite arts of seduction that she sought to captivate him. The court imitated its master and mistress. The city imitated the court. The country imitated the city, with the result that soon Egypt was nothing more than a vast theatre of prostitution. These depravities even infected the Jewish colony.

My grandfather would long since have retired to Jerusalem but the Parthians had just captured that city and driven out Herod, son of Antipas, who later was made King of Judaea by Antony.[2] So my grandfather was forced to prolong his stay in Egypt and did not know where to go, for Lake Mareotis was now crowded with gondolas day and night and was the scene of the most scandalous behaviour. In the end my grandfather decided to brick up the windows which overlooked the lake and to immure himself in his house with his wife, Melea, and a child whom he called Mardochee.

---

1 Symbols of prostitution and conjugal fidelity respectively.
2 Herod the Great (73 BCE–4 CE).

Otherwise his door was open to no one except his old friend Dellius. Some years passed, Herod was made king and my grandfather again thought of settling in Jerusalem.

One day Dellius came to my grandfather's house and said to him, 'My dear Hiskias, I have come to find out what I can do for you in Jerusalem. Antony and Cleopatra are sending me there. Give me a letter for Hillel, your father-in-law. I would like to consider him my host, although I am quite sure that I will be made to stay at court and not allowed to live in the house of a private citizen.'

My grandfather wept at the sight of someone who was setting off for Jerusalem. He gave Dellius a letter for Hillel, and the sum of thirty thousand darics, with instructions to buy on his behalf the finest house in Jerusalem. Dellius came back three weeks later. He informed my grandfather at once of his return, but let him know at the same time that he would not be able to see him for four days because he had business at court. When he eventually came to the house, he said:

'My dear Hiskias, here is the contract of sale relating to the finest house in Jerusalem, that of your father-in-law. All the judges have set their seal to it and the act is in due form. Here is a letter from Hillel, who will continue to live in the house until you get there and will pay you rent. As for my trip, it was highly enjoyable. Herod was not in Jerusalem when I got there. His mother-in-law, Alexandra, invited me to supper with her two children: Mariamne, who had just married Herod, and the young Aristobulus,[3] who was intended for the high priesthood but who found himself passed over in favour of a fellow from the gutter. Aristobulus looks like a god come down to earth. Picture the face of the most beautiful woman imaginable on the shoulders of the most handsome youth. As I have been speaking of nothing else since my return, Antony has said that they both simply must come here.'

'What a very good idea,' said Cleopatra in reply. 'Invite the wife of the King of Judaea here and in no time you'll have the Parthians swarming all over the Roman provinces.'

---

3 Aristobulus III (52–35 BCE), put to death by Herod.

'Well,' said Antony, 'at least let's have this handsome youth come. We'll make him first cupbearer. Although I am not concerned about how beautiful slaves are, I would like those who serve me to be from the very best Roman families, or if barbarians, at least sons of kings.'

'Splendid,' said Cleopatra. 'Let's summon Aristobulus.'

'Oh God of Israel and Jacob!' exclaimed my grandfather. 'Did I hear what you said? An Asmonean[4] of the purest blood of the Maccabees, a successor of Aaron, will be a page to the uncircumcised Antony? Antony, who has given himself over to every manner of impurity! I have lived too long, Dellius! I am going to retire, rend my garments, put on sackcloth and cover my head with ashes.'

My grandfather did as he said he would. He shut himself up in his house and wept over the tribulations of Zion; tears were his meat day and night. He would certainly have died of grief if Dellius had not arrived and shouted at his door, 'Aristobulus will not be Antony's page. Herod has made him high priest! Herod has made him high priest!'

My grandfather opened the door, took heart somewhat from this news and began to live with his family again as he had done before.

Some time later Antony left for Armenia and Cleopatra followed him, intending to procure Arabia Petraea and Judaea as gifts. Dellius undertook the journey with them and gave a detailed account of it.

Alexandra had been confined to her palace on Herod's orders and had decided to escape with her son to see Cleopatra who, if the truth were known, was curious to set eyes on the handsome high priest. A person called Gabion[5] discovered the plot and Herod had Aristobulus drowned in his bath. Cleopatra asked that his death be avenged but Antony replied that the king must be master in his own kingdom. To appease Cleopatra, however, he gave her a few towns that belonged to Herod.

'After that,' continued Dellius, 'we were witness to a great deal more. Herod, a real Jew at heart, leased back from Cleopatra the provinces she had taken from him. We went to Jerusalem to negotiate

4 The reigning dynasty in Judaea from 137 to 37 BCE.
5 The name is given as Kubion in Flavius Joseph's *History* (book 16).

this affair. Our queen wanted to give a seductive tone to the proceedings, but the good princess is fully thirty-five years old and Herod is in love with Mariamne, who is only twenty. Rather than respond to her blandishments he called the council together and proposed to have Cleopatra strangled, going so far as to assure them that Antony was tired of her and would be obliged to him if this were done. Fortunately, the council pointed out to him that although Antony would have been pleased to be rid of Cleopatra, he would still avenge her death; and they were quite right.

'On our return we learned other news: Cleopatra stands accused in Rome of having bewitched Antony. The trial has not yet begun but it will very soon. What have you to say about all this? Do you still want to retire to Jerusalem, my dear Hiskias?'

'Not at the moment,' replied my grandfather. 'I would not be able to hide my attachment to the blood of the Maccabees and I am sure that Herod would have all the Asmoneans killed one after the other.'

'Since you have decided to stay here,' Dellius went on, 'let me retire here with you. I left the court yesterday. We will live here together within these walls, and will only leave when this country shall again have become a Roman province, which cannot be long away. As for my fortune, I entrusted it to your father-in-law. It amounts to thirty thousand darics. He has also asked me to pass on to you the rent for your house.'

My grandfather accepted his friend Dellius's proposal with joy and lived an even more retiring life than before. Dellius would go out occasionally and bring back news from the city. The rest of the time he devoted to teaching Mardochee, my future father, about Greek literature. He also often read the Holy Scriptures, for my father was trying to convert Dellius.

You know how Antony and Cleopatra finished their days. Egypt became a Roman province exactly as Dellius had predicted. But our household was so used to living apart from the world that political events brought no changes to our way of life. Meanwhile there was no shortage of news from Palestine. Herod, who was expected to follow Antony in his fall, gained Augustus's favour. His lost territories were restored to him, he conquered others, created an army, amassed treasure and built inexhaustible grain-stores, with the result that already people were beginning to call him 'the Great'. And indeed he might well have been called if not great then at least happy, if there had not been family quarrels which tarnished the brilliance of so remarkable a career.

When peace had returned to Palestine my grandfather went back to his old plan of settling there with his dear Mardochee, then thirteen years old. Dellius was equally attached to his pupil and felt no desire whatsoever to leave him. One day a Jew arrived from Jerusalem, carrying the following letter:

Rabbi Sedekias, son of Hillel, miserable sinner and the least of the holy Sanhedrin of the Pharisees, sends greetings to Hiskias, husband of his sister Melea.

The epidemic which the sins of Israel have brought down on Jerusalem has carried off my father and my elder brothers. They are now in Abraham's bosom and share in his eternal glory. May heaven destroy the Sadducees and all those who do not believe in the resurrection!

I would be unworthy of the name of Pharisee if I dared to pollute my hands by taking possession of what belongs to another. That is why I have carefully examined whether my father had debts outstanding to anyone, and as I had heard it said that the house in which we live here in Jerusalem once belonged to you for a time, I went to see the judges but found nothing there to confirm my suppositions. The house is therefore mine without doubt. May heaven destroy the evil-doers! I am no Sadducee!

I also discovered that a certain uncircumcised person named Dellius at one time deposited thirty thousand darics with my father. By chance I came upon a somewhat faded document which I take to be the said Dellius's discharge of this sum. This man was in any case a follower of Mariamne and her brother Aristobule, and therefore an enemy of our great king. May heaven curse him together with all evil-doers and Sadducees!

Farewell, my dear brother. Greet my sister, Melea, tenderly from me. Although I was very young when you took her as your bride, I have always kept her memory alive in my heart.

It seems that the dowry she took with her into your house is somewhat greater than the share which was due to her. But we will speak of this another time. May heaven make you a true Pharisee!

My father and Dellius looked at each other for a long time in astonishment. Then Dellius broke the silence. 'This is the result of living away from the world,' he said. 'We hoped for peace but fate has decided otherwise. Men take you for a dead tree whose branches they can tear off at their leisure, and whose trunk they can uproot. They take you for an earthworm which they can crush. In short, they take you for a useless burden on the earth. In this world one must be either the hammer or the anvil. One must strike or be struck down. I was once the friend of several Roman prefects who chose Octavian's side. If I had not neglected their friendship, it would not be possible today to inflict this injustice on me. But I was tired of the world, and I left it to live with a virtuous friend. And now a Pharisee in Jerusalem turns up, strips me of my fortune and claims to have in his possession a yellowing document which he takes to be my discharge of debt. Your loss is not so great. The house amounts to barely a quarter of your fortune. But I have lost everything, and come what may I shall leave for Palestine.'

Melea came in as these words were uttered. She was told of the death of her father and two elder brothers and the despicable behaviour of her brother Sedekias was described to her. Emotions one suffers in solitude are usually very powerful. The grief which overtook the unhappy woman was compounded by an unknown illness which in six months carried her to her grave.

Dellius had already begun preparing for his journey when one evening, as he was returning from the suburb of Rakote, he was stabbed in the chest by a knife. He looked up and recognized the very Jew who had brought Sedekias's letter. It took a long time for him to recover from his wound. When he was better, he no longer felt any desire to journey to Palestine. But in case he went there after all, he decided to secure the support of those in power on this earth and reflected for a long time on how he could bring himself to the notice of his old protectors. Yet even Augustus followed the principle of letting kings reign as sovereigns in their own lands. So it was first necessary to discover what Herod's attitude to Sedekias was. It was thus decided to send a loyal and shrewd man to Jerusalem.

The messenger came back two months later. He reported that Herod's star was rising from one day to the next, that the astute monarch knew how to win Jews as well as Romans to his cause and that at the same time as erecting monuments to Augustus, he announced his intention to rebuild the temple of Jerusalem on an even more magnificent scale than before, which so delighted the people that Herod was being prematurely praised by some flatterers as the Messiah foretold by the prophets.

'These praises,' said the messenger, 'have been very well received at court. A sect has already been formed. Its members are called Herodians. Its head is Sedekias.'

You can well imagine that this news made my grandfather and Dellius abandon all further inquiries. But before I continue with their story I must tell you what our prophets said about the Messiah.

Suddenly the Wandering Jew fell silent. Then, casting a scornful glance at the cabbalist, he said, 'Impure son of Mamoun! A more powerful adept than you has summoned me to the Atlas mountains. Farewell!'

'You lie!' said the cabbalist. 'I am a hundred times more powerful than the Sheikh of Taroudant.'

'You lost your powers at the Venta Quemada,' retorted the Jew, who ran off so quickly that we soon lost sight of him.

The cabbalist was somewhat embarrassed by this, but said after a moment's reflection, 'I assure you that that insolent wretch doesn't know half of the formulae in my power. He will soon feel their effect. But let's speak of other matters. Señor de Velásquez, did you follow the thread of his story?'

'Certainly; I paid close attention to the Wandering Jew's words and believe them to conform to history. Tertullian mentions the Herodians as a sect.'

'Are you as versed in history as you are in geometry?' exclaimed the cabbalist.

'Not altogether,' admitted Velásquez. 'But my father, who applied

250

mathematical formulae to all reasoning, as I have told you, thought that geometry could be applied to history in order to determine the relationship between events which really occurred and those which might have occurred. He even took his theory further and thought in fact that it was possible to describe human action and emotion by geometrical figures.

'Here's an example to give you a clearer idea. My father would say:

"Take the case of Antony in Egypt. He is prey to two emotions: ambition, which incites him to rule, and love, which dissuades him from it. I represent these two movements by two lines, AB and AC, with an arbitrary angle between them. The line AB, representing the love of Antony for Cleopatra, is less than AC because at heart Antony has less love than ambition. Let us suppose he has three times less. So I take the line AB and produce it to three times the length of AC. Now I complete the parallelogram and draw in the resulting diagonal, which represents exactly the new direction produced by Antony's attraction to B and C. This diagonal will come closer to the line AB the greater we suppose love is. And contrarily it will come closer to the line AC the more ambition is supposed. Augustus, for example, who did not experience love, was not deflected from point C. And although less energetic he reached it more quickly."

'But as passions grow larger or diminish in turn, changing as a consequence the form of the parallelogram, the extremity of the resulting diagonal describes in every case a curve to which my father applied differential calculus, then called the calculus of fluxions. Apart from this the wise author of my life only looked upon all historical problems as pleasant absurdities which he employed to brighten up the dryness of his usual studies. But as the accuracy of solutions depends on the accuracy of data my father collected historical sources with great care. This storehouse was long denied to me, as were the books on geometry, for my father hoped that I would learn only the saraband, the minuet and other such absurdities. Happily, I managed to get into his library. It was only then that I was able to devote myself to history.'

'Please allow me, Señor de Velásquez,' said the cabbalist, 'to express again my admiration for your learning in history as well as in mathematics. For one of these fields of knowledge requires more thought, the other more memory. And these two mental faculties are the complete opposite of each other.'

'I venture not to share your opinion,' said the geometer. 'Thought assists memory in enabling it to order the material it has assembled. So that in a systematically ordered memory every idea is individually followed by all the conclusions it entails. However, I do not deny that memory and thought can only be effectively applied to a certain number of notions. For example, I myself have retained very well all that I learned about geometry and about human and natural history. Whereas I often forget what relationship I have at any time with the things around me. Or rather I don't see what is staring me in the eyes or hear what is ringing in my ears, which leads certain people to take me to be absent-minded.'

'I now understand how you came to fall in the water, Señor,' said the cabbalist.

'It is certain that I don't myself know why I found myself in the water at the very moment I least expected to,' said Velásquez. 'But this accident was a happy one for me since it afforded me the opportunity of saving the life of this noble young gentleman who is a captain in the Walloon Guards. However, I should be glad not to have to be of service in this way too often because I know no more disagreeable sensation than that felt by a man whose empty stomach fills up with water.'

Conversing in this way we reached our resting-place, where a meal awaited us. We ate voraciously and conversation languished because the cabbalist seemed worried. After the meal brother and sister spoke to each other for a long time. I did not want to disturb them so I went to a little cave in which a bed had been prepared for me.

The Twenty-third Day

The weather was beautiful. We rose with the sun and after a light meal set out once more. Around midday we stopped and sat down to table, or rather round a hide spread out on the ground. The cabbalist uttered some remarks which indicated that he wasn't altogether pleased with the superterrestrial world. After the meal he continued in the same vein until his sister, thinking that such monologues would bore the company, asked Velásquez to continue his story, which he did as follows:

✑ VELÁSQUEZ'S STORY CONTINUED ✑

I had the honour of relating to you how I came to be born and how my father took me in his arms, uttered a geometric prayer over me and then swore solemnly that he would never teach me geometry.

About six months after my birth my father saw a small vessel, a chebec, enter harbour, drop anchor and send out a longboat to the shore. From this longboat stepped out a man stooped with age, dressed in the manner of an officer of the late Duke of Velásquez's household, that is to say, in a green jacket, gold and scarlet braid, loose-hanging sleeves and Galician belt, and a sword suspended from his shoulder-harness. My father took up his telescope and thought he recognized old Alvarez. Indeed it was he. He was finding it difficult to walk. My father rushed all the way to the harbour to meet him and they both nearly died of the emotions they then felt. Then Alvar told my father that he had been sent by the Duchess Blanca, who had retired to an Ursuline convent. He gave him a letter couched in the following terms:

Señor Don Enrique,

A hapless person who caused the death of her father and the misery of your life ventures to remind you of her.

Prey to remorse, I have devoted myself to acts of penance whose severity would have shortened my days, but Alvar made me realize that my death, by restoring to the duke his freedom, might also allow him to have heirs, and that by prolonging my days I would be able to keep his inheritance for you. This thought made me decide to live. I gave up austere fasting, took off my hair shirt and restricted my acts of penance to solitude and prayer.

The duke, whose life is constantly filled with worldly dissipations, has suffered every year from some grave illness or other. On several occasions I thought that he was going to restore to you the title and fortune of our house. But heaven evidently has decreed that you remain in an obscurity which so ill befits your talents.

I have learnt that you have a son. Perhaps I may be able to preserve for him the advantages of which the errors of my ways have deprived you. Meanwhile I have watched over his and your interests. The allodial estates of our house have always belonged to the younger branch. Since you did not claim them they have been combined with those intended for my establishment. But by right they belong to you. Alvar will hand over to you the income of the last fifteen years, and with him you must make whatever arrangements you think suitable for the future.

Reasons connected with the character of the duke have prevented me from making this restitution earlier.

Farewell, Señor Don Enrique. No day passes when I fail to raise my voice in penance and call down heavenly benediction on you and your fortunate wife. Pray also for me and do not reply to this letter.

I have already described to you the power which memory exercised over Don Enrique's heart. You will not find it difficult to believe that this letter stirred them up again. It was more than a year before he could again take up his favourite pursuits, but the attentions of his wife, the affection he felt for me, and still more the general solution of equations with which mathematicians were then beginning to be preoccupied, together had the effect of bringing strength and peace to his soul. The rise in his income also allowed him to expand his library and his laboratory. He even managed to set up an observatory, which was very well equipped with instruments. I do not need to tell you that he indulged the philanthropic side of his nature. I can assure you that when I left Ceuta there was not a single individual in real distress because my father used all the resources of his genius to procure a decent subsistence for everyone. I could give you an account of all this which would, I am sure, interest you, but I have not forgotten that I undertook to tell you my story and I must not depart from the terms of my proposition.

As far as I can remember, curiosity was my first passion. There are no horses or carriages on the streets of Ceuta and there are no dangers for children. So I was allowed to go wherever I liked. I would satisfy my curiosity by going down to the harbour and climbing back up to the town a hundred times a day. I went into all the houses, shops, arsenals and workshops, observing the tradesmen, following the porters, questioning the passers-by. Everywhere people were amused by my curiosity and were happy to satisfy it. That wasn't the case in the paternal home, however.

My father had had constructed in the courtyard of his house a separate building in which his library, laboratory and observatory were housed. I was not allowed access to this building. At first I wasn't too concerned about this, but as time went by the fact that I was not allowed access excited my curiosity and was a powerful spur to my first steps in a scientific career. The first science to which I applied myself was that part of natural history known as conchology. My father often went down to the sea-shore, near a particular rock where in calm weather the sea was as transparent as glass. He observed the behaviour of marine animals and when he found a well-preserved shell he took it home with him. Children are mimics so I became a conchologist, but in the process I was bitten by crabs, burnt by sea-nettles and stung by sea-urchins. These unpleasant experiences put me off natural history and I became attached to physics.

My father needed a skilled worker to modify, repair or copy the instruments which arrived for him from England. He taught an armourer whom nature had endowed with some talent how to do this. I spent nearly all my time with this apprentice technician and helped him in his work. I acquired practical skills but still lacked one very essential one, that of reading and writing.

Although I was then eight years old, my father said that provided I knew how to sign my name and dance a saraband I need know no more. There was at Ceuta an old priest who had been exiled there for some monastic intrigue. He was highly thought of by everyone and often came to see us. This good cleric, seeing me thus neglected, pointed out to my father that I had not been instructed in my religion and offered to teach me himself. My father agreed to this. With this as a pretext Father Anselm taught me to read, write and count. I made swift progress, especially in mathematics, in which I soon outstripped my teacher.

So I reached my twelfth year, having a good deal of knowledge for my age, but I was careful not to show it off in front of my father, for if it ever happened that I did, he would unfailingly look at me severely and say, 'Learn to dance the saraband, my friend, learn to dance and don't meddle with things that will only bring you unhappiness!' At this, my mother would gesture to me to keep quiet and then change the subject.

One day, as we were sitting at table and my father was urging me once again to devote myself to the graces, we saw a man come in. He was about thirty years old and dressed in the French fashion. He bowed to us twelve times in succession. Then, trying to perform some pirouette or other, he bumped into a servant bringing in the soup, and made him drop it. A Spaniard would have apologized profusely. Not so this stranger. He laughed as much as he had bowed on arrival, after which he told us in bad Spanish that his name was the Marquis de Folencour; he had been obliged to leave France for having killed a man in a duel and asked permission to be given asylum until the affair had been settled.

Folencour had no sooner finished his speech than my father, jumping up in great animation, said to him, 'Monsieur le Marquis, you are the very man I have been waiting for for a long time. Treat my house as your own. Only please be so kind as to give some attention to the education of my son. If one day he could be like you, I should be the happiest of fathers.'

If Folencour had known the meaning my father attached to what he had said, he would perhaps not have been very flattered by it. But he took my father's compliment quite literally and seemed very pleased by it. Indeed, his impertinence became all the greater. He constantly alluded to the beauty of my mother and the age of my father, who for all this did not stop congratulating him and urging me to admire him.

At the end of the meal my father asked the marquis if he could teach me how to dance the saraband. At this my tutor started laughing even louder than he had done before. When he had recovered from his great outburst of mirth he told us that the saraband had not been danced for two thousand years. Only the passepied and bourrée. And then he drew from his pocket one of those instruments which dancing-masters call *pochettes*[1] and played these two dance tunes.

When he had finished my father said to him in great seriousness, 'Monsieur le Marquis, you can play an instrument that few noblemen can play, and you lead me to wonder whether you have not been a dancing-master in your time. But it doesn't matter. You will be all the more suitable to fulfil my purposes. I request you to begin tomorrow to educate my son and to make him like a nobleman of the French court.'

Folencour admitted that certain misfortunes had obliged him for a time to take on the profession of dancing-master, but that he was no less of a nobleman for all that and no less suited to educate a young gentleman. So it was decided that the following day I would have my first lesson in dancing and good manners. Before, however, I describe to you that fateful day I must tell you of a conversation which my father had the same evening with his father-in-law, Señor de Cadanza. I have hardly thought about it since, but it has just this instant come back to me and it may be of interest to you.

That day my curiosity kept me at the side of my new mentor and I did not think of roaming about the streets. Passing by my father's study, I heard him say to Cadanza with anger in his voice:

'My dear father-in-law, I warn you for the last time that if you continue your dispatches into the African interior, I shall denounce you to the minister.'

'My dear son-in-law,' replied Cadanza, 'if you want to be privy to

1 Pocket violins.

257

our secrets nothing will be easier. My mother was a Gomelez and my blood flows in the veins of your son.'

'Señor Cadanza,' continued my father, 'I am the king's lieutenant here and have nothing to do with the Gomelez and their secrets. You may be sure that tomorrow I shall let the minister know of this conversation.'

'And you may be sure that the minister will forbid you in future to make reports on things that are not your concern,' said Cadanza.

Their conversation went no further. The secret of the Gomelez preoccupied me all day and part of the night. But the next day the cursed Folencour gave me my first dancing lesson, which turned out altogether differently to what he had hoped and had the effect of directing my mind towards mathematics.

As Velásquez reached this point in his story, he was interrupted by the cabbalist, who said that he still had important business to discuss with his sister, so we dispersed and everyone went his own way.

The Twenty-fourth Day

We continued our meanderings across the Alpujarras mountains and at last we reached our resting-place. After a meal had reinvigorated us, we asked Velásquez to carry on telling us the adventures of his life, which he did as follows:

✑ VELÁSQUEZ'S STORY CONTINUED ✑

My father wanted to be present at Folencour's first lesson and wanted my mother to be there too. Encouraged by such signs of respect, Folencour quite forgot that he had passed himself off as a gentleman and discoursed at some length on the nobility of dancing, which he called his art. Then he observed that my toes were pointing inwards. He wished to point out to me that this habit was shameful and quite incompatible with the rank of gentleman. So I pointed my toes outwards and tried to walk in this way, even though it was against the laws of equilibrium. Folencour was not pleased with my attempt. He insisted, moreover, that my feet should point downwards. In the end, in a fit of spiteful impatience, he pushed me from behind. I fell on my nose and hurt myself badly. It seemed to me that Folencour owed me an apology. But far from giving me one he lost his temper with me and said the most disagreeable things, using turns of phrase of whose impropriety he would have been aware had he understood Spanish better. I was accustomed to being kindly treated by all the residents of Ceuta. Folencour's words seemed to me outrageous and not to be tolerated. Proudly, I went up to him, took his *pochette*, smashed it on the ground and swore never to be taught to dance by anyone so vulgar.

My father did not scold me. He rose gravely, took me by the hand, led me to a low room at one end of the courtyard and, as he locked me in, he said, 'Señor, you will not come out of there except to learn to dance.'

Accustomed as I was to complete freedom, prison seemed intolerable to me at first. For a long time I wept a great deal. But as I cried I looked towards a large square window, the only one in that low room, and started counting the panes. There were twenty-six across and as many down. I remembered Father Anselm's lessons, which went no further than multiplication.

I multiplied the panes down by the panes across and realized with surprise that I had the overall number of panes. My sobs grew less frequent, my sorrow less great. I repeated my calculation, taking off one or sometimes two rows of panes, either across or down. I then realized that multiplication is only repeated addition and that surfaces could be measured as well as length. Next, I did the same experiment with the tiles which formed the floor of the room. It worked just as well. I didn't cry any longer. My heart was beating with joy. Even today I cannot talk of this without feeling some emotion.

Towards midday my mother brought me a loaf of black bread and a jug of water. She begged me with tears in her eyes to bow to the wishes of my father and take lessons from Folencour. When she had finished her entreaties I kissed her hand with great affection. Then I asked her to bring me some paper and a pencil and not to concern herself about me any more because I was quite happy in that low room. My mother left me in bewilderment and sent in the things that I had asked for. Then I devoted myself to my calculations with indescribable ardour, convinced that I was making great discoveries from one moment to the next. And indeed the properties of numbers were veritable discoveries for me. I had had no notion of them.

Meanwhile, I noticed I was hungry. I broke the loaf and found that my mother had hidden inside it a roast chicken and a piece of bacon. This token of kindness added to my contentment and I took up my calculations again with renewed pleasure. In the evening a lamp was brought to me and I continued working late into the night.

The following day I halved the side of a pane, and saw that the product of a half and a half was a quarter. I divided the side of a pane into three and came up with a ninth, which made clear to me the nature of fractions. I confirmed this when I multiplied two and a half by two and a half, and together with the square of two I obtained a square whose value was two and a quarter.

I took my experiments with numbers further. I realized that by multiplying a number by itself and squaring the product I would obtain the same result as if I had multiplied the number four times by itself. All my fine discoveries were not expressed in algebraic language, of which I was ignorant. I had made up my own notation to apply to the window-panes, which lacked neither elegance nor precision.

At last, on the tenth day of my incarceration, my mother said when she brought me my meal, 'My dear child, I have good news to tell you. Folencour has been unmasked as a deserter. Your father, who abhors desertion, has had him put on a ship. I think you will soon leave your prison.'

I received the news of my release with an indifference which surprised my mother. Shortly afterwards my father came to confirm what she had said, and then added that he had written to his friends Cassini and Huygens[1] to ask them to send the steps of the most fashionable dances in London and Paris. He, as it happens, had a clear memory of the way his brother Carlos pirouetted on entering a room: it was which above all else that he wanted to teach me. As he spoke, my father saw a notebook sticking out of my pocket, and seized it. He was at first very surprised to see it covered with numbers and certain signs which were unknown to him. I explained them, as well as all my calculations. His surprise grew. It was mingled with a certain look of satisfaction which did not escape me. My father followed the account of my discoveries closely and then said to me:

'If I added two panes to the width of this window, which is twenty-six panes in both directions, how many panes would have to be added for it to keep the form of a square?'

I replied unhesitatingly, 'You will have added across and down two blocks each of fifty-two panes, with a little square of four panes at the corner where the two blocks meet, as well.'

---

1 Gian Domenico Cassini (1625–1712), and Christiaan Huygens (1629–95), prominent experimental scientists of their day.

This reply gave my father great joy, which he hid as best he could. Then he said to me, 'But if I added to the base of the window an infinitely small row, what would then be the resulting square?'

I thought for a moment and then said, 'You would have two blocks as long as the sides of the window but infinitesimally narrow, and as for the square in the corner, it would be so infinitesimally small that I cannot imagine it.'

At this point my father collapsed back in his chair, clasped his hands together, raised his eyes to heaven and said, 'Merciful Heaven, you are witness to him! He has worked out the law of binomials! If I let him continue, he will work out the differential calculus!'

The state that my father was in frightened me. I undid his cravat and called for help. He came to his senses, embraced me and said, 'My child, my dear child. Give up your calculations! Learn to dance the saraband, my friend, learn to dance the saraband!' There was no longer any question of prison. That evening I went all round the ramparts of Ceuta and as I walked I repeated to myself, 'He has discovered the law of binomials!' From then on, I can say, every day that went by was marked by some progress I made in mathematics. My father had sworn never to allow me to learn the subject, but one day I found on the ground in front of me the noble Don Isaac Newton's *Arithmetica Universalis*,[2] and I cannot help thinking that my father had mislaid it there almost by design. Sometimes, too, I found the library open and did not fail to profit from this. On other occasions, however, my father set out to prepare me for entry into polite society. He made me pirouette when I came into a room, hum a tune and pretend to be short-sighted. Then he would dissolve in tears and say, 'My child, you are not meant for a life of impertinence. Your days will be no happier than mine have been.'

Five years after the period of my incarceration, my mother discovered that she was pregnant. She gave birth to a daughter, who was called Blanca in honour of the beautiful and all-too-fickle Duquesa de Velásquez. Although that lady had not given my father permission to write to her, he believed it to be his duty to inform her of the birth

2 First published in 1707; Newton's own revision appeared in 1722.

of the child. He received a reply which revived old sorrows, but my father was growing older and was not so susceptible to such violent emotions.

Thereafter, ten years passed without anything to disturb the regularity of our lives, although for my father and myself they were given variety by the new knowledge which from day to day we were acquiring. My father had even given up his former aloofness with me. He had indeed not taught me mathematics; he had done all in his power to make me learn to dance the saraband. So he had nothing to reproach himself with and indulged himself with a clear conscience in talking to me about everything that related to the exact sciences. These conversations had the effect of stimulating my enthusiasm and increasing my efforts. But at the same time, by commanding all my attention, they developed my tendency towards absent-mindedness, as I have said. I have often had to pay dearly for this distraction, as you will soon learn, for one day I left Ceuta and found myself suddenly, without knowing how, surrounded by Arabs.

As for my sister, she grew in grace and beauty and our joy would have been complete if we still had had a mother with us, but a year earlier a violent illness had carried off the one we loved so much.

My father then took into his household a sister of his deceased wife, called Doña Antonia de Poneras. She was twenty years old and had been a widow for six months. She was not born of the same bed as my mother. When Señor de Cadanza married off his daughter, who was then his only child, he found his house too lonely and decided to remarry. His second wife died six years later giving birth to a daughter, who later married Señor de Poneras, who himself died in the first year of their marriage.

This young and pretty aunt took up residence in my mother's apartment and ran the household, which she did quite well. She was especially attentive to me. She would come into my room twenty times a day to ask whether I wanted chocolate, lemonade or something similar.

These visits were often unwelcome since they interrupted my calculations. Whenever it happened that Doña Antonia did not come, she was replaced by a chambermaid, a girl of the same age and humour as her mistress, whose name was Marita. I soon noticed that my sister liked neither the maid nor the mistress, and it was not long before I shared her antipathy for them, which was, however, in my case only founded on the annoyance I felt at being interrupted. But I wasn't always caught out by them. I had taken to substituting symbols for values as soon as one of these women entered my room, only to take up my calculations again when she had gone away.

One day, as I was looking up a logarithm, Antonia came into my room and sat down in an armchair next to my table. Then, complaining of the heat, she took off the kerchief she wore on her breast, folded it and put it on the back of my chair. I concluded from this activity that she was going to stay for some time, so I stopped my calculations, shut up my logarithm tables and started musing about the nature of logarithms and the extreme effort that drawing up the tables must have cost the famous Lord Napier.

Then Antonia, who only wanted to annoy me, went behind my chair, put her two hands over my eyes and said to me, 'Now do your calculations, Señor geometer!'

These words of my aunt seemed to me to contain a real challenge. Having latterly used the tables a great deal, I had retained many logarithms in my memory and knew them by heart, as it were. Suddenly, I had the idea of breaking down into three factors the number whose logarithm I sought. I found three factors whose logarithms I knew, I added them up in my head and, quickly breaking free of Antonia's hands, I wrote out the whole logarithm without missing a single decimal place. Antonia was irritated by this. She left the room, saying somewhat discourteously, 'What fools geometers are!'

Perhaps she wanted to raise the objection that my method could not be applied to prime numbers, which can only be divided by one. In this she was right, but what I had done proved none the less that I had a considerable facility with calculation and it certainly wasn't the moment to tell me that I was a fool. Soon after, her maid Marita arrived. She also wanted to pinch and tickle me. But her mistress's words still rankled and I sent her away somewhat peremptorily.

The thread of my story now leads me to a period of my life which was noteworthy for the new use to which I began to put my ideas, by directing them all towards a single goal. You will have observed that in the life of every scientist there comes a moment when, having grasped some principle, he develops its consequences and broadens its applications or, as people say, he builds a system. At such times his courage and strength increase. He goes over what he knows and finishes acquiring the knowledge that he lacked. He considers every notion from all its aspects, which he brings together and classifies. And if he is unable to establish his own system or even to convince himself that it really exists, at least when he abandons it he is more knowledgeable than he was before he conceived of it, and he salvages from it some truths which had not been known before. The moment of system-building had come for me, and this was the occasion which gave me the first inklings of it.

One evening I was working after supper and had just finished a very complex piece of differentiation when my aunt Antonia appeared in my room, dressed in little more than her nightdress. 'My dear nephew,' she said, 'I cannot sleep while I can still see a light in your room. Since geometry is such a fine thing I want you to teach me it.'

As I hadn't anything better to do I agreed to do as my aunt requested. I took my slate and demonstrated to her the first two propositions of Euclid. I was about to pass to the third when my aunt tore my slate from me and said, 'My clot of a nephew, hasn't geometry even shown you how babies are made?'

My aunt's words seemed absurd at first, but after some reflection I thought that she was perhaps asking me for a general expression which would cover all the modes of reproduction found in nature, from cedar trees to lichen and from whales to microscopic animals.

I remembered at the same time thoughts I had had about the smaller and greater mental capacities of every animal whose first cause I had found by investigating their procreation, gestation and manner of birth. In this case, the smaller or greater degree demonstrated to me the existence of increase and decrease, and this brought me back to the sphere of geometry. In the end, I conceived the idea of a particular notation for all the animal kingdom which might represent actions of the same kind but of different values. My imagination suddenly became inflamed. I thought I could glimpse the possibility of determining the geometric locus and the limit of every one of our ideas and the action which resulted from it. In a word, I thought I glimpsed the possibility of submitting the whole system of nature to the process of calculation. Overwhelmed by the ideas which crowded in upon me, I felt the need to breathe more freely in the open air. I rushed out on to the ramparts and went round them three times without knowing what I was doing.

Eventually my brain slowed down and the day began to dawn, which gave me the idea of writing down some of my principles. I got out my tablets and, as I was writing, walked back along the path to our house, or what I took to be the path to our house. But it turned out that instead of going to the right of the corner tower of the rampart I went to the left and walked down into the moat by a postern gate. There was little light and I could scarcely see what I was writing. I was in a hurry to return home so I walked twice as fast, thinking that I was on the way back to our house, but instead I went along a ramp which had been formed to move out cannon if a sortie was to be made, and soon I found myself on the outer slope. Still thinking that I was on my way home, and still scribbling on my slates, I walked as fast as I could, but hurry as I might I did not get there, as I had taken the direction that led away from the town. So I sat down and began further calculations.

After some time I looked up and saw I was surrounded by Arabs. I knew their language, which is generally known in Ceuta. I told them who I was and assured them that if they brought me back to my father they would receive from him a decent ransom. The word 'ransom' has something about it which never fails to flatter Arab ears. The nomads all around me looked at their chief ingratiatingly and seemed to expect a reply from him which would turn out to their financial benefit. The sheikh stroked his beard pensively and gravely for a long while and then said, 'Listen, young Nazarene, we know your father, who is a God-fearing man. We have also heard of you. It is said that you are as kind as your father but that Allah has deprived you of part of your reason. Let that not trouble you. God is great. He bestows intelligence and takes it away at his will. Imbeciles are a living proof of the power of God and the nullity of human wisdom. Imbeciles, not knowing good and evil, are also symbols of our original state of innocence. They possess, as it were, the first degree of holiness. We give imbeciles the name "marabout", which we also give to saints. This is fundamental to our religion, and so we would consider that we had sinned if we took the least ransom for you. We shall accompany you back to the nearest Spanish outpost and we will then withdraw.'

I confess to you that the Arab sheikh's words plunged me into the deepest consternation. 'Well,' I thought to myself, 'by following Locke and Newton I might be said to have reached the very frontiers of human intelligence. By applying to the principles of the former the calculus of the latter, I might be said to have taken several sure steps into the abyss of metaphysics. And where does all this lead me? To be classed as simple-minded! To be thought of as an imbecile who doesn't truly belong to the human race! A curse on differential calculus and all those integrations on which I depended for my reputation!'

With these words I took my tablets and smashed them into small pieces. I then continued my lamentations as follows: 'Oh my father, how right you were to have me learn the saraband and every other sort of impertinence since invented!' Then, without consciously wishing to, I started practising several steps of the saraband, as my father used to when he remembered his misfortunes.

The Arabs, who had seen me writing with great application on my tablets then smash them, and start to dance, exclaimed with an air of compassion, 'Praise be to Allah! Allah is kind! Al-Hamdu lillahi! Allah karim!' After that, they then took me gently by the arm and led me to the nearest Spanish outpost.

As Velásquez reached this point in his story, he became upset or absent-minded. Since we saw that he was finding it difficult to recover the thread of what he was saying, we asked him to stop and begin again the next day.

The Twenty-fifth Day

We set off again and crossed a pretty region, although only wilderness. Making my way round a hill, I parted company with the caravan. Suddenly I heard a groaning coming from a small valley full of lush vegetation which lay alongside our path. The groaning grew louder. I dismounted, tied up my horse, drew my sword and plunged into the undergrowth. The more I went on, the further away the groaning seemed to be. At last I reached a clearing and found myself surrounded by eight or ten men, who were pointing their muskets at me.

One of them ordered me to give him my sword. By way of reply, I leapt at him, hoping to run him through. But at that moment he put his musket down as if in surrender, and offered to make a deal with me if I gave myself up and agreed to make certain undertakings. I replied that I would not give myself up nor undertake anything.

At that moment the cries of my fellow travellers shouting for me were heard. The person who seemed to be the chief of the band said to me, 'Señor caballero, people are searching for you. We have no time to lose. In five days you must leave the camp and set off in a westerly direction. You will then meet persons who have an important secret to communicate to you. The groaning you heard was only a trick to lead you to us. Don't forget to come to the rendezvous at the appointed time.'

With these words he nodded to me, gave a whistle and disappeared with his companions. I went back to the caravan but didn't think it necessary to speak of my meeting. We soon reached our resting-place. After the meal we asked Velásquez to continue his story, which he did as follows:

ᖇ VELÁSQUEZ'S STORY CONTINUED ᖇ

I have told you how in reflecting on the order which reigns in the universe I thought that I had found an application of calculus that had not been noticed before. I also then described how my aunt Antonia, by her indiscreet and untoward utterances, had caused my scattered ideas to come together around one focus, as it were, and form themselves into a system. I finally related to you how I had fallen from the heights of exaltation to the depths of discouragement on learning that I was thought to be an imbecile. I will confess to you freely that this state of depression was long and painful. I did not dare to raise my eyes to anyone. My fellow men seemed to me in league to reject and revile me. The books which gave me such pleasure now filled me with deep disgust. All I could see in them was a confused mass of useless verbiage. I didn't touch my slate. I did no more calculations. The fibres of my mind had slackened; they had lost all tension. I was no longer able to think.

My father noticed my discouragement and urged me to tell him what had caused it. For a long time I refused, but eventually I told him what the Arab sheikh had said, and confessed how hurtful I had found it to be taken for someone who had lost his reason.

My father's head dropped on to his chest and his eyes filled with tears. After a long silence he looked at me with compassion and said:

'Oh my son, you are taken for a madman and I really was mad for three years. But your absent-mindedness and my love for Blanca are not the first causes of our sorrows. Our troubles have deeper roots.

'Nature is infinitely rich and diverse in her ways. She can be seen to break her most unchanging laws. She has made self-interest the motive of all human action, but in the great host of men she produces ones who are strangely constituted, in whom selfishness is scarcely perceptible because they do not place their affections in themselves. Some are passionate about the sciences, others about the public good. They are as attached to the discoveries of others as if they themselves had made them, or to the institutions of public welfare and the state as if they derived benefit from them. This habit of not thinking of themselves influences the whole course of their lives. They don't know how to use other men for their own profit. Fortune offers them opportunities which they do not think of taking up.

'In nearly all men the self is almost never inactive. You will detect their self-interest in nearly all the advice they give you, in the services they do for you, in the contacts they make, in the friendships they form. They are deeply attached to the things which affect their interests however remotely, and are indifferent to all others. When they encounter a man who is indifferent to personal interest they cannot understand him. They suspect him of hidden motives, of affectation, or of insanity. They cast him from their bosom, revile him and relegate him to a rock in Africa.

'Oh my son, we both belong to this proscribed race, but we also have our compensations, which I must tell you about. I have tried everything to make you a dandy and a fool. But heaven has not crowned my efforts, for you are a sensitive soul with an enlightened mind. So I must tell you that we too have our pleasures. They are private and solitary but are sweet and pure.

'What inner satisfaction I felt when I learnt that Don Isaac Newton approved of one of my anonymous pamphlets and wanted to know who the author was! I didn't make myself known but was spurred on to renewed efforts, which enriched my mind with a host of new thoughts. It was so full of these that it could not keep them in. So I went out to disclose them to the rocks of Ceuta. I entrusted them to the whole realm of nature. I offered them up as a tribute to my Creator. With these exalted sentiments the memories of my sufferings mingled sighs and tears which also had their pleasures, and which reminded me that there were ills about me which I could palliate. In my mind I became one with the purposes of providence, the work of creation, the progress of the human spirit. My mind, my person, my fate did not take on for me individual form but became part of a great unity.

'So passed the age of my youthful passion. Then I found myself again. The unflagging ministrations of your mother told me a hundred times a day that I myself was the sole object of her love. My soul, once turned in upon itself, now opened up to the feeling of gratitude and to the effusions of intimacy. Through the little events of your childhood and that of your sister I have become accustomed to these emotions.

'Now your mother lives on only in my heart, and my mind, weakened by age, can no longer add to the riches of the human spirit. But I see this treasure increasing daily and it gives me pleasure to plot its growth. The interest I take in it helps me forget my infirmity. Boredom has not yet touched my life.

'So you see, my son, that we too have our pleasures, and if you had become a fop, as I had always wanted, you would not have escaped life's woes. When Alvarez was here he spoke about my brother in a way which aroused more pity in me than envy.

'The duke, he said, knows the court well and has no difficulty in uncovering its intrigues, but when he tries himself to fulfil his ambition to rise in it he soon repents of having aspired to such heights. He has been ambassador and it is said that he represented the king with all possible dignity, but the first time a delicate situation arose he had to be recalled. You know that he had been given a ministry. He filled the vacant posts as did any other, but whatever care his secretaries took to spare him work, his own lack of application was still greater and he was forced to resign his portfolio. Now he has no power, but he has the knack of creating small opportunities which bring him close to the monarch and make him seem to be in favour. For the rest, boredom is destroying him. He has done everything to escape it, but he always falls back into the grim clutches of the monster which is crushing him. He escapes it by being ceaselessly preoccupied with himself and his person, but this excessive egoism has made him so sensitive to the least set-back that life has become a torment for him. And now frequent illnesses have warned him that this self, this unique object of all his attentions, may too slip away from him one day, and this thought poisons all of his pleasures.

'This is more or less what Alvarez said. From it I reached the conclusion that I have perhaps been happier in my obscurity than my brother has been in the midst of his fortunes and the splendour of which he deprived me. As you know, my dear son, the inhabitants of Ceuta have thought you a bit mad. That is because of their own simple-mindedness. One day, if you join polite society, you will certainly experience injustice, against which you must be forearmed.

The best defence would no doubt be to match insult with insult, calumny with calumny, to fight injustice with injustice, but this way of dealing with iniquity is not within the scope of people like us. So when you are afflicted by it, withdraw and turn in upon yourself. Feed off the substance of your own soul and you will know happiness.'

My father's words made a profound impression on me. My courage returned and I set to work again on my system. At that time, too, I began to become really absent-minded. It was seldom that I heard what was said to me except for the last few words, which imprinted themselves on my memory. I replied an hour or two after being spoken to. Sometimes I went for a walk not knowing where I was going. It was then said that I needed a guide like the blind. This distracted state of mind lasted, however, only as long as it took me to bring order to my system. As I devoted less attention to it I became less absent-minded. Today I am more or less cured.

'It had seemed to me that you did suffer occasionally from absent-mindedness,' said the cabbalist. 'But since you tell me that you are cured of it, please allow me to congratulate you.'

'With pleasure,' said Velásquez, 'for my system was no sooner finished when an unexpected occurrence produced a change in my fortune that will not only make it difficult for me to build a system, but may also, alas, not allow me to devote ten to twelve hours a day to my calculations. For, Señores, heaven has decreed that I be Duque de Velásquez, grandee of Spain and master of a considerable fortune.'

'What? Señor Duque,' said Rebecca, 'you tell us this as though it were an incidental detail in your story? I believe that in your place most people would have begun with it.'

'I admit,' said Velásquez, 'that such a coefficient multiplies an individual value, but I did not think I had to state it before its due place in the order of events. This is what it remains for me to tell you:

About four weeks ago Diego Alvarez, son of the other Alvarez, came to Ceuta to give my father a letter from Duquesa Blanca. These were its contents:

272

Señor Don Enrique,

These lines are to let you know that God will perhaps soon call to himself your brother, the Duque de Velásquez. The conditions of entailment of our succession do not allow you to inherit from a younger brother. The grandeeship must pass to your son. I am glad to be able to end forty years of penance by restoring to him the fortune which my imprudence took away from you. What I cannot give you back is the glory that your talents would have brought you. But we are both at the threshold of eternal glory and the glory of this world can scarcely move us now. For the last time I beg you to forgive guilty Blanca and to send us the son heaven has given you. The duke, whom I have been nursing for the last two months, wishes to meet his heir.

Blanca de Velásquez.

I may say that this letter brought joy to all Ceuta, where I had many well-wishers, but I was far from sharing in the public happiness. Ceuta was a whole world for me. I only left it in spirit to lose myself in abstract thoughts, and if I looked over the ramparts at the vast territories inhabited by the Moors, it was as though I was looking at a landscape painting. Being unable to walk about in it, the countryside seemed to me to be there to provide only visual pleasure. What would I do away from Ceuta? In that town there was no wall on which I had not scribbled some equation, and no seat which did not recall to me some meditation which had given me mental satisfaction. It is true that I was occasionally bothered by my aunt Antonia and Marita, her maid, but these were but small interruptions compared to the distractions to which I was now condemned. There would no longer be any long periods of reflection, nor any calculations, nor any happiness for me. That is how I thought, but I had to leave.

My father came down to the harbour with me. He placed both his hands on my head to bless me and said, 'My son, you will see Blanca. She is now not the striking beauty who once was destined to be the glory and happiness of your father. You will see her features consumed by age and worn away by penitence. Why did she continue so long to weep for a sin for which her father had forgiven her? As for me, I have never felt anger towards her. If I have not gloriously served my king in high office, I have for forty years at least been of service to a few good people on this rock. Such service is due to Blanca. People here have heard of her virtues and all bless her.'

My father was unable to say more. He felt sobs choking him. All of Ceuta's inhabitants were present to see me go. In their eyes could be seen the sorrow of losing me, mingled with the joy of my change in fortune.

I set sail and reached the port of Algeciras the next day. From there I went first to Córdoba and then to Andújar, where I spent the night. The innkeeper at Andújar told me some story or other about ghosts, of which I didn't understand a word. I slept at his inn and left early the next morning. I had two servants with me, one who went ahead of me and one who followed. The idea struck me that in Madrid I would not have the time to work so I got out my tablets and did some calculations which were incidental to my system. The mule on which I was riding walked at a regular pace, which favoured this sort of work. I don't know how long I was thus occupied. But suddenly my mule stopped. I found myself at the base of a gallows on which there were two hanged men whose faces seemed set in grimaces, which caused me to shudder in horror. I looked all around me but did not catch sight of my servants. I shouted for them but they did not come, so I decided to follow the path ahead of me. At nightfall I came to a vast, well-built inn, which was abandoned and empty.

I put the mule in the stable and went up to a room in which I found the remains of a supper: a partridge pâté, bread and a bottle of Alicante wine. I had not eaten since Andújar and thought that my need for food gave me the right to the pâté, which in any case had no owner. My throat was also very dry so I slaked my thirst, perhaps too fast, for the Alicante wine went to my head, as I discovered only too late.

There was a reasonably clean bed in the room. I undressed, lay down and fell asleep. Then something woke me with a start. I heard a bell strike midnight. I thought that there must be a monastery nearby and decided to go there the next day.

Soon after, I heard a noise in the courtyard. I thought that my servants had arrived. But you can imagine my surprise when I saw my aunt Antonia and Marita, her maid, come in. The maid carried a lantern with two candles and my aunt had a notebook in her hand.

'My dear nephew,' she said, 'your father has sent us to give you this document, which he says is important.'

I took the notebook and read on the cover, *Proof of how to square the circle.* I knew that my father had never bothered himself with this idle problem. Astonished, I opened the notebook, but soon saw with indignation that the so-called solution was no more than the well-known theory of Dinostrates, accompanied by a proof which I recognized to be in my father's handwriting but not to be the product of his mind. And indeed I demonstrated that the proofs on offer were no more than poor paralogisms.

Meanwhile my aunt pointed out to me that as I had taken possession of the only bed in the inn I was duty bound to give up half of it to her. The idea that my father could have committed such mathematical errors bothered me so much that I scarcely heard what she said. I automatically made room for her, and Marita lay down at my feet and rested her head on my knees.

I went back to the proof. I don't know whether the Alicante wine had gone to my head or whether my eyes had been bewitched, but in some way or other I lost sight of the error I thought I had detected at first, and having reread the proof a third time I was convinced that it was right.

I turned to the third page. I found a highly ingenious set of corollaries which had the effect of squaring and rectifying all curves; in other words, the solution to the problem of isochrones, using elementary rules of geometry. Delighted, amazed and stupefied, I believe, by the effects of Alicante wine, I cried out, 'Yes, my father has made the greatest of discoveries!'

'Well, then,' said my aunt, 'give me a kiss for the trouble I have taken in crossing the sea to bring you this scribbling.'

I kissed her.

'I crossed the sea, too,' said Marita.

So I had to kiss her as well.

I wanted to return to the problem but my two bedfellows hugged me so tightly in their arms that I could not release myself from them. Indeed, I no longer wanted to. I felt the stirrings of indescribable sensations in my person. Over the whole surface of my body a new feeling was growing, especially where it was in contact with the two women. I was reminded of some of the properties of osculating curves. I wanted to analyse what I was feeling but my brain could no longer follow through any line of reasoning. Eventually my feelings developed into a series ascending to infinity, which was succeeded by sleep and a very unpleasant awakening under the gallows on which I had seen the two hanged men smiling horribly.

And that is the whole story of my life. All that is missing from it is the theory of my system, that is to say, the application of mathematics to the general order of the universe. I hope however one day to be able to acquaint you with it, especially this fair lady who seems to have a taste for the exact sciences rarely to be found in her sex.

Rebecca thanked him for the compliment, then she asked Velásquez what had become of the papers that his aunt had brought him.

'I don't know where they have got to,' said the geometer. 'I didn't find them among the papers which the gypsies fetched for me, which I much regret, because in looking again at the so-called proof I am sure that I would have immediately spotted the error. As I told you, my blood was overheated that night. The Alicante wine, the two women, the irresistible sleep – all of this caused me to fail. But what surprises me still is that the handwriting was my father's. The way of writing symbols was unique to him.'

I was struck by Velásquez's words, above all his remark that he was unable to stop himself falling asleep. I guessed that he had been given a similar wine to that which my two cousins had served me at our first meeting in November, or a potion similar to the poison I had been ordered to drink in the underground cave, which was actually only a sleeping draught.

The company split up. As I was on the point of falling asleep, several thoughts came to me which might, it seemed, have explained my adventures by natural means. In the course of these reflections I fell asleep.

The Twenty-sixth Day

—————————— ∽ ——————————

The next day we devoted to rest. The life which the gypsies led and the contraband which was their principal means of subsistence required constant and tiring changes of camp. So I was delighted to stay for a whole day in the place where we had spent the night. Everyone smartened themselves up a little. Rebecca put on some jewellery. She might have been said to be trying to attract the attentions of the young duke, for that is what he was called from then on.

We found ourselves on a fine grass meadow shaded by tall chestnut trees. We partook of a somewhat more varied breakfast than usual, and then Rebecca said to the gypsy chief that as he was less busy than usual she would take the liberty of asking him to tell us more of his adventures. Pandesowna needed no persuasion and began as follows:

∽ THE GYPSY CHIEF'S STORY CONTINUED ∽

I have told you that I did not go to school until all my stratagems and excuses for putting off the day had run out. At first I was pleased to find myself in the company of so many companions of my age; but I found our continual subjection to our tutors intolerable. I had grown pleasantly accustomed to my aunt's caresses, her indulgence and her affection. I was also very flattered when she told me, as she did many times each day, that I had a nice nature. A nice nature was of no use at school. One had to pay attention all the time or suffer the rod. I hated both equally, so I ended up by altogether detesting anyone wearing a black cassock, and I showed my detestation by playing every imaginable trick on him.

There were pupils whose talents for observation were better than their character and who took pleasure in telling tales about their companions' doings. I founded a league against them and we arranged our tricks in such a way that suspicion always fell on the informers. In

277

the end, all those in black cassocks accused of being informers could bear us no longer.

I don't want to bore you with all the details of our childishness. Suffice it to say that during the four years I put my mind to devising them, our pranks took a more and more serious turn. In the end I was so carried away that I committed an act which, though perhaps innocent in itself, was despicable because of the means I employed. I very nearly paid for it by several years of imprisonment or even the permanent loss of my freedom. This is what happened.

Of the Theatines who treated us most harshly, none had shown us more pitiless severity than Father Sanudo, the teacher of the first class. Such hardness was not part of his nature, however. Quite the opposite. This monk had been born hypersensitive. His secret inclinations had always been contrary to his duties. Sanudo had reached the age of thirty without ceasing to struggle against and suppress his true nature.

He was without pity for himself and had become implacable towards others. The continual sacrifice which he made through his manner of behaving was all the more meritorious in that no one had ever seen a more striking case of natural instincts being opposed to the dictates of religion; for he was as handsome a man as you can imagine and few women were able to cross his path without giving him signs of their admiration for him. But Sanudo would lower his eyes, frown and pass by without seeming to notice. Such was, or rather such had long been, Father Sanudo. But so many victorious battles had exhausted his soul, which had lost some of its vigour. By being obliged to be wary of women he ended up by thinking about them all the time. The enemy he had fought against for so long never left his mind. In the end a grave illness followed by a difficult convalescence left behind a hypersensitivity which manifested itself as a perpetual state of impatience. Our smallest errors angered him. Our excuses could cause him to weep. He had become absent-minded, and in moments of distraction his eyes would stare at some object with a look of affection, and if someone interrupted him in one of these ecstasies his expression was one of pain rather than severity. We were too used to observing our mentor closely for such a change to escape our notice. But we did not fathom what caused it until we had occasion to notice something that put us on the scent. However, to make myself understood I shall have to start from a point further back in the story.

The two most famous families of Burgos were those of the Counts of Lirias and the Marquesses of Fuen Castilla. The former even belonged to that class in Spain called *agraviados*, to express the wrong done to them by their not being called grandees. So the other grandees would address them in the familiar form of address which they used in addressing each other, which was a way of assimilating them to their number.

The head of the house of Lirias was a seventy-year-old gentleman with the noblest and most gracious of characters. He had had two sons, both of whom had died, and his fortune fell to the young Condesa de Lirias, the only daughter of his elder son. The old count, having no heirs of his own name, had betrothed his granddaughter to the heir of the family of Fuen Castilla, who on marrying was to take the title Fuen de Lirias y Castilla. This union, though well matched in other respects, was also well matched as far as the age, looks and character of the engaged couple went. They loved each other passionately, and the elderly Conde de Lirias delighted in the sight of their innocent love, which brought back memories of the happier times of his own life.

The future Condesa de Fuen de Lirias resided in the convent of the Annunciads, but every day she went to dine at her grandfather's house, where she stayed in the company of her future husband until the evening. On these occasions she was accompanied by a duenna mayor called Doña Clara Mendoza, a woman of about thirty years of age who was very respectable but not at all morose. But the old count did not like people of that disposition.

Every day the young Condesa de Lirias and her duenna passed by our college because it was on the way to the old count's house. As they did so during our recreation time we were often at the windows, or we ran there when we heard the sound of the carriage.

The first to reach the windows had often heard Doña Mendoza say to her young pupil, 'There's the handsome Theatine.'

That's the name ladies gave Father Sanudo, and indeed the duenna had eyes only for him. As for her young charge, she looked at all of us, perhaps because our age recalled to her that of her lover, or because she was trying to recognize two of her cousins.

Sanudo, for his part, ran like the others to the window, but as soon as the women took notice of him he would look sombre and retreat disdainfully. We were struck by this contradiction.

If he really has a horror of women, we said to ourselves, why does he come to the window? And if he is curious to see them, he is wrong to turn his eyes away.

A young pupil called Veyras told me in this connection, that Sanudo was not the misogynist he had been in the past and that he would try to find a way of proving it. Veyras was the best friend I had in the college, that is to say, he aided and abetted me in all my tricks, of which he was in many cases the author.

At that time, a new novel, entitled *Leonce in Love*, appeared. The author's graphic description of love made the novel dangerous reading. Our teachers had strictly forbidden it. Veyras found a way of procuring a copy of *Leonce*, and put it in his pocket so as to let part of it be seen. Sanudo noticed it and confiscated it. He threatened Veyras with the most severe punishment if he ever were to commit the same fault again, and then disappeared on the pretext of some illness or other and did not appear again for evening lessons. We for our part pretended to be very concerned about the health of our teacher. We went into his room unannounced and found him there, in the middle of reading the dangerous novel with his eyes wet with tears, which proved how much the book had captivated him. Sanudo looked embarrassed; we pretended not to notice. Soon we had another indication of the great change that had taken place in the heart of the hapless monk.

In Spain, women are often very assiduous in fulfilling their religious duties, and ask for the same confessor on each occasion. The expression for this is 'buscar a su padre'.[1] This provides an opportunity for shameless cynics who exploit the ambiguity of the phrase to ask, when they see a child in church, whether he has come to 'buscar a su padre'.

---

1 'To look for one's father'.

The ladies of Burgos would have very much liked to confess to Father Sanudo, but the touchy cleric had said that he would not undertake to direct the consciences of persons of the fair sex. Yet on the day after the fateful reading of *Leonce*, when one of the prettiest women of the town asked for Father Sanudo, he went straight away to his confessional. Several suggestive compliments were paid to him as a result. In reply to them he gravely stated that he had nothing more to fear from an enemy against whom he had fought so valiantly. The other fathers may have believed him, but we schoolboys knew exactly what to make of this.

As each day passed Sanudo seemed to take greater interest in the secrets which the fair sex brought to the tribunal of penitence. His practice in the confessional was quite consistent. He would dispatch old ladies quickly, but detain younger women for longer, and he still ran to the window to see the fair Condesa de Lirias and her attractive companion, Doña Mendoza, go by. Then, when the carriage had disappeared from view, he would turn his eyes away disdainfully.

One day, when we had paid very little attention to our lessons and had incurred Sanudo's wrath, Veyras, looking secretive, took me aside and said, 'The time has come to take revenge on this accursed pedant who is spoiling the best days of our lives with his impositions of penance and seems to take pleasure in inflicting punishment on us. I have thought up an excellent trick to play on him, but we will have to find a young girl whose figure is similar to that of the Condesa de Lirias. Juanita, the gardener's daughter, is very helpful to us in our tricks but she isn't clever enough for this one.'

'My dear Veyras,' I replied, 'even if we find a person with a figure similar to that of Lirias, I can't see how we can give her a pretty face.'

'I don't see that as a problem,' said Veyras. 'The ladies here have just put on the lenten veils they call *catafalcos*. They are like lace flounces which lie one on top of the other and hide their faces so well that they do not even wear masks when they go to balls. Juanita will still be useful, if not to pass herself off as Lirias then at least for dressing up the supposed Lirias and her duenna.'

Veyras said no more about it that day, but one Sunday, when he was installed in his confessional, Father Sanudo saw two women

281

come in, covered in mantillas and crêpe. One sat down on a mat on the floor, as women do in Spanish churches, the other knelt in penitence beside Sanudo. The latter, who seemed very young, could not stop crying; her sobs were choking her. Sanudo did what he could to calm her but all she would say was, 'Father, I am in mortal sin.'

At last Sanudo said that she was in no state to unburden her soul to him and told her to come back the next day. The sinful young woman moved away, prostrated herself before the altar, prayed fervently for a long time and then left the church with her companion.

'I am not able to tell you this story,' the gypsy said, interrupting himself, 'without being overcome by remorse for these criminal tricks which can't be excused even by appeals to my youth. And if I could not hope for your indulgence, I would not dare to continue.'

We all tried to reassure the gypsy chief on this point as best we could, and so he began his story again as follows:

The two penitents came back the next day at the same hour. Sanudo had been waiting for them for a long time. The younger of the two took her place in the confessional and seemed to be a bit more in control of herself. There was, however, still much sobbing and many tears. At last in a silver-toned voice she uttered the following words:

'Father, until recently my heart was at one with my duty and seemed to be destined never to leave the path of virtue. I was betrothed to a nice young man and believed that I loved him.'

At this point the sobbing began again, but Sanudo was able to calm the young girl with words full of unction and piety. She began again, 'An imprudent duenna made me too aware of the merits of a man to whom I cannot belong and whom I must never contemplate: this sacrilegious passion, however, I cannot overcome.'

The word 'sacrilegious' seemed to alert Sanudo to the fact that a priest was in question, even perhaps himself.

'Señora,' said Sanudo in a trembling voice, 'you owe all your affections to the husband whom your parents have chosen.'

'Oh, Father,' replied the young girl, 'if only he looked like the man

I love! If only he had his tender yet severe gaze, his handsome and noble features . . .'

'Señora,' said Sanudo, 'this is no way to engage in confession.'

'It isn't a confession,' said the young girl, 'it's a declaration.'

And as if overcome with shame, she stood up and rejoined her companion. As the two of them left the church, Sanudo's eyes followed them. For the rest of the day he seemed preoccupied. He spent almost all the next day in the confessional but no one appeared, nor did they on the day after.

It was on the third day that the young woman came back with her duenna, knelt in the confessional and said to Sanudo, 'Father, last night I went through a crisis, I think. I felt myself overcome with shame and despair and, inspired by my bad angel, I put one of my garters round my neck. I was no longer able to breathe. Then I felt that my hand was stayed, my eyes were blinded by a bright light and I saw my patron saint, St Theresa, standing at the foot of my bed. "Daughter," she said, "go to confession tomorrow and ask Father Sanudo to give you a lock of his hair. You must carry it next to your heart and grace will enter it again."'

'Go away, Señora,' said Sanudo. 'Cast yourself before the altar and weep for your sinful folly. I shall for my part beg heaven to be merciful to you.'

Sanudo rose, left the confessional and withdrew to a chapel, where he stayed until evening in fervent prayer.

The next day the duenna came alone. She entered the confessional and said, 'Father, I have come to ask for your indulgence on behalf of a young sinner who is in danger of losing her soul. Yesterday you treated her with such severity that she is desperate. She tells me that you refused to give her a holy relic which is in your possession. She is losing her sanity and she is trying to find a way of doing away with herself. Come to our house, Father. Bring the relic which she asked of you. Do not refuse me this grace.'

Sanudo hid his face in a handkerchief, left the church and returned a little later. He held a small reliquary in his hand, which he presented to the duenna, saying, 'Señora, what I am giving you is a piece of the skull of our founder. A great number of indulgences are attached to this relic by a papal bull. We have no more precious relic here than this. Let your charge carry these holy remains next to her heart, and may heaven come to her aid.'

When the relic was in our hands we undid its case, hoping to find a lock of hair, but found nothing inside. Sanudo was only soft-hearted and gullible: he may have been a little vain too, but he was virtuous and faithful to his principles.

Veyras asked him after our evening class, 'Father, why are priests not allowed to marry?'

'For their unhappiness in this world and perhaps their damnation in the next,' Sanudo replied. Then, looking more austere, he added, 'Never ask me such questions again, Veyras.'

Next day there was no sign of Sanudo at the confessional. The duenna asked for him but another member of the order came in his place. We were close to despairing of the success of our detestable tricks when chance came to our aid in a way which exceeded our hopes.

The young Condesa de Lirias fell dangerously ill as she was on the point of being married to the Conde de Fuen Castilla. She suffered from a high temperature together with brain fever, or rather a sort of delirium. All Burgos took an interest in these two great houses: at the illness of Señora de Lirias there was great consternation throughout the town. The Theatine fathers were not the last to be informed of it. Sanudo received that evening the following letter:

Father,

St Theresa is angry. She says that you have betrayed me. She also reproaches Señora Mendoza. Why did she make me pass by the Theatine house every day? St Theresa loves me, unlike you. I have a terrible pain in my head. I am dying.

This letter was written in a trembling, almost illegible hand. Underneath, in different handwriting, the following had been added:

Father, she is writing twenty letters like this every day. Now she can no longer write. Pray for us, Father. That is all I can tell you at present.

Sanudo's poor brain could take no more. His distress knew no bounds. He went out, came back, left again, made inquiries, and turned things over again and again in his mind. The best part of it for us was that he didn't hold classes any more, or at least they were so short that we could put up with them without getting bored. At last, after a crisis which resulted in a happy outcome and some sudorific medicine, the life of sweet Señora de Lirias was saved. She was declared to be convalescent. Sanudo then received the following letter:

Father,

The danger is past, but sanity has not returned to the mind of the young person who is slipping away from me. Father, see if you could not receive us in your cell. Your cells are not locked until eleven o'clock. We could come at dusk. Perhaps your exhortations will be more effective than your relics. If this goes on much longer, I shall probably go mad too. In the name of heaven, Father, save the honour of two great houses.

This letter had such an effect on Sanudo that he had difficulty in finding his way back to his cell. There he went and shut himself in. We stood outside the door and listened to what was happening inside. At first we heard sobbing and weeping, then fervent prayer. Then he summoned the porter of the house and said to him, 'Brother, if two women come and ask for me, you are not to let them in under any pretext.'

Sanudo did not come to supper. He spent the evening in prayer, and towards eleven o'clock he heard a knock at his door. He opened it. A young lady rushed into his cell and upset his lamp, which instantly went out. At that moment the voice of the Father Prefect was heard, summoning Sanudo.

When the gypsy chief reached this point in his story one of his men came to discuss with him matters concerning his band. But Rebecca cried, 'Please, please do not break off your story at this point. I simply must know today how Sanudo extracted himself from this delicate situation.'

'Please allow me to give a few moments of my time to this man,' replied the gypsy chief. 'As soon as I have finished, I'll begin again.'

We all shared Rebecca's impatience. Then the gypsy chief, after his conversation with his man, continued his story as follows:

I have told you that we heard the voice of the Father Prefect calling Sanudo, who only had time to double-lock his door and go down to see his superior. It would be an insult to the intelligence of my listeners if I were to suggest that they had not already guessed that the supposed Mendoza was none other than Veyras, and that the pretty Lirias was the same person whom the Viceroy of Mexico wanted to marry, in other words, myself. So it was that I found myself in Sanudo's cell in the dark, not knowing how to bring the drama I was playing to an end, a drama that hadn't altogether turned out as we had wished. For we had indeed found out that Sanudo was gullible, but never weak or hypocritical. We would perhaps have done best to let our drama have no ending at all. The marriage of Señora de Lirias, which took place a few days later, and the happiness of the married couple, would have been for Sanudo inexplicable mysteries which would have tormented him for the rest of his life. But we wanted to enjoy our teacher's embarrassment, and I was only uncertain as to whether to finish the last act by shouting with laughter or by some witty and ironical comments. I was still preoccupied by this malicious plotting when I heard the door open.

Sanudo appeared. The sight of him made a deeper impression on me than I had expected. He was dressed in stole and surplice. In one hand he held a candlestick, in the other an ebony crucifix. He placed the candlestick on the table, held the crucifix in both hands and said to me, 'Señora, you can see that I have put on my holy vestments, which must remind you of the character of the priesthood imprinted on my whole person. As a priest of a redeeming God I can fulfil my ministry in no better way than to hold you back from the abyss. The evil one has disturbed your reason in order to lead you into evil ways. Turn your steps from them, Señora. Return to the paths of virtue. For you it was strewn with flowers. A young husband stretches out his hand to you. He is given to you by a virtuous old gentleman whose blood flows in your veins. Your father was his son, and that father, having gone before both of you to the place where pure souls dwell, is marking out for you the path to follow. Lift up your eyes to the light of heaven. Fear the spirit of untruth which has cast a spell on your eyes and drawn them to look upon the servants of the God of whom he is the eternal enemy . . .'

Sanudo said many other fine things designed to bring about my conversion, if I had been a certain Señora de Lirias, who was in love with her confessor, but I was only a young wretch decked out in a dress and a mantilla who was very keen to know how it would all end.

Sanudo caught his breath and then said, 'Come, Señora, a way of getting you out of the monastery has been found. I shall take you to the gardener's wife and we shall tell Señora Mendoza to take charge of you there.'

At the same time, Sanudo opened the door for me. I rushed forward to leave the cell and flee as fast as I could. That indeed is what I should have done, but at that very moment an evil demon gave me the idea of taking off my veil, throwing my arms around the neck of Sanudo and saying, 'Cruel heart. Do you want to put an end to the days of the lovesick Lirias?'

Sanudo recognized me. His consternation was at first very great. Then he wept and, showing signs of the deepest pain, he said again and again, 'My God, my God, have pity on me. Dispel my doubts. My God, what must I do?'

The poor teacher inspired me with pity. I embraced his knees, begged him to forgive me and swore that Veyras and I would not say a word about the matter.

Sanudo raised me up, bathed me with his tears and said, 'Unhappy child, do you think it is the fear of being laughed at which is making me so upset? Miserable child, I am crying for you. You have not shrunk from profaning what our religion holds most holy. You have mocked the holy tribunal of penitence. It is my duty to denounce you to the Inquisition. Imprisonment and torture will now be your lot.'

Then he embraced me with an expression of deep sorrow and said, 'No, my child, do not surrender your soul to despair. I may be able to have us administer your punishment. It will be severe but it will not mark you for the rest of your days.'

After these words Sanudo went out, double-locking the door behind him, and left me in a state of mental turmoil that you can easily imagine for yourselves. I will not try to describe it. The idea that what we were doing was criminal had not once entered my head. Our sacrilegious tricks had seemed to us like innocent pieces of mischief. The punishment with which I was threatened plunged me into a state of depression which even deprived me of the ability to weep. I do not know how long I remained in this state. Eventually the door was opened and the father prefect came in, followed by the father penitentiary and two lay brothers who took hold of me by the arms and led me along all the corridors of the house to a remote cell. They pushed me in but did not enter themselves, and I heard several bolts being shot, locking me in.

I caught my breath and inspected my prison. The moon shone right through the bars of the window. I could see only walls blackened by graffiti and some straw in the corner.

My window looked out on to a cemetery. Three bodies, wrapped in their shrouds and lying on biers, had been placed under a portico. The sight of them frightened me. I dared neither to look out of the window nor into my room.

Soon I heard noises in the cemetery. I saw a Capuchin monk and four grave-diggers enter it. They approached the portico. The Capuchin said, 'Here is the body of the Marqués de Valornez. You will place it in the embalming chamber.[2] As for these two Christians, you will throw them in the new grave that was dug yesterday.'

No sooner had the Capuchin finished his sentence than I heard a long wail and three dreadful ghosts appeared on the cemetery wall.

As the gypsy reached this point in his story the man who had already interrupted us once came back. He had a message for his chief. But Rebecca, spurred on by her recent success, said very gravely, 'Señor gypsy, I simply must know today what the meaning of those three ghosts is. Otherwise I shall not sleep a wink all night.'

The gypsy promised to fulfil her wish and indeed it was not long before he returned to take up the thread of his story as follows:

I have told you that three dreadful ghosts appeared on the cemetery wall. Their appearance and the wailing which accompanied it terrified the four grave-diggers and the Capuchin. They fled screaming. I was

2 The text reads *la chambre d'imbulsamation*. This is neither a French nor a Spanish word, but the sense seems to be clear.

frightened too but it had a different effect on me for I remained glued to the window in a state close to death.

I then saw two ghosts jump into the cemetery from the top of the wall and offer their hands to the third, who had some difficulty climbing down. Then other ghosts, up to ten or twelve of them, appeared and jumped down into the cemetery. The one who had been helped down then went under the portico to inspect the three dead bodies. He turned to the other ghosts and said, 'Friends, this is the body of the Marqués de Valornez. You have seen the treatment which those asses my colleagues made him undergo. But they were all wrong in taking the marqués's illness to be a hydropsy of the chest. I alone, Dr Sangre Moreno, hit the mark. I alone recognized his illness as angina polyposa, which the masters of our art have described so well.

'But I had no sooner identified this case of angina polypsosa than those prize asses my colleagues shrugged their shoulders and turned their backs on me as if I were unworthy to be one of their number. Yes, indeed! Dr Sangre Moreno was not born to be one of their number! It's the likes of Galician donkey-herds and Estremaduran muleteers whom they need to guide them and make them see sense. But heaven is just. Last year we saw a high mortality rate among beasts. If epizootia is seen again this year too you can be sure that none of my colleagues will survive it, whereas Dr Sangre Moreno will remain master of the battlefield and you, dear disciples, will arrive there to raise the banner of chemical medicine. You have seen how I saved the young Lirias girl simply by the effects of a happy mixture of phosphorus and antimony. For the heroic remedies whose property is to fight and overcome all diseases are semi-metals and well-balanced compounds of them, and not those herbal roots fit only for grazing on by those prize asses my honourable colleagues.

'My dear disciples, you have witnessed the attempts I made to persuade the Marquesa de Valornez to let me do no more than to pierce the artery of the trachea of the famous marqués with the point of my scalpel. Misled by my enemies, the marquesa refused to let me do this, but now I am at last able to offer proof that I am right. Ah – if only it were possible for the famous marqués to be present himself at the dissection of his own body! It would have been such pleasure to show

289

him the hydatic and polypous matter, with its roots in the bronchi and its branches extending as far as the larynx!

'But what can I say? That miserly Castilian, wholly indifferent to scientific progress, denies us things of which he himself has no further use. If the marqués had had the slightest taste for medicine he would have left us his lungs, liver and viscera, which aren't of any benefit to him. But, oh no! We must come here at the risk of our lives to violate the resting-place of the dead and disturb the peace of these tombs!

'Never mind, my dear disciples! The more obstacles we encounter, the greater will be our glory in overcoming them! Take courage! Let's bring this great undertaking to an end! When you whistle three times, your comrades on the other side will pass the ladders over the wall and we will abduct our famous marqués. Dying of so rare an illness was already a cause for self-congratulation; but falling into the hands of capable men who can recognize the illness and give it its proper name was even greater cause.

'The day after next we will be in a position to fetch from here a famous person who died from the effect of . . . shhh! There are things we mustn't say.'

As the doctor finished his speech one of his disciples whistled three times, and I saw ladders passed over the wall. Then the marqués's body was bound with ropes and passed across. The ghosts followed it and the ladders then disappeared.

When no one was left in sight I laughed heartily at the fright I had had.

Before going on, I must tell you about the manner of burial which is peculiar to some Spanish and Sicilian monasteries. Small, dark vaults are built, in which, however, the flow of air is very strong through the skilful creation of draughts. Bodies which are intended to be preserved are placed there. The darkness protects them from insects, and the air desiccates them. After six months the vault is opened. If all has worked well, the monks go in procession to the family to congratulate them on the outcome. Then they dress the body in a Capuchin habit and place it in a vault reserved for the bodies of saints, or at the very least for those who have reached a certain degree of beatitude. In the monasteries, the funeral procession accompanies the body to the cemetery, where lay brothers take charge of it and bury it according to the orders of their superiors. Normally, bodies are fetched in the evening. Superiors then deliberate about them and at night they are carried to their final resting-place. Many bodies are not suitable for preservation.

The Capuchins wished to desiccate the Marqués de Valornez's body and were on the point of setting about this process when the ghosts put the grave-diggers to flight. These tiptoed back at daybreak, huddling close together. They were extremely alarmed to discover that the marqués's body had disappeared, and decided that the devil had carried it off. Soon afterwards all the monks appeared, armed with aspergillae, and set about sprinkling holy water, exorcizing and braying at the tops of their voices. As for me, I was exhausted so I threw myself down on the straw and fell asleep at once.

The first thing I thought about the next day was the punishment with which I was threatened; the second was the way I could escape it. Veyras and I had so often stolen food from the pantry that we were very used to climbing up buildings. We also knew how to remove bars from a window and put them back without being noticed. I used the penknife I had in my pocket to take out a nail from the wooden part of my window. With the nail I worked away at the place where the bar had been set into the wall. I continued without a break until midday.

Then the peep-hole in the door opened and I caught sight of the face of the lay brother who served our dormitory. He passed me through some bread and a jug of water and asked me if he could do anything for me. I asked him to see Father Sanudo on my behalf and to ask him to give me sheets and a blanket since, although it was fair that I should be punished, I did not think it fair that I should not be clean. This point was well taken, and I was sent what I asked for, together with some meat to sustain me. I asked discreetly what Veyras was up to, and learnt that he had not been troubled. So it was that I found out that the guilty were not being sought. I asked when my punishment would begin. The lay brother answered that he did not know, but usually three days of meditation were left to go by. I did not need more than this, and was quite calm.

I used the water I had been given to wet the setting in the wall, which I wanted to loosen. The work went ahead at a good rate, and the bar was completely free on the morning of the second day. Then I cut up my sheets and blankets and made a cable which was quite like a rope-ladder. I waited for nightfall before making good my escape. It was not a moment too early, for the lay brother on duty at the door told me that I was to be sentenced the next day by a tribunal consisting of Theatine monks presided over by a member of the Inquisition.

Towards evening a body, covered by a black shroud decorated with a rich silver fringe, was brought in. I guessed that this was the great nobleman of whom Sangre Moreno had spoken.

When it had become quite dark and there was no noise to be heard I took out the bar, secured the end of the ladder and was on the point of climbing down when the ghosts appeared again on the wall. As you will have guessed, they were the doctor's pupils. They went straight to the dead nobleman and removed his body without disturbing the black, silver-fringed shroud.

When they had gone I opened my window and climbed down with ease. Then I decided to put one of the biers up against the wall to act as a ladder.

As I was on the point of doing this I heard the cemetery gate open. I ran and hid in the portico. I stretched myself out on the bier and covered myself with the silver-fringed sheet whose corner I folded over so I could see who was coming in.

First came an equerry dressed in black, holding a torch in one hand and his sword in the other, then valets wearing mourning; finally a remarkably beautiful woman dressed in black crêpe from head to toe.

The grieving beauty came up to my bier, fell to her knees and uttered the following pitiable words: 'Oh dear mortal remains of the dearest of husbands! If only, like Artemisia, I could mix your ashes with my libation they would circulate in my bloodstream and would revive a heart which beat only for you! But although my religion will not allow me to be your living sepulchre I want at least to remove you from this place of dusty death. I want daily to bathe with my tears the flowers which will grow on your grave, in which I shall soon join you when I breathe my last.'

Having uttered these words, the lady turned to her equerry and said, 'Don Diego, remove the body of your master. We will then bury it in the garden chapel.'

Four strong valets took hold of the bier. They thought they were carrying a corpse and were not far wrong, for I was half-dead with terror.

When the gypsy reached this point in his story he was told that the business of his band required his presence. He took his leave of us and that day we did not see him again.

The Twenty-seventh Day

The next day we stayed in the same place. As the gypsy chief had nothing to do, Rebecca seized the opportunity of asking him to continue the story of his adventures. He needed no persuasion and began as follows:

∽ THE GYPSY CHIEF'S STORY CONTINUED ∽

While I was being carried on the bier I had managed to undo a seam of the black shroud with which I was covered. I could see that the lady was riding in a black-draped litter, but her equerry was on horseback, and those who were carrying me were taking turns to do so in order to go faster. We had left Burgos by one of the gates and proceeded for about an hour. Then we stopped in front of a garden. We went in and I was finally put down in the summer-house, in the middle of a room draped in black and dimly lit by the light of several lamps.

'You may go now, Don Diego,' said the lady to her equerry. 'I want to be left to weep over these beloved remains with which my grief will soon reunite me.'

As soon as the lady was alone she sat down beside me and said, 'You monster! Look where your implacable rage has got you! You condemned us without even listening to us. How will you be able to answer this before the awful tribunal of heaven?'

At that moment another woman appeared, looking like a fury and carrying a dagger in her hand. 'Where are the vile remains of that monster with a human face?' she said. 'I want to know whether he has bowels. I want to rip them out. I want to tear his pitiless heart asunder. I want to crush it in my hands. I want to satisfy my rage.'

It seemed to me at that point that it was time to make myself known. I threw off my black sheet, clasped the knees of the woman with the dagger and said, 'Señora, take pity on a poor schoolboy who hid under this shroud to escape being beaten.'

'You little wretch,' she screamed. 'Where is the body of the Duke of Sidonia?'

'It's in the hands of Dr Sangre Moreno,' I replied. 'His pupils snatched it tonight.'

'Merciful heavens!' exclaimed the woman. 'He alone realized that the duke had been poisoned to death. I am lost!'

'Don't be frightened,' I said. 'The doctor will never dare admit to having snatched bodies from the Capuchin cemetery. And the Capuchins, who believe that the devil carried off the bodies which have disappeared, will not admit that Satan has acquired so much power within the walls of their monastery.'

Then the woman with the knife looked at me severely and said, 'And you, you little wretch, who is there to answer for your discretion?'

'Señora,' I replied, 'today I am to be sentenced by a tribunal of Theatines presided over by a member of the Inquisition. They will probably sentence me to a thousand strokes of the whip. I beg you to ensure my discretion by keeping me out of everyone's sight.'

Instead of replying, the lady opened a trap-door which had been fitted in the corner of the room, and indicated that I should go down through it. I obeyed, and the trap-door was shut above my head.

I went down stairs plunged in darkness which led me to an equally dark underground vault. I bumped into a post. My hands encountered chains. Then my foot struck the stone of a sepulchre on which stood a metal cross. These gloomy objects do not inspire slumber. But I was at that happy age when one sleeps in spite of everything. I lay down on the marble tomb and fell quickly into a deep sleep.

The next day I saw that my prison was lit by a lamp situated in another vault separated from mine by iron bars. Soon the lady with the knife appeared at the bars and put down a basket covered by a cloth. She wanted to speak but her weeping prevented her. She led me to understand by making signs that the place brought terrible memories back to her. I discovered an abundance of food and some books in the basket. I was safe from being beaten and safely out of the sight of any Theatine. These thoughts made my day pass by quite agreeably.

The following day it was the young widow who brought me food. She too tried to speak to me but didn't have the strength to do so. She went away unable to utter a single word.

The day after, she came back with her basket under her arm, which she passed through the iron bars. In the vault where she stood there was a large crucifix. She cast herself down on her knees before this image of our Saviour and prayed as follows: 'Oh God, underneath this marble slab lie the mutilated remains of a sweet, loving creature. He has no doubt already taken his place among the angels of whom he was the very image on earth. Doubtless he is begging you to spare not only his barbaric murderer but also the person who avenged his death and her unwitting accomplice, that unhappy victim of so many horrors.'

The lady then continued praying in a low, but very fervent voice. Eventually she rose, came up to the bars and said to me in a calmer tone, 'Tell me if you are lacking anything, or if there is anything we can do for you.'

'Señora,' I replied, 'I have an aunt called Dalanosa. She lives in the same street as the Theatine monastery. I would like her to know that I am alive and safe.'

'Such a mission could compromise us,' said the lady. 'None the less, I promise to try to find a way to reassure your aunt.'

'Señora,' I replied, 'you are goodness itself. The husband who caused you such unhappiness must indeed have been a monster.'

'Alas,' she said. 'You could not be more wrong. He was the best and the most affectionate of men.'

The next day the woman with the knife brought me food. She seemed less upset or at least more in control of herself.

'My child,' she said. 'I myself went to see your aunt. She seems to love you like a mother. No doubt you have lost your parents.'

I replied that I had indeed lost my mother, and that as I had had the misfortune to fall into my father's inkpot he had banished me for ever from his presence.

The lady asked me to explain what I had just said to her. So I told her my story, which appeared to draw a smile from her. She then said:

'My child, I think I laughed. I haven't done that for a very long time. I had a son. He is lying beneath the marble slab on which you are sitting. I would like to discover him again in you. I was the wet-nurse of the Duchess of Sidonia. I am only a woman of the common people but I have a heart which knows how to love and knows how to hate. People with such a character are never to be despised.'

I thanked the woman and assured her that my feelings towards her would always be those of a son.

Several weeks went by more or less in this way. The two ladies grew more and more used to me as the days passed. The nurse treated me as her son and the duchess showed me great kindness. She would often spend several hours in the vault.

One day, when she seemed a little less sad than usual, I ventured to ask her to tell the story of her misfortunes. She demurred for a long time but in the end she decided to give in to my entreaties. She spoke as follows:

∽ THE DUCHESS OF MEDINA SIDONIA'S STORY ∽

I am the only daughter of Don Emanuel de Val Florida, first secretary of state, who died a short time ago, a man honoured by the sadness of his master at his passing and regretted, moreover, in those European courts that are allied to our all-powerful monarch. I did not get to know this worthy man until the last years of his life.

My youth was spent in Asturias, in the company of my mother, who had separated from her husband early in their marriage and who lived with her father, the Marqués de Astorgas, of whom she was the sole heir.

I do not know to what extent my mother deserved to lose the affections of her husband, but I do know that the long sufferings of her life would have been sufficient to expiate the gravest of sins. She seemed steeped in melancholy. Her eyes were full of tears, her smile full of sorrow. Even her slumbers were not free from sadness: their peace was disturbed by sighs and sobs.

Not that the separation was total. My mother received letters regularly from her husband and replied to them. She had been twice to Madrid to see him but his heart was shut to her for ever. The marquesa had a loving and tender soul. All her affections, which she carried to the point of exaltation, she directed towards her father, and they brought some balm to the bitterness of her enduring sorrows.

As for me, I would find it difficult to define the feelings of my mother towards me. She certainly loved me, but she seemed to be frightened to involve herself in my destiny. Far from preaching at me, she scarcely dared to give me advice at all. In short, if you must know, she did not feel able to teach her daughter virtuous ways, having strayed from them herself. So my childhood was marked by a sort of neglect which would have deprived me of the advantages of a good education if I had not had la Girona, who was first my nurse and then my governess, at my side. You have made her acquaintance, and you know that she has a strong spirit and a cultivated mind. She has done all she could to make me the happiest of women, but inexorable fate defeated all her efforts. Pedro Girón, her husband, was known for his enterprising if dubious character. Having been forced to leave Spain, he had embarked for America and nothing more had been heard of him. La Girona had had only one son by him, with whom I had been suckled. He was a remarkably good-looking child, which caused him to be nicknamed 'Hermosito',[1] a nickname that he kept throughout his short life. We were nourished by the same milk, and we often slept in the same cradle. Up to the age of seven we grew closer and closer together. Then la Girona thought that it was time to tell her son about our difference of rank and the great distance which fate had set between himself and his young girlfriend.

One day, after we had had some childish squabble, la Girona called her son over to her and said with great gravity, 'Never forget that Señora de Val Florida is your mistress and mine and that we are no more than the first servants of her household.'

Hermosito did not question this. He made all my desires his own. He would make it his business to guess and anticipate them. His

---

1 The diminutive of *hermoso* (beautiful).

complete devotion seemed to have ineffable charm for him, and I took great pleasure in seeing him obey me in everything.

La Girona soon saw the dangers of the new relationship which had developed between us and decided to separate us once we reached the age of thirteen. Then she forgot all about it and turned her attention to other matters.

La Girona, as I have said, had a cultivated mind. When we were still very young she put the works of good Spanish authors into our hands and gave us a general notion of history. She also wanted to train our judgement, so she made us think about our reading and showed us how to use it as a basis for moral reflection. It is quite usual for children when they first begin to study history to enthuse over historical figures whose role in history is very brilliant. In such cases my hero became that of my young friend too, and if I changed my mind he too would at once adopt the object of my new enthusiasm.

I had grown so used to Hermosito's submissiveness that I would have been astonished had he shown any resistance to my wishes. But this was hardly to be feared, and I was obliged myself to place limits on my authority or at least use it very carefully. One day I wanted to have a bright shell which I could see lying in deep, clear water. Hermosito jumped in at once and almost drowned. Another time, as he tried to reach a nest that I wanted, a branch broke under him and he hurt himself badly. Thereafter I was very circumspect in expressing my desires, but I found it very agreeable simply to have such great power and not to use it. It was, if my memory serves me aright, the first time I felt pride. I think I have felt it on several occasions since then.

Our thirteenth year went by in this way. When Hermosito had completed it his mother said to him, 'My son, today we have celebrated the thirteenth anniversary of your birth. You are no longer a child and cannot live as close to Señora de Val Florida as you have up to now. Tomorrow you will leave and make your way to Navarre to live with your grandfather.'

La Girona had no sooner finished her sentence than Hermosito manifested the most terrible despair. He wept, fainted and, on coming to his senses, wept again. As for me, I consoled him more than I shared his distress. I looked on him as a being who was wholly dependent on me and who only breathed, as it were, with my permission. I found nothing unusual in his despair but I didn't feel the slightest obligation to reciprocate it. I was too young and too accustomed to the sight of his remarkable good looks for these to make any impression on me.

La Girona was not one of those persons who can be moved by the sight of tears. Those which Hermosito shed were to no avail. He had to leave. But two days later his muleteer returned, looking upset, to report that in going through a wood he had left his mules for an instant and had returned to find Hermosito gone. He had called to him, then searched the forest in vain. Apparently he had been eaten by wolves. La Girona seemed more surprised than distressed to hear this.

'You'll see,' she said. 'The wilful little wretch will come back to us.'

She was not wrong. We soon witnessed the return of the young fugitive. He clasped his mother's knees and said, 'I was born to serve Señora de Val Florida and I will die if you try to banish me from this house.'

A few days later la Girona received a letter from her husband, who had not been heard of for a very long time. He told his wife about the fortune he had made in Vera Cruz and expressed the desire to have his son with him. La Girona, who wanted at all costs to get Hermosito away, readily accepted this offer.

Since his return Hermosito had not been living in the castle. He had been lodged in a farm, which we owned by the sea. One day his mother went to fetch him and made him embark on the boat of a fisherman who had undertaken to escort him to a ship bound for America. During the night Hermosito threw himself overboard and swam to the shore. La Girona forced him to board ship again. These actions were so many sacrifices she made to her duty. It was easy to see at what cost to her heart they were done.

The events which I have just related all came one upon another in quick succession. They were followed by very sad occurrences. My grandfather fell ill and my mother, who had long been declining, mingled her last breath with that of the Marqués de Astorgas.

My father had been expected daily in Asturias but the king could not make up his mind to give him leave, as the state of affairs was not such as to allow him to absent himself. The Marqués de Val Florida wrote to la Girona in the most moving terms and told her to bring me as quickly as possible to Madrid. My father had taken into his service the whole household of the Marqués de Astorgas, of whom I was sole heir. They set off in my company and formed a splendid cortège. The daughter of a secretary of state is in any case pretty sure of being well received from one end of Spain to the other. The honours which I received on that journey contributed, I think, to engendering the ambitious feelings which since then have ruled my destiny. I felt a different sort of pride as I approached Madrid. I had seen that the Marquesa de Val Florida loved and idolized her father, living and breathing only for him, and that she had treated me with a sort of coldness. Now I was to have a father for myself. I promised myself to love him with my whole heart. I wanted to contribute to his happiness. This hope made me proud. I thought of myself as grown up even though I had not yet reached my fourteenth birthday.

These flattering thoughts still filled my mind when my coach entered the courtyard of our mansion. My father received me at the foot of the steps and embraced me affectionately a thousand times. Soon after, he was summoned to the court by order of the king. I withdrew to my apartment. I was very excited, and spent a sleepless night.

The next morning I was summoned by my father. He was drinking his chocolate and he had me take breakfast with him. Then he said to me, 'My dear Leonor, my heart is sad, and my humour has become somewhat melancholy. But since you have been restored to me I hope from now on to see happier days. My study will always be open to you. Bring some needlework with you. I have a more private study for meetings and secret negotiations. I shall try to find time to chat with you in the midst of my work. And I hope that I shall rediscover in such sweet conversation an image of the domestic happiness which I have long since lost.'

Having uttered these words, the marqués rang. His secretary came in, carrying two bags – one containing the letters which had arrived that day, the other letters whose dispatch had been held back.

I spent some time in the study and then came back at dinner time.

301

There I found some of my father's close friends, who, like him, were employed in the most important affairs of state. They spoke about them in my presence without much restraint. I added to their discussions a few naïve remarks which amused them. I saw, or so I believed, that they interested my father. I grew more bold as a result.

The next day I went back to his study as soon as I knew him to be there. He was drinking his chocolate and he said with a satisfied expression, 'It is Friday today. We will receive letters from Lisbon.' Then he rang. His secretary brought the two bags. My father hurriedly rummaged through one; he drew out a letter comprising two sheets, one in code, which he gave to his secretary, the other in writing, which he began to read himself with an expression of pleasure, affection and benevolence.

While he was busy reading, I picked up the envelope and looked at the seal. It was decorated with a fleece over which there was a ducal crown. Alas, those grandiose arms would one day be mine! The next day the French mail arrived, after which came mail from other quarters, but none interested my father as much as the mail from Portugal.

After a whole week had passed, I said to my father as he was drinking his chocolate, 'Today is Friday. The mail from Lisbon will come.'

The secretary came in, and I hurried to rummage in the bag. I drew out my father's favourite letter and ran to give it to him. He rewarded me with a tender kiss.

I repeated the same routine several Fridays in succession. Then, one day, I was brave enough to ask my father what the letter was that he treated differently from all the others.

'This letter,' he replied, 'is from our ambassador in Lisbon, the Duque de Medina Sidonia, my friend, benefactor, and even more than that, for I sincerely believe that my life depends on his.'

'In that case,' I said, 'the charming duke has claims on my attention. I must try and make his acquaintance. I will not ask you what he writes to you in code, but I beg you to read to me the letter written in plain handwriting.'

This suggestion seemed to whip my father into a real fury. He called me a spoiled, wilful, whimsical child. He said other hurtful things. Then he calmed down, and not only read me the Duke of Sidonia's letter but told me to keep it. I have it upstairs. I shall bring it to you the next time I come to see you.

When the gypsy had reached this point in his story, someone came to tell him that the affairs of his band required his presence, so he left and we did not see him again that day.

The Twenty-eighth Day

———————————— ∽ ————————————

We all met for breakfast very early. Seeing the gypsy chief to be at leisure, Rebecca asked him to continue his story, which he did as follows:

∽ THE GYPSY CHIEF'S STORY CONTINUED ∽

The duchess did indeed bring me the letter of which she had spoken the day before.

THE DUCHESS OF MEDINA SIDONIA'S STORY ∽ CONTINUED ∽

The letter read as follows:

The Duque de Medina Sidonia to the Marqués de Val Florida.

You will find, dear friend, in the coded dispatch an account of how our negotiations have progressed. In this letter I'd like to tell you about the devout and flirtatious court at which I am condemned to live. One of my people will take this letter to the frontier, which means that I shall be able to elaborate on the subject with greater confidence.

The king, Don Pedro de Braganza,[1] continues to make convents the scenes of his amorous intrigues. He has left the abbess of the Ursulines for the prioress of the Visitandines. His Majesty desires that I accompany him on his amorous pilgrimages, and for the good of our affairs I have to submit to his wishes. The king stands in the presence of the prioress, separated from her by a menacing grille, which it is said can be lowered by a

1 Reigned 1683–1706.

304

secret mechanism in the control of the omnipotent monarch.

The rest of us are distributed among other parlours, in which the young nuns receive us. The Portuguese take great pleasure in the conversation of nuns, which is scarcely more sensible than the warbling of cage-birds, whom they resemble, insofar as they live similarly enclosed lives. But the touching pallor of these holy virgins, their devout sighs, the amorous turn they give to the language of piety, their half-naïve remarks and their vague yearnings, these, I think, are what charm Portuguese gentlemen and what they would not find in the ladies of Lisbon.

Everything in these houses of retreat tends to intoxicate the heart and the senses. The very air which one breathes is balmy. There are rows upon rows of flowers in front of the images of saints. A glimpse beyond the parlour reveals solitary dormitories, decorated and perfumed in the same way. The sound of the profane guitar mingling with the chords of the sacred organ, drowns the sweet whisperings of young lovers glued to each side of the grille. Such is the way of life in Portuguese convents.

As for me, I can be induced to partake of such tender folly for a short time but then these seductive discussions of passion and love recall swiftly to mind thoughts of crime and murder. Yet I have only committed one. I killed a friend who saved your life and mine. The elegant ways of polite society led to those disastrous events which have caused my life to wither. I was then at that burgeoning age when the heart is open to happiness as well as to virtue. Mine would no doubt have been open to love, but such an emotion could not arise amid such cruel memories. I could not hear love spoken of without seeing my hands stained with blood.

Yet I felt the need to love. The feelings in my heart which would have become love turned into a sort of general benevolence which extended to all around me. I loved my country; I loved above all else the good Spanish people who were so loyal to their religion, their kings, their word. The Spanish people returned my affection, and the court then found that I was too well loved.

Since then I have been able to serve my country in honourable exile. I have also, although from afar, been able to do some good for my vassals. The love of my country and my fellow-man has filled my life with sweet emotions.

As for that other love which might have adorned the springtime of my life, what can I expect from it now? I have made my decision. I will be the last Duke of Sidonia.

I know that grandees' daughters aspire to marry me but they do not realize that the gift of my hand is a dangerous present. My humour cannot adapt itself to the ways of today. Our fathers considered their wives to be the depositories of their happiness and honour. Poison and the dagger, those were in old Castile the punishment for infidelity. I am far from blaming our ancestors but I would not wish to find myself in the position of imitating them. So, as I have said, it is better that I should be the last of my house.

As my father reached this point in the letter he seemed to hesitate and not to want to continue to read it out. But I persuaded him to pick it up again, and to read out the following:

I rejoice with you in the happiness you find in the company of dear Leonor. At her age reason must take on highly seductive forms. What you tell me proves to me that you are happy, and that makes me happy myself.

I could not listen to any more. I fell to my father's knees and embraced them. I made his happiness, I was assured of doing so and I was carried away with pleasure.

After these first moments of joy had passed, I asked what the age of the Duke of Sidonia was.

'He is five years younger than me, that is to say thirty-five,' said my father. 'But,' he added, 'his is one of those faces that look young until well on in years.'

I was of an age at which young girls have not yet thought about men's ages. A boy who, like me, was only fourteen years old would have seemed a mere child unworthy of my attention. My father did not seem old to me, and the duke, being younger than my father, seemed to me necessarily to be a young man. That was the idea I then formed and it helped subsequently to decide my fate.

Then I asked what the murders were of which the duke had spoken.

At this my father grew very grave, thought for a short while, and then said:

'My dear Leonor, those events are closely related to the separation which you witnessed between your mother and me. I should perhaps not tell you about it, but sooner or later your curiosity might lead you to speculate. Rather than let your thoughts brood on a matter which is as delicate as it is distressing, I prefer to tell you about it myself.'

After this preamble my father told me the story of his life, beginning as follows:

∽ THE MARQUÉS DE VAL FLORIDA'S STORY ∽

You know that your mother was the last member of the house of Astorgas. That house and the house of Val Florida are the most ancient houses in Asturias. It was by the general wish of the province that I was betrothed to Señora de Astorgas. We had accustomed ourselves early to the idea and the feelings we had formed for one another were such as to ensure a happy marriage. Circumstances delayed our union, however, and I only married when I reached the age of twenty-five.

Six weeks after our wedding I told my wife that as all my ancestors had embraced the profession of arms I believed myself obliged by honour to follow their example, and, besides, there were many garrisons in Spain where we could pass the time more agreeably than in Asturias. Señora de Val Florida replied that she would always be at one with me in matters in which I might think my honour to be involved. So it was decided that I should serve. I wrote to the court and obtained a company of horse in the regiment of Medina Sidonia; it was garrisoned at Barcelona, where you were born.

War broke out. We were sent to Portugal where we were to join up with the army of Don Sancho de Saavedra. This general opened hostilities at the famous skirmish of Vila Marga. Our regiment, at that time the strongest in the army, was ordered to wipe out the English troops who formed the enemy's left wing. Twice we threw ourselves at them without success, and were preparing to attack for a third time when an unknown officer appeared before us. He was in the first flush of youth and dressed in shining armour. 'Follow me!' he said. 'I am your colonel, the Duke of Sidonia.'

Indeed, he did well to identify himself because otherwise we might have taken him for the angel of battles or some other prince of the celestial host. His appearance really did have something divine about it.

This time the English troops were routed and the triumph of the day belonged to our regiment. I had reason to believe that next to the duke it was I who distinguished himself most by his actions. At least I had a flattering indication that this was so, in that my illustrious colonel did me the honour of asking me to be his friend.

It was no vain compliment on his part. We became real friends, without this friendship in the duke's case taking on any sign of patronage or in mine any hint of inferiority. Spaniards are criticized for a sort of gravity that they bring to their manner of behaviour, but it is by avoiding familiarity that we are able to be proud without arrogance, and combine deference with nobility.

After the victory of Vila Marga there were several promotions. The duke was made a general; I was promoted to the rank of lieutenant-colonel and to be first adjutant to the general. We were given the dangerous mission of stopping the enemy crossing the Douro river. The duke took up a position which gave him a fair advantage and held it for a long time. Eventually the whole English army advanced towards us. But even this overwhelming superiority did not cause us to retreat. There was a terrible carnage which would have ended with our being wiped out if a certain van Berg, the commander of the Walloon companies, had not unexpectedly come to our aid with three thousand men. He performed remarkable feats of bravery and not only averted the danger but left us masters of the field. In spite of that, we soon fell back to join the main body of the army.

When we, together with the Walloons, struck camp, the duke approached me and said, 'My dear Val Florida, the most appropriate number for a friendship is, I know, the number two. It cannot be exceeded without breaking its sacred laws, yet I think that the outstanding service which van Berg has done us justifies an exception being made. We owe him, I think, the offer of both our friendships, which would make him a third in the bond that unites us.'

I agreed with the duke, who then went to see van Berg and offered him friendship with a gravity which reflected the importance he attached to the title of friend. Van Berg seemed taken aback by this.

'Señor duque,' he said, 'Your Excellency does me great honour, but I am in the habit of getting drunk most days. Whenever by chance I am not drunk, I gamble as heavily as I can. If Your Excellency hasn't the same habits I don't believe that our bond of friendship would last very long.'

This reply at first took the duke aback, then it made him laugh. He assured van Berg of his complete esteem and promised to use his influence at court to procure for him a handsome reward. But van Berg wanted recompense in the form of money. The duke left for Madrid and obtained for our rescuer the barony of Deulen in the proximity of Malines. Van Berg sold it that very day to Walter van Dyck, a citizen of Amsterdam and a victualler of the army.

So it was that everyone prepared to spend the winter in Coimbra, one of the most important cities of Portugal. Señora de Val Florida came and joined me there. She enjoyed polite society and I willingly opened my house to the highest ranking officers of the army, but the duke and I took little part in the tumultuous social life. All our moments were filled with serious pursuits. Virtue was the idol of the young Duke of Sidonia. The public good was his dream. We made a special study of Spain's constitution, forming many plans for her future prosperity. To make her people good, we first decided to make them love virtue and then abandon their self-interest, which seemed to us a very easy task. We also wanted to revive the old chivalric spirit. A Spaniard, we thought, must be as faithful to his wife as to his king, and everyone must have a brother-in-arms. We were not far from thinking that one day the world would talk about our friendship, and that through our example men of honour forming similar unions would in future find the paths of virtue less arduous and more secure.

My dear Leonor, I would feel ashamed to tell you about such absurdities but it has long been observed that young gentlemen who have strayed into excessive zeal may in the fullness of time become great and valuable persons. On the other hand, youthful Catos, once age has cooled their ardour, can never rise above the strict calculations of self-interest. Their minds are circumscribed by their souls, which makes them wholly incapable of those thoughts which constitute the statesman or the man who serves his fellow-men. This rule admits few exceptions.

Thus, by giving our imagination free rein to pursue its virtuous objects, the duke and I hoped to bring about in Spain the reign of Saturn and Rhea. Meanwhile, however, van Berg was actually bringing back the age of gold. He had sold his barony of Deulen and had received eight hundred thousand livres in ready money for it. Then he had declared and sworn on his word of honour not only to spend all his money during the two months of our winter quarters but also to run up debts of a hundred thousand francs. Our prodigal Fleming then found that to keep his word he had to spend about one thousand four hundred pistoles a day, which wasn't all that easy in a city like Coimbra. He was afraid that he had given his word incautiously. It was suggested to him that he could use part of his money to help the poor and bring people happiness, but van Berg rejected this idea, saying that he had sworn to spend the money, not give it away. It was a point of honour with him not to use it on benefactions. Gambling didn't even count because he had the chance of winning, and losing money was not the same as spending it.

This cruel dilemma seemed to upset van Berg. For several days he seemed preoccupied. Finally he discovered a way which, so it seemed to him, did not compromise his honour. He brought together all the available cooks, musicians, actors and others who made their living from pleasurable pursuits. He gave feasts in the morning and put on plays in the evening. Fairs were held in front of his house, and if, in spite of all his efforts, the one thousand four hundred pistoles had not been spent, he threw the rest out of the window, declaring that such an act was not against the laws of prodigality.

As soon as van Berg had managed in this way to appease his

conscience, he recovered all his cheerfulness. He had a fund of native wit and used any amount of it to defend his bizarre behaviour, which was attacked from all quarters. This defence, which he often repeated, lent his conversation an air of brilliance which distinguished it from that of us Spaniards, who were all very reserved and grave.

Van Berg often visited me together with all the other high-ranking officers. He also came at times when I was not there. I knew this and did not take offence at it. I thought that his excessive self-confidence led him to believe that he was welcome everywhere at any time of day. The general public were more clear-sighted than I, and it was not long before rumours began to circulate which were injurious to my honour. I did not know of them but the duke had been told. He knew how much I was attached to my wife, and his friendship for me made him suffer vicariously in my place.

One morning the duke went to see Señora de Val Florida, threw himself at her knees and begged her to remember her duty and to refuse to receive van Berg at moments when she was alone. I don't know exactly what reply he received but van Berg dropped by that morning and no doubt was told of the exhortations to virtue which Señora de Val Florida had been given. The duke went to see van Berg, intending to speak to him in the same way and to bring him back to a more virtuous frame of mind. He found that he was out and came back after dinner. Van Berg's rooms were filled with visitors but van Berg himself was alone, sitting at a gaming-table, shaking dice in a cup. I was there too, talking to young Fonseca, the duke's brother-in-law and the much-adored husband of a sister of whom the duke was very fond.

Sidonia accosted van Berg in a friendly way and asked him with a laugh how his spending was going.

Van Berg gave him a look of anger and said, 'I spend my money to receive friends, not dishonourable people who interfere in affairs which do not concern them.'

Some of those present heard this exchange.

'Is it I,' said the duke, 'who is being called dishonourable? Van Berg, take back what you have said.'

'I don't take anything back,' said van Berg.

The duke knelt and said, 'Van Berg, you did me a very great service. Why do you want now to deprive me of my honour? I beg you, recognize me as a man of honour.'

Van Berg uttered the word 'coward'.

The duke rose calmly, drew his dagger from his belt, put it on the table and said, 'This affair cannot be settled by an ordinary duel. One of us must die, the sooner the better. We will each throw the dice in turn. The one who obtains the higher score will take up the dagger and plunge it into the heart of the other.'

'Excellent!' exclaimed van Berg. 'Now that's what I call a serious gamble; but I swear that if I win I shall not spare Your Excellency.'

Those looking on were transfixed with terror.

Van Berg picked up the cup and threw two twos. 'The devil!' he cried. 'It seems that I am out of luck.'

Then the duke shook the cup and threw a five and a six. He picked up the dagger, plunged it into van Berg's chest, turned to those who had witnessed the scene and said, 'Señores, I ask you to pay homage for the last time to this young gentleman, who, for his heroic courage, deserved a better fate. As for me, I shall go at once to the commissioner-general of armies to place myself at the mercy of the king's justice.'

You can imagine the stir caused by this incident. Not only the Spaniards, but even our enemies the Portuguese, held the duke in high esteem. When the news reached Lisbon the archbishop of that city, who was also patriarch of the Indies, established that the house where the duke was detained belonged to the chapter of the cathedral and had always been held to be a place of inviolable sanctuary, so that the duke could stay there without fearing the force of secular authority. The duke was deeply moved by this act of solicitude, but declared that he did not intend to take advantage of this privilege.

The commissioner-general indicted the duke, but the Council of Castile decided to intervene whatever the outcome. Furthermore, the High Marshal of Aragon, whose army had just been disbanded, claimed that it fell to him alone to judge the duke, since he had been born in his province and belonged to the ancient order of *Ricos Hombres*. In short, a number of persons fought for the privilege of saving the duke.

In all this turmoil I pondered long and hard what might have given rise to the quarrel between the duke and van Berg, and asked everyone about it. In the end a charitable soul took pity on me and informed me of what I would have preferred not to have known.

I had been convinced – why, I do not know – that my wife could feel affection only for me. It was some days before I could be persuaded to the contrary. In the end, having been enlightened by other circumstances, I went to see Señora de Val Florida and said to her:

'Señora, I have been informed by letter that your father is not well. I think it would be fitting for you to be at his side. Your daughter in any case requires your attention and I think that from now on you will have to live in Asturias.'

Señora de Val Florida lowered her eyes and accepted her sentence with resignation. You know how we have since lived. Your mother had many estimable qualities and even virtues, which I have always recognized.

Meanwhile the trial of the duke took a strange turn. Walloon officers turned it into a national issue. They claimed that since Spanish grandees felt at liberty to murder Flemings, they found themselves obliged to leave the service of Spain. The Spaniards replied that it was a matter of a duel, not an assassination. It reached the point where the king appointed a commission of twelve Spaniards and twelve Flemings, not to sit in judgement on the duke but to determine whether van Berg had been killed in a duel or had been murdered.

The Spanish officers voted first, and, as one might suppose, favoured the hypothesis of a duel. Eleven Flemings were of the opposite opinion. They did not justify their view but made a great deal of noise about it.

The twelfth, who, being the youngest, voted last, had already made a name for himself in affairs of honour. He was called Don Juan van Worden.

Here I interrupted the gypsy to say, 'I have the honour of being van Worden's son and I hope that there is nothing in your story liable to slight his honour.'

313

'I assure you,' replied the gypsy, 'that I will faithfully record the words that the Marqués de Val Florida uttered to his daughter.'

When it was the turn of Don Juan van Worden to cast his vote, he spoke and said, 'Gentlemen, I think there are two aspects of a duel which define its essence. First, the challenge, or in its place, the encounter; second, the equality of arms, or if not that, equal chances of killing the adversary. Thus, for example, a man armed with a musket could be opposed to another who only had a pistol, provided that the first fired from a distance of a hundred paces and the second from four paces, and on the condition that it had been settled in advance who should have the first shot. In the present case the same arm was at the disposal of both. No greater equality of arms could be required. The dice were not loaded so they had an equal chance of killing each other. So there is no objection to be made on that score. Finally, the challenge was clearly made and accepted by both parties.

'I confess that it is with great regret that I find the duel – that most noble of combats – reduced in this case to chance, to one of those games which gentlemen should only engage in with extreme discretion. But following the principles I have set out it seems to me indisputable that the affair which we must consider is a duel and not a murder.

'It is my conviction which makes me speak in this way, although I hate having to contradict the opinion of my eleven comrades. Being almost certain of having the misfortune of having lost their affection, and in the hope of forestalling in the least violent manner any manifestation of their displeasure, I ask all eleven of them to do me the honour of duelling with me, six tomorrow morning and five tomorrow afternoon.'

This argument gave rise to a general murmuring but the challenge had, in propriety, to be taken up. Van Worden wounded the first six, who came in the morning. He then began on the last five. The first three were wounded by van Worden, the tenth wounded him in the shoulder and the eleventh ran him through and left him for dead.

A skilful surgeon saved van Worden's life. After this, there was no more talk of commission or trial and the king pardoned the Duke of Sidonia.

War began again in the spring and we waged it honourably, although no longer with the same spirit as before. We had felt the first stirrings of unhappiness. The duke had had a great deal of respect for van Berg's courage and military talents. He accused himself of having been excessively concerned about my peace of mind, which he had troubled in so cruel a way. He learned that it was not enough to do good, one had to know how to do it. As for me, like many husbands I locked my sufferings inside myself, only to feel them all the more acutely. We made no more plans for Spain's prosperity.

At last, Don Luis de Haro negotiated the famous Paix des Pyrénées.[2] The duke decided to travel. Together we visited Italy, France and England. On our return, my noble friend was admitted to the Council of Castile and I was made recorder to the same council.

Travel and growing age had given maturity to the duke's mind. Not only had he renounced the ill-judged virtue of his youth but he had acquired a high degree of prudence. The public good was no longer his dream, it was his passion. He knew, however, that one cannot achieve everything at once; that it was necessary to predispose men's minds to accept things, and to hide carefully one's means and one's ends. His caution was such that at the council he seemed never to have an opinion of his own but always to follow that of others. Yet it was he who had inspired those opinions. The care the duke took to hide his talents and to stop others seeing them only served to make them more conspicuous. The Spanish people sensed them and loved him for them. The court became jealous of them. The duke was offered the embassy in Lisbon. He realized that he would not be allowed to refuse the offer so he accepted, on condition that I was made secretary of state.

Since then I have not seen him. But our hearts remain united.

When the gypsy chief reached this point in his story, someone came to tell him that his presence was required for business concerning his

---

2 The peace treaty of the Pyrenees was signed in 1659; this date does not fit the supposed age of the Duke of Medina Sidonia (according to the fiction, he would not yet have been born).

band. As soon as he left, Velásquez spoke and said, 'I have tried in vain to concentrate all my attention on the gypsy chief's words but I am unable to discover any coherence whatsoever in them. I do not know who is speaking and who is listening. Sometimes the Marqués de Val Florida is telling the story of his life to his daughter, sometimes it is she who is relating it to the gypsy chief, who in turn is repeating it to us. It is a veritable labyrinth. I had always thought that novels and other works of that kind should be written in several columns like chronological tables.'

'You are right,' said Rebecca. 'One would find in one column, for example, the story of the Marquesa de Val Florida being unfaithful to her husband, in the other the effects this event had on him. That would no doubt clarify the story.'

'That's not what I mean,' replied Velásquez. 'Take the example of the Duke of Sidonia, whose character I am about to find out about although I have already seen him laid out dead on his bier. Wouldn't it be better to start with the war in Portugal? I could then find in the second column Dr Sangre Moreno thinking about the medical arts, and so would not be surprised by his odd behaviour.'

'Yes, indeed,' interrupted Rebecca. 'Continual surprises don't keep one's interest in the story alive. One can never foresee what will happen subsequently.'

I then spoke, and said that my father was very young during the war in Portugal and that the intelligence he had shown in the affair of the Duke of Medina Sidonia was to be admired.

'That is indisputable,' said Rebecca. 'If your father hadn't duelled with eleven officers a quarrel might well have arisen. This he did very well to avoid.'

It seemed to me that Rebecca was making fun of all of us. I detected in her character an element of mockery and scepticism. 'Who knows,' I wondered, 'whether she might not relate to us adventures quite different from the story of the heavenly twins?' And I decided to ask her to one day. Meanwhile the time had come to disperse, and we all went on our own ways.

The Twenty-ninth Day

We reassembled early and as the gypsy chief was free, he took up once more the story of his adventures:

✍ THE GYPSY CHIEF'S STORY CONTINUED ✍

After telling me the story of her father, the Duchess of Sidonia did not come for several days. It was la Girona who brought me my basket. She also told me that my affair had been settled, thanks to my Theatine great-uncle on my mother's side, Fray Gerónimo Sántez. The fact that I had got off was generally well received. The decree of the Inquisition spoke only of imprudence and of two years' penance. I was only referred to by the initial letters of my name. La Girona passed on a message from aunt Dalanosa that I had to remain in hiding for the two years and that she would return to Madrid, where she would set about securing the income from the *quinta*, that is, the farm which had been assigned to me.

I asked la Girona if she thought I ought to spend the two years in the vault where I presently was. She replied that that would be safest and that in any case precautions had to be taken for her own safety.

The next day it was the duchess who came. I was delighted because I liked her better than her haughty nurse. I also was keen to hear more of her story. I asked her to continue, which she did as follows:

THE DUCHESS OF MEDINA SIDONIA'S STORY ✍ CONTINUED ✍

I thanked my father for the trust he had shown me in telling me about the most remarkable happenings of his life, and the following Friday I again handed him the letter of the Duke of Sidonia. He did not read it to me any more than he did those which he subsequently

317

received. But he spoke to me about his friend and I realized that no conversation interested him as much as this.

Some time later I received the visit of a lady who was an officer's widow. Her father had been born a vassal of the duke, and she was claiming a fief which was in the jurisdiction of the Duchy of Sidonia. Bestowing patronage had never happened to me before. I was flattered by this chance to do so. I wrote a memorandum in which I proved the widow's rights clearly and precisely. I took it to my father, who was pleased with it and sent it to the duke, as I had foreseen. The duke recognized the widow's claim and wrote me a letter full of compliments on my precocious intellectual powers.

Later I had another occasion to write to him and I received a second letter, in which he told me how charmed he was by my mind. And indeed I did all I could to cultivate my wit and intellect. I was helped in this by la Girona's intelligence, which is very great. I had just completed my fifteenth year when I wrote this second letter.

I was sixteen when one day I heard from my father's study a commotion in the street and what sounded like the cheers of an assembled crowd. I ran to the window. I saw many excited people triumphantly accompanying a gilded coach on which I recognized the arms of Sidonia. A crowd of *hidalgos*[1] and pages rushed to the coach doors and I saw a very handsome man step down. He was dressed in the Castilian fashion, which our court had just given up, that is to say, he wore a ruff, a short coat and a plume. What set off this beautiful costume was the diamond-studded fleece which he wore on his breast.

'It's him!' cried my father. 'I knew he would come!'

I withdrew to my apartment and did not see the duke until the following day. But thereafter I saw him every day, for he did not leave my father's house.

The duke had been recalled on very important business. It was necessary to quell violent unrest, which had been caused by the imposition of new taxes in Aragon. This kingdom had its own

1 Gentlemen.

constitutions, among which is that of the *Ricos Hombres*, who were once the equivalent of what Castile called grandees. The Dukes of Sidonia were the oldest of the *Ricos Hombres*, which alone would have earned the duke great respect, but he was also loved for his personal qualities. The duke went to Saragossa and was able to reconcile the interests of the court with the wishes of the Aragonese. He was allowed to choose a reward, and he asked for permission to breathe the air of his native land for a short while.

The duke, who was by nature very straightforward, did not hide the fact that he took pleasure in conversing with me. We were nearly always together while the other friends of my father resolved matters of state. Sidonia admitted to me that he was very jealous by nature and even sometimes violent. Usually he spoke to me about himself or about myself. When this sort of conversation becomes habitual between a man and a woman their relationship soon becomes intimate, so I was not surprised when my father called me into his study to tell me that the duke had asked for my hand in marriage.

I replied that I would not ask him for time for reflection, because I had foreseen that the duke might show a lively interest in the daughter of his friend, and I had thought in advance about his character and the difference in age between us. 'But Spanish grandees intermarry,' I added. 'How will they look on our union? They might go so far as to refuse the familiar form of address to the duke, which is the first sign of their disapproval.'

'That is an objection I myself made to the duke,' said my father. 'He replied that all he asked for was your consent. The rest was his affair.'

Sidonia was not far away. He put in a timid appearance, which contrasted with his natural pride. I was touched by this and I did not keep him waiting too long for my consent. I made two people happy thereby, for my father was more pleased than I can tell you. La Girona was wild with joy.

The next day the duke invited all the grandees then in Madrid to dinner. When they were all present he asked them to sit down and spoke to them as follows:

'Alba, I shall address myself to you since I look upon you as the

319

first among us, not because your house is more famous than mine but out of respect for the hero whose name you bear.[2]

'A presumption among us which does us honour requires us to choose our wives from the daughters of grandees, and without doubt I would despise anyone among us who entered into a *mésalliance* out of motives of wealth or lust.

'The case I wish to place before you is very different. You know that Asturians say that they are as noble as the king and even a bit more so. However exaggerated this expression may be, their titles mostly antedate the Moors and they have the right to look upon themselves as the highest noblemen in Europe.

'Well, the purest blood of Asturias flows in the veins of Leonor de Val Florida. In her it is combined with the rarest virtues. I maintain that such an alliance cannot but bring honour to the house of a Spanish grandee. If anyone is of a different opinion let him pick up this glove, which I now throw down in the midst of this assembly.'

'I shall pick it up,' said the Duke of Alba, addressing Sidonia by the familiar form of address, 'but it is only to give it back to you and to compliment you on so noble a union.'

He then kissed him, as did all the other grandees. When he told me of this scene my father said somewhat sadly to me:

'That's the Sidonia I knew of old, with his notions of chivalry. Be careful not to offend him, Leonor!'

I confess to you that I had in my character a tendency towards pride, but this haughty love of grandeur left me as soon as it was satisfied. I became the Duchess of Sidonia and my heart was full of the sweetest feelings. In private life the duke was the most amiable of men because he was the most affectionate. His kindness was unfailing, his benevolence steadfast, his love constant. His angelic soul was reflected in his features. Only on occasions when some severe emotion changed them did they take on a terrifying aspect which made me tremble. Then, without wishing to, I saw in him the murderer of van Berg. But few things were able to upset Sidonia, and everything about me was able to make him happy. He

2 i.e. Fernando Alvarez de Toledo, Duke of Alba (1507–82), the scourge of the Netherlands.

loved to see me talking and doing things. He guessed the least of my thoughts. I did not think that his love for me could possibly be greater, but the birth of a daughter increased his affection and crowned our happiness.

The day I rose from my confinement, la Girona said to me, 'My dear Leonor, you are a married woman and a happy mother. You have no further need for me. Duty calls me to America.'

I wanted her to stay.

'No,' she said. 'My presence there is necessary.'

La Girona went away and took with her all the happiness I had till then enjoyed. I have described to you this short period of heavenly felicity, which could not last, because apparently so much good fortune is not meant for this world. I haven't the strength today to tell you about my misfortunes. Farewell, young friend. Tomorrow you will see me again.

The story of the young duchess interested me deeply. I wanted to know how it continued, and to learn how so much happiness could change into such awful adversity. While I pondered on this, I thought also of what la Girona had said about my having to stay for two years in the vault. That wasn't what I had in mind at all and I set about preparing some means of escape.

The duchess brought me my provisions. Her eyes were red, and she looked as though she had wept a great deal. She told me, however, that she felt strong enough to tell me the story of her misfortunes. This is how she carried on:

I have told you that la Girona held the post of duenna mayor. She was replaced by a certain Doña Menzia, a thirty-year-old woman who was still quite pretty and whose mind was not altogether uncultivated, which from time to time earned her a place in our society. On those occasions she would behave as though she was in love with my husband. I only laughed at this, and he paid no attention to it. Otherwise la Menzia sought to please me and especially to get to know me well. Often she would bring the conversation round to frivolous topics or she told me the gossip of the town. More than once I was obliged to tell her to be silent.

I had breast-fed my daughter and was fortunate enough to wean her before the events which I still have to relate to you. My first misfortune was the death of my father. He suffered an attack of an acute and violent illness and died in my arms, giving me his blessing and little foreseeing any of what was going to happen to us.

There were uprisings in Biscay. The duke was dispatched there. I accompanied him as far as Burgos. We had estates in all the Spanish provinces, and houses in nearly all Spanish cities. But in Burgos the Dukes of Sidonia had only a country house about a league outside the city, the very house where you now are. The duke left me there with all his retinue and went away to his destination. One day, on returning home, I heard a commotion in the courtyard. I was told that a thief had been discovered; he had been knocked out by being hit on the head with a stone, but he was a young man more handsome than had ever been seen before.

Some valets carried him to where I was standing. I recognized Hermosito.

'Heavens!' I cried. 'This is no thief, but a young man from Asturias who was brought up in my grandfather's house.'

I then turned to the major-domo and told him to take him in and look after him carefully. I even think I said that he was la Girona's son, but I don't have a clear memory of having said so.

The next day Doña Menzia told me that the young man was feverish and that in his delirium he spoke a great deal about me in very passionate terms.

I replied to Doña Menzia that if she continued to speak to me in such a way I would have her dismissed.

'We'll see about that!' she replied. I ordered her then not to appear again in my presence.

The next day she sent word to me asking to be forgiven. She came and threw herself at my feet. I forgave her.

A week later, as I was alone, I saw la Menzia come in supporting Hermosito, who seemed extremely weak.

'You commanded me to come,' he said in a faint voice.

I gave la Menzia a surprised glance, but I did not want to upset la Girona's son, so I had a chair set down for him a few paces from me.

'My dear Hermosito,' I said. 'Your mother has never mentioned your name to me. I would like to know what has happened to you since we were separated.'

Hermosito found difficulty in speaking but he made a great effort and spoke as follows:

∾ HERMOSITO'S STORY ∾

When I saw our ship set sail I lost all hope of seeing the shores of my native land again and deplored the severity that my mother had displayed in banishing me, while being unable to understand the reasons for it. I had been told that I was your servant and I served you as zealously as I was able. I had never disobeyed you. 'Why then,' I asked myself, 'drive me away as though I had committed the gravest of faults?' The more I thought about it, the less I was able to understand it.

On the fifth day of our voyage we found ourselves in the middle of Don Fernando Arudez's squadron. We were told to steer to the stern of the admiral's vessel, where there was a gilded balcony decked out with flags of many colours. There I saw Don Fernando with the resplendent chains of several orders around his neck. Officers stood around him respectfully. He had a loudhailer in his hand, and asked us several questions about our encounters at sea before ordering us on our way. Once we had passed, the captain said to me, 'There's a marqués. But he began life like that ship's boy over there who is sweeping the cabin.'

As Hermosito reached this point in his story he repeatedly cast embarrassed glances at la Menzia. I thought him to be indicating that he was afraid of talking about himself in her company. So I asked her to leave. In doing this I thought only of my friendship for la Girona. The idea that I would be suspected of anything did not even enter my mind. When la Menzia had gone out Hermosito continued as follows:

I believe, Señora, that being nourished from the same springs as you were, my soul was formed in sympathy with yours. It cannot think except of you and through you. Everything which touches it relates to you. The captain told me that Don Fernando had become a marqués, having begun as a ship's boy. I remembered that you were a marquesa. It seemed to me that nothing could be finer than to become a marqués and I asked how Don Fernando had set about it. The captain explained that he had risen from one rank to the next, distinguishing himself by heroic deeds. From that moment on I decided to become a sailor, and I practised climbing the rigging. The captain in whose care I had been placed tried his best to stop me, but I resisted him and by the time we arrived in Vera Cruz I was not a bad sailor.

My father's house was by the sea. We reached it by longboat. My father received me surrounded by a group of young mulatto girls, whom he made me embrace one after the other. They danced for me and acted provocatively in many other ways. The evening was spent in great frivolity.

The next day the *corregidor* of Vera Cruz had my father told that if one lived in the style he did, one did not keep one's son at home, and that he had to send me to the Theatine college. My father obeyed, albeit reluctantly.

I found a teacher at the college who, in order to encourage us to study, told us often that the Marqués de Campo Salez, then second secretary of state, had like us begun life as a poor student, and that he owed his good fortune to his hard work. On learning that one could become a marqués by this means, I studied with great fervour for two years.

The *corregidor* of Vera Cruz was replaced. His successor had less rigid principles. My father thought that he could risk taking me back again.

Once again I found myself prey to the exuberance of the young mulatto girls, which my father encouraged in every conceivable way. I was far from pleased at this frivolity, but they instructed me in many things of which I had been ignorant up to then, and I realized at last why I had been banished from Asturias.

At the same time a most ominous change occurred in me. New emotions grew in my heart and revived in me the memory of the games I played when little. The thought of the happiness I had lost at the gardens of Astorgas in which I had run about with you, the hazy recollection of a thousand proofs of your kindness: too many enemies assaulted my frail sanity all at once and neither it nor my health were able to resist them. The doctors said that I had a wasting fever. As for me, I did not believe myself to be ill but the turmoil of my senses was such that I often believed that I could see things that were not in front of my eyes and that had no reality. It was you, Señora, who appeared most often to my deluded imagination; not as you are today but more or less as you were when I left you. At night I would wake up with a start and you would seem to pierce the darkness, and appear shining and radiant before me. If I went out the sounds of the countryside seemed to repeat your name again and again.

Sometimes you seemed to cross the plain before my eyes. If I looked at the heavens to beg that my torment cease, I saw there your image imprinted on the sky.

I discovered that I suffered less in churches and that prayer brought me relief above all else. I ended by spending whole days in these devout refuges. A monk whose hair had turned white in the practice of penance accosted me one day and said, 'Oh my son, your heart is full of an immense love which is not meant for this world. Come to my cell. I will show you the way to paradise.'

I followed him to his cell and saw hair shirts and other instruments of martyrdom, which did not frighten me much. I was suffering from a quite different pain. The monk read to me several passages from the lives of the saints. I asked him to let me take the book away and I read it all night. My head filled with new thoughts. In a dream I saw the heavens open and I saw angels who all looked rather like you, as a matter of fact.

News of your marriage to the Duke of Sidonia then reached Vera Cruz. For some time I had been thinking of devoting myself to the religious life. I found happiness in praying night and day for your felicity in this world and your salvation in the next. My devout teacher told me that in the monasteries of America there had been much relaxation of the rule and he advised me to undertake my noviciate in a monastery in Madrid.

I let my father know of my resolve. He had always frowned on my devotions, but not wanting to dissuade me from them openly he asked me to await the arrival of my mother, which was shortly due. I told him that I no longer had parents in this world and that heaven was now my family. To this he had no reply. Then I went to see the *corregidor*, who approved of my plans and embarked me on the next ship. On arriving in Bilbao I learnt that my mother had set sail for America. My letters of obedience were for Madrid. I set out on that road. In passing through Burgos, I learnt that you were residing not far from the city. I decided to see you for one last time before leaving the world. It seemed to me that, having seen you, I would be able to pray for your salvation with even greater fervour.

So I took the road to your country house. I entered the outer courtyard and decided to look for an old retainer, one of those whom you had in Astorgas for I knew that they had not left you. I wanted to make myself known to the first one who came by, and ask him to find me a place from which I could see you as you stepped into your carriage. For I wanted to see you, not to introduce myself to you.

The only people who came by were unknown to me and I began to feel ashamed at being there. I went into a quite empty room, then I thought I saw someone I knew go by. I went out and was knocked down by a blow from a stone . . . But Señora, I see that my story has made a deep impression on you . . .

'I can assure you,' said the duchess, 'that Hermosito's devout ramblings had only inspired me with pity.' She then continued as follows:

But when he had spoken of the gardens of Astorgas, and of my childhood games, the memory of the past, the thoughts of my present happiness, a sudden fear for the future and a vague feeling of sad melancholy had weighed down my heart and I found myself bathed in my own tears.

Hermosito got up and I thought that he wanted to kiss the hem of my dress. His knees buckled under him. His head fell on my knees and his arms held me in a strong embrace. At that moment I looked into a mirror in which I saw la Menzia and the duke; his features wore an expression of rage which was so frightening that it was hard to recognize him.

My senses froze in horror. I looked again into the same mirror and saw nothing. I freed myself from Hermosito's arms and cried out. La

Menzia came. I ordered her to look after the young man and withdrew into a study. The vision I had seen caused me deep worry but I was assured that the duke was absent.

The next day I asked for news of Hermosito. I was told that he was no longer in the house.

Three days later, as I was ready to retire to bed, la Menzia handed me a letter from the duke. It consisted only of the following words:

Do what Doña Menzia tells you to do. I, your husband and your judge, command you so to do.

La Menzia bound my eyes with a handkerchief. I felt my arms seized and I was led down to this vault.

I heard the rattle of chains. My blindfold was removed; I saw Hermosito attached by the neck to the pillar against which you are leaning. There was no life in his eyes. He was extremely pale.

'Is that you?' he said in a dying voice. 'I find it difficult to speak to you. I am not given any water. My tongue is stuck to my palate. My agony will not be long. If I go to heaven I shall speak there about you.'

As Hermosito uttered these words a gunshot, which came from the slit you see in this wall, shattered his arm. He cried out, 'Oh God, forgive my executioners.'

A second shot rang out from the same direction. I don't know what effect it had for I lost consciousness.

When I recovered the use of my senses I was surrounded by my ladies-in-waiting, who seemed to me to know nothing. All that they told me was that la Menzia had left the house. In the course of the morning an equerry came from my husband. He told me that the duke had gone to France on a secret mission and would not be back for some months. Left to myself I pulled myself together. I laid my case before the supreme judge of all and gave all my attention to my daughter.

Three months later la Girona appeared. She had come back from America and had already looked for her son in Madrid, in the monastery where he was to undertake his noviciate. Not having found him there, she had gone to Bilbao and had followed Hermosito's tracks to Burgos. Fearing her distress and her anger, I told her part of the truth. She was able to drag the rest out of me.

327

As you know, the woman has a hard and violent character. Fury, rage and every terrible, destructive feeling took hold of her heart. I was too distressed myself to be able to bring her relief from her sorrows.

One day la Girona, while rearranging her room, discovered a door hidden behind a wall-hanging, and through it went down to the vault. She recognized the pillar which I had described to her. It was still stained with blood. She came to see me in a state bordering on frenzy. Thereafter she shut herself away in her room, or rather she went down into that awful vault to think of ways of exacting vengeance.

A month later, I was told that the duke had returned. He came in in a calm and composed manner, greeted my daughter affectionately and then, asking me to sit down, seated himself beside me.

'Señora,' he said. 'I have thought long and hard about how I should behave towards you. I will not alter my behaviour. In the house you will be served with the same degree of respect and you will receive from me in appearance, at least, the same signs of esteem. This will last until your daughter reaches the age of sixteen years . . .'

'And when my daughter is sixteen, what will happen?' I asked the duke.

At this moment la Girona came in, bringing chocolate. The idea crossed my mind that it was poisoned.

But the duke spoke again and said, 'When your daughter is sixteen, I shall say to her, "Daughter, your features remind me of those of a woman whose story I shall tell you. She was beautiful and her soul seemed even more so. But her virtue was feigned. By putting on appearances, she managed to make the greatest match in Spain. One day her husband had to leave her for a few weeks. At once she summoned from her province a little wretch. They remembered their previous loves and fell into each other's arms. Daughter, there is that execrable hypocrite. She is your mother." Then I will banish you from my presence, and you will go away to shed tears on the tomb of a mother who was as unworthy as you are.'

The injustice of the situation so hardened my soul that this awful speech had little effect on me. I took my daughter up in my arms and withdrew to another room.

Unfortunately I forgot about the chocolate. As I learnt later the duke had eaten nothing for two days. The cup had been placed in front of him. He drained it to the last drop.

Then he went into his own apartment. Half an hour later he ordered Dr Sangre Moreno to be brought to the house and that no one else but him should be admitted.

Someone went to the doctor's house. He had left it for a house in the country where he practised dissection. This was quickly visited but he was no longer there. He was looked for on his usual round of visits, but arrived only three hours later and found the duke dead.

Sangre Moreno examined the body very carefully. He looked at the nails, eyes and tongue. He had a number of flasks brought for some purpose or other. Then he came to see me and said, 'Señora, you may be certain that the duke died from the effect of a detestable but skilful mixture of narcotic resin and a corrosive metal. It is not my profession to call for blood, and I leave the task of uncovering crimes to the supreme judge above. I shall announce that the duke died of apoplexy.'

Other doctors then came and confirmed Sangre Moreno's opinion.

I summoned la Girona and relayed to her what the doctor had said. Her distress betrayed her.

'You have poisoned my husband!' I said to her. 'How could a Christian commit such a crime?'

'I am a Christian,' she said. 'But I was a mother. If someone slit the throat of your child you would perhaps become more cruel than a raging lioness.'

I pointed out to her that she could have poisoned me instead of the duke.

'No,' she said. 'I was looking through the keyhole. If you had but touched the cup, I would have come in at once.'

Then the Capuchins arrived to ask for the duke's body. And as they brandished an order from the archbishop it could not be refused them.

La Girona, who up till then had shown great intrepidity, seemed all at once to be anxious and nervous. She was afraid that during the embalming of the body traces of poison would be found. She was haunted by this idea to the point where her very sanity was threatened. Her pleas forced me into the abduction which has procured for us the honour of having you with us. The exaggerated speech I made in the cemetery was designed to fool my servants. When we saw that it was you who had been carried off it was necessary to fool them again. Another body has been buried in the garden chapel.

But in spite of all these precautions, la Girona is not easy in her mind. She speaks of returning to America and wants you to be locked away until she has decided what to do. As for me, I have no fears. If ever I am questioned I shall tell the truth. I have let la Girona know that. The duke's injustice and cruelty rid me of all affection for him and I would never have been able to bring myself to live with him. All my hopes of happiness lie with my daughter and I am not worried about her future. Twenty grandeeships have accumulated in her person. That is enough to ensure that she will be well received into some family.

And that, young friend, is what you wanted to know. La Girona knows that I have told you the whole of our story. She thinks you should not be left knowing just half of it.

But the atmosphere of this vault is stifling. I am going upstairs to breathe more freely.

Having finished her sad story, the duchess left the vault, saying, as we have heard, that she was suffocating. After she had gone, I cast my eyes about me and found that the place really did have something stifling about it. The tomb of the young martyr and the pillar to which he had been bound seemed to me to be very gloomy furnishings. I had been pleased with that prison while I was still afraid of the Theatine tribunal, but since my affair had been settled I began no longer to like it. I laughed at la Girona's confident expectation that I could be kept in it for two years. The two ladies knew little about the profession of gaoler. They left the door of their vault open, believing perhaps that the iron grille which separated me from it was an insurmountable obstacle. I had, though, not only made a plan of escape but even worked out how I would spend the two years my penance should last. I'll tell you what my ideas were.

Throughout my time at the Theatine college I often thought about the good fortune which the few small beggars who stood at the door of our church seemed to enjoy. Their fate seemed clearly preferable to mine. Indeed, while I grew pale over my books without any chance of completely satisfying my masters, these young children of poverty roamed the streets and played cards for chestnuts on the steps of the church. They fought each other without being forcibly separated. They got dirty without being made to wash. They undressed in the street and washed their shirts in the gutter. Could there be any more pleasant way of passing the time?

These thoughts on the happy lives of these young urchins came back to me in my prison. And thinking about the best course of action for me to follow, it seemed to me to be that of adopting the profession of beggar for the time my penance was to last. It is true that I had had an education which might have given me away through my having more polished speech than my colleagues, but I hoped to take on their accent and manners without difficulty and return to my own in due course. This decision was odd but at bottom it was the best I could take in the situation in which I found myself.

Once I had made my mind up, I broke the blade of a knife and started working on one of the iron bars of the grille. It took me five days to work it free. I carefully collected up the bits of stone and put them back around the bar so nothing could be seen.

The day I finished this task la Girona brought me my basket. I asked her whether she wasn't afraid that it might come to be known that she was supplying food to a young man in the cellar of the house.

'No,' she replied, 'the trap-door through which you came down leads into a separate building, the one where you had been laid out. I have had the door bricked up on the pretext that it brought back sad memories to the duchess. The passage by which we come down ends in my bedroom and the entry to it is hidden by a wall-hanging.'

'I trust that there's a good iron door at that end,' I said.

'No,' she replied. 'The door is quite light but it's very well hidden. In any case, I keep my bedroom door locked. In this house I believe there to be other similar vaults, put there by other jealous husbands who have committed similar crimes.'

Having said this, la Girona seemed to want to go away.

'Why go away so soon?' I asked her.

'Because the duchess wants to go out. Today she has completed the first six weeks of her mourning and she wants to go for a ride.'

Having learnt what I needed to know, I did not detain la Girona any longer. She went away again without closing the vault door. I hastily wrote a letter of apology and thanks to the duchess, and put it on the bars. Next I loosened the iron bar and entered first the vault of the two ladies, and then a dark passage which ended in a door which I found shut. I heard the sounds of a coach and horses and concluded that the duchess had gone out and that the nurse was not in her room.

I set myself to the task of breaking the door down. It was half-rotten and yielded as soon as I tried to break it. I then found myself in the nurse's bedroom and, knowing that she took care to keep the door locked, I thought that I could stay there in safety.

I saw my face in a mirror and decided that my appearance did not yet correspond to the profession I was to embrace. I took a piece of charcoal from a grate and used it to dull the colour of my skin. After that I made some rents in my shirt and clothing. Then I went to the window. It looked out on to a small garden, once favoured by the presence of the masters of the house but now utterly abandoned. I opened the window and could see no other which looked out in the same direction. It wasn't very high and I could have jumped down into the garden but I preferred to use la Girona's sheets. After that, the frame of an old bower afforded me the means of climbing up on to the wall, from which I took flight into the countryside, delighted to be able to breathe the country air and yet more so to be free of Theatines, Inquisitions, duchesses and their nurses.

I saw the city of Burgos far off, but went in the opposite direction. I reached a low tavern. I showed the innkeeper's wife a twenty-real coin which I had carefully wrapped in paper, and told her I wanted to spend all the money in her inn. She began to laugh and gave me bread and onions worth double the sum. I had some money but was afraid of letting it be seen, so I went to the stable and there I slept as one sleeps when one is sixteen years old.

I reached Madrid without anything happening to me which is worth relating. I entered the city at nightfall. I was able to find my aunt's house and I leave it to your imagination how pleased she was to see me. But I only spent a moment there for fear of giving my presence away. I went right across Madrid, came to the Prado and there I lay down on the ground and fell asleep.

As soon as it was light I went around the streets and squares to select a place where I intended mainly to practise my profession. Passing by the Calle de Toledo, I met a servant girl carrying a bottle of ink. I asked her whether she wasn't from the house of Señor Avadoro.

'No,' she replied. 'I have come from the house of Don Felipe del Tintero Largo.'

So it was that I discovered that my father was still known by the same name and still passed his time in the same pursuits.

Meanwhile I had to think about a place to live. Under the portals of St Roch, I caught sight of a few urchins of my age with faces which predisposed me in their favour. I went up to them and said that I was a boy from the provinces; I had come to Madrid to commend myself to charitable souls, I had a small handful of reals left and if there was a common kitty I would willingly place this money in it.

This first speech predisposed them in my favour. They said that they indeed had a common kitty which was kept by a chestnut-seller whose pitch was at the end of the street. They took me to her and then we all came back to the portal, where we started playing tarot.

As we were engrossed in this game, which requires quite a lot of attention, a well-dressed man appeared and seemed to examine us all closely, first one then another. Then, apparently deciding on me, he called me over and told me to follow him. He led me into a quiet street and said, 'My boy, I have preferred you to your comrades because your face indicates that you have more wit than they and that will be needed for the task I want you to do for me. This is what it is about. Many women will pass by this spot, all wearing black velvet dresses and a black lace mantilla which hides their faces so well that it is impossible to see who they are. But luckily the patterns of the velvet and the lace are not the same and thus are ways of detecting who these unknown beauties are. I am the lover of one such person, who loves me and who seems to have a propensity to be inconsistent. I have decided to discover whether this is so or not. Here are two samples of velvet and two of lace. If two women go by whose clothes correspond, you will look closely to see whether they go into this church or into the house opposite, which is that of the Knight of Toledo. And then you will come to the tavern at the end of the street and tell me. Here is a gold piece. You will be given another if you acquit yourself well of this mission.'

While the man was speaking to me, I had examined him very closely. He didn't seem to me to look like a lover, but rather a husband. The rage of the Duke of Sidonia came back to my mind. I jibbed at sacrificing the interests of love to the dark suspicions of marriage. So I decided to accomplish only half the mission, that is to say, if the two women went into the church I decided that I would tell the jealous husband, but if they went elsewhere I would, on the contrary, warn them of the danger which threatened them. I returned to my comrades, telling them to continue their game without paying attention to me. Then I lay down behind them, keeping my eye on the samples of velvet and lace.

Soon many women came in pairs, and eventually two who were indeed wearing the materials of which I had samples. The two women made as if to go into the church, but they stopped under the portal, looked all around them to see if they were being followed and then hurried across the street as fast as they could and went into the house opposite.

When the gypsy had reached this point in his story, he was called away to his band.

Velásquez then spoke and said, 'Really, this story alarms me. All the gypsy's stories begin in a simple enough way and you think you can already predict the end. But things turn out quite differently. The first story engenders the second, from which a third is born, and so on, like periodic fractions resulting from certain divisions which can be indefinitely prolonged. In mathematics there are several ways of bringing certain progressions to a conclusion, whereas in this case an inextricable confusion is the only result I can obtain from all the gypsy has related.'

'In spite of that you derive great pleasure from listening to them,' said Rebecca. 'If I am not mistaken, you were to go directly to Madrid, yet you can't bear to leave us.'

'There are two reasons which keep me in this place,' replied Velásquez. 'First, I have begun important calculations which I want to finish here. Second, Señora, I must confess to you that I have never found so much pleasure in the company of a woman as I have in yours or rather, to be more precise, that you are the only woman whose conversation gives me pleasure.'

'Señor duque,' replied the Jewess, 'I would indeed be happy if the secondary reason became the primary one.'

'You shouldn't be too upset about whether I think of you before or after I think about geometry,' said Velásquez. 'What upsets me is something else – not knowing what to call you. I am reduced to designating you by the symbol x, y or z, which we use in algebra for unknown quantities.'

'I would willingly entrust to you the secret of my name,' said the Jewess, 'if I did not have to fear the results of your absent-mindedness.'

'There is nothing to fear,' interrupted Velásquez. 'Through the frequent practice of substitution in calculations I have acquired the habit of always designating the same values in the same way. As soon as you have given me your name you couldn't change it even if you wanted to.'

'Very well,' said Rebecca. 'Call me Laura de Uzeda.'

'With the greatest pleasure,' said Velásquez. 'Or fair Laura, clever Laura, charming Laura, for there are many mathematical exponents of your base value.'

As they were chatting I remembered the promise I had made to the brigand to meet him four hundred yards west of the camp. I took a sword with me and when I had gone a certain distance, I heard a pistol shot. I went towards the forest from which the shot had come and met the men with whom I had already had dealings. Their chief said to me, 'Welcome, Señor caballero. I see that you keep your word, and do not doubt that you are brave as well. Do you see that tunnel in the rock? It leads to an underground cave where you are very impatiently awaited. I hope that you will not disappoint the trust that has been placed in you.'

I went into the tunnel while the stranger stayed outside. After a few paces I heard a loud noise behind me and saw an enormous stone, which was moved by a secret mechanism, shutting off the entry. The dim light which came through the chink in the rock soon disappeared in that dark tunnel. But in spite of the darkness I went forward at a good pace, for the path was smooth and the slope gentle. I wasn't required to expend much effort, but I imagined that many another person would have felt terror as they went down without a visible goal into the bowels of the earth. I walked for two whole hours, one hand holding my sword, the other extended to protect me from bumping into things.

Suddenly I felt a breath close to mine, and a sweet, melodious voice said, 'By what right does a mortal dare to come down into the kingdom of the gnomes?'

An equally seductive voice replied, 'Perhaps he has come to rob us of our treasure.'

The first one then said, 'If he would consent to throw down his sword, we could come near him.'

After that I said, 'Charming gnomesses! I recognize you by your voices, if I am not mistaken. I may not throw down my sword but I have stuck its point into the earth so you can come near without fear.'

These chthonic divinities then threw their arms round me, though a secret instinct told me that they were my cousins. Suddenly there was bright light on every side and I saw that I was not mistaken. They led me towards a cave decorated with carpets and minerals shot through with countless opalescent colours.

'Well,' said Emina. 'Are you pleased to meet us again? You are now living in the company of a young Israelite who is as intelligent as she is charming.'

'I can assure you,' I replied, 'that Rebecca has made no impression on me. On the other hand, every time I meet you, I am anxious in case it may be the last. People have tried to convince me that you are evil spirits but I did not believe them. An inner voice tells me that you are creatures of my kind meant for love. It is always claimed that one can only truly love one woman. This is indisputably false because I love the two of you equally. My heart does not distinguish in any way between you. You both reign there in common.'

'Oh,' cried Emina, 'it is the blood of the Abencerrages that speaks in you because you can love two women at the same time; so adopt the sacred faith which permits polygamy.'

'You might then accede to the throne of Tunis,' added Zubeida. 'If only you could see that enchanting country, the harems of Bardo and Manouba, the gardens, fountains, marvellous baths and thousands of young slave girls even prettier than us!'

'Enough of kingdoms on which the sun shines,' I replied. 'We are in an abyss, and however close we might be to hell we can here know the sensual pleasures which the prophet, it is said, promises to his elect.'

Emina smiled nostalgically, and looked at me tenderly; and Zubeida put her arms round my neck.

The Thirtieth Day

When I awoke, my cousins were no longer at my side. I looked around uneasily and saw in front of me a long, dimly-lit corridor. I was able to guess that this was the way to go. I dressed as quickly as possible, strode briskly ahead and, after walking for half an hour, reached a spiral staircase that I could take either to return to the daylight or go deeper into the mountain. I followed the second route and came to a vault where I caught sight of an old dervish who was muttering prayers beside a tomb lit by four lamps.

The old man turned towards me and said in a soft voice, 'Welcome, Señor Alphonse, we have been waiting for you for some time.'

I asked him whether we were in the underground domain of Cassar Gomelez.

'You are not mistaken, noble Nazarene,' said the dervish. 'This tomb hides the famous secret of the Gomelez. But before I tell you anything about this important subject, let me offer you a light tonic. Today you will need all your spiritual and physical powers. And perhaps,' he added in a mocking tone, 'your body will be craving for rest.'

Then the old man led me into a neighbouring cave, where I found breakfast properly set out on a table. When I had taken refreshment my host asked me to pay close attention and said:

'Señor Alphonse, I know that your fair cousins have spoken to you of your ancestors and have explained the importance they attached to Cassar Gomelez's secret. Nothing in the world could be more important. He who possesses our secret could easily bring whole peoples under his sway, and perhaps even found a universal monarchy. On the other hand, these powerful means could become extremely dangerous in incautious hands, and destroy any order founded for a long time on obedience. The laws which have governed us for centuries require that the secret should only be revealed to men of the blood of

338

the Gomelez, and then only after they have provided convincing proof of their courage and integrity. Equally, it is required that a solemn oath reinforced by the full authority of religious ceremony be sworn. But knowing your character we will be satisfied with your word alone. May I therefore ask you to swear on your honour never to reveal to a living soul what you will hear and see in this place?'

As I was in the service of the King of Spain, I felt at first unable to give my word of honour, before being assured that I would not have to hear or see things in that cave which were incompatible with that dignity. I expressed my reservations to the dervish.

'Your caution, Señor, is quite understandable,' replied the dervish. 'Your arm belongs to the king whom you serve, but you are here in underground domains into which his power has never extended. The line of which you were born also imposes duties on you. And the promise which I ask of you is only the extension of that which you made to your cousins.'

I concurred with this reasoning, even though it seemed somewhat odd, and gave the word of honour which was expected of me.

Then the dervish opened up one face of the tomb and showed me a staircase which led to even greater depths.

'Go down there,' he said. 'It isn't necessary for me to accompany you. I'll come to fetch you this evening.'

So I went down and saw things which I would most happily tell you about if the word I gave did not constitute an insurmountable obstacle to my doing so.

Just as he promised, the dervish came to fetch me that evening. We made our way together to another cave in which a dinner had been prepared for us. The table was placed under a golden tree representing the genealogy of the Gomelez. The trunk split into two major branches, one of which, the Muslim Gomelez, seemed to unfold and flourish with all the force of a vigorous plant, while the other, representing the Christian Gomelez, was visibly withering and bristled with long and menacing pointed thorns. After dinner the dervish said:

'Don't be surprised at the difference you can see between the two principal branches. The Gomelez who remained faithful to the law of the prophet were rewarded with crowns, while the others lived in obscurity and only fulfilled some minor public offices. None of those were admitted to our secret, and if an exception has been made in your case you owe it to the respect due to you for having been able to win the favours of the two Princesses of Tunis. For all that, you have only a dim notion of our policies. If you are willing to cross over to the other branch, which is blossoming and which will blossom more and more as time goes by, you would possess all that you need to satisfy your personal ambitions and accomplish vast projects.'

I tried to reply to this but the dervish did not allow me the room to utter a single word and went on:

'Be that as it may, a share of the possessions of your family falls to you, as does a reward for the trouble you have taken in coming to this underground place. Here is a bill of exchange drawn up in the name of Esteban Moro, the richest banker in Madrid. The sum which figures there is apparently only one thousand reals but a single secret stroke of the pen will turn it into an unlimited amount. On signing it you will be given as much as you ask for. Now take the spiral staircase, and when you have counted to 1,500 steps you will reach a very low chamber in which you will crawl for fifty paces. Then you will be in the very heart of the castle of Alcassar or Cassar Gomelez. It will be best for you to spend the night there. The next day you will easily find the gypsy camp at the bottom of the mountain. Goodbye, dear Alphonse. May the prophet enlighten you and show you the path of truth.'

The dervish kissed me, took his leave and closed the door behind me. I followed his instructions to the letter. As I went up, I stopped often to catch my breath. Eventually I saw the starry sky above me. I lay down beneath a ruined vault and fell asleep.

The Thirty-first Day

On waking, I caught sight of the gypsy camp in the valley and discerned some movement which told me that they were going to leave that place and begin their wanderings again. So I hurried to join them. I expected some questions about my two nights' absence but no one asked any and everyone seemed only to be concerned about the preparations for departure.

Once we were on horseback the cabbalist said, 'On this occasion, I can promise you that we shall have the pleasure today of the Wandering Jew's conversation. My power has not yet been destroyed, as the rascal thinks it has been. He had almost reached Taroudant when I forced him to come back. He is showing his unwillingness by travelling as slowly as he can. But I have the means of making him go faster.' Then he drew a book from his pocket from which he read out some barbaric formulae. Soon after, we saw a man appear on a mountain top.

'Look at him,' said Uzeda. 'The sloth! The scoundrel! Just see how I'll deal with him!'

Rebecca begged pardon for the guilty party and her brother seemed to be mollified. When the Wandering Jew reached us he was let off with a few sharp reproaches uttered by the cabbalist in a language I did not understand. Then he told him to stay by my horse and take up the story again at the point where he had left off. The unhappy wanderer made no reply and began as follows:

∽ THE WANDERING JEW'S STORY CONTINUED ∽

I have told you that a sect of Herodians claiming Herod to be the Messiah had been formed in Jerusalem, and I promised to explain what meaning the Jews attach to this name, so I'll start by telling you that Messiah in Hebrew means 'anointed' or 'rubbed with oil' and

341

Christos is the translation of this term into Greek. When Jacob awoke after his famous vision, he poured oil on the stone on which his head had rested and he called the place 'Bethel' or 'House of God'. You may read in Sanchoniathon[1] that Sham invented betyles, or living stones. It was then thought that everything that was consecrated by anointing was filled at once with the divine spirit. Kings were anointed, and 'Messiah' became the synonym of 'king'. When David spoke of the Messiah he was thinking of himself, as can convincingly be seen from the second psalm onwards.

But after the kingdom of the Jews had been divided up and invaded, becoming the plaything of neighbouring powers, and above all when the people were led into captivity, the prophets consoled them by telling them that one day a king would be born of the race of David who would humble the pride of Babylon and make the Jews triumphant.

It didn't cost the prophets anything to have visions of splendid buildings, so they duly built a future Jerusalem worthy of being the place where so great a king would dwell, with a temple that had all that was needed to give the cult of religion dignity in the eyes of the people. The Jews listened to the prophecies with pleasure but without attaching much importance to them. After all, why should they show an interest in events which were not destined to happen until the time of the grandchildren of their great-nephews?

It seems that the prophets were more or less forgotten under the Macedonian empire, so that none of the Maccabees were considered as the Messiah although they had freed their country from foreign oppression. Their descendants, who bore the title of king, were also not taken to have been foretold by the prophets.

But under the elder Herod, things were different. Having in forty years run through all the flattering remarks that might please him, this prince's courtiers ended up by convincing him that he was the Messiah foretold by the prophets. Herod, who was tired of everything except the supreme power to which he grew daily more attached, thought that he had found in this claim a way of identifying those

1 A Phoenician historian of the twelfth century BCE.

who were loyal to him. So his friends formed a sect of Herodians whose head was the swindler Sedekias, the younger brother of my grandmother. You can well imagine that my grandfather and Dellius gave no more thought to settling down in Jerusalem. They had a small bronze chest made, and in it they locked the contract of sale of Hillel's house, his receipt for thirty thousand darics and an assignment made by Dellius in favour of my father. Then they sealed the coffer and promised each other to think no more about it until circumstances were more favourable.

Herod died and Judaea was prey to the most awful internal strife. Thirty heads of factions had themselves anointed and became as many messiahs. Some years later, Mardochee married the daughter of one of his neighbours and I, the sole fruit of this union, came into the world in the last year of Augustus's reign. My grandfather wanted to have the satisfaction of circumcising me himself, and he ordered a quite sumptuous feast to be prepared, but he was in the habit of living a retired life. The energy he had to expend on this occasion and perhaps also his great age were the early causes of an illness which carried him off within a few weeks. He breathed his last in the arms of Dellius, recommending that he should preserve the bronze coffer for us and not allow the evil-doer to benefit from his wickedness. My mother, whose labour had been difficult, only survived her father-in-law by a few months.

At that time it was the fashion among the Jews to take Greek or Persian names. I was called Ahasuerus. It was by this name that I made myself known to Antonius Colterus in Lübeck in 1603, as can be seen in the writings of Duduleus, and I also took this name in Cambridge in the year 1710, as you can read in the works of the discerning Tenzelius.

'Señor Ahasuerus, you are also mentioned in the *Theatrum Europaeum*,[2] said Velásquez.

'That may well be,' said the Jew. 'I am only too well known since

---

2 A journal founded in Frankfurt in 1627, which continued to appear until 1738.

cabbalists have got it into their heads to fetch me from the depths of Africa.'

I then spoke and asked the Jew what was the charm he found in such wildernesses.

'Not seeing any humans,' he replied. 'And if I do meet some lost traveller or a family of Arabs, I know the lair of a lioness who is rearing her young. I lead her towards her prey and have the pleasure of seeing her devour them under my very eyes.'

'You seem to have a somewhat bad character, Señor Ahasuerus,' said Velásquez.

'I warned you,' said the cabbalist. 'He's the greatest scoundrel on earth.'

'If you had lived eighteen hundred years,' said the wanderer, 'you wouldn't be any better than I am.'

'I hope to live longer and be better than you,' said the cabbalist. 'But enough of these disagreeable thoughts. Continue with your story.'

The Jew made no further reply but continued his story as follows:

The aged Dellius stayed with my father, who had been over-whelmed by so much loss. They continued to live in retirement from the world but Sedekias was uneasy. The death of Herod had deprived him of a sure protector. The fear that we might turn up in Jerusalem constantly tormented him. He decided to sacrifice us to his peace of mind. What is more, everything seemed to favour his plans, for Dellius became blind and my father, who was very fond of him, with-drew more than ever into retirement. Six years went by in this way.

One day someone came to tell us that the house adjoining ours had just been bought by Jews from Jerusalem and that it was full of unprepossessing characters who looked like assassins. My father, who had a natural love of retirement, found in this news fresh reasons for not going out.

At that point there was then a commotion in the caravan which interrupted the Wandering Jew's story. He took advantage of it to stride off, and we soon arrived at our resting-place. Our meal was prepared and then served. We ate with the customary appetite of travellers, and, when the cloth had been taken away, Rebecca turned to the gypsy and said, 'At the point where someone interrupted you, you were telling us, I believe, that the two ladies, having made sure that they were not being watched, crossed the road to go into the house of the Knight of Toledo.'

The gypsy chief, seeing that we wanted to hear the sequel to his story, took up its thread as follows:

✑ THE GYPSY CHIEF'S STORY CONTINUED ✑

I reached the two ladies while they were still on the steps and, having shown them the samples of cloth, I told them about the mission I had been given by the jealous husband. Then I said to them, 'Now, ladies, really go into the church. I will go and fetch the supposed lover, whom I believe to be the husband of one of you. When he has seen you, he will probably go away since he doesn't know that you know that he had you followed. Then you will be able to go wherever you wish.'

The two ladies were grateful for this advice. I went down to the tavern and said to the man that the two women had indeed gone into the church. We went there together and I pointed out to him the two velvet dresses which corresponded to the samples, as did the lace. He still seemed in doubt but one of the two ladies turned round and casually lifted her veil. At once an expression of conjugal complacency spread across the jealous husband's features. Soon after, he mingled with the crowd and left the church. I joined him in the street. He thanked me and gave me another gold piece. In accepting it I felt a pang of conscience but I was afraid to give myself away. I watched him as he went off, then fetched the two ladies, whom I accompanied to the knight's house. The prettier one wanted to give me a gold piece. 'No, Señora,' I said. 'I betrayed your supposed lover because I recognized him to be a husband and my conscience made me do this. But I am too honourable to be paid by both sides.'

I went back to the portal of St Roch and showed off my two gold pieces. My comrades were dazzled by them. They had often been given similar missions but no one had ever paid them so handsomely for them. I took the money to the kitty. My comrades came with me to enjoy the sight of the chestnut-seller's surprise. She really was astonished at the sight of the gold.

She declared that she would not only give us as many chestnuts as we wanted but also small sausages with the wherewithal to grill them. The expectation of such delicious food spread joy throughout our band, but I took no share in it, intending to find myself a better cook. Meanwhile we helped ourselves to chestnuts. We went back to the portal of St Roch and had our evening meal. Then we all wrapped ourselves in our coats and were soon asleep.

The next day one of the two ladies of the previous day accosted me and gave me a letter which she asked me to take to the knight. I went to his house and gave it to his valet. Soon after, I was myself admitted. The appearance of the Knight of Toledo predisposed me so greatly in his favour that I could easily understand why ladies were bound not to look at him with indifference. He was a young man with the most pleasant of faces. He did not need to laugh for all his features to express merriment; it was as if it were already imprinted on them. There was a certain grace which accompanied all his movements, but in his manner could be detected something of the inconstant libertine, which might not have stood him in good stead with women if they didn't all believe themselves born to cure even the most fickle of men of their inconstancy.

'Friend,' said the knight, 'I already am aware of your intelligence and integrity. Would you like to enter my service?'

'I cannot do that,' I replied. 'I was born a gentleman and cannot embrace a condition of servitude. I made myself a beggar because it is a state which does not break this rule.'

'Bravo!' said the knight. 'That way of thinking is worthy of a Castilian. But how can I be of use to you?'

'Señor caballero,' I said, 'I like my profession because it is honourable and provides me with a livelihood, but one doesn't eat well, so you would oblige me by allowing me to come here to eat with those who serve you and share your dessert.'

'With great pleasure,' said the knight. 'The days on which I expect the ladies I normally send my people away. If your noble birth can bear it, I should be grateful if you would come to serve me on such occasions.'

'Señor,' I replied, 'when you are with your mistress I will serve you with pleasure, because the pleasure I shall find in being of service to you will in my own eyes ennoble this action.'

Then I took my leave of the knight and went to the Calle de Toledo. When I asked after the house of Señor Avadoro no one was able to give me an answer. Then I asked for Don Felipe del Tintero Largo. A balcony was pointed out to me, on which I saw a man with very grave looks, smoking a cigar and appearing to count the tiles on the palacio de Alba. Although nature predisposed me to like him, I could not help marvelling that she had given so much gravity to the father and so little to the son. It seemed to me that she would have done better to give a little to both. But then the thought struck me that God must be praised for everything, as they say, and I went back to rejoin my companions. We went to try the chestnut-seller's sausages, and I found them so good that I forgot all about dessert at the knight's house.

Towards-evening I saw the two women go in. They stayed there a long time. I went to see whether I was needed but the ladies were already coming out. I paid the prettier one a somewhat dubious compliment for which she rewarded me by tapping me on the cheek with her fan.

A moment later I was accosted by a young man of imposing appearance, which was further dignified by a Maltese cross embroidered on his cloak. The rest of his dress indicated that he had been travelling. He asked me where the Knight of Toledo lived. I offered to take him there. We found no one in the antechamber so I opened the door and went in with him. The Knight of Toledo was extremely taken aback. 'What's this?' he said. 'You, my dear Aguilar? In Madrid? I am so happy, but what's going on in Malta? What are the grand prior, the *grand bailli*,[3] the master of novices up to? Let me give you a kiss!'

The Knight of Aguilar replied to these signs of friendship with the same warmth but with great gravity.

I surmised that the two friends would take supper together, so I

---

3 A rank in the order of the Knights of Malta.

found in the antechamber what was needed to lay the table and went to fetch the meal. When it was served, the Knight of Toledo told me to ask his butler for two bottles of French sparkling wine. I brought them to table and removed the corks.

The two friends had by then already said a lot to each other and recalled many memories. Then Toledo spoke. 'I cannot imagine how we can be so fond of each other, having such different characters,' he said. 'You have every virtue and yet I like you as if you were the worst sinner in the world. And the truth of the matter is that I have made no other friend in Madrid. You are still the only friend I have, but I have to admit I am not as constant in love.'

'Do you still have the same principles where women are concerned?' said Aguilar.

'The same principles? Not altogether,' said Toledo. 'Once I changed my mistresses as fast as I could. But I found that I lost too much time by this method. Now, when I begin a second affair before the first is finished, I am already planning a third.'

'So you propose never to renounce your libertine ways?' said Aguilar.

'Indeed not,' said Toledo. 'I am more afraid that they will give me up. The ladies of Madrid have something in their characters which is so insistent and so tenacious that very often one is forced to be more moral than one would wish.'

'Our order is a military one,' said Aguilar. 'But it is also religious. We take vows like monks and priests.'

'Quite so,' said Toledo. 'And like wives when they promise to be faithful to their husbands.'

'Who knows whether they won't be punished for this in the next world?' said Aguilar.

'My friend,' replied Toledo, 'I have all the faith a Christian should have but there is necessarily some misunderstanding in all this. How the devil can you expect the wife of the *oidor* Uscariz, who has just spent an hour in my company, to burn for that through all eternity?'

'Our religion tells us there are other places to expiate one's sins,' said Aguilar.

'You are referring to purgatory,' said Toledo. 'As for that, I think I have already been there. It was during the time that I was in love with that pest Inés Navarra, the most capricious, demanding and jealous of creatures. Because of her I have given up actresses. But you are neither eating nor drinking, my good friend. I have emptied my bottle and your glass is still full. What are you thinking about? What on earth are you thinking about?'

'I was thinking,' said Aguilar, 'that I had seen the sun today.'

'Now as for that, I believe you,' said Toledo. 'I, the very person now speaking to you, have seen it despite everything.'

'I was thinking too,' said Aguilar, 'that I wanted very much to see the sun again tomorrow.'

'You will,' said Toledo, 'unless it's foggy.'

'That's not certain,' said Aguilar, 'because I might die tonight.'

'It has to be said that you have brought back some very cheerful conversation from Malta,' said Toledo.

'Alas,' said Aguilar, 'we must all die. Only the hour of our death is not certain.'

'Wait,' said Toledo, 'who has told you all these pleasant novelties? It must be a mortal with an extraordinarily witty turn of conversation. Is he often invited out to supper?'

'Not at all,' said Aguilar. 'My confessor said all this to me this morning.'

'You arrive in Madrid and you go to confession the very same day?' said Toledo. 'So you have come to fight a duel.'

'Just that,' said Aguilar.

'Splendid,' said Toledo. 'It's been some time since I duelled. I'll be your second.'

'That is precisely what cannot happen,' said Aguilar. 'You are the only man in the world I cannot take as a second.'

'Heavens!' said Toledo. 'You have taken up your cursed quarrel with my brother again!'

'Just so,' said Aguilar. 'The Duke of Lerma has not agreed to the satisfaction I demanded. So we will fight tonight by torchlight on the banks of the Manzanares, below the great bridge.'

'Merciful heavens,' said Toledo sorrowfully. 'Must I lose either a brother or a friend this evening?'

'Perhaps both,' said Aguilar. 'We are fighting to the death. Instead of foils we are using short swords, with a dagger in the left hand. You know that these arms are merciless.'

Toledo, whose sensitive soul was very impressionable, went in an instant from the greatest jollity to the most extreme despair.

'I foresaw your distress,' said Aguilar, 'and I did not want to come to see you, but a voice from heaven made itself heard in me. It commanded me to tell you about the sufferings in the next world.'

'Be quiet!' said Toledo. 'That's enough about my conversion!'

'I am only a soldier,' said Aguilar. 'I don't know how to preach, but I obey heaven's voice.'

At that moment we heard eleven o'clock strike. Aguilar embraced his friend and said to him, 'Toledo, listen to me. An intuition deep inside me tells me that I am going to die. But I want my death to benefit your salvation. I have decided to put the duel off until midnight. So pay attention. If it is possible for the dead to communicate with the living by some sign or other you can be sure that your friend will give you news of the other world, but pay great attention at midnight exactly.' Then Aguilar embraced his friend again and left.

Toledo threw himself down on his bed and shed many a tear. I withdrew to the antechamber, more than a little curious to discover how it would all end.

Toledo would get up, look at his watch and then return, weeping, to his bed. The night was dark, and through the wooden planks of our shutters came the light from a few flashes of lightning in the distance. The storm came closer and added its terror to the sorrows of our situation. Midnight struck and we heard three knocks on our shutters.

Toledo opened the shutter and said, 'Are you dead?'

'I am dead,' said a sepulchral voice.

'Is there a purgatory?' said Toledo.

'There is, and I am there,' said the same voice. And then we heard something like a groan of pain.

Toledo fell down, his forehead pressed into the dust. Then he rose, took his coat and went out. I went after him. We followed the road to the Manzanares, but we had not yet reached the great bridge when we saw a crowd of people, some carrying torches. Toledo caught sight of his brother.

'Go no further,' said the Duke of Lerma, 'or you will come upon the body of your friend.'

Toledo fell in a faint. I saw all his retinue crowd around him and I returned to the portal. When I reached it I started to reflect on what we had heard. Father Sanudo had always told me that there was a purgatory, so I wasn't surprised to be told it again. All this did not make a very great impression on me. I slept as well as usual.

The next day the first man to enter the church of St Roch was Toledo. He was so pale and so discomposed as to be scarcely recognizable. He prayed and then asked for a confessor.

When the gypsy had reached this point in his story, someone came and interrupted him. He was obliged to leave us. We all went our own ways.

The Thirty-second Day

———————— ∽ ————————

We set off fairly early, following a track which led us into the valleys that penetrated deepest into the mountain range. After an hour had passed we caught sight of the Jew Ahasuerus. He took his place between Velásquez and myself and continued his story as follows:

∽ THE WANDERING JEW'S STORY CONTINUED ∽

One day we were told that an officer of the Roman court was at the door. He was admitted, and we learnt that my father was accused of high treason for having tried to deliver Egypt into the hands of the Arabs. When the Roman had gone, Dellius said to my father, 'My dear Mardochee, it is pointless trying to justify yourself for everyone is clearly convinced that you are innocent. But it will cost you half your goods, which you must give up with a good grace.'

Dellius was right. The affair cost us half our fortune.

The following year, on his way out of the house, my father discovered on the doorstep a man who seemed barely alive. My father had him taken into the house and tried to revive him but immediately officers of the law appeared in the house, together with those who were living next door, eight in all, who all swore that they had witnessed my father murdering the man. My father spent six months in prison, and only came out after having sacrificed the other half of his fortune, that is to say all that he had left.

His house still belonged to him, but he was scarcely home again when the house of our wicked neighbours caught fire. This was at night. My father's neighbours gained entry to his house, stole everything they could and spread the fire to those parts it had not yet reached.

By dawn our house was no more than a heap of ashes, in which the blind Dellius could be seen shuffling about, with my father, who was holding me in his arms, bemoaning his misfortune.

When the shops opened, my father took me by the hand to the baker who had up to then been our supplier. This man seemed moved to compassion and gave us three loaves. We rejoined Dellius, who told us that while we had been away a man whom he had not been able to see had said to him, 'Oh Dellius, may your misfortunes fall on the head of Sedekias! Forgive those in his employ. We were paid to kill you and we have spared your days. Here is something to sustain you for a little while.'

The man had then given him a purse containing fifty gold pieces.

This unexpected help cheered my father up. He merrily spread out a half-burnt mat over the ashes, put the three loaves on it and went to fetch water in a half-broken earthenware ewer. I was seven years old. I remember sharing with my father this moment of good cheer and having gone with him to the water trough. I also had my share of breakfast.

We had scarcely begun our meal when a child of my age appeared, weeping and begging for bread.

'I am the son of a Roman soldier and a Syrian woman,' he said. 'She died giving birth to me. The wives of the soldiers of the same cohort, who were sutlers, suckled me in turn. Obviously I was given some other sustenance for here I am now. But my father, who had been sent out against a group of shepherds, never came back, nor did any of his comrades. The bread which had been left for me ran out yesterday. I tried to beg some in the city but all the doors were shut to me. As you have neither a door nor a house I hope that you will not refuse me some.'

Old Dellius, who never missed an opportunity to be sententious, said, 'This shows that there is no human being so wretched that he cannot still do some good to someone, just as there is no person so powerful that he does not still have some need of others. Welcome, my child, share in our bread of misery. What is your name?'

'I am called Germanus,' said the child.

'Long may you live,' said Dellius. And this blessing of sorts became a prophecy, for the child lived long and is still alive now in Venice, where he is known as the Chevalier de Saint-Germain.[1]

'I know him,' said Uzeda. 'He has some knowledge of the cabbala.'

Then the Wandering Jew continued as follows:

When we had eaten, Dellius asked my father whether the door to the cellar had been broken down.

My father replied that the door was closed, as it had been before the fire, and that the flames had not been able to destroy the ceiling of the cellar. 'Well,' said Dellius, 'take two gold pieces from the purse which I was given, hire workmen and construct a cabin round the ceiling. It will certainly be possible to use some of the debris from the old house.'

And indeed a few beams and planks were found intact. They were attached to each other by some means or other, everything was covered with palm fronds and matting and we thus had a comfortable shelter. Nature does not require more than this in our happy climate. Under so clear a sky the vestige of a roof is sufficient and the simplest food is also the most healthy. So one can rightly say that poverty is not as much to be feared in our part of the world as in your latitudes, which you call temperate.

As our dwelling was being constructed, Dellius set down matting on the street, sat down on it and played a tune on the Phoenician cithara. Next he sang a grand aria he had composed for Cleopatra. The voice of this more than sixty-year-old man still had the power to attract to us a crowd of people, who took pleasure in hearing him. When he had finished his aria he said, 'Citizens of Alexandria! Give alms to poor Dellius, whom your fathers knew as Cleopatra's first musician and Antony's favourite!'

Then little Germanus took round a small earthenware bowl, in which everyone put his offering.

Dellius made it a rule only to sing and beg once a week. On those days the whole neighbourhood assembled and did not return home before leaving us with plentiful alms. We did not owe them all to

1 The Comte de Saint-Germain (1707–84) was a notorious adventurer.

Dellius's voice. We owed them also to his conversation, which was cheerful, instructive and full of anecdotes. So our lot was quite tolerable. Meanwhile my father, who had been too deeply hurt by the succession of misfortunes, fell into a decline which carried him to his grave in less than a year. We remained then in the sole care of Dellius, reduced to living on what his old and broken voice could bring in. The following winter a severe cough, which was followed by permanent hoarseness, took away even this resource. Then I inherited a small sum from a relative from Pelusium who had died. It amounted to five hundred gold pieces, not even the third of that which was due to me, but Dellius declared that justice was not meant for the poor, who should be content with what they were given as a favour. So he was content in my name with this sum, but he was able to deploy it so well that it met all my needs throughout my childhood.

Dellius did not neglect either my education or that of young Germanus besides. One or the other of us remained always in his company. The days I was not required, I went to a little Jewish school in the neighbourhood, and the days Germanus was free, he sat at the feet of a priest of Isis called Chaeremon. Subsequently he was made torchbearer during that goddess's mysteries and he would charm me with his description of the ceremonies.

As the Wandering Jew reached this point in his story we arrived at our resting-place, and he went off into the mountains. Towards evening, as we were all together and the gypsy chief seemed not to be needed, Rebecca asked him to continue his story, which he did as follows:

✑ THE GYPSY CHIEF'S STORY CONTINUED ✑

The Knight of Toledo had obviously allowed a large number of sins to accumulate on his conscience, because he detained his confessor for a very long time. He left him with tears streaming down his face and went out of the church showing all the signs of the most profound contrition. As he crossed the portal he caught sight of me and signalled that I should follow him.

It was still very early in the morning and the streets were deserted. The knight engaged the first mules for hire we came across and we

355

rode out of the city. I remarked to him that his household would be worried by such a long absence. But he replied, 'No, they have been forewarned and will not be expecting me back.'

'Señor caballero,' I said to him, 'may I be allowed to make an observation? The voice you heard yesterday told you something which you could just as well have found in your catechism. You have gone to confession and doubtless were not refused absolution. By all means amend your ways a bit but don't upset yourself to this extent.'

'Oh my friend,' said the knight, 'once one has heard the voice of the dead, one is not long for this world.'

I then realized that my young protector thought that he was going to die soon, and this idea had affected him. So I made the decision not to leave him.

We took a lonely road which crossed a wild stretch of countryside and led us to the doors of a Camaldolese monastery. The knight paid off the muleteers and rang at the door. A monk appeared. The knight made himself known and asked to be allowed to undertake a retreat lasting several weeks. We were led to a hermitage at the bottom of the garden and informed by sign language that a bell would announce the time to go to the refectory. Our cell was furnished with devout literature, which the knight read to the exclusion of all else. As for me, I found a Camaldolese who was sitting fishing with a rod; I joined him and that was the only way I had to amuse myself.

The silence which is part of the Camaldolese rule did not upset me too much the first day, but it had become unbearable by the third. As for the knight, his melancholy grew daily. Soon he stopped talking altogether.

We had been at the monastery for a week when I saw one of my comrades from the portal of St Roch arrive. He told us that he had seen us ride away on our hired mules and, having subsequently met the same muleteer, he had learnt from him where our retreat was. He told me at the same time that the sadness of having lost me had caused our little troop to begin to split up; for his part he had placed himself in the service of a Cadiz merchant who needed people to look after him, having suffered multiple fractures to his legs and arms in an unfortunate accident.

I told him that I couldn't bear it any longer in the Camaldolese monastery and asked him to take my place with the knight just for a few days.

He replied that he would willingly do so but that he was afraid of letting down the Cadiz merchant who had taken him into his service; he had been given the job under the portal of St Roch, and to let him down would do no good to those who foregathered there.

I told him in turn that I could take his place with the merchant. I had, as it happened, managed to impose my authority on my comrades and this one did not think he should refuse to obey me. I led him to the knight, whom I told that important affairs obliged me to return to Madrid for a few days and that during this time I would leave him a comrade whom I would answer for as for myself. The knight, who did not speak, let me know by signs that he agreed to the substitution.

So I went to Madrid and went at once to the inn which my comrade had indicated to me, but I found that the patient had been transferred to the house of the famous doctor who lived in the Calle St Roch. I had no trouble finding him. I said that I had come in the place of my comrade Chiquito, that I was called Avarito and that I would undertake the same services just as faithfully.

I was told that my services would be accepted but that I had to go at once to rest, as I would have to sit up with the patient for several consecutive nights. So I slept, and that evening presented myself to take up my duties. I was led to the patient, whom I found stretched out on a bed in a very awkward position, not having the use of any of his limbs except his left hand.

As it happens, he was a young man with an interesting face. He wasn't actually ill but, having had his limbs shattered, suffered terrible pain. I tried to make him forget his suffering by amusing and distracting him as best I could. Eventually I managed to get him to agree to tell me his story, which he did as follows:

∽ LOPE SOAREZ'S STORY ∽

I am the only son of Gaspar Soarez, the richest merchant in Cadiz. My father, who is of a naturally austere and unbending humour, required me to do nothing else but work at the counter of his

357

business. He refused to let me take part in the amusements in which the sons of the prominent families of Cadiz indulged. Since I wanted to please him in all that I did, I rarely went to the theatre and never took part in those festivities to which people in mercantile towns devote their Sundays.

Yet because the mind needs relaxation I sought this by reading those enjoyable but dangerous books we know as novels. The taste I had for them predisposed me to love but, as I rarely went out and as no women visited us, I did not have the opportunity of disposing of my heart.

My father discovered that he had business at court and thought that this would be a good opportunity for me to get to know Madrid, so he told me of his plan to send me there. Far from having any objections, I was delighted at being able to breathe a freer air away from the iron grilles of the counter and the dust of our shops.

When all the preparations for the journey had been made, my father summoned me to his study and spoke to me as follows:

'My son, you are going to a place where merchants don't play the leading role as they do in Cadiz. They need to adopt a very grave and modest demeanour in order not to bring into disrepute a profession which confers honour on them since it contributes greatly not only to the prosperity of their country but also to the real power of the monarch. Here are three precepts that you will faithfully observe on pain of incurring my wrath.

'First, I order you to avoid the company of nobles. They think they do us honour when they address words to us. This is an error in which they must not be left, since our reputation is altogether independent of anything they might have to say to us.

'Second, I order you to call yourself just Soarez, not Lope Soarez. Titles do not enhance the reputation of a merchant. That consists entirely in the range of his connections and the wisdom of his ventures.

'Third, I forbid you ever to draw your sword. Since it is the custom, I will allow you to carry one. But you must not forget that the honour of a merchant consists entirely in the scrupulousness with which he fulfils his engagements. This is why I have never wanted you to take a single lesson in the dangerous art of fencing.

'If you contravene any one of these three rules you will incur my wrath. But there is a fourth which you must also obey on pain of incurring not only my wrath but also my solemn curse, my father's curse and the curse of my grandfather, who is your great-grandfather and the founder of our fortune. The important point is never to enter into any direct or indirect relations with the house of the brothers Moro, the court bankers.

'The brothers Moro rightfully enjoy the reputation of being the most honest people in the world and this prohibition of mine may justifiably surprise you. But you will no longer be surprised when you learn of the grievances which our house has against theirs. That is why I must briefly tell you our story:

∽ THE STORY OF THE HOUSE OF SOAREZ ∽

The founder of our fortune was Iñigo Soarez, who, having spent his childhood sailing the seven seas, bought a sizeable share at the auction[2] of the Potosí mines and established a trading house at Cadiz.

As the gypsy reached this point of the story Velásquez pulled out his tablets and made some notes. The story-teller then turned to him and said, 'Señor duque perhaps intends to engage in some interesting calculations? My tale might distract him from them.'

'Not at all,' said Velásquez. 'It's your story which I am thinking about. Señor Iñigo Soarez will perhaps meet someone in America who will tell him the story of someone who has also a story to tell. So as not to lose my way, I have thought up a scale of relations which is like the one used for sequences given by recurrence relations, so called because they ultimately depend upon the first terms. Please go on.'

The gypsy went on as follows:

Intending to found a house, Iñigo Soarez sought the friendship of the principal merchants of Spain. The Moro brothers had a prominent role already at that time. He told them of his intention of establishing

2 Potocki uses here the word *apalte* (from the Italian *apalti*).

lasting relations with them. He obtained their consent and, to set things in motion, established funds in Antwerp on which he drew in Madrid. But imagine his indignation when he received a bill of exchange together with a legal protest. By the following post he received a letter of apology. Rodrigo Moro wrote to him to say that he had been at San Ildefonso with the minister, that the letter of confirmation from Antwerp had been delayed, that his head clerk had not thought that he should waive the established rule of the house and that meanwhile he would be ready to make any reparation required. But the insult had been delivered. Iñigo Soarez broke off all relations with the Moro brothers and on his deathbed he advised his son never to have any dealings with them.

My father, Ruiz Soarez, remained obedient to his for a long time, but a great bankruptcy which unexpectedly reduced the number of trading houses forced him, one might say, to have recourse to the Moro brothers. He had every reason to repent of this decision. I have told you that we had taken a great share in the Potosí mines at their auction. This meant that we had many ingots in our possession and it was our practice to settle bills with them, as they were not subject to fluctuations in rates of exchange. To do this we kept chests containing a hundred pounds of silver to a value of two thousand seven hundred and fifty-seven piastres fortes and six reals. These chests, some of which you may have seen, were bound in iron and sealed with lead seals bearing the mark of our house. Every chest had its own number. They went out to the Indies and back to Europe and out to America again without anyone thinking of opening them, and everyone was very happy to take payment in them. They were even well known in Madrid. Yet when someone had to make a payment to the house of Moro and took in four of these chests, not only did the head clerk have them opened but he even had the silver assayed. When the news of this insulting behaviour reached Cadiz my father became very indignant indeed. It is true that he received by the next post a letter full of apology from Antonio Moro, Rodrigo's son. Antonio wrote that he had been called away to Valladolid, where the court then was, and that on his return he had been furious about the actions of his clerk, who being foreign, did not know Spanish practice.

My father was not satisfied with this apology. He broke off all relations with the house of Moro and on his deathbed advised me never to have any dealings with them.

For a long time I remained obedient to my father's orders and things went well. But eventually a particular set of circumstances put me in contact with the house of Moro. I forgot my father's dying advice, or rather I did not have it in the forefront of my mind, and you will see what happened to me as a result.

I was forced by some business at court to go to Madrid. There I made the acquaintance of a certain retired merchant called Livardez, who lived off the income he received from considerable capital sums which had been invested in various places. There was something about this man's character which I found congenial. Our friendship was already close when I learnt that Livardez was the maternal uncle of Sancho Moro, then the head of the Moro house. I should have broken off all contact with Livardez then, but I did not. On the contrary, my friendship with him became even closer.

One day Livardez told me that, knowing how much I knew about commerce in the Philippines, he wanted to invest a million in shares in a venture there. I pointed out to him that as he was an uncle of the Moro family he ought really to entrust his money to them.

'No,' he replied. 'I do not like to have financial dealings with my close relatives.' In the end, he succeeded in convincing me to act for him. He was able to do this all the more readily because I was not entering into any relations with the Moro family itself. Once back in Cadiz, I added a ship to the two I sent every year to the Philippines and thought no more about it.

The following year poor Livardez died and Sancho Moro wrote to me that his uncle had placed a million with me and asked me to send it to him. I should perhaps have informed him of the conditions of the share agreement but I did not want to enter into any contact with the accursed house and so simply returned the million.

Two years later my ships returned and my capital investment tripled, so two millions were due to the late Livardez. I had therefore to engage in correspondence with the Moro brothers. I wrote to them that I had two millions to hand over to them.

They replied that the capital had been banked two years before and that they didn't want to hear any more about the matter. You can well imagine, my son, that I could not fail to be offended by so dreadful an insult. For it amounted to their wanting to make a present of two millions. I spoke about it to several Cadiz merchants, who told me that the Moro brothers were right, and that having banked the capital they no longer had any rights to the profits I had made. I for my part offered to prove by original documents that Livardez's capital was really on the ships, and that if they had not returned I would have had the right to reclaim the money that I had given to them. But I saw that the name of Moro impressed them too much and that if I had appealed to a cómmission of merchants, their expert opinion would not have been in my favour.

I consulted a lawyer, who told me that as the Moro brothers had withdrawn this capital without the permission of their dead uncle and as I had used it in the way the said uncle intended it to be used, the said capital was still really in my hands and that the million banked by the Moro brothers was another million which had nothing to do with the former sum. My lawyer advised me to summon the house of Moro to the court at Seville. This I did and in six years spent one hundred thousand piastres as plaintiff; but in spite of all this I lost my case and still had the two million pounds.

At first I wanted to use it to set up some pious foundation but I feared that the merit of this would be attributed in part to the cursed Moro brothers. I still do not know what I will do with this money. In the meantime when I draw up my accounts of credit and debit I place on the credit side two million less. So you see, my son, that I have sufficient reason to forbid you to have any contact with the Moro family.

The gypsy chief was at this point in his story when he was summoned elsewhere and we all went our own ways.

The Thirty-third Day

---⁊---

We set off again and were soon joined by the Wandering Jew, who continued his story as follows:

⁊ THE WANDERING JEW'S STORY CONTINUED ⁊

So we grew up under the gaze of good Dellius, who could no longer see but guided us by his prudence and directed us by his good counsel. Eighteen centuries have since passed and my childhood years are the only time of my long life that I recall with some pleasure. I loved Dellius like a father, and was deeply attached to my friend Germanus, but I used to have frequent arguments with him, always on the same subject, which was religion. Imbued with the intolerant principles of the synagogue, I would repeatedly say to him, 'Your idols have eyes but they see not; they have ears but they hear not. A goldsmith carves the first and mice make their nest in the second.' Germanus would always reply that they were not looked on as gods and that I had no idea about the religion of the Egyptians.

This frequently repeated reply made me curious. I asked Germanus to get Chæremon[1] the priest to instruct me himself in his religion, which could only be done in secret, for if it had been known in the synagogue I would have suffered the indignity of being excommunicated. Germanus was much liked by Chæremon, who was happy to agree to my request. And the very next night I made my way to a grove next to the temple of Isis. Germanus introduced me to Chæremon, who, having made me sit down beside him, joined his hands in devout meditation and then uttered the following prayer in the vernacular of Lower Egypt, which I understood perfectly:

---

1 A name found in Jamblichus's (*c.* 250–*c.*330) *On the Egyptian Mysteries.*

363

The Egyptian Prayer
O my God, father of all, you show yourself to your own
You are the holy one who has made everything by your word
You are the holy one of whom nature is the image
You are the holy one whom nature has not created
You are the holy one more powerful than any power
You are the holy one higher than any height
You are the holy one better than any praise
Receive the sacrifice of thanks of my heart and my tongue
You are ineffable and in silence do you speak to us
You have abolished the errors which are contrary to true
    knowledge
Commend me, strengthen me and extend your grace to those
    who are in ignorance as well as to those who know you and
    are thereby my brothers and your children.
I believe in you and openly acknowledge my belief
I rise to life and light
I desire to share in your holiness; and it is you who inspires this
    desire in me.

When Chæremon had finished his prayer he turned to me and said, 'My child, you see that we acknowledge as you do a God who created the world by his word. The prayer you have just heard is taken from the Pimander, a book we attribute to the thrice-great Thoth, whose works are carried in procession at all our feasts.[2] We possess twenty-six thousand codices which are taken as having been written by this philosopher, who lived two thousand years ago, but since only our priests are allowed to make copies of them it is possible that they have added much. Besides, the writings of Thoth are full of obscure and subtle metaphysics which has given rise to very divergent interpretations. I shall therefore limit myself to instructing you in the most generally accepted dogmas, which are more or less consistent with those of the Chaldeans. Like everything in this world, religions

---

2 In fact, a neoplatonist text of much later date attributed to Hermes Trismegis-tus (Egyptian Thoth).

are subject to a slow, continuous force which tends continually to change their form and nature, with the result that after some centuries a religion that is still thought of as the same ends up by offering different things for men to put their faith in: allegories whose meaning has been lost, dogmas which no longer are fully believed.

'I cannot therefore assure you that I will teach you the old religion whose ceremonies you can still see depicted on the bas-relief of Ozymandias[3] at Thebes. But I will transmit to you the lessons of those who taught me in the way I give them to my pupils.

'The first thing I will recommend to you is not to become attached to any image or emblem, but to strive to grasp the spirit of all such things. Thus, earth represents all that is material, and a god sitting on a lotus leaf floating on mud represents thought, which rests on matter without touching it. This is the emblem your lawgiver used when he said that the spirit of God was borne on the waters. It is claimed that Moses was brought up by priests in the town of On or Heliopolis; and your rites are in fact very similar to ours. Like you, we have priestly families and prophets, circumcision is practised, pork is not eaten and there are many other similarities.'

When Chæremon had reached this point in his lesson, an acolyte of the cult of Isis struck the hour which marked the middle of the night. Our master told us that religious duties called him to the temple and that we could come back at nightfall the next day.

'And you will soon reach your resting-place,' said the Wandering Jew. 'Allow me therefore to put off the next part of my story until tomorrow.'

After the wanderer had gone away, I reflected on what he had said to us, and I thought I detected in it the more or less blatant desire to weaken our religious principles and thereby to abet the plans of those who wanted me to change mine. But I knew very well what course honour prescribed for me in this respect and that however one went about it, it would be impossible to succeed.

Meanwhile, we reached the resting-place. The meal took place in

3 Rameses II (*c.* 1279–1213 BCE).

365

the usual way and then the gypsy chief, having nothing else to do, took up again the thread of his story:

∽ THE GYPSY CHIEF'S STORY CONTINUED ∽

When young Soarez had finished the story of his house he seemed to want to rest, and as I knew sleep was very necessary for his recovery I asked him put off to the next night the sequel to his story. He did, in fact, sleep well, and the following night he seemed to me to be better. But seeing that he could not sleep, I asked him to continue his story, which he did as follows:

∽ LOPE SOAREZ'S STORY CONTINUED ∽

I have told you that my father had forbidden me to take the title of don, to draw my sword or to frequent the nobility, but above all else I had to have no contact with the house of Moro. I have also told you of the exclusive taste I had for reading novels. I took care to engrave in my memory the precepts of my father and then I went to all the booksellers in Cadiz to supply myself with works of this kind, promising myself great pleasure from them during my journey.

At last I embarked on a pink, and it was with no little satisfaction that I left our little, arid, dusty, scorched island. On the other hand, I was entranced by the flowery banks of the river Andalusia. I sailed into the Guadalquivir and landed at Seville. I only stayed in that city as long as it was necessary to find muleteers. One presented himself with a reasonably comfortable coach instead of the usual chaise. I chose him and, having filled my carriage with the novels I had bought in Cadiz, I left for Madrid.

The pretty countryside through which one passes as far as Córdoba, the picturesque sights of the Sierra Morena, the pastoral ways of the inhabitants of La Mancha, all that met my eyes added to the effect of my favourite reading. My soul became more sensitive and I nourished it with exalted and elegant sentiments. In short, I can tell you that as I arrived in Madrid I was already madly in love without having a particular object yet to be in love with. On reaching the capital I stayed at the Cross of Malta. It was midday and the table was soon laid for me. Then I put away my belongings as is usual for travellers to do when they take possession of a room at an inn. I heard and saw the handle of my door move. I went across and opened the door suddenly. I felt some resistance, which led me to believe that I had hit someone. And indeed I saw a quite well-dressed man behind my door, rubbing his nose, which had been grazed.

'Señor Don Lope,' the stranger said to me, 'I heard in the inn that the honoured son of the famous Gaspar Soarez had arrived and I came to pay you my respects.'

'Señor,' I said, 'if you had simply intended to come in, I would have given you a bump on the forehead with the door. But as you have got a grazed nose I think that you perhaps had your eye to the keyhole.'

'Bravo!' said the stranger. 'Your intelligence is remarkably sharp. It is true that, wishing to make your acquaintance, I wanted in advance to get some idea of the sort of person you were. And I have been charmed by your noble way of walking round your room and putting away your belongings.'

Having said this, the stranger entered my room without being invited and, continuing his discourse, said to me, 'Señor Don Lope. You see in me the famous scion of the family of Busqueros of Old Castile, not to be confused with the other Busqueros who come from León. As for me, I am known by the name of Don Roque Busqueros. But from now on I want only to be known for the devotion with which I shall serve your lordship.'

I then recalled the order of my father and said to him, 'Señor Don Roque, I must tell you that when I took leave of Gaspar Soarez, whose son I am, he forbade me ever to allow myself to be given the title of "don". He added to this prohibition that of never frequenting the nobility, by which your lordship will understand that it will no longer be possible for me to benefit from his obliging disposition.'

At this, Busqueros looked very grave and said, 'Señor Don Lope, your lordship has deeply embarrassed me by what he has said, for my own father on his deathbed commanded me always to call famous merchants by the title of "don" and to seek their company. Your lordship can thus see that he cannot obey his father without my having to contravene the last wishes of my own, and that however

367

much you try to avoid my company I must try to my utmost to seek yours.'

Busqueros's arguments confounded me. Besides, he looked very grave and, as my father had forbidden me to draw my sword, I had to do all I could to avoid quarrels.

Meanwhile Don Roque had found some pieces of eight on my table which were worth eight Dutch ducats. 'Señor Don Lope,' he said. 'I collect these pieces of eight and it so happens that I am missing those struck in the years I see you have here. You know what the craze for collecting is and I'm sure I shall delight you by offering you the opportunity of obliging me; or rather it is chance which offers you this opportunity, for I have all these pieces since the year 1707, when they were first struck, and it so happens that only these two are missing.'

I made Don Roque a present of the two pieces of eight with an eagerness made greater by the thought that he would then go away; but that was not his intention.

Busqueros looked grave and said to me, 'Señor Don Lope, I think it would not be fitting for us to eat out of the same plate or be reduced to passing the spoon or fork one to the other. I shall therefore have a second place-setting brought.'

Busqueros gave the necessary orders. Then we were served, and I had to admit that the conversation of my importunate guest was quite amusing, and that, but for the distress of having disobeyed my father I would have taken pleasure in having him at my table.

Busqueros went away immediately he had finished his meal. I let the heat of the day go by and then had myself taken to the Prado. I marvelled at the beauty of the place but was impatient to see the Buen Retiro. This lonely walk is well known in our novels and some premonition told me that I too would find there the opportunity of forming a tender relationship.

The sight of that beautiful garden delighted me more than I can say and I would have been for a long time lost in admiration of it if I had not been roused from my ecstasy by the sight of something which flashed in the grass a few yards from where I stood. I picked it up and saw it to be a portrait attached to a gold chain. The portrait was of a very handsome man and on the back of the medallion was a lock of hair held in a gold band on which these words had been engraved: 'I am altogether yours, dear Inés.' I put the piece of jewellery in my pocket and continued on my walk.

Having returned to the same spot, I came across two women, of whom one – a very young and beautiful person – was searching the ground with the distressed look which one has when one has lost something. I had little difficulty guessing that she was looking for the portrait. I went up to her respectfully and said to her, 'Señora, I think I may have found the object which you are looking for but prudence makes me hold on to it until you have been so kind as to give me some sort of description of it which will prove your ownership of it.'

'Señor,' said the pretty stranger, 'I am looking for a portrait attached to a gold chain of which this is the remaining piece.'

'But was there not some inscription with the portrait?' I asked her.

'There is one,' said the stranger, blushing somewhat. 'It would have told you that my name is Inés and that the subject of the portrait is altogether mine. Well, what is stopping you giving it back to me?'

Señora,' I said, 'you have not told me in what way that happy mortal belongs to you.'

'Señor,' said the stranger, 'I thought it was necessary to answer your scruples but not to satisfy your curiosity. And I don't know what right you have to ask me such questions.'

'My curiosity,' I replied, 'would more accurately have been called interest. As for my right to ask you such questions, I must point out to you that those who give back something which was lost usually receive an honourable reward. The reward I ask of you is to tell me what will perhaps make me the unhappiest of men.'

The pretty stranger looked somewhat grave and said to me, 'You are very bold for someone at their first meeting. It is not always the surest way to have a second. But I am willing to satisfy you on this point. The subject of the portrait is . . .'

At that moment Busqueros emerged unexpectedly from a neighbouring walk and accosted us in a gallant way. 'I compliment you, Señora,' he said, 'on getting to know the famous son of the richest merchant of Cadiz.'

The girl's features expressed very great indignation. 'I did not think that I was the kind of person to be addressed without it being known

369

who I am.' Then, turning to me, she said, 'Señor, please hand me back the portrait you found.'

At that, she climbed into her coach and passed from our sight.

Someone came to find the gypsy and he asked our permission to postpone telling us more of his story until the next day. When he had left us, the fair Jewess, now only called Laura, turned to Velásquez and said to him, 'What is your opinion, Señor duque, about the exalted sentiments of young Soarez? Have you ever bothered to turn your mind to what is commonly called love?'

'Señora,' Velásquez replied, 'my system embraces all of nature and therefore it must include all the feelings which she has put into the human heart. I have had to study and define all of them. I have been especially successful with love, for I have found it possible to express it in algebraic terms and, as you know, questions that can be approached through algebra yield solutions which are completely satisfactory.

'Now let us suppose love to have a positive value marked by a plus sign; hate, which is the opposite of love, will have a minus sign; and indifference, which is no feeling at all, will be equal to zero.

'If I multiply love by itself, whether I love love, or love to love love, I still have positive values, for a plus multiplied by a plus always makes a plus.

'But if I hate hate, I come back to feelings of love or positive quantities, for a minus multiplied by a minus makes a plus. But if on the contrary I hate the hate of hate, I come back to feelings which are the opposite of love, that is to say, negative values, just as the cube of a minus is a minus.

'As for the product of love and hate, or hate and love, they are always negative, just as are the products of a plus and a minus or a minus and a plus. So whether I hate love or love hate my feelings are always opposed to love. Can you think of any argument against my reasoning, fair Laura?'

'None at all,' said the Jewess, 'and I am convinced that there is not a woman who would not yield when faced by such arguments.'

'That wouldn't suit me,' continued Velásquez, 'for in yielding so quickly she would lose track of the corollaries or consequences which can be drawn from my principles. So I'll take my reasoning further. Since love and hate behave exactly like positive and negative values, it follows that I can write in the place of hate minus-love, which must not be confused with indifference, whose property is equal to zero.

'Now let us examine the behaviour of lovers. They love each other, then they hate each other, then they hate the hate they felt; they love each other more than before, then the negative factor changes all these feelings to hate. Now it is impossible to fail to identify here the alternative powers of plus and minus. Finally, you hear that the lover has stabbed his mistress. You are in a quandary as to whether it is a product of love or hate. Well, just as in algebra, you will reach a plus or minus root x when the exponents are odd.

'The truth of this is such that you will often see love beginning by a sort of aversion, a small negative value, that we can represent by $a - b$. This aversion will lead to a tiff, which we will represent by $a - c$. And the product of these two values will give $+bc$, that is to say, a positive value, a feeling of love.'

At this, the person known as Laura de Uzeda interrupted Velásquez and said to him, 'Señor duque, if I have understood you aright, love cannot be better represented than by the development of the powers of $x - a$, the latter being much less than x.'

'Dear Laura,' said Velásquez, 'you have read my thoughts. Yes, entrancing creature, the formula of the binomial invented by the noble Don Newton must be our guide in our investigation of the human heart as in all other calculations.'

We then dispersed. From then on it was easy to see the fair Israelite had made a deep impression on the mind and heart of Velásquez. As he was a descendant of the Gomelez, just as I was, I did not doubt that the power that the charming creature had over him would be used to try to convert him to Islam. What happened subsequently will show that I was not wrong in my conjectures.

The Thirty-fourth Day

We were already in the saddle early in the morning. The Wandering Jew, who did not think that we would be able to leave so early, had taken himself far off. We waited for him a long time. At last he reappeared, took his place beside me and began as follows:

∽ THE WANDERING JEW'S STORY CONTINUED ∽

'Emblems have never prevented us from believing that there is a God above all others,' Chæremon told us the next night. 'Thoth's text is clear on this point. This is what he says:

> This God is immobile and alone in his unity. He cannot be joined in thought nor can anything unite itself with Him. He is His own father and He is His own son and only father of God. He is the good; He is the source of all ideas and all elemental beings. This one God explains Himself by Himself because He is self-sufficient. He is the beginning, the God of Gods, the monad of unity and the origin of essence. And because He existed before thought He is called Noetarch.[1]

So you see, my friends,' continued Chæremon, 'that it is impossible to have more lofty notions of the divinity than ours. But we have believed it possible to deify part of the attributes of God and a part of His dealings with us to make of them, as it were, so many divinities, or rather divine virtues.

'So we call divine thought Emeph, and when it manifests itself in speech we call it Thoth (persuasion) or Ormeth (interpretation).

---

1 This passage, and much of what follows, is loosely translated or paraphrased from Jamblichus, *On the Egyptian Mysteries*. vii. 2–6.

'When divine thought, the guardian of truth, descends to earth and unleashes its creative power, it is called Amun. When divine thought brings to this the aid of art, it is called Ptah or Vulcan.

'When this thought appears most eminently benevolent it is called Osiris.

'We look upon God as one, but the huge number of beneficial dealings that God deigns to have with us leads us to think that we can without impiety look upon Him as many, for He is indeed multiple as well as immensely diverse in the qualities which we can perceive.

'As for demons, we believe that each of us has two: a good one and a bad one. The souls of heroes are of a similar nature to demons, especially those who are foremost in the spiritual order.

'The nature of gods can be compared to ether, the nature of heroes and demons to air, and simple souls seem to us to have something material about them. Divine providence is compared by us to light, which fills all the space of the universe.

'Ancient traditions speak of angelic powers, or powers of annunciation, whose task it is to transmit the orders of God and of other higher powers, which hellenizing Jews call archontoi, or archangels.

'Those among us who have been ordained priests believe that they have the power to summon up the real presence of gods, demons, angels, heroes and spirits. But such theurgy cannot be brought about without the order of the universe being disturbed in some way. When gods descend to earth the sun or moon hides for a short time from the sight of mortals.

'Archangels are surrounded by a more dazzling light than that of angels. The spirits of heroes have less brilliance than that of angels but more than that of simple mortals, which are dimmed by the effects of shadow. The princes of the Zodiac appear in very majestic shapes. There is also an infinite number of special circumstances which accompany the apparition of these different beings and are a means of distinguishing one from another. Evil demons, for example, can be recognized by the malign influence which never leaves them.

'As for idols, we believe that if they are made under certain celestial conjunctions and accompanied by certain theurgic ceremonies, some part of the divine essence can be brought down into them. But this art is so delusory and so unworthy of true knowledge of God that we

373

leave it to a much lower order of priests than that to which I have the honour of belonging.

'When one of our priests invokes the gods he somehow makes himself part of their essence. For all that, he does not cease being human; but the divine nature dwells in him to a certain degree. He is united in some way with his God. When he is in this state, he finds it easy to hold sway over animal or terrestrial demons and to cause them to leave the bodies they have entered.

'By mixing together stones, herbs and animal matter, our priests sometimes create a compound worthy of receiving the divinity, but prayer is the true bond which unites the priest with his God.

'All these rites and dogmas which I have explained to you are not attributed by us to Thoth, or the Third Mercury, who lived in the reign of Ozymandias. Their real author, according to us, is Bytis the prophet, who lived some two thousand years earlier and who explained the opinions of the First Mercury. But as I have already told you, time has changed and added to them, and I do not believe that this ancient religion has come down to us unadulterated.

'Finally, to hide nothing from you, our priests sometimes dare to utter threats to the gods. On these occasions during the sacrifice they say:

' "If you do not give me what I ask of you, I will reveal what Isis most jealously hides. I will disclose the secrets of the abyss. I will break open the casket of Osiris and scatter his members."

'I will confess to you that I do not approve of these formulae and Chaldeans abstain from them completely.'

As Chæremon reached this point in his lesson the acolyte struck midnight; and as you are now close to your resting-place please allow me to stop now and continue my story tomorrow.

The Wandering Jew went off, and Velásquez declared to us that he had learnt nothing new, and that all that we had heard was in the work of Jamblichus. 'It's a book I have read very carefully,' he said, 'and I have never understood why the critics who have taken Porphyry's letter to the Egyptian Anebon to be genuine consider the reply made by the Egyptian Abammon to have been made up by Porphyry. On the contrary, it seems to me that Porphyry had done

374

nothing other than incorporate Abammon's reply into his work, adding a few observations on Greek philosophers and on Chaldeans.'[2]

'Be that as it may as far as Anebon and Abammon are concerned,' said Uzeda, 'I assure you that the Jew has only told you the pure truth.'

We reached the resting-place. We made a light meal and the gypsy, having nothing else to do, began his story again:

✑ THE GYPSY CHIEF'S STORY CONTINUED ✑

When young Soarez had told me about the way the conversation in the garden ended, he seemed to be in need of sleep. Rest was necessary for the recovery of his health so I left him free to enjoy it. But the following night he began his story again:

✑ LOPE SOAREZ'S STORY CONTINUED ✑

I left the Buen Retiro, my heart full of love for the beautiful stranger and full of indignation towards Busqueros. As the next day was Sunday, I thought that by going to all the churches in turn I might meet the lady of my thoughts. I visited three in vain but I found her in the fourth. When Mass was over, she left the church and, deliberately passing close to me, said to me, 'The portrait was of my brother.'

She had already gone by but I was still transfixed to the spot, entranced by those few words I had heard. Indeed the care she had taken to set my mind at rest could only arise from a burgeoning interest in me.

Back in my inn I ordered dinner to be brought and hoped that Busqueros would not appear. But he came in with the soup and said, 'Señor Don Lope, I have turned down twenty invitations, but as I have told you I am utterly devoted to serving your lordship.'

I was very tempted to say something disagreeable to Señor Don Roque, but I remembered my father's order that I should not draw

2 All this is indeed taken from Jamblichus, loc. cit.

my sword and thought that I must avoid a quarrel for that reason.

Busqueros had a place laid for himself, sat down and then said to me in a highly self-satisfied and smug way, 'You must agree, Señor Don Lope, that I did you a great service yesterday. Without apparently intending to, I let the lady know that you were the son of a rich merchant. She pretended to feel great anger but it was to convince you that her heart was unmoved by the lure of wealth. Don't believe it, Señor Don Lope. You are young and have some wit and a handsome face. But when you are loved by another, money will play its part in it. But in my case, as it happens, that is not to be feared. When people like me, they like me for what I am, and I have never inspired passions in which self-interest played a part.'

Busqueros went on and on in the same vein, and when he had finished his meal he left. That evening I went to the Buen Retiro with a secret premonition that I would not see the pretty stranger there. And indeed she did not come but Busqueros did, and stayed with me the whole evening.

The next day he came to dine and, as he departed, he told me that he would join me at the Buen Retiro. I told him I would not be going there and, when evening came, as I was quite convinced he would not believe what I said, I hid in a shop on the way to the Buen Retiro. I had not been there long when I saw Busqueros go by. He went to the Buen Retiro, did not find me there and I saw him come away again. Then I went there myself. I took several turns around the garden and at last the pretty stranger appeared. I greeted her in a respectful way, which did not seem to displease her. I did not know whether I should thank her for what she had said to me in church.

She decided herself to save me from my predicament. Smilingly, she said, 'You claim that one has the right to a reward when one has found an object which has been lost. And for having found this portrait you wanted to know what my connection was with its subject. Now you know it, so don't ask me more unless you find some other piece of property which belongs to me. For in that case you would have a right perhaps to further rewards. It is not, however, proper that we should often be seen to walk together. Farewell. I do not forbid you to accost me when you have something to say to me.'

The girl then bade me farewell graciously, to which I replied with a deep bow. After that, I directed my steps to a nearby path parallel with the walk I had just left, towards which I allowed my eyes to stray. The stranger herself took a few more turns before leaving the garden, and in stepping into her carriage, she threw me a last glance in which I thought I could detect some benevolence.

The next morning I was still imbued by the same feeling, and was thinking all the while about how it might develop. It seemed that the moment might not be far off when the beautiful Inés would accord me the right to write to her. As I had never written any love-letters I thought it appropriate to practise so as to catch the style. So I put my hand to my pen and wrote the following letter:

Lope Soarez to Inés.

My trembling hand, in concert with the timidity of my feelings, is not able to form the letters of these words. And indeed what can they express? What mortal can write to love's dictation? No pen can follow it.

I would like to convey my thoughts on this paper but they flee and wander off into the groves of the Buen Retiro. They linger on the sand bearing the imprint of your foot and cannot tear themselves away.

Is this garden of our kings really as beautiful as it seems to me? No – its charm is surely in my eyes and it is you who have put it there. And would this place ever be deserted if others saw the beauties that I have found there?

In this garden the grass is more fresh, the jasmine strains to breathe out its perfume, and the grove where you have passed, jealous of its amorous shade, resists with ever greater vigour the burning rays of the noonday. And all you did was to pass. What will you do in this heart of mine in which you dwell?

Having finished this epistle, I read it back and found it to be full of extravagance. I didn't therefore want either to present it or to send it, but so as to indulge an agreeable day-dream I sealed it and wrote on it, 'To fair Inés . . .' Then I threw the letter in a drawer.

That evening I felt like going out. I wandered the streets of Madrid and, passing by the Inn of the White Lion, thought that it would be pleasant to dine there and thus avoid the accursed Busqueros. So I

377

took my meal there and returned afterwards to my inn. I opened the drawer where I had put my amorous epistle. I could not find it. I asked my servants about it: they said that no one other than Busqueros had come. I was sure that he had taken it and I was very worried about what he would do with it. That evening I did not go directly to the Buen Retiro but lay in waiting in the same shop in which I had been before. Soon the carriage of the fair Inés appeared, with Busqueros running after it, waving a letter he had in his hand. He made so much fuss with his gestures and cries that the carriage was stopped, and he took advantage of this to place the letter into the very hands of the addressee. Then the carriage went on its way towards the Buen Retiro and Busqueros went on his.

I did not know how this scene would end and walked on slowly towards the garden. There I found fair Inés sitting with her companion on a bench set in front of a bower.

She indicated that I should approach her and invited me to sit down. Then she said, 'Señor, it is necessary that I speak frankly to you. First, I beg you to tell me why you have written to me such absurdities. Then, why did you give them to that man whose brazenness greatly displeased me, as you were able to witness?'

'Señora,' I replied, 'it is indeed true that I wrote that letter to you but I did not intend you to be given it. I wrote it for the pleasure of writing it and then I placed it in a drawer, whence it was taken by the detestable Busqueros, who has been the bane of my life since my arrival in Madrid.'

Inés started to laugh and read my letter with an indulgent air. Then she said to me, 'Your name is Don Lope Soarez? Are you related to the great and rich merchant of Cadiz?'

I replied that I was his very son.

Inés then spoke of unimportant matters and went back to her carriage. Before stepping in, she said to me, 'It is not proper that I should keep such absurdities so I shall give them back to you. But do not lose them, for I may ask you for them back one day.' And in giving me back my letter Inés squeezed my hand.

Until then no woman had squeezed my hand. I knew of examples of this in novels, but I had not been able accurately to assess what pleasure it produced simply by reading about it. I found this way of expressing one's feelings quite charming and returned to my inn the happiest of men.

The next day Busqueros again did me the honour of dining with me. 'Well,' he said, 'the letter reached its destination. I can see from the way you look that it made a good impression.'

I was forced to agree that I had some obligation towards him.

Towards evening I went to the Buen Retiro and on going in saw Inés, who was about fifty paces ahead of me. She was without her companion and was followed a long way behind by a lackey. She turned, then continued to walk on, then let her fan fall to the ground. I took it back to her and she accepted it graciously and said, 'I promised you an honourable reward whenever you bring back to me some lost possession. Let us sit on that bench and settle this great affair.'

She led me to the same bench which we had sat on the evening before and said to me, 'Well, when you brought back this portrait you learnt that it was that of my brother. What do you wish to know now?'

'Oh Señora,' I replied, 'I want to know who you are, what you are called and to whom you are related.'

'Listen,' said Inés to me, 'you might be led to believe that your riches are such as to dazzle me, but you will banish this thought when you discover that I am the daughter of a man as rich as your father, Moro the banker.'

'Heavens above!' I cried. 'Have I heard correctly? Oh Señora, I am the unhappiest of men. I may not think of you without incurring my father's curse and that of my grandfather and my great-grandfather, Iñigo Soarez, who, having sailed the seven seas, established a trading house in Cadiz. All that remains for me is to die.'

At that moment Busqueros stuck his head out of the bower against which our bench was set and, placing it between Inés and myself, he said to her, 'Don't believe a word of it, Señora. He always uses this trick when he wants to get rid of someone. As he wasn't keen on making my acquaintance, he alleged that his father had forbidden him to frequent the nobility. Now he's afraid of upsetting his great-grandfather, Iñigo Soarez, who, having sailed the seven seas, established a trading house in Cadiz. Don't be put off, Señora, little

Croesuses like him always find it difficult to take the bait, but they have to in the end.'

Inés stood up with a look of extreme indignation and made her way to her carriage.

As the gypsy reached this point in his story, someone came and interrupted him and we did not see him again that evening.

The Thirty-fifth Day

We mounted our horses again and set off into the mountains. After about an hour's ride the Wandering Jew appeared. He took his usual place between Velásquez and me and continued his story as follows:

↶ THE WANDERING JEW'S STORY CONTINUED ↷

The following night the venerable Chæremon received us with his usual kindness and spoke to us as follows:

'The many matters which I dealt with yesterday did not allow me to tell you about a dogma which is universally received among us and which enjoys even greater fame among the Greeks, thanks to the vogue given to it by Plato. I am referring to the belief in the logos or divine wisdom which we sometimes call Mander, sometimes Meth and sometimes Thoth, or persuasion.

'There is another dogma which I want to mention to you. It was established by one of the three Thoths, called Trismegistus, or Thrice Great, because he had thought of the divinity as being divided between three great powers: God Himself, to whom he gave the name of father, the word and the spirit.

'Such are our dogmas. As for our precepts, they are just as pure, especially for us priests. The exercise of virtue, fasting and prayer is what goes to make up our lives.

'The vegetarian diet to which we restrict ourselves, makes the blood which flows in our veins less easily inflamed and we have less difficulty in controlling our passions. The priests of Apis abstain altogether from intercourse with women.

'Such today is our religion. It differs from the ancient religions in several important ways, including metempsychosis, which has few adherents today although it had many followers seven hundred years ago, when Pythagoras visited our country. Our ancient mythology

381

also makes much of the gods of the planets, known as guardians. But today this doctrine has been left to those who cast horoscopes. As I told you, religions change like everything else in this world.

'It only remains for me to speak to you about our holy mysteries. I will tell you all that you need to know about them. First, you can be sure that if you were initiated you would not know more about the origins of our mythology. Open the histories of Herodotus: he was initiated and boasts about it on every page; yet he investigated the origins of the gods of Greece as someone who knew no more than the common people.

'What he calls sacred discourse has nothing to do with history. It is what the Romans call "turpiloquens", or speaking indecently. To every initiate a story is told which is shocking to ordinary ideas of decency. At Eleusis it is about Baubo, who received Ceres in her house. In Phrygia it is about Bacchus's loves.

'In Egypt we believe this turpitude to be an emblem which indicates to what extent the essence of matter is vile in itself, and we learn no more than this from it. A famous consul called Cicero has just written a book on the nature of the gods.[1] He admits that he does not know where Italy got its religious cult from. And yet he was an augur and hence initiated into all the mysteries of the Etruscan religion. The ignorance which is apparent in all works of initiates shows you that initiation does not lead us to know more about the origins of our religion. All that is indeed very ancient. On the bas-relief of Ozymandias you can see a procession of Osiris. The cult of Apis and Mnevis[2] was introduced into Egypt by Bacchus more than three thousand years ago.

'So initiation throws no light either on the origins of religion or on the history of the gods or on the meaning of emblems; but the establishment of mysteries has none the less been very useful to mankind. The man who accuses himself of some grave fault or whose hands are sullied by murder goes to see the priests of the mysteries, confesses his sins and then is purified by baptism. Before the era of this salutary institution many men, not being able to approach the altar, were rejected by society and became brigands.

1 i.e. the *De natura deorum*.
2 The sacred bulls of Memphis and Heliopolis respectively.

382

'In the mysteries of Mithras, the initiate is given bread and wine and this meal is called the eucharist. The sinner, reconciled with God, begins a new, more innocent life than that he had lived up till then.'

At this point I interrupted the Wandering Jew and remarked to him that I thought the eucharist to belong only to the Christian religion.

Velásquez then spoke and said, 'Forgive me, but what he has said in this respect is very consistent with what I read in Justin Martyr, who even adds that he detected in it the evil-doing of demons, in that they imitated in advance what the Christians were to do one day. But please go on, Señor Wandering Jew.'

The Jew then picked up the thread of his story as follows:

'Mysteries,' said Chæremon, 'have another ceremony which is common to all of them. A god dies, he is buried, and mourned for several days. Then the god comes back to life and there is great rejoicing. Some say that this emblem represents the sun, but it is generally thought to refer to seeds in the ground.

'And that, my young Israelite, is more or less all I can tell you about our dogmas and rites,' said the priest. 'You see that we are not idolaters, as your prophets have accused us of being from time to time, but I confess to the belief that your religion and mine are beginning no longer to be sufficient for the nations. If we cast our eyes about us, we can see unease and the taste for novelty on every side.

'In Palestine whole crowds are going out into the desert to listen to this new prophet who is baptizing in the Jordan. Here you can see therapeuts, healers and magi who bring together the cult of the Persians with our own. Young Apollonius goes from one town to the next with his fair hair and tries to pass himself off as Pythagoras. Street acrobats are calling themselves priests of Isis, the old cult is abandoned, the temples are deserted and there is no longer any incense burning on the altars.'

As the Wandering Jew reached this point in his story he noticed that we were nearing our resting-place and went off into a valley in which he was soon lost to sight.

I took the Duke of Velásquez aside and said to him, 'Let me ask your opinion on what the Wandering Jew has told us. There are things which it is not proper for us to hear and seem to me contrary to the faith which we profess.'

'Señor Alphonse,' Velásquez replied, 'these pious sentiments must do you honour in the eyes of any thinking person. I dare say that my faith is more philosophical than yours but it is no less fervent and pure. And the proof of this is in my system, about which I have spoken to you on several occasions and which is only a series of reflections on providence and its infinite wisdom.

'So I believe, Señor Alphonse, that what I can hear without qualms you can listen to without scruple.'

Velásquez's reply set my mind altogether at rest and during the evening the gypsy, having nothing else to do, continued his story as follows:

∽ THE GYPSY CHIEF'S STORY CONTINUED ∽

When young Soarez had told me the story of his discomfiture in the Buen Retiro gardens he seemed to feel the need for sleep. I let him enjoy the rest which was indispensable to his state of health and when I came next evening to sit with him during the night he continued his story as follows:

∽ LOPE SOAREZ'S STORY CONTINUED ∽

My heart was still full of love for Inés and, as you may well imagine, full of wrath towards Busqueros, which didn't prevent that importunate boor appearing before me next day as the soup was being brought to me. When he had taken the edge off his hunger, he said to me, 'Señor Don Lope, I imagine that at your age you have no desire to get married. It's a folly that is always committed when one is young. But to offer to a girl as an excuse the anger of your great-grandfather Iñigo Soarez, who, having sailed the seven seas, established a trading house at Cadiz, that's really very eccentric. You are lucky that I was able to patch matters up a bit.'

'Señor Don Roque,' I replied. 'Please do me another service to add

384

to all those you have already done me, that is, not to go to the Buen Retiro gardens this evening. I think it likely that the fair Inés will not go there and even if she does she won't speak to me. But I want to go to the same bench where I saw her yesterday, to weep over my misfortunes and to sigh as much as I wish.'

Don Roque looked very grave and said, 'Señor Don Lope, the words your lordship has just addressed to me are deeply insulting and might lead one to suppose that my devotion to you does not have the honour of being approved by you. It is true that I could, without impropriety, allow you to lament alone and weep over your misfortunes, but the fair Inés might come, and if I am not there, who will take on the task of making good your imprudence? No, Señor Don Lope, I am too devoted to you to obey you.'

Don Roque withdrew immediately after the meal. I let the heat of the day go by and then took the road to the Buen Retiro; but I made sure to hide in the usual shop. I soon saw Busqueros go by. He went to the Buen Retiro, but not finding me there retraced his steps and appeared to me to go off in the direction of the Prado. Then I left my vantage-point and went to the very place where I had experienced already so much joy and so much sadness. I sat down on the bench where I had been the day before, and shed many tears.

Suddenly I felt a tap on my shoulder. I thought it was Busqueros and turned round angrily; but whom should I see but Inés, who smiled at me with ineffable grace. She sat down next to me, told her companion to go on a little way and then spoke to me as follows:

'My dear Soarez, I was very angry with you yesterday because I did not understand why you were speaking to me about your grandfather and great-grandfather. But I have informed myself of these things. I learnt that for a century your house has refused to have any dealings with ours, all because of grievances which, it is said, are of very small moment in themselves. But if you have difficulties on your side, I have them also on mine. My father has long since disposed of my hand and is afraid that I might have different ideas about my future than he has. He does not like me to go out often, and does not allow me to go to the Prado or the theatre at all. It is only the absolute need that I have to take the air from time to time which obliges him to let me come here with my duenna. This walk is so

385

little frequented that he believes that I can be seen here without any risk. My future husband is a Neapolitan gentleman called the Duke of Santa Maura. I believe that his only motive for marrying me is to enjoy my fortune and repair his own. My feelings for this party have always been very distant and since I have met you they are even more so. My father has a very decisive nature. But his younger sister, Señora de Avalos, has a great deal of influence over his mind. This dear aunt is very fond of me and she is very much against the Neapolitan duke. I have spoken about you to her, and she would like to meet you. Come with me as far as my carriage. You will find at the gate to the gardens one of Señora de Avalos's servants, who will take you to her.'

The words of the adorable Inés filled my heart with joy and I formed many sweet hopes. I followed her to her carriage and then went to her aunt's house. I had the good fortune to be approved of by Señora de Avalos. On the following days I went back at the same time and each time I encountered her niece there.

My happiness lasted six days. On the seventh, I was informed of the arrival of the Duke of Santa Maura. Señora de Avalos told me not to lose heart, and a female member of her household secretly gave me the following letter:

Inés Moro to Lope Soarez.

The hateful man to whom I am betrothed is in Madrid and his people occupy our whole house. I have obtained permission to withdraw to a part of the building one window of which looks out on to the Calle de los Agustinos. The window is not very high and we will be able to speak to each other for a short time. I have things to say to you which concern our happiness. Come at nightfall.

It was five o'clock in the evening when I received this note and, as sunset was at nine o'clock, there were four hours which I didn't know how to occupy. I decided to go to the Buen Retiro. The sight of that place duly filled me with sweet reveries, which allowed me to pass the time without noticing how slowly it was going by. I had already walked round the garden several times when I saw Busqueros arrive. My first impulse was to climb up into a knotty oak tree which I saw close by. But I wasn't nimble enough to manage this so I climbed back down and went to sit on a bench, where I made my stand against the enemy.

Don Roque accosted me in his familiar and self-satisfied way and said, 'Well, Señor Don Lope, I think that the fair Moro girl will end up by softening the heart of your great-grandfather, Iñigo Soarez, who, having sailed the seven seas, established a trading house at Cadiz. What? Not a word from you, Señor Don Lope? Well, since you refuse to speak I will sit down on this bench and tell you my story. You will find quite singular aspects to it which may well be a lesson to you.'

I had decided to put up with anything until sunset. So I offered no resistance to Busqueros, who began as follows:

∾ DON ROQUE BUSQUEROS'S STORY ∾

I am the only son of Don Blas Busqueros, who is the younger son of the younger brother of another Busqueros, who himself was a younger son of the cadet branch.

My father had the honour of serving the king for thirty years as *alfier*, that is, ensign, in an infantry regiment but, realizing that his perseverance could not bring him promotion to the rank of sub-lieutenant, he left the service and set up house in the small village of Allazuelos, where he married a noble lady whose uncle, a canon, had left her a life rent of six hundred piastres. I was the only fruit of this union, which did not last long as my father died when I was only eight years old.

So I was left in the care of my mother, who, however, did not take much care of me. Doubtless believing that to be active was good for children, she let me run about the streets from morning to night without showing much concern about what I got up to. The other children of my age didn't have the freedom to go out whenever they wanted to, so I went to see them. Their parents were used to my visits and paid little attention to them. So I found thereby a way of slipping into all the houses of the village at any time of day.

My naturally observant mind led me to note carefully what happened in the privacy of all these households and I faithfully retailed this to my mother, who enjoyed hearing my stories. I must even admit that it is thanks to her guidance that I owe my happy talent of involving myself in the affairs of others, more for their benefit than for my own.

For a short time I thought that I would please my mother by telling the whole neighbourhood everything that took place in our own house. Not a visitor was received, not a conversation took place, no matter how personal, which the whole village was not instantly informed of. But this publicity did not enjoy the favour of pleasing her and a somewhat sharp punishment indicated to me that it was necessary to import items of news from outside without exporting those from within.

After some time I noticed that in all the houses people hid from me. I was stung by this. The obstacles which were erected against my curiosity only excited it further. I discovered countless ways of looking even into the intimacy of bedrooms. The flimsy style of house construction which was common in the village helped me in my ploys. Ceilings consisted only of juxtaposed planks. At night I would slip into the attics, drill a hole through the planks and soon know all the secrets of the marriage. I relayed them to my mother, who passed them on to all the inhabitants of Allazuelos, or rather to each of them in turn.

People guessed to whom my mother owed this information and I was daily more detested. All the houses were closed to me but the roof-lights were not. And as I crouched in the attics I was in the midst of my compatriots without their knowing it. They gave me shelter without wanting to, and I inhabited their houses in spite of them, more or less as rats do. Like those animals too, I would slip into larders when I could and nibble at the provisions kept there.

When I reached the age of eighteen my mother told me that it was time for me to choose a career, but my choice had long been made. I wanted to be a lawyer and have thereby countless opportunities of knowing the secrets of families and involving myself in their affairs. So it was decided that I would study law and I left for Salamanca.

What a difference there was between the city and the village where I was born! What vast scope for my curiosity! But also what new obstacles! The houses were several storeys high. They were scrupulously locked at night and, as if to annoy me further, those living on the second and third floors left their windows open at night to be able to breathe more freely. I saw straight away that I could not do anything by myself and that I needed to ally myself with friends who were worthy of abetting me in my enterprises. So I began to follow the law course and at the same time studied the characters of my comrades, to know where to place my trust. At last I found four who seemed to have the necessary qualities, and I began to roam around at night with them, just engaging in a little rowdiness in the streets.

At last when I thought that they were more or less ready, I said to them, 'Dear friends, aren't you amazed at the audacity with which the inhabitants of this city leave their windows open all night? What? Because they are twenty feet above our heads do they think they have the right to cock a snook at us students? Their sleep is an insult to us; their rest makes me restless. So I have decided first to find out what goes on up there and then to show them just what we are capable of.'

These words were well received but no one realized what I was getting at. Then I explained myself more clearly. 'My dear friends,' I said. 'First we must have a ladder just fifteen feet long. Three of you wrapped up in your cloaks will easily carry it, looking like people walking in single file, especially if you walk on the darker side of the street and carry the ladder next to the wall. When we decide to use it, we will lean it against the window, and while one of us climbs to the apartment we want to look into, the others will stand a little way off to keep watch and ensure our common safety. When we find out what is happening above the ground floor we will see what is to be done about it.'

This plan was approved and I ordered a light but strong ladder. As soon as it was ready we started using it. I chose a decent-looking house with a not-too-high window. I put my ladder up against it, and climbed up so that only my head could be seen from inside the bedroom.

There was a full moon. None the less for a moment I couldn't see anything. Then I saw a man in his bed, staring at me with a haggard expression. Fear seemed to have deprived him of the power of speech. When he recovered it he said to me, 'Ghastly and bloody head! Stop persecuting me and reproaching me for an involuntary crime!'

★

As Don Roque reached this point in his story, it seemed to me that the sun was going down quickly. Not having brought a watch with me, I asked him what the time was.

This quite simple question seemed to offend him deeply. 'Señor Don Lope Soarez,' he said somewhat angrily. 'It seems to me that when a member of polite society has the honour of telling you a story, to interrupt him at the most interesting point in order to ask him the time, is almost to lead him to understand that he is what we Spaniards call *pesado*, that is, boring. I do not believe that I can be accused of that. So in that conviction I shall continue my story.'

Seeing that I had been taken for a ghastly and bloody head, I put on the most terrifying expression I could manage. The man could not bear it. He leapt out of his bed and rushed out of the bedroom. He wasn't alone in bed: a young woman woke up and stretched out two very plump arms from under the covers. Catching sight of me, she got up and bolted the door by which her husband had gone out, and then indicated that I should climb in. My ladder was a little short, so I had recourse to some architectural carving, on which I placed a foot and jumped into the apartment. On looking at me more closely, the lady seemed to notice that she had made a mistake, and I realized too, that I was not the man she was expecting. But she asked me to sit down and slipped on a skirt.

Then she came back to where I was, sat down on a chair a few paces from me and said, 'Señor, I was expecting a relation who was to speak to me about some family affairs, and you can well imagine that if he came through the window he had good reasons for doing so. As for you, Señor, I do not have the honour of knowing you and do not know why you have presented yourself in my house at this time, which is not the time for visiting people.'

'Señora,' I replied, 'my intention was not to enter your house but only to raise my head to the level of your bedroom to see what was going on there.' I then took the opportunity of telling the young lady about my tastes, my childhood pastimes and the association I had formed with four young men whose role it was to help me in my enterprises.

The lady seemed to pay close attention to what I said. Then she said, 'Señor, what you have just told me restores you completely to my esteem. You are quite right; there is nothing nicer in the world than to know what others get up to, and I have always shared your view of this. I cannot keep you here any longer, but we will meet again.'

'Señora,' I said, 'before you woke up, your husband did me the honour of taking my face for a ghastly head that had come to reproach him for an involuntary crime. Please do me the honour of informing me of the circumstances of all this.'

'I approve of your curiosity,' said the lady. 'Come tomorrow at five o'clock in the evening to the public garden and you will find me there with one of my friends. But for this evening, farewell.'

The lady graciously accompanied me to the window. I climbed down the ladder, rejoined my companions and told them what had happened. Next day I went to the public garden at exactly five o'clock.

As Busqueros reached this point in his story, it seemed to me that the sun was going down fast and I said impatiently, 'Señor Don Roque, I can assure you that an affair of importance obliges me to leave you. It will be easy for you to pick up the thread of your story when next you do me the honour of dining with me.'

Busqueros looked very grave and said, 'Señor Don Lope Soarez. It is becoming clear to me that it is your intention to insult me. If that is the case, you would do better to tell me plainly that you look on me as an impudent gossip and a bore. But no, Señor Don Lope, I cannot bring myself to believe that that is how you think about me and so I'll continue with my story.

'I found the lady in question in the public garden with one of her friends, a tall, attractive lady of about her age. We sat down on a bench and the lady, wanting me to know her more intimately, began to tell the story of her life as follows:

✑ FRASQUETA SALERO'S STORY ✑

I am the younger daughter of a brave officer whose services were so meritorious that on his death his full salary was paid to his widow as a pension. My mother, who had been born in Salamanca, retired there with my sister, called Dorothea, and me, whom people at that time called Frasqueta. She owned a house in a very quiet part of town, which she had repaired and decorated, and we settled ourselves there, living with a frugality which corresponded well to the modest exterior of our house.

My mother did not let us go either to the theatre, or to the bullfight, or to the public gardens. She neither visited others nor received visitors. Having no other form of amusement, I spent nearly all my time at the window.

As I had a great natural inclination to courtesy, if anyone well dressed went by in the street, I would follow him with my eyes and look at him in such a way as to suggest that he inspired some interest in me. Passers-by were not indifferent to the attention I paid them. Some greeted me, some shot me approving glances, yet others walked up and down the street several times, their only motive being that of seeing me again. When my mother noticed what I was up to she would say, 'Frasqueta, Frasqueta! What are you doing? Be modest and solemn, like your sister, or else you won't find a husband.'

My mother was wrong, for my sister is still a spinster and I have been married for a year.

Our street was very deserted and I rarely had the pleasure of seeing passers-by whose outward appearance prejudiced me in their favour. I was, however, helped by a particular circumstance. Very near our windows was a tall tree with a stone seat. Those who wanted to look at me at their leisure could sit there without appearing suspicious or drawing attention to themselves.

One day, a much better-dressed man than those I had seen till then sat down on the seat, drew out a book from his pocket and began to read. But as soon as he caught sight of me, he paid little attention to his book, and looked into my eyes. The young man came back the following days. Once he came close to my window and seemed to be looking for something; then he said, 'Señora, haven't you dropped something?'

I said that I had not.

'A pity,' he said, 'for if, for example, you had dropped the little cross that you are wearing around your neck, I would have picked it up and taken it back to my house. By having in my possession something which had belonged to you, I could flatter myself with the thought that you were not as indifferent to me as you are to other people who come and sit on this seat. The effect you have had on my heart perhaps earns me the right to be distinguished by you from the crowd.'

As my mother came in at that moment I was not able to reply to the young man. But I deftly undid my cross and let it fall.

That evening I saw two ladies arrive with a lackey in a fine livery. They sat down on the seat and lifted their mantillas. Then one drew a small piece of paper from her pocket, undid it and removed from it a small golden cross, after which she shot me a somewhat mocking glance. Convinced that the young man had sacrificed the first sign of my affection to the lady, I flew into a terrible rage and did not sleep all that night.

The next day the inconstant young man sat down again on the seat and I was very surprised to see him draw from his pocket a little piece of paper, unfold it, take out a little cross and kiss it fervently.

That evening two lackeys in the livery of the day before appeared. They carried a table with them, which they laid. Then they went away and came back with ices, chocolate, orangeade, biscuits and other such things. Then the two ladies of the day before appeared. They sat down on the seat and were served with the food which had been brought.

My mother and sister, who never sat at the window, could not remain indifferent to the sound of glasses and bottles. One of the two ladies, having caught sight of them, and finding them of an amenable disposition, invited them to share their repast, asking them only to bring some chairs.

My mother needed no persuasion. She had chairs carried into the street. We added a few ornaments to our attire and went to join the lady who had anticipated our wishes so obligingly. In greeting her, I noticed that she looked very like the young man. I supposed that she was his sister. From that I concluded that he had spoken to her about me, had given her my cross and that she had sat down on the seat the day before simply to observe me. It was soon discovered that there was a shortage of spoons and my sister went to fetch some. Immediately after it transpired that there were no napkins and so my mother went for those. As soon as she had gone, I said to the lady, 'Am I right in thinking, Señora, that you have a brother who looks much like you?'

'No, Señora,' she replied. 'The brother to whom you refer is myself. Listen carefully. I have another brother, whose name is the Duke of San Lugar. I am soon to be the Duke of Arcos, because I am marrying the heiress to that title. I cannot abide my future wife but if I refuse to enter into this marriage there will be lugubrious scenes in my family as a result, for which I have no taste. Since I cannot dispose of my hand as I would wish, I have decided to save my heart for someone more worthy of love than the young Señora de Arcos. I am far from wishing to suggest anything dishonourable to you, Señora, but you are not leaving Spain and nor am I. Chance could unite us and if it doesn't I shall be able myself to bring about opportunities for us to meet again. Your mother is about to come back. Here is a ring in which is set a valuable solitaire. I have chosen one of considerable value to convince you that I am not trying to impress you with my birth. I beg you to be so kind as to accept this token of my thoughts for you, which is intended to recall me to yours.'

I had been brought up by a mother whose principles were of the most austere, and I knew well enough that honour required me to refuse this gift. But I was persuaded to accept it by considerations that I then had and which I cannot now recall. My mother came back with napkins and my sister with spoons. The unknown lady was very friendly throughout the evening and we separated on the best of terms. But the pleasant young man did not reappear under my window. He had probably married the Arcos heiress.

Next Sunday it occurred to me that the ring would sooner or later be found in my room. Consequently, as I was in church at the time, I pretended to have found it under my seat and showed it to my mother. She told me that it was probably a piece of glass that had been set in the ring but that I should none the less put it in my pocket. A jeweller lived nearby. He was shown the ring and valued it at eight thousand pistoles. This high valuation delighted my mother. She told me that it would be fitting to present it to St Anthony of Padua, who was the protector of our family, but that if we sold it, it could produce two good dowries: enough to marry both of us.

'Forgive me, dear mother,' I replied. 'It seems to me that we should first make it known that we have found the ring, without specifying its value. If the rightful owner comes forward we will give the ring back. Otherwise my sister has no right to it any more than St Anthony of Padua. As I found the ring it will indubitably belong to me.'

My mother had no answer to this. It was made known in Salamanca that a ring had been found but the value was kept secret and, as you may well imagine, no one came forward.

The young man to whom I owed so precious a gift had left a deep impression on my heart and for a week I was not seen at the window. But eventually I would sit there again as before, from force of habit, and would spend nearly all my time there.

The stone seat on which the young duke used to place himself to see me was then filled by a large man of what seemed to be an imperturbably calm and tranquil humour. He caught sight of me at the window and my presence there seemed to displease him. He turned his back on me. But even when he could not see me, I troubled him, for he would turn round uneasily from time to time. Soon he went away, indicating by his looks that he felt some indignation. But he returned the next day and played out the same scene. In the end he turned away and returned so often that when two months had passed he asked for my hand in marriage.

My mother told me that one did not find such parties every day of the week and ordered me to accept his offer. I obeyed and changed my name from Frasqueta Salero to Doña Francisca Cornádez and came to live in the house in which you met me yesterday.

Once I became the wife of Señor Cornádez I devoted all my time to making him happy. I succeeded rather too well. At the end of three months I found him to be happier than I hoped, and what was worse, he believed that he made me perfectly happy. His smug expression did not suit his face. Moreover, it displeased and annoyed me. Happily, however, this state of beatitude did not last long.

One day Cornádez, on his way out of the house, met a boy with a letter in his hand, looking bewildered. He decided to help him and discovered that the letter was addressed to 'Adorable Frasqueta'. Cornádez made a face that put the errand boy to flight. Then he took the precious document home and read the following:

Is it possible that my wealth, my courage, my reputation are not able to bring me to your attention? I am ready to do anything, give anything, undertake anything, only for you to show me some interest. Those who undertook to serve me must have deceived me, for I have obtained no sign of recognition from you. But boldness is part of my character. Nothing deters me when passion is in question and my passion, even in its earliest infancy, knows no bridle nor measure. My only fear is to remain unknown to you.

Conde de Peña Flor.

Reading this letter dispelled in an instant all of Cornádez's happiness. He became uneasy, suspicious and did not allow me to go out unless accompanied by one of our neighbours, of whom he had become fond because of her exemplary piety.

Cornádez meanwhile did not dare mention his suffering to me, for he did not know how I stood with the Conde de Peña Flor, nor even whether I knew of his love. In the meanwhile a thousand circumstances increased his anxiety. On one occasion he found a ladder propped up against the garden wall, on another a stranger seemed to be hidden somewhere in the house. On others frequent serenades were heard, and that is a kind of music which jealous husbands detest. Eventually the Conde de Peña Flor's boldness knew no bounds. One day I went to the Prado with my devout neighbour. We stayed late, and were almost by ourselves at the end of a long walk. The count accosted us, formally declared his love for me and said that he was determined to possess me or to die. Then he took my hand by force and I don't know what that man would have done if we had not cried out.

We returned home in a terrible state. Our devout neighbour told my husband that she refused to go out with me again and that it was all very regrettable. Who would call Peña Flor to account since I had a husband who was so little capable of making others respect me? Although it was true that religion forbade us to avenge ourselves, the honour of a loving and faithful wife was worthy of being better protected; and she finally said that the Conde de Peña Flor only acted as he did because someone had probably told him of Señor Cornádez's indulgent temperament.

My husband was coming back the following night by a narrow street which he frequently took on his way home, when he found it barred by two men, one of whom was practising lunges against the wall with a disproportionately long sword. The other was saying to him, 'Bravo, Señor Don Ramiro. If you go the same way about it with the famous Conde de Peña Flor, he won't be the terror of brothers and husbands much longer!' The hated name of Peña Flor caught Cornádez's attention and he hid himself in a dark alley-way.

'My dear friend,' said the man with the long sword, 'I am not at all bothered about bringing the Conde de Peña Flor's good fortunes to an end. I have decided not to kill him but just to leave him in a state in which he will not take up his old tricks again. It's not for nothing that Ramiro Caramanza is said to be the best swordsman in Spain. But what bothers me are the consequences of my duel. If only I had a hundred doubloons I would spend some time away in the islands.'[3]

The two friends spoke to each other for some time in the same vein and were about to go away when my husband emerged from his hiding-place, accosted them and said, 'Señores, I am one of those husbands whose peace of mind has been disturbed by the Conde de Peña Flor. If your intention had been to kill him I would not have interrupted your conversation. But since you just want to teach him a lesson, it is my pleasure to offer the hundred doubloons necessary for the journey to the islands. Stay here. I'll go and fetch the money.'

So he went home and came back with the hundred doubloons, which he gave to the terrible Caramanza.

Two evenings later we heard a peremptory knock on our door. We opened it and saw there an officer of the law with two *alguaziles*. The officer of the law said to my husband, 'Señor, we have come at night out of consideration for you so that our appearance here would not do your reputation any harm or alarm the neighbourhood. It's about the Conde de Peña Flor, who was murdered yesterday. A letter which, it is alleged, fell from the pocket of one of the murderers may lead people to believe that you gave them a hundred doubloons, to incite them to commit this crime and to assist their escape.'

3 i.e. the Spanish West Indies.

397

My husband answered with a presence of mind of which I wouldn't have thought him capable. 'I have never met the Conde de Peña Flor. Two men with whom I was not acquainted gave me yesterday a bill of exchange for a hundred doubloons which I issued a year ago in Madrid. I paid them the sum. If you like, I'll go and fetch the bill of exchange.'

The officer of the law drew a letter from his pocket and said, 'It says here, "We are off to San Domingo with the hundred doubloons of good old Cornádez."'

'Well,' said my husband, 'those are the hundred doubloons of the bill of exchange. It was an open bill and I did not have the right to defer payment or ask for the name of the bearers.'

'Criminal justice is my business,' said the officer of the law, 'and I am not competent in commercial affairs. Farewell, Señor Cornádez. Please forgive us for having troubled you.'

As I said to you, the presence of mind which my husband showed on this occasion surprised me. But I had already noticed at other times that he could be brilliant when his self-interest or personal safety was in question.

When all these alarms were over I asked my dear Cornádez if he had really had the Conde de Peña Flor murdered. At first he refused to admit anything, but in the end he admitted that he had given a hundred doubloons to Caramanza the swordsman, not to kill the count, but only to punish him for his impudence; the idea of having been an accessory to his murder nevertheless weighed on his conscience and he wondered whether he might not go on a pilgrimage to Santiago de Compostela, or even further afield, to procure still more indulgences.

This confession by my husband heralded, as it were, the most extraordinary and supernatural events. For nearly every night was marked by some terrifying apparition of a kind to disturb an already tortured conscience. They were nearly always about the hundred doubloons. Sometimes in the darkness a voice was heard to say, 'I am going to give you back the hundred doubloons.' At others one could hear money being counted out. Once a servant girl found a pot full of doubloons in a corner. She tried to get her hands on them but only picked up dried leaves, which she brought to us with the pot.

The next evening my husband, passing through a bedroom dimly lit by the light of the moon, thought he saw in a corner a man's head in a pot. He came out terrified and told me what had caused his terror. I went in and found only the dummy head for keeping his wig in shape, which by chance had been placed on his shaving-dish. As I didn't want to contradict him, and even wanted to keep him in a state of terror, I screamed horribly and assured him that I had seen the same head covered in blood and full of menace.

Since then the same head has appeared to nearly all the members of the household and my husband was so distressed by it that we began to fear for his reason. I do not, however, need to tell you that all these apparitions are my invention. The Conde de Peña Flor was, as I said, a hypothetical being, only thought up to worry Cornádez and to make him lose his smug air. The officer of justice as well as the swordsman were members of the household of the Duke of Arcos, who had returned to Salamanca immediately after his marriage.

Last night I planned on giving my husband a great fright, because I was sure that he would leave his bedroom and go into his study, where he has a prayer-stool. Then I intended to bolt the door and the duke was to come in through the window. I was not afraid that my husband would see him enter or find the ladder, for the house is scrupulously locked every night and I keep the key at my bedside. Suddenly your head appeared at the window and my husband took it to be that of Peña Flor, who had come to reproach him about the hundred doubloons.

Finally, it only remains for me to tell you about my devout and quite exemplary neighbour, in whom my husband had so much confidence. Alas, this neighbour was the duke himself, and here he is with us in women's clothing, which really suits him very well. I am still a faithful wife but I cannot bring myself to send away my dear Arcos, for I am not sure that I may not one day abandon my virtue, and if I decided to take a step down that road, I would like to have Arcos by me.

Here Frasqueta ended her story, and the duke spoke up and said, 'Señor Busqueros, it is not by chance that you have been taken into our confidence. It is important to hasten Cornádez's journey. We even want him not to stick to a simple pilgrimage but to decide to do penance in some pious retreat. For this I shall need you and the four students at your disposal. I'll explain my plan to you.'

As Busqueros reached this point in his story, I noticed that the sun was on the point of setting, and the thought crossed my horrified mind that I might miss the rendezvous that charming Inés had given me. So I interrupted the storyteller and begged him to postpone to the next day the account of the Duke of Arcos's intentions. Busqueros replied with his customary insolence, but I was beside myself with anger and said to him, 'Busqueros, you loathsome man, prepare to rob me of the days, days which you fill with bitterness, or prepare to defend your own.' At the same time I drew my sword and made him draw his.

As my father had never let me handle a foil I didn't know what to do with my sword. So I twirled it round and round in the air, which seemed to amaze my adversary. But then he feinted somehow and ran through my arm, and his point even wounded me in the shoulder.

My sword fell from my hands and I was instantly bathed in my own blood. But the most distressing thing was that I was failing to keep my rendezvous and would not be able to discover the things that dear Inés wanted to tell me.

As the gypsy reached this point in his story someone came to call him away. After he had gone, Velásquez said, 'I was right to foresee that the stories of the gypsy would get entangled one with another. Frasqueta Salero has just told her story to Busqueros, who told it to Lope Soarez, who told it to the gypsy. I hope that the gypsy will tell us what became of fair Inés. But if he interpolates yet another story, I'll fall out with him just as Soarez fell out with Busqueros. Meanwhile I don't believe that our storyteller will be coming back this evening.'

And indeed the gypsy did not reappear, and we all went to bed.

The Thirty-sixth Day

———————— ✑ ————————

We set off again. The Wandering Jew soon joined us and continued his story as follows:

✑ THE WANDERING JEW'S STORY CONTINUED ✑

The lessons of wise Chæremon had much greater scope than the sort of résumé I have given of them. Their gist was that a prophet called Bytis had demonstrated in his works that God and angels exist, and that another prophet, called Thoth, had enveloped his ideas in very obscure and at the same time even more sublime-sounding metaphysics.

In this theology God, who is called the father, was only praised in silence. However, when one wished to express to what degree He was self-sufficient one said, 'He is his own father, He is his own son.' He was also thought of in terms of son, and then He was called 'Reason of God' or Thoth, which in Egyptian means persuasion.

Finally, as nature was thought to consist of spirit and matter, the spirit was looked upon as an emanation of God and He was represented as floating on mud, as I have told you elsewhere. The inventor of this metaphysics was called Thrice Great. Plato, who spent eighteen years in Egypt, took the doctrine of the Word back to the Greeks, which won him from them the epithet 'divine'.

Chæremon claimed that all this wasn't entirely in the spirit of the ancient Egyptian religion, that it had changed and that all religions were bound to change. This opinion of his was shortly confirmed by what happened in the synagogue of Alexandria.

I had not been the only Jew to study Egyptian theology. Others had developed a taste for it. They had been particularly attracted to the enigmatic spirit which pervaded all Egyptian literature and which probably had its origin in hieroglyphic writing and in the Egyptian precept never to dwell on the emblem but on the hidden sense it contained.

Our rabbis in Alexandria also wanted enigmas to interpret. They took pleasure in supposing that although they told the story of facts and real events, the works of Moses were none the less written with such sublime skill that besides their historical sense they concealed another hidden and allegorical one. Some of our scholars worked out this hidden sense with a subtlety which brought them much honour at the time. But of all the rabbis none was better at this than Philo.[1] Long study of Plato had trained him in spreading false ideas, using the obscurity of metaphysics. So for this reason he was called 'the Plato of the synagogue'. The first work of Philo dealt with the creation of the world and especially with the properties of the number seven. In this work God is called Father, which is very much in the spirit of Egyptian theology but not at all in the style of the Bible. It also says that the serpent is an allegory of sensual pleasure and that the story of the woman created from the rib of man is also allegorical.

The same Philo wrote a work on dreams, in which he says that God has two temples; one of these temples is the world and the high priest of that temple is the word of God. The other temple is the rational soul whose high priest is man. In his work on Abraham, Philo expresses himself in a style even more Egyptian, for he declares, 'He whom our sacred writings call a being, or He who is, is He who is the father of all. On each side He is flanked by the oldest and most intrinsic powers of the Great Being: the Creator Power and the Guardian Power. One is called God and the other Lord. So that the Great Being who is always accompanied by these two powers is present sometimes as a simple form, sometimes as a triple form: the former when the completely purified soul rises above all numbers and even the binary, which is so close to the one, and reaches at last the sublime and simple abstract image; the latter, which is triple, presents itself to the soul which is not entirely initiated into the great mysteries.'

This Philo, who could platonize as far as the eye and mind could

---

1 i.e. Philo Judaeus (who flourished in the first century of the Common Era). Potocki is drawing on his works *On Dreams* and *On Abraham*.

see, is the same Philo who was subsequently a delegate sent to the Emperor Claudius. He was held in high esteem in Alexandria and the beauty of his style and the love of novelty which is found in all men helped to win nearly all hellenizing Jews over to his opinion. Soon they were Jews in name only, as it were. For them the books of Moses were no more than a sort of canvas on which they sketched their allegories and mysteries at will, especially that of the triple form.

At this time the Essenes had already formed their bizarre fellowship. They did not take wives and all their goods were held in common. In short, new religions were emerging on all sides, mixtures of Judaism, magism, sabeism[2] and Platonism, and everywhere a great deal of astrology. The old religions were collapsing on every side.

As the Wandering Jew reached this point in his story we came close to our resting-place; the sad wanderer left us and was soon lost to sight in the mountains. Towards evening the gypsy, having nothing else to do, took up the thread of his story again:

∾ THE GYPSY CHIEF'S STORY CONTINUED ∾

Young Soarez, having told me the story of his duel with Busqueros, seemed to want to rest. I let him surrender his senses to sleep, and when I asked him the next day to continue his story he went on as follows:

∾ LOPE SOAREZ'S STORY CONTINUED ∾

Having run through my arm, Busqueros declared that he was delighted to have a new opportunity of proving his devotion to me. He tore a strip off my shirt, bound my arm, wrapped me up in a cloak and took me to a surgeon, who gave first aid to my wounds; and then I summoned a carriage and went back to my room. Busqueros had a bed brought up to my antechamber. The failure of my attempt to get rid of him had so depressed me that I did not put up any

2 An astrological cult of the ancient world.

resistance. The next day I ran a fever, as often happens with those who are wounded, and Busqueros was unfailingly dutiful. He did not leave my side either on that day or on those which followed. On the fourth day I was able to go out with my arm in a sling. On the fifth a man appeared after dinner, who came from the house of Señora de Avalos and brought me a letter, which Busqueros immediately snatched. This is what he read:

Inés Moro to Lope Soarez.

My dear Soarez, I have learnt that you have fought a duel and have been wounded in the arm. You can imagine what agonies my heart has gone through. However, now is the time for a last endeavour. I want my father to find you in my room. This is a risky undertaking but my aunt de Avalos is protecting us and is telling me what to do. Trust the man who brings you this letter. Tomorrow will be too late.

'Señor Don Lope,' said the detestable Busqueros, 'you can see that you cannot now dispense with my services, and you will at least concede that as this is a matter involving initiative it falls within my competence. I have always thought of you as lucky to have me as a friend, but it is on occasions like this that you must really be congratulated. Ah by St Roch, my patron saint! If you had let me finish my story you would have seen what I did for the Duke of Arcos, but you rudely interrupted me. None the less, I shall not complain because the blow with the sword which I gave you, procured for me new opportunities of proving my devotion to you and now, Señor Don Lope, I only ask you one favour, which is not to get involved in anything until the moment comes to put the plan into action: not a single question, not a word. Just leave it to me, Señor Don Lope, leave it to me.'

Having said these words, Busqueros went next door with the trusted servant of Señora Moro. They conferred for a long time, after which Busqueros came back by himself, carrying a sort of map of the Calle de los Agustinos in his hand.

'Here's the end of the street which leads towards the Dominicans' house,' he said. 'There you will find the man you have already seen, with two others he will answer for. As for me, I shall be at the opposite end with the pick of my friends, who are also yours, Don Lope. No, no, I am wrong. There will be a couple there, and the pick of them will be by this back door to keep the Duke of Santa Maura's people at bay.'

I thought that all these explanations gave me the right to say a few words and to ask what I would be doing while all this was going on. But Busqueros interrupted me imperiously and said, 'Not one question, Señor Don Lope, not one word! That was the condition and if you have forgotten already, I haven't.'

For the rest of the day Busqueros did nothing but come and go. It was the same in the evening. Sometimes the house next door was too well lit; at others there were suspicious characters in the street; or again the agreed signals had not been seen. Sometimes Busqueros came himself; sometimes he sent reports by one of his henchmen. Eventually he came to get me, and I dutifully followed him. My heart was thumping, as you may well imagine. The thought that I was disobeying my father added to my worries; but love conquered all other feelings.

On entering the Calle de los Agustinos, Busqueros showed me where his trusted friends were posted and gave them the password. If someone came by, he told me, my friends would seem to pick a quarrel with him and the passer-by would quickly take another route. 'Now we're here,' he continued, 'here's the ladder you must climb up. As you can see, it is securely propped up against a pile of building-stones. I will look out for the signal and when I clap, you must climb up.'

Who would believe that after all these plans and arrangements Busqueros picked the wrong window? But that's what he did. And you will see what became of it.

I had my right arm in a sling but when he gave me the signal I climbed up nimbly with the help of only one arm. When I reached the top of the ladder I could not find the half-open shutter I had been promised. I risked knocking with my remaining arm, supporting myself only on my legs. At that moment a man opened the shutter violently, pushing it against me. I lost my balance and fell from the top of the ladder on to the building-stone below. I broke my already injured arm in two places. A leg which was trapped in the rungs was also broken and the other one dislocated; and I was lacerated from my neck to my hips. The man who had opened the shutter, and who apparently wanted me to die, shouted to me, 'Are you dead?'

Fearing that he would come to finish me off, I replied that I was dead.

Then the same man shouted, 'Is there a purgatory?'

As I was suffering appalling pain I replied that there was certainly a purgatory and that I was there already. Then I think I fainted.

At this point I interrupted Soarez and asked him whether there had been a storm that evening.

'There had certainly been thunder and lightning,' he replied. 'Perhaps it was that which made Busqueros mistake the house.'

'Ah,' I cried, 'there can't be any doubt. You are a soul from purgatory. You are poor Aguilar.'

I immediately ran out into the street and as dawn was just breaking I hired mules and went quickly to the Camaldolese monastery. There I found the Knight of Toledo prostrated in front of an image. I prostrated myself beside the knight and, as one is not allowed to speak aloud in the Camaldolese monastery, I put my lips to his ear and told him Soarez's story. At first this had no effect on him but then Toledo turned to me and mouthed in my ear, 'My dear Avarito, do you think that the wife of the *oidor* Uscariz still loves me and has remained faithful to me?'

'Bravo!' I replied. 'Shhh! Let's not shock these good hermits. Say your prayers as usual, and I'll let it be known that we have completed our period of retreat.'

When the superior learned that it was our intention to return to the world he was no less fulsome for all that about the knight's piety.

As soon as we had left the monastery the knight recovered all his jollity. I told him about Busqueros. He told me that he knew him, that he was a gentleman in the household of the Duke of Arcos and that he was looked on as unbearable throughout Madrid.

As the gypsy reached this point in his story, someone called him away and he did not reappear that evening.

The Thirty-seventh Day

The next day was given over to rest. Breakfast was more copious and better prepared. No one was absent. The fair Jewess had taken some care with her appearance, but this effort was pointless if her intention was to please the duke. It wasn't her face that entranced him. He saw in her a woman different from others of her sex in her greater powers of thought and her mind, whose education had culminated in the exact sciences.

Rebecca had long wanted to know what the duke thought about religion, for she had a decided aversion for Christianity and she was involved in the plot to encourage us to embrace the Muslim faith. So she addressed the duke in a tone half-way between the serious and the playful and asked him if there were no awkward equations in his religion.

Velásquez had become very solemn once religion had been mentioned. But when he realized that the question was a sort of joke he looked angry. He thought for a few moments and then replied as follows:

✑ VELÁSQUEZ'S IDEAS ON RELIGION ✑

I can see what you are driving at. You are challenging my geometry. So I shall reply to you in geometry. When I want to indicate the infinitely great, I write a sideways '8' over '1'. When I want to indicate the infinitely small, I write a '1' which I divide by the symbol for infinity. These symbols which I use give me no idea at all of what I am expressing. The infinitely great is the number of fixed stars multiplied *ad infinitum*; the infinitely small an infinite subdivision of the smallest of atoms.

I can therefore indicate the infinite, but I cannot comprehend it. Now, if it is the case that I cannot comprehend, cannot express but

407

can only indicate the infinitely great and the infinitely small, how can I express what is simultaneously infinitely great, infinitely intelligent, infinitely good and the creator of all infinities? Here the Church comes to the aid of my geometry. She gives me the expression of three contained in one without breaking it down. What can I object to that, which is beyond my powers of conception? All I can do is offer my submission.

It is not science which leads to unbelief but rather ignorance. The ignorant man thinks he understands something provided that he sees it every day. The natural philosopher walks amid enigmas, always striving to understand and always half-understanding. He learns to believe what he does not understand, and that is a step on the road to faith. Don Newton and Don Leibniz were true Christians, and even theologians, and both acknowledged the mystery of numbers which they could not comprehend.

If they had been born into our Church they would also have confessed another no less inconceivable mystery, which consists in the possibility of an intimate union between man and his creator. In problem form this possibility does not afford any direct data because it gives us only unknowns. But it affords us some grasp of it in that it indicates to us that man is completely separated from other material intelligences. For if man really is alone in his species in this world, if we are firmly convinced of his isolation in the whole animal kingdom, then we can accept with less difficulty that he can achieve union with his God. After these preliminaries, let us now turn for a moment to the intelligence of animals.

An animal wills, remembers, combines, weighs up alternatives and decides. It thinks but it doesn't think about its thinking, which is the force of the intellect raised to the power of two. An animal does not say, 'I am a thinking being.' This abstraction is so far from its nature that one never sees an animal endowed with the idea of number, although this is the simplest of abstractions.

The magpie does not leave its nest as long as it suspects a man to be hiding nearby. It was decided to test the extent of its intelligence. Five hunters went into a hide and the magpie only left its nest after seeing the fifth emerge from it. When six or seven hunters came, the magpie lost count, so that it always left the nest after the fifth. Some have deduced from this that the magpie can count up to five. They are wrong. The magpie had retained the image of all five men but it had not counted them. To count is to abstract the number from the material circumstance.

We see charlatans put ponies on show which tap with their hooves the number of spades or clubs on a card. But it is a sign from their master which makes them tap or stop tapping. They have no idea of numeration and this abstraction, which is the simplest of all abstractions, may be considered to mark the limit of animal intelligence.

Doubtless the intelligence of animals often comes close to our own. The dog soon recognizes the master of the house and his friends and those who are neither friends nor enemies. It is fond of the former and tolerates the latter. It hates evil-looking people. It gets upset and gets excited. It hopes and fears. It is ashamed if it is found doing what it has been told not to do. Pliny says that elephants have been taught to dance, and that once they were found rehearsing in the moonlight.

The intelligence of animals surprises us when it is applied to particular circumstances. They do what they are told, they avoid doing what they are told not to do and what would be harmful to them in other ways. But they do not distinguish the general idea of the good from the particular idea associated with one action or another. So they cannot classify their actions. They cannot divide them into good and bad actions. This abstraction is more difficult than numeration. They are not capable of the easier form so they will not be of the more difficult.

Conscience is partly man's own creation, since what is bad in one country is good in another. But in general, conscience warns of what abstraction has placed under the one or the other sign, that is, good or evil. Animals are incapable of such abstraction. They therefore have no conscience and cannot be guided by it. So they are therefore not susceptible of reward or punishment other than that which we inflict on them for our convenience and not for theirs.

So man is alone in his species in a world where we find nothing which does not fit into a general scheme. Man alone knows his thought and alone can abstract and generalize qualities. He alone is susceptible to merit or demerit, since abstraction, generalization and division into good and evil have shaped his conscience.

But why should man have qualities which distinguish him from all the other animals? Here analogy leads us to say that everything in this world has a well-specified goal. Conscience must have been given to man for a purpose. And thus we are brought by reasoning to natural religion. And where does that lead us? Nowhere other than to the same goal as revealed religion, that is, to future rewards. For where the products are the same, the factors cannot be very different.

But the reasoning on which natural religion is based is a dangerous instrument which can easily harm the person using it. What virtue has not been attacked by reason? What crime have people not tried to justify by it? Could eternal providence have exposed the fate of ethics to the mercy of sophistry? Certainly not. Faith, supported by the habits of childhood, filial love, and the needs of the human heart, offers man a surer mainstay than reason. Conscience itself, which distinguishes us from brute beasts, has been doubted, and sceptics have made it their plaything. They have insinuated that man is not different from the countless other material intelligences which inhabit this world. But in spite of them man senses that he has a conscience, and the priest uttering the words of consecration says to him, 'a God comes down to this altar and unites Himself with you.' Then man understands clearly that he does not belong to brute nature. He withdraws inside himself and there he guards his conscience.

But you will say that it isn't a question of proving to me that natural religion tends to the same end as revealed religion. If you are a Christian, you must believe in revealed religion and in the miracles which have established it. But wait a moment. Let us first be clear about the difference between revealed and natural religion.

According to theologians, God is the author of the Christian religion. He is this also according to philosophers, since nothing happens, according to them, without divine permission. But the theologians base their arguments on miracles, which are exceptions to the general laws of nature and with which philosophers have some difficulty. In so far as they study nature, the latter tend to believe that God, the author of our holy religion, decided to establish it only by human means and without setting aside the general laws which govern the natural and spiritual world.

Here the difference is slight, but natural philosophers attempt to make a yet more delicate distinction. They say to theologians, 'Those who have seen miracles have no difficulty in believing in them. The merit of faith is yours, since you have come eighteen centuries later. And if faith is a merit, yours is also tested, whether miracles really occurred or whether a sacred tradition transmitted knowledge of them to you. If the test is the same, then the merit is also the same.'

At this point theologians abandon the defensive and say to natural philosophers, 'But who has revealed to you the laws of nature? How do you know whether miracles, instead of being exceptions, are not rather manifestations of phenomena unknown to you? For you do not know the laws of nature with which you dare to challenge the decrees of religion. How do the rays of light, which you have postulated in the laws of optics, pass through each other in all directions without colliding with each other? Whereas, if they strike a mirror, they bounce off it as though they were elastic bodies? Sounds pass through each other in the same way and they are sent back in the form of echoes. They obey more or less the same laws as rays of light, yet they seem only to be a way of being whereas rays of light seem substantial. You don't understand it for at bottom you don't understand anything.'

Natural philosophers are forced to admit that they know nothing. But they can say, 'If we are not able to define a miracle, and are very far from being able to deny it, you theologians don't have the right to reject the declarations of the Church fathers, who admitted that our dogmas and mysteries existed already in earlier religions. Now as these were not given to ancient religions by revelation, you must incline to our opinion and concede that the same dogmas could have been established without the help of miracles.' Finally, these natural philosophers add, 'If you want us clearly to state our opinion on the origins of Christianity, here it is.

'The temples of the ancients were slaughterhouses and their gods shameless adulterers, but some congregations of religious men had purer principles and less repellent sacrifices. Philosophers called the divinity *theos*, without specifying Jupiter or Saturn. Rome, then, was subduing the world by its arms and subjugating it to its vices. A divine master appeared in Palestine. He preached love of one's fellow-man, contempt for riches, forgiveness of trespasses, resignation to the will of a Father who is in heaven.

'Simple men had followed him during his lifetime. They came together after his death. Other more enlightened men chose from among pagan rituals that which was best adapted to the new cult. Finally, Church fathers made heard from the pulpit a more persuasive eloquence than that which up till then had been heard in public. And thus by apparently human means Christianity was formed from the purest elements of pagan and Jewish religions. But that is also how the will of heaven is accomplished. Doubtless, the creator of the universe could have written His holy law in letters of fire across the starry night sky, but He did not do so. He hid the rites of a more perfect religion in ancient mysteries, just as in the acorn He hid the forest which one day is going to give shade to our descendants. Unknown to us, we live in the midst of causes whose effects will surprise posterity. Therefore we give to God the name providence. We would call him only power if He acted otherwise.'

Such is the idea that natural philosophers have formed of the origins of Christianity. It is far from pleasing to the theologians, but they have not got the courage to contest it, since they see in the opinions of their antagonists true and great ideas which make them indulgent towards forgivable errors.

Thus, rather like the lines we call asymptotes, the opinions of philosophers and theologians can converge, without ever meeting, to within a distance which is smaller than any given distance. That is to say, that difference becomes less than any given distance or perceptible quantity. Now does a difference which I cannot perceive give me the right to set my convictions up in opposition to my brothers and to my Church? Does it give me the right to sow my doubts in the faith that they possess and which they have made the basis of their ethics? Certainly not. I haven't got that right. So I submit heart and soul. Don Newton and Don Leibniz were Christians and even theologians; the latter even strove for the reunion of the churches. As for me, who am not worthy to be named after such great men, I study theology in the works of creation and find in it new reasons for adoring the creator.

*

Having thus spoken, Velásquez took off his hat, seemed to meditate and then sank into contemplation which might have been taken for ecstasy in an ascetic.

Rebecca seemed a bit disconcerted by this and I realized that those who wanted to weaken our religious principles and turn us into Muslims would find it no easier with the geometer than they had with me.

The Thirty-eighth Day

———————— ∽ ————————

The previous day's rest had been beneficial. We all set off again in better spirits. The Wandering Jew had not been seen the previous day because, not being able to remain static for a moment, he could only tell us his story when we too were on the move. So we hadn't gone a quarter of a league before he appeared, took up his usual place between Velásquez and myself and began again as follows:

∽ THE WANDERING JEW'S STORY CONTINUED ∽

Dellius was growing old and, sensing his end was near, he summoned Germanus and myself and told us to dig in the cellar near the door, where we would find a bronze casket which we should bring to him. We did as he asked, found the casket and brought it to him. Dellius drew out a key from his bosom, opened the casket and then said to us:

'Here are two signed and sealed parchments. One of these parchments will secure for my dear son the possession of the finest house in Jerusalem. The other is a deed worth thirty thousand darics together with many years' interest.'

He next told me the whole story of my grandfather, Hiskias, and my forebear, Sedekias. Then he added, 'This rapacious and unjust man is still alive, which goes to prove that remorse does not kill. My children, as soon as I die, you will go to Jerusalem. But do not make yourself known until you have found protectors. Perhaps it may be best to wait for Sedekias to die, which, given his great age, must happen very soon. Meanwhile you can live on your five hundred darics. You will find them sewn into this pillow, which never leaves me.

'I have only one piece of advice to give you. Live a life free from reproach and you will be rewarded by the serenity which a clear

414

conscience will give to the evening of your lives. As for me, I shall die as I have lived, that is, singing. This will be my swan-song, as they say. Homer who, like me, was blind, wrote a hymn to Apollo, who is the very sun whom he could not see and whom I also can no longer see. I once set this hymn to music. I shall intone it but I doubt whether I shall be able to reach the end.'

So Dellius sang the hymn that begins, 'Greetings, happy Latona.' But when he reached 'Delos, if you wish my son to live on your shores,' Dellius's voice faded away. He leant on my shoulder and breathed his last.

We long mourned for our old friend. At last we left for Palestine, and reached Jerusalem on the twelfth day after our departure from Alexandria. For safety's sake we changed our names. I took the name Antipas and Germanus was known as Glaphyras. We first stayed at an inn outside the city gates. When we asked where Sedekias lived, we were told at once, for it was the finest house in Jerusalem, a veritable palace worthy of a prince. We rented a poor room in the house of a cobbler who lived opposite Sedekias. I did not go out much; Germanus roamed all over the city and set about finding things out.

Several days later, he came to me and said, 'My friend, I have just made an excellent discovery. The brook Cedron broadens into a magnificent sheet of water behind Sedekias's house. The old man spends all his evenings there in a bower of jasmine. He is there now. I'll show you your persecutor.'

I followed Germanus and we reached the bank of the stream opposite a beautiful garden in which I could see an old man asleep. I sat opposite him and looked at him. How different was his sleep from that of Dellius! Troublesome dreams seemed to disturb it and make him shudder from time to time. 'Dellius,' I cried, 'how right you were to praise the life of innocence!'

Germanus made the same observation as I did.

As we were still looking, an object met our eyes which soon made us forget our observations and moral reflections. It was a young girl between sixteen and seventeen years old, of marvellous beauty which was enhanced by her rich attire. On her neck and calves she wore pearls and gem-studded chains. Otherwise she was dressed only in a gold-hemmed linen tunic. Germanus cried out, 'It's Venus herself!' I instinctively prostrated myself before her. The beautiful young girl caught sight of us and seemed somewhat disturbed. But then she regained her composure, picked up a peacock-feather fan and wafted it to and fro above the old man's head to refresh him and prolong his rest.

Germanus opened a book which he had specially brought with him, and pretended to read. I pretended to listen. But all our attention was fixed on what was happening in the garden.

The old man woke up. The questions he put to the young girl indicated to us that his sight was very dim and he couldn't see us where we were, which pleased us greatly, for we proposed to come there often. Sedekias went away, leaning on the beautiful girl, and we returned to our room. Having nothing else to do, we got our landlord the cobbler to gossip to us. From him we learnt that Sedekias didn't have a son still alive but his fortune was to pass to the daughter of one of his sons: she was called Sara and her grandfather was very fond of her.

After we had retired to our room, Germanus said to me, 'Dear friend, I have thought up a way of bringing matters to a head with your great-uncle: it will be to marry his granddaughter. A great deal of prudence will be needed to succeed.'

I was very taken by this idea. We discussed it for a long time and I dreamed about it that night.

The next day I returned to the stream, and went back again on the following days. I rarely failed to see my young cousin, sometimes alone, sometimes with her grandfather, and without my having to speak the beautiful young girl guessed in the end that I was there only because of her.

As the Jew reached this point in his story we arrived at our resting-place and the unhappy wanderer was soon lost to sight in the mountains.

Rebecca was careful not to set the duke off again on the subject of religion. But as she wanted to hear about what he called his system, she seized the first opportunity to speak to him about it and even pressed him with questions.

★

416

∽ VELÁSQUEZ'S ACCOUNT OF HIS SYSTEM ∽

'Señora,' Velásquez replied, 'we are blind men who can feel some walls and know the ends of several roads. But we mustn't be expected to know the map of the whole city. However, since you wish it, I shall try to give you an idea of what you call my system and what I would rather call my way of seeing things.

'Now everything that our eyes can see, all that vast horizon which stretches out at the foot of the mountains, in short, all of nature which can be perceived by our senses, can be divided into dead matter and organic matter. The latter differs from the former by its organs but belongs to it absolutely by its elements. Thus, Señora, the elements which go to make you up can also be found in the rocks on which we are sitting or the grass which covers them. Indeed, you have chalk in your bones, siliceous earth in your flesh, alkali in your bile, iron in your blood, salt in your tears. Your fatty parts are a combination of combustible material with an element of the atmosphere. So that if you were put in a reverberatory furnace you could be reduced to a glass bottle and if some metallic chalk were added you could be turned into a nice telescopic lens.'

'Señor duque,' said Rebecca, 'what a very droll picture you are painting. But please go on.'

The duke thought that he had, without being aware of it, paid a compliment to the fair Jewess. He graciously raised his hat, put it back on his head and continued as follows:

We can see in the elements of dead matter a spontaneous tendency, if not towards organization, then at least combination. Elements come together and separate to unite themselves with others. They take on certain forms. It can be supposed that they are intended for organization but they do not organize themselves of themselves. Unless there is a germ they could not pass to the other kind of combination which results in life.

Like magnetic fluid, life is only ever seen by its effects. Its first effect in organized bodies is to stop an interior fermentation known as putrefaction, which begins in bodies having organs as soon as life has

417

left them. For this reason an ancient philosopher dared to affirm that life was a salt.

Life can be preserved for a long time in a fluid, as in an egg, or in a solid, as in seeds, and it develops once conditions are favourable.

Life extends to all parts of the body, even fluids, and even blood, which putrefies once it leaves our veins. Life is in the walls of the stomach, protecting them from the effect of gastric juices, which dissolve dead things that are admitted to the stomach.

Life is preserved for varying amounts of time in members cut off from the body.

Finally, life possesses the property of self-propagation. That is what is called the mystery of generation, which is a mystery like everything else in nature.

Organized beings are divided into two great classes: one which through combustion gives a fixed alkali, the other which abounds in volatile alkali. Plants form the first class, animals the second.

There are animals which, in respect of their degree of organization, seem much inferior to plants, such as living mucilages, which can be seen floating on the sea, or hydatids, which live in sheep's brains. There are animals with a higher form of organization in which, none the less, what we call a will cannot be easily detected. Thus when coral extends its capsule to swallow up the small animals which it eats, it is possible to suppose that this act is an effect of the way it is organized, just as we see flowers which close up at night and turn to the light during the day.

The sort of will which a polyp manifests when it stretches out its tentacles and opens up its capsule can be compared with some justice to the will of a child who has just been born and who doesn't yet think, but who wills; for in children will, being the immediate result of need and pain, precedes thought.

Similarly a limb with cramp wants to stretch out and inspires that will in us. The stomach often refuses the diet imposed upon it. The salivary glands swell in the presence of the desired dish, and the palate also has a will. Often reason has great difficulty in gaining the upper hand.

If one pictures a man who has long not eaten or drunk, has shrunken limbs and has lived a celibate existence, one may see that several parts of his body will make him simultaneously will different things.

These appetites which derive directly from need are found in the adult polyp and new-born child. They are the first elements of the higher will, which develops later in virtue of the organization being perfected.

The will of a new-born child precedes thought but not by much. And thought too has its elements, which I shall describe.

As Velásquez reached this point in the exposition of his ideas, someone came and interrupted us. Rebecca indicated to the duke all the pleasure she had taken in listening to him, and we put off to the next day the next part of a lecture in which I also was deeply interested.

The Thirty-ninth Day

We set off once more and were soon joined by the Wandering Jew, who took up the thread of his story as follows:

∽ THE WANDERING JEW'S STORY CONTINUED ∽

While I was occupied with the fair Sara, Germanus, who did not take the same interest in her, had spent several days listening to the teaching of a master called Josuah, who subsequently became so famous under the name of Jesus. For Jesus is in Greek the same name as Jehoschuah in Hebrew, as one can see in the translation of the Septuagint.

Germanus even wanted to follow his master to Galilee, but the thought that he could be of use to me made him stay in Jerusalem.

One evening Sara took off her veil and tried to tie it to the branches of the balsam tree. But the wind caught hold of the light fabric and made it flutter up and fall into the Cedron. I threw myself into the stream, seized the veil and hung it on some branches below the terrace. Sara threw me a gold chain which she had taken from around her neck. I kissed it and swam back across the stream.

Old Sedekias had been woken by the noise and wanted to know what had happened. Sara began to tell him. He thought himself near the balustrade, but he was standing on rocks where there was none because bushes took its place. The old man lost his footing, the bushes gave way and he rolled down into the stream. I jumped in after him, caught hold of him and brought him back to the bank. All this took but an instant.

Sedekias regained his senses and, seeing himself in my arms, realized that he owed me his life. He asked me who I was. I told him that I was an Alexandrian Jew called Antipas and that, having neither money nor parents, I had come to Jerusalem to try to make my fortune.

420

'I wish to take the place of your father,' said Sedekias to me. 'You will live in my house.'

I accepted the invitation without mentioning Germanus. He found it not to be a bad idea and continued to live at the cobbler's house. So it was that I was installed in the house of my great enemy, and every day grew a little in the esteem of the man who would have murdered me if he had known that I was the legitimate heir to the greater part of his fortune. For her part, Sara was more and more pleased to see me as the days went by.

Money-changing was then practised in Jerusalem, as it still is throughout the East. If you go to Cairo or Baghdad, you will see men at the doors of mosques, sitting on the ground with little tables on their knees, with a groove in one of the corners into which money that has been counted rolls away. Next to them are bags of gold and silver, which they disburse to those needing this or that currency. Nowadays these money-changers are called *sarafs*. The writers of your gospels called them *trapesitos*, because of the little tables I mentioned. Nearly all the money-changers of Jerusalem worked only for Sedekias, who had an understanding with Roman tax-farmers and customs-men to raise or lower the value of a given currency at will. I soon realized that the surest way to win the good graces of my uncle would be to become a clever money-changer and to follow the rise and fall of rates of exchange. I succeeded so well in this that after two months no operation was undertaken without my first being consulted.

At about that time there was a rumour that Tiberius had ordered a general reminting of all the moneys of the empire; silver money would not be currency any longer and would be melted down into ingots to constitute the imperial treasury. I had not invented this story but I thought that it was within my rights to spread it about. You can well imagine the effect it was bound to have on those involved in money-changing. Sedekias himself did not know what to think, and could not make up his mind about it.

I have told you that throughout the East money-changers can still be seen near the doors of mosques. In Jerusalem we were inside the temple. This was a vast place, and in the corner we occupied we did not get in the way of divine service. But for several days money-changers had not appeared because of the general alarm. Sedekias did not ask my opinion, but he seemed to want to read it in my eyes. Eventually, when I thought that silver money had been sufficiently devalued, I presented my plan to my great-uncle. He listened attentively and looked hesitant and pensive for a long time. At last he said to me, 'My dear Antipas, I have two million gold sesterces in my vaults. If your speculation succeeds you may aspire to the hand of Sara.'

The hope of possessing fair Sara and the sight of the gold, which is always seductive to a Jew, sent me into a state of ecstasy from which I recovered only to go through the city decrying silver money still more. Germanus helped me as best he could. I won over several merchants who refused to be paid in silver. At last things reached the point at which the inhabitants of Jerusalem acquired a sort of horror and disgust for silver. When we thought that this feeling was running high enough we got ready to put our plan into action.

On the appointed day I had all my gold carried to the temple in covered bronze pots. I let it be known that Sedekias, having a payment to make in silver, had decided to buy two hundred thousand sesterces at the rate of one ounce of gold for twenty-five of silver. That meant that he was making a profit of a hundred per cent or more. Moreover, the rush to profit from this good deal was such that I soon had to change half of all my gold. Our porters carried away the silver as it was changed, and it was thought that I had acquired only twenty-five thousand or thirty thousand sesterces in this way. So all was going well and I was on the point of doubling Sedekias's fortune when a Pharisee came to tell us that . . .

When the Wandering Jew reached this point in his story, he turned to Uzeda and said, 'A more powerful cabbalist than you is forcing me to leave you.'

'Really?' said the cabbalist. 'Or is it that you don't want to tell us about the fight in the temple, and the blows you received?'

'The Old Man of Mount Lebanon is calling me,' said the Jew, and disappeared before our eyes. I confess that I wasn't too upset and did not want him to come back, because I suspected him of being a fraud who was well-versed in history and who was telling us things which it was not proper for us to hear on the pretext of relating to us the story of his life.

Meanwhile we reached the resting-place and Rebecca asked the duke to be so kind as to continue to instruct us in his system. He thought for a few moments and then began as follows:

VELÁSQUEZ'S ACCOUNT OF HIS SYSTEM
∽ CONTINUED ∽

I tried yesterday to impart to you the elements of will and how it precedes thought, and we had decided to go back to the elements of thought.

One of the most profound philosophers of antiquity showed us the true way to follow in metaphysical research. And those who have thought that they have added to his discoveries have not, in my opinion, made any progress at all.

Long before Aristotle the word 'idea' meant 'image' in Greek. The word 'idol' also comes from it. Aristotle, having carefully examined all of his ideas, realized that all came from an image, that is, an impression made on our senses. From this it can be deduced that the most inventive of geniuses cannot invent anything. Mythologists combined a man's torso with a horse's body, or the body of a woman with the tail of a fish. They removed an eye from Cyclops and added some arms to Briareus, but they invented nothing. For that is not in the power of man. And since Aristotle it has been accepted that nothing is in thought which was not previously in the senses.

In our time, however, there have been philosophers who believe themselves more profound and who have said, 'We agree that the soul could not have developed its faculties without the mediation of the senses. But once its faculties have been developed the soul can conceive of things which would never have been in the senses, such as space, eternity and mathematical truths.

I must confess to you that I do not like this new doctrine. Abstraction seems to me to be no more than a subtraction. To abstract you must remove something. If I mentally take away from my room everything that encloses it, even to the point of subtracting air, I have pure space. If I remove from a length of time its beginning and its end I have eternity. If from an intelligent being I take away the body I have the idea of an angel. If from lines I mentally take away their width, only to be left with their length and the two-dimensional figures that they enclose, I have the elements of Euclid. If I take away an eye from a man and I add to his height I am left with the figure of a Cyclops. All of these are images received by the senses. If these new thinkers can provide me with a single abstraction which I cannot reduce to a subtraction I shall declare myself their disciple. Until then I'll stick to old Aristotle.

The word 'idea' or 'image' does not refer uniquely to things which make an impression on our sight. Sound strikes our ears and gives us the idea which belongs to the sense of hearing. Lemon sets our teeth on edge and gives us the idea of acidity.

But note that our senses benefit from the faculty of having things impress them in the absence of the object which caused the impression. If it is suggested that we bite into a lemon the mere idea produces saliva and sets our teeth on edge. Loud music resonates in our ears long after the orchestra has stopped playing. In the present state of physiology we can't yet explain sleep and therefore we cannot yet explain dreams. But we can say that the involuntary activity of our organs puts them in the same state in which they have been put by the impression made on our senses, or rather, to put it in different terms, by the idea once it has been conceived.

From this it follows that, as we wait for advances in physiological knowledge, it is helpful to accept the theory that ideas are impressions made on the brain, impressions in which organs can involuntarily or voluntarily take the place of an absent object. Note that the impression will be less marked if one thinks only of the object, but that in a state of fever it can be as strong as the impression when first received.

After this series of definitions and consequences, which was somewhat difficult to follow, we will turn to certain thoughts which by their nature will throw some new light on the subject.

Animals which are closest in organization to man and which show more or less intelligence all have, as far as I know, the viscera called the brain; but one cannot find this organ in animals whose organization is similar to that of plants.

Plants live, and some have powers of movement, or rather, just move. Among marine animals there are some creatures which, like plants, do not possess locomotive movement or power of displacement. I have seen other marine animals whose movement is always uniform, like that of our lungs, and does not appear to come from any act of will.

The best organized animals have a will and conceive ideas. Man alone possesses the power of abstraction.

But not all men have this faculty to the same degree. A weakness in the glandular system deprives goitrous mountain-dwellers of it, and the deprivation of one or more senses has the effect of making abstraction very difficult.

The deaf and dumb, who are like animals in that they do not have the power of speech, have great difficulty in understanding abstractions. But if they are shown five or ten fingers when fingers themselves are not in question, they can grasp an idea of number. They can see that people pray and prostrate themselves, and from that they derive the idea of an invisible being.

It is much easier with blind people because abstractions are given to them ready-made, as language is the great instrument of intelligence. Besides, an absence of distraction gives blind people a quite particular aptitude for combination.

But if you think about a child born deaf and blind, we can clearly affirm that he will never be capable of a single abstraction. He will have ideas which come to him through taste, smell and feeling. He will be able to dream those same ideas. If he is punished for a piece of misbehaviour he may well desist from it because he is not entirely bereft of memory. But I don't believe that any degree of persistence by men could introduce into his mind the abstract idea of evil. He won't have a conscience and will not be susceptible of merit or demerit. If he were to be guilty of a murder he could not in justice be punished for it. Here then are two souls, two very different emanations of the divine breath, and why so different? For the lack of two senses.

A smaller but still considerable difference divides the Eskimo and the Hottentot from the man with the cultivated mind. What causes this difference? It isn't the lack of a sense. It is the smaller or greater quantity of ideas and the number of combinations. The man who has seen the whole world through the eyes of travellers and has read about[1] all the events of history really has an infinity of images in his head which the peasant hasn't got, and if he combines ideas, associates them and compares them, then this man really has knowledge and intellect.

Newton was perpetually in the habit of combining ideas, and in the mass of ideas he assembled there was found the combination of the apple falling and the moon held in its orbit.

From all this I conclude that difference in intellect lies in the quantity of images and the facility of combining them. Or, if I may be permitted to express myself in this way, it is a ratio of the number of the images to the ease of combining them. Here I must crave your attention.

Animals with mixed organization may have neither will nor ideas. Their movements are involuntary, like those of sensitive plants. But one can always suppose that when the freshwater polyp stretches out its tentacles to swallow up worms, it eats one which it enjoys more than others and which gives it the idea of good, better or bad. And if it has the faculty to reject bad worms, it may also be thought to have a will. The first will was the need which made it stretch out its tentacles. The organisms it devoured gave it two or three ideas. To reject an organism and to swallow another is a will to choose which resulted from one or several ideas.

If we apply the same reasoning to new-born children we will see that their first will is the direct result of need. That is, the will which makes them put their mouth to their nurse's breasts. But as soon as they have tasted the nurse's milk they have an idea. Another impression is made on their senses; they acquire another idea, then a third, then a fourth. Ideas are therefore susceptible of enumeration. But we have already seen that they are also susceptible of combination. To them one can therefore apply, if not the method of calculating combinations, then at least the principles of this calculation. What I call combination is aggregation, not transposition. Thus *ab* is the same combination as *ba*. So two letters can be aggregated in only one way.

1 The French text has *vu* for *lu* at this point.

Three letters taken two by two can be aggregated or combined in three ways, and all three can be taken together as well. That makes four ways.

Four letters taken two by two give six combinations, three by three they give four, all four together one. That makes eleven.

Five letters give sixteen combinations in all.

Six letters give fifty-seven combinations in all.

Seven letters give 121 combinations in all.

Eight letters give 236 combinations in all.

Nine letters give 495 combinations in all.

Ten letters give 1,013 combinations in all.

Eleven letters give 2,035 combinations in all.[2]

So one can see that one idea more (than two) doubles the number of combinations, and that combinations of five ideas are to combinations of ten ideas as sixteen is to 1,013, or as one is to sixty-nine.

I am not claiming by this material calculation to reduce the mind to numbers, but only to demonstrate the law governing all that is susceptible of combination.

We have said that the difference in minds is a compound ratio of the quantity of ideas to the facility with which they are combined.

We can now represent all these different minds as a scale. Let us suppose Newton is the top of the scale, with a mind represented by the figure 1,000,000, and that a peasant in the Alps has a mind represented by the figure 100,000. We can place an infinite number of proportionals between these two numbers, which will designate minds superior to the peasant but inferior to Newton. In this scale your minds and mine will find their place.

The attribute of minds which are at the top of the scale will be, for example:

to add to Newton's discoveries,

to understand them,

to understand a part of them,

to show brilliance in combining ideas.

2 These figures are in fact incorrect in some instances (5:26, not 5:16; 7:120, not 7:121; 8:247, not 8:236; 9:502, not 9:495; 11:2,036, not 11:2,035).

But one can imagine a declining scale which goes from the peasant, represented by 100,000, to minds designated by sixteen, eleven, five, then down to intelligences which have four ideas and six combinations and three ideas and four combinations.

The child having only four ideas and six combinations does not yet abstract, but between this number and 100,000, the ratio will be found between the number of ideas and their combinations, the product of which is abstraction.

Now it is this compound ratio which animals and deaf and blind children never reach, the latter because of a lack of images, the former because of a lack of combinations.

Perhaps the simplest abstraction is that of numbers. It consists in separating objects from their mathematical quantity. Until they can do so, children have not achieved abstraction; they reach abstraction by the analysis of qualities, which is also a sort of abstraction. They reach it gradually. When they get past this first abstraction, they then can abstract by combining and acquiring ideas.

This series from the least to the highest intelligence therefore always consists of dimensions of the same genus, or values of the same species, in respect of the number of images, and according to the laws governing combination. These elements are always the same.

So intelligences of different orders can really be regarded as belonging to a single species, just as the most complicated of calculations can be considered as a species of additions and subtractions and every mathematical treatise, when it is complete, is really a scale of abstractions from the simplest to the most transcendent.

Velásquez then developed this comparison in other ways, the brilliance of which Rebecca seemed to appreciate, after which they went their own ways, reciprocally convinced of the other's merits.

The Fortieth Day

I awoke early and left my tent to enjoy the coolness of the morning. Velásquez and the girl we knew as Laura de Uzeda, had gone out with the same purpose.

We went in the direction of the high road to see whether any travellers might appear. But when we reached a point above a deep ravine set between the rocks we decided to sit down.

Soon we saw a caravan coming into the pass, which went by about fifty feet below the rocks where we were sitting. The nearer the company came to us, the more surprised we were. At the front of the column were four Americans. All that they wore were single long garments fringed with lace. On their heads they had straw hats decorated with long multi-coloured feathers, and they were armed with long rifles. Then came a herd of vicuña, each with a monkey on its back. After this there was a mounted troop of well-armed negroes. Then came two old gentlemen mounted on fine Andalusian horses and wrapped up in their blue velvet cloaks, which were embroidered with Calatrava crosses. Then came a Chinese palanquin carried by eight Moluccan islanders. In the palanquin could be seen a young lady dressed in the Spanish manner and a young man on horseback was prancing gallantly at its doors.

Then there was a young person lying unconscious on a litter, and a priest on the back of a mule was throwing holy water on the young person and seemed to be exorcizing her. Then came a long file of men of every hue from ebony-black to olive-brown, there being none of paler shade.

While the company was processing by, we did not think to ask who these people could be. But when the last of them had gone by, Rebecca said, 'We really ought to have asked who they were.'

As Rebecca spoke, I saw a member of the column who had

remained behind the rest. I risked climbing down the rocks and ran after the laggard.

He threw himself on his knees, looked frightened and said to me, 'Señor Bandit, may your grace have pity on a gentleman who was born amid gold-mines but who hasn't a penny to his name.'

I replied that I wasn't a thief and wanted only to know the names of the illustrious gentlemen whom I had seen go by.

'If that's all you want,' said the American, rising proudly to his feet, 'I shall satisfy you. If you like, we may climb to this spur of rock, from which we will be able to see more easily the whole line of the caravan in the valley. First, Your Lordship can see those oddly-dressed men at the front. They are highlanders from Cuzco and Quito, whose job it is to look after the fine vicuña which my master expects to present to His Majesty the King of Spain and the Indies.

'The negroes are slaves, or rather they were slaves, of my master, for on Spanish soil slavery is not tolerated any more than is heresy. From the moment their feet touched this sacred soil these blacks have been as free as you and I.

'The old gentleman that you see on the right is the Conde de Peña Vélez, a nephew by blood of the famous viceroy of that name and a grandee of the first class.

'The other old gentleman is Don Alonso, Marqués de Torres Rovellas, son of a Marqués de Torres, who became husband of the heiress of the Rovellas family. These two gentlemen have always had the most intimate of friendships, which will become even more so with the marriage of young Peña Vélez with the only daughter of Torres Rovellas – and there you see the charming couple. The young groom is mounted on a superb, spirited horse, and the young bride-to-be is in the gilded palanquin, which was a present that the King of Borneo once made to the late Viceroy de Peña Vélez.

'Finally, the young girl carried in the litter, being exorcized by a priest, is as unknown to me as to you. Yesterday morning curiosity prompted me to go to the gallows which is just off the highway. There I found this young person lying between two hanged men. I called everyone over to show them this bizarre circumstance. The count, my master, perceiving that the young person was still alive, had her carried to the place where we spent the night. He even decided that we would spend the whole day there so that the patient could be cared for, and indeed she deserves it, for she is a striking beauty. Today we risked putting her in that litter, but she keeps fainting.

'The gentleman following the litter is Don Alvar Massa Gordo, first cook, or rather, major-domo of the count. Next to him you see Lemado, the pastry cook, and Lacho, the confectioner.'

'That, Señor, is already more than I wanted to know,' I said.

'Finally, the person bringing up the rear, who has the honour to address you, is Don Gonzalo de Hierro Sangre, a Peruvian nobleman born into the families of Pizarro and Almagro and heir to their valour.'

I thanked the illustrious Peruvian and rejoined my own company, to whom I told what I had learnt. We all returned to the camp, and we told the gypsy chief that we had seen his little Lonzeto and the daughter of the young Elvira, whose place he had taken with the viceroy.

The gypsy replied that they had long planned to leave America, that they had landed in Cadiz the previous month, that they had left there the week before and had spent two nights on the banks of the Guadalquivir, quite close to the gallows of the Zoto brothers, where they had come upon a young girl lying between two hanged men.

Then he added, 'I have reason to believe that the young person has nothing to do with the Gomelez. I don't know her at all.'

'What?' I exclaimed with surprise. 'This young girl is not an instrument of the Gomelez? And yet she was found under the gallows? Could the hauntings be true?'

'Perhaps,' said the gypsy.

'We must detain these travellers for a few days,' said Rebecca.

'I have already thought of that,' replied the gypsy. 'Tonight I shall have half their herd of vicuña stolen.'

The Forty-first Day

This way of detaining the strangers seemed to me very odd. I was going to say so but the chief went on to give the order to strike camp. From the tone of his voice I could tell that my observations would have been fruitless. On this occasion we only moved camp a few times the range of a musket to a place where rocks seemed to have split after an earthquake. There we dined and everyone retired to his tent.

Towards evening I went to the chief's tent, where I came upon a commotion. The descendant of the house of Pizarro was there with two foreign servants and was haughtily demanding that the vicuñas be returned to them. The gypsy chief listened to him very patiently, which emboldened Señor Hierro Sangre, who started to shout even louder and was not sparing in his use of such epithets as 'scoundrel', 'bandit' and the like. At this the chief began to whistle at a very shrill pitch. The tent filled up gradually with armed gypsies, whose successive appearance caused a gradual diminution in the Peruvian's tone. Indeed he finished up trembling so much that one could hardly hear what he said.

When the chief saw that he had calmed down he offered him his hand with a smile and said to him, 'Forgive me, brave Peruvian, the appearances are against me and you have some cause to be angry; but go to the Marqués de Torres Rovellas. Ask him whether he recalls a Señora Dalanosa, whose nephew agreed out of pure kindness to become the wife of the Viceroy of Mexico in the place of Señora de Rovellas. If he remembers him, let him come here to meet me.'

Don Gonzalo de Hierro Sangre seemed delighted that a drama, whose outcome he had feared, had ended so well and he promised to acquit himself of the mission.

When he had left us the chief said to me, 'The Marqués de Torres Rovellas used to have a prodigious appetite for novels and pastorals.

432

We must receive him in surroundings which may please him.'

We went down into the fissure in the rock, which was shaded by thick bushes. Suddenly I was struck by the sight of natural scenery different from any I had seen up till then. A lake of dark green waters, transparent into its very depths, was surrounded by precipitous cliffs which were separated from each other by sunny beaches covered in flowering shrubs, which had been planted artistically although not in any pattern. Wherever the foot of the cliffs met the water, a path hollowed out through the rock led from one beach to the other. The waters of the lake flowed into grottoes decorated like those of Calypso. These were so many retreats where one could enjoy the coolness, and even bathe. The silence, which was total, indicated that this place was not known to men.

'Here is a province of my little empire where I have spent several years of my life, perhaps the happiest ones,' said the chief to me. 'But the two Americans are about to come. Let us find a pleasant refuge in which to await their arrival.'

We went into one of the prettiest grottoes, where Rebecca and her brother joined us. Soon the two old gentlemen appeared.

'Is it possible,' said one of them, 'that after such a long period of time I have found again the man who in his childhood did me so great a service? I have often sought information about you but in vain. Satisfactory reports never reached me in America.'

'Nor could they,' said the gypsy. 'I have undergone so many transformations and I have lived my life under so many different guises that it would have been difficult to catch up with me. But now we have found each other again at last, do me the honour of spending a few days in this retreat. Here you will enjoy a rest from the fatigues of your journey, of which you must be in need.'

'But this is a magical place,' said the marqués.

'It has that reputation,' replied the gypsy. 'Under Arab domination it was called Afrid Hamami, or the Devil's Bath. Now it's called La Frita. The inhabitants of the Sierra Morena do not dare come near it, and of an evening tell each other tales about the strange happenings which occur here. I do not want to enlighten them too much, and I would ask that the greater part of your retinue should stay outside this valley in the one where I have pitched my camp.'

'My old friend,' said the marqués, 'I ask for an exception to be made in the case of my daughter and future son-in-law.'

The gypsy bowed low and ordered those two persons, with a small number of servants, to be fetched.

While the gypsy showed his guests round the valley Velásquez looked all round him with surprise, picked up a stone, examined it and said, 'This is meltable in a glass-blower's furnace without any additive. We are in the crater of an old volcano here. The inner wall of this inverse cone provides us with a way of knowing its depth and hence of calculating the expansive force which hollowed it out. It is a subject worth considering.'

Velásquez thought for a moment, drew out tablets from his pocket and wrote something on them. Then he said, 'My father had a good theory about volcanoes. According to him, the expansive force which develops a core is higher than that which can be attributed either to steam or to the combustion of saltpetre and he inferred from that, that one day we will come to know about fluids whose effects will explain a great proportion of the phenomena of nature.'

'So you think that this lake has been hollowed out by a volcano?' said Rebecca.

'Yes, Señora,' replied Velásquez. 'The nature of the stone proves it, and the shape of the lake is a strong clue, too. From the way I can see objects on the opposite bank I estimate the diameter to be about 300 fathoms, and as the average incline of the lower cone is more or less sixty-six degrees, I estimate that the core may have been at a depth of 413 fathoms, which would give a displacement of 9,734,455 cubic fathoms of matter. And as I have told you, no forces in man's power could produce a similar effect, no matter in what quantity they were brought together.'

Rebecca wanted to add something to this line of reasoning but at that moment the marqués came back with his own people. As this conversation would not have interested everyone to the same degree, the chief wanted to put an end to Velásquez's geometrical proofs, so he turned to his guest and said, 'Señor, when I knew you, you lived and breathed love and were as fair as love itself. Your union with Elvira must have been nothing other than a series of delights and pleasures. You have breathed in the perfumes of life without knowing its thorns.'

'Not altogether,' said the marqués. 'It is true that love has perhaps taken up too much of my time but, as I have otherwise neglected none of the duties of a gentleman, I can confess to this foible without shame. And since we are in a place very well suited to romantic tales, I will, if you would like me to, tell you the story of my life.'

The whole company greeted this proposal with acclaim, and the narrator began as follows:

☙ THE MARQUÉS DE TORRES ROVELLAS'S STORY ❧

When you joined the Theatines, we were living, as you know, quite near your aunt Dalanosa. My mother sometimes went to see young Elvira but she didn't take me with her. Elvira had entered the convent pretending to want to become a nun and visits from a boy of my age would not have been proper. So we were prey to all of the ills of absence, which we softened by a correspondence whose Mercury my mother agreed to be, although she did this a little unwillingly, for she claimed that dispensation from Rome was not that easy to obtain and according to the usual rules we should not have written to each other until the dispensation had been granted. But in spite of these scruples she carried the letters and the replies. As for Elvira's wealth, we were very careful not to touch it. She was destined to become a nun and as soon as that happened all her goods would revert to Rovellas's collateral.

Your aunt spoke to my mother about her uncle the Theatine, referring to him as a shrewd and wise man who would give her good advice about the dispensation. My mother showed deep gratitude to your aunt. She wrote to Father Sántez, who thought the affair to be so important that instead of replying, he came himself to Burgos, with an adviser to the nunciature, who bore an assumed name because of the secrecy which those involved in the negotiation wanted to maintain.

It was decided that Elvira would spend six more months in the noviciate, and that afterwards, when her vocation had altogether disappeared, she would have the status of a highly distinguished,

435

paying resident in the convent, with private service provided; that is, with women cloistered with her, and a house set up outside as if she lived in it. My mother would stay there with some lawyers, who would deal with the details of the guardianship. As for me, I was to leave for Rome with a tutor, and the adviser was to follow; this did not in fact happen, for I was thought too young to solicit a dispensation and two years went by before I left.

And what years they were! I could see Elvira in the parlour every day and spend the rest of my time writing to her or reading novels. This reading matter greatly helped me to write my letters. Elvira read the same works and replied in the same vein. There was little of ourselves in this correspondence. Our turns of phrase were borrowed but our love was very real, or at least we had a very marked taste for each other. The insurmountable obstacle of the grille, which always came between us, excited our desire. Our blood burned with all the fire of youth and the turmoil of our senses added to that which was already ruling our heads.

The time came when I had to leave. The moment of saying farewell was cruel. Our sorrow was neither rehearsed nor feigned and was close to frenzy. People feared for Elvira's life. My sorrow was no less powerful but I was better able to resist it than was she. The distractions of the journey did me a great deal of good. I also owed a great deal to my mentor, who wasn't a pedant plucked from the dust of a school but a retired officer who had even spent some time at court. He was called Don Diego Sántez and was quite closely related to the Theatine of that name. This man, who was as shrewd as he was urbane, used indirect means to bring my mind back to reality, but the habits of fiction were too deeply rooted in it.

We arrived in Rome, and our first task was to pay our respects to Monsignor Ricardi, a very influential man, especially well looked-on by the Jesuits, who were then setting the style in Rome. He was a grave, proud person with an imposing figure, which was set off by a cross of enormous diamond which sparkled on his chest.

Ricardi told us that he had been informed of our affair, that it required discretion and that we should not move much in polite society. 'Meanwhile,' he said, 'you would do well to come to my house. The interest I shall be seen to have in you will prove on your

436

part a modesty which will count in your favour. I have decided to sound out the minds of the sacred college on your behalf.'

We followed Ricardi's advice. I spent my mornings visiting Roman antiquities, and in the evenings I went to see the auditor in a villa which he had, close to the villa Barberini. The Marchesa Paduli presided over the house. She was a widow and lived with Ricardi because she had no closer relative. At least, that is what was said, because no one really quite knew. Ricardi was from Genoa and the person called the Marchese Paduli had died on service abroad.

The young widow possessed all the qualities to make the house pleasant: a great deal of amiability and a general air of politeness mixed with modesty and dignity. None the less I thought I saw in her a preference or even a fondness for me, which betrayed itself constantly, though only by signs invisible to the rest of the assembled company. I recognized in those signs the secret sympathies of which novels are formed and I felt sorry for La Paduli for directing such a feeling to a person who could not reciprocate it.

Meanwhile, I sought the conversation of the marchesa and was happy to set her on to my favourite subjects, that is, love, the different ways of loving and the differences between affection and passion, and between fidelity and constancy. But as I spoke of these grave matters to the pretty Italian the idea did not cross my mind that I could ever be unfaithful to Elvira and the letters which went off to Burgos were as ardent as before.

One day I was at the villa without my mentor. Ricardi was not at home. I walked in the gardens and entered a grotto in which I found La Paduli, plunged in deep reverie, from which she was roused by some sound I made as I came in. Her great surprise in seeing me appear might have almost made me suspect that I had been the subject of her dreams. She even had the frightened look of a person who wants to escape from some peril.

She composed herself, however, made me sit down and addressed to me the courteous inquiry customary in Italy: 'Lei a girato questa mattina?'[1]

---

1 'Have you been for a walk this morning?'

I replied that I had been to the Corso, where I had seen many women, the most beautiful of whom was the Marchesa Lepri.

'Don't you know a more beautiful woman?' said La Paduli.

'Forgive me,' I replied. 'In Spain I know a young lady who is much more beautiful.' This reply seemed to upset Signora Paduli. She relapsed into her reverie, lowered her beautiful eyes and stared down at the ground with an expression of sadness.

To distract her I began another conversation, on the subject of affection.

At that she raised her languid eyes, looked at me and said, 'Have you ever experienced these feelings you are so adept at describing?'

'Yes, certainly,' I replied. 'And feelings a thousand times more intense and a thousand times more tender for the same young lady whose beauty is so superior.' I had scarcely said these words when a deathly pallor covered La Paduli's face. She fell flat on the ground just as if she were dead. I had never seen a woman in such a state and had absolutely no idea what to do with this one. Fortunately, I caught sight of two of her servants walking in the garden. I ran to them and told them to come to their mistress's aid.

Then I left the garden, reflecting on what had just happened, marvelling at the power of love and how a spark that it lets fall in a heart produces such ravages. I felt sorry for La Paduli. I blamed myself for being the cause of her unhappiness but I could not think of being unfaithful to Elvira for La Paduli or any other woman in the world.

The next day I went to the villa Ricardi, but guests were not received as Signora Paduli was ill. The day after, all that was talked about in Rome was her indisposition, which was by all accounts grave. For this I felt the same remorse as for an ill of which I was the cause.

On the fifth day of her illness I saw a young woman appear where I was staying, with a veil covering her face. She said to me, 'Signor forestiere,[2] a dying woman begs to see you. Follow me.'

I suspected that it was Signora Paduli but did not believe that I

2 Stranger.

could refuse the wishes of a person on the verge of death. A carriage awaited me at the end of the street. I climbed in with the veiled girl. We reached the villa by the back of the garden. We went down a dark walk, then a corridor, then through some dark bedrooms, which led to that of Signora Paduli. She was in her bed and held out her hand to me. It was burning, which I took to be an effect of her fever. I lifted my eyes to the patient and saw that she was half-naked. Until then I had only seen women's faces and hands. My sight grew clouded and my knees buckled under me. I was unfaithful to Elvira without knowing how this had happened to me.

'God of love!' cried the pretty Italian. 'Another of your miracles! The one I love has restored me to life!'

From a state of complete innocence I suddenly passed to the most pleasurable sensual pursuits. Four hours went by in this way. At last the maidservant came to warn us that it was time to part, and I went back to the carriage with some difficulty, forced to accept the support of the arm of the young girl, who was quietly laughing. As she was on the point of leaving me, she clasped me in her arms and said, 'I'll have my turn!'

No sooner was I in the carriage than the idea of pleasure gave way to the most harrowing remorse. 'Elvira!' I cried. 'Elvira, I have betrayed you! Elvira, I am no longer worthy of you! Elvira, Elvira, Elvira . . .' In short, I said everything that one says on such occasions and retired to bed determined not to return to the marchesa's house.

As the Marqués de Torres Rovellas reached this point in his story, some gypsies arrived in search of their chief. As he was very interested in the story of his old friend, he asked him to stop and continue it the next day.

The Forty-second Day

We assembled in a grotto no less resplendent than the one of the day before, and the Marqués de Torres Rovellas, seeing that we were waiting with impatience to hear him continue to relate to us his adventures, took up the thread of his story as follows:

THE MARQUÉS DE TORRES ROVELLAS'S STORY
∽ CONTINUED ∽

I have told you how remorseful I was about the infidelity of which I had been guilty. I did not doubt that Signora Paduli's maidservant would come the next day to lead me to her mistress's bed, and I promised myself that I would not receive her well. But Sylvia did not come the next day, nor the days after that, which surprised me a little.

Sylvia came a week later. She was dressed with a care which her person could well have done without, for in herself she was prettier than her mistress.

'Sylvia!' I said to her. 'Sylvia, go away. You have made me unfaithful to the most adorable of women. You have deceived me. I thought I was going to see a dying woman and you led me to a woman who emanated sensuality. My heart is not guilty but I am not innocent.'

'You are innocent, and more than just a little innocent,' replied Sylvia. 'Set your mind at rest on that point. But I have not come to take you to the marchesa, who at this moment is in Ricardi's arms.'

'Her uncle!'

'No, Ricardi is not her uncle. Come with me and I will explain everything.'

I followed Sylvia out of pure curiosity. We climbed into the carriage, arrived at the villa and went in through the gardens. Then the pretty messenger took me up to her room, a real grisette's den bedecked with pots of pomade, combs and items of toiletry. There was a little snow-white bed there too, under which there was a remarkably fine pair of slippers. Sylvia took off her gloves, her veil and then the kerchief she wore on her breast.

'Stop!' I cried. 'Go no further. That's the way your mistress made me unfaithful.'

'My mistress,' replied Sylvia, 'has recourse to crude means which up to now I have been able to forgo.'

As she said this, she opened a cupboard and took out some fruit, some biscuits and a bottle of wine. She put them on a table, which she drew over to the bed, and then said, 'My charming Spaniard, maidservants are badly off for furniture. There used to be a chair in this room, but it was taken away this morning. Sit down here on the bed next to me and don't spurn this little collation, which I am happy to give you.'

Such gracious offers had to be accepted. I sat down next to Sylvia, ate the fruit, drank her wine and asked her to tell me the story of her mistress, which she did as follows:

THE STORY OF MONSIGNOR RICARDI AND LAURA CERELLA, ⌖ KNOWN AS LA MARCHESA PADULI ⌖

Ricardi, the younger son of a famous Genoese family, had entered orders early and soon after became a priest. A handsome face and violet stockings were taken at that time in Rome to be strong recommendations by the fair sex. Ricardi used these advantages and even abused them, as did all his young prelate colleagues. When he reached the age of thirty he became bored with pleasures and wanted to play a role in politics.

He did not wish altogether to give up women. He would have liked to form a liaison in which he would find nothing but enjoyment, but he did not know how to go about it. He had been the *cavaliere servente* of the most beautiful princesses in Rome but these princesses were beginning to favour younger prelates. Besides, he was tired of those assiduous courtships which require an intolerable degree of continual discomfort. Kept women also have their drawbacks. They don't know what is happening in polite society and one doesn't know what to talk to them about.

Amid all this uncertainty, Ricardi conceived of a plan which many people before and after hit upon – that of educating a young girl, altogether to his taste, who thereby would be able to make him perfectly happy. And indeed, what pleasure there is in seeing in someone already endowed with all the graces, the charms of the mind blossom with those of the face; what pleasure there is in showing this person society and the world, in enjoying her surprise, in witnessing the first stirrings of passion, in endowing her with all her ideas and in making of her a being entirely suited to oneself. But what shall one then do with such charming creatures? Many marry them in order to avoid the problem. Ricardi could not. While pursuing his libertine plans our prelate had not stopped working for his advancement. He had an uncle, an auditor at the *Rota Romana*[1], who had been promised a cardinal's hat and who had been assured by his cardinal that he could pass on his position as auditor to his nephew. But all that was not to take place for four or five years. Ricardi reckoned that in the meanwhile he could return to his homeland or even travel.

One day, as Ricardi was walking in the streets of Genoa, he was accosted by a girl of thirteen carrying a basket of oranges, who offered him one in a charming and graceful way. Ricardi's libertine hand parted the unkempt locks which fell across the face of the girl and revealed features which promised to become perfectly beautiful. He asked the orange-seller who her parents were. She replied that only her mother was left, a poor widow called Bastiana Cerella. Ricardi had her take him to her mother and began by saying who he was. Then he said to Bastiana that he had a female relative, a very charitable lady, who took it upon herself to educate poor young girls and then give them a dowry, and that he would undertake to place little Laura with her.

Her mother smiled and said, 'I don't know your relative, who certainly must be a respectable lady. But your charity towards young

1 The Supreme Court for Ecclesiastical and Secular causes in Rome.

girls is widely known and you may take this one into your charge. I don't know whether you bring them up virtuously, but you will certainly save her from poverty, which is worse than any vice.'

Ricardi offered to make some arrangement in favour of the mother. 'No,' she replied. 'I won't sell my daughter. But I'll accept any gifts you may send me. Staying alive is the first law of all and often hunger prevents me from working.'

On that very day little Laura was given lodgings by one of Ricardi's clients. Her hands were covered with almond paste, her hair with curl-papers, her neck with pearls, her bosom with lace. The girl looked at herself in all the mirrors and could not recognize herself but from the beginning she understood what she was destined for and adopted the appropriate attitude of her estate.

However, the girl had had childhood companions who did not know what had become of her and were very worried. The one who was most concerned to find her again was Ceco Boscone, a boy fourteen years of age, the son of a porter, already well built and already in love with the little orange-seller, whom he often met in the street or in our house, because he was related to us distantly. If I say 'our house' it's because I am also called Cerella, and have the honour of being my mistress's first cousin.

We were all the more worried about our cousin because not only did no one talk to us about her, but we were even forbidden to speak of her or to mention her name. My usual occupation was with household laundry and my cousin ran errands in the port until he was ready to carry bales. When I had finished my work for the day I went to join him in the porch of a church and we wept many tears over our cousin's fate.

One evening Ceco said to me, 'I've had an idea. These last few days it has been pouring and Signora Cerella has not been able to go out. But on the first fine day she won't be able to restrain herself and if her daughter is in Genoa she will go to see her. All we have then to do is to follow her and we will find out where Laura is hidden.'

I gave this idea my approval. The next day it was fine. I went to Signora Cerella, saw that she was extracting from an old wardrobe an even older veil, said a few words to her and then ran to warn Ceco. We lay in wait and soon saw Signora Cerella leave the house. We followed her to a distant part of the town and when she went into a house we hid again. She came out and went away. We went into the house, climbed the stairs, or rather ran up them, and opened the door to a fine apartment. I recognized Laura and threw my arms round her neck. Ceco pulled me away, took her in his arms and pressed his lips to hers. But then another door opened. Ricardi appeared, slapped me twenty times and gave Ceco as many kicks. His servants appeared and in the twinkling of an eye we found ourselves in the road, slapped, beaten and very clear in our minds that we were not to make any further investigation into what was happening to our cousin.

Ceco went off to become a ship's boy on a Maltese privateer. I haven't heard any more of him since.

As for me, the desire to see my cousin again never left me, but you might say the desire grew as I did. I was in service in several houses and eventually in that of the Marchese Ricardi, the elder brother of our prelate. Signora Paduli was often mentioned there and no one had any notion where the prelate had found this relative. For the time being she escaped investigation by the family but nothing escapes the curiosity of valets. We made our own inquiries and soon learnt that the so-called marchesa was none other than Laura Cerella. The marchese advised us to be discreet, and sent me to his brother to warn him to be twice as careful if he did not want to do himself considerable harm.

But it's not my story I am telling and I have strayed from the Marchesa Paduli, having left the little Laura in the house of one of the prelate's clients. She did not stay there long. She was moved to a little town on the Genoan coast. Monsignor went to see her there from time to time and always returned yet more satisfied with the work of his hands.

Two years later Ricardi went to London. He travelled under an alias and passed himself off as an Italian merchant. Laura went with him and was thought to be his wife. He took her to Paris and other cities, where it was easier to preserve one's incognito. She became daily more agreeable, adored her benefactor and made him the happiest of men. Three years passed like a flash. Then the uncle of Ricardi was about to obtain the cardinal's hat and urged him to come back to Rome.

Ricardi took his mistress to an estate he possessed near Gorizia. The day after their arrival he said to her, 'Signora, I have news to give you which will please you. You are the widow of the Marchese Paduli, who has just died in the service of the emperor. Here are the papers which prove it. Paduli was a relative of ours. You will not, I hope, refuse to join me in Rome and do the honours in my house.'

Ricardi left a few days later.

Left to her own thoughts, the new marchesa reflected deeply about Ricardi's character, her relations with him and what she could get out of them. When three months had gone by, she was summoned to join her so-called uncle and found him in all the splendour attached to the offices he now filled. Part of this glory reflected on to her and homage was addressed to her from many quarters. Ricardi announced to his family that he had taken into his house the widow of Paduli, who was a cousin of the Ricardi on their mother's side. The Marchese Ricardi, who had never heard of Paduli's marriage, made the inquiries I have already mentioned and sent me to the new marchesa to advise her to be extremely circumspect.

I travelled by sea, disembarked at Civitavecchia and made my way to Rome. I presented myself to the marchesa. She asked her servants to withdraw and threw herself into my arms. We spoke of our childhood, of my mother, of hers, of the chestnuts we ate together. Little Ceco was not forgotten. I told her that he had embarked on a privateer and had not been heard of since. Laura, who was already in an emotional state, burst into tears and had great difficulty in composing herself. She asked me not to make myself known to the prelate but to pass myself off as her maidservant. She added that my Genoese accent might betray me and that I was to say I was born in the state of Genoa and not in the capital.

Laura had her plan. She remained equitable and cheerful for a fortnight, but then she took on a serious, reflective, capricious, world-weary look. Ricardi tried hard to please her, but in vain. He couldn't restore her mood to what it was before.

'My dear Laura,' he said to her one day, 'what are you lacking? Compare your present state to the one from which I saved you.'

'And why did you save me from it?' replied Laura with great vehemence. 'It's my poverty that I am missing. What am I doing

445

among all these princesses? Their insinuations, though they are couched in polite language, are just so many bitter insults. Oh, how I miss you, my rags, my black bread, my chestnuts! I can't think of you without my heart breaking. And you, my dear Ceco, who was to have married me when you were strong enough to be a porter! With you I would have known poverty but not the vapours, and princesses would have envied me my fate.'

'Laura, Laura!' cried Ricardi. 'What's this new manner of speech?'

'It's the voice of nature,' replied Laura. 'She makes women to be wives and mothers in an estate in which heaven has caused them to be born, not to be the nieces of libertine priests!'

Then Laura went into her study and closed the door behind her.

Ricardi was in an awkward position. He had introduced Signora Paduli as his niece. If she rashly disclosed the truth, he was lost and his career was finished. What is more, he loved the hussy and he was jealous of her. Everything contributed to his unhappiness.

But the next day a trembling Ricardi presented himself at Laura's door and was agreeably surprised to receive the tenderest of welcomes.

'Forgive me!' she said to him, 'dear uncle, dear benefactor. I am an ingrate who is unworthy to see the light of day. I am the work of your hands, you have cultivated my mind, I owe you everything. Forgive a whim in which my heart had no part.'

Peace was soon made.

Some days later Laura said to Ricardi, 'I cannot be happy with you. You are too much my master. Here everything belongs to you and I am in a state of complete dependency. The lord who has just left us has given his mistress the most beautiful estate in the duchy of Urbino. *That's* what I call a lover. And if I ask you for that baronial estate in which I spent three months you would refuse, and yet it's a legacy from your uncle Cambiosi and you are free to dispose of it.'

'You want to have your independence,' said Ricardi, 'so that you can leave me.'

'It's to love you all the more,' replied Laura.

Ricardi didn't know whether to make the gift or to refuse to. He was in love; he was jealous; he feared that his dignity would be compromised; he feared himself becoming dependent on his mistress.

Laura read his mind and would have driven him to a decision but Ricardi had immense power in Rome. One word from him and four *sbiri* would have seized his niece and taken her to a convent where she would have done long penance. This thought held Laura back. She eventually decided to pretend to be ill, to get Ricardi where she wanted him. This plan was occupying her mind when you entered the grotto.

'What? It wasn't me she was thinking about?' I asked, astonished.

'No, my child,' said Sylvia, 'she was thinking of a good baronial estate with an income of four thousand scudi. But suddenly she hit on the idea of feigning illness or even death. She had already practised this by copying actresses she had seen in London. She wanted to know whether she could persuade you of the illusion. So you see, my little Spaniard, that up to now you have been completely fooled. But you haven't the right to complain about what happened subsequently, and my mistress has no complaints about you. As for me, I found you charming when you sought my arm to support you in your weakness. Then I swore that I would have my turn.' That is how the soubrette expressed herself.

What can I say? I was astounded by what I had just heard. I had been stripped of my illusions. I didn't know where I was. Sylvia profited from my confusion to bring turmoil to my senses. She had no difficulty in succeeding. She even abused the advantages she had. At last, when she put me back in my carriage, I didn't know whether to feel fresh remorse or not to think any more about it.

As the Marqués de Torres Rovellas reached this point in his story the gypsy was forced to leave us and asked him to be so kind as to stop at that point and continue the next day.

The Forty-third Day

―――――――――――――― ✆ ――――――――――――――

We assembled as on the previous day and duly asked the Marqués de Torres Rovellas to continue his story. He took it up again as follows:

THE MARQUÉS DE TORRES ROVELLAS'S STORY
✆ CONTINUED ✆

I have told you how I was twice unfaithful to the fair Elvira; how I felt terrible remorse after the first time; and how after the second I didn't know whether I should feel remorse or whether it was better not to think any more about it. I can assure you that otherwise my love for my cousin was still the same and my letters still as passionate. My mentor, who wanted at all costs to cure me of my romantic ideas, permitted himself sometimes to take measures which went somewhat beyond what was expected of his office. Without seeming to be any part of it, he would expose me to temptation, to which I always succumbed, but my passion for Elvira was still the same and I was very impatient for the dispensation to emerge from the apostolic registry.

Eventually Ricardi summoned Sántez and me one day. His expression was somewhat solemn, heralding the great news which he had to impart to us. He tempered his gravity, however, with an affable smile and said to us, 'Your affair is concluded, although not without difficulty. We give dispensation quite freely to certain Catholic countries but much less freely to Spain, because the faith is purer there and observance stricter. However, His Holiness, considering the pious foundations established in America by the house of Rovellas, and considering also that the venial fault of the two children was a consequence of the misfortunes of that house, His Holiness, as I say, has loosed on earth the blood ties that existed between you. They will equally be loosed in heaven. However, so that other young persons

448

do not use this example as an excuse to commit similar faults, it is enjoined on you as penitence to carry a rosary of a hundred beads round your neck and to recite it every day for three years, also to build a church for the Theatines in Vera Cruz. And thereupon I have the honour to congratulate you and your future wife.'

I can leave you to imagine my joy. I hurried to secure His Holiness's brief and we left Rome two days later.

Travelling fast by day and night I reached Burgos and saw Elvira again. She was yet more beautiful. All that remained for us to do was to have the marriage approved by the court but Elvira had taken possession of her fortune and we were not short of friends. Those looking after our interests obtained the permission we desired and to it the court added for me the title of the Marqués de Torres Rovellas.

Then all that was thought about was dresses, jewellery, caskets, the delightful paraphernalia of a girl who is about to become a bride. But the tender Elvira was not touched by it all. She was only moved by her lover's attentions.

At last the day came on which we were to be united. It seemed desperately long to me, for the ceremony was not to take place until the evening, in the chapel of a country house we possessed close to Burgos.

I wandered through the garden to while away the impatience with which I was devoured. Then I sat on the seat, where I began to think about my behaviour, which was so unworthy of the angel to whom I was going to be united. For, counting all the times I had been unfaithful to her, I reached the number of twelve. At that, remorse once more entered my soul and, reproaching myself bitterly, I said to myself, 'Ingrate! Wretch! Have you thought of the treasure which is destined to be yours, of that divine being who sighs and even breathes for no one else but you and who never addressed a single word to another?'

While I was engaged in this act of contrition, I heard two of Elvira's maids of honour sit down on a bench behind the bower against which mine was set and begin a conversation which captured all of my attention.

'Well, Manuela,' said one of them. 'Our mistress will be very happy today, for she will love in reality and give real tokens of her love, instead of the minor favours she would grant so generously to her suitors at the grille.'

'Oh!' said the other maid of honour. 'You are referring to her guitar master, who furtively kissed her hand while seeming to place it on the strings.'

'Not at all,' replied the first maid of honour. 'I am talking about the dozen or so beautiful passions – wholly innocent, it is true – which she enjoyed as a game and which in her own way she encouraged. First, the little bachelor of arts who taught her geography. He was head-over-heels in love with her so she gave him a sizeable lock of her hair, which I found missing when I combed her the next day. After him came the sweet talker who informed her of the state of her fortune and apprised her of her income. He knew what he wanted. He overwhelmed her with the most flattering praise and even intoxicated her with his eulogies. She gave him her portrait in silhouette, let him kiss her hand a hundred times through the bars and gave him gifts of flowers and exchanged bouquets with him.'

The rest of the conversation has gone from my memory but I can assure you that the dozen were all there. I was devastated. Certainly Elvira had only accorded innocent favours, or rather they were really childish acts. But the Elvira of my imagination could never have permitted even these shadows of infidelity. No doubt this was not very rational. Since her childhood Elvira had stammered words of love, even before she pronounced them correctly. I ought to have realized that, being so fond of the subject itself, she would practise it with persons other than myself, but I would never have believed this even if I had been told it. Now I was convinced of it, disillusioned, overcome by my sorrow. At that point I was summoned to the ceremony. I entered the chapel with a face so distraught that it surprised my mother and filled my bride with anxiety and sadness. Even the priest was disconcerted and did not know whether he should marry us. But marry us he did, and I can assure you that never did a day awaited with such impatience fulfil less well what it seemed to promise.

That was not true of the night. Hymen extinguished his torches and hid us in the protective veil of his first pleasures. Then all the flirtation at the grille disappeared from Elvira's memory. Unknown ecstasies filled her heart with love and gratitude. She gave herself altogether to her husband.

The next day we looked very happy. How could I have still nurtured any sorrow? Men who have lived their life know that among the good things that it can offer, none is comparable with the happiness that a young bride gives, bringing, as she does, to the nuptial bed so many secrets to be revealed, so many dreams to be realized, so many loving thoughts. What is the rest of existence beside days like these, spent between the recent memory of such sweet emotions and the deceptive illusions of a future which hope paints in the most flattering hues?

Our family friends left us several months to drink deep of our happiness. Then, when they thought that we were in a fit state to listen to them, they sought to awaken in us the passion of ambition.

The Conde de Rovellas had had some expectation of becoming a grandee and they said that we should continue with his plans. This we owed as much to ourselves as to the children which heaven might give us. In short, it was pointed out to us that whatever the effects of our representations, we would repent one day of not having made them, and that it is always a good thing to spare oneself feelings of regret.

We were of an age at which one's will is scarcely one's own, being dictated by those around one; and we let ourselves be taken off to Madrid. When the viceroy was told of our intentions he wrote on our behalf in the most pressing terms. Soon appearances were in our favour; but they were only appearances. And although these appearances took on all the protean shapes of the court, they never became realities.

These frustrated hopes upset my friends and also unfortunately my mother, who would have given anything in the world to see her little Lonzeto become a Spanish grandee. Soon the poor woman went into a decline and realized that she did not have long to live. She looked to the salvation of her soul and wanted first of all to show her gratitude to the decent folk of the village of Villaca, who had helped us in such a friendly way when we were in need. Above all else, she would have wanted to do something for the *alcalde* and the priest. My mother had no personal fortune but Elvira was glad to be in a position to help her in her noble plan and made them gifts which even exceeded my mother's wishes.

As soon as our old friends learned of the good fortune which had befallen them, they came to Madrid and crowded round the bedside of their benefactress. When my mother left us we still loved each other and we were still rich and happy. She passed away into eternal life in a peaceful sleep, having already received on earth a part of the rewards which her virtues and especially her infinite goodness deserved.

Soon after, misfortune struck us down. The two sons which Elvira had given me died after a short illness. Then also the grandeeship lost all its attraction for us. We decided to put an end to our solicitations and to go to Mexico, where the state of our fortunes required our presence. The health of the marquesa had suffered a great deal, and her doctors assured us that a sea voyage might make her better.

So we departed and arrived at Vera Cruz after a sea voyage lasting six weeks, which had the full, promised, favourable effect on Elvira's health. She arrived in the New World not only well but more beautiful than she had ever been.

At Vera Cruz we met one of the senior officers of the viceroy, whom he had sent to pay his compliments to us and to take us to the city of Mexico. This man spoke a great deal about the magnificence of the Conde de Peña Vélez and the gallant style he had introduced into his household. We knew something of this from the connections we had in America. We were aware that once his ambitions had been completely satisfied, his predilection for the fair sex had been rekindled and, not being able to find happiness in marriage, he had sought pleasure in that discreet and refined amorous intercourse which used once to be the distinctive mark of Spanish society.

We did not stay long at Vera Cruz and had the most comfortable of journeys to Mexico. As you know, the capital city is situated in the middle of a lake. We reached its outskirts at nightfall and soon caught sight of a hundred gondolas bearing lanterns. The most sumptuously bedecked gondola forged ahead and reached us first. From it the viceroy appeared and addressed my wife.

'Incomparable daughter of the woman whom my heart has never stopped loving!' he said. 'I thought that heaven had taken you from my honourable aspirations. But it did not want to deprive the world of its most beautiful jewel and for that I give it thanks. Come and be the ornament of our hemisphere. In possessing you it can envy the Old World nothing.'

Then the viceroy did me the honour of embracing me and we took our places in his gondola. I soon noticed that the count was staring at the marquesa and looking surprised.

At last he said to her, 'I thought, Señora, that I had kept the image of your features in my memory, but I must confess that I would not have recognized you. However, if you have changed, it is very much to your advantage.'

We then remembered that the viceroy had never met my wife and that it was your features which had remained in his memory.

I said to him that the change was indeed so great that those who had seen Elvira at that time would have had the greatest difficulty in recognizing her now.

After about half an hour on the water, we reached a floating island, which, by cunning artifice, had been given the appearance of a real island covered with orange trees and other trees and bushes, but which still floated on the surface of the water. It could be moved to all parts of the lake and benefit successively from its different aspects. Such constructions are not rare in Mexico. They are called *chinampas*.

A well-lit rotunda was in the middle of the island. The sound of loud music could be heard from afar. Soon through the lanterns we could pick out the letters of 'Elvira'. As we reached the shore we saw two troupes of men and women in the most magnificent but strangely decorated costumes, on which the bright colours of different plumages vied in brilliance with sumptuous jewellery.

'Señor,' said the viceroy, 'one of these troupes is composed of Mexicans. The fine lady you see at their head is the Marquesa de Montezuma, the last of that great name which the sovereigns of this country once bore. It is the policy of the Council of Madrid not to allow her to perpetuate rights which many Mexicans still consider wholly legitimate. We console her for this disgrace by proclaiming her the queen of our festivities. Those in the other troupe are taking the parts of Peruvian Incas. They have learnt that a daughter of the Sun has landed in Mexico and have come to pay homage to her.'

As the viceroy was addressing this compliment to my wife, I was looking closely at her. I saw in her eyes a fire which was born of a spark of vanity which in the seven years of our marriage had not had time to develop. Indeed, in spite of all our wealth we had been far from playing a leading role in Madrid society. Elvira had been preoccupied by my mother, her children, her own health and had had few chances to shine. But the journey had given her back all of her beauty at the same time as restoring her health, and placed now in the forefront of a new theatre she seemed inclined to take an exalted view of herself and attract to herself the attention of the world.

The viceroy installed Elvira as Queen of the Peruvians, then said to me:

'You are certainly the first subject of this daughter of the Sun. But as we are all in costume I would ask you to acknowledge the rule of another sovereign until the end of the ball.'

As he said this he presented me to the Marquesa de Montezuma and put her hand in mine.

We then reached the main part of the ball. The two troupes danced sometimes apart, sometimes together. The desire of each to outdo the other brought the festivity alive and it was decided to prolong the masquerade until the end of the season.

So I remained the subject of the pretender to the throne of Mexico and my wife treated her own subjects with a familiarity which did not escape my notice. I must at this point paint you a portrait of the daughter of the caciques, or rather give you some idea of her looks, for it will be impossible for me to describe to you her savage grace and the fleeting impressions which the emotions of her passionate soul imprinted on her features.

Tlascala de Montezuma was born in the mountainous region of Mexico and did not have the dark complexion of those living in the plain. Hers was not fair, but it had its delicacy, and her jet-black eyes increased its lustre. Her features were less sharp than those of Europeans, but were not flattened in the way one sees in some American races. Tlascala resembled these only in her somewhat full lips, which looked enchanting when a smile lent them its fleeting grace. As for her figure, I have nothing to say on that score. I leave it to your imagination, or rather to that of an artist wanting to paint Atalanta or Diana.

Her whole posture was also unusual. In the way she moved could be detected an initial passionate impulse which was repressed by self-control. In her, immobility did not look like repose but hid some inner turmoil.

Too often the blood of the Montezumas reminded Tlascala that she had been born to reign over a vast region of the world. People who addressed her would be met by the haughty air of an outraged queen. But before she had even opened her mouth to make a gracious reply her tender gaze already enchanted them. When she entered the viceroy's state rooms, she seemed to be indignant at finding herself among equals but soon she had no equals. Hearts formed for love had recognized their sovereign and crowded round her. Tlascala was no longer a queen; she was a woman, and basked in their homage.

I detected her haughty temperament from the very first ball. I thought it incumbent on me to address a compliment to her which related to the character of her mask and my role as her subject allotted to me by the viceroy, but Tlascala did not receive me well. 'Señor,' she said, 'royal status conferred by a mask can only flatter those who have not been called to the throne.'

At the same moment she glanced at my wife. Just then Elvira was surrounded by Peruvians who were offering her their service on their knees. Her vanity and joy almost reached the point of ecstasy and I felt a sort of shame for her. I spoke to her about it that very evening. She received my counsel distractedly and my advice frostily. Vanity had entered her soul and driven out love.

The intoxication which the incense of flattery instils takes a long time to dissipate. Elvira's could only grow. All Mexico was divided between her perfect beauty and the incomparable charms of Tlascala. Elvira's days were spent glorying in yesterday's successes and preparing those of the morrow. A precipitous slope swept her down to every form of pleasurable pastime. I wanted to stop her but could not. I was myself being drawn down but in a different direction, very far from the flowery paths on which, as my wife trod them, pleasure after pleasure was springing up.

I was not yet thirty years old, nor even twenty-nine. I was at that age at which feeling still has the freshness of youth and passions the force of the grown man. My love, which had come into being close to Elvira's cradle, had never grown up; and her mind, nourished from the first by romantic folly, had never acquired maturity. My own mind had not progressed much further, but my reason had advanced enough to allow me to see that Elvira's thoughts turned around petty interests, petty rivalries and often petty backbiting in the narrow circle in which women are confined, not so much by the limits of their character as by those of their mind. Exceptions to this are rare, and I had thought that there were none at all. I was, though, completely disabused of this when I came to know Tlascala. No rivalry born of jealousy had found its way into her soul. The fair sex seemed all to have a claim on her benevolence and those who brought honour to it by their beauty, their grace or their tenderness aroused the keenest interest in her. She would have liked to have them about her, to earn their trust and to win their friendship. As for men, she seldom spoke about them and then always with reserve, unless she found noble and magnanimous acts to praise. Then her admiration was expressed openly and even with warmth. Otherwise her conversation turned on general topics and only became very animated when it was a question of the prosperity of the New World or the happiness of its inhabitants: her favourite subjects, to which she returned whenever she thought she could do so without impropriety.

Many men seem destined by the influence of fate and no doubt of their characters to live their lives governed by that sex which dominates all those who are not able to master it. Indubitably I am one of those men. I had been Elvira's humble worshipper, then a quite submissive husband. But she had loosened my chains by the small worth she seemed to place on them.

Masquerade followed masquerade and the social round obliged me to follow the marquesa everywhere; but much more than this, my heart made me follow her. The first change I noticed in myself was to sense my thoughts grow more lofty and my soul swell. My character took on greater decisiveness and my will more energy. I felt the need to turn my feelings into actions and to influence my fellow-men. I solicited an office and obtained it.

The duties with which I was entrusted placed several provinces under my authority. I saw natives oppressed by their conquerors, and took their side. I had powerful enemies and incurred the minister's wrath. The court itself seemed to threaten me. I put up the most spirited resistance. I won the love of Mexicans, the respect of the Spaniards and, what was of greatest value in my eyes, I inspired a deep interest in the person who already governed my whole heart. In truth, Tlascala was just as reserved with me, if not more so; but her eyes sought mine, looked into them with pleasure, then uneasily looked away. She said little to me even about what I had done for the Americans. But when she spoke to me she found it difficult to breathe. Her respiration was agitated and her timid, sweet voice endowed even the most unimportant speech with a tone of growing intimacy.

Tlascala thought that she had found in me a soul kindred to hers; she was wrong. Her soul had occupied me. She inspired me and she it was who determined my actions.

As for me, I deluded myself about the force of my character. My dreams became reveries, and my ideas about the happiness of America risky schemes. My pastimes took on a heroic hue. I hunted jaguar and puma in the forest, or even fought with these ferocious animals. But what I did most often was to go down into wild valleys amid solitary echoes which were the only confidants of a love which I feared to confess to the person who had inspired it.

But Tlascala had seen through me. I began to divine her feelings, and we might easily have betrayed ourselves to the eyes of a discerning public but we escaped its attention. The viceroy had to deal with serious matters, which put an end to the series of splendid festivities for which he had developed a very marked taste, and all of Mexican society a veritable passion. Everyone then adopted a less dissipated form of life. Tlascala retired to a house she possessed on the north side of the lake. I started by going there frequently; in the end I went to see her every day. I cannot explain to you very clearly how we behaved together. On my side it was a cult bordering on fanaticism; on hers it was a sacred fire whose flame she nurtured in fervent and deep contemplation. We were always on the point of confessing our passion for each other but did not dare to utter it. This was an exquisite state of affairs. We appreciated its sweetness and feared changing it.

*

457

As the Marqués de Torres Rovellas reached this point in his story, the gypsy was forced to give his attention to the affairs of his band and asked the marqués to stop, and continue his story the next day.

The Forty-fourth Day

We assembled as we had on the previous days. The Marqués de Torres Rovellas was asked to continue his story, which he did as follows:

THE MARQUÉS DE TORRES ROVELLAS'S STORY
∾ CONTINUED ∾

I have told you about my love for the adorable Tlascala and have described her soul and person. The rest of my story will make her better known to you.

Tlascala was persuaded of the truths of our holy faith, but at the same time she was imbued with respect for the memory of her ancestors, and in her mitigated faith she had provided a separate paradise for them, which was not heaven but was in some other region between that place and earth. She shared to a certain degree her compatriots' superstitions. She believed that the illustrious ghosts of the kings of her race came back to earth on dark nights and haunted an old cemetery situated in the mountains. Nothing in the world would have been able to persuade Tlascala to go there at night. But we sometimes would go there during the day and spend many hours there. She would decipher the hieroglyphs engraved on the tombs of her forefathers and elucidate them by traditions which she knew all about.

We soon were acquainted with most of the inscriptions and, by extending our investigations, we would find new ones from which we would remove the moss and thorns growing over them.

One day Tlascala showed me a spray of a spiny shrub and told me that it was not where it was by chance. The person who had planted it had had the intention to call down celestial vengeance on enemy spirits. She told me that I would be doing a good action by destroying the ominous plant. I took an axe which a Mexican had with him and

459

cut down this ill-starred shrub. We then came upon a stone covered with more hieroglyphs than those we had seen up to that point.

'This was written after the conquest,' said Tlascala. 'At that time the Mexicans mixed some letters of the alphabet, copied from the Spaniards, with their hieroglyphs. Inscriptions of this period are the easiest to read.'

Tlascala then began to read, but as she read her features showed growing anguish; then she fell unconscious on the stone which for two centuries had hidden the cause of her sudden horror.

Tlascala was carried back to her house and regained consciousness to some degree, but only to utter disconnected words which expressed no more than her mental anguish. I returned home sick at heart and the next day received the following letter:

> Alonso, I have gathered my strength and thoughts together to write these few lines to you. They will be delivered to you by old Xoaz, who was my teacher in our ancient language. Take him to the stone that we discovered and have him translate the inscription.
>
> My sight is clouded and my eyes are shrouded in a dark mist.
>
> Alonso, terrible spectres come between us.
>
> Alonso, I shall not see you again.

Xoaz was a priest, or rather a descendant of the old priests. I took him to the cemetery and showed him the fateful stone. He copied the hieroglyphs down and took the transcription home with him. I went to Tlascala's house; she was delirious and did not recognize me. That evening her fever seemed less high but her doctor asked me not to go in to see her.

The next day Xoaz came to my house and brought me the translation of the Mexican inscription, which read as follows:

> I, Koatril, son of Montezuma, have brought here the infamous body of Marina, who yielded her heart and her country to the hateful Cortez, chief of the sea-brigands.
>
> Spirits of my ancestors, who return here on dark nights, restore life to these inanimate remains long enough to make them suffer the agony of death.

Spirits of my ancestors, hear my voice, hear the curses which my voice utters in the name of the human victims whose blood still reeks on my hands.

I, Koatril, son of Montezuma, am a father. My daughters wander on frozen mountain peaks, but beauty is the attribute of our illustrious blood. Spirits of my ancestors, if ever a daughter of Koatril or the daughter of his daughters and of his sons, if ever a daughter of my blood gives her heart and her charms away to the perfidious race of the sea-brigands, if among the daughters of my blood there should be another Marina, spirits of my ancestors, who return here on dark nights, punish her with horrible torments.

Come in the dark night in the shape of burning vipers, rip her body apart, scatter it in the bosom of the earth and let every fragment that you tear off her feel the agony of death. Come in the dark night in the shape of vultures whose beaks are red-hot iron. Rip her body apart. Scatter it across the sky and let every fragment that you tear off feel mortal pain and the agony of death.

Spirits of my ancestors, if you should refuse to do this I invoke vengeful gods, gorged on the blood of human sacrifices, to rise up against you. May they make you suffer the same torments.

I, Koatril, son of Montezuma, have inscribed these curses and I have planted a mescusxaltra bush on this tomb.

This inscription had very nearly the same effect on me as on Tlascala. I tried to convince Xoaz of the absurdity of Mexican superstitions but I soon saw that that was not the way to win him over. And he himself showed me another way of bringing consolation to Tlascala's soul.

'Señor,' said Xoaz, 'it cannot be doubted that spirits of the kings return to the cemetery in the mountains and that they have the power to torment the dead and living, especially when they are solicited to do so by the curses which you saw on the stone. But many circumstances have weakened their dreadful effects. In the first place, you have destroyed the evil shrub which had been deliberately planted on that fateful tomb. And then, what do you have in common with the wild companions of Cortez? Continue to be the protector of the Mexicans

461

and trust that we are not altogether ignorant of the art of appeasing the spirits of the kings, and even of the terrible gods once worshipped in Mexico which your priests call demons.'

I advised Xoaz to be discreet about his religious opinions and decided to seize any opportunities to be of service to the natives of Mexico. These were not slow to arise. A revolt broke out in the provinces conquered by the viceroy. It wasn't in fact any more than justified resistance to oppressive measures which were not at all what the court intended. But the severe Conde de Peña Vélez, prejudiced by false reports, made no such distinction. He placed himself at the head of an army, entered New Mexico, dispersed the mobs and brought back two caciques, whom he intended to put to death on the scaffold in the capital of the New World. Their sentence was about to be read when I stepped forward in the judgement hall and put my hands on the two accused men, saying the words, 'Los toco por parte del rey.'[1] This ancient formula of Spanish law even today has such force that no tribunal would dare oppose it, and it suspends the execution of any decree, but at the same time the person using it offers his own person as surety. The viceroy was furious and, rigorously exercising his rights, had me thrown into a dungeon intended for criminals. There I passed the happiest moments of my life.

One night – and all was night in that dark place – I noticed a pale, dim glow at the end of a long corridor. It came towards me and by it I recognized Tlascala's features. This sight alone would have been enough to make my prison a place of delight. But not content with beautifying it by her presence she had the sweetest of surprises for me: the confession of a passion equal to mine.

'Alonso,' she said, 'virtuous Alonso, you have won. The spirits of my forefathers are appeased. This heart, which no mortal was to possess, has become yours and is the reward of the sacrifices which you ceaselessly make for the happiness of my unfortunate compatriots.'

Scarcely had Tlascala uttered these words when she fell unconscious, almost lifeless, into my arms. I attributed her state to the shock she

---

1 'I touch them on behalf of the king.'

had suffered. But, alas, the cause was more remote and more dangerous. The horror that had gripped her in the cemetery and the
delirious fever which had followed it had weakened her constitution.

Meanwhile Tlascala's eyes opened again to the light. Celestial
brilliance seemed to change my dark prison into a place of radiance.
Oh god of love, whom men in ancient time adored because they
were the children of nature, divine love, your power never appeared
in Cnida or in Paphos as it did in our New World dungeons! My
prison had become your temple, the executioner's block your altar,
my irons your garlands. This magic has still not faded. It lives on
complete in my heart, now cold with age. And when I want my
thoughts as they are stimulated by memories to revert to images of
the past, they do not seek out Elvira's nuptial bed or the couch of the
libertine Laura but the walls of a prison.

I have told you that the viceroy was very angry with me. His
impetuous character had swept away his principles of justice and his
friendship for me. He sent a light vessel to Europe and his report
described me as a trouble-maker.

But scarcely had the ship set sail when the goodness and sense of
justice of the viceroy regained the upper hand. He saw the affair in a
very different light. If he had not been afraid of compromising
himself, he would have sent a second report contradicting the first.
He did, however, send a second vessel carrying dispatches designed to
mitigate the effect of the earlier ones.

The Council of Madrid, which is slow in its deliberations, received
this second report in plenty of time. Its reply was long coming. It
was, as one could have predicted, characterized by the most consum-
mate prudence. The decree of the council seemed to be motivated by
the most extreme severity and sentenced to capital punishment the
authors and instigators of the revolt, but by following strictly the
terms of the decree it was difficult to find out which persons were
guilty and the viceroy received secret instructions which forbade him to
look for them.

But the ostensible part of the decree was known first and delivered
a fatal blow to Tlascala's frail life. First she vomited blood, after
which, a fever, at first weak and slow, then high and persistent . . .

★

The tender-hearted old man was not able to say any more. Sobs choked his voice and he left us to weep freely by himself while we remained deep in solemn silence. Every one of us lamented the fate of the fair Mexican.

The Forty-fifth Day

We assembled at the usual time and asked the marqués to continue his story, which he did as follows:

THE MARQUÉS DE TORRES ROVELLAS'S STORY
✑ CONTINUED ✑

In telling you of my disgrace I haven't spoken of the share Elvira took in it, nor how she expressed her sorrow. First, she had several dresses of a sombre colour made. Then she retired to a convent whose parlour became her salon. But she only appeared there with a handkerchief in her hand and her hair unkempt. Twice she came to see me in my prison. I could not but be grateful for these tokens of interest. Although I had been exonerated, legal formalities and the natural slowness of the Spanish caused me to remain four more months in prison. As soon as I was released I went to the marquesa's convent and brought her back to our house, where her return was celebrated by a festivity.

But, righteous heaven, what a festivity! Tlascala was no more. Even those most indifferent to her thought of her and honoured her memory with their regrets. By their affliction you can gauge the extent of my distress. I was absorbed in my sorrow and saw nothing of what was going on around me.

I was drawn out of this state by a new and flattering feeling. A young man with a good nature wants to distinguish himself. At thirty years of age he feels the need for the esteem of others. Later, he wants their respect. I was still at the stage of esteem and I would perhaps not have been given it if it had been known what role love played in all my actions. They were instead attributed to rare virtue sustained by a strong character. To this was added a little of that zealousness of which people are willing to approve in those who have attracted the

465

attention of the public. The Mexican public made known to me the high opinion it had formed of me and its flattering homage drew me out of my deep sorrow. I felt that I had not yet earned this measure of esteem but I hoped to make myself worthy of it. So it is that when we are struck down by suffering and can only see a dark future ahead of us, providence, solicitous of our fate, rekindles an unexpected glow which sets us back on the path of light.

So I decided to earn the esteem of others. I had offices which I exercised with an integrity which was as scrupulous as it was active. But I was born to love. The image of Tlascala still filled my heart, yet left there a great emptiness which I sought opportunities to fill.

When one is past the age of thirty one can still feel deep love and even inspire it, but woe to the man of that age who decides to involve himself in the sport of youthful passion. Gaiety is no longer on his lips, tender joy no longer in his eyes, the folly of love no longer in his speech. He seeks the means to please and no longer has the easy instinct by which they are to be found. The shrewd and the frivolous recognize him for what he is, and flee swiftly to join the company of the young.

In short, to speak prosaically, I had mistresses who returned my love, but their affection was usually motivated by a sense of what was fitting, which did not prevent them from giving me up for younger lovers. I was sometimes annoyed but never upset by this. I exchanged light chains for ones which were no heavier, and these affairs, all in all, gave me more pleasure than sorrow.

My wife reached the age of forty and remained beautiful. She was besieged by homages but they were homages of respect: people were eager to speak to her but they did not speak about her. Polite society had not yet abandoned her but to her eyes it was not as delightful as before.

The viceroy died. The marquesa had formed a regular circle of acquaintances. She liked to see guests in her house. I still enjoyed the company of women. It delighted me to meet the marquesa, even coming down a staircase. She became almost a new acquaintance for me. She looked charming, and I made a point of being so.

My daughter, who is here with me, is the fruit of this reunion. The late confinement of the marquesa had a disastrous effect on her health.

Different afflictions followed one upon the other. Eventually she fell into a decline which bore her to the tomb. I wept heartfelt tears for her. She had been my first mistress and my last friend. Blood united us. I owed her my fortune and my rank. How many reasons I had to regret her passing! When I lost Tlascala I was still compassed about by all of life's illusions. The marquesa left me without consolation, alone, in a state of dejection from which nothing could raise me.

Yet I did emerge from it. I went to my estates and lodged with one of my vassals. His daughter, who was too young to appreciate the difference in our ages, conceived a feeling for me which resembled love a little and which allowed me to gather some roses in the last days of my late autumn.

Age has in the end cooled my senses but my heart still feels affection and I have a fondness for my daughter more intense than were my passions. To see her happy and to die in her arms is my daily wish. I have no reason to complain. My dear child rewards me with her heartfelt love. What lies ahead of her does not cause me anxiety; circumstances are favourable to her. I believe that I have ensured her future in so far as one can ensure anything on this earth. I leave this world in peace but not without regrets – a world in which I, like any man, have known much adversity but also much happiness.

You wanted to know my story: there it is. But I fear that it has bored our friend the geometer. He has just pulled out his tablets and written numbers all over them.

'You must forgive me,' said the geometer. 'Your history has deeply interested me. In following you along the path of your life and in seeing the driving force of passion raise you up as you went along, sustain you in the middle of your career and support you in the declining years of your existence, I thought I saw the ordinates of a closed curve progress along the axis of abscissae, grow according to a given law, remain almost stationary towards the middle of the axis, then decline in proportion to its rate of growth.'

'To tell the truth,' said the marqués, 'I had thought that one could draw some moral from the story of my life, but not turn it into an equation.'

'It's not a matter here of your life,' said Velásquez, 'it's a matter of human life in general. Physical and mental energy grow with age. Ceasing to grow and then declining is *ipso facto* identical to other forces and subject to analogous laws; that is to say, to a certain proportion between the number of years and the quantity of energy measured by moral elevation. I shall explain myself more clearly. I have considered the course of your life as the major axis of an ellipse divided into ninety equal parts, and I have taken half the minor axis so that the ordinate of 45 is greater than the ordinate of 40 and that of 50 by only two tenths. These ordinates, which represent degrees of energy, are not values of the same kind as the parts of the major axis, which are years, but are none the less functions of them. So, by the very nature of the ellipse, we shall obtain a curve which will rise rapidly at first, remain then more or less stationary, and will decline as it rose.

'The moment of your birth is the origin of the coordinates, at which point y and x are still equal to 0. You were born, Señor, and after a year the ordinate has a value of 31/10. The following ordinates will not also grow by 31/10 for the gap between 0 and that being who can barely stammer out a few elementary notions is far greater than any of those which follow. The human being aged 2, 3, 4, 5, 6 and 7 years has as ordinates for his energy values of 47/10, 57/10, 65/10, 73/10, 79/10 and 85/10. The differences between these are 16/10, 10/10, 8/10, 8/10, 6/10 and 6/10.

'The ordinate of the age of 14 years is 115/10 and the sum of the differences between the seventh and the fourteenth years is only 30/10. At fourteen, man begins to be an adolescent, which he still is at twenty-one. But the sum of the differences of these seven years is only 19/10. Between the twenty-eighth and twenty-first years we obtain a difference of 14/10. I am bound to remind you that my curve represents only the life of men of moderate passions, whose energy reaches its highest point when they have passed the age of forty years and are approaching the age of forty-five. Love being your motive, passion, the greatest ordinate must naturally be brought forward by ten years. I calculate your ellipse as having a long axis of 70, and so your greatest ordinate will fall in your thirty-fifth year. That is why the ordinate of age fourteen, which for the moderate

468

man is 115/10, has in your case the value of 127/10. At twenty-one your ordinate measures 144/10 instead of 134/10.[2] Whereas for a moderate man energy continues to grow after the forty-second year, in your case, Señor, it is already declining.

'At fourteen, you love a girl. After the age of twenty, you become the best of husbands. Once past the age of twenty-eight, you are strikingly unfaithful to your wife. But the woman whom you love has a noble soul which exalts yours. And at the age of thirty-five you play a glorious role in society. Soon you fall back into the taste for happiness that you had already at the age of thirty-eight, whose ordinate is equal to that of age forty-two. Then you become a good husband again as you were at the age of twenty-one, whose ordinate corresponds to that of age forty-nine. Finally you go to live with one of your vassals and there you love a very young girl just as you loved one at the age of fourteen, whose ordinate corresponds to that of age fifty-six. I hope, Señor Marqués, that the long axis of your existence will not stop at seventy and will go on to a hundred. But in that case the ellipse will gradually change into a different curve which will probably resemble the catenary.'

On uttering these words, Velásquez rose to his feet, waved his arm in the air with a terrible expression on his face and grabbed hold of his sword, with which he began to draw great figures in the sand. He would no doubt have rehearsed the whole theory of catenaries if the marqués, who like the rest of us, as it happens, was little interested in the proofs of our geometer friend, had not asked leave to withdraw to take some rest. Only Rebecca remained with Velásquez. He took not the slightest notice of those who left. The presence of the pretty Jewess was enough for him. So he began to explain his system to her. I listened for a while before, exhausted by the number of scientific expressions and figures which I have never found particularly attractive, I could no longer resist sleep and so took myself off to bed. Velásquez meanwhile was still holding forth.

2 As in the previous case of calculation (above, day thirty-nine, p. 427) some of these figures are incorrect.

The Forty-sixth Day

The Mexicans, who had stayed longer with us than planned, decided to leave. The marqués tried to persuade the gypsy chief to go to Madrid with him and lead a life compatible with his birth. But the gypsy would have none of it. He even asked that his name should not be mentioned anywhere and that the secret with which he surrounded his life should be kept. The travellers expressed their profound respects to the future Duke of Velásquez and did me the honour of offering me their friendship.

We accompanied them to the end of the valley and watched them for a long time as they rode off. On the way back it struck me that someone was missing from the caravan. I then remembered the girl who had been found at the foot of the accursed gallows of Los Hermanos. I asked the chief what had become of her and if it wasn't a matter of another extraordinary adventure, or perhaps a trick of damned spirits from hell who had so often made a sport of us.

The gypsy smiled mockingly and said, 'This time you are mistaken, Señor Alphonse, but it is part of human nature to relate even the most ordinary events of life to the supernatural once one has had a taste of it.'

Velásquez broke in and said, 'You are right. One can apply to these notions the theory of geometric progression, the first term being represented by a believer in some dark superstition, the last by the alchemist or astrologer. Between the two there is room for a mass of prejudices which oppress humanity.'

'I can't contradict this argument,' I said. 'But it doesn't tell me who the girl was.'

'I sent one of my men to find out about the young girl,' replied the gypsy. 'He reported to me that she happened to be a poor orphan who had lost her reason after the death of her lover, and, not having anywhere to go, lives on the charity of travellers and the sympathy of shepherds. She is always by herself, wanders in the mountains and sleeps wherever night overtakes her. The day before yesterday she certainly was under the gallows of Los Hermanos and, not noticing how horrible the place was, must have peacefully fallen asleep. The marqués, overcome by pity, had her looked after but, as the demented girl had recovered her strength, she fled and disappeared in the mountains. I'm surprised that you haven't yet met her. The poor girl will end up by falling from some cliff and dying a pitiable death. But I must confess that I would think it mad to shed tears for so miserable a life. At night when the shepherds light their fires they sometimes see her approaching. Then Dolorita – that's the name of the unfortunate girl – calmly sits down, stares at one of them with a piercing gaze, throws her arms round his neck and calls him by the name of her dead lover. At first they fled from her but then the shepherds got used to her, and now they let her wander about wherever she wants to and even give her food.'

As soon as the gypsy had finished, Velásquez began to elaborate a theory of opposing forces which consume each other: passion, which after a long struggle with reason ends up by overcoming it, snatching the sceptre and reigning tyrannically over the brain. As for me, I was amazed as I listened to the gypsy's words, for I had thought that he would seize the opportunity of telling us yet another long story. Perhaps he had only abridged the adventures of Dolorita because the Wandering Jew was in sight. He was striding down the mountainside, and the cabbalist began to murmur terrible imprecations but in vain – for the Wandering Jew took no notice of them. At last he came close as if out of simple courtesy towards our company and nothing more. He said to Uzeda, 'Your reign is over. You have lost the power which you have shown yourself unworthy to possess. A terrifying future awaits you.'

The cabbalist roared with laughter. But his laugh did not seem to come from his heart, for he spoke to the Jew in an unknown language, entreating him, almost begging him.

'Very well,' replied Ahasuerus, 'today as well but for the last time. You will not see me again.'

'Well,' said Uzeda, 'we will see what will happen, but today take advantage of our journey, you old wretch, and continue your story.

We will see whether the Sheikh of Taroudant possesses more power than I do. Besides, I know very well why you are avoiding us and you may be sure that I will reveal your reason to everyone.'

The unhappy wanderer shot a murderous glance at the cabbalist but, seeing that he could not refuse, he positioned himself as usual between Velásquez and myself, remained silent for a moment and then continued his story as follows:

∽ THE WANDERING JEW'S STORY CONTINUED ∽

I have told you how the moment I thought I would reach my most ardently desired goal, a commotion occurred in the temple. A Pharisee came up to me and accused me of deception. I replied, as was normally done in such cases, that he was a slanderer and that if he didn't immediately go away I would have him thrown out by my servants.

'Enough,' cried the Pharisee, and, turning to the crowd, he shouted, 'Enough. This unworthy Sadducee is deceiving you. He has spread a false rumour to make himself rich at your expense. He is taking advantage of your credulity. It's high time to tear his mask from his face. To prove to you the truth of what I say, I will offer twice as much gold for your silver as he does.'

In this way the Pharisee was still profiting by twenty-five per cent but the people, drunk with cupidity, pressed round him in a crowd, called him the benefactor of the city and insulted me in the most hateful way. Gradually tempers became heated, actions succeeded words and suddenly there was such an uproar in the temple that one could no longer hear oneself speak. Seeing that something awful was about to happen, I had all the gold and silver that I could muster transported to our house, but before the servants had taken all of it away, the people, now out of control, threw themselves on the tables and began to carry off the money. I defended it as best I could but my efforts were in vain; my adversaries were stronger. In an instant the temple was transformed into a battlefield. I have no idea what the outcome would have been. I might not have come away alive from it because my head was already bloody, but at that moment the prophet from Nazareth came into the temple with his disciples.

I shall never forget that severe, solemn voice, which stilled the noise in a moment. We waited to find out whose side he would take. The Pharisee was sure of having won his case, but the prophet turned in indignation against both sides and reproached us for polluting the temple, for dishonouring the house of God and spurning the creator for the goods of the devil. His words had a profound effect on the assembled crowd. The temple gradually filled up with the common people, among whom were many disciples of the new sect. Both sides realized that the prophet's intervention would have disastrous consequences for them and we were not wrong, for soon the cry rang out as from one breast, 'Out of the temple.'

This time the mass of the people did not think about their own advantage, but in the grip of a fanatical passion began to throw out the tables and drive us out too. Once we were in the street the crowd became denser but the mass paid more attention to the prophet than to us, and so I was thus able in the general confusion to return home by slipping along little alley-ways. At our door I noticed our servants fleeing with the money which had been saved.

A glance at the money-bags allowed me to see that my hopes of profit had not been realized but that we hadn't made any losses either. I breathed a sigh of relief at this thought. Sedekias had already been told about everything. Sara had uneasily awaited my return. When she saw me covered with blood, she threw herself in my arms. The old man stared at me for a long time in silence and eventually said:

'I promised to give you Sara if you doubled the sum which was entrusted to you. What have you done with it?'

'It isn't my fault,' I replied, 'if an unforeseen event destroyed my plans. I have defended your money at the risk of my life. You can count your money. You have lost nothing, quite the contrary. But what there is in comparison with what we were hoping for isn't worth speaking about.'

Then suddenly I had a happy inspiration. I decided to throw everything into fortune's scales, and said, 'If, however, you want me to stay to bring you profit I can compensate for your loss in another manner.'

'How?' cried Sedekias. 'I think I see. It must be another plan which will be as successful as this one.'

'Not at all,' I replied, 'you will be convinced yourself that what I am giving you has a very real value.'

Having said this, I quickly went out, and soon came back with my bronze casket under my arm. Sedekias observed me, and a smile of hope came about Sara's lips. I opened the casket, brought out the document which was inside, tore it in half and handed it to the old man. Then Sedekias recognized what it was, convulsively screwed up the document and a terrible rage contorted his features. He half-rose, and tried to say something but the words stuck in his throat. My destiny was about to be decided. I fell at the old man's feet and bathed them with my tears.

Seeing all this, Sara knelt next to me and, without knowing why, wept and began to kiss her grandfather's hands. The old man let his head drop on to his breast. A thousand emotions struggled with each other in his heart and wordlessly he ripped the documents up in a thousand pieces. Then he jumped to his feet and rushed out of the room. We remained alone, a prey to painful uncertainty. I must confess that I had lost all hope. I realized that after all that had happened I could no longer remain in Sedekias's house. I looked back one last time at the weeping figure of Sara and went out, but suddenly noticed a commotion in the corridor. I asked what had caused it and was smilingly told that it was less appropriate for me than for anyone else to ask such a question.

'It's to you that Sedekias has decided to give his granddaughter in marriage. He has commanded that preparations for a lavish wedding should be made as quickly as possible.'

You can well imagine how I passed from the deepest despair to indescribable joy. A fortnight later I married Sara. All that was missing was my friend, who ought to have had a share in this brilliant turning-point in my fortunes. But Germanus was fully imbued with the doctrine of the prophet from Nazareth and was among those who had driven us out from the temple. So I was obliged, in spite of my friendship, to break off all relations with him and I have lost sight of him since.

After knowing many adversities, I thought that I had a peaceful life in front of me – all the more so because I had abandoned money-changing, which had led me to undertake such dangerous ventures. I wanted to live off my fortune, but so as not to remain idle I decided to lend money. And indeed, as there was no shortage of people having need of money, I made considerable profits. Sara was daily making my life more and more pleasant when an unforeseen event suddenly changed this state of affairs.

But the sun is already going down and it will soon be time for you to rest. As for me, a powerful form of incantation which I cannot resist is calling me away. My heart is filled with a strange foreboding. Might the end of my suffering be nigh? Farewell!

At this, the wanderer disappeared into a nearby gorge. His last words intrigued me. I asked the cabbalist what they meant.

'I don't think that we will ever hear the end of the Wandering Jew's story. That wretch disappears whenever he reaches the time when he was condemned for ever to wander for having insulted the prophet. And no power in the world can then call him back. His last words do not surprise me. For some time I have noticed that he has aged a great deal, but this will probably not lead to his death, for what would then become of your legend?'

As I realized that the cabbalist intended to speak about topics not suitable for the ears of a good Catholic, I broke off the conversation, left the company and returned alone to my tent. Soon others came too, but apparently they didn't go to bed at once, for I could hear for a long time Velásquez's voice explaining to Rebecca some geometric formula.

The Forty-seventh Day

The next day the gypsy announced to us that he was expecting another delivery of merchandise and for reasons of security he intended to remain where we were. We greeted this news with joy, for it would have been difficult to find a more enchanting place in the whole mountain range of the Sierra Morena. In the morning I went hunting with some of the gypsies. In the evening I joined the assembled company and listened to the next part of the gypsy chief's adventures. He spoke as follows:

THE GYPSY CHIEF'S STORY CONTINUED

I returned to Madrid with Toledo, who swore he would make up for the time he had lost at the Camaldolese monastery. Lope Soarez's adventures, which I related to him on the journey, greatly interested him. He listened very attentively and then said, 'If it is true that, having done penance, one begins in some way or other a new life, it is appropriate to inaugurate it with some charitable act. I pity that poor fellow. He is stuck in bed without friend or acquaintance, ill, abandoned, in love and incapable, moreover, of protecting himself in a strange city. Avarito, you will lead me to Soarez; perhaps I may be able to be of use to him.'

Toledo's plan didn't surprise me at all. I had long been aware of his nobility of spirit and his devotion to others.

As soon as we reached Madrid the knight at once visited Soarez. I followed him. Soarez was running a high fever; his eyes were wide open but unseeing. But from time to time his lips did form a haggard smile. No doubt he was dreaming about his beloved Inés. Close beside him was Busqueros, in an armchair, who did not even turn round when we came in. Toledo went up to the man who had caused the misfortunes of poor Soarez and shook him by the shoulder.

476

Don Roque woke up, rubbed his eyes and exclaimed, 'What's this? Señor Don José! Yesterday I had the honour of meeting His Excellency the Duke of Lerma in the Prado, who looked closely at me. Perhaps he wishes to make my acquaintance. If His Excellency were to have need of my services please explain to your brother, Señor, that I am always at his disposal.'

Toledo interrupted the interminable flow of Busqueros's words and said to him, 'It's not a matter of that at the moment. On the contrary, what I want to know is how the patient is and whether he needs anything.'

'The patient is not doing well,' replied Don Roque. 'He needs care, consolation and the hand of fair Inés.'

Toledo interrupted him. 'On the first point, I shall go immediately to see my brother's doctor. He is the most skilful surgeon in Madrid.'

'On the second,' Busqueros added, 'you can scarcely help him. For you cannot bring his father back to life again; and as for the third, I can assure you that I am sparing no effort to bring this plan about.'

'Is it possible?' I exclaimed. 'Is the father of Don Lope dead?'

'Yes,' said Busqueros. 'The very grandson of the Iñigo Soarez who, having sailed the seven seas in his youth, established a trading house in Cadiz. Our patient was already getting better and would soon have been cured if the news of his father's death hadn't laid him low again. Since you are interested in the fate of my friend, Señor,' Busqueros continued, 'allow me to accompany you to the doctor and at the same time offer you my services.'

After he had spoken they both left, and I remained alone with the patient. For a long time I gazed at his ashen face, on which suffering had etched such deep lines in so short a time, and I cursed the meddler who had caused his misfortunes. The patient had fallen asleep again and I was breathing quietly so as not to disturb his rest when there was a knock at the door.

I got up angrily, tiptoed to the door and opened it. I saw before me a woman no longer in the first flush of youth but of pleasant appearance. Seeing that I had a finger on my lips to indicate that she should remain silent, she drew me out on to the landing.

'My young friend,' she said, 'can you tell me how Señor Soarez is today?'

'Not well, I think,' I said in reply. 'But he has just fallen asleep and I hope that this will restore some strength to him.'

'I was told that he was very ill,' the unknown lady said. 'A person who has a sincere interest in his welfare asked me to find out how he was. Please be so kind as to give him this letter when he wakes up. I shall come back tomorrow to see if he is better.'

Having uttered these words, she went away. I put the letter in my pocket and went back to the invalid.

Shortly after, Toledo came back with the doctor. The goodly disciple of Aesculapius reminded me by his manner of Dr Sangre Moreno. He looked at the patient, shook his head and then said that he was unable to pronounce on him, but he would spend the night by his bedside and would give his definitive diagnosis the next day. Toledo embraced him in a friendly way and begged him to spare no effort. Then we left, swearing to return at daybreak. As we went along I told the knight about the visit of the stranger. He took the letter and said, 'I am sure that it is from fair Inés. If Soarez feels better you may give him the letter tomorrow. If I could, I really would give half my life to secure the happiness of a man to whom I have done so much harm. But it's getting late. After our journey we too need rest. Come, you will sleep in my house.'

I joyfully accepted the invitation of this man for whom I felt growing esteem. Having eaten, I fell asleep.

Next morning we went to see Soarez. The doctor's expression showed that his art had conquered the illness. The patient was still weak but he recognized me and greeted me warmly.

Toledo told him how he had caused his fall. He assured him that he would do all in his power to make up for the suffering he had endured and asked Soarez to look on him as a friend. Soarez generously accepted and extended his still weak hand to the knight. Then Toledo went with the doctor into the adjoining room. I seized the opportunity to give the letter to the patient. The words it contained were certainly a powerful remedy, for Lope Soarez sat up in bed, and tears streamed down his cheeks. He pressed the letter to his heart and cried out through his sobs, 'Almighty God, so you have not abandoned me and I am not alone in all the world. Inés, my dear Inés, has

478

not forgotten me and she loves me. That dear Señora de Avalos came in person for news of the state of my health.'

'Quite right, Señor Lope,' I replied. 'But for the love of God, calm down. A sudden shock could hurt you.'

Toledo had overheard these last words. He came in with the doctor, who prescribed rest and cool drinks above all else. Then he left, promising to return.

After a moment the door opened and Busqueros came in. 'Bravo!' he exclaimed. 'As I can see, our patient is much improved. So much the better, for soon we shall have to exercise all our ingenuity. There is a rumour in town that the banker's daughter will soon marry the Duke of Santa Maura. Let them talk! We shall see who's right! I have just met a member of the duke's household at the Golden Hart Inn and I let it be understood that their journey has been in vain.'

Toledo interrupted at this point and said, 'Whatever is the case, I believe that Señor Don Lope need not despair. None the less, my good friend, I hope that you will not intervene in this affair.'

The knight uttered these words in such a firm tone that Don Roque did not dare to contradict him. None the less I noted with what glee he saw Toledo leave the patient a moment later.

'It's not fine words that will get us any further,' said Don Roque when we were alone. 'We must act, and the sooner the better.'

After the meddler had said this, I heard a knock at the door. Supposing it to be Señora de Avalos, I whispered in Soarez's ear that Busqueros must be made to leave by the back door. But he said indignantly, 'I say again we must act now. So if you are receiving a visitor who is connected with our affair, I must be present or at least hear the whole conversation from the adjoining room.'

Soarez looked imploringly at him. Realizing that his presence was unwelcome, he went into the neighbouring room and stood behind the door. Señora de Avalos did not stay long. She was delighted to see the patient better and assured him that Inés hadn't stopped loving him and thinking about him. Her present visit had been at Inés's request. She had found out about his new misfortunes, was very worried and had decided to come that evening with her aunt to exhort him with words of consolation and hope to endure his fate.

As soon as Señora de Avalos had gone, Busqueros rushed into the room and cried, 'What's all this? The fair Inés wants to visit us this evening? Now that's what I call a real proof of love. The poor girl doesn't even consider whether or not this unthinking act may have ruined her reputation, but we will do the considering on her behalf, Señor Don Lope. I shall immediately go to fetch my friends. I shall post them in front of this house and order them to let no stranger in. Don't worry. I shall take full charge of things.'

Soarez tried to reply, but Don Roque had already run out as though the ground was burning the soles of his feet. Realizing that a new catastrophe was brewing, and that Busqueros was about to commit another folly, I hurried off to see Toledo to tell him what had happened, without saying anything to the invalid. The knight frowned. After some reflection he told me to go back to Soarez's bedside and tell him that he would do all he could to put a stop to the meddler's lunacy. Towards evening we heard a carriage go by in the street. Soon after, Inés came in with her aunt. Not wishing to meddle myself, I slipped out. Suddenly I heard noises in the street. I went down and found Toledo in a heated exchange with a stranger.

'Señor,' the stranger was saying, 'I declare to you that I shall succeed in going in here. My fiancée has a rendezvous with a Cadiz merchant in this house. I am certain of it. A friend of this ne'er-do-well, in the presence of my major-domo, enlisted several wretches in the Golden Hart Inn, whom he instructed to ensure that these turtle doves are not disturbed.'

'Excuse me, Señor,' replied Toledo. 'I shall not allow you to enter this house under any pretext. I do not deny that a young lady has just gone in but it is one of my relations and I shall not allow her to be insulted by anyone.'

'That's a lie!' exclaimed the stranger. 'This lady is called Inés Moro and is my fiancée.'

'Señor, you have called me a liar,' said Toledo. 'I am not concerned whether you are right or not. In either case you have insulted me, and before you can leave this very spot you will give me satisfaction. I am the Knight of Toledo, brother of the Duke of Lerma.'

The stranger raised his hat and said, 'Señor, the Duke of Santa Maura is at your service.'

Whereupon he threw off his cloak and drew his sword. The lantern above the door cast a dim light over the adversaries. I flattened myself against the wall and waited for this disastrous adventure to end. Suddenly the duke let his sword fall, clasped his chest and fell. By pure chance the Duke of Lerma's doctor came by at that moment to visit Soarez. Toledo pointed to Santa Maura and asked him anxiously whether the wound was fatal.

'Not at all,' said the doctor. 'Have him carried to his house and dress his wound quickly. He will be cured in about a fortnight. The sword has not even grazed his lung.'

As he said this, he administered smelling-salts to the wounded man and Santa Maura opened his eyes. The knight approached him and said, 'Your Excellency, you are not mistaken. Fair Inés is here with a young man whom she loves more than life itself. After what has happened between us, I believe you to be too noble to want to force a young girl to enter a bond which her heart does not want.'

'Señor caballero,' Santa Maura replied in a weak voice, 'I do not doubt that what you say is true but I am surprised not to have heard from fair Inés herself that her heart is not free. Some words from her mouth or some lines from her hand . . .'

The duke tried to continue but lost consciousness again. He was carried off to his lodgings. Meanwhile Toledo hurried to Inés to let her know what her suitor required for him to renounce her hand and to leave her in peace.

What more need I say? The rest of the story isn't difficult to guess. Soarez, assured of his mistress's fidelity, recovered quickly. He had lost his father, but on the other hand had gained a wife and a friend. For the father of Inés, who had never shared the hate which had set the late Gaspar Soarez so passionately against him, generously gave them his blessing.[1] The young couple married and immediately left for Cadiz. Busqueros accompanied them out of Madrid for several miles and managed to extort a purse of gold from the young couple for services he claimed to have rendered. As for me, I thought that fate would never cause me to meet again that insufferable man who

---

1 In the alternative version of the forty-seventh day, Lope Soarez's father is given a more prominent role, and his forgiveness is given a motivation.

inspired me with unspeakable loathing. But things turned out otherwise.

I had noticed that Don Roque had mentioned my father's name from time to time. I foresaw that his acquaintance would scarcely be profitable to our family and started spying on Busqueros. I soon discovered that he had a female relative called Gita Cimiento, whom he was trying hard to get my father to marry. For he knew that Señor Avadoro had money, perhaps even more than was generally thought. The lady in question was already living in a nearby house on the other side of the side-street, exactly opposite my father's balcony.

My aunt had come back to Madrid to live. I could not resist going to greet her. The good Señora Dalanosa was moved to tears to see me but she urged me not to show myself in public before the end of my penance. I spoke to her about Busqueros's plans. She thought it imperative to stop the marriage. She spoke about it to her uncle, the worthy Theatine Fray Gerónimo Sántez. But the monk absolutely refused to have anything to do with an affair which looked too much like a society intrigue. He said that he only ever involved himself in family affairs to bring about a reconciliation or prevent a scandal, and that in all other cases this kind of business did not fall within his ministry. Thrown back on our own resources, I would have liked to have won the friendly Knight of Toledo over to my side, but I would have had to tell him who I was and I was not allowed to do that. So I started carefully spying on Busqueros who, since Soarez's departure, had attached himself to the Knight of Toledo, though admittedly in a less interfering way. But he still appeared every morning to ask whether the knight had need of his services.

When the gypsy reached this point in his story, his men came to discuss the day's business and that was the last we saw of him that day.

The Forty-eighth Day

———————— ✑ ————————

When we had assembled again the next day we asked the gypsy to continue his story, which he did as follows:

✑ THE GYPSY CHIEF'S STORY CONTINUED ✑

Lope Soarez had been happily married for a fortnight to the charming Inés, and Busqueros, who believed himself to have made the greatest contribution to this fine match, had now attached himself to Toledo's service. I recommended the knight to be careful about his follower's interfering nature, but Don Roque on some occasions did not lack a sort of tact. The knight had allowed him to pay court to him at his house and Busqueros felt that to retain this right it was necessary not to abuse it.

One day the knight asked Busqueros what the love affair was with which the Duke of Arcos had been occupied for so many years, and whether the woman in question was attractive enough to have held his attention for so long.

Busqueros looked very solemn and said to Toledo, 'In asking me to divulge my patron's secrets, Your Excellency proves to me that he knows how devoted I am to him. On the other hand, I have the advantage of knowing Your Excellency well enough to realize that a certain inconstancy which can be detected in his behaviour has never had any unfortunate consequences except for women who, as it happens, have forgiven him for it, and furthermore of knowing that Your Excellency is incapable of compromising his faithful servant.'

'Señor Busqueros,' the knight said, 'I didn't ask you for my eulogy.'

'I know,' said Busqueros, 'but the praises of Your Highness spring naturally to the lips of those who have the honour of knowing him. I had begun to tell the story that Your Excellency asks of me, using

483

assumed names, to the young merchant whom we've just married to fair Inés . . .'

'I know the story up to that point,' said the knight. 'Lope Soarez told little Avarito, who told me. You had reached the point where Frasqueta had told you her story in the garden, after which the Duke of Arcos, dressed up as Frasqueta's lady friend, had approached you to tell you that it was imperative to hasten Cornádez's departure. The Duke even hoped Cornádez would not stick just to the pilgrimage but that he would do penance for a certain time at some shrine or other.'

'Your Excellency,' Busqueros broke in, 'has a remarkable memory. His Highness the Duke of Arcos really did utter those words to me. Since Your Excellency already knows the story of the wife, it is necessary – to keep things in their historical order – to acquaint you with the husband and to tell you how he came to know Hervas, that terrible pilgrim.'

The Knight of Toledo sat down and told us that he envied the Duke of Arcos a mistress like Frasqueta, that he had always loved brazen women and that she was the most brazen of them all. Busqueros smiled an equivocal smile and began his tale as follows:

✑ CORNÁDEZ'S STORY AS TOLD BY BUSQUEROS ✑

The husband, whose name is as illuminating as a rebus,[1] was the son of a citizen of Salamanca. He had long held a somewhat obscure position in the magistracy, which he combined with a small wholesale business supplying a few retailers. Having come into a large legacy, he decided, like many Spaniards, to do nothing at all other than go often to church and other public places and to smoke cigars.

You will tell me that having a taste for nothing other than complete tranquillity, Cornádez should not have married the first mischievous girl to make faces at him from a window. But therein

1 i.e., it is reminiscent of the French word for a cuckold (*cornu*). The original name given to this character (Cabrónez) related in the same way to the equivalent Spanish term (*cabrón*).

lies the great mystery of the human heart. No one does what he should do. One person may imagine there to be no happiness except in marriage and dies single; another, who swears never to take a wife, marries and remarries. So Cornádez was married. He congratulated himself on it at first, but then he repented. When he found himself not only with the Conde de Peña Flor on his hands but also his ghost, which had come back from hell to torment him, he became worried and introspective. Soon he had his bed moved into his study, where his prayer-stool was, together with a basin of holy water. During the day he would see little of his wife and would spend more time than usual at church.

One day he found himself there beside a pilgrim, who stared at him in such a disturbing way that he was forced to leave the church. That evening he came across him again while out walking, and then discovered him everywhere he went; and everywhere the pilgrim's fixed and penetrating stare caused him indescribable anguish.

At last Cornádez, overcoming his natural shyness, said to him, 'Señor, I'll go and complain to the *alcalde* if you continue to haunt me.'

'Haunt, haunt!' said the pilgrim in a sepulchral voice. 'Yes, you are haunted, much haunted. A hundred doubloons; a head; a murdered man who died without taking communion. Well, have I guessed correctly?'

'Who are you?' said Cornádez, petrified with fear.

'I am a reprobate, but I trust in divine mercy. Have you heard of Hervas the scholar?'

'I know his story more or less. He had the misfortune of being an unbeliever and came to a bad end.'

'Quite so. I am his son and I was imprinted at birth with the sign of reprobation. But I have been given the power to recognize the sign on the foreheads of sinners and to bring them back to the paths of salvation. Come with me, wretched plaything of the devil, I shall make myself better known to you.'

The pilgrim led Cornádez to one of the lonely walks in the garden of the Celestine fathers. He sat down with him on a seat and spoke to him as follows:

485

THE STORY OF DIEGO HERVAS TOLD BY HIS SON, ∽ THE REPROBATE PILGRIM ∽

My name is Blas Hervas. My father, Diego Hervas, was sent while still very young to the university of Salamanca, where he quickly distinguished himself by his extraordinary hard work. Soon he was unrivalled by any of his comrades and some years later he knew more than his teachers. Then, ensconced in his study with the masters of every branch of knowledge, he conceived the seductive hope of attaining the same glory and seeing his name one day inscribed among theirs. Diego combined this hardly modest ambition with another. He wanted to publish anonymous works, which, when they were known, he would acknowledge and thereby obtain an instant reputation. While engaged on this plan, he decided that Salamanca was not a horizon on which the glorious star of his destiny would shine brightly enough, so he turned his eyes to the capital. There, perhaps, men distinguished by their genius enjoyed the respect due to them, and the homage of the public, the confidence of ministers, even the favour of the king.

So Diego thought that only in the capital would his talents be recognized for what they were worth. Our young scholar scrutinized Descartes's geometry, Harriot's analysis and the works of Fermat and Roberval.[2] He realized that while these great minds were blazing the trail of science, they were still advancing unsteadily. He brought together their discoveries, added solutions which up till then had not been tried, and suggested modifications to the algorithm which then was still the most used. Hervas spent more than a year writing his text. Geometry books were then always written in Latin. Hervas wrote his in Spanish to make it more accessible and to bring it out with a title which would excite curiosity. He called it *The Secrets of Analysis Revealed, together with the Science of Infinite Dimensions*.

When the manuscript was ready, my father was on the point of

---

2 These three mathematicians are, respectively, Thomas Harriot (1560–1628), Pierre de Fermat (1601–65), and Gilles Personne de Roberval (1602–75).

attaining his majority and he was informed of this by his guardians. They told him at the same time that his fortune, which seemed as though it ought to be of the order of eight thousand pistoles, was reduced to eight hundred through a variety of circumstances, and that this sum would be handed over to him when he had signed a legal release for his guardians. Hervas considered that eight hundred pistoles was exactly the sum required to have his book printed and transported to Madrid. So he hurriedly signed the document discharging his guardians, accepted the eight hundred pistoles and submitted his manuscript to the censors.

The theological censors made certain difficulties on the grounds that the analysis of infinitesimals seemed to entail the atoms of Epicurus, whose doctrines were condemned by the Church. It was pointed out to them that what was in question was abstract quantities and not material particles, and they withdrew their objection.

From the censor the text passed to the printer. It was quite a thick quarto book, for which it was necessary to cast the algebraic characters which were lacking and even make new punches, with the result that the publication costs for a printing of a thousand copies was seven hundred pistoles. Hervas paid this sum all the more willing because he expected to sell the copies for three pistoles each. Hervas was not at all acquisitive but the thought of owning this little capital sum certainly pleased him.

The printing took more than six months. Hervas corrected the proofs himself, and this fastidious task took him longer than composing the work itself. At last the biggest cart that could be found in Salamanca brought the heavy bales, on which his present reputation and future immortality were based, to his house.

The very next day a deliriously happy Hervas, full of expectations, loaded his books on to eight mules, mounted the ninth himself and took the road to Madrid. On his arrival in the capital he went straight to Moreno the bookseller's and said to him:

'Señor, these eight mules have brought nine hundred and ninety-nine copies of a book. Here is the thousandth. One hundred copies sold on your account will bring in three hundred pistoles. You will be kind enough to credit the remainder to me. I am bold enough to think that the whole edition will be sold out in a few weeks and

I will be able to produce a new edition to which I shall add a few clarifications which I thought of while the work was being printed.'

Moreno seemed to doubt that the work would sell as quickly as that, but as he noticed that there was a licence from the Salamanca censors he didn't object to the bales being stored in his shop and a few copies being displayed in front of it. Hervas went off to find lodgings in an inn and without delay he began to work on the notes and appendices which were to accompany the second edition of his work.

Three weeks went by in this way and our mathematician thought that it was time to go to see Moreno and recover the money from the sale, which must amount at least to a thousand pistoles or so. He went there, and was very mortified to discover not a single copy had yet been sold.

Soon he had an even more painful reason to be mortified. For on returning to his inn he found an *alguazil* from the court, who obliged him to step into a closed carriage and took him to the tower of Segovia. It is surprising for a mathematician to be treated as a state prisoner but this is what had happened. The two or three copies put on sale by Moreno soon fell into the hands of curious people who frequented the shop. One of them read the title, *The Secrets of Analysis Revealed*, and said that it might well be an anti-governmental pamphlet. Another, scrutinizing the same title-page, said with a sly smile that the satire must be directed towards Don Pedro Alanyes, the minister of finance, because analysis was the anagram of Alanyes;[3] and the second part of the title, *Infinities of All Dimensions*, was also directed at the minister, who was physically infinitely small and infinitely fat, and mentally infinitely low and infinitely high. It is easy to deduce from this joke that Moreno's customers had a licence to say whatever they liked and that the government tolerated this small satirical assembly.

Those who know Madrid know that its common people are in a certain respect equal to the highest classes, are interested in the same events and share the same opinions, and that the witticisms of high society soon find their way down to the streets, where they circulate

3 The anagram only works perfectly in French (*analyse*).

freely. So Moreno's customers' jokes were soon repeated in all the barbers' shops and eventually at all the crossroads.

It wasn't long, either, before the minister Alanyes was called Señor Analysis, Infinite in Every Dimension. This financier was quite inured to the people's criticisms and paid them no attention. But when the same nickname came to his ears more than once he asked his secretary to explain why. He in turn replied that the origin of the joke was an alleged book of geometry on sale at Moreno's shop. Without making further inquiries, the minister first had the author arrested and then confiscated the whole edition.

Locked up in the tower of Segovia, Hervas was not aware of this and was deprived of pen and ink. He did not know when his detention would come to an end, and in order to dispel his boredom decided to recall all his knowledge, that is to say, to recall all that he knew about every science. He then realized, to his great satisfaction, that he had really altogether grasped the whole range of human knowledge and that he would have been able like Pico della Mirandola to defend a thesis *De omni scibili*.

Hervas was ambitious to make a scientific name for himself and conceived of the project of a work in a hundred volumes, which was to contain all that men knew in his time. He decided to publish it anonymously. The public would not fail to be duped by this into believing that it was the work of a learned society; then Hervas would reveal that he was the author and would obtain immediately a reputation and the title of Universal Man. Hervas had a mind whose power was equal to such a vast enterprise. He had a belief in it and gave himself entirely up to a project which flattered the two passions of his soul: vanity and the love of knowledge.

Six weeks went swiftly by for Hervas. At the end of this period he was summoned by the castle governor. There he met the first secretary of the minister of finance. This man greeted him with a sort of respect and said:

'Don Diego Hervas, you decided to enter society without a protector, which is extremely imprudent. For when you were accused no one presented himself to defend you. You are accused, in your *Analysis of Infinities*, of having had the minister of finance in mind. Don Pedro Alanyes, rightly angered, has had the whole edition of your work consigned to the flames. But his honour is satisfied, and he has decided to pardon you, and offers you a post as *contador*[4] in his department. You will be given calculations to do whose complicated nature occasionally causes us problems. Leave this prison and make sure that you never return to it.'

Hervas was at first extremely upset that nine hundred and ninety-nine copies of a work which had cost him so much effort had been burned. But as he had staked his reputation on other projects, he was soon consoled and went to take up his post in the ministry. There he was given the register of annuities, the accounts concerning deductions for payment in cash and other calculations, which he managed with a facility which earned him the respect of his superiors. He was given an advance of a quarter of his annual salary and assigned a place to live in a house in the gift of the minister.

When the gypsy had reached this point in his story, he was summoned to his band, so we had to wait until the next day for our curiosity to be satisfied.

4 Comptroller of accounts.

The Forty-ninth Day

We reassembled in the cave at dawn. Rebecca observed that Busqueros had presented his story very skilfully.

'An ordinary intriguer,' she explained, 'would, to frighten Cornádez, have introduced phantoms dressed in winding-sheets to his house, and these would, it is true, have had a certain effect on him. But this would have been dispelled when he had thought about it a little. Busqueros proceeds in a different way. He tries to act on Cornádez entirely through words. Everyone knows the story of the atheist Hervas, which the Jesuit Granada[1] recorded in the notes to his work. The reprobate pilgrim claims to be his son to make an even greater impression on Cornádez's mind.'

'Your judgement is premature,' said the old chief. 'The pilgrim could well be the son of Hervas the atheist and it is certain that the facts which he relates are not to be found in the legend you mention, where what we mainly find are a few details about the circumstances of his death. So please have the patience to listen to the end of the story.'

∽ THE STORY OF DIEGO HERVAS CONTINUED ∽

So Hervas was restored to himself, and his livelihood was assured. The work required of him could only occupy him for a few hours in the morning and he had before him an immense project which would bring into play all the powers of his genius and give him all the enjoyment which knowledge affords. Our ambitious polygraph decided to write an octavo volume on every branch of knowledge. Noting that speech is the distinctive attribute of man, he devoted the first

1 It is not clear to whom Potocki is here referring.

491

volume to universal grammar. There he revealed the infinitely varied artifice of grammar, by which different parts of speech are expressed in every language and different forms are given to the fundamentals of thought.

Then, passing from the inner thoughts of man to the ideas which come to him from things about him, Hervas devoted the second volume to natural history in general; the third to zoology, which is the study of animals; the fourth to ornithology, which is the study of birds; the fifth to ichthyology, which is the study of fish; the sixth to entomology, which is the study of insects; the seventh to scoleology, which is the study of worms; the eighth to conchyliology, or something like it, which is the study of shells; the ninth to botany; the tenth to geology or knowledge of the earth's structure; the eleventh to lithology, or the study of stones; the twelfth to oryctology, or the study of fossils; the thirteenth to metallurgy, or the art of extracting and working metals; the fourteenth to docimastics, or the art of assaying.

The fifteenth volume, bringing the study of man back to himself, dealt with physiology, or the study of the human body; the sixteenth volume dealt with anatomy; the seventeenth was devoted to myology, or the study of muscles; the eighteenth to osteology; the nineteenth to neurology; the twentieth to phlebology, or the study of the system of veins.

The twenty-first volume was devoted to medicine. This was then divided into parts: in the twenty-second volume nosology, or the study of illnesses; in the twenty-third aetiology, or the study of their causes; in the twenty-fourth pathology, or the study of the ills which they give rise to; in the twenty-fifth semiotics, the knowledge of symptoms; in the twenty-sixth clinical medicine, or study of the procedures to be followed at the patient's bedside; in the twenty-seventh therapeutics, or the art of curing patients – the most difficult part of all; the twenty-eighth volume dealt with dietetics or the study of diet; the twenty-ninth with hygiene or the art of staying healthy; the thirtieth, surgery; the thirty-first, pharmacology; and the thirty-second veterinary medicine.

Then, in the thirty-third volume, came general physics; in the thirty-fourth, specific physics; in the thirty-fifth, experimental physics;

in the thirty-sixth, meteorology; in the thirty-seventh, chemistry and the pseudo-sciences which are derived from it, such as alchemy in the thirty-eighth volume and hermeticism in the thirty-ninth. After these natural sciences came those which arise from the state of war, which is also believed to be a state natural to man. Thus the fortieth volume dealt with strategy, or the art of war; the forty-first, castramentation, or the art of siting camps; the forty-second, fortification; the forty-third, underground warfare, or the art of the sapper; the forty-fourth, pyrotechnics, which is the artificer's art; the forty-fifth, ballistics, or the art of projecting heavy bodies. The artillery had lost this art but Hervas had, as it were, brought it back to life through his learned researches on the machines used in antiquity.

From there Hervas returned to the arts of peace and devoted the forty-sixth volume to civil architecture; the forty-seventh to naval architecture; the forty-eighth to shipbuilding; the forty-ninth to navigation.

Then Hervas turned to man in society and devoted the fiftieth volume to legislation; the fifty-first to civil law; the fifty-second to criminal law; the fifty-third to international law; the fifty-fourth to history and the fifty-fifth to mythology; the fifty-sixth to chronology; the fifty-seventh to biography; the fifty-eighth to archaeology, or the study of antiquity; the fifty-ninth to numismatics; the sixtieth to heraldry; the sixty-first to diplomatics, which is the study of documents; the sixty-second to diplomacy, which is the study of embassies and the art of negotiation; the sixty-third to idiomatology, which is the general study of languages; the sixty-fourth to bibliography, which is the study of books and publishing.

Then Hervas returned to the arts of thought and dealt with logic in his sixty-fifth volume; rhetoric in the sixty-sixth; ethics, which is moral philosophy, in the sixty-seventh; aesthetics, which is the analysis of the impressions we receive through our senses, in the sixty-eighth.

Then came the sixty-ninth volume, containing philosophy, which is the study of wisdom in relation to religion; the seventieth contained theology in general, which was then divided into parts: dogmatics in the seventy-first volume; polemics, which is the faculty of considering general points in a discussion, in the seventy-second; ascetics, which teaches the exercise of piety, in the seventy-third. Then, in the seventy-fourth, came exegesis, which is the exposition of Holy Writ; in the seventy-fifth, hermeneutics, which is its interpretation; in the seventy-sixth, scholastics, that is, the art of conducting a proof completely independently of common sense; and in the seventy-seventh, the theology of mysticism or the pantheism of spiritualism.

From theology, in a transition which looked too daring, Hervas passed to oneirocritics, or the explanation of dreams. This was not the least interesting volume. Hervas demonstrated in it how misleading and irresponsible errors had been allowed to govern the world for many centuries, for we can see from history that the dream of the fat cows and the lean cows changed the constitution of Egypt, whose territorial possessions became at that period royal domains. Five hundred years later we can see Agamemnon telling his dream to the assembly of Greeks. Finally, six centuries after the Trojan war, the Chaldeans of Babylon and the oracle of Delphi were explaining dreams.

The seventy-ninth volume dealt with ornithomancy, or the science of augury, which is divination by birds, practised principally by the Etruscan haruspices. Seneca recorded their rites for us.

The eightieth volume, more learned than the rest, went back to the origins of magic, in the time of Zoroaster and Ostanes.[2] In it was found the history of that deplorable science which to the shame of our era infected its beginning and has still not altogether been abandoned.

The eighty-first volume was devoted to the cabbala as well as other means of divination, such as rhabdomancy or divination by wands, hydromancy, geomancy etc.

From all these lies, Hervas passed suddenly to the incontestable truths. Thus the eighty-second volume was devoted to geometry; the eighty-third to arithmetic; the eighty-fourth to algebra; the eighty-fifth to trigonometry; the eighty-sixth to stereometry, which is the study of solids applied to the cutting of gemstones; the eighty-seventh to geography; the eighty-eighth to astronomy and its false applications, known as astrology; the eighty-ninth to mechanics; the ninetieth to dynamics, the science of living forces; the ninety-first to statics, or

2 A legendary magus.

forces in equilibrium; the ninety-second to hydraulics; the ninety-third to hydrostatics; the ninety-fourth to hydrodynamics; the ninety-fifth to optics and perspective; the ninety-sixth to dioptrics; the ninety-seventh to catoptrics; the ninety-eighth to analytical geometry; the ninety-ninth to the first principles of differential calculus and the hundredth to analysis, which, according to Hervas, was the science of sciences and marked the extreme limit of human knowledge.

A deep knowledge of the hundred different sciences may appear to some people to be necessarily beyond the mental powers given to man. But it is certain that Hervas wrote a volume on each which began with the history of the science and finished with reflections full of wisdom on how it might be added to and how the frontiers of knowledge might, as it were, be driven back.

Hervas was equal to the whole task thanks to an economical use of his time and to a great regularity in its distribution. He would rise with the sun and prepare himself for work in his office by reflections pertaining to the task he had to do there. He would attend the minister half an hour before the rest and would wait for the office hour, pen in hand and his brain free from anything to do with his great work. When the hour struck he would begin his calculations and get through them with amazing speed; then he would go to the bookshop kept by Moreno, whose trust he had been able to gain, would take away the books he needed and carry them home. He would go out again to eat a light meal, return home before one o'clock and work until eight o'clock in the evening. After this he would play *pelota*[3] with small children in the neighbourhood, would go home, consume a cup of chocolate and go to bed. On Sundays he would spend the whole day out, thinking about the work of the coming week. Hervas was thus able to devote about three thousand hours a year to the production of his universal work, which at the end of fifteen years came to forty-five thousand hours, at which point the amazing work was actually finished without anyone in Madrid knowing about it; for Hervas was not at all communicative and spoke

3 An outdoor ball game.

to no one about his work, wanting to astonish the world by displaying all at once his vast mass of knowledge.

Hervas's work was therefore finished as he completed his thirty-ninth year, and he congratulated himself on entering his fortieth with a great reputation ready to blossom forth. But he felt at the same time a certain sadness, for the habit of work supported by his expectations had been for him a sort of pleasant companion which filled every instant of his day.

He had lost this companionship, and now boredom, which he had never experienced, began to make itself felt. This state, so new to Hervas, made him act completely out of character. Far from seeking solitude, he was seen everywhere in public places. Once there he would look as though he was going to accost everyone, but knowing no one and not having the habit of conversation, he would go by without saying a word. However, he thought inwardly that soon all Madrid would know him, would seek his company and that his name would be on everyone's lips.

Tormented by the need for distraction, Hervas hit on the idea of going back to his birthplace, an obscure village in Asturias which he hoped he would make famous. For fifteen years he had allowed himself no other amusement than playing *pelota* with the boys of his neighbourhood, and he promised himself the great delight of playing it in the place where he had spent his early childhood.

Before leaving, Hervas wanted to enjoy the sight of his hundred volumes arranged in a row on a single shelf. He possessed a copy in the same format that the volumes were to have once they had been printed. He gave his manuscripts to a printer, instructing him that the spine of every volume should bear longways the name of the science and the number of the volume, from the first, which was universal grammar, to the hundredth, which was analysis.

The binder delivered the work three weeks later. The shelf which was to receive it had already been made. Hervas placed the imposing series on it and ceremonially burned all his rough drafts and incomplete copies. Then he double-locked his room, sealed it up and left for Asturias.

The sight of his birthplace indeed gave Hervas all the pleasure he hoped it would. A host of innocent and sweet memories brought tears of joy to his eyes, whose springs had been dried up by the twenty years of arid thinking. Our polygraph would willingly have spent the rest of his days in his native hamlet but the hundred volumes called him back to Madrid. He took the road to the capital, arrived home, found the seal fixed to the door still intact, opened the door ... and saw his hundred volumes torn to pieces, stripped of their bindings, with all their pages loose and out of order on the floor.

This terrible sight drove him out of his mind. He fell down amid the debris of his book and even lost all sensation of life.

Alas! The cause of the disaster was this. Hervas never had meals in his own room. Rats, which are found in such great numbers in all the houses in Madrid, took good care not to visit his, where they would only have found a few quill pens to gnaw at. But that was not the case when a hundred volumes all glued with fresh glue were brought to his room and the room was on the same day abandoned by its master. The rats were attracted by the smell of the glue, emboldened by his absence and came there in great numbers to create chaos, gnawing and devouring.

On regaining his senses, Hervas saw one of these monsters dragging the last pages of his analysis into a hole. Anger had perhaps never before entered Hervas's soul, but he then felt a first spasm of it, rushed at the destroyer of his transcendental geometry, struck his head against the wall and fell down unconscious once again.

Hervas came round a second time, picked up the shreds which covered the floor of his room and put them into a chest. Then he sat on the chest and succumbed to sad thoughts. Soon after, he was seized by shivering which the very next day degenerated into a bilious, comatose, and malignant fever. He was placed in the care of doctors.

When the gypsy chief had reached this point in his narration he was summoned to join his band, so he put off until the next day the continuation of his story.

The Fiftieth Day

———————————— ∽ ————————————

The next day the company reassembled and the gypsy chief continued his story as follows:

∽ THE STORY OF DIEGO HERVAS CONTINUED ∽

Having been robbed of his glory by rats, and given up by his doctors, Hervas was not however abandoned by his nurse. She continued to care for him, and soon after a crisis with a happy outcome, his life was saved. The nurse was a girl aged thirty years called Marica. She had come to look after him out of the kindness of her heart because he used sometimes to converse in the evening with her father, who was a local cobbler. As Hervas was recovering, he realized all that he owed to this kind girl.

'Marica,' he said to her, 'you have saved my days and have smoothed my path back to life. What can I do for you?'

'Señor,' the girl replied, 'you can make me happy but I dare not say how.'

'Speak, speak, and rest assured that if it is in my power I shall do it.'

'But suppose I were to ask you to marry me?'

'I will do so very willingly. You will feed me when I am well, look after me when I am sick and protect my work from rats in my absence. Yes, Marica, I will marry you whenever you want and the sooner that is, the better.'

While still not completely restored to health, Hervas opened the chest which contained the debris of his polymathesis. He tried to put the single sheets back together again and suffered a relapse which left him very weak. When he was strong enough to go out he went to see the minister of finance, and pointed out that he had worked for fifteen years; he had trained pupils who were capable of replacing him, and his health was ruined. He asked to be allowed to retire with a pension equivalent to half his salary. In Spain it is not difficult to obtain these sorts of favours; Hervas was granted what he wanted and married Marica.

Our scholar then changed his way of life. He took lodgings in a quiet part of town and vowed not to leave them until he had reconstructed the manuscript of his hundred volumes. The rats had nibbled away the paper which was stuck to the spines of the books, leaving only the other half of each page; and even that half was torn to shreds; but they enabled Hervas to recall the whole text. In this way he set about rewriting the whole work. At the same time he produced one of quite another kind, for Marica brought me into the world: me, a sinner and a reprobate. Oh, surely on the day of my birth there was rejoicing in hell! The eternal fires of that awful place blazed with a new intensity, and the demons there increased the torments of the damned so as to revel all the more in their wailing.

As he uttered these words, the pilgrim seemed to succumb to despair. He shed many tears and then, turning to Cornádez, said:

'I am unable today to continue my story. Come back here tomorrow at the same time and be sure to do so without fail, for your salvation depends on it.'

Cornádez returned home, his soul filled with new terrors. That night he was woken by the dead Peña Flor, who counted the hundred doubloons in his ears without a single coin missing from the count.

The next day he went to the gardens of the Celestine fathers. There he found the pilgrim, who continued his story as follows:

I was born, and my mother survived my birth by only a few hours. Hervas had never known love or friendship except through a definition of these two emotions which he had included in the sixty-seventh volume. The loss of his wife showed him that he had been born to feel friendship and love. It distressed him more than the loss of his hundred volumes that the rats had devoured. Hervas's house was small and every cry that I gave reverberated right through it. It was clearly not possible to keep me there. I was taken in by my grandfather, Marañon, who seemed very flattered to have his grandson, the son of a *contador* and a gentleman, in his house. For all his humble estate, my

499

grandfather was very comfortably off. He sent me to school as soon as I was old enough to go. When I reached the age of sixteen years he gave me elegant clothes and the wherewithal to wander about at my leisure in Madrid. He thought himself well rewarded for his outlay as he could say, 'Mi nieto, el hijo del contador.'[1] But let us turn to my father and his sad fate, which is all too well known. May it serve as a lesson and a terrible warning to the ungodly!

Diego Hervas spent eight years repairing the damage done by the rats. His work was nearly complete when foreign journals which fell into his hands revealed to him that great progress had been made in the sciences, without his knowledge. Hervas sighed at this increase in his labours but, not wishing to leave his work in an imperfect state, he added to every science the discoveries which had been made. This took him four years, so he spent twelve years without leaving his house, glued to his work nearly all the time. This sedentary life finally destroyed his health. He suffered from chronic sciatica, kidney pains, gravel in the bladder and all of the early symptoms of gout. But at last the polymathesis in a hundred volumes was complete. Hervas summoned Moreno the bookseller – the son of the Moreno who had put on sale his ill-fated *Analysis* – to his house.

'Señor,' he said. 'Here are a hundred volumes which contain all that men presently know. This *Polymathesis* will bring honour to your presses and, if I may say so, to Spain. I want nothing for myself, but I beg you of your charity to print my work so that my historic labours will not be entirely lost.'

Moreno opened all the volumes, examined them carefully and then said, 'Señor, I will undertake the work, but you must bring yourself to reduce it to twenty-five volumes.'

'Go away, go away!' replied Hervas in the deepest indignation. 'Go back to your shop and print the romantic or pedantic rubbish which are the shame of Spain! Leave me, Señor, with my kidney stones and my genius, which if it had been better known would have won general esteem. I have nothing left to ask of mankind and still less of booksellers. Go away!'

1 'My grandson, the son of the *contador*.'

Moreno withdrew and Hervas fell into the blackest of melancholy. He constantly kept in his sight his hundred volumes, the children of his genius, conceived in rapture, born of pain mingled with pleasure and now consigned to oblivion. He saw his whole life wasted, his present and future existence destroyed. It was then also that his mind, trained to understand all the mysteries of nature, unfortunately turned to the abyss of human misery. By measuring its depth he saw only evil everywhere, and said in his heart, 'Who are you, author of evil?'

He was himself filled with horror at this thought and decided to investigate whether evil, to exist, must have been created. Then he examined the same question in a broader context. He turned his attention to natural forces and attributed to matter an energy which seemed to him to have the property of explaining everything without having to have recourse to the Creation.

As far as animals and men were concerned, they owed their existence, according to him, to a generative acid which by making matter ferment, gave it constant forms, in more or less the same way that acids crystallize alkaline and earthy bases in polyhedra which are always the same. He considered fungus substances produced by wet wood as the link connecting the crystallization of fossils to the reproduction of plants and animals, indicating if not their identity then at least the analogy between them.

Learned as he was, Hervas had no trouble supporting his false system with sophistical proofs designed to lead men's minds astray. He found for example that mules, which are a mixture of two species, could be compared to salts with a mixed base whose crystallization is of a compound type. The effervescence produced by mixing some earths with acid appeared to him to be comparable to the fermentation of mucous tissue in plants; according to him this constituted the beginnings of life that had not been able to develop due to lack of propitious circumstances.

Hervas had observed that crystals as they formed accumulated in the lightest parts of the test-tube and were difficult to form in darkness. And as light is equally favourable to vegetable growth, he considered luminous fluid to be one of the elements of which the universal acid, which gave life to all nature, consisted. Besides, he had seen light turn blue-coloured paper red over a period of time, and that was another reason for considering it to be an acid.

Hervas knew that in high latitudes near the pole, blood, lacking sufficient heat, was exposed to alcalaemia, which could only be halted by the internal use of acids. He concluded that heat, being able in some cases to be replaced by an acid, must also be a sort of acid, or at least one of the elements of the universal acid.

Hervas knew that thunder had been seen to cause wine to ferment and turn to vinegar. He had read in Sanchoniathon that when the world began, those things destined to be living beings had been, so to speak, brought to life by violent thunder-claps, and our hapless scientist had ventured to rely on the authority of this pagan cosmogony in order to declare that the matter of lightning had had the capacity to activate the generative acid which was infinitely varied but which consistently reproduced the same forms.

In his attempt to understand the mysteries of creation, Hervas was duty-bound to attribute it in all its glory to the Creator. Would to Heaven that he had done so! But his good angel had left him, and his mind, led astray by the presumption of knowledge, delivered him up defenceless into the hands of the spirit of pride, whose fall led to that of the whole world.

Alas! As Hervas's guilty speculations were rising above the sphere of human intelligence, his mortal coil was threatened by imminent dissolution. He was struck down by a number of acute diseases, which added themselves to his chronic afflictions. His sciatica became severe and deprived him of the use of his right leg. His kidney stones became larger and tore at his bladder. Arthritis deformed the fingers of his left hand and threatened the joints of his right. Finally the darkest of hypochondrias destroyed his mental powers at the same time as those of his body. He hated the idea of witnesses to his lamentable state and ended up by rejecting my ministrations and refusing to see me. His household consisted only of an infirm old man who devoted all his remaining energy to serving him but he too fell ill and my father was then forced to put up with having me with him.

Marañon, my grandfather, was struck down soon after by a high fever. His illness lasted only five days. Sensing his end to be near, he summoned me and said:

'Blas, my dear Blas, receive my last blessing. You were born the son of a learned father: would that he were less so! Fortunately for you, your grandfather is a simple man, simple in his faith and works, and he has brought you up in that same simplicity. Do not let yourself be led astray by your father. For some years he has fulfilled few of his religious duties and his opinions are such that heretics would be ashamed of them. Blas, beware of human wisdom. In a few instants I shall know more than all the philosophers. Blas, Blas, bless you, I am passing away.'

And die he did. I paid my last respects to him as was due and returned to my father's house, from which I had been absent for four days. In that time the infirm old servant had also died and a charitable fraternity had undertaken to bury him. I knew that my father was alone and intended to devote myself to serving him. But on going into his room an extraordinary spectacle met my eyes and I remained in the antechamber, transfixed with horror.

My father had taken off his clothes and had dressed himself up in a bed-sheet as if it were a shroud. He was seated watching the setting sun. Having looked at it for some time, he raised his voice and said, 'Oh star whose dying beams have met my eyes for the last time, why did you shine upon me on the day of my birth? Did I ask to be born? Why was I born? Men told me that I had a soul and I have nurtured it even at the expense of my body. I have cultivated my mind but rats have devoured it and booksellers have disdained it. Nothing of me will remain. All of me will die, in as great obscurity as if I had never been born. So, nothingness, receive your prey.'

Hervas remained for a few moments plunged in sombre thoughts. Then he took a goblet that looked to me to be filled with old wine, lifted his eyes to heaven and said, 'Oh God, if there is one, have pity on my soul, if I have one.'

After that he drained the goblet, put it on the table and placed his hand to his heart as though he felt some anguish there. Hervas had prepared another table, on which he had placed cushions. He lay down on it, crossed his hands on his breast and did not utter another word.

You will be surprised that, seeing all these preparations for suicide, I did not fling myself at the goblet or call for help. I am surprised myself, or rather I am sure that a supernatural power held me rooted to the spot where I was standing, leaving me no freedom of movement. The hairs of my head stood on end.

The charitable fraternity who had buried our old servant found me in this position. They saw my father stretched out on the table, covered with a shroud, and asked me whether he was dead. I replied that I did not know. They asked me who had put the shroud on him; I replied that he had dressed himself in it. They examined the body and found it lifeless. They saw the goblet with the dregs of a liquid in it, and took it away to examine it. After that they went away, making their displeasure clear to me, and left me in a state of utter dejection. Then people from the parish came, asked me the same questions and went away saying, 'He died as he lived. It is not for us to bury him.'

I remained alone with the body, and my depression reached the point where I had lost all power to act or to think. I slumped into the chair in which I had seen my father sitting and relapsed into the same immobility in which the people from the parish had found me.

Night came. Clouds covered the heavens. A sudden gust of wind blew open my window, a bluish light seemed to flash across the room, leaving it darker than it was before. In the midst of all this darkness I thought I saw some fantastic shapes. Then I thought I heard my father's body utter a long groan, which echoed and was repeated across night and space. I tried to get up, but was transfixed where I was, unable to make the slightest movement. An icy chill pierced my limbs. I shivered as if in a high fever. My visions became dreams and sleep conquered my senses.

I awoke with a start and saw six tall, yellow candles lit around the body of my father and a man sitting in front of me who seemed to be watching for the moment of my awakening. His face was majestic and imposing. He was tall; black, somewhat wavy hair fell across his forehead. His look was keen and penetrating, yet also soft and seductive. For the rest he was dressed in a ruff and a grey cloak, much as gentlemen dress in the country.

When the stranger saw that I was awake he smiled at me affably and said, 'My son – I call you this because I look on you as though you were already mine – you have been forsaken by God and man and the earth has closed itself to the remains of this scholar who gave you life. But we will not forsake you.'

'Señor,' I replied, 'you said, I believe, that I was forsaken by God and man. This is true of man but I do not believe God can ever forsake one of his creatures.'

'Your remark is correct in some respects,' said the stranger. 'I will explain this to you another time. Meanwhile, to convince you of our concern for you, I am giving you this purse. You will find a thousand pistoles in it. A young man must have desires and the means of satisfying them. Spend this gold freely, and count on us always.'

Then the stranger clapped his hands. Six masked men appeared and took away Hervas's body. The candles went out and deep darkness fell. I did not stay long where I was. I felt my way to the door, reached the street and, on seeing the starry sky, imagined that my breathing became easier. The thousand pistoles that I could feel in my pocket also contributed to raising my spirits. I crossed Madrid and reached the far end of the Prado at the spot on which a statue of Cybele has since been placed. There I lay down on a seat and soon fell asleep.

When the gypsy had reached this point in his story, he asked for leave to stop and continue it on the morrow. We did not see him again that day.

The Fifty-first Day

We assembled at the usual time. Rebecca addressed the old chief and said to him that the story of Diego Hervas, although already known to her in part, had made a deep impression on her.

'But it seems to me,' she added, 'that too much trouble was taken to fool the poor husband. One could have misled him more easily. Doubtless the story of the atheist was told to that timid soul, Cornádez, to frighten him even further.'

'Allow me to draw attention to the fact that your judgement on the adventure which I have had the honour to relate to you is too hasty. The Duke of Arcos was a member of the high nobility, and one might have thought of, or even acted out, certain roles to do him a service, but there is nothing to suggest that the story itself of Hervas's son, which you haven't yet heard, was told to Cornádez for that reason.'

Rebecca assured the gypsy chief that that story itself also interested her deeply. The old man then continued his story as follows:

THE STORY OF BLAS HERVAS,
THE REPROBATE PILGRIM

I was telling you that I lay down on a bench at the end of the main avenue of the Prado and fell asleep. The sun was already quite high in the sky when I awoke. What roused me was, I think, a light flick of a handkerchief which I received in my face for, on waking up, I saw a young girl who was using her handkerchief as a fly-whisk and was brushing away those flies which might have disturbed my slumbers. But the most peculiar thing of all was that my head was resting very gently on the knees of another girl, whose sweet breath I could feel caressing my hair. In waking up, I had scarcely moved at all, and was at liberty to prolong this situation by pretending still to be asleep. So I closed my eyes again and soon after heard a slightly disapproving, but not sharp, voice address those who were cradling me, and say:

'Celia, Zorrilla, what are you doing here? I thought you were in church, and here I find you engaged in a fine form of piety!'

'But Mama,' said the young girl who was acting as my pillow, 'didn't you say that good works were meritorious as well as prayer? And isn't it a charitable act to prolong the rest of this poor young man, who must have spent a very unpleasant night?'

'Certainly,' said a voice which laughed more than it scolded. 'Certainly, that is very meritorious, and that's a thought which proves your innocence, if it doesn't prove your piety. But now, my charitable Zorrilla, put the young man's head down very gently on the seat and follow me home.'

'Oh dear Mama!' the young girl replied, 'look how softly he is sleeping! Rather than wake him up you should help me, Mama, to undo the ruff which is choking him.'

'Should I indeed?' said their mother. 'That's a fine task you have given me! But, on closer inspection, doesn't he look very sweet?' At the same time, the mother's hand slipped softly under my chin and undid my ruff.

'He is even better now,' said Celia, who up till then hadn't spoken, 'and he is breathing more easily. I can see that there's a sweetness in doing good works.'

'That remark shows much discernment,' said their mother, 'but charity must not be taken too far. Come, Zorrilla, put the young man's head back on the seat and let us go.'

Zorrilla slipped her two hands gently under my head and removed her knees. I then thought that there was no longer any point in feigning sleep. I sat up and opened my eyes. The mother let out a cry and the girls wanted to run away. I stopped them.

'Celia, Zorrilla,' I said. 'You are as pretty as you are innocent. And as for you, who only look like their mother because your charms have blossomed further, please spare me a few moments before you leave me to enjoy the admiration which all three of you inspire in me.'

What I said to them was true. Celia and Zorrilla would have been perfect beauties if it had not been for their extreme youth and their mother, who was not yet thirty years old, looked as though she had not yet reached her twenty-fifth year.

'Señor caballero,' said the mother, 'if you have only been pretending to sleep, you must have been persuaded of the innocence of my daughters and must have formed a good opinion of their mother. I therefore am not afraid of losing reputation in your eyes in asking you to accompany me home. An acquaintance which begins in such a singular fashion seems destined to become closer.'

I followed them. We reached their house, which looked out on to the Prado. The girls went away to preside over the preparation of the chocolate. The mother sat me down beside her and said, 'You see here a house somewhat better appointed than is appropriate to our present situation. I took it in happier times. Now I would like to sub-let the first floor but dare not do so, for circumstances in which I find myself require me to live in strict seclusion.'

'Señora,' I replied, 'I also have reason to live a very retired life. And if it suited you, I would willingly come to an agreement about the *cuarto principal*, or best rooms.'

As I spoke, I drew out my purse, and the sight of the gold dispelled any objections the lady might have put to me. I paid three months' rent and board in advance. It was agreed that my dinner would be brought up to my room and that I would be served by a trusty manservant, who would also run errands for me. Zorrilla and Celia were told of the conditions of the agreement when they reappeared with the chocolate, and their eyes seemed to take possession of my person. But those of their mother appeared to lay a rival claim to it. This little battle of coquetry did not escape my notice, but I left the outcome to fate and thought only about settling into my new lodgings.

It was not long before it was furnished with all that could contribute to making it pleasant and convenient for me. At one moment it was Zorrilla bringing me a writing desk; at another Celia came to furnish my table with a lamp or some books. Nothing was forgotten. The two pretty girls came separately, but when they met in my room, endless giggling ensued. The mother also took her turn. She attended to my bed, supplying it with sheets of Dutch linen, a fine silk coverlet and a pile of cushions. These arrangements took up my morning. Noon came; a place was laid for me in my room. I was delighted. It charmed me to see three enchanting persons trying to please me and vying for a share of my goodwill. But there is a time for everything and I was glad to satisfy my appetite without distraction or disturbance.

So it was that I dined. Then I took my cloak and sword and went out for a walk in town. I had never felt so much pleasure. I was independent, my pockets were full of gold, I was in good health and full of energy and, thanks to the attentions of the three ladies, full also of a high opinion of myself. For it is normal for young men to rate themselves at the value the fair sex sets on them.

I went into a jeweller's shop and bought several jewels. Then I went to the theatre and eventually back to my lodgings. I found the three ladies sitting by the door of their house. Zorrilla was singing and accompanying herself on the guitar. The two others were making *redicilla*, or lace.

'Señor caballero,' the mother said to me, 'you have taken lodgings with us and have shown great confidence in us without knowing who we are. But it would be only fitting to tell you. You should know, Señor caballero, that I am called Inés Santarez, widow of Don Juan Santarez, the *corregidor* of Havana. He took me penniless and has left me penniless with two daughters, as you see. I was in great difficulty because of my poverty and widowhood when I unexpectedly received a letter from my father. You will permit me not to name him. Alas! He also had struggled against misfortune all his life, but at last, as his letter informed me, he had found a splendid post as army paymaster. His letter included a remittance of two thousand pistoles and a summons to come to Madrid. So here I came, only to discover that my father had been accused of misappropriation, even high treason, and was being held prisoner in the castle of Segovia. But in the meanwhile this house had been rented for our use. So here I live in strict seclusion, receiving nobody except a young man employed in the war office. He comes to tell me what he is able to find out about my father's trial. Apart from him, no one knows we are related to the hapless prisoner.'

As she uttered these last words, Señora Santarez shed a few tears.

'Don't cry, Mama,' said Celia, 'there is an end to everything, and surely there must be an end to our suffering. Already here's a young gentleman with very auspicious looks. Meeting him seems to me to be a favourable omen.'

509

'In truth,' said Zorrilla, 'since he has been here our solitude seems no longer to be joyless.'

Señora Santarez gave me a look in which I detected sadness and affection. The girls looked at me too, lowered their eyes, blushed and became embarrassed and dreamy. So I was loved by three charming persons. This state of affairs seemed delightful to me.

As this was going on, a tall, well-built young man came up to us, took Señora Santarez by the hand, led her a few steps away from us and had a long conversation with her. She then brought him to me and said to me:

'Señor caballero, this is Don Cristoforo Sparadoz, about whom I have spoken to you, and who is the only man we see in Madrid. I would like to procure for him the benefit of your acquaintance but although we live in the same house I don't know to whom I have the honour of speaking.'

'Señora,' I said, 'I am an Asturian of noble birth. My name is Leganez.' I thought that I ought not to mention the name of Hervas, which might be known.

Young Sparadoz looked me up and down arrogantly, and seemed not even to want to acknowledge my presence. We entered the house and Señora Santarez had a collation of fruits and light pastries served. I was still the main centre of attention of the three ladies but I noted that much simpering and many glances were directed at the new arrival. I was hurt by this, and in an attempt to draw all the attention to myself, I was as charming and witty as I was able to be.

At the height of my triumph Don Cristoforo placed his right foot on his left knee and, looking at the sole of his boot, said, 'In all truth, since the death of Marañon the cobbler, it isn't possible to find a well-made boot in Madrid.' He then looked at me with a sneering and disdainful expression.

Marañon the cobbler was my maternal grandfather, who had brought me up, and I owed the greatest of obligations to him. But he was a blot on my genealogical tree, or so at least I thought. It seemed to me that I would be much diminished in the esteem of the three ladies if they discovered that I had a cobbler for a grandfather. My gaiety vanished altogether. I shot Don Cristoforo glances which were sometimes angry, sometimes proud and disdainful. I decided to forbid him to set foot in the house.

He left. I followed him, intending to tell him this. I caught up with him at the end of the street and uttered the offensive greeting that I had rehearsed. I thought that he was going to lose his temper, but on the contrary, he assumed a friendly manner, put his hand under my chin as if to caress me but then suddenly jerked me off my feet and kicked me, or rather tripped me, causing me to fall flat on my face in the gutter. I was stunned, and got back to my feet covered with mud. Full of rage, I went back to the house.

The ladies had retired. I went to bed but could not sleep. Two passions, love and hate, kept me awake. The latter was entirely directed at Don Cristoforo, but that was not the case with the love with which my heart was filled. It was not fixed on any one object. Celia, Zorrilla and their mother occupied my thoughts in turn. Their alluring images, which grew confused with each other in my dreams, haunted me for the rest of the night.

I woke late. On opening my eyes, I saw Señora Santarez sitting at the foot of my bed. She seemed to have been weeping.

'My good young Sir,' she said, 'I have come to take refuge in your room. There are people upstairs who are asking me for money and I have none to give them. Alas! I am in debt. But did I not have to feed and dress those poor children? They are deprived of enough as it is.'

At this, Señora Santarez began to sob, and her eyes, full of tears, involuntarily turned to my purse, which was next to me on my bedside table. I understood this mute language. I poured out the gold on to the table, made two piles, which I judged to be equal, and presented one to Señora Santarez. She was not expecting this generous gesture. At first she seemed to be petrified by astonishment, then she took my hands and kissed them effusively and pressed them to her heart; finally she picked up the gold, saying, 'Oh my children, my dear children.'

The girls came in next and kissed my hands. All these expressions of gratitude succeeded in inflaming my blood, which was already burning from my dreams.

I dressed quickly and decided to take the air on one of the house's terraces. As I went by the bedroom of the two girls I heard them sobbing and tearfully embracing each other. I listened for a moment and then went in.

Celia said to me, 'Listen, dear, kind guest. You find us in the greatest distress. Since we were born no cloud has cast its shadow on our feelings for each other. We were united by affection, even more than by blood. But that isn't any longer the case since you have been here. Jealousy has crept into our souls, and we might have reached the point of hating each other. Zorrilla's good nature has prevented this terrible calamity. She threw herself into my arms, our tears mingled with each other's and our hearts have grown closer. And now, dear guest, it is for you to complete our reconciliation. Promise us not to love one more than the other, and if you have caresses to distribute, share them equally between us.'

What reply could I give to this heartfelt and pressing invitation? I held them one after the other in my arms. I wiped away their tears and their sadness gave way to playful affection.

We went out together on to the terrace and Señora Santarez came to join us there. The delight at having settled her debts made her drunk with joy. She asked me to dinner and begged me to give the rest of the day to her. Our meal was eaten in an atmosphere of intimacy and trust. The servants were sent away. The two girls waited at table one after the other. Señora Santarez, drained by the emotion she had suffered, drank two glasses of powerful Rotha wine. Her somewhat unfocused eyes shone the more brightly. She became very animated and her daughters came close to feeling jealous again. However, they respected their mother too much for such an idea to cross their minds. But even though her blood, exhilarated by the wine, betrayed her feelings, she was far from engaging in any immodest behaviour.

As for me, conscious thoughts of seduction did not even cross my mind. We were seduced by our age and our difference of sex. The sweet impulses of nature infused our intercourse with an indescribable charm. We found it difficult to take leave of each other. The setting sun would finally have separated us if I had not ordered refreshments from a neighbouring lemonade-seller. We were pleased when they came because they afforded us an excuse to remain in each other's company. All was going well. We had just sat down to table when

Cristoforo Sparadoz appeared. The entry of a French gentleman in the harem of a sultan would not have produced a more disagreeable sensation than that which I experienced on the arrival of Don Cristoforo. Señora Santarez and her daughters were not really my wives, and did not constitute my harem, but my heart had taken possession of these ladies in a certain way and seeing my rights compromised caused me real distress.

Don Cristoforo took no notice either of this or of my person. He greeted the ladies, led Señora Santarez to the end of the terrace and had a long conversation with her, then sat down at table without being invited to do so. He ate, drank and said not a word. But when the conversation turned to bullfighting he pushed away his plate, thumped the table with his fist and said:

'Oh, by St Christopher, my patron! Why am I only a simple clerk in the minister's office? I would prefer to be the humblest *torero* in Madrid than president of all the *cortes* of Castile.'

As he said this, he extended his arm as if to transfix a bull and made us admire the size of his muscles. Then, to show how strong he was, he had the three ladies sit in an armchair, put his hand underneath it and carried it all round the room. Don Cristoforo found these games so amusing that he carried them on for as long as he could. Then he gathered up his cloak and sword to go. Up till then he had paid no attention to me, but then he turned to me and said, 'My noble friend. Since Marañon the cobbler has died, who makes the best boots?'

These words seemed to the ladies to be no more than a silly joke of the same kind as those often uttered by Don Cristoforo. But I was enraged by them. I went to fetch my sword and ran after him.

I caught up with him in a side-street and placed myself in front of him. I drew my sword and said to him, 'You insolent wretch! You will now pay me back for so many cowardly insults!'

Don Cristoforo put his hand on the hilt of his sword. Then, noticing a stick on the ground, he picked it up and, striking my sword with it, knocked it out of my hand. Then he came close to me, grabbed hold of me by the hair, carried me to the gutter and threw me into it as he had done the day before, only this time so violently that I was stunned for longer.

Someone helped me up. I recognized the gentleman who had had my father's body taken away and had given me a thousand pistoles. I threw myself at his feet. He raised me up in a kindly manner and told me to follow him. We walked in silence and arrived at the Manzanares bridge, where we found two black horses, on which we galloped for half an hour along the bank. We reached a lonely house, whose doors opened by themselves. The room we entered was hung with brown serge wall-hangings, and decorated with silver torches and a brazier of the same metal. We sat down next to this in two armchairs and the stranger said to me:

'Señor Hervas, that is the way of the world, whose much admired order does not excel in distributive justice. Some have received from nature the strength to lift eight hundred pounds, others only sixty. It is true that treachery has been invented, which restores the balance somewhat.'

As he spoke, the stranger opened a drawer, drew out a dagger and said, 'Look at this instrument. The end, shaped like a button, finishes in a point thinner than a hair. Put it in your belt. Farewell, caballero, and never forget your good friend Don Belial de Gehenna. Whenever you need me, come after midnight to the Manzanares bridge, clap your hands three times and you will see the black horses appear. By the way, I have forgotten the most important thing. Here is a second purse. Don't deny yourself anything.'

I thanked generous Don Belial and remounted my black horse. A negro mounted the other. Together we reached the bridge, where I had to dismount. I then went back to my lodgings.

Once there, I went to bed and fell asleep, but my dreams were troubled. I had put the dagger under my pillow; it seemed to me that it came out from under it and pierced me in the heart. I also dreamed that Don Cristoforo took the three ladies away from me and from the house.

The next morning I was in a sombre mood. The presence of the girls did not set my mind at rest. The efforts they made to cheer me up produced a different effect. My caresses grew less innocent. When I was alone again, I held my dagger in my hand and went through the motions of threatening Don Cristoforo, whom I imagined I could see before me.

That formidable character reappeared that evening and did not pay the slightest attention to my person. But he pressed his attentions on the ladies. He teased them one after the other, made them angry, then made them laugh. In the end his clumsy antics were more pleasing to them than my kindness.

I had had a supper delivered which was more elegant than it was copious. Don Cristoforo ate nearly all of it himself. Then he gathered up his cloak as he prepared to go. Before leaving he suddenly turned to me and said, 'Noble sir, is that a dagger I can see in your belt? You'd do better to put a cobbler's awl there.'

Thereupon he went out and left us, roaring with laughter. I followed him and caught up with him at the end of a street. I went to his left side and struck him with the dagger with the full force of my arm, but I felt it repelled with as much force as I had used to strike him, and Don Cristoforo, turning round with great sang-froid, said to me, 'You wretch. Don't you realize that I am wearing a breastplate?'

Then he grabbed me by the hair and threw me into the gutter. But for once I was pleased to be there and to have been saved from committing a murder. I got up with a sort of pleasure. This feeling stayed with me until I went to bed and my night was calmer than the preceding one.

In the morning, the ladies found me less agitated than I had been the day before and complimented me on this, but I didn't dare to spend the evening with them. I feared the man whom I had wanted to murder and I thought that I would not dare to look him in the face. I passed the evening walking round the streets, feeling enraged whenever I thought of the wolf that had found his way into my fold.

At midnight I went to the bridge, I clapped my hands and the black horses appeared. I mounted the one intended for me and followed my guide to Don Belial's house. The doors opened by themselves, my protector came to meet me and led me to the brazier where we had been the previous day.

'Well,' he said in somewhat mocking tones, 'well, caballero, the murder didn't come off! But that doesn't matter; you will be credited with the intention. Moreover, we have taken care to rid you of such a tiresome rival. The indiscretions of which he was guilty have been denounced, and he is now in the same prison as the father of Señora

515

Santaréz. So it is up to you to profit from your good fortune somewhat more successfully than you have done up to now. Accept this sweet-box as a gift. It contains pastilles made to an excellent recipe. Offer them to your ladies and eat some yourself.'

I took the sweet-box, which gave off a pleasant scent, and then said to Don Belial, 'I am not sure what you mean by "profit from my good fortune". I would be a monster if I could bring myself to abuse the trust of a mother and the innocence of her daughters. I am not as perverse as you seem to suppose.'

'I don't suppose you to be more or less wicked than any of the sons of Adam,' said Don Belial. 'They feel scruples before they commit crimes and suffer remorse afterwards. Thereby they flatter themselves into thinking that they still cling to virtue to some degree; but they would be able to spare themselves these tiresome feelings if they chose to examine what virtue is, that abstract quality whose existence they accept without question. That alone should put it in the category of prejudices, which are opinions accepted without a prior act of judgement.'

'Señor Don Belial,' I replied to my protector, 'my father placed in my hands his sixty-seventh volume, which dealt with ethics. According to him, a prejudice is not an opinion accepted without a prior act of judgement but an opinion already considered before we came into the world and transmitted as if by inheritance. These childhood habits sow the first seeds of virtue into our souls. Example develops it; the knowledge of the law fortifies it. By conforming to it we are honourable men. In doing more than the law requires we are virtuous men.'

'That is not a bad definition, and does your father honour. He wrote well and thought even better,' said Don Belial. 'Perhaps you will do as he did. But to come back to your definition, I agree with you that prejudices are opinions which have already been considered. But that isn't a reason for not considering them again once one's judgement has developed. A mind curious to understand things deeply will question prejudices, and question whether laws are equally binding on everyone. Indeed you will note that the rule of law seems to have been thought up for the sole benefit of those cold, indolent characters who expect to obtain their pleasures from marriage and their well-being from frugality and hard work. But what does the social order do for the brilliant geniuses and passionate characters, burning for gold and for pleasure, who want eagerly to devour their allotted span? They will spend their lives in prisons and end them in a torture chamber. Fortunately, human institutions are not really what they seem to be. Laws are barriers; they are sufficient to turn aside passers-by but those who want to cross them get over them or under them. This subject would lead me too far. It is getting late. Farewell, caballero. Use my sweet-box and count always on my protection.'

I took my leave of Señor Don Belial and returned home. The door was opened to me; I went to bed and tried to go to sleep. The sweet-box was on a bedside table. It gave off a delicious scent. I could not resist the temptation; I ate two pastilles, fell asleep and had a very disturbed night.

My young friends appeared at the usual time. They found something very odd about the way I looked at them and indeed I saw them with different eyes. All their movements seemed to me to be deliberately provocative and intended to give me pleasure. I attributed the same meaning to their most casual remarks. Everything about them attracted my attention and made me think of things which I had previously never thought about.

Zorrilla found the sweet-box. She ate two pastilles and offered some to her sister. Soon what I had imagined became reality. The two sisters were overcome by an inner sensation and, without being aware of it, succumbed to it. They became alarmed and left me with vestiges of a timidity which had something wild about it.

Their mother came in. Since I had saved her from her creditors she had adopted an affectionate manner towards me. Her caresses calmed me down for a short time, but soon I saw her with the same eyes that I had seen her daughters. She noticed what was happening to me and felt embarrassed. Her eyes, avoiding mine, fell on the fatal sweet-box. She took some pastilles from it and went away. Soon she came back, caressed me again, called me her son and clasped me in her arms. After struggling with herself she dragged herself away. The turmoil of my senses reached the point of frenzy. I could feel fire circulating in my veins. I could scarcely focus on objects about me. A mist covered my eyes.

I went out towards the terrace. The young girls' door was ajar; I could not stop myself going in. Their senses were in even greater turmoil than mine: they alarmed me. I wanted to tear myself free from their arms but did not have the strength to do so. Their mother came in. Reproaches were on her lips, but she soon lost the right to address any to us.

'Forgive me, Señor Cornádez,' added the pilgrim. 'Forgive me if I say things which even to speak of is a mortal sin. But this story was necessary for your salvation. I have undertaken to save you from perdition and have to succeed. Be here tomorrow at the same time without fail.'

. Cornádez went home and was disturbed again that night by the ghost of Peña Flor.

When the gypsy had reached this point in his story he had to leave us and postpone its sequel to the next day.

The Fifty-second Day

We reassembled at the usual hour. The old gypsy gave in to the impatience of his listeners and continued his story, or rather Busqueros's, in the terms in which the latter had told it to the Knight of Toledo.

THE GYPSY CHIEF'S STORY CONTINUED

The next day, after Cornádez had gone to the place appointed by the pilgrim, Hervas continued his story as follows:

THE REPROBATE PILGRIM'S STORY CONTINUED

My sweet-box was empty and I had no pastilles left, but our glances and sighs seemed to express our desire to see our quenched fires revive. Our thoughts were fuelled by guilty memories and our languor had its guilty pleasures.

Crime has the property of stifling the sentiments of nature. Having given herself up to unbridled desire, Señora Santarez forgot that her father was languishing in a dungeon, perhaps under sentence of death; and if she thought little about him, I thought even less.

But one evening a man, carefully wrapped up in his cloak, appeared in my rooms, causing me some alarm, and I was hardly reassured when I noticed that he had put on a mask the better to hide his identity. The mysterious person indicated that I should sit down, sat down himself and said to me:

'Señor Hervas, you seem to me to be attached to Señora Santarez. I want to speak frankly to you about something that concerns her. Since the matter is a serious one, it would be painful for me to discuss it with a woman. Señora Santarez once put her trust in a rash fellow

519

called Cristoforo Sparadoz. Today he is in the same prison as Señor Goranez, the father of the said lady. This mad fool, Sparadoz, believed that he was in the confidence of certain powerful men, but I am the person who has their confidence. This, briefly, is what I know. In a week from now, half an hour after sunset, I shall go by this door and say the name of the prisoner three times: Goranez, Goranez, Goranez. The third time, you will give me a bag containing three thousand pistoles. Señor Goranez is no longer in Segovia but in prison in Madrid. His fate will be decided before the middle of that same night. That is what I have to say. My mission is accomplished.' As he said this, the masked man rose and left.

I knew, or I thought I knew, that Señora Santarez had no financial means. So I decided to have recourse to Don Belial. All I said to my charming hostess was that Don Cristoforo didn't come any more to her house because he had become suspect in his superior's eyes, but I myself had sources of information in the ministry and I had every reason to expect complete success. Señora Santarez was overjoyed at the prospect of saving her father. She added gratitude to all the emotions which I had already inspired in her. The surrender of her person seemed to her less reprehensible. So great a service seemed necessarily to absolve her. New pleasures occupied all of our time. I tore myself away from them one night to go and see Don Belial.

'I was expecting you,' he said. 'I knew full well that your scruples would not last long and your remorse would be even shorter lived. All the sons of Adam are made of the same clay. But I didn't expect that you would be so quickly tired of pleasures the like of which the kings of this little globe, who have not had my sweet-box, have never tasted.'

'Alas, Señor Belial,' I replied, 'part of what you say is all too true, but it isn't that I am tired of my present state. On the contrary, I fear that if it were to come to an end, life would have no more charms for me.'

'Yet you have come to ask me for the three thousand pistoles to save Señor Goranez, and as soon as he is declared innocent he will take his daughter and his granddaughters home with him. He has already promised his granddaughters' hands to two clerks in his office. You will see in the arms of those fortunate husbands two charming persons who have sacrificed their innocence to you and who as a price for such an offering asked only for a share in the pleasures of which you were the focal point. Inspired more by rivalry than jealousy, each of them was happy in the happiness she had given you, and enjoyed without envy the happiness which you owed to the other. Their mother, more knowledgeable but no less passionate, could look on her daughters' pleasures without resentment, thanks to my sweet-box. After such moments what will you do with the rest of your life? Will you seek the legitimate pleasures of matrimony? Or sigh away your love in the company of a coquette who will not be able to promise you even the shadow of the sensual pleasures that no mortal before you has known?'

Then Don Belial changed his tone and said, 'No: I am wrong! The father of Señora Santarez is really innocent and it is in your power to save him. The pleasure of doing a good action should take priority over all the others.'

'Señor, you speak very coldly about good works but with great warmth about pleasures, which after all are sinful ones. You seem to want my eternal damnation. I am tempted to think that you are . . .'

Don Belial did not let me finish but said, 'I am one of the principal members of a powerful society whose aim is to make men happy by curing them of the vain prejudices which they suck in with the milk of their wet-nurse, and which afterwards get in the way of all their desires. We have published very good books in which we demonstrate admirably well that self-love is the mainspring of all human action, and that gentle compassion, filial piety, ardent, tender love, and clemency in kings are so many refinements of egoism. Now if self-love is the mainspring of all our actions, it follows that the satisfaction of our own desires must be its natural goal. Legislators have clearly felt this: they have written laws so that they can be evaded. And self-interested people rarely fail to do so.'

'What, Señor Belial!' I said. 'Don't you regard just and unjust to be real qualities?'

'They are relative qualities. I will make you see this with the help of a moral fable:

'Some tiny insects were crawling about on the tips of tall grasses. One said to the others, "Look at that tiger near us. It's the gentlest of

521

animals. It never does us any harm. The sheep, on the other hand, is a ferocious beast. If one came along it would eat us with the grass which is our refuge. But the tiger is just. He would avenge us." You can deduce from this, Señor Hervas, that all ideas of the just and the unjust, or good and evil, are relative and in no way absolute or general. I agree with you that there is a sort of inane satisfaction to be had from what you call good works. You will certainly find it by saving good Señor Goranez, who is unjustly accused. You must not hesitate to do this if you are tired of living with his family. Think about it. You have the time. The money has to be handed over on Saturday, half an hour after sunset. Be here on Friday night. The three thousand pistoles will be ready at exactly midnight. Farewell. Please let me give you another sweet-box.'

I went back home and ate a few pastilles on the way. Señora Santarez and her daughters were waiting for me and had not gone to bed. I wanted to speak about the prisoner but I was not given time ... But why should I reveal so many shameful crimes? You need only know that we gave full rein to our desires, and that it was not in our power to measure the passage of time or count the days. The prisoner was completely forgotten.

Saturday was on the point of ending; the sun, which had set behind clouds, seemed to me to cover the sky with blood-red hues. Sudden flashes of lightning made me tremble. I struggled to recall my last conversation with Don Belial. Suddenly I heard a hollow, sepulchral voice say three times, 'Goranez, Goranez, Goranez.'

'Merciful heavens,' cried Señora Santarez. 'Was that a spirit from heaven or hell? It was telling me that my father is no more.'

I fainted; when I came round I took the road to Manzanares to make one last appeal to Don Belial. I was arrested by *alguaziles* and taken to a part of the town which I did not know at all, and into a building which I knew no better but which I soon saw to be a prison. I was clapped in irons and pushed into a dark dungeon.

I heard the sound of chains rattling near me. 'Are you young Hervas?' my companion in misfortune asked me.

'Yes,' I said. 'I am Hervas. And I can tell from the sound of your voice that you are Cristoforo Sparadoz. Do you have any news of Goranez? Was he innocent?'

'He was innocent,' said Don Cristoforo. 'But his accuser had hatched his plot with a skill which placed Goranez's condemnation or his salvation in his control. He demanded three thousand pistoles from him. Goranez was not able to procure them and has just hanged himself in prison. I was also given the choice of either hanging myself or spending the rest of my days in the castle of Larache on the African coast. I have chosen the latter course, and have decided to escape as soon as I am able and turn Muslim. As for you, my friend, you will be cruelly tortured to make you confess to things you know nothing about; but your affair with Señora Santarez gives rise to the presumption that you know all about them and are an accomplice of her father.'

Imagine a man whose soul as well as his body had been softened by pleasure; a man threatened with the horrors of protracted and cruel torture. I thought I could already feel its pains; my hair stood up on my head. A shudder of terror ran through my limbs, which no longer obeyed my will but were jerked by sudden convulsions.

A gaoler came into our prison to fetch Sparadoz. As he went away, Don Cristoforo threw me a dagger. I did not have the strength to grasp it and would have been even less able to stab myself with it. My despair was such that death itself could not bring me comfort.

'Oh Belial,' I cried. 'Belial, I know who you are and yet I invoke you.'

'Here I am,' the vile spirit cried. 'Take this dagger. Draw blood and sign the paper I am giving to you.'

'Oh my guardian angel,' I then cried. 'Have you altogether forsaken me?'

'It is too late to invoke your angel,' cried Satan, grinding his teeth and vomiting out flames.

At the same time he scored my forehead with his claw. I felt a burning pain and fainted, or rather fell into a trance.

A sudden light illuminated the prison. A cherubim with shining wings held up a mirror to me and said, 'Behold on your forehead the inverted *Thau*. It is the sign of reprobation. You will see it on other sinners. If you bring twelve back to the path of salvation you will return there yourself. Take up this pilgrim's habit and follow me.'

I woke up, or I thought I did, and in truth I was no longer in prison but on the high road to Galicia. I was dressed as a pilgrim.

Soon after, a company of pilgrims came by. They were going to Santiago de Compostela. I joined them and went with them to all the holy places in Spain. I wanted to go into Italy and visit Loreta. I was in Asturias and took the road to Madrid. Once I reached this city I went to the Prado and looked for Señora Santarez's house. I could not find it even though I recognized all those in the neighbourhood. These hallucinations proved to me that I was still in Satan's power. I did not dare pursue my researches further.

I visited several churches and then went to the Buen Retiro. The garden was completely deserted. I saw only one man sitting on a seat. The great Maltese cross embroidered on his cloak told me that he was one of the principal members of that order. He seemed lost in thought and plunged in so deep a reverie that he seemed to have lost all power of movement. As I came closer I thought I saw under his feet an abyss in which his face was depicted upside-down as if in a pool of water, but in this case the abyss looked as though it was filled with fire.

As I came still closer, the vision disappeared, but in looking at the man I saw that he bore on his forehead the inverted *Thau*, the sign of reprobation which the cherubim had made me see on my own forehead in the mirror.

When the gypsy reached this point in his story a man came to discuss the day's business with him. So he had to leave us.

The Fifty-third Day

The next day the old chief, taking up Busqueros's story, continued to tell it as follows:

THE REPROBATE PILGRIM'S STORY
CONTINUED

It was easy for me to realize that before my eyes was one of the twelve sinners who had to be led back by me to the path of salvation. I tried to gain his confidence; I did not succeed until I convinced him that my motive was not idle curiosity. It was necessary for him to tell me his story. I asked him for it, and he began as follows:

THE COMMANDER OF TORALVA'S STORY

I entered the order of the Knights of Malta before the end of my childhood, having been received into it, as they say, as a page. The protection I enjoyed at court obtained for me the favour of a galley command at the age of twenty-five and in the following year the grand master, having offices to distribute, conferred on me the best commandery in the 'langue'[1] of Aragon. So I could, and still can, aspire to the highest positions in the order. But as these are not reached until one is of an advanced age, and as I had nothing to do in the meanwhile, I followed the example of our first *bailli*, who perhaps should have set me a better one. In a word, I spent my time in love affairs, which I thought then to be the most venial of sins. Would that I had not committed any more serious ones! The sin for which I reproach myself was a guilty excess which made me defy what our

---

1 The Knights of Malta were divided into 'nations'.

religion holds most sacred. I can only think about it with terror. But I must not get ahead of myself.

You will know that on Malta we have noble families of the island who do not enter the order or have any contact with the knights of whatever rank, recognizing only the grand master, who is their sovereign, and the chapter, which is their council.

Below this class, there is an intermediate one whose members take offices and seek the protection of the knights. The ladies of this class are independent and are designated by the title of *onorate*, which means 'honoured' in Italian. And they certainly deserve this title through the propriety of their behaviour and, to be perfectly frank with you, through the secretiveness in which they shroud their love affairs.

Long experience has taught the lady *onorata* that discretion is incompatible with the character of French knights, or at least that it is extremely rare to find discretion combined with all the other fine qualities which distinguish them. The result of this is that young gentlemen of that nation who are used to enjoying brilliant success with the fair sex, have to make do with prostitutes in Malta.

The not very numerous German knights are those who please the *onorate* most. I believe this to be because of their pink and white complexions. After them come the Spanish knights, and I believe we owe this to our character, which is justly reputed to be honest and dependable.

The French knights, and especially the caravanists,[2] take revenge on the *onorate* by making fun of them in all sorts of ways, most especially by revealing their secret liaisons. But as they stick together and do not bother to learn Italian, which is the language of the country, whatever they say makes little impression.

So it was that we were living together peacefully, as were our *onorate*, when a French vessel brought us the Commander de Foulequère, of the ancient house of the Seneschals of Poitou, themselves descended from the Counts of Angoulême. He had previously spent time in Malta and had often been involved in affairs of honour. He

2 A junior rank in the order.

526

had now come to solicit the post of grand admiral. He was over thirty-five years old. He was therefore expected to be of steadier character, and indeed the commander did not seek quarrels and make trouble as he had done before, but he was haughty, imperious, even factious, aspiring to more consideration than the grand master himself.

The commander kept open house. The French knights flocked there. We seldom would go there, and ended up by not going at all because we found the conversation would turn on subjects which we found distasteful, including the subject of the *onorate* whom we loved and respected.

When the commander appeared in public he was accompanied by a crowd of young caravanists. He would often lead them to the *via stretta*,[3] show them the places where he had fought and retail to them all the details of his duels.

I must tell you that according to our customs duelling is forbidden in Malta except in the *via stretta*, which is an alley not overlooked by any windows. It is only wide enough to allow two men to take guard and cross swords. They cannot step back. The adversaries face each other across the street. Their friends stop passers-by and prevent the duellists from being disturbed. This custom was introduced in former times to prevent murders, for a man who believes himself to have an enemy does not go down the *via stretta*, and if a murder was committed elsewhere it couldn't be passed off as a duel. Besides, the death penalty is passed on anyone who comes to the *via stretta* with a dagger. So duelling is not only tolerated in Malta but even permitted. However, this permission is, so to speak, a tacit one. And far from being abused, it is spoken of with a sort of shame, as though it were offensive to Christian charity and improper in the headquarters of a monastic order.

The commander's strolls down the *via stretta* were altogether out of place. They had the bad effect of making the French caravanists very quarrelsome, which they were anyway very inclined to be.

The bad atmosphere grew worse. The Spanish knights became

3 The French text has *rue étroite*.

more reserved than before. In the end, they came together to my house and asked me what was to be done to put a stop to this wild behaviour, which was becoming altogether intolerable. I thanked my compatriots for the honour they had done me by placing their trust in me, and I promised to speak to the commander about it and point out to him that the behaviour of the young Frenchmen was a sort of abuse to which he alone could put a stop because of the great consideration and respect in which he was held in the three 'langues' of his nation. I promised myself to be as circumspect as was possible in the way I expressed this, but I had no hope of ending the affair without a duel. However, as the issue of this single combat did me honour I was not too upset about it.

In a word, I believe that I was motivated by an antipathy which I felt for the commander.

We were then in Holy Week, and it was agreed that my conversation with the commander would not take place for a fortnight. I think that he knew what had taken place in my house, and he wanted to forestall me by picking a quarrel with me.

We reached Good Friday. According to Spanish custom, as you know, if one has an attachment to a lady, one follows her on that day from church to church to offer her holy water. This is partly done out of jealousy in case someone else might offer it to her and take the opportunity to make her acquaintance. This Spanish custom had been introduced into Malta. So it was that I was following a young *onorata* to whom I had been attached for some years. But at the very first church which she entered the commander accosted her before me, placing himself between us, turning his back on me and stepping backwards from time to time, treading on my toes, all of which was noticed.

On the way out of church I accosted my man in a casual way as if to exchange views with him. I then asked him which church he intended to go to. He named it. I offered to show him the shortest way and I led him without his noticing into the *via stretta*. Once there I drew my sword, quite certain, as it happened, that no one would disturb us on such a day when everyone is in church.

The commander also drew his sword but he lowered his guard. 'What?' he said. 'On Good Friday?'

528

I resolutely paid no attention.

'Look here,' he said, 'it is more than six years since I fulfilled my religious duties. I am horrified by the state of my conscience. In three days . . .'

I am of a pacific temperament and, as you know, once people of such a nature lose their temper they will not hear reason. I forced the commander to take guard, but terror was written on his features. He retreated to the wall as if foreseeing that he would be struck down. He was already looking for support; and indeed with my first pass I ran him through with my sword.

He lowered his guard, leant against the wall and said in a dying voice, 'I forgive you. May heaven forgive you! Take my sword to Tête-Foulque and have a hundred masses said for me in the castle chapel.'

He died. I did not at that moment pay great attention to his last words. If I have retained them it was because I have since heard them repeated. I made my declaration in the usual form. I am able to say that in the eyes of men the duel did me no harm. Foulequère was detested and was thought to have deserved his fate, but it seemed to me that in the eyes of God my action was very reprehensible because the sacraments had not been taken. My conscience reproached me cruelly. This lasted a week.

In the night between Friday and Saturday I was woken with a start and, looking round me, seemed no longer to be in my room, but lying on the stones in the middle of the *via stretta*. I was still feeling surprised at finding myself there when I distinctly saw the commander leaning against the wall. The spectre seemed to make an effort to speak. He said to me, 'Take my sword to Tête-Foulque and have a hundred masses said for me in the castle chapel.'

No sooner had I heard these words than I fell into a lethargic sleep. Next day I awoke in my own room and bed but I had a perfect recollection of my vision.

The next night I had a valet sleep with me in my room and I saw nothing, either then or the following nights. But on the night between Friday and Saturday I had the same vision again, the only difference being that I saw my valet lying on the stones a few yards from me. The spectre of the commander appeared to me and said the same things. The same vision repeated itself every Friday. On such occasions my valet dreamed that he was lying in the *via stretta* but, that apart, he neither saw nor heard the commander.

At first I did not know what this Tête-Foulque was to which the commander wanted me to take his sword. Some knights from Poitou told me that it was a castle three leagues from Poitiers in the middle of a forest; many extraordinary things were told about it in that part of the country; it contained many curious objects such as the armour of Foulque-Taillefer and the arms of the knights he had killed; and it was a custom of the house of Foulequère to deposit there the arms they had used either in war or in single combat. I found all this interesting but I had to look to my conscience.

I went to Rome and confessed to the grand penitentiary. I revealed to him my vision, which still haunted me. He did not refuse me absolution but he made it conditional on the performance of my penance. The hundred masses in the castle of Tête-Foulque formed part of it, but heaven accepted this offering and from the moment of my confession I stopped being haunted by the spectre of the commander. I had brought his sword from Malta with me and as soon as I could I set out for France.

When I reached Poitiers I discovered that the commander's death was already known and that his passing was no more regretted there than in Malta. I left my coach and horses in the town, dressed as a pilgrim and took a guide. It was appropriate to go to Tête-Foulque on foot and in any case the road was not practicable for carriages.

We found the door of the keep locked. For a long time we rang at the belfry. Eventually the castellan appeared. He was the only inhabitant of Tête-Foulque other than a hermit who ministered in the chapel, whom we found at prayer. When he had finished I told him that I had come to ask him to say a hundred masses. At the same time I put my offering on the altar and wanted also to leave the commander's sword there, but the castellan told me that it had to be put in the armoury with all the other swords, both of members of the Foulequère family killed in duels and of those killed by them. That was the sacred custom.

I followed the castellan into the armoury and indeed found there swords of every shape and size, together with family portraits beginning with the portrait of Foulque-Taillefer, Count of Angoulême, who built Tête-Foulque for a *manzier* of his, that is to say, a bastard, and who became Seneschal of Poitou and progenitor of the Foulequère de Tête-Foulque.

The portraits of the seneschal and his wife were on either side of a great fireplace in the corner of the armoury. They were very lifelike. The other portraits were equally well painted, although in the style of their age. But none was as striking as that of Foulque-Taillefer. He was dressed in a buff coat with his sword in his hand, grasping his rondache, which a squire was presenting to him. Most of the swords were attached to the bottom of this portrait, where they formed a sort of bundle.

I asked the castellan to light a fire in the room and to bring me my supper there.

'As for supper,' he replied, 'I am quite happy to do that, but, dear pilgrim, I entreat you to sleep in my room.'

I asked him the reason for this precaution.

'I know what I am doing,' said the castellan. 'I shall in any case make up a bed for you next to mine.'

I was all the more pleased to accept his proposal as it was Friday and I feared a recurrence of my vision.

The castellan went away to attend to my supper and I started to look at the arms and the portraits. These were, as I have said, very lifelike. As the daylight faded, the dark hangings became indistinguishable in the shadows from the dark background of the pictures, and the firelight picked out only the faces, which was somewhat frightening; or perhaps it seemed frightening to me because my conscience left me in a perpetual state of fear.

The castellan brought me my supper, which consisted of a dish of trout which had been caught in a nearby stream. I had a very reasonable bottle of wine as well. I asked the hermit to join me at table but he lived solely off boiled herbs.

I have always read my breviary punctiliously, which is obligatory for professed knights, at least in Spain, so I took it out of my pocket together with my rosary and said to the castellan that, as I did not feel drowsy, I would stay where I was to pray until later in the night. All he need do was to show me my bedroom.

'Very well,' he said. 'The hermit will come to pray in the adjoining chapel at midnight. Then you will go down the small staircase and you cannot miss my bedroom; I shall leave the door open. Do not stay here after midnight.'

The castellan went away. I started praying and from time to time put a log on the fire, though I did not dare to look too closely around the room because the portraits seemed to me to be coming to life. If I stared at them for a few seconds they looked as though they blinked and twisted their mouths, especially the seneschal and his wife, who were on either side of the fireplace. I fancied that they were casting angry glances at me and then looking at each other. A sudden gust of wind added to my terror. Not only did it rattle the windows, it also shook the bundle of swords, whose clinking made me tremble. Meanwhile I was praying fervently.

At last I heard the hermit intoning a psalm. When he had finished I went down the stairs towards the castellan's bedroom. I had the stub of a candle in my hand. The wind blew it out, and I went upstairs to light it again. You can imagine my astonishment on seeing that the seneschal and his wife had come down from their picture frames and were sitting by the fire. They were talking in familiar tones to each other, and one could hear what they were saying.

'My Lady,' the seneschal said, 'what think you of the Castilian who hath slain the commander but granted him not leave to seek shrift?'

'Methinks,' said the female ghost, 'methinks, my love, that he hath thereby committed felony and wickedness. Thus think I that Messire Taillefer will not let the Castilian hie away from the castle but that he throw down the gauntlet.'

I was terrified and rushed headlong down the stairs. I searched for the castellan's door but could not find it by feeling my way to it. In my hand I still held the candle which had gone out. I thought of lighting it again and took heart somewhat. I tried to convince myself that the two figures I had seen by the fire had only existed in my imagination. I went back up the stairs and, pausing outside the door of the armoury, saw that the two figures were indeed not by the fireside where I had imagined seeing them. So I boldly went in, but had not taken more than a few paces when I saw before me in the middle of the room Messire Taillefer, who had taken guard and was presenting the point of his sword to me.

I wanted to retreat to the staircase but the door was blocked by a squire, who threw down a gauntlet. Not knowing what to do next, I seized a sword from the bundle of arms and fell upon my fantastical enemy. I thought I had split him in two, but at once I was pierced by a blow below the heart which burned me like a red-hot iron. My blood spilled all over the room and I fainted.

I woke up in the morning in the castellan's bedroom. Seeing that I had not come down, he had armed himself with holy water and gone to fetch me. He found me lying on the floor, unconscious but without any wound. The wound I thought I had suffered was only sorcery. The castellan asked me no questions but merely advised me to leave the castle.

I left and set off for Spain. It took me a week to get to Bayonne, which I reached on a Friday. I lodged in an inn. In the middle of the night I awoke with a start and saw Messire Taillefer at the bottom of my bed, threatening me with his sword. I made the sign of the cross and the spectre seemed to dissolve into smoke. But I felt a blow the same as the one I imagined having received in the castle of Tête-Foulque. I seemed to be bathed in my own blood. I tried to cry out and leave my bed, but I could do neither. This indescribable anguish lasted until cockcrow, when I fell asleep again. But the next day I was ill and in a pitiable state. I have had the same vision every Friday since. No acts of devotion have been able to rid me of them. Melancholy will drive me to my grave, and I will be laid there before I am able to free myself from Satan's power. A vestige of hope in divine mercy still sustains me and helps me endure my ills.

That is how the Commander of Toralva's story finished, or rather, how the reprobate pilgrim's account of it to Cornádez ended. Then he once more took up the thread of his own story:

The Commander of Toralva was a devout man. Although he had offended against his religion by fighting a duel without letting his adversary put his conscience in order, I had no trouble in making him see that if he wanted to free himself from diabolical hauntings it was necessary to visit the holy places that sinners never visit without finding the consolation of grace. Toralva was easily persuaded of this. We visited together the holy places of Spain. Then we went to Italy and saw Loreto and Rome. The grand penitentiary gave him not just conditional but general absolution, together with a papal indulgence. Toralva, now completely freed of his hallucinations, went to Malta, and I have come to Salamanca.

From the first time I set eyes on you, I saw on your forehead the mark of reprobation and your whole story has been disclosed to me. The Conde de Peña Flor had indeed had the intention of seducing and possessing all women but he had neither seduced nor possessed any of them, so having committed only sins of intention his soul was not in danger. But for two years he had neglected his religious duties and was on the way to fulfil them when you had him murdered, or at least were an accessory to his murder. This is the reason for the haunting which torments you. There is only one way to be rid of it, which is to follow the commander's example. I will serve as your guide. As you know, my own salvation depends on it.

Cornádez was convinced. He visited the shrines of Spain, then those of Italy. He spent two years in pilgrimage. Señora Cornádez spent this time in Madrid, where her mother and sister had settled.

Cornádez came back to Salamanca. He found his house in excellent order and his wife agreeable, sweet-natured and yet more beautiful. Two months later she went again to Madrid to see her mother and sister, and then came back to Salamanca, where she ended by staying permanently when the Duke of Arcos was appointed to the embassy in London.

At this point the Knight of Toledo spoke up and said, 'My dear Busqueros, I don't think you have fully acquitted yourself yet. I want to hear the end of this story and know what has become of Señora Cornádez.'

'She became a widow,' said Busqueros. 'Then she remarried, and her conduct is exemplary. But look, here she comes. I think she is on her way to your house.'

'What!' exclaimed Toledo. 'The person you are pointing out is

Señora Uscariz. What a woman! She had convinced me that I was her first love. She'll pay for that!' The knight, wishing to be alone with his mistress, hurriedly dismissed us.

'And I am forced to leave you to look to the affairs of my little people,' added the gypsy.

The Fifty-fourth Day

The next day we reassembled at the usual hour and asked the gypsy to take up the thread of his story again, which he did as follows:

∽ THE GYPSY CHIEF'S STORY CONTINUED ∽

Toledo, knowing now the true story of Señora Uscariz, indulged for some time in the mischievous pleasure of speaking to her of Frasqueta Cornádez as a charming woman whose acquaintance he would love to make, the only woman who could make him happy and secure his affections for good. But in the end he lost interest in all love affairs including that with Señora Uscariz.

As his family enjoyed the favour of the court, the office of Prior of Castile was destined for Toledo. It became vacant, so the knight hurried off to Malta. For a time I lost a protector who could oppose Busqueros's plans for my father's great inkpot. I was a spectator of the whole intrigue without being able to put obstacles in its way. This is how it came about.

At the beginning of my story I told you that every morning my father would go out on to a balcony overlooking the Calle de Toledo to take the air. He then would go to another balcony which looked out over a narrow street, and when he saw his neighbours opposite he would greet them by saying 'Agour'. He did not like to go back into his house without having given this greeting. His neighbours would hurry out to receive his compliment in order not to hold him up too long. Otherwise he had no contact with them.

These good neighbours moved away and were replaced by the Señoras Cimiento, who were distant relatives of Don Roque Busqueros. The aunt, Señora Cimiento, was a person of forty years of age with a fresh complexion and a calm, gentle manner. Her niece,

536

Señorita Cimiento, was tall and well-built, with quite nice eyes and very beautiful arms.

The two ladies took possession of their apartment as soon as it was empty and, when the next day my father came to the balcony over-looking the narrow street, he was charmed to see them on the balcony opposite. They received his greeting and returned it most graciously. This surprise was a pleasant one for him. None the less, he withdrew again into his apartment and the ladies withdrew on their side.

This polite exchange remained on the same footing for a week. At the end of this period my father caught sight of an object in Señorita Cimiento's room which excited his curiosity. It was a small, glazed cupboard containing jars and crystal bottles. Some looked as though they were filled with the brightest colours for use in dyeing, others with gold dust, silver dust or powdered lapis lazuli, others with a golden varnish. The cupboard was placed near the window. Señorita Cimiento, dressed in a plain bodice, would come to fetch first one bottle then another. But what did she do with them? My father was unable to guess, and he wasn't in the habit of seeking information. He preferred not to know about things.

One day Señorita Cimiento was writing near the window. Her ink was thick; she poured water into it and made it so thin that it was impossible to use. Moved by feelings of courtesy, my father filled a bottle with ink and sent it to her. His maid came back with thanks and a cardboard box containing twelve sticks of sealing-wax, all of different colours. On them had been impressed ornaments and devices in a most accomplished way. So my father found out how Señorita Cimiento spent her time; and her work, analogous to his, was, as it were, its complement. The quality of the manufacture of the waxes was even higher than that of his ink. Full of approbation, he folded down an envelope, wrote an address on it with his fine ink and sealed it with his new wax, which took the impression perfectly. He put the envelope on the table and did not tire of contemplating it.

That evening he went to Moreno's shop. A man he did not know brought a box similar to his, with the same number of sticks. They were tried out and aroused universal admiration. My father thought about them the whole evening and that night he dreamed about sealing-wax.

The next morning he uttered his customary greeting. He even opened his mouth to say more, but in the end he said nothing and went back into his apartment, where he took up a position from which he could observe what was going on in that of Señorita Cimiento. The young lady was examining with a magnifying glass all the furniture being cleaned by the servant and whenever she discovered a speck of dust she made her begin again. The cleanliness of his room mattered a great deal to my father. The trouble he saw his nice neighbour taking gave him a great deal of respect for her.

I have said that my father's main pastime was to smoke cigars and to count either the passers-by or the tiles on the palacio de Alba. But already, instead of spending hours doing this, he spent hardly a few minutes. A powerful force of attraction constantly drew him to the balcony overlooking the narrow street.

Busqueros was the first to notice this change and in my presence said confidently several times that Don Felipe Avadoro would soon recover his real name and lose the nickname del Tintero Largo. Although little versed in legal matters, I supposed that a second marriage by my father would scarcely be to my advantage, so I rushed to see Aunt Dalanosa and begged her to do something to avert this calamity. Genuinely saddened by the news I brought her, my aunt went back to see Uncle Sántez. The Theatine replied, however, that marriage was a divine sacrament with which he could not interfere, although he promised to see that my interests would not be harmed by it.

The Knight of Toledo had been living for some time on Malta, so I was forced to be an impotent spectator of the progress of this affair, and had sometimes to hasten its progress when Busqueros entrusted me with letters to his relatives, whom he never visited himself.

Señora Cimiento neither made nor received visits. For his part, my father went out less frequently. He would not readily have changed the pattern of his days and given up attending the theatre, but the least cold gave him the excuse of staying at home. On those days he would rarely leave the side of his apartment looking out on to the narrow street and he would look at Señorita Cimiento lining up the bottles and even the sticks of sealing-wax. Her beautiful arms, which

538

were continually on view, captivated his imagination. He could think of nothing else.

A new object appeared to excite his curiosity. It was a jar quite like that in which he put his ink, but it was much smaller and was placed on an iron trivet. Lamps burning underneath kept it at a moderate heat. Soon two other similar jars were set up alongside the first. The next day, when my father appeared on the balcony and said 'Agour', he opened his mouth in order to ask what the jars were for. But as he was not in the habit of speaking he said nothing and went back inside.

Tormented by curiosity, he decided to send Señorita Cimiento another bottle of ink. Three crystal bottles filled with red, green and blue ink were sent back to him.

The next day my father went to Moreno's the bookseller's. A man appeared, a clerk in the ministry of finance, who carried under his arm a statement of balances in tabular form; some columns were in red ink, the headings were in blue ink and the lines in green ink. The clerk of finances said that he alone knew the composition of his inks and he challenged anyone to show him similar ones.

Someone whom my father did not know turned to him and said, 'Señor Avadoro, you who can make black ink so well, could you make inks of such colours?'

My father did not like to be challenged and was easily embarrassed. He opened his mouth to reply but said nothing. He preferred to go home to fetch the three bottles. Their contents were much admired and the clerk of finances asked permission to take samples of them. Overwhelmed with praises, my father privately accorded the glory to fair Señorita Cimiento, whose name he did not yet know. Once home, he fetched his recipe book and found three recipes for green ink, seven for red and two for blue. They all became confused in his head, but the beautiful arms of Señorita Cimiento were clearly etched in his imagination. His dormant senses were aroused and made him aware of their power.

The next day, as he greeted the ladies, my father finally felt a resolute wish to know their names and he opened his mouth to ask them; however, he said nothing and went back inside. Then he went to the balcony overlooking the Calle de Toledo and saw quite a well-dressed man holding a black bottle in his hand. He realized that he had come to ask him for ink and stirred the contents of the jar well to give him some of good quality. The tap on the jar was a third of the way up so that there was no risk of drawing off the lees. The stranger entered and my father filled his bottle, but instead of going away the man put the bottle on a table, sat down and asked for permission to smoke a cigar. My father wanted to reply but said nothing. The stranger took a cigar from his box and lit it from a lamp which was on the table.

The stranger was none other than the implacable Busqueros. 'Señor Avadoro,' he said to my father, 'you make up a liquid here which has done much evil in the world. So many plots, so much treachery, so much trickery, so many wicked books – all have flowed from ink, not to speak of love-letters and all those little conspiracies against the happiness of husbands and against their honour. What do you say to that, Señor Avadoro? You say nothing, but it's your habit to say nothing. Never mind, I'll speak for both of us. That's my habit more or less. Now, Señor Avadoro, sit down on that chair and let me explain my idea to you. I claim that from this bottle of ink there will come out . . .'

As he said this, Busqueros pushed the bottle and ink spilled all over my father's knees; he went off to dry himself and change his clothes. On returning, he found Busqueros waiting to say goodbye, hat in hand. My father, delighted to see him go, went to open the door for him, and indeed Busqueros went out, but immediately returned.

'Well, Señor Avadoro,' he said, 'we are forgetting that my bottle is empty. But don't put yourself out, I'll fill it myself.'

Busqueros took a funnel, put it in the neck of the bottle and opened the tap. When the bottle was full my father went again to open the door, and Busqueros was quick to leave, but suddenly my father noticed that the tap was open and that ink was running into the room. My father rushed to turn off the tap. Then Busqueros came back in and, apparently without noticing the mess he had caused, put the bottle of ink on the table, sat down on the chair where he had sat before, took a cigar from his box and lit it.

'Now, Señor Avadoro,' he said to my father, 'I have heard it said that you had a son who drowned in this jar. Bless me, if he had known how to swim he would have survived. But where did you get this jar from? I think it's from Toboso. There is excellent soil there which is used in the manufacture of saltpetre. It's as hard as rock. Allow me to put it to the test with this pestle.'

My father tried to prevent the test but Busqueros hit the jar, which broke. The ink flooded out and covered my father and everything else in the room, Busqueros not excepted, who was bespattered from head to foot.

My father, who rarely made a sound, on this occasion made a very great sound indeed. His two lady neighbours appeared on their balcony.

'Oh, ladies!' cried Busqueros. 'A terrible accident has occurred. The great jar has broken. The room is awash with ink and Señor Tintero is at his wits' end. It will be an act of Christian charity if you would let us come over to your room.'

The ladies seemed very willing to consent to this and, in spite of his distress, my father felt some pleasure when he realized that he was going to be united with the pretty lady who from afar seemed to hold her beautiful arms outstretched to him and smile at him so graciously.

Busqueros threw a cloak over the shoulders of my father and led him across to the house of the Señoras Cimiento. He had hardly got there when he received a very unpleasant message. A cloth merchant whose shop was under his apartment came to tell him that the ink had gone through to his shop and that he had summoned a lawyer to certify the damage. The landlord had him informed at the same time that he would no longer put up with him in his house.

Banished from his house and bathed in ink, my father looked as woebegone as it is possible to look.

'Don't be upset, Señor Avadoro,' said Busqueros. 'These ladies have a complete apartment facing the courtyard which they do not use. I'll have your effects brought over. You will be very comfortable here and you'll find red, green and blue inks which are equal to your black. But I advise you not to go out in the near future, for if you go to Moreno's bookshop everyone will make you tell the story of the broken jar and you don't care much for talking. And see there, all the idlers of the district are now in your apartment to see the flood of ink. Tomorrow nothing else will be talked about all over Madrid.'

My father was dismayed but a gracious glance from Señorita Cimiento gave him new heart, and he went off to take possession of his apartment. He did not stay there long. Señora Cimiento went to see him and say that, having consulted with her niece, she would let him have the apartment that overlooked the street. My father, who took pleasure in counting the tiles on the roof of the palacio de Alba, was happy to agree to this change. He was asked whether he would allow the coloured inks to be left where they were. He expressed his consent by a nod. The jars were in the middle of the room. Señora Cimiento would come and go without making a sound, fetching the colours. The deepest silence would reign in the house. Never had my father been so happy.

Eight days went by in this way. On the ninth Don Busqueros called on him and said, 'Señor, I can tell you of a piece of good fortune which you hoped for without daring to declare yourself. You have touched the heart of Señorita Cimiento. She agrees to give you her hand. I have brought you a document to sign if you want the banns to be published on Sunday.'

Astonished, my father tried to reply but Busqueros did not leave him time.

'Señor Avadoro,' he said, 'your coming marriage is no longer a secret. All Madrid is informed of it, so if you intend to put it off the relatives of Señorita Cimiento will assemble in my house and you will come there and divulge to them the reasons for the delay. That is a courtesy you cannot dispense with.'

My father was thrown into consternation by the idea of addressing a whole family assembly. He was about to say something but Busqueros forestalled him.

'I know what it is, and I can understand you. You want to learn of your happiness from the very lips of Señorita Cimiento. I can see her coming. I'll leave you alone together.'

Señorita Cimiento came in, looking somewhat bashful and not daring to raise her eyes to my father. She took some colours and mixed them in silence. Her timidity gave heart to my father. He stared at her and could not look away. He saw her with different eyes.

Busqueros had left the document about the publication of banns on the table. Tremblingly, Señorita Cimiento went up to it, picked it up and read it, then she put her hand over her eyes and shed some tears. Since the death of my mother, my father had not wept and still less caused anyone else to weep. The tears which were addressed to him moved him all the more because he only dimly understood their cause.

Was Señorita Cimiento crying about the document itself or the lack of signature on it? Did she, or did she not, want to marry him? Meanwhile she went on crying. Leaving her to cry was altogether too cruel. Asking her to say what she thought would lead to a conversation. My father picked up a pen and signed the paper. Señorita Cimiento kissed his hand, took the paper and went away.

She came back to the drawing-room at the usual time, kissed my father's hand in silence and began to make sealing-wax. My father smoked cigars and counted the tiles on the palacio de Alba. My great-uncle, Fray Gerónimo Sántez, arrived towards midday and brought a marriage contract in which my interests were not neglected. My father signed it, Señorita Cimiento signed it, kissed my father's hand and went back again to making sealing-wax.

Since the destruction of his great ink-bottle, my father had not dared to show himself at the theatre, still less to appear at Moreno's bookshop. This reclusion wearied him. Three days had passed since the signature of the contract. Don Busqueros came to propose to my father a ride in a calèche. My father accepted. They went beyond the Manzanares and when they reached the little church of the Franciscans, Busqueros had my father step down. They went into the church and found Señorita Cimiento there, waiting for them in the porch. My father opened his mouth to say that he thought he was just going for a ride but he said nothing, took Señorita Cimiento's hand and led her to the altar.

Having left the church, the newly-married couple stepped into a fine carriage, returned to Madrid and went into a pretty house where a ball was being held. Señora Avadoro opened the ball, partnered by a very handsome young man. They danced a fandango and were much applauded. In vain my father searched in his wife for the sweet and calm person who kissed his hand with such a submissive air. What he saw on the contrary was a lively, noisy, flibbertigibbet.

543

Otherwise he said nothing to anybody and nobody spoke to him. This way of things did not displease him too much.

Cold meats and refreshments were served: then my father, who was exhausted, asked if it wasn't time to go home. He was told that he was there already, and that the house he was in belonged to him. My father supposed that the house was part of his wife's dowry; so he had himself shown to his bedroom and went to bed.

The next morning Señor and Señora Avadoro were woken by Busqueros.

'Señor, dear cousin,' he said to my father, 'I call you this because your good wife is the closest relative I have in the world, her mother being a Busqueros from the León branch of my family. Up to now I have not wanted to talk to you about your affairs but I expect from now on to attend to them more than I attend to my own, which will be all the easier for me since I haven't actually any particular business of my own. As far as you are concerned, Señor Avadoro, I have taken the trouble of informing myself in detail of your revenues and the use you have made of them over the last sixteen years. Here are all the relevant papers. At the time of your first marriage you had an income of four thousand pistoles and, by the way, you didn't manage to spend it all. You only kept for yourself six hundred pistoles and two hundred for the education of your son. So you had three thousand, two hundred pistoles over, which you placed in the Gremios bank. You gave the interest to Gerónimo the Theatine to be used for charitable purposes. I don't blame you on this account, but, bless me! (and I feel for the poor over this), they cannot count on this revenue any longer. First, we will manage to spend your annual income of four thousand pistoles and, as for the fifty-one thousand, two hundred deposited with the Gremios bank, this is how we will dispose of them. Eighteen thousand for this house. It's a lot, I admit, but the seller is one of my relatives and my relatives are yours, Señor Avadoro. The necklace and the earrings that you see on Señora Avadoro are worth eight thousand pistoles. As we are brothers we will put down ten thousand. I'll tell you why some day. That leaves us twenty-three thousand, two hundred pistoles. Your devil of a Theatine has reserved fifteen thousand for your urchin of a son, if he's ever found again. Five thousand to set up your house, for between ourselves your wife's trousseau consists of six shifts and as many stockings. You'll tell me you still have five thousand pistoles left, which you don't know what to do with. Well now, to get you out of your difficulty I'll agree to borrow them from you at a rate of interest to be agreed between us. And here's a power of attorney, which you will be so kind as to sign, Señor Avadoro.'

My father could not get over the surprise that Busqueros's words caused him. He opened his mouth to reply but, not knowing where to begin, he turned over in bed and pulled his nightcap over his eyes.

'Splendid!' said Busqueros. 'You're not the first person who thought that he could get rid of me by putting on his nightcap and pretending to want to sleep. I'm used to these ways and always keep a nightcap in my pocket. I shall just settle down on that sofa and when we've all had a little nap we'll come back to the power of attorney. Or, if you prefer, we'll bring together your relatives and mine and we'll see what there is to be done.'

With his head buried in his pillow, my father thought seriously about the situation and the policy he should adopt to ensure his tranquillity. He saw that if he left his wife completely free, he might be allowed to live after his own manner: to go to the theatre, then to Moreno's bookshop and he might even make some ink. Somewhat consoled, he opened his eyes and indicated that he would sign the power of attorney.

So he actually signed it and made as if to get up.

'Wait a moment, Señor Avadoro,' said Busqueros. 'Before you get up, it will be appropriate for me to inform you of the programme of your day. I believe that it won't displease you, as today, like those which will follow, will be nothing but a series of lively and varied pleasures. First, I have brought you a fine pair of embroidered gaiters and a complete riding outfit. A decent palfrey awaits you at your door. We will go together and parade a bit around the Prado. Señora Avadoro will come in a *chaise roulante*. You will discover that she has illustrious friends in society who will be yours too, Señor Avadoro. To tell you the truth, they had grown rather cool towards her but seeing her married to a man of your quality they'll change their mind about their attitude. I'm telling you the highest gentlemen of the

545

court will seek you out, will wait on you and will embrace you. More than that, they'll throttle you with embraces.'

At this my father fainted, or at least fell into a state of stupor very similar to a faint.

Busqueros did not notice but continued to speak. 'Some of these gentlemen will do you the honour of inviting themselves to your table to eat your soup. Yes, Señor Avadoro, they will do you this honour and that's where I'll expect you to be. You'll see how well your wife will do the honours of the house. Ah, bless me! You won't recognize the person who made sealing-wax. You're not saying a word, Señor Avadoro! You're right to leave me to speak. Now, for example, you like the Spanish theatre but you've never been to the Italian opera, which is all the rage at court. Well, you'll go this evening and guess in whose box you'll be? In that of the Duke of Ihar, Master of the Horse, no less. From there we'll go on to the *tertulia*[1] of His Highness, where you'll see all the court. Everyone will speak to you. Make sure that you have an answer ready!'

My father had recovered the use of his senses, but a cold sweat emanated from all his pores. His arms stiffened, the back of his neck grew tense, his head fell back, his eyelids opened abnormally wide, his constricted chest gave out stifled groans and he began to have convulsions. Eventually Busqueros noticed the state he was in and called for help, then rushed off to the Prado, where he was joined by my stepmother.

My father had fallen into a state of lethargy. When he emerged from it, he recognized no one except for his wife and Busqueros. When he saw them, fury was written all over his features. Otherwise, he was calm, remained silent and refused to leave his bed. When he was absolutely obliged to do so, he seemed pierced through with cold and shivered for half an hour. Soon the symptoms grew more troublesome. The patient could only take food in very small quantities. A convulsive spasm constricted his throat, his tongue was stiff and swollen, his eyes were dull and haggard, his skin was dark yellow, covered with white tubercles.

1 Soirée.

I had slipped into the house in the guise of a servant and I sadly charted the course of his illness. My Aunt Dalanosa was in my confidence and spent many nights by his bedside. The patient did not seem to recognize her. As for my stepmother, it was clear that her presence was very bad for the patient. Father Gerónimo encouraged her to leave for the provinces and Busqueros followed her there.

I thought of a last resort which might just lift the unhappy man out of his hypochondria. And indeed it had a short-lived success. One day, through a half-open door, my father caught sight of a jar very similar to the one which had once been used to manufacture his ink. Next to it was a table on which there were various ingredients and scales to weigh them. A sort of hilarity crossed my father's features. He got out of bed, went up to the table and asked for a chair. As he was very weak, others performed the operations in front of him and he followed the various procedures. The next day he was able to take part in the work and the day after there were even more hopeful signs.

But a few days later a fever manifested itself which had absolutely nothing to do with his illness. The symptoms were not distressing, but the patient's weakness was such that he could not resist the slightest affliction. He passed away without having been able to recognize me, however hard people had tried to make him remember his son. And that was the end of a man who wasn't born with even the degree of physical and mental strength sufficient to give him an average amount of energy. A sort of instinct had led him to choose a way of life which was proportionate to his powers. He was killed by people wishing to propel him into active life.

It is time to return to my affairs. My two years of penance were nearly over. In deference to Fray Gerónimo, the Inquisition allowed me to take my name back on the condition that I would do a spell as a caravanist on the galleys of Malta, which I accepted joyfully, hoping that I would encounter the Knight of Toledo, not as a servant but more or less as his equal. And to tell you the truth I was tired of wearing rags. I kitted myself out with luxury, trying on all my clothes at my Aunt Dalanosa's house, who died of joy at the sight of them. I left very early one morning to keep my transformation from the eyes of the curious. I embarked at Barcelona and reached Malta after a short voyage. My meeting with the knight gave me even more pleasure than I expected.

The knight assured me that he had never been fooled by my disguise and that he had always counted on making me his friend once I had reverted to my original rank. He was captain of a galley. He took me on board and we sailed the seas for four months without inflicting much harm on the Barbary pirates, whose light vessels could easily outrun us.

That is the end of the story of my childhood. I have related it to you in all its details for they have remained engraved on my memory. It still seems to me that I can see the cell of the Theatine teacher at Burgos, and the stern profile of Father Sanudo. I can still feel what it was like to eat chestnuts in front of the portal of St Roch and to hold out my hand to the noble Knight of Toledo. I won't tell you the story of my early manhood in the same detail. Whenever my imagination transports me back to the most brilliant part of my life, all I can perceive is a hotchpotch of all kinds of passions, their tumult and their turmoil. The feelings which then filled my soul and raised it up towards a secret happiness have sunk into the deepest oblivion. It is true that I can still see, shining through the mist, the rays of requited love, but those to whom this love was directed have merged into a single blurred image, in which I see only tender, beautiful women and merry girls with their snow-white arms around my neck. I can even see gloomy duennas unable to resist this moving sight, bringing together lovers they should have kept for ever apart. I can see the light I so fervently watched for signalling to me from a window, and the secret staircases leading me to hidden doors. How supremely blissful those moments were! Four o'clock strikes, the day dawns and lovers must part. Alas! Even partings had their sweetness. The story of youthful love is, I believe, the same all over the world. My amorous adventures could not really interest you, but I think you will be willing to listen to the story of my first real passion. The circumstances are astonishing. They might even be thought to be miraculous. But the day is growing late and I have still to think about the business of my band. Please allow me to begin again tomorrow.

The Fifty-fifth Day

We reassembled at the usual hour and the gypsy, having nothing else to do, continued his story as follows:

✑ THE GYPSY CHIEF'S STORY CONTINUED ✑

The following year the Knight of Toledo was made the supreme commander of the galleys, and his brother sent him six hundred piastres for his expenses. The order then possessed six galleys: Toledo himself paid for two others to be equipped. Six hundred knights, the flower of European youth, assembled. The practice of giving uniforms to soldiers, which hadn't been the case before, began at that time in France. Toledo gave us half-Spanish, half-French costumes. We wore scarlet habits, black breastplates with the Maltese cross at the middle, ruffs and Spanish hats. This costume suited us very well. Wherever we appeared, women never left their windows and duennas came running to us with love-letters, often delivered to the wrong person. Such confusion led to the most amusing incidents. We visited all the ports in the Mediterranean and were fêted everywhere.

Amid these revels I attained my twentieth year. Toledo was ten years older.

The Knight of Toledo had become *grand bailli* and sub-prior of Castile. Arrayed in his new honours, he left Malta and invited me to travel with him round Italy. I happily consented. We embarked for Naples, which we reached without incident. We would have found it more difficult to leave if pretty women had found it as easy to keep, as it was to catch, charming Toledo in their snares. But Toledo's greatest art was to abandon the ladies without their ever having the heart to be angry with him for it. So he left his Neapolitan loves and accepted new chains in Florence, Milan, Venice and Genoa in turn. It was the following year before we reached Madrid.

As soon as we had arrived, Toledo went to pay court to the king. Then he took the finest horse from the stable of his brother, the Duke of Lerma. I was given one which was scarcely less fine, and we went to join the company parading alongside the carriage-doors of the ladies in the Prado.

A superb coach and horses met our eyes. It was an open carriage occupied by two ladies in half-mourning. Toledo recognized the proud Duchess of Avila and at once paid court to her. The other lady turned towards him. He did not know her and seemed struck by her beauty.

This stranger was none other than the beautiful Duchess of Sidonia, who had just abandoned her retirement and rejoined society. She recognized her former prisoner and put a finger to her mouth to recommend that I should remain silent. Then she turned her beautiful eyes to Toledo, whose own took on a certain grave and shy expression which I had never seen before when he looked at women. The Duchess of Sidonia had declared that she would never marry again, the Duchess of Avila that she would never marry at all. Knights of Malta were exactly what they required as company. They made advances to Toledo, who accepted them with the best grace in the world. The Duchess of Sidonia, without letting it be seen that she knew me, managed to have me accepted by her friend. We formed a sort of foursome, who were always to be found in the hurly-burly of any festivity. Toledo was loved for the hundredth time in his life; he loved for the first. I set out to pay respectful homage to the Duchess of Avila. But before speaking to you about my relations with this lady, I should say a few words about the situation she found herself in at that time.

Her father, the Duke of Avila, had died during our time on Malta. The end of an ambitious man always causes a great stir. His fall is great; people are moved and surprised by it. In Madrid people recalled the Infanta Beatriz and her secret union with the duke. There was talk of a son on whom rested the future of the house of Avila. The will of the late duke was expected to shed some light on matters, but this expectation was frustrated. The will made nothing any clearer. The court spoke no more about the affair, but the proud Duchess of Avila returned to society more haughty, more disdainful and less inclined to marry than before.

I was born of good gentlemanly stock, but in Spanish eyes there could be no sort of equality between the duchess and me and if she deigned to have me near her it could only be as a protégé whose fortunes she wished to advance. Toledo was the knight of the sweet Duchess of Sidonia. I was, as it were, the squire of her friend.

This degree of servitude did not displease me. Without betraying my love, I was able swiftly to anticipate Manuela's desires, to carry out her orders – in short, to devote myself to her every wish. In serving my sovereign lady, I took good care that no word, look or sigh betrayed the feelings of my heart. The fear of offending her, and still more of being banished from her presence, gave me the strength to master my passion. Throughout the period of this sweet bondage the Duchess of Sidonia missed no opportunity of raising me in her friend's esteem. But the favours she obtained for me extended at most to an affable smile which expressed no more than protection.

This lasted more than a year. I would see the duchess in church, and in the Prado; I would take her orders for the day; I never went to her palace.

One day she summoned me. She was surrounded by her ladies and was engaged in needlework. She made me sit down and, adopting a haughty tone, said to me, 'Señor Avadoro, I would do little honour to the blood of which I was born if I did not use my family's influence to reward the respects which daily you pay me. My Uncle Sorriente has himself made this remark to me and has offered you the brevet of colonel in the regiment of his name. Will you do him the honour of accepting? Think about it.'

'Señora,' I replied, 'my fortunes are bound up with those of my friend, Toledo, and I seek only the employment which he will obtain for me. As for the respects which I am happy enough to pay you each day, their sweetest reward would be the permission to continue to pay them.'

The duchess did not reply but indicated by a slight bow that I should withdraw.

A week later I was summoned again to the house of the haughty duchess. She received me as before and said to me, 'Señor Avadoro, I cannot allow you to be more noble and generous than the Avilas, the

551

Sorrientes, and all the grandees whose blood flows in my veins. I have new proposals to put to you, to the advantage of your fortune. A gentleman whose family is connected with ours has made a great fortune in Mexico. He has an only daughter whose dowry is a million . . .'

I did not allow the duchess to finish her sentence, rose somewhat indignantly and said to her, 'Señora, although the blood of the Avilas and the Sorrientes does not run in my veins, the heart which they nourish is set too high for a million to touch it.'

I was about to retire, but the duchess asked me to sit down again. She first commanded her ladies to withdraw to the next room and to leave the door open. Then she said to me, 'Señor Avadoro, there is only one reward left for me to offer you, and your zeal for my interests leads me to hope that you will not refuse me. You will be doing me an essential service.'

'Indeed,' I replied, 'the happiness of serving you is the only reward that I shall ask you for my services.'

'Come closer,' said the duchess. 'We might be heard in the other room. Avadoro, you know, no doubt, that my father was secretly the husband of the Infanta Beatriz and perhaps you will have been told in great confidence that he had a son by her. My father actually spread that rumour, but it was to throw the courtiers off the scent. The truth is that he had a daughter, who is still alive. She was brought up in a convent near Madrid. On his deathbed my father revealed to me the secret of her birth, which she still does not know. He also explained what he had planned for her, but his death has brought all that to nothing.

'It would be impossible today to weave again the ambitious web of intrigue he had spun around her. The complete legitimation of my sister would, I think, be impossible to obtain and the first step we would take might lead to the perpetual reclusion of the poor girl. I have been to see her. Leonor is a nice girl, simple and gay, and I felt real fondness for her, but the abbess said so often that she looked like me that I have not dared to go back. However, I have declared myself to be her protector and let it be thought that she is one of the fruits of the many love affairs my father had while a young man. Recently the court has been having inquiries made in the convent, which make me uneasy and I have decided to have her brought to Madrid.

'I possess a modest house in the Calle Retrada. I have rented a house opposite. What I ask of you is to live there and to watch over the treasure which I am entrusting to you. Here is the address of your new lodgings and here is a letter which you will give to the abbess of the Ursulines del Peñón. You will take four horsemen and a chaise drawn by two mules. A duenna will accompany my sister and will stay with her. The duenna is the only person with whom you may have dealings. You will not have the right to enter the house; the daughter of my father and of an infanta should have at least a spotless reputation.'

After these words the duchess gave a slight nod, which for her was the signal to withdraw. So I left her and went to see my new lodgings. It was comfortable and well-appointed. I left two trusted servants there and kept the rooms I had in Toledo's house. As for the house I had inherited from my father, I let it go for four hundred piastres.

I also looked at Leonor's house. I found two maids, who were there to serve her, and an old retainer of the Avila family, who was not wearing livery. The house was generously and elegantly appointed with all that is necessary for living in town.

The next day I took four horsemen and went to the convento del Peñón. I was taken to the abbess's parlour.

She read my letter, smiled and sighed. 'Dear Jesus!' she said. 'Many sins are committed in the world. I am glad to have left it. For example, Señor caballero, the young lady you have come to fetch looks just like the Duchess of Avila. She's the very image of her! Two images of our sweet saviour do not look more alike. And who are the young lady's parents? It's not known. The late Duke of Avila, God rest his soul . . .'

It is probable that the abbess's chattering would have gone on much longer but I pointed out to her that I was in a hurry to fulfil my mission. The abbess shook her head, uttered many an 'Alas!' and a 'Dear Jesus!' and told me to speak to the sister gatekeeper. This I did. The gates of the convent were opened, two heavily veiled ladies came out and stepped into the chaise without uttering a word. I mounted my horse and followed them in silence. When we were near Madrid I took the lead and received the ladies at the door of their house. I did not go up but went to my lodgings across the street, from where I saw them take possession of theirs.

Leonor did indeed seem to me to bear a strong resemblance to the duchess, but her complexion was fairer. She had very blonde hair and looked plumper. So much I could tell from my window but Leonor was too restive to allow me to examine her features closely. She was so delighted to have escaped from the convent that she abandoned herself to unfettered joy. She ran all over the house from the attic to the cellar, uttering joyful cries at the sight of simple domestic objects, entranced by a fine poker or a cooking pot. She put a thousand questions to the duenna, who could not keep up with her. Soon after, the duenna had the blinds put up, locked them in place and I could see no more.

After dinner, I went to see the duchess and told her what I had done. She received me in her usual cold manner.

'Señor Avadoro,' she said, 'the plan is that Leonor should marry. According to our customs you could not be admitted into her house even if you were going to be her husband. However, I shall tell the duenna to leave a blind open on the side facing your windows. But I insist that your blinds must remain closed. You must report to me all that Leonor does. It will be dangerous for her to know you, especially if you have the distaste for marriage that you showed me the other day.'

'Señora,' I replied, 'I only said to you that self-interest would not make me marry. However, you are right. I do not expect to marry.'

I left the duchess and went to see Toledo, whom I did not make privy to our secrets, and from there I went to my lodgings in the Calle Retrada. The blinds of the house opposite and even the windows were open. Androdo, the old retainer, was playing the guitar. Leonor was dancing the bolero with a vivacity and grace which I would not have expected of a person who had been cloistered with the Carmelites, for she had been brought up by them, and had not entered the Ursuline house until after the death of the duke. Leonor was very wanton and playful. She tried to make her duenna dance with Androdo. I could not get over my astonishment at discovering that the grave Duchess of Avila had a sister of such a lively temperament. Otherwise the resemblance was remarkable. I was very much in love with the duchess and her living image could not fail to interest me deeply. I was indulging in the pleasure of watching her when the duenna closed the blind.

The next day I went to see the duchess. I told her what I had seen. I did not hide from her the great pleasure that the artless amusements of her sister had given me. I even dared to attribute my excessive joy to the strong family resemblance she bore.

As this seemed to be something a little like a declaration of love, the duchess looked angry. She grew yet more grave.

'Señor Avadoro,' she said, 'whatever the similarity between the two sisters I must ask you not to confuse them in the praises you may wish to make of them. However, you may come back tomorrow. I must make a journey and wish to see you before I leave.'

'Señora,' I said, 'even if your anger were to destroy me, your features are imprinted on my soul as might be the image of a goddess. You are too far above me for me to raise a single amorous thought towards you. But today I can find your divine features in a young lady who is gay, straightforward, simple, natural and who will prevent me from loving you in her.'

As I spoke the duchess's face grew more severe. I expected to be banished from her presence but I was not. She simply told me to come back the next day.

I dined with Toledo and went back to my post in the evening. The windows in the house opposite were open and I could see right into the apartment. Leonor was herself preparing an *olla podrida*. Every moment she asked the advice of her duenna. She cut the meat and arranged it on a plate. With bursts of laughter Leonor herself covered the table with a white cloth and laid two simple places. She was wearing only a plain bodice with the sleeves of her blouse rolled up to her shoulders.

The windows and blinds were then shut. But what I had seen had left a deep mark on me. What young man can gaze with indifference into the privacy of a young household? Such scenes are the reason why people get married.

I don't quite know what I stammered to the duchess the next day. She seemed to fear that it was a declaration of love and, hurriedly breaking in, she said, 'Señor Avadoro, I must leave, as I told you yesterday. I must spend some time in my duchy of Avila. I have allowed my sister to go for a walk after sunset without going too far from the house. If you want to accost her then, the duenna has been forewarned and will allow you to converse as much as you wish. Try to discover the mind and character of this young person. You will give me an account of them on my return.'

At that, a nod indicated that I should withdraw. It cost me dear to leave the duchess. I was really in love with her. Her extreme pride did not put me off: on the contrary, I thought that if she did decide to take a lover she would choose him from amongst those below her station, which in Spain is not uncommon. In short, something told me that the duchess might love me one day. But I really don't know where this feeling came from. Her behaviour towards me could not have given rise to it. I thought all that day about the duchess. Towards evening I began to think of her sister. I went to the Calle Retrada. In the bright moonlight I recognized Leonor and her duenna sitting on a seat near the door of their house. The duenna recognized me too, came towards me and invited me to sit down next to her charge. She then withdrew a little distance.

After a moment Leonor said, 'So you are the young man I am allowed to see. Will you like me?'

I replied that I already liked her a great deal.

'Well then, do me the pleasure of telling me my name.'

'Your name is Leonor.'

'That's not what I asked you. I must have another name. I am not as naïve as I was when I was with the Carmelites. I then thought that the whole world was inhabited only by nuns and confessors. But now I know that there are husbands and wives who do not leave each other night and day and that children bear the name of their father. That is why I want to know my name.'

As the Carmelites, especially in some of their houses, have a very strict rule, I was not surprised to see that Leonor had been kept in such ignorance up to the age of twenty. I replied to her that I knew her only by the name of Leonor. I then said that I had seen her dancing in her room and that she had certainly not learnt to dance with the Carmelites.

556

'No,' she replied. 'It's the Duke of Avila who put me in the Carmelite house. After his death I entered an Ursuline house, where one of the girls who resided there taught me how to dance and another to sing. As for the manner in which husbands live with their wives, all the girls in the Ursuline house spoke to me about it. It's no secret to them. As far as I'm concerned, I would like to have a name, and for that I shall have to marry.'

Then Leonor spoke to me about the theatre, about promenades, about bullfighting and evinced a great desire to see all these things. I had a few more conversations with her, always in the evening. After a week I received the following letter from the duchess:

> In bringing you together with Leonor, I hoped that she would form an attachment to you. The duenna assures me that my wishes have been fulfilled. If the devotion you have for me is genuine, you will marry Leonor. Consider that I shall take offence if you refuse.

I replied as follows:

> Señora,
> My devotion to Your Highness is the only feeling which can occupy my heart. The feelings which are due to a wife might find no more room there. Leonor deserves a husband whose thoughts are for her alone.

I received the following reply:

> It is futile to hide this from you any longer. You are dangerous for me. Your refusal of the hand of Leonor has given me the greatest pleasure I have ever felt in my life, but I am determined to triumph over myself. I therefore give you the choice of marrying Leonor or being for ever banished from my presence and perhaps from the shores of Spain. My power at court is great enough for that. Do not write to me again. The duenna has received my orders.

As much as I was in love with the duchess, so much arrogance justifiably angered me. For a moment I was tempted to confess all to Toledo and place myself under his protection, but Toledo was still in love with the Duchess of Sidonia, who was very much devoted to her friend and would not have supported me against her. So I decided to keep quiet and that evening went to the window to look at my future wife.

The windows were open and I could see right to the back of the room. Leonor was surrounded by four women, who were busy dressing her. She had a robe of white satin embroidered with silver, a crown of flowers and a necklace of diamonds. Over all that was placed a white veil, which covered her from head to toe.

All this surprised me somewhat. Soon my surprise increased. A table was carried from the back to the room and dressed like an altar. Candles were placed on it. A priest appeared, accompanied by two gentlemen who seemed to be there only as witnesses. The groom was still missing.

I heard a knock at my door: the duenna appeared. 'You are awaited,' she said. 'Did you think that you could resist the duchess's wishes?'

I followed the duenna. The bride did not lift her veil. Her hand was placed in mine. In a word, we were married.

The witnesses congratulated me and also my wife, whose face they had not seen, and withdrew. The duenna led us to a bedroom dimly lit by moonlight and shut the door behind her.

When the gypsy had reached this point in his story, one of his men asked to speak to him. He left us and we did not see him again that day.

The Fifty-sixth Day

We reassembled at the usual hour and the gypsy, having nothing else to do, continued his story as follows:

✍ THE GYPSY CHIEF'S STORY CONTINUED ✍

I have told you how my marriage was concluded. The manner in which I lived with my wife corresponded to the bizarreness of the wedding. After sunset the blinds would open and I could see into the whole of her apartment. She no longer went out at night and I had no means of accosting her. Towards midnight the duenna came to fetch me and accompanied me back to my house before daybreak.

A week later the duchess came back to Madrid. I went to see her again with some embarrassment. I had profaned her cult and reproached myself for it. She on the other hand treated me with extreme friendliness. Her pride disappeared when we were alone together. I was her brother and her friend.

One evening, as I reached home and was closing the door behind me, I felt a tug at my coat-tails. I turned round and saw Busqueros.

'Ah, I've caught you!' he said. 'Monsignor of Toledo told me that he wasn't seeing anything of you any more and that he wasn't informed of your comings and goings. I asked him to give me twenty-four hours to discover them and I have succeeded. Now, my boy, you owe me respect, for I have married your stepmother.'

These few words reminded me of how much Busqueros had contributed to the death of my father. I was unable to prevent myself showing him ill will. I got rid of him.

The next day I went to the duchess and told her of this tiresome encounter. She seemed very upset about it.

'Busqueros is a ferret; nothing escapes him,' she said. 'Leonor must be shielded from his curiosity. I shall have her leave for Avila this very day. Don't be angry with me, Avadoro. It's to ensure your happiness.'

'Señora,' I said to her, 'the idea of happiness seems to imply the fulfilment of one's desires and I never desired to be Leonor's husband. But it is true that I am now devoted to her and love her more each day – if I can use that word, for I never see her by day.'

The same evening I went to the Calle Retrada but found no one there. The door and shutters were closed.

Some days later Toledo summoned me to his study and said, 'Avadoro, I have spoken about you to the king. His Majesty is giving you a mission in Naples. That nice Englishman, Temple, has had me make overtures to him. He wants to see me in Naples and if I can't go, then he wants it to be you. The king does not think it appropriate that I should make the journey and wants to send you. But,' Toledo added, 'you don't seem very flattered at the prospect.'

'I am deeply flattered by the kindness of His Majesty. But I have a noble lady who protects me and I would not wish to do anything without her approval.'

Toledo smiled and said to me, 'I have spoken to the duchess. Go and see her this morning.'

I went. The duchess said to me, 'My dear Avadoro. You are aware of the present position of the Spanish monarchy. The king is close to death, and with him the line of Austria comes to an end. In such critical circumstances every good Spaniard should forget his own interests, and if he can serve his country he should not fail to grasp any opportunities of doing so. Your wife is in safety. She won't write to you for the Carmelites did not teach her to write. I shall act as her secretary. If I am to believe her duenna, I shall soon be in a position to give you news of something which will attach you even more closely to Leonor.'

As she uttered these words the duchess lowered her eyes, blushed and then indicated that I should withdraw. I took my instructions from the minister. They concerned foreign affairs and covered also the administration of the Kingdom of Naples, which it was hoped more than ever to tie to Spain. I left the next day and undertook the journey with all possible speed.

I devoted all the zeal to the performance of my mission that one

560

devotes to one's first employment, but in the intervals between my work memories of Madrid would dominate my thoughts. The duchess loved me in spite of what it cost her. She had admitted as much to me. Having become my sister-in-law, she had cured herself of the passionate side of her feelings, but she had preserved an attachment for me which she proved in countless ways. Leonor, the mysterious goddess of my nights, had presented me through marriage with the cup of sensual bliss. The memory of her ruled my senses as much as my heart. My regret at her absence turned almost to despair but except for these two ladies I felt only indifference for the fair sex.

The duchess's letters reached me in the official mail. They were not signed and the handwriting was disguised. From them I learnt that Leonor's pregnancy was progressing but that she was ill and above all else listless. Then I learnt that I was a father and that Leonor had suffered a great deal. What I was told about her health seemed couched in such a way as to prepare me for even sadder news.

Eventually Toledo appeared at the moment when I least expected him. He threw himself in my arms. 'I have come on royal business,' he said, 'but it's the duchesses who have sent me.'

As he said this he gave me a letter. I trembled as I opened it. I foresaw its contents. The duchess gave me the news of Leonor's death and offered me all the consolations of her most affectionate friendship.

Toledo, who for long had had a great influence over me, used it to restore calm to my mind. In a way I had not known Leonor at all, but she had been my wife and the idea of her was inseparable from the memory of the pleasures of our short union. My sorrow left me very melancholy and dejected.

Toledo took upon himself the running of affairs and as soon as they were concluded we returned to Madrid. When we were near the gates of the capital he had me get out and, taking a roundabout route, led me to the Carmelites' cemetery. There he showed me a black urn. On its base was written 'Leonor Avadoro'. I bathed this monument with my tears. I went back to it several times before going to see the duchess. She was not angry with me for this. On the contrary, on the first occasion I saw her she showed me an affection which resembled love. In due course she took me to her inner apartments and showed me a child in a cradle. I felt the most intense emotion. I knelt. The duchess held out her hand to help me up; I kissed it. She indicated that I should withdraw.

The next day I went to see the minister and with him the king. In sending me to Naples, Toledo had been seeking an excuse to have me granted honours. I was made Knight of Calatrava. This decoration, without promoting me to the first ranks of society, brought me none the less nearer to them. With Toledo and the two duchesses I was on a footing which no longer smacked of inferiority. Besides, I was their handiwork and they seemed to rejoice in my elevation.

Soon after, the Duchess of Avila gave me the task of following through an affair of hers in the Council of Castile. You can imagine with what zeal and care I did this. It increased the esteem I had already inspired in my patroness. I saw her every day, and daily she became more affectionate. And here the miraculous part of my story begins.

On my return from Italy I had taken up lodgings again with Toledo but the house that I had in the Calle Retrada had remained in my care. I had a servant called Ambrosio sleep there. The house opposite, the one in which I had been married, belonged to the duchess. It was closed and no one lived there. One morning Ambrosio came to ask me to put someone else in his place, someone who had to be courageous, since after midnight it was not good to be there, any more than in the house across the street.

I tried to find out from him what sort of apparitions there were but Ambrosio confessed to me that fear had prevented him from seeing anything clearly. Moreover he was determined never to sleep again in the Calle Retrada, either alone or in company. What he said excited my curiosity. I decided to venture there myself that same night. The house was still partially furnished. I went across to it after supper. I had a valet sleep on the staircase and myself occupied the room which looked on the street and was opposite Leonor's former house. I drank a few cups of coffee to keep myself from falling asleep and heard midnight strike. Ambrosio had told me that this was the hour at which the ghost appeared. In order not to frighten anything away I extinguished my candle. Soon I saw a light in the house opposite. It wandered from room to room and floor to floor. The blinds prevented me from seeing where the light was coming from. The next day I asked in the duchess's household for the keys to the house and went there. I found it completely empty and confirmed that it was not occupied. I unfastened the blind on every floor and then went about my normal business.

The next night I returned to my post and when midnight struck the same light appeared; this time I saw where it was coming from. A woman dressed in white, with a lamp in her hand, walked slowly through all the rooms on the first floor, went up to the second floor and then disappeared. The lamp threw too feeble a light on to her features for me to be able to see them clearly but I recognized Leonor by her blonde hair.

I went to see the duchess as soon as it was daylight. She was not there. I went to see my child. I discovered the women attending her to be agitated and uneasy. At first they were unwilling to say why. Finally the nurse told me that a woman dressed all in white had come in that night, holding a lamp in her hand. She had looked at the child for a long time, had blessed her and then had gone away.

The duchess came home. She summoned me and said:

'I have reasons to wish your child to be here no longer. I have given orders that the house in the Calle Retrada be made ready to receive her. She will stay there with her nurse and the woman who passes for her mother. I would happily suggest also that you might live there too, but there might be drawbacks.'

I replied that I would keep the house opposite and sleep there from time to time.

The duchess's wishes were carried out. I was careful to see that my child slept in the bedroom which looked out over the street, and that the blind was not shut again.

Midnight struck. I went to the window and saw in the room opposite the child asleep with her nurse. The woman dressed in white appeared, a lamp in her hand. She went up to the cradle, gazed at the child for a long time, then blessed her. Then she came to the window and looked for a long time in my direction. After that she went out of the bedroom and I saw light on the next floor. Finally, the woman appeared on the roof, ran lightly along the ridge and on to a neighbouring roof and then disappeared from sight.

I confess that I was bewildered. I slept little and next day waited impatiently for midnight. When it struck I was at my window. Soon I saw not a woman in white but a sort of dwarf come in, with a bluish face, a wooden leg and a lantern in his hand. He went up to the child whom he looked at intently, then he went to the window, sat down, crossed his legs and started to stare at me. After that, he jumped down from the window into the street, or rather seemed to slide down, came to my door and knocked.

I asked him from my window who he was.

Instead of replying he said to me, 'Juan Avadoro, get your cloak and sword and follow me.'

I did as he said. I went down into the street and saw the dwarf about twenty paces ahead of me, hobbling along on his wooden leg and showing me the way with his lantern. After about a hundred paces he turned left and led me into a lonely district which extends from the Calle Retrada to the River Manzanares. We went under an arch and came out on to a patio in which several trees were planted. In Spain what are called patios are inner courtyards into which carriages cannot enter. At the end of the patio was a little Gothic façade which looked like the portal of a chapel. The woman in white came out; the dwarf lit her face with his lantern.

'It's he!' she cried. 'It's he – my husband, my dear husband!'

'Señora,' I said, 'I thought you were dead!'

'I am alive!' And it really was Leonor. I recognized her by the sound of her voice and more still by her ardent embraces, which were those of a wife. So passionate was she that I had no time to ask questions about our miraculous meeting. Leonor tore herself from my arms and escaped into the darkness. The limping dwarf offered me the aid of his small lantern. I followed him across some ruins and through completely deserted parts of the town. Suddenly the lantern went out. The dwarf, whom I tried to call back, did not answer my shouts. The night was pitch-black. I decided to lie down on the ground and wait for the day. I fell asleep.

When I awoke it was broad daylight. I found myself lying by a black marble urn. On it I read in gold letters the name 'Leonor Avadoro'. In a word, I was lying beside my wife's tomb. I then recalled the events of the night and was troubled by their memory. For a long time I had not approached the tribunal of penitence. I went to the Theatine house and asked for my great-uncle, Father Gerónimo. He was ill. Another confessor appeared. I asked him whether it was possible for demons to assume human form.

'Without doubt,' he replied. 'Succubi are mentioned by name in St Thomas's *Summa*. It's a special case. When a man has not partaken of the sacraments for a long time demons gain a certain control over him. They appear in the shape of women and lead him into temptation. My son, if you think you have met succubi, go and see the grand penitentiary. Go at once. Waste no time.'

I replied that a strange adventure had befallen me in which I had been misled by visions. I asked for permission to break off my confession.

I went to Toledo's house. He told me that he would take me to dine with the Duchess of Avila and that the Duchess of Sidonia would be there too. He found me preoccupied and asked me the reason. I was indeed abstracted and could not marshal my ideas in any reasonable order. I was melancholy at dinner with the duchesses. But they were so lively and gay and Toledo responded so well to their mood that I ended up by sharing it myself.

During dinner I noticed conspiratorial signs and some laughter which seemed to have something to do with me. We left the table and instead of going to the salon the four of us went to the inner apartments. When we reached them Toledo locked the door and said:

'Illustrious Knight of Calatrava. Kneel down before the duchess. She has been your wife for more than a year! Don't say that you suspected it. The people to whom you will tell your story will guess perhaps, but the great art is to prevent suspicions from forming and that is what we have done. Actually the secretiveness of the ambitious Duke of Avila has helped us. He really did have a son, whom he hoped to have recognized. This son died and so he ordered his daughter not to marry in order that his estates would revert to the Sorriente, who are a branch of the Avila family. The haughty character of our duchess made her not want to have a master but since our return from Malta this same pride didn't quite know what was happening to it and ran the risk of suffering a notable shipwreck. Happily for the Duchess of Avila, she has a friend who is also yours, my dear Avadoro. She took her into her complete confidence and we have worked together in the interests of those who are so close to our hearts.

'We then invented a Leonor, daughter of the duke and the infanta, who was none other than the duchess herself, dressed in a blonde wig and lightly made-up; but you never thought of recognizing your haughty mistress in the naïve girl who had been brought up in the Carmelites' house. I was present sometimes when this role was being rehearsed and I assure you that I would have been just as deceived as you were.

'Seeing that you had refused the most brilliant matches simply to remain attached to her, the duchess decided to marry you. You are married before God and his Church, but you are not married before men, or at least you would search in vain for proof of your marriage. In this way the duchess has not broken any engagement she has made.

'So you were married and the duchess had to spend some months in her country estate to avoid the eyes of the curious. Busqueros had just reached Madrid. I put him on your trail and, on the pretext of throwing that ferret off the scent, we had Leonor leave for the country. Then it suited us to have you leave for Naples, for we didn't know any more what to tell you about Leonor, and the duchess was unwilling to make herself known to you until a living proof of your love had added to your rights.

'At this point, my dear Avadoro, I must implore your forgiveness. I plunged a dagger into your breast by announcing to you the death of a person who never existed. But you did not lose by reacting with such feeling. The duchess is touched that you have loved her so perfectly under two so different guises. For a week she has been eager to declare herself, and here I am again the guilty party. I was determined to call Leonor back from the other world. The duchess agreed to act the woman in white, but it wasn't she who ran so lightly along the ridge of the neighbouring house. That Leonor was just a little chimney sweep.

'The same lad came back the next night dressed as the limping devil.[1] He sat on the window and slipped down a rope which had been already tied in place. I don't know what happened in the patio of the former Carmelite convent but I had you followed this morning and knew that you had made a lengthy confession. I don't like to have dealings with the Church and I feared the consequences of a joke which might be taken too far. So I didn't oppose the duchess's wish and we decided that her declaration should be made today.'

That was what my friend Toledo said. But I hardly listened to him. I was at Manuela's feet. A delightful shy blush coloured her face, in which I saw the clear expression of her complete submission. My victory had then and was only ever to have two witnesses, but it was no less dear to me for that.

I was thus fulfilled in love, in friendship and even in self-esteem. What a moment for a young man!

When the gypsy reached this point in his story, he was told that the affairs of his band required his presence and he had to leave us. I turned to Rebecca and said to her that we had heard an account of extraordinary adventures which none the less had all been explained by natural means.

'You're right,' she said. 'Perhaps yours will be explained in the same way.'

1 The eponymous protagonist of Guevara's novel *El diablo cojuelo* (1641), better known through Lesage's adaptation of it of 1707 (*Le diable boiteux*).

The Fifty-seventh Day

———————————— ✧ ————————————

We were expecting important events. The gypsy had sent messengers out in different directions and was impatiently awaiting their return. When he was asked when we would strike camp, he shook his head and replied that he was not yet able to give a precise time. Our stay in the mountains was beginning to bore me. I would have been happy to join my regiment as quickly as possible, but I had to stay on for some time in spite of this wish. The days were quite monotonous, but the evenings on the contrary were very pleasant, thanks to the company of the gypsy chief, in whom I was discovering new qualities. I was quite curious to know what his next adventures were and on this occasion asked him myself to satisfy my curiosity, which he did as follows:

✧ THE GYPSY CHIEF'S STORY CONTINUED ✧

You will recall my dinner with the Duchess of Avila, the Duchess of Sidonia and my friend, Toledo. I told you that it was only then that I learned the proud Manuela was my wife. The horses were harnessed to the carriages and we went to the castle of Sorriente. A new surprise awaited me there. The same duenna who had lived with the supposed Leonor in the Calle Retrada presented my little Manolita to me. The duenna was called Doña Rosalba and passed for the mother of the child.

Sorriente is on the banks of the Tagus in one of the most enchanting regions of the world. But the charms of nature only impressed me for a short time. Paternal feelings, love, friendship, tender trust and a deep courteousness shown by all made every day a new delight. What we in this brief life call happiness filled every moment. As far as I can remember, this state lasted six weeks; then we had to go back to Madrid. It was already late in the evening when we reached the capital. I accompanied the duchess to the steps of her palace. She was very emotional.

'Don Juan,' she said, 'in Sorriente you were Manuela's husband; here you are Leonor's widower.'

No sooner had she uttered these words than I saw a shadow cross the rail of the staircase. I grabbed the man by the collar and brought him into the light. I saw it was Busqueros. I was on the point of giving him the reward due for his spying when a single glance from the duchess stopped me. This look had not escaped Busqueros's notice. He adopted his usual impertinent manner and said:

'Señora, I could not resist the temptation of admiring the charm of your person for a moment, and perhaps nobody would have discovered me in my hiding-place if the light of your beauty had not illuminated the staircase like the sun.'

Having produced this well-turned compliment, Busqueros bowed low and left.

'I fear that my words may have reached the ears of that wretched man,' said the duchess. 'Go after him and try to banish from his mind any unwelcome suppositions.'

The incident seemed deeply to have upset the duchess. I left her and rejoined Busqueros in the street.

'Dear stepson,' he said, 'just now you nearly struck me with your stick, which would certainly have done you no good at all. First, you'd have failed to show the respect you owe to me as the husband of your former stepmother; secondly, you will discover that I am not the idler that you once knew. I have been promoted, and both in the ministry and at court my talents have been recognized. The Duke of Arcos has returned from his post as ambassador and enjoys the favour of the court. Señora Uscariz, his former mistress, has become a widow and shares a close friendship with my wife. We carry our heads high and fear no one.

'But tell me, dear stepson, what the duchess was confiding in you. You were terribly afraid that I would hear. I warn you that we don't like either the Avilas or the Sidonias or your friend, that spoilt child Toledo, very much. Señora Uscariz can't forgive him for having left her. I don't understand why you all went to Sorriente. People have been much concerned about you in your absence without your

569

knowing about it. You are as innocent as new-born children. The Marqués de Medina, who is a descendant of the Sidonia family, is soliciting the title of duke and the hand of the young Duchess of Sidonia, for his son. It's true that the young duchess is scarcely eleven years old but that doesn't matter. The marqués has long been a friend of the Duke of Arcos and enjoys the favour of Cardinal Portocarrero.[1] As he is omnipotent at court the affair will go ahead. You can tell the duchess. Wait, dear stepson. Don't think that I haven't recognized you as the little beggar beneath the portal of St Roch. You then had problems with the holy Inquisition, but I am not keen to come up against that tribunal. Look after yourself! Farewell!'

Busqueros went off, and I realized that he was still the same inquisitive meddler that he had always been, except that he exercised his talents in higher spheres.

Next day I dined with the Duchess of Avila, the Duchess of Sidonia and Toledo. I reported to them my conversation with Busqueros. This made more of an impression than I would have expected. Toledo, who was now less handsome and did not pay court to the ladies with the same assiduity as of old, would willingly have solicited an honorific post, but unfortunately Count Oropesa[2], the minister on whom he was counting, had left government service. That is why he was hesitating between different options. The Duke of Arcos's return, and the favour he enjoyed with the cardinal, were not events calculated to please him.

The Duchess of Sidonia seemed to fear the moment that she would have only a life rent to live on. On the other hand, every time the subject of the court and court favours came up, the Duchess of Avila took on an even more haughty air than usual. I was amazed to realize that differences of rank remained a sensitive matter, even among close friends.

A few days later, as we were dining with the Duchess of Sidonia, a gentleman of the Duke of Velásquez's retinue announced a visit of his master. Velásquez was then in the full vigour of manhood. He was a

---

1 Manuel Fernandez de Portocarrero, statesman (1629–1709).
2 Prime Minister 1685–91, and again in 1698–9.

handsome man, who always dressed in the French manner, which he refused to abandon for the Spanish style because it stood out well from the crowd. His eloquence also set him apart from Spaniards, who say little and clearly for that reason take refuge in cigars and guitars. Unlike them Velásquez passed easily from one subject to another and always found an opportunity to address a compliment to the ladies.

Toledo was certainly more intelligent, but intelligence only shows itself intermittently, whereas eloquence is inexhaustible. Velásquez's chatter gave pleasure. He saw himself that he charmed his listeners. He turned to the Duchess of Sidonia, burst out laughing, and said:

'Really, I must confess to you that nothing more curious and more ravishing could be thought of.'

'And what's that?' asked the duchess.

'It's true, Señora, that you share your beauty and youth with many women,' replied Velásquez, 'but you will certainly be the youngest and most beautiful of mothers-in-law!'

The duchess hadn't thought about this. She was twenty-eight years old. To pass for being very young, one had to be younger in years, but there existed artifices by which to become younger.

'Believe me, Señora,' added Velásquez, 'I am speaking nothing but the truth. The king has instructed me to ask you for the hand of your daughter for the Marqués de Medina. His Majesty is very keen that your famous name should not die out. All the grandees share his concern. As for you, Señora, what could be more charming than to see you lead your daughter to the altar? The general admiration will have to be shared between your two persons. If I were you, I would present myself in a dress similar in all respects to that of your daughter – in white satin embroidered with silver. If I may allow myself to give you a piece of advice, I would have cloth brought from Paris. I'll recommend the best houses to you. I have already promised to dress the young groom in the French way with a white wig. Farewell, Mesdames! Portocarrero wants to appoint me ambassador. May my embassies always be as agreeable!'

With these words, Velásquez threw a glance at the two ladies, which led each one to believe that she had made a greater impression on him. He bowed a few times, did a pirouette and left. That was what was then called *savoir vivre* in France.

When the Duke of Velásquez had gone, a long silence ensued. The ladies dreamed of robes embroidered with silver, whereas Toledo thought about the present state of the country and exclaimed, 'Is it really possible? Does the king want to rely only on the services of men like Arcos and Velásquez, the most vapid beings in all Spain? If that's how the French party see things we shall have to turn to Austria.'

And in fact Toledo went straight away to Graf Harrach,[3] who was then the emperor's ambassador in Madrid. The ladies went to the Prado and I followed them on horseback.

We soon encountered a magnificent coach in which Señora Uscariz and Señora Busqueros were preening themselves. The Duke of Arcos was prancing beside it. Busqueros, who was following the duke in a servile way, had that very day received the Cross of Calatrava and wore it on his chest. This sight dumbfounded me. I possessed the same decoration. I thought that I had received it as a reward for my merit and especially for my integrity, which had won me noble and powerful friends. I confess to you that I was crestfallen to see that cross on the chest of a man whom I despised above all others. I remained rooted to the spot where I had encountered Señora Uscariz's carriage.

After Busqueros had taken one turn round the Prado and saw me still in the same place he came up to me in a familiar way and said, 'You see, my friend, that different paths lead to the same goal. Like you, I am a Knight of the order of Calatrava.'

I was utterly outraged. 'So I see,' I replied. 'But knight or no, my dear Busqueros, I warn you if I find you nosing about in one of the houses I frequent I'll treat you like a common criminal!'

Busqueros put on his sweetest air and said, 'My dear stepson, your words call for an explanation between gentlemen. But with the best will in the world I can't be angry with you. I am, and will remain, your friend. To prove it to you I'd like to talk to you about certain

3 Ferdinand Bonaventura von Harrach (1637–1706).

matters which concern you all, particularly you and the Duchess of Avila. If you would like to know more, put your horses in the hands of the groom and accompany me to the nearest confectioner's.'

As I was curious, and feared for the peace of mind of the person who was most dear to me, I allowed myself to be persuaded. Busqueros ordered some refreshment and began to speak about things which were completely unrelated one to another. We were alone, but soon some officers from the Walloon Guards came into the shop, sat down and had chocolate brought to them.

Busqueros leaned towards me and said in a low voice, 'Dear friend, you were a little annoyed because you thought that I had wormed my way into the house of the Duchess of Avila. Now I heard there some words which I can't get out of my head.'

At this Busqueros burst out laughing and looked at the Walloon officers. Then he carried on: 'Dear stepson, the duchess said to you, "There the husband of Manuela, here the widower of Leonor."' With these words Busqueros burst out laughing again while looking at the Walloon officers. This trick was repeated several times. Suddenly Busqueros jumped up and left without saying a word. The Walloons came over to my table and one of them said to me very politely, 'My comrades and I would be happy to know what your neighbour found so funny about us.'

'Señor caballero,' I replied, 'your question is quite justified. My companion did indeed almost explode with laughter but I cannot guess the reason. I can, however, assure you that our conversation had absolutely nothing to do with you, but concerned family matters about which it would be impossible to find anything the slightest bit funny.'

'Señor caballero,' replied the Walloon officer, 'I confess that your reply does not wholly satisfy me although it indubitably does me honour. I shall transmit it to my comrades.'

The Walloons seemed to disagree amongst themselves and not to share the opinion of the officer who had spoken.

After a moment he came back to me and said, 'Señor caballero, my comrades and myself have not been able to reach agreement about the conclusions which it is appropriate to draw from the explanation which you were kind enough to give us. My comrades are of the opinion that we should be satisfied with it. Unfortunately, I am of the opposite opinion. This upsets me to the point that in order to avoid a quarrel I have offered satisfaction to each of them separately. As for you, Señor caballero, I admit that I should really lay the blame on Señor Busqueros. But I must say that his reputation scarcely allows me to take glory from a duel with him. On the other hand, Señor, you were with Don Busqueros and you even glanced fleetingly at us when he laughed. That is why I think that it would be right, without giving too much importance to this affair, to end this explanation with our swords.'

The comrades of the captain tried again to convince him that he had no reason to fight either them or me. But knowing with whom they were dealing, they abandoned their efforts and one of them offered to be my second.

We went to the place of the duel. I inflicted a light wound on the captain but received simultaneously a blow to my right lung which felt like a pinprick. A moment later I was convulsed by a mortal shudder and fell to the ground unconscious.

When the gypsy reached this point in his story, he was interrupted and had to leave to see to the affairs of his band.

The cabbalist turned to me and said, 'If I am not mistaken, the officer who wounded Avadoro was your father.'

'You are not mistaken,' I replied. 'The chronicle of my father's duels mentions it, and my father notes that, fearing a futile quarrel with the officers who did not share his point of view, he fought three of them that very evening and wounded them.'

'Señor capitano,' said Rebecca, 'your father thereby proves his remarkable foresight. The fear of a pointless quarrel incited him to fight four duels in one day!'

Rebecca's jest at the expense of my father displeased me greatly, and I was preparing to reply to her when at that very moment the company dispersed and did not reassemble until the next day.

The Fifty-eighth Day

That evening the gypsy took up the thread of his story as follows:

∾ THE GYPSY CHIEF'S STORY CONTINUED ∾

When I recovered consciousness I noticed that I was being bled in both arms. As if through a mist I could see the Duchess of Avila, the Duchess of Sidonia and Toledo. All three were in tears. I fainted again. For six weeks I remained in a state similar to an uninterrupted sleep or even death. As my sight was feared for, the shutters were kept closed the whole time, and when my wound was treated a blindfold was placed over my eyes. Eventually I was able to see and speak. My doctor brought me two letters: one from Toledo, who told me that he had just gone to Vienna, on what mission I could not guess; the other was from the Duchess of Avila, but not in her handwriting. She informed me that I was being spied on in the Calle Retrada and people had even started searching my house. She had lost patience and withdrawn to her estates, or as they say in Spain, *a sus tierras*.

After I had read the two letters the doctor ordered me to close the shutters again and left me to my thoughts. This time I really started to think seriously. Till then life had seemed to me like a path strewn with roses. Only then did I begin to know its thorns.

After two more weeks I was allowed to go to the Prado in a carriage. I decided to get down and walk, but weakness overcame me and I had to sit down on a seat.

A little later, the Walloon officer who had been my second came up to me. He told me that during the whole time I had been in danger, my adversary had been terribly upset, and that he begged permission to embrace me. I granted it. He threw himself at my feet, then hugged me and said in a voice choked with tears, 'Señor

Avadoro, give me the opportunity to fight a duel for you. It will be the happiest day of my life.'

Shortly afterwards I saw Busqueros, who came up to me with his usual insolence.

'My dear stepson,' he said, 'the lesson you received has been a little too severe. Doubtless I ought to have administered it myself to you but I wouldn't have succeeded so well.'

'Dear stepfather,' I replied, 'I have no complaints about the wound that the brave officer gave me. I carry a sword for I know such an adventure may befall me. But as for the role you played in this affair, it is my opinion that it merits a good beating.'

'That's enough, dear stepson,' said Busqueros. 'Don't speak of beatings. In the present circumstances they will be altogether out of place. Since I last left your company I have become an influential person: a sort of deputy minister of the second rank, and I must tell you in some detail how this came about.

'His Eminence the Cardinal Portocarrero noticed me on a few occasions in the suite of the Duke of Arcos and deigned to address me a particularly benevolent smile. Seeing myself encouraged, I paid court to him on his days of giving audience.

'One day His Eminence came up to me and said in a low voice, "I know, dear Busqueros, that no one is better informed than you about what goes on in this town."

'I replied, with a surprising presence of mind, "Your Eminence, the Venetians, who are said to be masters in state administration, number this art among the indispensable qualities of any man who wishes to engage in affairs of state."

'"And they are right!" added the cardinal, upon which he spoke to some other persons and then left. A quarter of an hour later the palace marshal came up to me and said:

'"Señor Busqueros, His Eminence has instructed me to invite you to dinner and it seems that he even intends to speak to you after the meal. As you will know, you should not prolong this conversation too much, as His Eminence eats a great deal and cannot stop himself from drowsing afterwards."

'I thanked the palace marshal for his friendly advice and remained behind to dine with more than ten other people. The cardinal ate nearly a whole pike.

'After dinner he invited me into his study. "Well, Señor Busqueros! Haven't you done something interesting these last few days?"

'The cardinal's question threw me into the deepest embarrassment, for in fact I hadn't learnt anything interesting either that day or the preceding ones. I thought for a moment and then replied, "Your Eminence, these last few days I learnt of the existence of a child of Austrian blood."

'The cardinal was extremely surprised.

'"Yes," I added. "Your Eminence will no doubt remember that the Duke of Avila was secretly united in marriage with the Infanta Beatriz. After his death a daughter called Leonor was born of this union. She married later and had a child. Leonor died and was buried in the Carmelite convent. I saw her tomb, which has since, however, disappeared without trace."

'"This could do the Avilas and the Sorrientes a great deal of harm," the cardinal said.

'His Eminence would perhaps have said more if the pike had not brought on his slumbers. I decided that it would be best to withdraw. All this happened three weeks ago and indeed, dear stepson, the tomb had disappeared from where I had seen it, and yet I perfectly recall the inscription "Leonor Avadoro". I abstained from uttering your name before His Eminence, not to protect your secret but to save up this news for later.'

The doctor, who was accompanying me on my outing, had withdrawn a few paces. He saw me suddenly blench and nearly faint. He told Busqueros that it was his duty to interrupt the conversation and take me home again. So I went home. The doctor gave me cool drinks and closed the shutters. Then I succumbed to my thoughts. certain of Busqueros's remarks had humiliated me to the utmost.

'That's what it is really like,' I said to myself, 'when you spend time with those set above you. The duchess has entered into a marriage with me that isn't really one. Because of an imaginary Leonor I have aroused the suspicions of the authorities and on top of that have to listen to the gossip of a man I despise. But I cannot

577

justify myself without betraying the duchess and she is far too proud even to admit to her liaison with me.'

Then I thought of little Manolita, then two years old, whom I had pressed to my heart at Sorriente but dared not call my daughter. 'My dear child!' I exclaimed. 'What does the future hold in store for you? The convent, perhaps? But no, I'm your father and if it's a matter of your future I am prepared to fly in the face of prudence. I shall be your protector even at the expense of my life.'

Thinking about my child had upset me. I was bathed in my tears and soon also in my blood, for my wounds had opened up again. I called for the surgeon and he dressed me again. Then I wrote to the duchess and had the letter taken to her by one of the servants she had left behind with me.

Two days later I went back to the Prado and noticed everywhere great excitement. I was told that the king was dying. I concluded that my affair would be forgotten, in which I was not mistaken. The king died the following morning. I immediately sent a second letter to inform the duchess of this.

The king's will was read two days later, and it was learnt that Philippe d'Anjou had been called to the throne. The secret of this had been closely guarded, and when the news spread it gave rise to great astonishment. I sent a third message to the duchess. She replied to my three letters, and asked me to join her at Sorriente. As soon as I was strong enough I hurried there. The duchess arrived two days later.

'I was lucky to get away,' she said. 'That worm Busqueros was already on the right path and would certainly have ended up finding out about our marriage. I would have died of chagrin. I truly feel that this is not fair, and I know that in scorning marriage I am placing myself above my sex and even yours. A disastrous pride has taken hold of my soul. But even if I were to employ all my strength to overcome it, I swear to you that it would not be possible.'

'But what about our daughter?' I asked. 'What will be her fate? Must I never see her again?'

'You will see her,' said the duchess. 'But don't speak about it now. Believe me, it hurts me more than you can imagine to have to hide her from the eyes of the world.'

The duchess was indeed suffering, but to my sufferings she had added humiliation. My love for the duchess was also bound up with my pride. I then received due punishment for this.

The Austrian party had designated Sorriente as the place for a general assembly. I saw a procession of famous names: Count Oropesa, Prince Infantado, Count Melzar and many others, not to speak of less noble figures, some of whom looked suspicious to me. Among these I noticed a certain Uzeda, who passed himself off as an astrologer and who assiduously sought my friendship.

Eventually an Austrian called Berlepsch arrived. He was the widowed queen's[1] favourite and the representative at the embassy since Graf Harrach's departure.

Several days were spent in discussions, which culminated in a solemn session around a great table draped in green cloth. The duchess had access to the deliberations, and I became convinced that pride, or rather a desire to involve herself in the affairs of state, had taken complete control of her mind.

Count Oropesa addressed Berlepsch and said, 'Señor, you see assembled here all the people with whom the last Austrian ambassador discussed Spanish affairs. We are neither French nor Austrians, but Spaniards. If the King of France recognizes the will, his grandson will no doubt become our king. It is true that we cannot always foresee future events but I can assure you that none of us here will begin a civil war.'

Berlepsch declared that the whole of Europe would take up arms and would not allow the Bourbons to take control of such vast territories. He then asked that the nobles who formed the Austrian party should send their representative to Vienna.

Count Oropesa's eyes rested on me and I thought he was going to propose me, but he became thoughtful and said that the moment for so decisive a step had not yet come.

Berlepsch declared that he would leave a confidential agent in the country. In any case he could easily see that the nobles taking part in that session were only waiting for the favourable moment to protest in public.

After the session I went into the garden to join the duchess and tell

1 Marie-Anne de Neubourg (1667–1740), sister of Leopold I, wife of Charles II.

her that Count Oropesa had looked in my direction when the question of sending a representative to Austria had arisen.

'Don Juan,' she said, 'I must admit that we have already spoken of you in this respect and it was I who proposed you. You seem disposed to upbraid me for what I have done. I am doubtless guilty but at least I want to explain my situation to you before you pass judgement on me. I was not meant for love, but yours succeeded in moving my heart. I wanted to know the joys of love before renouncing them for ever. What do you imagine? I learnt to know you and you haven't changed my opinion. However, the rights I have accorded you to my heart and my person, however slight they may be, can no longer continue. I have wiped out every trace of them. It is my intention to spend some years in the great world and if possible to influence Spain's destiny. Then I will found an order for noble ladies whose first mother superior I shall become.

'As for you, Don Juan, you ought to rejoin Prior Toledo, who has left Vienna and gone to Malta. But as the party to which you belong at present may expose you to danger, I shall purchase all that you own and will transfer its value to my Portuguese possessions in the Kingdom of the Algarve. That isn't the only precaution you should take, Don Juan. There are unknown places in Spain where one can spend one's whole life in safety. I shall recommend you to someone who will show you them. What I am saying seems to surprise you, Don Juan. I once showed you more affection. But Busqueros's spying has alarmed me and my decision is irrevocable.'

With these words the duchess left me to my own thoughts, which were not very charitable towards the high-born of this world.

'Let them be swallowed up in hell!' I exclaimed. 'These demi-gods for whom other mortals do not count! I've been the plaything of a woman who wanted to use me as an experiment to see whether her heart was meant for love, who now is sending me to exile, and who furthermore thinks that I shall be overjoyed at this opportunity of sacrificing myself for her cause and that of her friends. But that won't happen. Thanks to my little importance I shall no doubt be able to live in peace.'

I had said all this out loud and suddenly a voice replied: 'No, Señor Avadoro, you will not be able to live in peace!'

I turned round and saw under the trees Uzeda, the same astrologer of whom I have already spoken.

'Don Juan,' he said, 'I have heard part of your monologue and I can assure you that no one in these troubled times can find peace. You find yourself under powerful protection and you should not reject it. Go to Madrid. Arrange the sale which the duchess has suggested to you and then come to my castle.'

'Don't speak to me about the duchess,' I cried indignantly.

'Well then,' said the astrologer, 'let's speak about your daughter, who is at present in my castle.'

The desire to hold my child in my arms dispelled my anger. Besides, it wasn't proper to break with my protector. I went to Madrid and pretended that I was leaving for America. I put my house and all my possessions into the hands of the duchess's lawyer, and set out with a servant whom Uzeda had found for me. By a very circuitous route we reached Uzeda's castle, which you have seen, where he still lives with his son, the honourable cabbalist who is one of our present company.

The astrologer greeted me at his gate and said, 'Señor Don Juan, in this place I am not Uzeda, but Mamoun ben Gerson, a Jew by religion and race.'

Then he took me to see his observatory, his workshop and all the hidden quarters of his mysterious residence.

'Please tell me,' I asked him, 'whether your art has a basis in reality, for you have been said to be an astrologer and even a magician.'

'Would you like to put it to the test?' said Mamoun. 'Look in this Venetian mirror. Meanwhile I shall close the shutters.'

At first I saw nothing, but after a moment the surface of the mirror slowly cleared and I saw the Duchess Manuela with our child in her arms.

After the gypsy had said these words and we were all listening intently, curious to know what was going to happen, a man from his band came to discuss the day's business with him. The gypsy chief left us and we didn't see him again that evening.

The Fifty-ninth Day

We impatiently awaited the evening. When the gypsy appeared, we had long been assembled. Pleased with the interest we were showing in him, he needed little persuasion to continue his story as follows:

∽ THE GYPSY CHIEF'S STORY CONTINUED ∽

I was telling you that I was staring into the Venetian mirror in which I could see the duchess with the child in her arms. An instant later the vision disappeared. Mamoun opened the shutters and I said to him, 'Señor magician, I don't think that you have any need of demons to deceive my eyes with spells. I know the duchess. She has already played one trick on me of an even more surprising kind. In a word, having seen her image in the mirror I don't doubt that she is herself present in the castle.'

'You are not mistaken,' said Mamoun. 'We'll go directly to dine with her.'

He opened a little secret door and I fell at the feet of my wife, who could not hide her own feelings.

She regained control of herself and said, 'Don Juan, what I said to you at Sorriente had to be said once and for all because it is the truth, and my plans are irrevocable. But after you went away I reproached myself for my lack of tenderness. The inner instinct of my sex is repelled by behaviour which arises from heartlessness. Guided by this instinct, I decided to await you here and say goodbye to you one last time.'

'Señora,' I replied to the duchess, 'you have been, and still are, the only dream of my life and you will always take precedence over reality for me. Pursue your destiny by all means, and forget Don Juan for ever. But remember that I leave a child with you.'

'You will soon see her,' said the duchess, 'and together we will entrust her to those who will attend to her education.'

What more can I tell you? It then seemed to me and even now still seems to me that the duchess was right. Would I have been able to live with her, I who was her husband yet without being so? Even if our liaison had escaped the prying eyes of the public, it could not have remained hidden from the eyes of our household, and the secret could not have been kept for long. Perhaps the duchess's fate would have been entirely different. That is why it seemed to me that she was acting within her rights and so I gave in. I was to see my little Ondina,[1] who was so called because she had only been baptized in a water and not anointed.

We met again at dinner. Mamoun said to the duchess, 'Señora, I believe that Don Juan should be informed of certain things he needs to know. If you agree, I shall do this.'

The duchess gave her consent. Mamoun turned to me and said, 'Señor Don Juan, you find yourself here on lands whose deep places are hidden from profane eyes; lands in which everyone has a secret to keep. There are vast caves and extensive underground workings in this chain of mountains. They are inhabited by Moors who have never left them since they were driven out of Spain. In the valley which stretches out before your eyes you will meet bogus gypsies, some of whom are Muslim, others Christian, yet others who confess no religion. On the pinnacle of that rock over there you can see a tower to the top of which a cross is fixed. It is a Dominican monastery. The holy Inquisition has its reasons for shutting its eyes to everything that goes on there, and the Dominicans make it their duty to see nothing. The house in which you find yourself is lived in only by Jews. Every seven years Portuguese and Spanish Jews gather to celebrate the sabbatical year.[2] This will be the four hundred and thirty-eighth time since Joshua celebrated it. I have already said, Señor Avadoro, that among the gypsies some are Muslims, some

---

1 The child has previously been referred to as Manolita – little Manuela, that is, the Duchess Manuela's daughter. (See above, pp. 568, 577.)

2 Prescribed by Leviticus 25:2–7.

Christians and some confess no religion. These last are pagans who are the descendants of Carthaginians. In the reign of Philip II,[3] some hundreds of these families were burnt at the stake. A few only found refuge near a small lake of volcanic origin. The Dominicans have a small chapel there.

'Now, Señor Avadoro, listen to what we have arranged for little Ondina, who will never know what her origins are. The duenna, who is completely devoted to the duchess, is taken to be her mother. A pretty little house is being built for your daughter beside the lake. Dominicans from the monastery will teach her the first principles of religion. For the rest, we shall trust to providence. No ferreting spy will be able to find his way to the shores of the lake of la Frita.'

As he spoke, the duchess shed some tears, and I too could not stop myself from crying. The following day we went to the shores of the same lake where we find ourselves today, and took little Ondina there.

Next day the duchess had recovered her pride and her haughtiness, and I confess that our farewell was not very affectionate.

I did not stay long at the castle. I took a ship, landed in Sicily and arranged with Captain Speronara to be taken to Malta.

I went to see Prior Toledo. My noble friend embraced me warmly, took me to a room well apart from the others and closed the door behind me. Half an hour later the prior's marshal brought me a copious meal and towards evening Toledo came with a great wad of letters, or as they say in political circles, of dispatches. The next day I was already on my way to the Archduke Don Carlos with a message.

I met his Imperial Majesty in Vienna.[4] Immediately I had handed over my dispatches, I was shut up in a room well apart from the others, as I had been in Malta. An hour later the archduke came to see me in person, took me to the emperor and said:

'I have the honour to present to your Imperial and Apostolic Majesty Marchese Castelli, a Sardinian gentleman, and to ask that he be given the key of chamberlain.'

3 Reigned 1556–98.
4 i.e. Leopold I (reigned 1658–1705).

584

The Emperor Leopold twisted his lower lip into as pleasant an expression as he could manage, and asked me in Italian when I had left Sardinia.

I was not in the habit of speaking to monarchs, and still less of lying to them, so by way of reply I restricted myself to a deep bow.

'Good!' said the emperor. 'I hereby attach you to the household of my son.'

And so I became, without wishing to, Marchese Castelli, a Sardinian gentleman.

That evening I had a terrible headache, the next day a fever, and two days later smallpox. I must have caught it in some inn in Carinthia. My illness was violent and extremely grave. Yet I recovered from it, and even benefited by it. Castelli no longer looked in the least like Don Juan. In changing my name I had also changed my outward appearance. No one would ever have recognized in me the Elvira who once was going to become the wife of the Viceroy of Mexico. As soon as I was better, I was entrusted with communications with Spain. Meanwhile, Philippe d'Anjou was reigning in Spain, in the Indies and even in the hearts of his subjects. But heaven alone knows what demon intervenes at such moments in the affairs of princes. King Philippe and the queen, his wife, became, as it were, the first subjects of the Princesse des Ursins.[5] Moreover, the Cardinal des Estrées, the French ambassador, was admitted to the council of state, which enraged the Spaniards. Finally King Louis XIV, thinking that he could do as he liked, made Mantua a French garrison. The Archduke Don Carlos's hopes of acceding to the throne were rekindled.

One evening, right at the beginning of the year 1703, the archduke summoned me. He walked a few steps towards me and deigned even to embrace me affectionately. This greeting heralded something extraordinary.

'Castelli,' said the archduke, 'haven't you had news from Prior Toledo?'

I replied in the negative.

'He was a remarkable man,' added the archduke after a moment.

5 Anne-Marie de la Trémoille (1643–1715), widow of Flavio degli Orsini.

'What do you mean, "was"?' I exclaimed.

'Yes,' said the archduke, 'he was. Prior Toledo died of typhus on his island of Malta. But you will find in me a second Toledo. Mourn for your friend, and remain loyal to me.'

I wept bitter tears at the loss of my friend and realized that I had for ever to remain Castelli. By the force of destiny I became the docile instrument and the slave of the archduke.

Next year we went to London. From there the archduke went to Lisbon, while I joined the troops of Lord Peterborough,[6] whom I had had the honour of meeting in Naples. I was at his side when he secured the surrender of Barcelona and on this occasion he revealed his character by a noble and famous action. While the terms of surrender were being negotiated, some allied troops had entered the city and started looting it. The Duke Popoli, who commanded the army in the name of King Philippe, complained of this to the English lord.

'Allow me to enter the city for a moment with my English troops,' said Peterborough, 'and I give you my word that order will be restored.'

He did as he promised. He left the city and offered it honourable terms of surrender.

Soon after, the archduke, who had conquered nearly all of Spain, arrived in Barcelona. I regained my place in his household, still under the name of the Marchese Castelli. While walking one evening with members of the archduke's household in the main square, I saw a man whose gait – now crawling, now scuttling – reminded me of Don Busqueros. I had him watched, and was told that he wore a false nose and was known as Dr Robusti. I didn't doubt an instant that it was Busqueros, and that the wretch had slipped into the town with the intention of spying on us.

I informed the archduke of this, who gave me full powers to do as I saw fit with the villain. First, I ordered him to be locked up in our central guardhouse. Then, as the guard was being relieved, I lined up two ranks of grenadiers, each armed with a switch of birch, from

6 Charles Mordaunt, Earl of Peterborough (1658–1735).

there to the port. The men were spaced apart so that they could move their right arm. When Busqueros came out of the guardhouse he at once realized that these preparations had been made for him, and that he was to be the king of the festivities, as we say. He ran as fast as he could and avoided half the blows but none the less received at least two hundred. At the port he threw himself into a longboat, which took him on board a frigate, where he had the leisure to tend to his back.

The moment for the gypsy to attend to the affairs of his band had come, so he left us and put off the sequel to his story until the next day.

The Sixtieth Day

———————————— ∽ ————————————

The next evening the gypsy carried on his story as follows:

∽ THE GYPSY CHIEF'S STORY CONTINUED ∽

I stayed at the archduke's side for ten years. The best years of my life were spent in sadness but they were in fact no more joyful for other Spaniards. Every day disorder seemed to be ending, and every day it broke out again. King Philippe's supporters despaired of his weakness for the Princesse des Ursins. Don Carlos's party also had no reasons for rejoicing. Both sides had committed numerous errors. There was a general feeling of exhaustion and disillusionment.

The Duchess of Avila, who had long been thought to be the soul of the Austrian party, would perhaps have won over that of King Philippe if she had not been thwarted by the insurmountable pride of the Princesse des Ursins. The latter had eventually to leave the theatre of her exploits and return to Rome, but she soon came back, more triumphant than ever. At that the Duchess of Avila left for the Algarve and set about founding a convent. The Duchess of Sidonia lost her daughter and her son-in-law one after the other; the Sidonia line died out altogether and its possessions passed to the Medina Celi family. The duchess herself retired to Andalusia.

In 1711 the archduke succeeded his brother Joseph[1] on the throne and as emperor took the name of Charles VI. Europe's covetousness was no longer directed at France but at the new emperor. People no longer wanted Spain to remain under the same sceptre as Hungary. The Austrians withdrew from Barcelona, leaving behind the Marchese Castelli, whom the inhabitants honoured with their complete trust. I

1 Joseph I reigned from 1705 to 1711.

588

did not spare any effort to make them see reason, but my efforts were in vain. A madness had taken hold of the Catalans. They thought that they could defy the whole of Europe.

Amid all these events I received a letter from the Duchess of Avila. She already signed it as the Prioress of Val Santo. The letter consisted of these few words:

Go as soon as you can to Uzeda and try to see Ondina. Be sure to speak first to the prior of the Dominican monastery.

Duke Popoli, King Philippe's commander-in-chief, was besieging Barcelona. The first thing he did was to raise a fifty-feet-high gallows which was intended for the Marchese Castelli. I gathered the leading citizens of Barcelona together and said to them:

'Señores, I appreciate the honour that you do me in placing your trust in me, but I am not a soldier and am therefore not capable of being your commander. Besides, if you were ever forced to surrender, the first condition which would be imposed on you would be to hand me over, which would no doubt be very distressing for you. For these reasons it is best for me to bid you farewell and leave you for good.'

But when people are committed to the ways of folly, they carry with them the greatest number and even think that there is an advantage to be had in refusing to grant safe passes out of the city. So I was not given permission to go, but I had long since made my own plans. A boat awaited me on the beach; I boarded it at midnight and the next evening landed at Floriana, an Andalusian fishing village.

I rewarded the sailors generously, sent them back and went up into the mountains. After a long time trying to find my way, I finally reached Uzeda's castle and its owner hardly recognized me in spite of his astrological powers.

'Señor Don Juan, or rather Señor Castelli,' he said, 'your daughter is healthy and indescribably beautiful. As for the rest, you must speak to the Dominican prior.'

Two days later an aged monk approached me and said, 'Señor Castelli, the holy Inquisition, to which I belong, thinks it its duty to shut its eyes to much that occurs in these mountains. It does so in the hope of converting lost sheep, who are very numerous in these parts.

The example of these lost sheep has had a bad influence on young Ondina. She is in any case a girl with strange ideas. When we instructed her in the principles of our holy religion she listened attentively and did not show any signs of doubting the truth of what we said, but a moment later she was saying Muslim prayers with the others and participating in pagan festivals. Go to the lake of la Frita, Señor, and try to fathom her heart, over which you have some authority.'

I thanked the venerable Dominican and set off for the shores of the lake. My path took me to a promontory situated to the north. From there I saw a sailing boat gliding over the water at lightning speed. I was amazed at the way the boat was constructed: tapered like a skate, it was equipped with two beams whose counterweights stopped it capsizing. The sail was attached to a solid mast; beside it, a girl seemed to glide over the surface of the water, scarcely touching it. The curious craft came to land where I was standing. The girl got out. Her shoulders and legs were bare and a green silk dress clung to her body. Her hair fell down in great curls on to a snow-white neck. Sometimes she shook them like a mane; her appearance reminded me of the natives of America.

'Manuela, oh Manuela!' I exclaimed. 'Is this our daughter?'

It was indeed she. I went to her apartment. The duenna of Ondina had died some years previously. The duchess herself had then come and had entrusted her daughter to a Walloon family, but Ondina refused to recognize any authority. She spoke little, climbed trees, scaled rocks and swam in the lake. She was not unintelligent. She it was, for example, who had designed the gracious boat I have just described to you. Only one word would induce her to be obedient. It was the name of her father, and if something was required of her she was told to do it in her father's name. When I reached her lodgings it was decided to summon her at once. As she arrived, her whole body was trembling. She knelt before me. I pressed her to my heart, covered her with caresses, but did not succeed in extracting a single word from her.

After breakfast Ondina went back to her boat. I climbed in with her; she took the oars and rowed to the middle of the lake. I tried to engage her in conversation. She let the oars go and seemed to listen attentively to me. We were on the east side of the lake, very close to the precipitous cliffs which surround it.

'Dear Ondina,' I cried. 'Have you, I wonder, zealously followed the pious precepts of the monastery fathers? You are after all a rational being, Ondina. You possess a soul and religion should be your guide in the paths of life.'

As I was in the process of remonstrating with her as a father, Ondina suddenly jumped into the water and disappeared from sight. Full of fear, I immediately returned to her lodging and called for help. I was told that there was no reason to be alarmed, as there were hollows in the rock and caves that were linked one with the other; Ondina knew all these passages; she would disappear in one place only to reappear in another and often would not return for several hours. On this occasion she returned quite quickly, but I decided from then on not to remonstrate with her further. As I have said, Ondina was not lacking in intelligence, but having been brought up in solitude and left to her own devices, she had no idea of normal behaviour.

Some days later a monk came to see me in the name of the duchess, or rather Prioress Manuela. He gave me a habit similar to his to conduct me to her. We followed the coast to the mouth of the Guadiana, where we reached the Algarve and eventually Val Santo. The convent was almost built. The prioress received me in her usual dignified way, but when the witnesses to our meeting had withdrawn she was overcome by emotion. Her haughty dreams had flown away. All that remained was a nostalgic regret for love that was lost for ever. I wanted to speak to her about Ondina but the prioress, sighing, asked me to defer the matter till the next day.

'Let us rather speak about you,' she said. 'Your friends have not forgotten you. Your fortune has doubled in their hands. It's a matter now of what the name will be under which you will have the enjoyment of it. It's impossible for you still to pass as the Marchese Castelli. The king will not pardon those who took part in the uprising in Catalonia.'

We talked about it for a long time without reaching a decision. Some days later Manuela secretly gave me a letter which she had received from the Austrian ambassador. It was flatteringly suggested that I should return to Vienna. I confess that few things in life have given me as much pleasure. I had served the emperor devotedly and his gratitude seemed to me to be the sweetest of rewards.

But I did not succumb to false hopes. I knew the customs of the court too well. People had tolerated my receiving favours from the archduke while he vainly struggled to accede to the throne, but I could not expect them to tolerate me at the side of the greatest monarch of all Christendom. Above all else I feared an Austrian gentleman who never stopped trying to harm me. He was Graf Altheim, who came later to possess considerable influence. In spite of that I went to Vienna and embraced the knees of His Apostolic Majesty. The emperor was gracious enough to consider with me whether it wasn't better to keep the name of Castelli rather than assume my own again, and offered me an important post in his empire. His kindness touched me, but a secret foreboding prevented me from taking advantage of his offer.

At that time some Spanish noblemen left their country and established themselves in Austria, among whom were the Counts Larios, Oyas, Basquez and Taruca. They knew me well and urged me to follow their example. I intended to do so, but the secret enemy of whom I spoke was watching carefully. He had learnt all that had been said at my audience and had immediately told the Spanish ambassador. The latter thought that he was fulfilling a diplomatic duty by persecuting me. Important discussions were still going on at that time. The ambassador invented obstacles and linked the difficulties that arose to questions about my person and the role I had played in affairs. He succeeded in his aim. I soon noticed that my situation had changed completely. Courtiers seemed embarrassed by my presence. As I had foreseen this change before my arrival in Vienna, I was not too upset by it. I solicited a valedictory audience. I was granted it without anything being referred to.

I left for London, and it was some years before I returned to Spain.

I found the prioress listless and pale. 'Don Juan,' she said, 'you can see how the years have changed me. To tell the truth, I can feel that a life which holds no more charms for me is nearing its end. Merciful heavens, how many reproaches you will be justified in making to me! Listen to me. My daughter died a pagan, my granddaughter is a

Muslim. Take this and read it.' As she said this she held out a letter from Uzeda, which read as follows:

Señora, Venerable Prioress,

While visiting the Moors in their caves I learnt that a woman wanted to talk to me. She led me to where she lived and said to me, 'Señor astrologer, you who know everything, explain to me an adventure which has happened to my son. Having walked all day in the gorges and ravines of our mountains, he discovered a magic spring. A girl of marvellous beauty met him there and he fell in love with her, even though he took her to be a fairy. My son has gone on a long journey and has asked me to clarify this mystery at all costs.' Such were the Moorish lady's words and I guessed at once that the fairy was our Ondina, who was in the habit of disappearing into a certain cave to reappear on the other side of it, where water wells up like a powerful spring. To calm the woman down I said a few words of no significance and went to the lake. I tried to question Ondina but in vain. You know her aversion to speaking. But soon there was no longer any need to question her. Her silhouette betrayed her secret. I took her to the castle, where she gave birth to a daughter but, prompted by a desire to return to her lake, she took up her previous wild style of life and a few days later an illness carried her off. To be completely frank, I cannot remember whether she had ever professed this or that religion. As for Ondina's daughter, whose father is of the purest Moorish stock, she ought incontestably to become a Muslim. Otherwise we will draw down on ourselves the vengeance of the inhabitants of the underground domain.

'You can imagine, Don Juan,' added the duchess in the greatest despair, 'how unhappy I am. My daughter died a pagan, my grand-daughter must remain a Muslim. Almighty God, how severely you have punished me!'

As the gypsy uttered these words, he noticed that it was already late and he rejoined his men. We for our part went to bed.

The Sixty-first Day

We waited for evening all the more impatiently because we sensed that the gypsy's adventures were almost over. And we listened all the more attentively when the gypsy chief took up his story again as follows:

∽ THE GYPSY CHIEF'S STORY CONTINUED ∽

The venerable Prioress of Val Santo would not have collapsed under the weight of her worries if she had not imposed upon herself a severe penitential regime which her exhausted organism could not sustain. I saw her slowly fade away and did not have the heart to leave her. My monk's habit gave me access to the convent at all times, and one day the unhappy Manuela breathed her last in my arms. The duchess's heir, the Duke of Sorriente, was staying at that time in Val Santo. He spoke to me most frankly.

'I know of your links with the Austrian party, to which I also belong,' he said. 'If ever you need help you can always count on me. I would take it to be a favour. As for open friendship, you will realize that I cannot engage in it in any event, without exposing both of us needlessly to danger.'

The Duke of Sorriente was right. The party had abandoned me. I had been pushed to the fore, so that I could be dropped at will. I was still left with a considerable fortune, which could easily be transferred to my name because it was in the hands of the Moro brothers. I intended to travel to Rome or to England, but when it was necessary finally to settle on plans I was unable to make up my mind. The very idea of returning to the world made me shudder with horror. An aversion for social relationships has become in a certain way a sort of obsession with me.

Uzeda, who noticed that I was hesitating and didn't know what to do, advised me to enter the service of the Gomelez.

'What does this service consist in?' I asked. 'Isn't it a threat to the peace of my country?'

'Not at all,' he replied. 'The Moors hidden in these mountains are planning an Islamic revolution, which is driven by political interests and fanaticism. They have unlimited means, thanks to which they hope to attain their goal. Some of the most famous Spanish families have entered into contact with them for their personal profit. The Inquisition receives considerable sums from them and allows things to go on in the depths of the earth that it would not tolerate on the surface. In a word, trust me, Don Juan, and try living with us in our valleys.'

I was tired of the world and decided to follow Uzeda's advice. The Muslim and pagan gypsies greeted me like a man destined to be their chief and swore me unshakeable loyalty. But it was the gypsy women who confirmed me in my decision. Two of them I found particularly attractive: one called Quita, the other Zita. Both were beautiful and I didn't know which one to choose.

They noticed my hesitation and released me from my predicament by telling me that among their people a man could have several wives and to get married there was no need for a religious ceremony.

To my shame I must confess that I allowed myself to be seduced into such libertine ways. There is only one way of keeping to the path of virtue: it is to avoid all acts which are not clearly enlightened by it. When a man conceals his name, his actions and his plans, he will soon be obliged to hide his whole life. My liaison with the duchess was only blameworthy in that I had had to hide it, but all the secretiveness of my life followed necessarily from this first act of dissimulation. A much more innocent spell kept me in the valleys: the attraction of the life lived there. The vault of the heavens above our heads, the coolness of caves and forests, the sweet air – in a word, nature with all her marvels brought peace to my soul, which had been tormented by the world and its turmoil.

My wives gave me two daughters. I then began to listen more closely to the voice of my conscience. I had seen the sorrow which had carried Manuela to her tomb, and I decided that my daughters would be neither Muslim nor pagan. I could not therefore leave them to their own devices. I hadn't any choice. I had to remain in the service of the Gomelez. I was entrusted with affairs of the greatest importance, and with vast sums. I was rich and wanted nothing for myself but with the sheikh's permission devoted myself as much as I could to charitable works. I often succeeded in saving people from great misfortune.

All in all, I carried on in the depths of the earth the life I had led on its surface. I became a diplomatic envoy again. I went to Madrid several times, and on several occasions travelled beyond the frontiers of Spain. This active life restored my lost energies, and I became more and more attached to it.

Meanwhile my daughters grew up. On my last journey I took them with me to Madrid. Two young noblemen contrived to win their hearts. The families of these gentlemen have links with the inhabitants of our caves, so we don't have to fear that they will divulge what my daughters might tell them about our valleys. As soon as I have married them I will look for a holy place of retreat where I shall peacefully live out my life, which, although it was not altogether free from faults, cannot be called a criminal one.

You wanted me to tell you my story; I hope that you do not rue your curiosity.

'I really would like to know,' said Rebecca, 'what has become of Busqueros.'

'You shall know at once,' replied the gypsy. 'The beating in Barcelona cured him of spying, but as he had received it in the name of Robusti he thought that it hadn't damaged the honour of Busqueros in any way, so he brazenly offered his services to Cardinal Alberoni[1] and became under this minister a mediocre intriguer, a sort of shadowy image of his protector, who was himself a celebrated one.

'Later another adventurer, called Ripperda,[2] governed Spain. Under his reign Busqueros knew more good times, but age, which puts an end to the most brilliant careers, deprived Busqueros of the use of his

---

1 Spanish politician (1664–1752).

2 Johann Wilhelm von Ripperda, adventurer (1690–1737).

legs. After he became paralysed he had himself carried to the Plaza del Sol and there he carried on his singular activities by stopping passers-by and meddling if possible in their affairs. Recently I saw him in Madrid beside the most comic person in the world, whom I recognized as Agudez the poet.[3] Old age had deprived him of sight, and the poor fellow consoled himself with the thought that Homer too had been blind. Busqueros was bringing him scraps of gossip and Agudez was turning them into verse; sometimes people would listen to it with pleasure although he had only a shadow of his former talent.'

'Señor Avadoro,' I then asked, 'what has happened to Ondina's daughter?'

'That you will learn later. Please be kind enough to prepare to move on.'

We continued on our way and after much travelling reached a deep valley enclosed by rocks. When the tents had been put up the gypsy chief came up to me and said, 'Señor Alphonse. Get your cloak and sword and follow me.'

We walked for a hundred paces and reached an opening in the rock, through which I could see a long, dark tunnel.

'Señor Alphonse,' said the gypsy chief, 'we all know how intrepid you are. Besides, you are taking this path not for the first time. Follow the tunnel and go down into the depths of the earth as you did the time before. I shall leave you now. Here we must go our own ways.'

Recalling my first visit to those caves, I calmly walked in the darkness for several hours. Eventually I glimpsed the light and reached the tomb, where I saw again the dervish in prayer.

Hearing my steps he turned round and said, 'Welcome, young man! It gives me pleasure to see you come back. You have been able to keep your promise and remain silent about a part of the secrets which we revealed to you. Now we are going to reveal more of them and we no longer need to swear you to secrecy. Meanwhile, rest and recover your strength.'

I sat down on a stone and the dervish brought me a basket in

---

3 Ramón Agudez is a character in the alternative version of the forty-seventh day.

which I found meat, bread and water. I ate. Then the dervish pushed a panel in the tomb, made it pivot on its hinges and showed me the spiral staircase.

'Go down there,' he said. 'You will see what you have to do.'

I counted nearly a thousand steps in the darkness and then reached a cave lit by lamps. I saw a stone bench on which chisels and steel mallets were carefully arranged. In front of the bench there was a shining seam of gold about the size of a man. The metal was dark yellow and seemed quite pure. I realized what was expected of me: I had to extract as much gold as I could. I seized hold of a chisel in my left hand and a mallet in my right, and in a short time became quite a skilled miner. But the chisels became blunt and I had to change them often. Three hours later I had extracted more gold than a man can carry.

I then noticed that the cave was filling up with water. I climbed up some of the steps, but the water continued to rise and I was forced to leave the cave. I went to the dervish. He blessed me and showed me another spiral staircase leading upwards. I climbed it and, when I had once more gone up about a thousand steps, I found myself in a round chamber. It was lit by countless lamps and their glow was reflected in sheets of mica and opal, which decorated its walls.

At the back of the chamber there was a raised throne of gold on which was sitting an old man wearing a snow-white turban. I recognized him to be the hermit in the valley; my cousins, dressed in rich attire, stood near him. He was surrounded by dervishes dressed in white.

'Young Nazarene,' the sheikh said to me, 'you have recognized in me the hermit who gave you shelter in the valley of the Guadalquivir and you have guessed that I am the Great Sheikh of the Gomelez. You surely can recall your two wives. The prophet has blessed their pious love. Both are going to be mothers and found the line destined to bring back the caliphate to the descendants of Ali. You have not disappointed the hopes we had placed in you. You returned to the camp without breathing a word of what happened to you in our tunnels. May Allah moisten your forehead with the dew of happiness!'

Then the sheikh stepped down from his throne and kissed me.

My cousins did the same. The dervishes were dismissed and we passed into a second chamber, at the back of which a dinner had been prepared. There were no solemn speeches, no attempts to convert me to Islam. We gaily spent the rest of the night together.

The Sixty-second Day

The next morning I was sent back down the mine and I extracted the same amount of gold as on the previous day. That evening I joined the sheikh and found my two wives with him. I asked him to explain to me certain things which were bothering me and especially to tell me the story of his own adventures.

The sheikh replied that the time had indeed come for the secret to be completely revealed to me and began his story as follows:

✺ THE GREAT SHEIKH OF THE GOMELEZ'S STORY ✺

You see in me the fifty-second successor of Massoud ben Taher, the first Sheikh of the Gomelez, who built the Cassar and who disappeared the last Friday of every month only to reappear the following Friday. Your cousins have already informed you of certain things. I shall complete their account and reveal to you all our secrets.

The Moors had been in Spain for several years when they decided to settle in the valleys of the Alpujarras mountains. A people called Turdules or Turdetains then lived in these valleys. The natives called themselves Tarsis and claimed to have lived formerly in the region of Cadiz. They still used several words of their ancient language, which they could even write. The letters of their alphabet were what are known in Spain as *desconocidas*.[1] Under Roman and later Visigoth domination the Turdetains paid considerable tribute and were able in return to retain their liberty and their old religion. They worshipped God under the name of Jahh and made sacrifices to him on a mountain called Gomelez Jahh, which in their language means Jahh mountain. The Arab conquerors, who were the enemies of

---

1 Unknown.

600

the Christians, hated pagans, or those taken to be pagans, even more.

One day Massoud discovered in the subterranean tunnels of the castle a stone covered in archaic writing. He lifted it up and saw a spiral staircase leading down into the mountain. Massoud had a torch brought and went down by himself. He found chambers, passages, corridors; but as he was afraid of losing his way he turned back. The next day he went back underground and noticed dust that glinted under his feet. He collected it together, took it to his apartment and was convinced that it was pure gold. He made a third expedition and, following the trail of gold dust, he reached the very seam which you have been working. He was dumbfounded by the sight of such treasure. He quickly returned to his apartment and took every conceivable precaution to hide the treasure from the eyes of the world. At the entrance to the underground domains he built a little mosque and claimed to wish to live the life of a hermit there in prayer and meditation. Meanwhile he worked tirelessly at his seam, extracting as much gold as possible. The work went ahead at a snail's pace, not only because he could not risk enlisting help but also because he had to procure the requisite steel tools secretly.

Massoud then realized that wealth by itself does not confer power. Before him he had more gold than all the princes of the world put together. He had expended untold energy on extracting the mineral, and didn't know what to do with his gold or where to hide it.

Massoud was a fervent disciple of the prophet and a fanatical supporter of Ali. He thought that the prophet himself had shown him this gold and given it to him so that the caliphate would return to his family, that is to say, the descendants of Ali, and the whole world be converted by them to Islam. This idea took hold of his mind. He embraced it all the more enthusiastically because the reign of the Ommayad of Baghdad was on the point of collapse and there was hope that the descendants of Ali would again succeed to the throne. Indeed, the Abbasids exterminated nearly all the Ommayads, but the descendants of Ali gained no advantage from this. On the contrary, one of the Ommayads even came to Spain and became the Caliph of Córdoba.

Massoud saw himself more than ever surrounded by enemies. By taking precautions he was able to avoid their attention. He abandoned any thought of implementing his project at once but rather gave his plans a shape which in some way kept them alive for the future. He chose six chiefs of tribes, made them swear a solemn oath, revealed to them the secret of the seam of gold and then said to them:

'For ten years I have owned this treasure and have not been able to profit at all by it. If I were younger I would have been able to raise an army and reign by this gold and by the sword. But I discovered my treasure too late. I am known to be a supporter of Ali and I would certainly have been murdered before being able to bring a party together. I have not abandoned hope that one day our prophet will return the caliphate to his family and that the whole world will then go over to his faith. That moment has not yet come but we must prepare for it. I am in contact with Africa and secretly give support to the Alids, but we must also reinforce the power of our family in Spain. Above all else we must keep the secret of our wealth. We must not all bear the same name, so, cousin Zegris, you will settle in Granada with your family and mine will remain in the mountains and keep the name Gomelez. Others will go to Africa and marry the daughters of the Fatimids. We must pay special attention to our young men. We must examine their hearts and put them to all sorts of tests. If one day one of our young men is found to have exceptional qualities of courage, he will set out to overthrow the Abbasids, wipe out the Ommayads and restore the caliphate to Ali's descendants. In my opinion this future conqueror should take the name of Mahdi – that is, the twelfth imam – and apply to himself the words of the prophet which declare that the sun shall rise in the west.'

These were Massoud's plans. He wrote them down and, from that time on, did nothing without taking the advice of the six chiefs of tribes. Eventually he gave up his position and entrusted to one of them the dignity of great sheikh and the castle of Cassar Gomelez.

Eight sheikhs succeeded one another. The Zegris and Gomelez acquired the most beautiful properties in Spain; other families went to Africa, occupied important posts and allied themselves by marriage to the most influential families.

At the end of the second century of the Hegira, a Zegris dared to proclaim himself mahdi, that is, legitimate chief. He made his capital at Kairouan, a day's journey from Tunis, conquered the whole of

Africa and became the first of the line of Fatimid caliphs.[2] The Sheikh of Cassar Gomelez sent him a great deal of gold but had to be more than ever careful to keep his secret because the Christians were beginning to win victories and it was feared that the Cassar might fall into their hands. Soon other worries preoccupied the sheikh, namely the sudden rise of the Abencerrages, a family which was hostile to us and whose outlook was opposed to ours. The Zegris and Gomelez were shy, reserved but keen on spreading the faith. The Abencerrages, on the other hand, were gentle, courteous to women and friendly towards Christians. They had discovered some of our secrets and encompassed us with snares.

The mahdi's successors conquered Egypt[3] and were recognized in Syria and Persia. The power of the Abbasids collapsed. Turcoman princes conquered Baghdad.[4] But in spite of this the doctrine of Ali scarcely spread and the Sunnis still held sway.

In Spain the example set by the Abencerrages started a progressive moral decline. Women appeared in public without veils, men sighed at their feet, the sheikhs of the Cassar no longer left their castle and did not touch the gold. This state of affairs went on for a long time. In their desire to save the faith and the kingdom, the Zegris and the Gomelez formed a league against the Abencerrages and slaughtered them in the Court of the Lions in their own palace, which they called the Alhambra.[5]

This disastrous event deprived Granada of a considerable number of its defenders and precipitated its fall. The valleys of the Alpujarras followed the example of the region and surrendered to the victors. The Sheikh of Cassar Gomelez destroyed the castle and took refuge in the underground dwellings in which you met Zoto's brothers. Six families hid with him in the depths of the earth. Others fled to surrounding caves, which open out on to other valleys.

2 This event took place in 910.

3 This event occurred in 973.

4 This event took place in 1055 (although the Turcoman dynasty did in fact continue to recognize the Abbasids until 1258, when Moguls sacked Baghdad and assassinated the last Abbasid caliph).

5 This event took place in 1485.

Some members of the Zegris and Gomelez families adopted the Christian faith or pretended to be converted. Among those was the Moro family, which before had had a trading house in Granada. Members of this family later became court bankers. They did not have to fear running short of money because the treasures of the mines were at their disposal. Contacts with Africa, especially Tunis, were maintained. So all went tolerably well until the time of Charles, the Emperor and King of Spain. The faith of the prophet, which was no longer as widespread in Asia as at the time of the caliphs, spread on the other hand through Europe, thanks to the Ottoman conquests.

At this time discord, which destroys everything on earth, reached below its surface too. That is to say, it reached our caves. Moreover, the small amount of living space exacerbated rivalries. Sefi and Billah fought over the position of sheikh, which was indeed worth coveting since it also conferred on its holder the right to have at his disposal an inexhaustible gold-mine. Sefi saw that he was weaker and sought to ally himself with the Christians. Billah plunged a dagger into his heart. Then he began to think about the whole issue of security. The secret of the underground domain was written down on a parchment and this was cut into six vertical strips so the page could not be read except by bringing together the six strips. All six chiefs of the tribes received one and were forbidden on pain of death to give it to anyone else. The initiate carried the strip on his right shoulder. Billah kept the power of life and death over all the inhabitants of the caves and of the region. The dagger he had plunged into Sefi's heart became the symbol of his power and was handed down to his successor. Having thus established a harsh regime in the caves, Billah devoted his indefatigable energies to Africa, where the Gomelez occupied several thrones. They reigned in Taroudant and Tlemcen. But Africans are fickle: men who listen above all to the voice of their passions. And Billah's undertakings on that continent did not result in the hoped-for success.

At about this time there began the persecution of the Moors who had stayed in Spain. Billah skilfully turned these circumstances to his advantage. With great shrewdness he established between the caves and high dignitaries of the state a system of mutual help. The latter thought that they were protecting a few Moorish families who wanted to be left to live in peace; in reality they were furthering the plans of the sheikh, who opened his purse to them in recompense. I also note in the annals that Billah introduced, or rather revived, the ordeals which young men had to undergo to show their strength of character. Before Billah's time they had fallen into oblivion.

Shortly after, the Moors were expelled. The sheikh of the caves was then called Kader. He was a wise man who used all the means at his disposal to ensure the safety of the inhabitants of the caves. Moro the bankers founded a society of highly-placed people who pretended to feel pity for the Moors. Under this cover they did many services for which they were handsomely paid.

The Moors who were banished to Africa were filled with a spirit of vengeance which constantly spurred them on. The whole continent looked as though it would rise up and overrun Spain but the African states were set against the interests of the exiled Moors. Much blood was pointlessly shed in civil wars. In vain did the sheikhs of the caves spend untold sums of money. The ruthless Moulay Ismael[6] took advantage of the age-old discord and founded the state of Morocco which still exists today.

I have reached the time of my own birth and will speak about myself from now on.

When the sheikh had said this he was told that dinner was served. The evening was spent in the same way as the previous one.

6 Reigned 1672–1727.

The Sixty-third Day

I was sent back down the mine in the morning. I set about extracting as much gold as I could. By now I was used to this work, having spent whole days at it. In the evening I went to see the sheikh, where I met my cousins again. I asked him to continue his story, which he did as follows:

THE GREAT SHEIKH OF THE GOMELEZ'S STORY CONTINUED

I have told you what I know of the story of our underground domains. Now I shall tell you about my own adventures. I was born in a spacious cave next to the one in which we find ourselves. It was lit by indirect light. The sky could not be seen, but we sometimes went out into clefts in the rock to breathe fresh air, and from there we could see a narrow part of the vault of the heavens and often even the sun. Above ground we had a small plot of land where we grew flowers. My father was one of the six tribal chiefs; that is why he lived with all his family underground, while his collateral relatives who were reckoned as Christians lived in the valley. Some had settled at Albicín on the outskirts of Granada. As you know, there are no houses there and the population lives in caves on the mountainside. Some of these strange dwellings were connected to certain caves which extended as far as our own underground domains. Some of those who lived close at hand came to pray with us every Friday. Those who lived further afield came only on great feast-days.

My mother spoke to me in Spanish, my father in Arabic, so from the beginning I knew both languages but principally Arabic. I learned the Koran by heart and made a deep study of its commentaries. From my earliest childhood I was a fervent Muslim and a follower of Ali. I had been inculcated with a deep hatred of Christians. All these feelings were more or less innate and grew as I grew in the darkness of the caves.

I reached my eighteenth year. For a long time it had seemed to me that the roof of the underground dwelling was oppressing my soul and crushing me. I was thirsty for pure air. This feeling made me ill. I lost my strength and grew visibly listless. My mother was the first to notice what was happening. She began questioning me and I confided to her all my feelings. I described to her the oppressive sensation which tormented me and the strange restlessness of my heart, which I could not express. I added that I wished absolutely to breathe a different air, to see the sky, the forests, the mountains, the sea, other men, and that I would die if this wish was not granted.

My mother shed some tears and said, 'Dear Massoud, your illness is common among us. I myself have suffered from it, and I was then allowed to make a few excursions. I went to Granada, and even further afield. But for you it's different. There are great plans for you. Soon you will be launched into the world and you will go much further away than I would like. But come and see me very early tomorrow and I shall see to it that you can breathe some pure air.'

The next day I joined my mother at the appointed hour.

'Dear Massoud,' she said, 'you want to breathe fresher air than that which you can breathe in these caves. Be patient. If you crawl for a certain time under this rock you will reach a deep, narrow gorge. The air is freer there than it is here. In places you can even climb the rocks and see a limitless horizon spreading out at your feet. This hollow passage was in the beginning only a crack in the rock, from which fissures have since run out in various directions. Today you will see before you a labyrinth of intersecting paths. Take some pieces of charcoal with you and at every fork mark the path you have followed. That is how to avoid getting lost. Here is a bag with provisions. You'll find no shortage of water. I hope that you don't meet anyone, but slip a *yatagan*[1] into your belt in case you do. I am putting myself in great danger in satisfying your wishes so don't stay away too long.'

1 A Turkish dagger.

I thanked my kind mother, started crawling and reached a narrow passage hollowed out in the rock but still covered with vegetation. Later I saw a little lake with clear water and several paths crossing one another. I walked for most of the day. The noise of a waterfall attracted my attention. I followed the downward path of the stream and reached the point where it flowed down into a bay. It was a magical place. For a moment I was silent in admiration, then hunger gnawed at me. I got out the provisions from my bag, proceeded to perform the ablutions prescribed by the prophet and eagerly set about my food. When I had finished my meal I performed my ablutions again, prepared to return to the caves and followed the path by which I had come. Suddenly I heard a strange rustling. I turned round and saw a woman emerging from a spring. Her wet hair covered her nearly completely, but she was wearing a green silk dress, which clung to her body. After the fairy had emerged from the water, she hid in the bushes and came out again dressed in dry clothes, with her hair held back by a comb.

She climbed on to a rock, no doubt to enjoy the view, and then went back to the spring from which she had come. Without knowing why, I instinctively blocked her path. She was frightened at first but I fell to my knees. This humble attitude seemed to reassure her somewhat. She came up to me, took me by the chin and kissed me on the forehead. Then, as fast as lightning, she threw herself in the lake and disappeared from sight. I was convinced that she was a fairy or, as they are called in our stories, a *peri*. But in spite of this I went up to the bush where she had hidden and found there the dress hung up to dry.

I had no other reason to linger there and returned to the cave. I greeted my mother with a kiss but did not tell her of the adventures which had befallen me, for I had read in our *ghasels*[2] that fairies like their secrets to be kept. My mother noticed that I was extremely lively and was glad that the liberty she had given me had had such a beneficial effect.

The next day I went back to the spring and, as I had marked the

2 The *ghasel* is a poetic form.

way with charcoal, I found it without difficulty. Once there I called out to the fairy at the top of my voice and asked her to excuse me for having performed my ablutions in her spring. However, I performed them again and then spread out my provisions. Guided by a secret instinct, I had brought enough for two people. I hadn't begun eating when I heard a rustling coming from the spring. The fairy emerged from it and laughed as she shook water over me.

She ran to the bush, put on a dry dress and sat down next to me. Then she ate like an ordinary mortal, but didn't say a word. I thought that this was the custom of fairies and was not surprised.

Don Juan Avadoro has already told you his story, so you have guessed that my fairy was his daughter Ondina, who dived into the passages under the rock and swam from her lake to mine. Ondina was innocent, or rather, she was unaware of innocence or sin. Her face was so enchanting, her behaviour so simple and engaging that I fell deeply in love with her and imagined that I had become the husband of a fairy. This lasted for one month.

One day the sheikh summoned me. In his company I discovered the six chiefs of the tribes, including my father.

'My son,' he said, 'you are going to leave our caves and go to those happy regions where people profess the faith of the prophet.'

These words made the blood run cold in my veins. To be parted from the fairy meant death to me. 'Dear father,' I cried, 'allow me never to leave these caves.'

I had no sooner uttered these words than I saw six daggers pointing at me. My father seemed to want to be the first to strike me in the heart.

'I accept that I must die,' I said, 'but let me first speak to my mother.'

This favour was granted me. I threw myself in her arms and told her of my adventure with the fairy. My mother was amazed and said, 'Dear Massoud, I didn't think there were any fairies on earth. In any case I don't know anything about them, but there's a wise Jew living nearby whom I'll ask about them. If the one whom you love is a fairy, she will be able to find you wherever you are. Moreover, you must also consider that in this place the least sign of disobedience is punished by death. Submit yourself to their wishes, and try to earn their good graces.'

My mother's words made a deep impression on me. I thought to myself that the fairy was indeed bound to be an omnipotent being and that she would be able to find me even at the very ends of the earth. I went to see my father and swore him blind obedience.

The next day I set off on my journey with a Tunisian called Sid Ahmed. He first took me to his native city, one of the most enchanting in the world. From Tunis we went to Zaghouan, a little town famous for the manufacture of the red beret called the fez. I was told that near the town there was a strange building composed of a temple and a colonnade forming a semicircle around a lake. The water springs from the temple like a fountain and runs into the lake. It was said that in ancient times the waters of the lake were piped as far away as Carthage. It was also said that the temple was dedicated to an aquatic deity. Deranged as I was, I thought that this deity was my fairy. I went to the fountain and started shouting for her as loud as I could, but all that replied was an echo.

Later, still at Zaghouan, I was told about a castle of ghosts, whose ruins were a few miles off in the desert. I went there and saw a circular edifice built in an unusual but fine style. A man was sitting in the ruins and drawing. I asked him in Spanish whether it was true that the palace had been built by ghosts. He smiled and said that it was a theatre in which the ancient Romans organized fights between wild animals. The place was called el Djem and had once been famous under the name of Zama. The traveller's explanation didn't interest me in the slightest. I would have preferred to meet a ghost there who might have brought me news of my fairy.

From Zaghouan we went on to Kairouan, the old capital of the mahdi. There I saw an immense town of a hundred thousand violent and passionate inhabitants, ready to rise up at any moment. We spent a whole year there. From Kairouan we went to Ghadames, a little independent state which is part of the Bled el Djerid, or the country of the date palms. That is what the region which stretches from the Atlas mountains to the Sahara, the desert of sand, is called. The date palms are so productive in this region that one tree is enough to feed a man of moderate appetite (as all the men of that race are) for a whole year. But there is no lack of other food. A cereal called *doura* is found there too, and tall sheep with no fleece whose flesh is succulent.

At Ghadames we met many Moors who had come from Spain. There were no Zegris or Gomelez among them but many families who were deeply devoted to us. It was a country of refugees.

Less than a year had gone by when I received a letter from my father, which ended as follows:

> Your mother asked me to tell you that fairies are ordinary women and that they even bear children.

I then realized that my fairy was a mortal like myself, and this thought calmed my imagination somewhat.

When the sheikh had reached this point in his story, a dervish came to say that dinner was served and we merrily sat down to table.

The Sixty-fourth Day

The next day I went back down the mine and practised the trade of miner for a few hours. In the evening I went to the sheikh and asked him to continue his story, which he did as follows:

THE GREAT SHEIKH OF THE GOMELEZ'S STORY CONTINUED

I told you that I had received a letter from my father, who informed me that my fairy was a woman. I was then at Ghadames. Sid Ahmed then took me to Fezzan, a bigger but less fertile region than Ghadames, all of whose inhabitants were black. From there we went to the oasis of Amnon, where we had to wait for news from Egypt. A fortnight later our messenger came back with eight dromedaries. The way these animals walked made riding unbearable, but we had to bear it eight hours without a break. Then we stopped. Each dromedary was given a ball made up of rice, gum Arabic and coffee. We rested for four hours and then set off again.

On the third day we stopped at Bahr Bila maa, that is, the sea without water. It is a large sandy valley covered in shells. We did not see any trace of plants or animals there. Towards evening we reached a lake rich in soda, which is a kind of salt. We dismissed our escort with his dromedaries and I spent the night alone with Sid Ahmed. At dawn eight strong men came to carry us across the lake on stretchers. Where the way across seemed narrow they went ahead in single file; the soda crackled under their feet, which they had wrapped in animal skins to protect them. We were transported in this way for more than two hours. The lake opened out into a valley, which was flanked on both sides at its entrance by two white granite rocks. It then stretched out into the distance and passed into a cave which was of natural origin although human hands had helped to fashion it.

Here the guides lit a fire and carried us another hundred paces to a sort of jetty, where a boat was waiting for us. They gave us a light meal. They themselves recovered their strength by drinking and by smoking hashish, a drug derived from hemp seed. Then they lit a resin torch, which threw light for a good distance all around, and fixed it to the rudder. We climbed into the boat, our porters turned themselves into oarsmen and all day we advanced along the underground waterway. Towards evening we reached a bay where the waterway divided into several branches. Sid Ahmed said that it was the beginning of the labyrinth of Ozymandias, which was famous in the ancient world. Nowadays only the underground part which is connected to the caves of Luxor and the underground areas of Thebes has been preserved.

They brought the boat to a halt at the entrance to one of the inhabited caves. The helmsman went to fetch food. Then we wrapped ourselves up in our *haiks*[1] and slept in the boat.

The next day they rowed on. Our boat advanced along long tunnels lined with slabs of dressed stone of extraordinary dimensions. Some were completely covered with hieroglyphs. At last we reached a port, where we declared ourselves to the local garrison. The officer in charge took us to his superior, who presented us to the Sheikh of the Druze.

The sheikh extended his hand to me in a friendly manner and said, 'Young Andalusian, our brothers in Cassar Gomelez have written good things about you to me. May the prophet send down his blessing on you.'

The sheikh seemed to know Sid Ahmed of old. Dinner was served, but at that moment strangely dressed men rushed into the room and spoke to the sheikh in an incomprehensible language. They spoke with vehemence and pointed to me as though accusing me of a crime. I looked towards my travelling companion to find out what was happening, but he had disappeared. The sheikh became violently angry with me; I was seized, my hands and feet were put in chains and I was thrown in a dungeon.

1 Cloaks.

613

This was a cave, hollowed out of the rock, which was linked to other tunnels by several corridors. A lamp lit the entry to my prison. Here I saw two horrible eyes and, just below, a terrifying mouth armed with monstrous teeth. A crocodile walked half-way into my cave and threatened to swallow me up. I was bound and couldn't move, so I prayed and waited for death.

The crocodile, however, was attached to a chain. This was a test of courage. The Druze then formed a great sect in the East. Their origins went back to a fanatic called Darasi, who in reality was nothing but a tool in the service of Al Hakim bi-Amr-Allah, the third caliph of the Egyptian Fatimids.

This monarch, famous for his impiety, tried by every means at his disposal to reintroduce the ancient cult of Isis. He commanded that he be considered an incarnation of the deity and indulged in the most abominable debauchery, which he tolerated also in his followers. At that time the ancient mysteries had not been altogether abolished. They were celebrated in a subterranean labyrinth. The caliph had himself initiated but was later defeated in his wild enterprises. His followers were persecuted and sought refuge in the labyrinth.

Nowadays they profess the purest of Muslim faiths, like that practised by the sect of Ali, which had formerly been adopted by the Fatimids. They took the name of Druze to avoid the universally hated name of Hashemites. Of all their ancient mysteries, all that the Druze have kept is their test of courage.

I have been present at some of these tests and have seen physical means employed which would give the best European scientist cause to ponder. Moreover, it seems to me that the Druze had several degrees of initiation which do not all relate to the Muslim faith but to things I know nothing about. I was then too young anyway to understand them. I spent a whole year in the caves of the labyrinth and often went to Cairo, where I stayed with people who kept secret links with us.

At bottom we only undertook these journeys to get to know the secret enemies of the Sunni faith, which was then dominant. We set out for Mascate, whose imam declared himself firmly against the Sunnis. This eminent priest received us with exquisite courtesy, showed us the list of Arab tribes who believed in him and claimed that he could drive the Sunnis out of Arabia. But as his faith was opposed to that of Ali we couldn't expect anything from him.

From Mascate a sailing boat took us to Bassora and, passing through Chiras, we reached the Seferid kingdom. It is true that there we saw the disciples of Ali to be in the majority. But the Persians indulged in sensual pleasures, tore themselves apart in internal quarrels and took little care to propagate Islam in their own country. We were recommended to go to see the Isids who inhabit the hills of Lebanon. Several sectarian groups were called Isids; those of the Lebanon were really known by the name Mutawali. From Baghdad we crossed the desert and reached Tadmora, which you call Palmyra. From there we wrote to the Sheikh of the Isids. He sent us horses, camels and an armed escort.

The whole population gathered in a valley near Baalbec; there we experienced real satisfaction. A hundred thousand fanatics uttered curses against Omar and screamed the praises of Ali. A funeral ceremony was celebrated in honour of Hussain, son of Ali. The Isids slashed their arms with knives, some cut their veins in the grip of madness and died, wallowing in their own blood.

We stayed with the Isids longer than planned. Eventually we received news from Spain. My parents had died and the sheikh intended to adopt me.

After four years of travel I was glad at last to return to Spain. The sheikh adopted me with all the usual ceremonies. Soon I was told of plans which even the six chiefs of tribes did not know about. It was hoped to make me a mahdi. I was first to have myself recognized in the Lebanon; the Egyptian Druze would declare themselves in my favour; Kairouan would also rally to me and when I had brought to this the wealth of Cassar Gomelez, I would be the most powerful monarch on earth.

All that wasn't badly thought out, but first, I was far too young, and second, I had no idea about military matters. So it was decided that I should immediately join the Ottoman army that was then fighting the Germans. Being of a gentle nature, I wanted to oppose these plans but I had to obey. Suitably equipped as a noble warrior, I went to Istanbul and joined the vizir's household. A general called Eugene defeated us and forced the vizir to fall back behind the Tana, that is to say, the Danube. We tried then to return to the attack and invaded Transylvania. We followed the course of the Pruth but the Hungarians attacked us from behind, cut us off from the Turkish frontier and slaughtered us. I was shot twice in the chest and was left for dead on the battlefield.

Nomad Tatars retrieved me, dressed my wounds and fed me exclusively on soured mare's milk. I am able to say that this drink saved my life. But I remained so weak for a year that I couldn't ride a horse and when the nomads moved camp, I was laid out on a cart with some old women, who looked after me.

My mind was as enfeebled as my body. I was incapable of learning a single word of Tatar. After two years I met a mullah who knew Arabic. I told him that I was a Moor from Andalusia, and begged to be allowed to return to my own country. The mullah interceded on my behalf with the khan, who gave me money for the journey.

At last I reached the caves where I had long been thought dead. My return gave rise to general rejoicing. Only the sheikh was sad, for he could see to what degree I was weakened and diminished. I was less able than ever to become the mahdi, but in spite of that a messenger was sent to Kairouan to test opinion because it was decided to act as soon as possible.

The messenger came back six weeks later. Everyone was extremely curious and crowded round him, but in the middle of his report the man collapsed and seemed to lose consciousness. He was given aid, came to, tried to speak but was unable to collect his thoughts. All that could be understood was that the plague was rife at Kairouan. It was decided to isolate him but it was already too late. People had touched him and carried his baggage. So all the inhabitants of the caves succumbed to a terrible epidemic.

That happened on the Saturday. When, on the next Friday, the Moors from the valleys came to pray and to bring us food, they found only corpses, among which I was crawling about with a great bubo on my left breast. But I escaped death.

As I no longer risked contagion, I set about burying the dead. In undressing the six chiefs of tribes, I discovered the six strips of parchment. I put them together and thus discovered the secret of the inexhaustible gold-mine.

The sheikh had opened the sluices before dying. I drained off the water and for some time stared in wonderment at my wealth without daring to touch it. My life had been so tumultuous that I needed peace, and I wasn't in the slightest bit tempted by the dignity of mahdi. I did not know the secret means of communication with Africa. The Muslims in the valley had decided to pray at home from then on, so I was left alone in my underground domains. I flooded the gold-mine again, collected together all the jewels I had found in the caves, washed them carefully in vinegar and went to Madrid, passing myself off as a Moorish jeweller from Tunis.

There, for the first time, I saw a Christian city. The freedom of the women amazed me, and I was enraged by the inconstancy of the men. I thought nostalgically about settling in a Muslim city. I wanted to go to Istanbul and live very comfortably in obscurity and return from time to time to the caves to replenish my wealth.

Those were my plans. I thought that no one knew who I was but I was mistaken. To appear more credible as a merchant I went to busy avenues and set out my jewels there. I had settled on fixed prices and refused to bargain. This procedure earned me general respect and assured me a profit that I wasn't at all concerned about.

However, I was being followed. Wherever I went – to the Prado, to the Buen Retiro, everywhere – a man was watching me whose stern, sharp eyes seemed able to read my soul. This man's persistent stare plunged me into the greatest anxiety.

The sheikh fell into a reverie, as if succumbing to his memories. Just then we were told that dinner was served and so he put off to the next day the sequel of his story.

The Sixty-fifth Day

I went back down the mine and set to work again. I had extracted an appreciable quantity of very pure gold. As a reward for my zeal the sheikh continued his story that evening as follows:

THE GREAT SHEIKH OF THE GOMELEZ'S STORY
∽ CONTINUED ∽

I had told you that wherever I went in Madrid a stranger kept me in his sight and his continual surveillance plunged me into indescribable anguish. One evening I decided at last to speak to him.

'What do you want from me?' I asked him. 'Are you trying to devour me with your gaze? What is your business with me?'

'I have no business with you,' the stranger replied. 'I simply intend to murder you if you betray the secret of the Gomelez.'

These few words made my situation clear to me. I realized that I must give up all peace of mind and a dark anxiety, the inevitable companion of all wealth, overwhelmed me.

It was already late. The stranger invited me to his house, had a meal prepared and carefully shut the door. Then he fell to his knees before me and said, 'Sovereign of the caves, receive my homage! But if you fail in your duty, I will kill you as once Billah Gomelez killed Sefi.'

I asked my strange vassal to rise, then sit down and tell me who he was. The stranger did as I wished and spoke as follows:

∽ THE STORY OF THE UZEDA FAMILY ∽

Our family is one of the most ancient in the world but as we don't like boasting about our lineage we restrict ourselves to tracing our origins to Abishua, son of Phinehas, grandson of Eleazar and great-grandson of Aaron, who was Moses's brother and high priest of Israel.[1] Abishua was the father of Bukki, the grandfather of Uzzi, the great-grandfather of Zerahiah and great-great-grandfather of Meraioth, who was the father of Amariah, the grandfather of Ahitub, the great-grandfather of Zadok and the great-great-grandfather of Ahimaaz, who was the father of Azariah, the grandfather of Johanan and the great-grandfather of Azariah II.

Azariah held the office of high priest in the famous temple of Solomon and left chronicles which some of his descendants continued. Solomon, who had done so much for the house of Adonaï, tarnished his old age by allowing his wives publicly to worship their idols. Azariah was justly angry, and wanted to oppose this sacrilege, but eventually on reflection realized that ageing monarchs have to show their wives some understanding, so he shut his eyes to these excesses which he had been unable to prevent and died high priest.

Azariah was the father of Amariah II, the grandfather of Ahitub II, the great-grandfather of Zadok II and the great-grandfather of Shallum, who was the father of Hilkiah, the grandfather of Azariah III, the great-grandfather of Seriaiah and the great-great-grandfather of Jehozadak, who was led into exile in Babylon.

Jehozadak had a younger brother called Obadiah and it is precisely from him that we are descended. He was not yet fifteen years old when he was made a page in the king's household and changed his name to Sabdek. There were other young Hebrews there whose names were also changed. Four of them refused to have any contact with the king's kitchens because of the unclean meat that was served there. So they lived on water and roots, and yet were well nourished, while Sabdek, who ate the portions intended for all four of them, despite this became thinner every day.

Nebuchadnezzar was a great king although he was too much ruled by his ambitions. In Egypt he had seen colossi sixty feet high, which is why he commanded that his own statue should be erected in the same dimensions, that it should be gilded and that everyone

1 Many of the names which follow are taken from genealogies in the Old Testament (notably 1 Chronicles 6:1–15).

should prostrate themselves before it and worship it. The young Israelites who would not eat unclean meat refused also to bend the knee before a statue. Sabdek, on the other hand, did so fervently and in his memoirs, written in his own hand, he commanded his descendants to bow before kings, their statues, their favourites, their mistresses and even their lap-dogs.

Obadiah, or Sabdek, was the father of Salathiel, who lived in the time of Xerxes, whom we Jews called Ahasuerus. This King of Persia had a favourite called Hamman, an extraordinarily arrogant and haughty man. Hamman had it proclaimed that any person who did not prostrate himself before him would be hanged. Salathiel was the first to pay this homage to him. But when Hamman was hanged himself Salathiel was also the first to bow before Mardochee.

Salathiel was the father of Malachiel and the grandfather of Zaphad, who lived in Jerusalem at the time when Nehemiah was governor. The Jewish women and girls were not very attractive. Moabites and Ashdodites were preferred to them. Zaphad married two Ashdodites. Nehemiah cursed him, hit him with his fist and, as that holy man reports himself in his chronicle, tore out the hair of his beard. In spite of this, Zaphad recommended to his descendants in his memoirs that if other women should please them no note should be taken of the opinion of the Jews.

Zaphad was the father of Naasson, the grandfather of Elphad, the great-grandfather of Zorobabel, who in turn engendered Elhuan and was the grandfather of Jehosabhebet. He lived at a time when the Jews rebelled against the Maccabees. Jehosabhebet, being by nature opposed to war, sought refuge in Kassiat, a Spanish town then inhabited by the Carthaginians.

Jehosabhebet was the father of Jonathan and the grandfather of Kalamil, who went back to Jerusalem when he discovered that peace had returned to that country. But he kept his house at Kassiat and the other property he had acquired in the vicinity of the town. As you will remember, our family divided into two branches during the exile in Babylon. Jehozadak, the head of the senior line, was a decent, pious Israelite and all his descendants have followed his example. I don't know why there was such hate between the two branches, but the elder line had to emigrate to Egypt, where it served the God of Israel in the temple founded by Onias. This line died out, or rather it lived on only in the person of Ahasuerus, known as the Wandering Jew.

Kalamil was the father of Eliphas, the grandfather of Elishua and the great-grandfather of Ephraim. In his time the Emperor Caligula wanted to erect a statue of himself in the temple at Jerusalem. The whole sanhedrin assembled. Ephraim, one of its members, was of the opinion that not only the emperor's statue, but that of his horse, which was already a consul, should be erected. But Jerusalem rose up in revolt against Petronius, the pro-consul, and the emperor had to abandon his project.

Ephraim was the father of Nebayoth. In his time Jerusalem rose up against Vespasian. Nebayoth did not wait to see how events turned out, but came to Spain, where our family, as I have already said, had considerable possessions. Nebayoth was the father of Jehosub, grandfather of Simran and the great-grandfather of Rephaiah, who was the father of Jeremiah. Now Jeremiah became astrologer to the court of Gonderic, the King of the Vandals.

Jeremiah was the father of Ezbon, the grandfather of Uzego and the great-grandfather of Jeremoth, who was the father of Anathot and the grandfather of Alemeth. In Alemeth's time Youssouf ben Taher invaded Spain with a view to conquering and converting the country. Alemeth presented himself to the Moorish chief and asked his permission to be converted to the religion of the prophet.

'You well know, my friend,' said the chief, 'that on judgement day all the Jews will be transformed into donkeys and will have to carry believers to paradise. So if you adopt our faith we will risk one day finding ourselves short of mounts.'

This was not a very courteous reply, but Alemeth found consolation in the way he was treated by Massoud, brother of Youssouf. Massoud kept him by him and entrusted him with several missions to Africa and Egypt. Alemeth was the father of Sufi, the grandfather of Gumi and the great-grandfather of Jeser, who was the father of Shalloum, the first *sarraf* or paymaster of the court of the mahdi.

Shalloum settled at Kairouan and had two sons, Makir and Mahab. The first remained at Kairouan, the other came to Spain, entered the service of the Cassar Gomelez and maintained contact with the Gomelez in Africa and Egypt.

Mahab was the father of Jehophelet, the grandfather of Malkiel, the great-grandfather of Behrez and the great-great-grandfather of Dehod, who was the father of Sachamer, the grandfather of Shova, the great-grandfather of Achieg and the great-great-grandfather of Bereg, who had a son, Abdon.

Realizing that the Moors were being driven out of all of Spain, Abdon became a convert to Christianity two years before the fall of Granada. King Ferdinand was his godfather. In spite of that, Abdon remained in the service of the Gomelez, abjured the prophet from Nazareth in his old age, and reverted to the faith of his ancestors.

Abdon was the father of Mehrital and the grandfather of Asael. In Asael's time Billah, the last legislator of the inhabitants of the caves, murdered Sefi. One day Sheikh Billah summoned Asael and spoke to him as follows:

'You know that I have killed Sefi. His death was predestined by the prophet, who desires the caliphate to revert to the descendants of Ali. I have therefore formed an alliance of four families. The Isids of Babylon, the Kabyles of Egypt, and the Benazars of Africa. The chiefs of these three families undertake, in their own name and in that of their descendants, to send in turn every three years a courageous, intelligent, experienced, prudent – even cunning – man to our caves. His task will consist in verifying that all that happens in our caves is according to the laws. In cases where they are broken, he has the right to kill the sheikh, the six chiefs of the tribes living in the caves – in short, all those who have brought guilt upon themselves. As a reward for his services, he will receive seventy thousand pieces of pure gold or one hundred thousand sequins converted into your currency.'

'Powerful sheikh,' replied Asael, 'you have only named three families. Which will be the fourth?'

'Yours,' said Billah, 'and for that you will receive thirty thousand gold pieces a year. But you must undertake to maintain contact and write letters. You will even take part in the running of the caves. If, on the other hand, you should fail in any way, one of the families is charged with the task of killing you at once.'

Asael wanted time to think but his cupidity triumphed and so he accepted this commitment for himself and his descendants.

Asael was the father of Gerson. The three families received every three years seventy thousand gold pieces. Gerson was the father of Mamoun, that is to say, of me. Faithful to the obligations of my grandfather, I have assiduously served the sovereign of the caves. After the epidemic of the plague I drew on my own fortune to pay the Benazars the seventy thousand pieces which were their due. I have just paid homage to you and sworn you unswerving loyalty.

'Honourable Mamoun,' I said. 'Have pity on me. I have already two bullets in my chest and am not suitable to be sheikh or mahdi.'

'As for mahdi,' Mamoun replied, 'you can put your mind at rest. No one is considering it any more. You cannot, however, refuse the dignity and the duties of sheikh if you do not want the Kabyles to kill you in three weeks' time – and not only you but also your daughter.'

'My daughter!' I exclaimed in amazement.

'Yes,' said Mamoun, 'the daughter which the fairy bore you.'

We were told then that dinner was ready and the sheikh interrupted his story.

The Sixty-sixth Day

———————— ✑ ————————

I spent another day in the gold-mine. In the evening, at my request, the sheikh continued his story as follows:

THE GREAT SHEIKH OF THE GOMELEZ'S STORY
✑ CONTINUED ✑

I had no choice. With Mamoun, I resumed the old activities of Cassar Gomelez and resumed contact with Africa and the great families of Spain. Six Moorish families had newly settled in the caves. But things were not going well for the African Gomelez. Their children of the male sex died or were born feeble-minded. I had myself only two sons from my twelve wives, both of whom died. Mamoun urged me to choose from among the Christian Gomelez, even from among those who are of our blood only on the maternal side but who might be converted to the faith of the prophet.

Hence Velásquez's claim to be introduced into our family. For him I intended my daughter Rebecca, whom you have already come to know. She was brought up by Mamoun, who has taught her all sorts of sciences and cabbalistic terms.

After the death of Mamoun, his son succeeded to the castle of Uzeda. I settled with him all the details of your own reception. We hoped that you would be converted to the Muslim religion or at least that you would become a father. On this latter point our hopes have been fulfilled. The children which your cousins bear in their wombs will be able to pass for descendants of the purest blood of the Gomelez. It was necessary for you to come to Spain. Don Enrique de Sa, the Governor of Cadiz, is an initiate. It was he who recommended to you Lopez and Mosquito, who abandoned you near the spring at Los Alcornoques. In spite of that you went courageously on as far as the Venta Quemada, where you met your cousins. With the help of a somnifer we succeeded in carrying you under the gallows of Zoto's brothers, where you woke up the next day. From there you came to my hermitage, where you met the demoniacal Pacheco, who in reality is only an acrobat from Biscay. The poor fellow lost an eye while executing a dangerous jump and has since lived off our charity. I thought that his sad story would make an impression on you and that you would betray the secret you swore to your cousins to keep. But you loyally kept your word. The next day we made you undergo a much more frightening test: the supposed Inquisition, which threatened you with the most horrible tortures but still did not succeed in undermining your courage.

We then wanted to get to know you better and had you brought to the castle of Uzeda. From the top of its terrace you thought that you recognized your two cousins. It was indeed they. But when you went into the gypsy's tent you only saw his daughters, with whom, you may be assured, you had no more intimate intercourse!

We had to retain you longer among us and we feared that you would grow bored. That is why we thought up various distractions for you. Thus Uzeda had an old man of my band memorize the story of Ahasuerus, the Wandering Jew, which he took from his family chronicles and which the old man recited to you. In this case we were combining business with pleasure.

You now know all the secrets of our underground life, which certainly will not last much longer. Soon you will learn that an earthquake has wrought destruction in these mountains. For this to happen, we have brought immense quantities of explosives and that will be our very last flight.

So go, Alphonse, where the world calls you. You have received from us a letter of credit, left blank. The sum which you will write on it must be high enough to recompense you for what we have asked of you. You should reflect that there will soon no longer be an underground domain. Do not fail to ensure yourself an independent future. The Moro brothers will help you to do this. Once again, farewell. Kiss your wives. These two thousand steps will lead you up to the ruins of the Cassar Gomelez, where you will find guides to take you to Madrid. Farewell, farewell.

*

I went up the spiral staircase. I had scarcely caught sight of the light of the sun when I also saw my servants, Lopez and Mosquito, who had abandoned me near the spring of Los Alcornoques. Both were delighted to see me and kissed my hand. They led me to the old tower, where a meal and a comfortable billet were waiting for me.

The next day we resumed our journey without delay, and that evening reached the Venta de Cardeñas, where I met Velásquez again. He was deep in a problem that looked just like that of squaring the circle. The famous geometer did not recognize me at once, and first I had to remind him one by one of the events which had occurred during our stay in the Alpujarras mountains. But then he embraced me and manifested the joy which our renewed meeting gave him. At the same time he told me how painful it had been to have to part from Laura de Uzeda, which was how he now referred to Rebecca.

Epilogue

———————— ✍ ————————

I arrived in Madrid on the twentieth day of June, 1739. The day after my arrival I received from the Moro brothers a letter sealed in black, which made me apprehend a sad event. And indeed I learnt that my father had died from a sudden heart attack. My mother had leased our property of Worden and had gone to a convent near Brussels where, with the help of her life annuity, she wished to live in peaceful retirement.

The next day Moro himself came and asked me to breathe not a single word about what he was going to say to me. 'Up to now, Señor,' he said, 'you know about only a part of our secrets. But soon you will know them all. As we speak, all of those who are initiated into the secret of the caves are busy placing their money in different countries. If one of them should by some unfortunate chance suffer a loss we would all come to his assistance. You had an uncle in the Indies, Señor. He died and left you practically nothing. In order that no one would be surprised by your sudden wealth, I have spread the rumour about that you have come into a considerable inheritance. You must buy property in Brabant, in Spain and even in America. Please allow me to see to this. As for you, Señor, I know how brave you are and do not doubt that you will embark on the San Zacarias, which is due to bring reinforcements to Cartagena, which is threatened by Admiral Vernon.[1] The English minister does not want war but public opinion is pushing him in that direction. None the less peace is close at hand, and if you let this occasion to take part in a war go by, you won't easily find another.'

The plan suggested by Moro had long been settled upon by my protectors. I embarked with my company. It formed part of a

———

1 Edward Vernon (1684–1757) besieged Cartagena in 1741.

627

battalion made up of soldiers chosen from different regiments. The crossing went well. We arrived in time and barricaded ourselves in the fortress with the brave Eslada. The English abandoned the siege and I returned to Madrid in March 1740.

One day, while I was in service at court, I saw in the queen's entourage a young woman in whom I immediately recognized Rebecca. I was told that it was a princess from Tunis who had fled her country to be converted to our faith. The king had been her godfather and had given her the title of Duchess of the Alpujarras, and the Duke of Velásquez had asked for her hand in marriage. Rebecca noticed that I was being told about her and cast me an urgent glance, by which she seemed to implore me not to betray her secret.

Later, the court went to San Ildefonso, while I took up quarters with my company in Toledo. I leased a house in a narrow street close to the market. Opposite me lived two women who each had a child. It was said that their husbands, who were naval officers, were both at sea. These women lived in complete retirement and seemed to do nothing other than look after their children, who were truly as pretty as little angels. Throughout the day they cradled them, fed them, bathed them and dressed them. This touching picture of maternal love made such an impression on me that I never left the window. It is true that I was also moved by curiosity, for I wanted to see the faces of my neighbours, which were always carefully veiled. Two weeks went by in this way. The room which faced the street was occupied by the children and the women did not eat there, but one evening I saw that the table was being laid in that room and that a feast was being prepared.

At the end of the table a chair decorated with flowers marked the place of the king of the feast. High chairs were put on either side, in which the children were placed. Then my neighbours indicated that I should join them. I hesitated, not knowing what I ought to do. At that they lifted their veils and I recognized Emina and Zubeida. I spent six months with them.

Meanwhile the Pragmatic Sanction and the struggles over the succession of Charles VI unleashed a war in Europe[2] in which Spain

2 The War of the Austrian Succession (1741–8), one of the consequences of the provisions of the Pragmatic Sanction of 1713.

soon took an active part. I left my cousins and became adjutant to the infante, Don Felipe. During the whole war I remained at the prince's side. When peace was signed I was made a colonel.

We were then in Italy. An agent from the Moro bank came to Parma to recover funds and settle the finances of the duchy. One night this man came to see me and told me that I was impatiently awaited at the castle of Uzeda and that I should set out at once. He named an initiate to me whom I was to meet in Málaga.

I bade farewell to the infante, embarked at Livorno and arrived at Málaga after ten days at sea. The man in question, who had been informed of my arrival, was waiting for me on the jetty. We continued on our journey that very day and reached the castle of Uzeda on the next.

There I found a notable gathering: the sheikh, his daughter Rebecca, Velásquez, the cabbalist, the gypsy with his two daughters and sons-in-law, Zoto and his two brothers, the fake demoniac Pacheco and lastly a dozen Muslims belonging to the three initiated families. The sheikh announced that now we were all assembled we would go to the cave at once. We set out at nightfall and arrived at dawn. We went down to the underground mine and rested a while.

Then the sheikh brought us all together and uttered the following words, which he repeated in Arabic for the benefit of the Muslims: 'The gold-mine, which for a thousand years constituted the fortune of our family, seemed inexhaustible. Strong in this belief, our ancestors decided to use this gold to spread the faith of Islam and especially to support the followers of Ali. They were the only guardians of this treasure, and this guardianship cost them infinite pain and effort. I have myself known countless torments. In order finally to free myself from this anguish, which was becoming more and more difficult to bear, I decided to discover for myself if the mine really was inexhaustible. I drilled into the rock in various places and have discovered that everywhere the seam is coming to its end. Señor Moro has undertaken to assess the remaining wealth and to calculate the share due to each of us. This calculation gives to each of the principal heirs a million sequins and to the other participants fifty thousand. All the gold has already been extracted and is hidden in a distant cave. I want first to accompany you into the mine, where you can convince yourselves of the truth of what I am saying. Then everyone will receive his share.'

We went down the spiral staircase, reached the tomb and then the mine, which was indeed completely worked out. The sheikh urged us to go back up again. When we were again on the mountainside we heard a terrible explosion. The sheikh told us that part of the underground workings, which we had just left, had been blown up. Then we went to the cave in which the remaining gold was piled up. The Africans took away what was their due, Moro took charge of my share and that of most of the Europeans.

I returned to Madrid and offered my services to the king,[3] who received me with remarkable graciousness. I bought considerable properties in Castile; I was given the title of Conde de Peña Florida, and sat with the highest Castilian *titulados*.

Together with my fortune, my honours also grew. I became a general at the age of thirty-six.

In 1760, I was entrusted with the command of the fleet; my mission was to make peace with the Barbary states. I first set sail for Tunis. I hoped that I would encounter fewer difficulties there and that the example of that state would be followed by others. My boat dropped anchor in the roads, and I sent an officer ashore to announce my arrival. The news had already reached the town and the Bay of La Goulette was swarming with boats, which had been decorated, and which were to accompany me to Tunis with my retinue.

Next day I was presented to the bey. He was a young man of twenty years of age, with a most charming face. I was received with every imaginable honour and was invited that evening to the castle of Manouba. I was led into a pavilion set aside from the rest and the door was closed behind me. The bey entered, knelt and kissed my hand.

Then I heard a second door creak open and three veiled ladies appeared. They lifted their veils. I recognized Emina and Zubeida. Zubeida was leading by the hand a girl: my daughter. Emina was the young bey's mother. I cannot describe the power of the paternal

3 i.e. Ferdinand VI (reigned 1746–59).

instincts which were awakened in me then. The only thing which spoiled my joy was the thought that my children belonged to a religion hostile to mine. I expressed this painful thought.

The bey confessed to me that he was very attached to his religion but that his sister Fatima, who had been brought up by a Spanish slave, felt herself to be Christian in her soul. We decided that my daughter would come to Spain, be baptized there and become my heiress.

All this was accomplished in the space of a year. The king stood godfather to Fatima, and gave her the title of Princess of Oran. A year later she married the elder son of Velásquez and Rebecca, who was two years younger than her. I ensured that she would have my whole fortune by showing that I had no close relative on my paternal side and that the Moorish girl, who was related to me through the Gomelez, was my sole heir. Although I was still at the height of my powers I started to think about a post which would allow me to enjoy the charms of a quiet life. The post of Governor of Saragossa was vacant; I solicited and obtained it.

Having thanked His Majesty and taken leave of him, I next went to see the Moro brothers and asked them to give me back the sealed scroll which I had deposited with them twenty-five years earlier. It was the diary of the first sixty-six days of my stay in Spain.

I have copied it out in my own hand and put it in an iron casket, in which one day my heirs will find it.